THE COMPLETE MAPP AND LUCIA
VOLUME ONE

Queen Lucia, Miss Mapp
& Lucia in London

The Complete
MAPP AND LUCIA

VOLUME ONE
(THE FIRST OF TWO VOLUMES)

Queen Lucia, Miss Mapp &

Lucia in London

———————◆———————

with an Introduction by
KEITH CARABINE

WORDSWORTH CLASSICS

For my husband
ANTHONY JOHN RANSON
with love from your wife, the publisher.
Eternally grateful for your unconditional love.

Readers who are interested in other titles from
Wordsworth Editions are invited to visit our website at
www.wordsworth-editions.com

This edition first published in 2011 by
Wordsworth Editions Limited
8B East Street, Ware, Hertfordshire SG12 9HJ

ISBN 978 1 84022 673 7

Text © Wordsworth Editions Limited 2011
Introduction © Keith Carabine 2011

Wordsworth® is a registered trade mark of
Wordsworth Editions Limited

Wordsworth Editions
is the company founded in 1987 by
MICHAEL TRAYLER

Typeset in Great Britain by Antony Gray
Printed and bound by Clays Ltd, Elcograf S.p.A.

Contents

Contents

GENERAL INTRODUCTION

Wordsworth Classics are inexpensive editions designed to appeal to the general reader and students. We commissioned teachers and specialists to write wide-ranging, jargon-free Introductions and in some cases to provide Notes that would assist the understanding of our readers rather than interpret the stories for them. In the same spirit, because the pleasures of reading are inseparable from the surprises, secrets and revelations that all narratives contain, we strongly advise you to enjoy this book before turning to the Introduction.

General Adviser: KEITH CARABINE
Rutherford College, University of Kent at Canterbury

THE AUTHOR'S LIFE

'Fred' Benson, as he was always called, was born on 24 July 1867 at Wellington College in Berkshire, where his father was the first headmaster. Edward Frederic was the fifth of six children born to Mary Sidgwick Benson and Edward White Benson, who later became successively Chancellor and Canon of Lincoln Cathedral, Bishop of Truro, where he supervised the construction of Truro Cathedral, and finally Archbishop of Canterbury (1883–96). A more extraordinary family than the Bensons is difficult to imagine. Aged twenty-three, White Benson sat the eleven-year-old 'Minnie' on his knee and proposed to her, and after seven years of self-righteous letters outlining what he expected from a wife, they married when she was eighteen. He was a workaholic, an autocrat and a depressive with a firm sense of his own and his teenage wife's duties and Minnie, who was very intelligent with a marked sense of fun, quickly discovered that she did not love him and they often quarrelled. From 1896, after her husband's sudden death, she shared the marital bed and subsequently a house, Tremans, with an old friend Lucy Tait, daughter of the previous Archbishop of Canterbury.

Minnie bore five children in the first seven years of her marriage, four of whom survived into adulthood; all of them were intensely literate and accomplished, all remained unmarried because they were drawn to their own sex, and all, except Fred, inherited their father's manic depression. Arthur Christopher Benson (1862–1925) was a prolific, popular and financially successful author, most famous now for his poem 'Land of Hope and Glory'; he kept a diary, running to millions of words, that confirms his homosexuality, but suggests he had few, if any, sexual relationships. He taught at Eton (1885–1903) and from 1903 he lectured in English at Magdalene College, Cambridge, becoming Master in 1915. Margaret Benson ('Maggie', 1865–1918) was always mentally unstable, but she was one of the first women to be accepted at Oxford and the first to be granted a concession to excavate in Egypt; with her lover, Janet Gourlay, she wrote *The Temple of Mut in Asher* (1899). Deeply resentful of her mother's relationship with Lucy Tait, she attacked them with a carving-knife and was admitted to The Priory Hospital, Roehampton, where she spent the last ten years of her life. Robert Hugh Benson (1871–1914), the youngest child, was ordained in the Church of England, but in 1903 he was received into the Catholic Church, became a priest in 1904 and a Monsignor in 1911. He worked in a kind of perpetual frenzy, writing over thirty books, including a number of propagandist novels devoted to the Roman cause, historical fiction, devotional works and sermons.

Fred attended an élite prep school, Temple Grove, then Marlborough College, where he excelled at games and developed a passion for music; aged twenty, he entered Kings College, Cambridge, where he studied archaeology and fell in love with all things Greek, including a succession of beautiful young men. He attended the British School of Archaeology in Athens where he encountered Lord Alfred Douglas, who was embroiled in a disastrous relationship with Oscar Wilde, and then he accompanied Maggie on a dig in Egypt. His first novel *Dodo* (1893), about a glamorous, amoral, humorous woman who charmed many and distressed others, was an instant success. During the Graeco-Turkish War (1897), he administrated a Red Cross fund for the relief of Greek refugees. He returned to England via Capri, and was enchanted by the island, which was a favourite resort of the European homosexual community; and, subsequently, during the pre-war years, he shared a lease with a resident, John Ellingham Brooks, an ex-lover of Somerset Maugham's. Though Fred associated with homosexuals, his biographers stress that he was deeply afraid of the sexual impulse and may, therefore, have remained chaste throughout his life.

Fred's connection with Rye began in 1900, when he first visited Henry James in Lamb House; as his memoir *As We Are* (1932) shows, he was a keen admirer of James's fictional methods. In 1913 he found a new home in a beautiful Georgian terrace, at 25 Brompton Square, Knightsbridge, and it remained his London address for the rest of his life. It is the model for Lucia's rented house in *Lucia in London* (1927). In 1920, four years after James's death, Fred took over the lease of Lamb House and lived there until his own death in 1940. During these years his arthritis severely restricted his movements but he stoically coped with the more or less constant pain. He became a generous benefactor to the town, notably paying for the restoration of the organ of St Mary's Church; he also commissioned and designed a large stained-glass west window in honour of his parents (incorporating portraits of his collie, his manservant Charlie Tomlin, disguised as a shepherd, and of himself in mayoral robes) and a north window memorialising his brother Arthur who had lived in Lamb House for the last three years of his life (1922–5). Fred proved to be a good magistrate and served three successful terms as Mayor of Rye (1934–7). He died on 29 February 1940, a few days after finishing his fine memoir *Final Edition*.

Fred was astonishingly prolific throughout his career, often writing several books a year and composing novels in three to six weeks. He published well over one hundred books in several genres, including – apart from scores of feeble, justly forgotten novels – memoirs, short stories, biographies, pamphlets and books on subjects as diverse as golf, cricket, winter sports and Christian Science (*The House of Defence*, 1906). Brian Masters provides a bibliography in *The Life of E. F. Benson* (pp. 296–300) and Geoffrey Palmer and Noel Lloyd include a useful and judicious survey of his *oeuvre* in their Appendix to *E. F. Benson: As He Was* (1988). Worth remembering are *David Blaize* (1916), a tender, if confused, study of the love between two boys based on his own schooldays; *Raven's Brood* (1934), a very strange, fetid book set in Cornwall heaving with lust, fertility rituals, and religious bigotry, and containing the most overtly homosexual character in his fiction, Willie Polhaven; several fine comic novels, including *Mrs Ames* (1912), the series reprinted in these volumes, beginning with *Queen Lucia* (1920) and ending with *Trouble for Lucia* (1939), *Paying Guests* (1929) and *Secret Lives* (1932); several interesting, discursive memoirs, most particularly *As We Were* (1930) and *As We Are* (1932); atmospheric ghost stories gathered in *Visible and Invisible* (1923) and *Spook Stories* (1928); and biographies of writers (notably *Charlotte Brontë*, 1932) and of historical figures (notably *Queen Victoria*, 1935).

INTRODUCTION

The six novels gathered in these two volumes are rightly regarded as Benson's richest and most subtle comedies of manners. They appeared sporadically during the last nineteen years of his life – *Queen Lucia* (1920), *Miss Mapp* (1922), *Lucia in London* (1927), *Mapp and Lucia* (1931), *Lucia's Progress* (1935) and *Trouble for Lucia* (1939). We see them now as a series, but the two early works have separate cast-lists and are set respectively in the villages of Riseholme, based on Broadway in the Cotswolds, and Tilling, which is closely modelled on the town of Rye on the East Sussex coast. Each of the two works centres around one of the two outrageous hypocrites and fabricators, Mrs Lucas (Lucia) and Elizabeth Mapp, who see themselves as the social and cultural leaders of their respective societies. *Lucia in London* is designed as a sequel to *Queen Lucia*, but the novels only became a series when Benson decided in *Mapp and Lucia* to stage a war between the pair for social supremacy in Tilling and discovered that its skirmishes were endless and enjoyable, not least for the odd collection of Tillingites for whom the 'tensions' proved 'a very agreeable rack of suspense' (p. 198).

'Light literature' is easy to read and praise, but notoriously difficult to write about; and I am conscious that in these Introductions I am in danger of throwing the baby out with the bath water as I try to *show* why the Mapp and Lucia books 'are rich, subtle and devastating comedies of manners'[1] and why they deserve respectful attention. Thus, rather than move from one novel to another in turn, dwelling on (say) their farcical plots, I have chosen through an extensive use of quotation to dwell on specific aspects and sequences in order to share with the reader Benson's 'rich' and 'subtle' humour, both generated by and brought to bear on his central characters and perceivers, Lucia and Miss Mapp; and in so doing to highlight his moral vision and his distinctly odd view on, and 'camp' treatment of, his characters' fear and loathing of sex.

---

1 Geoffrey Palmer and Noel Lloyd in *E. F. Benson: As He Was*, p. 153. In common with all the writers on Benson I have read, their brief is bio-graphical and they do not attempt to prove their case.

In 1905 Benson and Philip Burne-Jones, son of the artist, formed a lasting friendship, based largely on their common urge 'to puncture the pompous and turn a frivolous light upon so-called serious matters'.[2] Together, as Masters records, they compiled a scrapbook called 'The Book of Fearfuljoy', which included a collection of cuttings, pictures and letters relating to Marie Corelli (1855–1924), by far the best-selling and most popular writer of her day. Corelli was a preposterous figure who claimed descent from the Venetian musician Arcangelo Corelli, but her real name was Mary Mackay, and she was the illegitimate daughter of a well-known Scottish poet, Charles Mackay. Corelli, as Masters shows, is 'the source of all the sillinesses and pretensions of Lucia', including: claiming to speak Italian, indulging in coy baby-talk, and waging a lifelong campaign of self-promotion, even complaining to newspaper editors if her name was omitted from the guestlists of fashionable parties (Masters, pp. 80–1). Benson based the village of Riseholme upon the Cotswold village of Broadway, the home of the actress Mary Anderson, who had captured Benson's heart when, as an undergraduate, he had seen her play Hermione and Perdita in *The Winter's Tale*. He visited her in the late 1890s and 'got to know her well'.[3]

Benson never took these novels seriously and recognised that 'the foe by my fireside was the facility with which I could write readably' (*Final Edition*, p. 250). Thus, as Masters reports, he wrote *Lucia in London* in six weeks between 27 November and 14 January. He was, however, formidably well read in the English classics and, though prolific, he was a serious craftsman. Palmer and Lloyd remark of the Mapp and Lucia series: 'The standard of comic writing remains constant, invention never flags, the character-drawing is as scathingly accurate in the last as in the first.'[4] This is true, but they do not explain why. Little has been written on the craft of these volumes, but it is evident from the fine opening pages of *Queen Lucia* that he has a very sure sense of the nature of, and his relationship to, his

---

2 *The Life of E. F. Benson*, 1991, p. 178. Henceforward, referred to as 'Masters' in brackets after the quotation.

3 Palmer and Lloyd, op. cit., also report: 'He had kept her photograph in his pocket and thought of little else but her for a long time' (p. 123). For full details see the Bibliography at the end of this Introduction.

4 Palmer and Lloyd, op. cit., p.153

central character and of both the substance and the parameters of his carefully contrived fictional kingdom.[5] The novel opens with a simple, seemingly insignificant event:

> Though the sun was hot on this July morning, Mrs Lucas preferred to cover the half-mile that lay between the station and her house on her own feet, and sent on her maid and her luggage in the fly that her husband had ordered to meet her. After those four hours in the train a short walk would be pleasant, but, though she veiled it from her conscious mind, another motive, subconsciously engineered, prompted her action. It would, of course, be universally known to all her friends in Riseholme that she was arriving today by the twelve twenty-six, and at that hour the village street would be sure to be full of them, and they would see the fly with luggage draw up at the door of The Hurst, and nobody except her maid would get out.
>
> That would be an interesting thing for them: it would cause one of those little thrills of pleasant excitement and conjecture which daily supplied Riseholme with its emotional bread. They would all wonder what had happened to her . . .   [p. 43]

From the outset we are invited to watch and to listen to Lucia think (as with Georgie and later Miss Mapp), and our attention is held and rewarded because of the humour generated by Benson's mastery of what we have come to know as 'the free indirect style', whereby, as in Jane Austen's *Emma*, a character's thoughts are represented by a third-person narrator, ensuring (in this case) that the reader shares the entranced, self-absorbed, musings and 'dramatic perception' (p. 44) of the novel's heroine, the self-styled queen of

---

5 I deliberately invoke the title of Percy Lubbock's pioneering *The Craft of Fiction* (1921), which is based upon an appreciation of Henry James's 'Prefaces' to the New York Edition of his works. Benson knew both men. Lubbock was a pupil of Arthur's at Eton and was deputed in a codicil of his will to be the sole reader of his huge (2,000,000-plus words) diaries and told that he should 'undoubtedly' destroy some volumes. He seems to have suppressed one (Masters, p. 258). James, as both Lubbock and Benson appreciated, invented a very difficult 'method' whereby 'the author no longer tells his story directly . . . but presents it as it presented itself to a person in the story itself, the whole of which is seen through his eyes' (*As We Are*, pp. 258–9). In the Mapp and Lucia novels, as I go on to show, we often look through the characters' eyes and watch them think, but we are always aware of the monitoring author, as in Jane Austen.

Riseholme, while always aware of the monitoring, detached, amused narrator. Thus, Lucia's complacent self-centredness ('universally known to all her friends') and natural, vigorous condescension are wonderfully caught ('interesting for them', 'little thrills', 'emotional bread'), but these terms also belong to the narrator who mockingly invokes the familiar language of the Lord's Prayer ('Give us this day our daily bread') to register the trivialities that happily satisfy all his characters' needs.[6] Moreover, Benson drolly establishes that the very substance of the artificial world of Riseholme (as later Tilling) is made up of the latest 'news', and the curiosity and the promise of 'a good gossip' it readily engenders causes Georgie's face to beam like ' a drunkard's when brandy is mentioned' (p. 63). In Benson's worlds news is power and, therefore, all his characters are primarily motivated by a greedy quest for it and by the thrill of being the first to acquire it and therefore to pass it on. Correspondingly, they all participate in an elaborate, superficial game of one-upmanship as to who knows what and how; and with any particular gossip they either feel triumphant if they are the first to relay it or humiliated if they do not know the news or learn that theirs is old hat.

In Chapter Seven of *Lucia in London*, Lucia attends a lecture by Professor Bonstetter on psychoanalysis, 'dreams and the unconscious self', and thinks, 'How curious that if you dreamed about boiled rabbit, it meant that sometime in early childhood you had been kissed by a poacher in a railway-carriage, and had forgotten all about it!' (p. 571). Though Benson robustly satirises Freud's distinction between the conscious and unconscious minds, he uses it to establish that Lucia's unconscious mind (in common with all the characters in the novels) is most definitely not (as Freud would have it) a repository for socially unacceptable ideas, desires or wishes and traumatic memories and painful feelings that are put out of mind by the

6 Benson was formidably well read and all these novels, particularly when Lucia is the central consciousness, are drenched in implicit (as here) or explicit quotations from a host of literary sources that often (again as here) mock the inhabitants of his toy kingdoms. Benson consciously plays with his readers, inviting us to recognise (or not) his joking literary allusions. I early took the decision not to gloss Benson's many allusions because to draw attention to his witty deployment of his literary predecessors would interrupt the reading experience and exterminate his humour. Lovers of Benson who think they detect a hidden literary allusion can always, of course, type the phrase into Google and enjoy or bemoan the fruits of their labours.

mechanism of psychological repression. Indeed, Benson alerts us to an amusing truth that Lucia prefers not to entertain, namely that she so fully exists in her designs on and presumed effects on the minds and reactions of others that even her subconscious motives are entirely socialised. Lucia, therefore, in common with all Benson's characters, is never perturbed by dreams; rather she is sustained by her irrepressible fantasies of social domination and of universal adoration. Thus, Benson cleverly suggests from the outset that his characters are not only superficial, but deep down, like Lucia, they are all (except Olga Braceley) shallow. Incapable of self-knowledge, lacking psychological complexity and incapable of change, they are perfectly fitted to enter Benson's farcical kingdoms of Riseholme and Tilling.

Lucia's dramatic conceit ('as by right divine') that the village of Riseholme is 'her kingdom' is readily embellished by Benson's urbane narrator:

Riseholme might perhaps, according to the crude materialism of maps, be included in the kingdom of Great Britain, but in a more real and inward sense it formed a complete kingdom of its own, and its queen . . . ruled it with a secure autocracy pleasant to contemplate at a time when thrones were toppling, and imperial crowns whirling like dead leaves down the autumn winds. [p. 45]

The tongue-in-cheek narrator mocks Lucia and alerts the reader to the turbulent world (in 1920) outside the novel, while simultaneously establishing that the kingdom he pleasantly contemplates and describes is not to be confused with the real world because it is immune to 'the heady poison of Bolshevism'. Lucia's kingdom is untouched by the Great War and the Great Depression, and poverty, social discontent, class warfare and national politics rarely impinge. Moreover, nobody in these novels (other than the servants and Olga, who is a world-class opera singer) works because as with Lucia and Peppino their 'materialistic needs' are 'provided for by sound investments' (p. 46) or as with the Quantocks by the steadily rising value of 'Roumanian oils'. Riseholme and subsequently Tilling are toy kingdoms, and in the former Peppino is Lucia's 'prince-consort' (p. 55), her home 'The Hurst' is 'her court', Georgie her 'gentleman-in-waiting', the village green functions as a 'parliament' and the villagers are her subjects. In keeping with this grand, hyperbolic conceit all attempts to dislodge Lucia as 'leader of all that was advanced and cultured in Riseholme society' (p. 79), such as Daisy's

inept attempt to dispense her Guru in 'small doses', are conceived as
challenging 'darling Lucia to mutual combat'; and they always strike
the febrile Georgie (in a running gag) as 'sheer Bolshevism'.

We are also immediately introduced in the first chapter to Lucia's
cultural pretensions which prove an inexhaustible source of comedy
throughout the series. They are encapsulated in Benson's pleasing,
innovative riffs on her devotion to her favourite composer 'the noble
Beethoven':

> and many were the evenings when with lights quenched and only
> the soft effulgence of the moon pouring in through the uncurtained
> windows, she sat with her profile, cameo-like (or liker perhaps to
> the head on a postage stamp) against the dark oak walls of her
> music-room, and entranced herself and her listeners, if there were
> people to dinner, with the exquisite pathos of the first movement
> of the 'Moonlight Sonata'. Devotedly as she worshipped the Master,
> whose picture hung above her Steinway Grand, she could never
> bring herself to believe that the two succeeding movements were
> on the same sublime level as the first, and besides they 'went' very
> much faster. But she had seriously thought, as she came down in
> the train today . . . of trying to master them, so that she could get
> through their intricacies with tolerable accuracy.   [pp. 44–5]

Here, as ever, Lucia continually delights us because we inhabit her
mind ('the exquisite pathos of the first movement') and see the moon's
effulgence through her eyes while always aware of the monitoring
satirical voice of the author ('with tolerable accuracy'). Lucia's
'dramatic instincts' are fully displayed, but her romantic view of the
Sonata is inseparable from her ineptitude as a pianist even though,
we learn, she practised everyday. Similarly, Lucia's fastidious ideas
about music are subtly mocked, as with her fixed conviction of ' "the
impossibility of hearing music at all, if you are stuck in the middle of
a row of people" ' (p. 50). Her (unconscious) *non-sequitur* suggests
that all concerts are a waste of time and elegantly hints that unlike
'the noble Beethoven', the self-entranced Lucia is deaf because she is
incapable of listening. Similarly, Lucia's entranced, obtuse conviction
that she has transformed the remote Elizabethan village of Riseholme
into 'the palace of culture' (p. 46) continually inspires Benson's flights
of drollery. Thus, the 'quaintnesses' and 'humorous touches' of
Lucia's home The Hurst are 'whimsicalities' designed to amuse her
guests and to provide light and amusing topics of conversation as

they enter her drawing-room. However, such objects as 'a china canary in a Chippendale cage' and the dovecote surrounded by 'several pigeons of Copenhagen china' and 'the mechanical nightingale in a bush' invite the reader to collaborate with the author's satirical registering of his heroine's lowbrow vulgarity.

2

Masters refers to Lucia's subjects and all subsequent minor characters in the Mapp and Lucia series, as 'an enchanting cast of one-note grotesques' and rightly attributes the 'sunny qualities of these novels' to their 'unchanging simplicity'.[7] Because we can identify them through their 'tags' (Mr Wyse's bows, Benjy's 'ejaculation of "*Quai-hai*" to his maid') they inevitably recall Dickens's caricatures. But, as the opening pages of *Queen Lucia* clearly establish, Benson's characters are not warped or shaped as in Dickens by either toil, the environment, oppressive bureaucracies, political élites or the excesses of capitalism. They resemble, rather, as Benson signals, 'The Characters of Theophrastus' which Lucia enjoys perusing at the end of *Lucia's Progress*, in that they are pure characters who are disengaged from history and lack either an ethical or political dimension, and are defined only by 'the master impulse which characterises them'.[8] Lucia reads to Georgie 'in the English version the sketch of Benjy's prototype' (*Lucia's Progress* in Volume Two, p. 451), namely 'The Fabricator', who also makes up 'untrue stories' that rely on 'the kind of sources nobody could check' (*The Character Sketches*, p. 35). Similarly, Mr Wyse represents 'The Flatterer', Mr Quantock 'The Shamelessly Greedy Man', Miss Mapp combines 'The Penny-Pincher' and 'The Slanderer', and Lucia is a supreme 'Show-Off'; and because all the characters are hypocrites and fibbers they qualify as variations of 'The Insincere Man'. They never cease to amuse because of Benson brilliant variations on their defining gestures, habits and speech patterns.

Disengaged from history and politics, the gullibilities of these characters are not fashioned by the lure of the varieties of legal, political and financial 'humbug' that Dickens explores in (say) *Little*

7 Introduction to *Mapp and Lucia*, Penguin Modern Classics, 2004, pp. 7–8
8 Theophrastus, *The Character Sketches*, translated, edited and introduced by Warren Anderson, p. xvii. Theophrastus was a student of Aristotle and his thirty character sketches (c.319 BC) became the core of the character as a genre.

Dorrit. Rather they are (Daisy especially) attracted to fads and are hoodwinked by charlatans such as the Guru (yoga and meditation) and the Princess (séances) in *Queen Lucia*: and subsequently, throughout these novels, Benson delightfully mocks all his characters' strenuous attempts to tap their 'unconscious minds' through say meditation, ouija boards, planchettes or spiritism, all of which offer, through such processes as the emptying of the self, random association and automatic writing, the possibilities of discovering alternative ways of being and acting. They all fail, usually hilariously, because their random thoughts are utterly preoccupied by, and are saturated in, the trivia of the everyday. They may glimpse like Lucia (in her usual high-toned manner) that 'the world and its empty vanities had been too much with her' (p. 571), but they cannot have 'too much' of the 'emotional bread' their queen and the circulation of gossip in their small kingdom continually supplies. Similarly, Benson ridicules all attempts to improve health and slim waistlines through vegetarianism and the 'pursuance of the simple life' which leads Isabel Poppitt to sleep 'between blankets in the back-yard' and to eat 'uncooked vegetables out of a wooden bowl like a dog' (*Mapp and Lucia* in Volume Two, p. 88).

'Among the limbo of her [Daisy's] discarded beliefs' it is her 'Uric-Acid fad' which most appeals to Benson's love of the ridiculous.[9] Daisy and her husband Robert are a wonderfully ill-matched pair, because like characters out of Theophrastus they are governed by opposing master impulses, faddism (in this instance about diet) and greed. Hence:

Well might poor Robert remember the devastation of his home when Daisy, after the perusal of a little pamphlet . . . called 'The Uric Acid Monthly', came to the shattering conclusion that her buxom frame consisted almost entirely of waste-products which must be eliminated. For a greedy man the situation was frankly intolerable, for when he continued his ordinary diet . . . she kept pointing to his well-furnished plate, and told him that every atom of that beef or mutton and potatoes, turned from the moment he swallowed it into chromogens and toxins, and that his apparent

9 Masters reports that Benson's album, 'The Book of Fearfuljoy', included 'A copy of an unlikely magazine published in Connecticut, *The Uric Acid Monthly* . . . juxtaposed with an announcement that "A handsome widow has been unveiled in memory of the late vicar" ' (p. 180).

appetite was merely the result of fermentation . . . Tea and coffee were taboo, since they flooded the blood with poisons, and the kitchen boiler rumbled day and night to supply the rivers of boiling water with which (taken in sips) she inundated her system. Strange gaunt females used to come down from London, with small parcels full of tough food that tasted of travelling-bags and contained so much nutrition that a portmanteau full of it would furnish the daily rations of an army. Luckily even her iron constitution could not stand the strain of such ideal living for long, and her growing anaemia threatened to undermine a constitution seriously impaired by the precepts of perfect health.   [pp. 78–9]

Benson's satire is superbly controlled, mixing hyperbole ('shattering conclusion', 'rivers of boiling water'), wit ('taken in sips') and sarcasm ('such ideal living') and ending with an elegant aphorism that debunks all dietary faddists.

Benson was aware that as a writer 'my chief faculty lies in teasing the gilding off things which appear to be distinguished and are really common' (cited, Masters, p. 146). From the moment the Guru is first described in Daisy's letter to Lucia – ' "I don't even know his name, and his religion forbids him to tell it me . . . " ' (p. 58) – we know he is a fraud and sit back and enjoy the farcical battle between Daisy and Lucia to manage and own an evident charlatan who is certain to make 'such sillies' of them all (p. 135). The Guru's Eastern philosophy, his 'Great Message, a Word of Might, full of Love and Peace' (p. 127), is rather crudely rendered 'common' when Hermy reveals that the 'Word' that so moved Riseholme was delivered by a mere cook from an Indian Restaurant in London who first gulls and then robs Daisy, Lucia and Georgie. In the weightless world of Riseholme there are, of course, no repercussions because they all prefer to lose their possessions rather than be exposed as fools. The Guru's yoga exercises also yield much incidental mirth. Thus, they prove too much for Daisy who, struggling to stand on one leg in the middle of her lawn, 'looked like a little round fat stork, whose legs had not grown, but who preserved the habits of her kind' (p. 68). This exercise later prompts a hilarious conversation when the Guru admits it is ' "difficult for globe" ', but he assures Georgie that Daisy will be fine because ' "she has white soul" ' (p. 99).

In *Lucia in London* the heroine is a wonderful conduit for Benson's free-wheeling satirisation of the Post-Cubists because she is so desperate to be *au fait* and, as ever, is prone to error. Consider the following passage where she 'revelled in the works of these remarkable artists' in the company of Mrs Allingsby, who 'was tall and weird and intense, dressed rather like a bird-of-paradise that had been out in a high gale, but very well connected':

> Some were portraits and some landscapes, and it was usually easy to tell which was which, because a careful scrutiny revealed an eye or a stray mouth in some, and a tree or a house in others. Lucia was specially enthusiastic over a picture of Waterloo Bridge, but she had mistaken the number in the catalogue, and it proved to be a portrait of the artist's wife.   [p. 512]

Mrs Allingsbury also prompts two of my favourite jokes in the whole Mapp and Lucia series. The first combines a waspish, camp observation about the inhabitants of a *demi-monde* with a beautifully balanced aphorism about the back-scratching interrelationship between any élite, modish clique and the fawning media: '[S]he had collected round her a group of interesting outlaws, of whom the men looked like women, and the women like nothing at all, and though nobody knew what they were talking about, they themselves were talked about.' The second, following Benson's superb mockery of Mrs Allingsbury's swaying response to Sigismund's 'most rhythmical' painting of his wife, is her unconventional invitation to Lucia to meet him: ' "Breakfast about half-past twelve. Vegetarian with cocktails" ' (p. 512).

3

The most important character (after Lucia) in *Queen Lucia* and *Lucia in London* is the famous diva Olga Braceley, who differs from all the other characters because she is an adult and her manners and behaviour are always exemplary. She resembles, rather, her author in that they are both highly successful and famous artists, both are aware (in Olga's words) that ' "[t]here are big things in the world . . . seas, continents, people, movements, emotions" ', both are urbane and sophisticated, and both share an interest in, and a moral code that is alien to, the ' "darling twopenny place" ' of Riseholme (p. 232). When Olga first arrives in Riseholme she anticipates a quiet retreat to a place where ' "[n]othing ever happens" ', but by the end she laughingly admits to her devotee Georgie that ' "I never knew before how terribly interesting little things were. It's all wildly exciting . . . Is it all of you who take such a tremendous interest in them that makes them so absorbing, or is it that they are absorbing in themselves ... ?" ' (p. 231). At such moments Olga functions as Benson's ideal reader and we are steered, even bribed, to answer 'yes' to both questions because, as we have seen, the characters are totally immersed in the latest 'news' of each other's doings, and their incorrigibly curious conjectures and reactions to them, which the reader is invited to share, constitute the stuff of the novel.

From the moment Olga enters *Queen Lucia* the novel becomes rather schematic because Lucia is in every respect her opposite and inferior. Lucia is a fake and all her actions are calculated whereas Olga is natural and we admire the 'candour and friendliness of that beautiful face' (p. 112); Lucia is malicious, selfish and obtuse, whereas Olga is good-natured, kind and intelligent; Lucia is a bungling pretentious pianist, whereas Olga is a serious professional who manifests a 'concentrated seriousness' which Lucia does not understand (p. 129); Lucia's parties centre around herself and are carefully staged and formal, whereas Olga's are invitations to 'be silly for an hour or two' (p. 153) and her 'intense enjoyment of her own party' galvanises 'everybody into a much keener gaiety than was at all usual in Riseholme' (p. 157), and she 'causes others to talk' rather than seeking their admiration; and, finally, Lucia is an appalling snob who defers to Ladies and Countesses whereas Olga finds Lady Ambermere ridiculous. The greatest difference, however, is that of social status, most evident in *Lucia in London* where Lucia shamelessly uses people to clamber into the most fashionable and artistic circles that Olga, as a diva, serenely inhabits.

Inevitably, in *Queen Lucia*, Lucia views Olga as a rival, but there can be no contest, not only because Olga is her manifest superior but because Lucia is the inevitable victim of her own pretentiousness. Consequently she submits herself to a succession of humiliations, including the exposure in Chapter Twelve of her lack of Italian when Olga, taking Lucia and Peppino's Italian for granted, asks them to dinner to talk to Signor Cortese who has written a new opera, *Lucretia*, especially for her. The first of several humiliations connected to her lack of musicality occurs when the great diva quite naturally assumes from all she has heard that the leader of culture in Riseholme is a good pianist. Thus when she arrives late at Lucia's party and realises that the gathered guests are longing to hear her sing she graciously asks her hostess, ' "Do you play?" ' and inadvertently unleashes a terrible fiasco:

Lucia could not smile any more than she was smiling already.

'Is it very diffy?' she asked. 'Could I read it, Georgie? Shall I try?' She slid on to the music-stool.

'Me to begin?' she asked, finding that Olga had opened the book at the salutation of Brünnhilde [from Wagner's *Siegfried*], which Lucia had practised so diligently all the morning.

She got no answer. Olga, standing by her, had . . . some air of intense concentrated seriousness which Lucia did not understand at all. She was looking straight in front of her, gathering herself in, and paying not the smallest attention to Lucia or anybody else.

'One, two,' said Lucia. 'Three. Now,' and she plunged wildly into a sea of demi-semi-quavers. Olga had just opened her mouth, but shut it again.

'No,' she said. 'Once more,' and she whistled the *motif*.

'Oh! it's so diffy!' said Lucia, beginning again. 'Georgie! Turn over!'

Georgie turned over, and Lucia, counting audibly to herself, made an incomparable mess all over the piano.

Olga turned to her accompanist.

'Shall I try?' she said.

She sat down at the piano, and made some sort of sketch of the accompaniment, simplifying, and yet retaining the essence. And then she sang.   [p. 129]

Benson's adoration of Olga almost matches Georgie's and Lucia is reduced to a quivering child who retreats into baby-talk, counts audibly like a beginner, and then relieves herself 'all over the piano'. This is the first and most excruciating example of what Olga, talking to Georgie towards the end of the novel, calls Lucia's making ' "such a dreadful ass of herself" ' while thinking ' "it was my fault" '. Olga rightly insists the fault is primarily Lucia's because ' "she's quite the stupidest woman I ever saw" ' (p. 210), but she also feels embarrassed for her. In *Middlemarch*, George Eliot famously stated, with regard to Dorothea's failure to imagine how being Mr Casaubon feels to Mr Casaubon: 'We are all of us born in moral stupidity.' Clearly Olga has grown up and is able to sense Lucia's 'equivalent centre of self', but the case is always very different with Lucia, as when, for example, she tosses and turns in her bed and reflects on a sequence of 'unlucky affairs' (p. 186). Inevitably, Olga's invitation to meet and talk Italian to Signor Cortese surfaces:

She should have been told what was expected of her, so as to give her the chance of having a previous engagement. Lucia hated underhand ways, and they were particularly odious in one whom she had been willing to educate and refine up to the highest standards of Riseholme. Indeed it looked as if Olga's nature was actually incapable of receiving cultivation . . . Olga clearly meant mischief: she wanted to set herself up as leader of Art and Culture in Riseholme. Her conduct admitted of no other explanation.

[p. 187]

Georgie wryly calls such thinking 're-christened' (p. 189), but the process leaves the reader wincing with laughter at Lucia's unconscious hypocrisy and at her outrageous, self-regarding, mean-spirited mis-reading of Olga. Lucia becomes an embarrassment to Georgie and a figure of fun for the reader when she constantly carps about Olga's 'commonness' and her 'romping'; and she is always hoist with her own petard, as when she has the gall to bitch that Olga's singing is 'theatrical'. In the artificial worlds of the Mapp and Lucia series, Lucia's 'moral stupidity' is, however, the norm; and, indeed, much of the novels' excruciating comedy derives from our participation (as here) in Lucia's inability to assess the relationship between her incorrigible impulses and her disastrous behaviour and in her strenuous, ludicrous attempts to justify herself to herself, while trashing the motives of others.

During her conversation with Georgie, Olga also generously recognises that she is partly to blame for ' "poor Mrs Lucas . . . feeling out of it, and neglected and dethroned" ' (p. 210) because she has inadvertently exposed her pretensions, but she also acts as Georgie's moral compass when she points out his ' "selfishness" ' in allowing their new friendship to supplant his old relationship with Lucia. From this point on Olga stage-manages the ending of the novel when she orders him to ' "comfort her and make her feel you can't get on without her" ' by organising a party at his house on Christmas night (to which, pointedly, she will be not invited), which will culminate after dinner, at his special request, with a replay of Lucia's tableau of Brünnhilde, ' "and then I think you must ask me in afterwards" ' to admire it (p. 212). Georgie does not find this 'mission' easy because Lucia acts in a 'bright and unreal' manner, professing concern for Miss Bracely: ' "Not overtired with practising that new opera? *Lucy Greecia*, was it? Oh, how silly I am! *Lucretia*; that was it, by the extraordinary Neapolitan" ' (p. 217). The sheer malice and envy in Lucia's 'unrehearsed speech' (a great rarity) prompts Georgie's equally rare moral recognition that he had never 'conjectured how she must have suffered before she attained to so superb a sourness' (p. 217). This appeal to the reader's compassion for Lucia's suffering derives, of course, from Olga's moral instruction and Benson palpably uses her to solicit our sympathy for a monster of selfishness who is driven by desires that she can neither acknowledge nor control and that are, as we have seen, tied to her ambitions and not to her emotions.

It is easy for Olga to forgive Lucia because her 'rudeness' and 'absurd patronising airs' (p. 210) do not hurt her; they amuse her, rather, as they do her creator. Moreover, Olga's dethronement of Lucia was accidental and not the result of her subjects' Bolshevism. Lucia quite simply is as out of her depth with Olga as Mapp proves to be with her. Olga, therefore, like a fairy godmother ensures that Lucia regains control of her toy kingdom, replays her dreadful tableau of Brünnhilde, and organises once again, as always assisted by Georgie, 'all manner of edifying gaieties' at The Hurst. The closing pages are delightful because Lucia, entirely unconscious of Olga's generosity and Georgie's collusion, is thankfully released from her sourness to make an ass of herself again, to condescend to her benefactor, and generally to astonish and amuse through the sheer scale of her obtuseness. Thus, Lucia's musical incompetence and tin ear resurface brilliantly when her prejudice against carols and carol-singers (so inferior to Beethoven!) cause her to confuse Olga's beautiful solo with that of "the small red-headed boy who nearly deafens me in church ... Don't you hope his voice will crack soon?" ' (p. 225). Then, discussing her Brünnhilde performance with Olga, she inadvertently reveals how absolutely dire it was and how utterly ignorant she is about opera when she concedes that, ' "Singing, of course, as you say, helps it out: you can express yourself so much by singing. You are so lucky there" ' (p. 226). Finally, as promised, Olga attends all Lucia's parties and allows her to trespass on her good nature by always accepting her condescending invitations to sing. Georgie, however, is now (wisely) the pianist, and Olga and the reader are rewarded with Lucia's sublimely obtuse and irrepressibly hopeful introduction to the performance: ' "I declare I am jealous of him: I shall pop into his place someday!" ' (p. 230).

Lucia arrives in London in *Lucia in London* determined to become 'the supreme arbiter' of taste as she had been in Riseholme (p. 513), and like any modern would-be celebrity she immediately exploits the media, through Stephen Merivall the gossip-columnist 'Hermione', ensuring that her arrival and every subsequent move up the social ladder is reported. Thus we learn that Lucia was 'as all the world knew, a most accomplished musician and Shakespearian scholar' and Hermione assures his readers that 'nobody would suspect the blue-stocking in the brilliant, beautiful and witty hostess whose presence would lend an added gaiety to the London season' (p. 482-3). This is all great fun, as is her first letter to 'Georgino Mio' wherein she professes her hatred of vulgar publicity and recounts her pleasant chat with the Prime Minister who, of course, like everybody else mentioned in the letter, sought her out. Georgie sees through this pretence and ascribes her success to 'her moral force that made them powerless in her grip' (p. 488). Georgie's conviction signals again the absence of any ethical standards in the insulated, morally stupid kingdom of Riseholme. Lucia, rather, grips her social prey because she judges and uses people according to their 'value', and it is precisely her extravagant, transparent, 'undaunted and indefatigable' pursuit of social status that appeals to (Lady) Adele Brixton, 'a lean, intelligent American of large fortune who found she got on better without her husband', and who ruefully acknowledged: ' "I've been a climber myself . . . But I was a snail compared to her" ' (p. 554).

Lady Brixton is so amused by Lucia's vain enthusiastic prattling about her social triumphs, by such fatuous cultural observations as ' "there is something primitive about the flute. So Theocritan!" ' and especially by her 'curtsey' to the telephone when she pretends that Peppino's voice was that of ' "your Highness" ', that she founds and becomes 'high priestess' of 'the secret society of the Luciaphils'. All members must at all times show 'complete goodwill towards Lucia' (p. 557), and, as Adele advises an initiate, ' "You mustn't laugh at her ever. You must just richly enjoy her" ' (p. 590). At this point the Luciaphils take over the London plot, beginning in Chapter Seven with Adele's sly acceptance of Lucia's pretence that she is viewing Herbert Alton's exhibition of caricatures for the first time when she 'knew she had been here before' (p. 567). Similarly, Adele secretly facilitates Lucia's 'stunt' of Stephen as her lover and she arranges

for ' "people she [Lucia] will revel in" ' to attend her house party
(p. 591). We are assured by the narrator that this was all 'splendid
stuff for Luciaphils' such as Adele, who is said to be 'entranced' by
Lucia's swanking, but I'm not sure it is for the reader. Their aim
(like Benson's) is to ensure that she is 'at the top of her form' (p.
592), and their secret manoeuvres culminate in Marcia's invitation
to Lucia to join her in her bedroom after dinner where her fellow
Luciaphils, Aggie and Adele, actively encourage the 'blissfully unconscious' Lucia to preen while struggling to contain their sniggers
over her preposterous pretensions and fundamental chasteness. Lucia
is reduced to a sad, pathetic figure because she ecstatically regards 'a
good-night talk' with a duchess (Maria) as nearer 'Nirvana' than
even 'the paradise' of the earlier ball and vainly thinks that after
'months of strenuous effort' she now has three women hanging on
her every word, 'just as Riseholme'. Instead she is induced to indulge
in high-sounding confused twaddle about ' "our runnings-about" '
as ways of ' "widen[ing] our horizons" ' and extending ' "our very
souls" ' in a ' "multiplication of experience" ' (p. 597). The scene has
an uncomfortable edge because the Luciaphils are snobs who enjoy
toying with a foolish woman who desperately wages a futile campaign
to join their ranks. Thus, Lucia may at such moments be 'at the top
of her form', but the Luciaphils supplement the narrator's ridicule of
the hapless heroine's delusions of grandeur. In marked contrast to
Olga, at the end of *Queen Lucia*, who is embarrassed by her part in
Lucia's capacity for making an ass of herself and who richly enjoys,
along with the reader, seeing Lucia restored to her Queenship, the
Luciaphils are an unattractive bunch of cynics whose professed
'reverent affection' for Lucia is shallow and condescending.

Lucia is out of her depth in London and because she functions as
the Luciaphils' 'stunt' and fails to engage their feelings, her urgent
need to fill her days and her non-stop strivings for social consequence
induce a sense of pity and of waste. The end of the social season and
Peppino's illness prompt a return to Riseholme where she belongs.
Georgie and all her subjects know Queen Lucia is 'a poseuse, a sham
and a snob', but while she is in London he and Riseholme 'miss her
dreadfully' because 'though she might infuriate you, she prevented
your being dull' (p. 488). On her return she soon 'excites interest
and keeps people on the boil' (p. 605) as only she can, organising
golf tournaments, revitalising their play with 'planchette' and giving
a new urgency to the spirit messages, and laying 'down the law a
good deal on auction bridge' (p. 625). Order is restored in her

kingdom and even Daisy's accidental burning down of the town's junk-filled museum, established during Lucia's absence, proves a godsend, because the insurers more than cover the costs.

5

Benson candidly recognised in his last book and memoir, *Final Edition* (1940), that 'I made my people bustle about [but] they lacked the red corpuscle' (p. 182). As his biographers stress, Benson, like all his siblings, was 'deeply afraid of the sexual impulse' (Masters, p. 245) and could not bear to be touched. He was, perhaps, a repressed rather than active homosexual, but his distrust and fear of sex vitiates and distorts his portrayals of human relationships whether heterosexual in (say) *Mike* (1916) or *Lovers and Friends* (1921) or between piano teacher and pupil in *The Challoners* (1904) or public-school boys in *David Blaize* (1916). Thus, in the former Mike is paralysed by the thought of sex with Sybil and they settle for loving 'as only brother and sister can love, without trouble' (*Mike*, p. 153), and in the latter David's 'white innocence' (*David Blaize*, p. 149), Maddox admits, enables him to overcome his own beastly, 'filthy' feelings towards his own sex. As Brian Masters wryly observes, 'the love between the two boys is celebrated precisely for its purity and control, as if self-denial were the high road to ecstasy' (Masters, p. 245). Benson's inability or reluctance to explore his characters' sexuality ensures that most of his serious novels about human relationships are mediocre, confused and sentimental.

Benson's Mapp and Lucia novels, however, are farces and it is a given that all the characters lack 'the red corpuscle', and that marriage as in P. G. Wodehouse's Jeeves series is always to be avoided. But, whereas Bertie Wooster fears women such as Cynthia 'who wants a fellow to sort out a career and what not',[10] almost all the characters in the Mapp and Lucia novels have no interest in or yearnings for either marriage, sex or intimacy. Among the four notable bachelors, two of them, Georgie Pilson and 'Hermione' (Stephen Meriall, who appears only in *Lucia in London*), are extremely effeminate and are terrified of women's sexuality, whereas Major Benjy and his drinking partner Captain Puffin are cartoon bachelors. The Captain avoids and distrusts women, but the Major has cultivated 'no end of a reputation in amorous and honourable affairs' and for 'deeds of blood-thirsty

10 Wodehouse, *The Inimitable Jeeves*, Penguin, p. 125

gallantry' (p. 380). He is, of course, as Miss Mapp realises, a coward
and when he calls round in formal wear to apologise for his drunken
lack of chivalry towards her, she forgives him, but her punishment
reduces him to a buffoon in a farce: she inveigles him to accompany
her on her 'little shoppings' and the hapless Major, 'attired as for
marriage – top-hat, frock-coat and buttonhole' (p. 385), as if by ' "a
conjuring trick" ' (p. 389) is slowly paraded through the streets: 'She
allowed him (such was her firmness in "spoiling" him) to carry her
shopping basket, and when that was full, she decked him like a
sacrificial ram with little parcels hung by loops of string' (p. 386). As
Miss Mapp rightly recognises, in Tilling 'the men don't count'.
Similarly, the single women are either riotously masculine, like
Georgie's two plain strapping sisters Hermy and Ursy, who 'liked
pigs and dogs and otter-hunting and mutton chops' and who are
regarded as 'rather a discordant element in Riseholme' (p. 62), or,
like the wonderfully raucous, outrageous post-impressionist painter,
'quaint Irene', who adores Lucia, they are lesbians.[11]

   These one-note caricatures are farcical and never cease to entertain
because they all act according to type. Lucia's lack of passion and
fear of sex, however, are more complicated and disquieting, and
they are raised at the beginning of *Queen Lucia*, where she gushes
that ' "it is only in loneliness, as Goethe says, that your perceptions
put forth their flowers" ' (p. 50). Lucia amuses because her desires
in common with all the Riseholmites and subsequently the Tillingites
are entirely social, and we are told that 'she dedicated all that she
had of ease, leisure and income' (p. 53) 'to the permanence and
security of her own throne as queen of Riseholme'. Lucia's total
commitment prompts Benson to stand apart from his creation and
acknowledge that the inspiration for and butt of his wit and humour
misses out on 'the ravages of emotional living . . . such emotions as
she was victim of were the sterile and ageless ecstasies of art; such
desires as beset her were not connected with her affections, but her
ambitions' (p. 53). Benson's melancholic, compassionate reflections
on Lucia's etiolated emotional life are surprising, but they explain
why sex, passion and love whether for others or for God ('she
believed in God in much the same way as she believed in Australia')
are not to be found in the kingdom of Riseholme; and 'passion,
except in the sense of temper, did not exist in Tilling' (p. 339).

11 Irene's sexuality and love for Lucia is discussed in my Introduction to
   Volume Two of the Wordsworth Classics edition of the series (pp. 23–5).

Romance, also, is inconceivable because the characters' besetting desires, like Lucia's, are not compatible with such emotions: in Mapp's case they are extinguished by her insatiable craving to manipulate others; in Georgie's case they are expended upon his effeminate love of clothes and valetudinarian needs for creature comforts and pampering; and in Diva's case they are eclipsed by her obsessive pursuit of the newest fads. Moreover, of course, all the inhabitants display an unappeasable, competitive appetite for the latest 'news' and gossip that usually (except in the case of 'quaint Irene') banishes both erotic and kind thoughts of others.

In Chapter Two of *Queen Lucia* Benson archly informs us, 'In order to save subsequent disappointment', that even 'the smallest approach to a flirtation' between Lucia and Georgie Pillson, her gentleman-in-waiting and ADC, her devoted subordinate, will not occur. Their relationship is wittily described as a 'bloodless idyll': bloodless because 'neither of them . . . had ever flirted with anybody at all' – and never will because Lucia is a prude and chaste by nature and Georgie in a fey construction is, as Riseholme recognises, not 'an obtrusively masculine sort of person'; an 'idyll' because they both collude in and benefit from one of Riseholme's 'polite and pleasant fictions', namely 'that Georgie was passionately attached to her' (p. 61). Their 'bloodless idyll' invites Benson's unsettling, sly mirth as he records their delight in baby-language (' "Me vewy sowwy" ') which 'was the utmost extent of their carnal familiarities, and with bright eyes fixed on the music, they would break into peals of girlish laughter'.

This pattern and uneasy 'camp' humour recur in *Lucia in London* where her desires are inseparable from her social ambitions. Thus, though 'The idea of having a real lover was, of course, absolutely abhorrent to her whole nature . . . the reputation of having a lover was a wholly different matter . . . and most decidedly it gave a woman a certain cachet' (p. 559). She settles on Stephen Meriall who reminds her of Georgie. All will be well, Lucia thinks, provided he 'did not yield to one of those rash and turbulent impulses of the male', but Stephen is a safe choice because, as Adele bitchily observes, he looks ' "as if he had been labelled 'Man' by mistake when he was born, and ought to have been labelled 'Lady' " ' (p. 555). Adele and her fellow Luciaphils see through and encourage Lucia's 'stunt' of annexing Stephen as a 'lover'; and blissfully unaware of their amusement at her public gestures of affection that rub so excruciatingly against the grain of her chaste temperament ('She was a shade too close at first, and edged slightly away'), she is reduced to a ludicrous and rather pathetic figure. Similarly, Stephen's bewilderment and distaste for the female sex make for an excruciating 'camp' comedy as he struggles to make sense of her 'little signals of intimacy' when (truly!) 'he could not accuse himself of thought, word or deed which could possibly have given rise to any disordered fancy of hers that he observed her with a lascivious eye' (p. 564).

The culmination of Lucia's 'stunt' of 'advertising the guilt of their blameless relationship' occurs at Adele's house-party where she arranges for the pair to sleep in adjoining rooms and, of course, as in farce, Lucia accidentally enters Stephen's bedroom:

> Two yards in front of her, by the side of the bed, was standing Stephen, voluptuous in honey-coloured pyjamas. For one awful second – for she felt sure this was her room (*and so did he*) – they stared at each other in dead silence.
>
> 'How dare you?' said Stephen, so agitated that he could scarcely form the syllables.
>
> 'And how dare *you*?' hissed Lucia. 'Go out of my room instantly.'
>
> 'Go out of mine!' said Stephen.
>
> Lucia's indignant eye left his horror-stricken face and swept round the room.   [p. 599]

Hilarity, merriment and embarrassment are notably absent in this singular reworking of a stock scene in farces. The humour is camp ('voluptuous') and disconcerting as the pair evince a startling mutual disgust and loathing of sex. Lucia is humiliated and left to contemplate that Stephen would think that she had come to his room 'on the sinister errand of love', and the latter is moved to consider whether 'this pleasant public stunt' had become 'a need of her nature' (p. 600). Stephen's guess is shrewd and the same need to be the centre of attention that prompts Lucia to pretend to have a lover even though she fears sex, motivates all Mapp's vain actions, including such palpable fictions as that Major Benjy and Captain Puffin had fought a duel over her and, when married to the former, that she is pregnant – much to his and everybody's understandable surprise.

Lucia and Stephen's loathing of and panic over the possibility of sex strain the boundaries of farce, and the vein of bitchiness evident in the portrayal of the latter is disquieting.[12] It is, however, in keeping

---

12 I discuss the repetition of this pattern and the edgy humour in *Lucia's Progress*, when Georgie and Lucia contemplate and negotiate their marriage, in my Introduction to Volume Two (pp. 21–3).

with Benson's persistently negative presentation of marriage, manifest in Miss Mapp's successful plan to shame Benjy-boy into marriage at the end of *Mapp and Lucia* by forgiving him for his hasty spending of her bequest to him. 'And then,' Miss Mapp crows, 'Lulu [her demeaning name for Lucia] will only be a widow, and I a married woman with a well-controlled husband' (p. 266). Fortunately, given these ugly motives, Benjy's drinking is never controlled and his alcoholic misdemeanours never cease to amuse throughout the series.

6

Miss Mapp, published two years after *Queen Lucia*, is the first of the four novels set in Tilling, which as Benson genially acknowledges in his brief Preface is actually modelled on the town of Rye, where as a resident he shares his view from the garden-room of his home, Lamb House, with the titular central character. As the Map of Tilling (pp. 38–9) shows, the houses and the narrow cobbled streets in the novels are clearly identifiable, and the latter's sharp, steep turns are still as difficult to negotiate by car as they were when the Poppits with Susan in her sables ostentatiously insisted on driving 'the Royce' very short distances to shop, thereby 'extinguishing' Miss Mapp's 'survey' and inconveniencing the novels' pedestrians and artists marooned on the pavements.[13]

Benson had a sure sense of Mapp, as a letter to George Plank illustrates:[14]

> I outlined an elderly atrocious spinster and established her at Lamb House. She should be the centre of social life, abhorred and dominant, and she should sit like a great spider behind her curtains in the garden-room, spying on all her friends. . . . Of course, it would all be small beer, but one could get a head upon it of jealousies, malignities and devouring inquisitiveness.

In the opening of *Miss Mapp* Benson consciously recalls *Queen Lucia*, because both begin on a hot July morning and focus upon the central character, but as the titles alone indicate, the latter has a

---

13 I would like to thank Terry Harvey of the splendid Martello Bookshop, 26 High Street, Rye, for his kind permission to reproduce the 'Tilling Map' (in a slightly adapted form).

14 Cited, Masters, p. 254. Plank designed the bookplate and illustrated *The Freaks of Mayfair* (1916); he was a close friend (see Masters, pp. 250–2).

public status while the other is a spinster. However, whereas Lucia
happily anticipates a short pleasant walk that will provide her subjects
with 'little thrills of pleasant excitement', Miss Mapp sits isolated
'like a large bird of prey' ominously spying on 'all her friends'.
Disturbingly, her 'vivifying emotions' are 'chronic rage and curiosity'
that have 'preserved . . . an astonishing activity of mind and body . . .
anger and the gravest suspicions about everybody had kept her young
and on the boil' (p. 241). This bleak witticism encapsulates an endemic
nastiness and meanness of spirit that make such fictional counterparts
as Mrs Norris in *Mansfield Park* seem angels of mercy. Miss Mapp is
a monstrous hypocrite, who 'wore a practically perpetual smile when
there was the least chance of being under observation', and a paranoid
who always ascribes foul motives to others because she is certain that
everybody on all occasions is out either to exploit or demean her.
For these reasons she would not be out of place in a Dostoevsky
novel, but as with all Benson's characters her self-consciousness
precludes self-analysis and self-knowledge and in the toy kingdom
of Tilling her malice is always thwarted, and her successive disappointments and small humiliations generate the farcical plot; and
Benson mockingly transmutes her 'chronic rage', 'malignant curiosity
and cancerous suspicions' (p. 253) into the stuff of comedy.

Miss Mapp's shopping in the opening chapter is carried out in a
spirit of militant meanness which is often represented through
Benson's deft exploitation of the 'free indirect style'. Consider for
instance her (perennial) suspicion that she has been overcharged:
'There was an item for suet which she intended to resist to the last
breath of her body, though her butcher would probably surrender
long before that' (p. 252). On the one hand we register Mapp's
embattled, heroic self-conception and smug knowledge that her
butcher (as ever) will cave in; on the other the hyperbole registers
the narrator's sense that Mapp is demented and the long-suffering
butcher would rather not go to battle with a crazy woman over
such 'small beer' as a piece of suet. The narrator drolly assures us
that 'All these quarrelsome errands were meat and drink to Miss
Mapp' (p. 253) – a very different diet from the Riseholmites' whose
'daily bread', courtesy of Lucia's extravagant behaviour and treats,
is made up of those 'little thrills of pleasant excitement and
conjecture' (p. 43).

From such 'small beer' Benson weaves the narrative of *Miss Mapp*,
as in, for example, her reactions in the first chapter to the telephone
call from the Poppits inviting her to tea and a game of bridge that

afternoon. Nothing would seem more innocuous than this sociable invitation, but it causes a 'flood of lurid light' to pour 'into Miss Mapp's mind' (p. 250). 'Lurid light', of course, always shines on wicked witches and other devilish pantomime villains, but Benson obliges the reader to share both 'the lurid light' of Miss Mapp's mind and his hyperbolic version of it. The 'lurid light' is generated by Miss Mapp's righteous, smug envy of the Poppits' wealth and ostentation (she 'suspected them of being profiteers'), and of Mrs Poppit's thoroughly undeserved MBE for services to the local hospital ('entirely confined to putting her motor car at its disposal when she did not want it herself'), and by her conceited, snobbish conviction that 'she alone upheld the dignity of the old families' (p. 249). Nourished by her jealousy and envy, Miss Mapp deduces 'as if by special revelation' that this request is belated and a veiled insult, and her imagined grievance generates a lurid fantasy of the butler's 'brazen impudence' as he turns her away from the Poppits' door. But she still 'had to settle whether she was going to be delighted to accept, or obliged to decline' (p. 250). Her dilemma is utterly trivial, but we are obliged to share her mean-spirited ecstasy when 'A bright . . . joyous . . . diabolical idea struck her' that if she prevaricated she would 'put Isabel in a hole' because she would never be sure whether she should find another player, in which case Miss Mapp would turn up and embarrass her, or risk Miss Mapp not turning up and finding herself a player short. To Mapp's immense satisfaction and the reader's horrified amusement we learn that 'Isabel wouldn't have a tranquil moment all day'.

The joke, however, is on Miss Mapp because she can only ensure Isabel's maximum discomfort if she can ascertain whether there will be seven or eight players, and therefore her strategic shopping trip is fraught because each person she meets and obliquely quizzes alters the equation. The narrator archly assumes our collusion in his protracted teasing of Miss Mapp when he acknowledges that, 'as every reader will have perceived', her fey talk of butterflies and swallows with the Padre camouflages her urgent need to know whether he will be one of the eight bridge players. Our amusement is corroborated by Irene Coles, 'the Disgrace of Tilling and her sex, the suffragette, post-impressionist artist . . . the socialist and the Germanophil', who always leaves Miss Mapp quaking in her shoes because she publicly teases her about her meanness and hypocrisy. Miss Mapp's meeting with 'Quaint Irene' completely upsets her plans because the latter now makes an eighth player, obliging her to set up an easel near the church to enable her to spy on the Poppits' house to check the number of visitors because 'she had made up her mind to "squeeze it in" so that there would be nine gamblers', and so 'Isabel or her mother, if they had any sense of hospitality to their guests, would be compelled to sit out for ever and ever'. Mapp's hypocrisy and sanctimonious appeal to a value ('hospitality') that is inimical to her very being, and her lingering gratification over their discomfort ('ever and ever') are at once odious and very funny. Fortunately, the most obvious alternative, that the aggrieved, untranquil Mapp is simply unable to envisage as she counts the players entering the Poppits' house, is that one of the Poppits would not be there and that their invitation was genuine. Hence to her intense irritation and our gratified amusement she discovers, 'She had completed, instead of spoiling, the second table' (p. 262).

I dwell at some length over this sequence because it is altogether typical of both the narrator's amused toying with his unpleasant creation and of the pattern of the narrative. The novel is constructed out of a series of farcical humiliations ranging from the tiny, such as her failure to detect the brandy and champagne in the redcurrant fool the Poppits serve, to the very public revelation of her secret hoarding of groceries that she limply struggles to pass off as ' "my poor little Christmas presents for your needy parishioners, Padre" ' (p. 313); and as in all good farces Miss Mapp and her guests step into the mess made by the broken bottle of apricots.

Miss Mapp is less engaging and less amusing than *Queen Lucia* and *Lucia in London* because the reader is less active: too often we are privy to the secret facts that Miss Mapp feverishly struggles to decipher, such as the evening preoccupations of Major Benjy and Captain Puffin, and their cowardly flight from the duel is not for us, as for her, 'the great insoluble mystery'. Thus the fundamental incentive to turn the page to discover what happens next, as in (say) Miss Mapp's need to know the number of bridge players, is lacking. The Major and the Captain are, also, pure buffoons and their farcical night-time drinking bouts and their quarrels over worm-casts on golf greens are amusing in themselves, but they are so ludicrous that Miss Mapp's fervent speculations about their 'naughty' evening activities and her designs upon the gallant Major quickly become, as Georgie would say, ' "taresome" '. Moreover, nobody, least of all the author, likes or has a good word to say for Miss Mapp: her main rival Diva sees through her and openly teases her, and the reader like the characters is always invited to snigger at her humiliations and consequent squirmings. In contrast to the sociable Lucia, Mapp is an *isolato*: she doesn't have a faithful husband who admires her attempt to set up a salon in London; she has no Georgie ever-anxious to assist her schemes and to talk to and play duets with; and of course there is no Olga to appeal to our sympathies for the sufferings driving her sourness. Finally, Miss Mapp's 'extraordinary activity of mind' and her energy are entirely negative, feeding off the discomfort and misery she (hopes) to inflict on others, whereas Lucia's energy is positive, expansive and energising, designed (on her own terms of course) to give pleasure to others.[15]

KEITH CARABINE

15 For a continuation of this argument, see my Introduction to Volume Two (pp. 18–19).

BIBLIOGRAPHY

Anderson, Warren (trans.), *Theophrastus: The Character Sketches*, Kent State University Press, 1970

Benson, E. F., *The Challoners*, William Heinemann, London, 1904

—— *David Blaize*, Hodder & Stoughton, London, 1916

—— *Mike*, Cassell, London, 1916

—— *Lovers and Friends*, T. Fisher Unwin, London, 1921

—— *Paying Guests*, Hutchinson, London 1929; reprint, Hogarth Press, London, 1984

—— *As We Were*, Longmans, London, 1930

—— *As We Are*, Longmans, London, 1932

—— *Final Edition*, Longmans, London, 1940

Masters, Brian, *The Life of E. F. Benson*, Chatto and Windus, London, 1991

Palmer, Geoffrey and Lloyd, Noel, *E. F. Benson: As He Was*, Leonard Publishing, Luton, 1988

Revell, Cynthia (compiler), *E. F. Benson as Mayor of Rye, 1934–1937* (Reports from the *Sussex Express* Newspaper), Tilling Society, Martello Bookshop, Rye, 1993

Williams, David, *Genesis and Exodus: A Portrait of the Benson Family*, Hamish Hamilton, London, 1979

1 **Mallards** which is Lamb House in Rye

2 **The Garden-Room**

3 **Captain Puffin's house** which is Little Sussex House in Rye

4 **Major Flint's house** which is opposite Little Sussex House in Rye

5 **Mallards Cottage**

6 **Poppits' house** which is the Old Customs House in Rye

7 **the Padre' house** which is the Old Vicarage in Rye

8 **Diva's house (Wasters, later Ye Olde Tea-House)** which is the Mariners tea-room in Rye

9 **the King's Arms** which is the George in the High Street in Rye

10 **Twistevant's (*greengrocer*)** which is No. 97 in the High Street in Rye

11 **Twemlow's (*grocer*)** which is No. 99 in the High Street in Rye

12 **Worthington's (*butcher*)** which is No. 100 in the High Street in Rye

13 **the Stationer's** which is Barclays Bank in the High Street in Rye

14 **Mr Rice's (*poulterer*)** which is No. 21 in the High Street in Rye

15 **the Post-Office** which is No. 18 & No. 19 in the High Street in Rye

16 **Irene's house Taormina** which is No. 2 in West Street in Rye

17 **Hopkins's (*fishmonger*)** which is Santa Maria in West Street in Rye

18 **the Fruiterer's** which is The Other House in West Street in Rye

19 **the Dentist's in Porpoise Street** which is the first house on the left in Mermaid Street in Rye

20 **the Wyses' house in Porpoise Street** which is Hartshorn House in Mermaid Street in Rye

21 **Dr Dobbie's in Malleson Street** which is Market Road in Rye

22 **Woolgar & Pipstow in Malleson Street** which is Market Road in Rye

23 **the Trader's Arms in Curfew Street** which is the Hope Anchor in Watchbell Street in Rye

24 **the Suntrap in Curfew Street** which is Watchbell Corner in Watchbell Street in Rye

25 **the Norman Tower** which is the Ypres Tower in the Gun Gardens in Rye

26 **Grebe** which is Playden Cottage on the Military Road beyond Rye

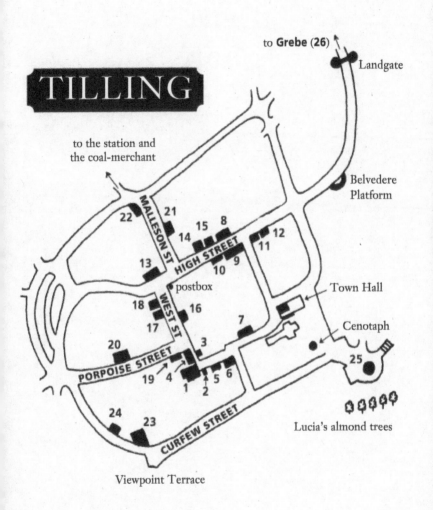

TILLING

to **Grebe** (**26**)

Landgate

to the station and
the coal-merchant

Belvedere
Platform

MALLESON ST
22
21
15 8
14
13
HIGH STREET
11 12
10 9

postbox

Town Hall

WEST ST
18
17
16
7
Cenotaph

20
PORPOISE STREET
3
25
19 4
1 2 5 6

Lucia's almond trees

24 23
CURFEW STREET

Viewpoint Terrace

QUEEN LUCIA

Chapter One

THOUGH THE SUN WAS HOT on this July morning, Mrs Lucas preferred to cover the half-mile that lay between the station and her house on her own brisk feet, and sent on her maid and her luggage in the fly that her husband had ordered to meet her. After those four hours in the train a short walk would be pleasant, but, though she veiled it from her conscious mind, another motive, subconsciously engineered, prompted her action. It would, of course, be universally known to all her friends in Riseholme that she was arriving today by the twelve twenty-six, and at that hour the village street would be sure to be full of them. They would see the fly with luggage draw up at the door of The Hurst, and nobody except her maid would get out.

That would be an interesting thing for them: it would cause one of those little thrills of pleasant excitement and conjectural exercise which supplied Riseholme with its emotional daily bread. They would all wonder what had happened to her, whether she had been taken ill at the very last moment before leaving town, and with her well-known fortitude and consideration for the feelings of others, had sent her maid on to assure her husband that he need not be anxious. That would clearly be Mrs Quantock's suggestion, for Mrs Quantock's mind, devoted as it was now to the study of Christian Science, and the determination to deny the existence of pain, disease and death as regards herself, was always full of the gloomiest views as regards her friends, and on the slightest excuse, pictured that they, poor blind things, were suffering from false claims. Indeed, given that the fly had already arrived at The Hurst, and that its arrival had at this moment been seen by or reported to Daisy Quantock, the chances were vastly in favour of that lady's having already started in to give Mrs Lucas absent treatment. Very likely Georgie Pillson had also seen the anticlimax of the fly's arrival, but he would hazard a much more probable though erroneous solution of her absence. He would certainly guess that she had sent on her maid with her luggage to the station in order to take a seat for her, while she herself, oblivious of the passage of time, was spending her last half-hour in contemplation of the Italian masterpieces at the

National Gallery, or the Greek bronzes at the British Museum. Certainly she would not be at the Royal Academy, for the culture of Riseholme, led by herself, rejected as valueless all artistic efforts later than the death of Sir Joshua Reynolds, and a great deal of what went before. Her husband with his firm grasp of the obvious, on the other hand, would be disappointingly capable, even before her maid confirmed his conjecture, of concluding that she had merely walked from the station.

The motive, then, that made her send her cab on, though subconsciously generated, soon penetrated into her consciousness, and these guesses at what other people would think when they saw it arrive without her, sprang from the dramatic element that formed so large a part of her mentality, and made her always take, as by right divine, the leading part in the histrionic entertainments with which the cultured of Riseholme beguiled or rather strenuously occupied such moments as could be spared from their studies of art and literature, and their social engagements. Indeed she did not usually stop at taking the leading part, but, if possible, doubled another character with it, as well as being stage-manager and adapter, if not designer of scenery. Whatever she did – and really she did an incredible deal – she did it with all the might of her dramatic perception, did it in fact with such earnestness that she had no time to have an eye to the gallery at all, she simply contemplated herself and her own vigorous accomplishment. When she played the piano as she frequently did (reserving an hour for practice every day), she cared not in the smallest degree for what anybody who passed down the road outside her house might be thinking of the roulades that poured from her open window: she was simply Emmeline Lucas, absorbed in glorious Bach or dainty Scarlatti, or noble Beethoven. The latter perhaps was her favourite composer, and many were the evenings when with lights quenched and only the soft effulgence of the moon pouring in through the uncurtained windows, she sat with her profile, cameo-like (or liker perhaps to the head on a postage stamp) against the dark oak walls of her music-room, and entranced herself and her listeners, if there were people to dinner, with the exquisite pathos of the first movement of the 'Moonlight Sonata'. Devotedly as she worshipped the Master, whose picture hung above her Steinway Grand, she could never bring herself to believe that the two succeeding movements were on the same sublime level as the first, and besides they 'went' very much faster. But she had seriously thought, as she came down in the train today and planned her fresh activities at home, of trying to master them, so that she could get through their intricacies with tolerable accuracy. Until then, she would assuredly stop at the end of the first movement in these moonlit séances, and say that the other two were more like morning and afternoon. Then with a sigh she would softly shut the piano lid, and perhaps wiping a little genuine moisture from her eyes, would turn on the electric light and taking up a book from the table, in which a paperknife marked the extent of her penetration, say: 'Georgie, you must really promise me to read this life of Antonio Caporelli the moment I have finished it. I never understood the rise of the Venetian School before. As I read I can smell the salt tide creeping up over the lagoon, and see the campanile of dear Torcello.'

And Georgie would put down the tambour on which he was working his copy of an Italian cope and sigh too.

'You are too wonderful!' he would say. 'How do you find time for everything?'

She rejoined with the apophthegm that made the rounds of Riseholme next day.

'My dear, it is just busy people that have time for everything.'

* * *

It might be thought that even such activities as have here been indicated would be enough to occupy anyone so busily that he would positively not have time for more, but such was far from being the case with Mrs Lucas. Just as the painter Rubens amused himself with being the ambassador to the Court of St James's – a sufficient career in itself for most busy men – so Mrs Lucas amused herself, in the intervals of her pursuit of Art for Art's sake, with being not only an ambassador but a monarch. Riseholme might perhaps, according to the crude materialism of maps, be included in the kingdom of Great Britain, but in a more real and inward sense it formed a complete kingdom of its own, and its queen was undoubtedly Mrs Lucas, who ruled it with a secure autocracy pleasant to contemplate at a time when thrones were toppling, and imperial crowns whirling like dead leaves down the autumn winds. The ruler of Riseholme, happier than he of Russia, had no need to fear the finger of Bolshevism writing on the wall, for there was not in the whole of that vat, which seethed so pleasantly with culture, one bubble of revolutionary ferment. Here there was neither poverty nor discontent nor muttered menace of any upheaval: Mrs Lucas, busy and serene, worked harder than any of her subjects, and exercised an autocratic control over a nominal democracy.

Something of the consciousness of her sovereignty was in her mind, as she turned the last hot corner of the road and came in sight of the village street that constituted her kingdom. Indeed it belonged to her, as treasure trove belongs to the Crown, for it was she who had been the first to begin the transformation of this remote Elizabethan village into the palace of culture that was now reared on the spot where ten years ago an agricultural population had led bovine and unilluminated lives in their cottages of grey stone or brick and timber. Before that, while her husband was amassing a fortune, comfortable in amount and respectable in origin, at the Bar, she had merely held up a small dim lamp of culture in Onslow Gardens. But both her ambition and his had been to bask and be busy in artistic realms of their own when the materialistic needs were provided for by sound investments, and so when there were the requisite thousands of pounds in secure securities she had easily persuaded him to buy three of these cottages that stood together in a low two-storeyed block. Then, by judicious removal of partition-walls, she had, with the aid of a sympathetic architect, transmuted them into a most comfortable dwelling, subsequently building on to them a new wing, that ran at right angles at the back, which was, if anything, a shade more inexorably Elizabethan than the stem on to which it was grafted, for here was situated the famous smoking-parlour, with rushes on the floor, and a dresser ranged with pewter tankards, and leaded lattice-windows of glass so antique that it was practically impossible to see out of them. It had a huge open fireplace framed in oak beams with a seat on each side of the iron-backed hearth within the chimney, and a genuine spit hung over the middle of the fire. Here, though in the rest of the house she had for the sake of convenience allowed the installation of electric light, there was no such concession made, and sconces on the walls held dim iron lamps, so that only those of the most acute vision were able to read. Even then reading was difficult, for the bookstand on the table contained nothing but a few crabbed black-letter volumes dating from not later than the early seventeenth century, and you had to be in a frantically Elizabethan frame of mind to be at ease there. But Mrs Lucas often spent some of her rare leisure moments in the smoking-parlour, playing on the virginal that stood in the window, or kippering herself in the fumes of the wood-fire as with streaming eyes she deciphered an Elzevir Horace rather late for inclusion under the rule, but an undoubted bargain.

The house stood at the end of the village that was nearest the

station, and thus, when the panorama of her kingdom opened before
her, she had but a few steps further to go. A yew-hedge, bought
entire from a neighbouring farm, and transplanted with solid lumps
of earth and indignant snails around its roots, separated the small
oblong of garden from the road, and cast monstrous shadows of the
shapes into which it was cut, across the little lawns inside. Here, as
was only right and proper, there was not a flower to be found save
such as were mentioned in the plays of Shakespeare; indeed it was
called Shakespeare's garden, and the bed that ran below the windows
of the dining-room was Ophelia's border, for it consisted solely of
those flowers which that distraught maiden distributed to her friends
when she should have been in a lunatic asylum. Mrs Lucas often
reflected how lucky it was that such institutions were unknown in
Elizabeth's day, or that, if known, Shakespeare artistically ignored
their existence. Pansies, naturally, formed the chief decoration –
though there were some very flourishing plants of rue. Mrs Lucas
always wore a little bunch of them when in flower, to inspire her
thoughts, and found them wonderfully efficacious. Round the
sundial, which was set in the middle of one of the squares of grass
between which a path of broken paving-stones led to the front
door, was a circular border, now, in July, sadly vacant, for it
harboured only the spring-flowers enumerated by Perdita. But the
first day every year when Perdita's border put forth its earliest
blossom was a delicious anniversary, and the news of it spread like
wildfire through Mrs Lucas's kingdom, and her subjects were very
joyful, and came to salute the violet or daffodil, or whatever it was.

The three cottages dexterously transformed into The Hurst
presented a charmingly irregular and picturesque front. Two were
of the grey stone of the district and the middle one, to the door of
which led the paved path, of brick and timber; latticed windows with
stone mullions gave little light to the room within, and certain new
windows had been added; these could be detected by the observant
eye, for they had a markedly older appearance than the rest. The
front door, similarly, seemed as if it must have been made years
before the house, the fact being that the one which Mrs Lucas had
found there was too dilapidated to be of the slightest service in
keeping out wind or wet or undesired callers. She had therefore
caused to be constructed an even older one made from the oak-
planks of a dismantled barn, and had it studded with large iron nails
of antique pattern made by the village blacksmith. He had arranged
some of them to look as if they spelled AD 1603. Over the door hung

an inn-sign, and into the space where once the sign had swung was now inserted a lantern, in which was ensconced, well hidden from view by its patinated glass sides, an electric light. This was one of the necessary concessions to modern convenience, for no lamp nurtured on oil would pierce those genuinely opaque panes, and illuminate the path to the gate. Better to have an electric light than cause your guests to plunge into Perdita's border. By the side of this fortress-door hung a heavy iron bell-pull, ending in a mermaid. When first Mrs Lucas had that installed, it was a bell-pull in the sense that an extremely athletic man could, if he used both hands and planted his feet firmly, cause it to move, so that a huge bronze bell swung in the servants' passage and eventually gave tongue (if the athlete continued pulling) with vibrations so sonorous that the whitewash from the ceiling fell down in flakes. She had therefore made another concession to the frailty of the present generation and the inconveniences of having whitewash falling into salads and puddings on their way to the dining-room, and now at the back of the mermaid's tail was a potent little bone button, coloured black and practically invisible, and thus the bell-pull had been converted into an electric bell-push. In this way visitors could make their advent known without violent exertion, the mermaid lost no visible whit of her Elizabethan virginity, and the spirit of Shakespeare wandering in his garden would not notice any anachronism. He could not in fact, for there was none to notice.

Though Mrs Lucas's parents had bestowed the name of Emmeline on her, it was not to be wondered at that she was always known among the more intimate of her subjects as Lucia, pronounced, of course, in the Italian mode – La Lucia, the wife of Lucas; and it was as '*Lucia mia*' that her husband hailed her as he met her at the door of The Hurst.

He had been watching for her arrival from the panes of the parlour while he meditated upon one of the little prose-poems which formed so delectable a contribution to the culture of Rise-holme, for though, as has been hinted, he had in practical life a firm grasp of the obvious, there were windows in his soul which looked out on to vague and ethereal prospects which so far from being obvious were only dimly intelligible. In form these odes were cast in the loose rhythms of Walt Whitman, but their smooth suavity and their contents bore no resemblance whatever to the productions of that barbaric bard, whose works were quite unknown in Rise-holme. Already a couple of volumes of these prose-poems had been published, not of course in the hard businesslike establishment of London, but at Ye Sign of Ye Daffodil, on the village green, where type was set up by hand, and very little, but that of the best, was printed. The press had only been recently started at Mr Lucas's expense, but it had put forth a reprint of Shakespeare's sonnets already, as well as his own poems. They were printed in blunt type on thick yellowish paper, the edges of which seemed as if they had been cut by the forefinger of an impatient reader, so ragged and irregular were they, and they were bound in vellum. The titles of these two slim flowers of poetry, *Flotsam* and *Jetsam*, were printed in black-letter type and the covers were further adorned with a sort of embossed seal and with antique-looking tapes so that when you had finished with Mr Lucas's *Flotsam* you could tie it up with two bows before you turned to untie *Jetsam*.

Today the prose-poem of 'Loneliness' had not been getting on very well, and Philip Lucas was glad to hear the click of the garden-gate, which showed that his loneliness was over for the present, and looking up he saw his wife's figure waveringly presented to his eyes through the twisted and knotty glass of the parlour window, which had taken so long to collect, but which now completely replaced the plain, commonplace unrefracting stuff which was there before. He jumped up with an alacrity remarkable in so solid and well-furnished a person, and had thrown open the nail-studded front door before Lucia had traversed the path of broken paving-stones, for she had lingered for a sad moment at Perdita's empty border.

'*Lucia mia!*' he exclaimed. '*Ben arrivata!* So you walked from the station?'

'*Si, Peppino, mio caro,*' she said. '*Sta bene?*'

He kissed her and relapsed into Shakespeare's tongue, for their Italian, though firm and perfect as far as it went, could not be considered as going far, and was useless for conversational purposes, unless they merely wanted to greet each other, or to know the time. But it was interesting to talk Italian, however little way it went.

'*Molto bene,*' said he, 'and it's delightful to have you home again. And how was London?' he asked in the sort of tone in which he might have enquired after the health of a poor relation, who was not likely to recover. She smiled rather sadly.

'Terrifically busy about nothing,' she said. 'All this fortnight I have scarcely had a moment to myself. Lunches, dinners, parties of all kinds; I could not go to half the gatherings I was bidden to. Dear good South Kensington! Chelsea too!'

'*Carissima*, when London does manage to catch you, it is no wonder it makes the most of you,' he said. 'You mustn't blame London for that.'

'No, dear, I don't. Everyone was tremendously kind and hospitable; they all did their best. If I blame anyone, I blame myself. But I think this Riseholme life with its finish and its exquisiteness spoils one for other places. London is like a railway-junction: it has no true life of its own. There is no delicacy, no appreciation of fine shades. Individualism has no existence there; everyone gabbles together, gabbles and gobbles: am not I naughty? If there is a concert in a private house – you know my views about music and the impossibility of hearing music at all if you are stuck in the middle of a row of people – even then, the moment it is over you are whisked away to supper, or somebody wants to have a few words. There is always a crowd, there is always food, you cannot be alone, and it is only in loneliness, as Goethe says, that your perceptions put forth their flowers. No one in London has time to listen: they are all thinking about who is there and who isn't there, and what is the next thing. The exquisite present, as you put it in one of your poems, has no existence there: it is always the feverish future.'

'Delicious phrase! I should have stolen that gem for my poor poems, if you had discovered it before.'

She was too much used to this incense to do more than sniff it in unconsciously, and she went on with her tremendous indictment.

'It isn't that I find fault with London for being so busy,' she said with strict impartiality, 'for if being busy was a crime, I am sure there are few of us here who would escape hanging. But take my life here, or yours for that matter. Well, mine if you like. Often and often I am alone from breakfast till lunchtime, but in those hours I get through more that is worth doing than London gets through in a day and a night. I have an hour at my music, not looking about and wondering who my neighbours are, but learning, studying, drinking in divine melody. Then I have my letters to write, and you know what that means, and I still have time for an hour's reading so that when you come to tell me lunch is ready, you will find that I have been wandering through Venetian churches or sitting in that little dark room at Weimar, or was it Leipzig? How would those same hours have passed in London?

'Sitting perhaps for half an hour in the Park, with dearest Aggie pointing out to me, with thrills of breathless excitement, a woman who was in the divorce court, or a coroneted bankrupt. Then she would drag me off to some terrible private view full of the same people all staring at and gabbling to each other, or looking at pictures that made poor me gasp and shudder. No, I am thankful to be back at my own sweet Riseholme again. I can work and think here.'

She looked round the panelled entrance-hall with a glow of warm content at being at home again that quite eclipsed the mere physical heat produced by her walk from the station. Wherever her eyes fell, those sharp dark eyes that resembled buttons covered with shiny American cloth, they saw nothing that jarred, as so much in London jarred. There were bright brass jugs on the window sill, a bowl of potpourri on the black table in the centre, an oak settee by the open fireplace, a couple of Persian rugs on the polished floor. The room had its quaintness, too, such as she had alluded to in her memorable essay read before the Riseholme Literary Society, called 'Humour in Furniture', and a brass milk-can served as a receptacle for sticks and umbrellas. Equally quaint was the dish of highly realistic stone fruit that stood beside the potpourri and the furry Japanese spider that sprawled in a silk web over the window.

Such was the fearful verisimilitude of this that Lucia's new house-maid had once fled from her duties in the early morning, to seek the assistance of the gardener in killing it. The dish of stone fruit had scored a similar success, for once she had said to Georgie Pillson, 'Ah, my gardener has sent in some early apples and pears, won't you take one home with you?' It was not till the weight of the pear (he swiftly selected the largest) betrayed the joke that he had any notion that they were not real ones. But then Georgie had had his revenge, for waiting his opportunity he had inserted a real pear among those stony specimens and again passing through with Lucia, he picked it out, and with lips drawn back had snapped at it with all the force of his jaws. For the moment she had felt quite faint at the thought of his teeth crashing into fragments . . . These humorous touches were altered from time to time; the spider for instance might be taken down and replaced by a china canary in a Chippendale cage, and the selection of the entrance-hall for those whimsicalities was intentional, for guests found something to smile at, as they took off their cloaks and entered the drawing-room with a topic on their lips, something light, something amusing about what they had seen. For the gong similarly was sometimes substituted a set of bells that had once decked the collar of the leading horse in a waggoner's team somewhere in Flanders; in fact when Lucia was at home there was often a new little quaintness for quite a sequence of days, and she had held out hopes to the Literary Society that perhaps some day, when she was not so rushed, she would jot down material for a sequel to her essay, or write another covering a rather larger field on 'The Gambits of Conversation Derived from Furniture'.

On the table there was a pile of letters waiting for Mrs Lucas, for yesterday's post had not been forwarded her, for fear of its missing her – London postmen were probably very careless and untrustworthy – and she gave a little cry of dismay as she saw the volume of her correspondence.

'But I shall be very naughty,' she said, 'and not look at one of them till after lunch. Take them away, *caro*, and promise me to lock them up till then, and not give them me however much I beg. Then I will get into the saddle again, such a dear saddle, too, and tackle them. I shall have a stroll in the garden till the bell rings. What is it that Nietzsche says about the necessity to *Mediterraniser* yourself every now and then? I must *Riseholmer* myself.'

Peppino remembered the quotation, which had occurred in a review of some work of that celebrated author, where Lucia had also seen it, and went back, with the force of contrast to aid him, to his prose-poem of 'Loneliness', while his wife went through the smoking-parlour into the garden, in order to soak herself once more in the cultured atmosphere.

In this garden behind the house there was no attempt to construct a Shakespearian plot, for, as she so rightly observed, Shakespeare, who loved flowers so well, would wish her to enjoy every conceivable horticultural treasure. But furniture played a prominent part in the place, and there were statues and sundials and stone-seats scattered about with almost too profuse a hand. Mottos also were in great evidence, and while a sundial reminded you that *'Tempus fugit'*, an enticing resting-place somewhat bewilderingly bade you to 'Bide a wee'. But then again the rustic seat in the pleached alley of laburnums had carved on its back, 'Much have I travelled in the realms of gold', so that, meditating on Keats, you could bide a wee with a clear conscience. Indeed so copious was the wealth of familiar and stimulating quotations that one of her subjects had once said that to stroll in Lucia's garden was not only to enjoy her lovely flowers, but to spend a simultaneous half-hour with the best authors. There was a dovecote of course, but since the cats always killed the doves, Mrs Lucas had put up round the desecrated home several pigeons of Copenhagen china, which were both imperishable as regards cats, and also carried on the suggestion of humour in furniture. The humour had attained the highest point of felicity when Peppino concealed a mechanical nightingale in a bush, which sang 'Jug-jug' in the most realistic manner when you pulled a string. Georgie had not yet seen the Copenhagen pigeons, or being rather short-sighted thought they were real. Then, oh then, Peppino pulled the string, and for quite a long time Georgie listened entranced to their melodious cooings. That served him out for his 'trap' about the real pear introduced among the stone specimens. For in spite of the rarefied atmosphere of culture at Riseholme, Riseholme knew how to '*desipere in loco*', and its strenuous culture was often refreshed by these light refined touches.

Mrs Lucas walked quickly and decisively up and down the paths as she waited for the summons to lunch, for the activity of her mind reacted on her body, making her brisk in movement. On each side of her forehead were hard neat undulations of black hair that concealed the tips of her ears. She had laid aside her London hat, and carried a red cotton Contadina's umbrella, which threw a rosy glow on to the oval of her thin face and its colourless complexion. She bore the weight of her forty years extremely lightly, and but for the droop of skin at the corners of her mouth, she might have passed as a much younger woman. Her face was otherwise unlined and bore no trace of the ravages of emotional living, which both ages and softens. Certainly there was nothing soft about her, and very little of the signs of age, and it would have been reasonable to conjecture that twenty years later she would look but little older than she did today. For such emotions as she was victim of were the sterile and ageless ecstasies of art; such desires as beset her were not connected with her affections, but her ambitions. Dynasty she had none, for she was childless, and thus her ambitions were limited to the permanence and security of her own throne as queen of Riseholme. She really asked nothing more of life than the continuance of such harvests as she had so plenteously reaped for these last ten years. As long as she directed the life of Riseholme, took the lead in its culture and entertainment, and was the undisputed fountainhead of all its inspirations, and from time to time refreshed her memory as to the utter inferiority of London, she wanted nothing more. But to secure that she dedicated all that she had of ease, leisure and income. Being practically indefatigable the loss of ease and leisure troubled her but little, and being in extremely comfortable circumstances, she had no need to economise in her hospitalities. She might easily look forward to enjoying an unchanging middle-aged activity, while generations of youth withered round her, and no star, remotely rising, had as yet threatened to dim her unrivalled effulgence. Though essentially autocratic, her subjects were allowed and even encouraged to develop their own minds on their own lines, provided always that those lines met at the junction where she was station-master. With regard to religion finally, it may be briefly said that she believed in God in much the same way as she believed in Australia, for she had no doubt whatever as to the existence of either, and she went to church on Sunday in much the same spirit as she would look at a kangaroo in the Zoological Gardens, for kangaroos come from Australia.

A low wall separated the far end of her garden from the meadow outside; beyond that lay the stream which flowed into the Avon, and it often seemed wonderful to her that the water which wimpled by would (unless a cow happened to drink it) soon be stealing along past the church at Stratford where Shakespeare lay. Peppino had written a very moving little prose-poem about it, for she had royally presented him with the idea, and had suggested a beautiful analogy between the earthly dew that refreshed the grasses, and was drawn up into the fire of the Sun, and Thought, the spiritual dew that refreshed the mind and thereafter, rather vaguely, was drawn up into the Full-Orbed Soul of the World.

At that moment Lucia's eye was attracted by an apparition on the road which lay adjacent to the further side of the happy stream which flowed into the Avon. There was no mistaking the identity of the stout figure of Mrs Quantock with its short steps and its gesticulations, but why in the name of wonder should that Christian Scientist be walking with the draped and turbaned figure of a man with a tropical complexion and a black beard? His robe of saffron yellow with a violently green girdle was hitched up for ease in walking, and unless he had chocolate-coloured stockings on, Mrs Lucas saw human legs of the same shade. Next moment that debatable point was set at rest for she caught sight of short pink socks in red slippers. Even as she looked Mrs Quantock saw her (for owing to Christian Science she had recaptured the quick vision of youth) and waggled her hand and kissed it, and evidently called her companion's attention, for the next moment he was salaaming to her in some stately Oriental manner. There was nothing to be done for the moment except return these salutations, as she could not yell an aside to Mrs Quantock, screaming out 'Who is that Indian?' for if Mrs Quantock heard the Indian would hear too, but as soon as she could, she turned back towards the house again, and when once the lilac bushes were between her and the road she walked with more than her usual speed, in order to learn with the shortest possible delay from Peppino who this fresh subject of hers could be. She knew there were some Indian princes in London; perhaps it was one of them, in which case it would be necessary to read up Benares or Delhi in the Encyclopaedia without loss of time.

Chapter Two

As she traversed the smoking-parlour the cheerful sounds that had once tinkled from the collar of a Flemish horse chimed through the house, and simultaneously she became aware that there would be macaroni au gratin for lunch, which was very dear and remembering of Peppino. But before setting fork to her piled-up plate, she had to question him, for her mental craving for information was far keener than her appetite for food.

'*Caro*, who is an Indian,' she said, 'whom I saw just now with Daisy Quantock? They were the other side of *il piccolo* Avon.'

Peppino had already begun his macaroni and must pause to shovel the outlying strings of it into his mouth. But the haste with which he did so was sufficient guarantee for his eagerness to reply as soon as it was humanly possible to do so.

'Indian, my dear?' he asked with the greatest interest.

'Yes; turban and burnous and calves and slippers,' she said rather impatiently, for what was the good of Peppino having remained in Riseholme if he could not give her precise and certain information on local news when she returned. His prose-poems were all very well, but as prince-consort he had other duties of state which must not be neglected for the calls of Art.

This slight asperity on her part seemed to sharpen his wits.

'Really, I don't know for certain, Lucia,' he said, 'for I have not set my eyes on him. But putting two and two together, I might make a guess.'

'Two and two make four,' she said with that irony for which she was feared and famous. 'Now for your guess. I hope it is equally accurate.'

'Well, as I told you in one of my letters,' said he, 'Mrs Quantock showed signs of being a little off with Christian Science. She had a cold, and though she recited the True Statement of Being just as frequently as before, her cold got no better. But when I saw her on Tuesday last, unless it was Wednesday – no, it couldn't have been Wednesday, so it must have been Tuesday – '

'Whenever it was then,' interrupted his wife, brilliantly summing up his indecision.

'Yes; whenever it was, as you say, on that occasion Mrs Quantock was very full of some Indian philosophy which made you quite well at once. What did she call it now? Yoga! Yes, that was it!'

'And then?' asked Lucia.

'Well, it appears you must have a teacher in Yoga or else you may injure yourself. You have to breathe deeply and say "Om" – '

'Say what?'

'Om. I understand the ejaculation to be Om. And there are very curious physical exercises; you have to hold your ear with one hand and your toes with the other, and you may strain yourself unless you do it properly. That was the general gist of it.'

'And shall we come to the Indian soon?' said Lucia.

'*Carissima*, you have come to him already. I suggest that Mrs Quantock has applied for a teacher and got him. *Ecco!*'

Mrs Lucas wore a heavily corrugated forehead at this news. Peppino had a wonderful *flair* in explaining unusual circumstances in the life of Riseholme and his conjectures were generally correct. But if he was right in this instance, it struck Lucia as being a very irregular thing that anyone should have imported a mystical Indian into Riseholme without consulting her. It is true that she had been away, but still there was the medium of the post.

'*Ecco* indeed!' she said. 'It puts me in rather a difficult position, for I must send out my invitations to my garden-party today, and I really don't know whether I ought to be officially aware of this man's existence or not. I can't write to Daisy Quantock and say "Pray bring your black friend Om", or whatever his names proves to be, and on the other hand, if he is the sort of person whom one would be sorry to miss, I should not like to have passed over him.'

'After all, my dear, you have only been back in Riseholme half an hour,' said her husband. 'It would have been difficult for Mrs Quantock to have told you yet.'

Her face cleared.

'Perhaps Daisy has written to me about him,' she said. 'I may find a full account of it all when I open my letters.'

'Depend upon it you will. She would hardly have been so wanting in proper feeling as not to have told you. I think, too, that her visitor must only have just arrived, or I should have been sure to see him about somewhere.'

She rose.

'Well, we will see,' she said. 'Now I shall be very busy all afternoon, but by teatime I shall be ready to see anyone who calls. Give me my letters, *caro*, and I will find out if Daisy has written to me.'

She turned them over as she went to her room, and there among them was a bulky envelope addressed in Mrs Quantock's great sprawling hand, which looked at first sight so large and legible, but on closer examination turned out to be so baffling. You had to hold it at some distance off to make anything out of it, and look at it in an abstracted general manner much as you would look at a view. Treated thus, scattered words began to leap into being, and when you had got a sufficiency of these, like glimpses of the country seen by flashes of lightning, you could hope to get a collective idea of it all. The procedure led to the most promising results as Mrs Lucas sat with the sheets at arm's length, occasionally altering the range to try the effect of a different focus. 'Benares' blinked at her, also 'Brahmin'; also 'highest caste'; 'extraordinary sanctity', and 'guru'. And when the meaning of this latter was ascertained from the article on 'Yoga' in her Encyclopaedia, she progressed very swiftly towards a complete comprehension of the letter.

When fully pieced together it was certainly enough to rivet her whole attention, and make her leave unopened the rest of the correspondence, for such a prelude to adventure had seldom sounded in Riseholme. It appeared, even as her husband had told her at lunch, that Mrs Quantock found her cold too obstinate for all the precepts of Mrs Eddy; the True Statement of Being, however often repeated, only seemed to inflame it further, and one day, when confined to the house, she had taken a book 'quite at random' from the shelves in her library, under, she supposed, the influence of some interior compulsion. This then was clearly a 'leading'.

Mrs Lucas paused a moment as she pieced together these first sentences. She seemed to remember that Mrs Quantock had experienced a similar leading when first she took up Christian Science. It was a leading from the sight of a new church off Sloane Street that day; Mrs Quantock had entered (she scarcely knew why) and had found herself in a Testimony Meeting, where witness after witness declared the miraculous healings they had experienced. One had had a cough, another cancer, another a fractured bone, but all had been cured by the blessed truths conveyed in the Gospel according to Mrs Eddy. However, her memories on this subject were not to the point now; she burned to arrive at the story of the new leading.

Well, the book that Mrs Quantock had taken down in obedience to the last leading proved to be a little handbook of Oriental Philosophies, and it opened, 'all of its own accord', at a chapter called Yoga. Instantly she perceived, as by the unclosing of an inward eye, that Yoga was what she wanted and she instantly wrote to the address from which this book was issued asking for any guidance on the subject. She had read in 'Oriental Philosophies' that for the successful practice of Yoga, it was necessary to have a teacher, and did they know of any teacher who could give her instruction? A wonderful answer came to that, for two days afterwards her maid came to her and said that an Indian gentleman would like to see her. He was ushered in, and with a profound obeisance said: 'Beloved lady, I am the teacher you asked for; I am your guru. Peace be to this house! Om!'

Mrs Lucas had by this time got her view of Mrs Quantock's letter into perfect focus, and she read on without missing a word.

Is it not wonderful, dearest Lucia [it ran] that my desire for light should have been so instantly answered? And yet my guru tells me that it always happens so. I was sent to him, and he was sent to me, just like that! He had been expecting some call when my letter asking for guidance came, and he started at once because he knew he was sent. Fancy! I don't even know his name, and his religion forbids him to tell it me. He is just my guru, my guide, and he is going to be with me as long as he knows I need him to show me the True Path. He has the spare bedroom and the little room adjoining where he meditates and does Postures and Pranayama, which is breathing. If you persevere in them under instruction, you have perfect health and youth, and my cold is gone already. He is a Brahmin of the very highest caste, indeed caste means nothing to him any longer, just as a Baronet and an Honourable must seem about the same thing to the King. He comes from Benares where he used to meditate all day by the Ganges, and I can see for myself that he is a person of the most extraordinary sanctity. But he can meditate just as well in my little room, for he says he was never in any house that had such a wonderful atmosphere. He has no money at all which is so beautiful of him, and looked so pained and disappointed when I asked him if I might not give him some. He doesn't even know how he got here from London; he doesn't think he came by train, so perhaps he was wafted here in some astral manner. He looked so bewildered too when I said the word 'money', and evidently he had to think what it was, because it is so long since it has meant anything to him. So if he wants anything, I have told him to go into any shop and ask that it shall be put down to me. He has often been without food or sleep for days together when he is meditating. Just think!

Shall I bring him to see you, or will you come here? He wants to meet you, because he feels you have a beautiful soul and may help him in that way, as well as his helping you. I am helping him too he says, which seems more wonderful than I can believe. Send me a line as soon as you get back. *Tante salute!*

Your own,

DAISY

The voluminous sheets had taken long in reading and Mrs Lucas folded them up slowly and thoughtfully. She felt that she had to make a swift decision that called into play all her mental powers. On the one hand it was 'up to her' to return a frigid reply, conveying, without making any bones about the matter, that she had no interest in nameless gurus who might or might not be Brahmins from Benares and presented themselves at Daisy's door in a penniless condition without clear knowledge whether they had come by train or not. In favour of such prudent measures was the truly Athenian character of Daisy's mind, for she was always enquiring into 'some new thing', which was the secret of life when first discovered, and got speedily relegated to the dust-heap. But against such a course was the undoubted fact that Daisy did occasionally get hold of somebody who subsequently proved to be of interest, and Lucia would never forget to her dying day the advent in Riseholme of a little Welsh attorney, in whom Daisy had discovered a wonderful mentality. Lucia had refused to extend her queenly hospitality to him, or to recognise his existence in any way during the fortnight when he stayed with Daisy, and she was naturally very much annoyed to find him in a prominent position in the Government not many years later. Indeed she had snubbed him so markedly on his first appearance at Riseholme that he had refused on subsequent visits to come to her house at all, though he several times visited Mrs Quantock again, and told her all sorts of political secrets (so she said) which she would not divulge for anything in the world. There must never be a repetition of so fatal an error.

Another thing inclined the wavering balance. She distinctly wanted some fresh element at her court, that should make Riseholme know that she was in residence again. August would soon be here with its

languors and absence of stimulus, when it was really rather difficult
in the drowsy windless weather to keep the flag of culture flying
strongly from her own palace. The guru had already said that he
felt sure she had a beautiful soul, and — The outline of the scheme
flashed upon her. She would have Yoga evenings in the hot August
weather, at which, as the heat of the day abated, graceful groups
should assemble among the mottos in the garden and listen to high
talk on spiritual subjects. They would adjourn to delicious moonlit
suppers in the pergola, or if the moon was indisposed – she could
not be expected to regulate the affairs of the moon as well as of
Riseholme – there would be dim séances and sandwiches in the
smoking-parlour. The humorous furniture should be put in cupboards, and as they drifted towards the front hall again, when the
clocks struck an unexpectedly late hour, little whispered colloquies
of 'How wonderful he was tonight' would be heard, and there
would be faraway looks and sighs, and the notings down of the
titles of books that conducted the pilgrim on the Way. Perhaps as
they softly assembled for departure, a little music would be suggested
to round off the evening, and she saw herself putting down the soft
pedal as people rustled into their places, for the first movement of
the 'Moonlight Sonata'. Then at the end there would be silence,
and she would get up with a sigh, and someone would say, 'Lucia
mia!' and somebody else, 'Heavenly music,' and perhaps the guru
would say, 'Beloved lady,' as he had *apparently* said to poor Daisy
Quantock. Flowers, music, addresses from the guru, soft partings,
sense of refreshment . . . With the memory of the Welsh attorney
in her mind, it seemed clearly wiser to annex rather than to repudiate
the guru. She seized a pen and drew a pile of postcards towards her,
on the top of which was printed her name and address.

> Too wonderful [she wrote]. Pray bring him yourself to my little
> garden-party on Friday. There will be only a few. Let me know if
> he wants a quiet room ready for him.

All this had taken time, and she had but scribbled a dozen
postcards to friends bidding them come to her garden-party on
Friday, when tea was announced. These invitations had the mystic
word 'Hightum' written at the bottom left-hand corner, which
conveyed to the enlightened recipient what sort of party it was to
be, and denoted the standard of dress. For one of Lucia's quaint
ideas was to divide dresses into three classes, 'Hightum', 'Tightum'
and 'Scrub'. 'Hightum' was your very best dress, the smartest and

newest of all, and when 'Hightum' was written on a card of invitation, it implied that the party was a very resplendent one. 'Tightum' similarly indicated a moderately smart party, 'Scrub' carried its own significance on the surface. These terms applied to men's dress as well and as regards evening parties: a dinner party 'Hightum' would indicate a white tie and a tail coat; a dinner party 'Tightum' a black tie and a short coat, and a dinner 'Scrub' would mean morning clothes.

With tea was announced also the advent of Georgie Pillson, who was her gentleman-in-waiting when she was at home, and her watch-dog when she was not. In order to save subsequent disappointment, it may be at once stated that there never had been, was, or ever would be the smallest approach to a flirtation between them. Neither of them, she with her forty respectable years and he with his blameless forty-five years, had ever flirted, with anybody at all. But it was one of the polite and pleasant fictions of Riseholme that Georgie was passionately attached to her and that it was for her sake that he had settled in Riseholme now some seven years ago, and that for her sake he remained still unmarried. She never, to do her justice, had affirmed anything of the sort, but it is a fact that sometimes when Georgie's name came up in conversation, her eyes wore that 'faraway' look that only the masterpieces of art could otherwise call up, and she would sigh and murmur, 'Dear Georgie!' and change the subject, with the tact that characterised her. In fact their mutual relations were among the most Beautiful Things of Riseholme, and hardly less beautiful was Peppino's attitude towards it all. That large-hearted man trusted them both, and his trust was perfectly justified. Georgie was in and out of the house all day, chiefly in; and not only did scandal never rear its hissing head, but it positively had not a head to hiss with, or a foot to stand on. On his side again Georgie had never said that he was in love with her (nor would it have been true if he had), but by his complete silence on the subject coupled with his constancy he seemed to admit the truth of this bloodless idyll. They talked and walked and read the masterpieces of literature and played duets on the piano together. Sometimes (for he was the more brilliant performer, though as he said 'terribly lazy about practising', for which she scolded him) he would gently slap the back of her hand, if she played a wrong note, and say 'Naughty!' And she would reply in baby language 'Me vewy sowwy! Oo naughty too to hurt Lucia!' That was the utmost extent of their carnal familiarities, and with bright eyes fixed on the music

they would break into peals of girlish laughter, until the beauty of
the music sobered them again.

Georgie (he was Georgie or Mr Georgie, never Pillson to the
whole of Riseholme) was not an obtrusively masculine sort of person.
Such masculinity as he was possessed of was boyish rather than adult,
and the most important ingredients in his nature were womanish.
He had, in common with the rest of Riseholme, strong artistic tastes,
and in addition to playing the piano, made charming little watercolour
sketches, many of which he framed at his own expense and gave to
friends, with slightly sentimental titles, neatly printed in gilt letters
on the mount. 'Golden Autumn Woodland', 'Bleak December',
'Yellow Daffodils' and 'Roses of Summer' were perhaps his most
notable series, and these he had given to Lucia, on the occasion of
four successive birthdays. He did portraits as well in pastel; these
were of two types, elderly ladies in lace caps with a row of pearls, and
boys in cricket shirts with their sleeves rolled up. He was not very
good at eyes, so his sitters always were looking down, but he was
excellent at smiles, and the old ladies smiled patiently and sweetly,
and the boys gaily. But his finest accomplishment was needlework
and his house was full of the creations of his needle, wool-work
curtains, petit-point chair seats, and silk embroideries framed and
glazed. Next to Lucia he was the hardest-worked inhabitant of
Riseholme, but not being so strong as the Queen, he had often to go
away for little rests by the seaside. Travelling by train fussed him a
good deal, for he might not be able to get a corner seat, or somebody
with a pipe or a baby might get into his carriage, or the porter might
be rough with his luggage, so he always went in his car to some
neighbouring watering-place where they knew him. Dicky, his
handsome young chauffeur, drove him, and by Dicky's side sat
Foljambe, his very pretty parlour-maid who valetted him. If Dicky
took the wrong turn his master called 'Naughty boy' through the
tube, and Foljambe smiled respectfully. For the month of August,
his two plain strapping sisters (Hermione and Ursula, alas!) always
came to stay with him. They liked pigs and dogs and otter-hunting
and mutton-chops, and were rather a discordant element in
Riseholme. But Georgie had a kind heart, and never even debated
whether he should ask Hermy and Ursy or not, though he had to do
a great deal of tidying up after they had gone.

There was always a playful touch between the meetings of these
two when either of them had been away from Riseholme that very
prettily concealed the depth of Georgie's supposed devotion, and

when she came out into the garden where her Cavalier and her husband were waiting for their tea under the pergola, Georgie jumped up very nimbly and took a few chassée-ing steps towards her with both hands outstretched in welcome. She caught at his humour, made him a curtsey, and next moment they were treading a little improvised minuet together with hands held high, and pointed toes. Georgie had very small feet, and it was a really elegant toe that he pointed, encased in cloth-topped boots. He had on a suit of fresh white flannels and over his shoulders, for fear of the evening air being chilly after this hot day, he had a little cape of a military cut, like those in which young ladies at music-halls enact the part of colonels. He had a straw-hat on, with a blue riband, a pink shirt and a red tie, rather loose and billowy. His face was pink and round, with blue eyes, a short nose and very red lips. An almost complete absence of eyebrow was made up for by a firm little brown moustache clipped very short, and brushed upwards at its extremities. Contrary to expectation he was quite tall and fitted very neatly into his clothes.

The dance came to an end with a low curtsey on Lucia's part, an obeisance hat in hand from Georgie (this exposure showing a crop of hair grown on one side of his head and brushed smoothly over the top until it joined the hair on the other side) and a clapping of the hands from Peppino.

'Bravo, bravo,' he cried from the tea-table. 'Capital!'

Mrs Lucas blew him a kiss in acknowledgement of this compliment and smiled on her partner. '*Amico!*' she said. 'It is nice to see you again. How goes it?'

'*Va bene,*' said Georgie to show he could talk Italian too. '*Va* very *bene* now that you've come back.'

'*Grazie!* Now tell us all the news. We'll have a good gossip.'

Georgie's face beamed with a 'solemn gladness' at the word, like a drunkard's when brandy is mentioned.

'Where shall we begin?' he said. 'Such a lot to tell you. I think we must begin with a great bit of news. Something really mysterious.'

Lucia smiled inwardly. She felt that she knew for dead certain what the mysterious news was, and also that she knew far more about it than Georgie. This superiority she completely concealed. Nobody could have guessed it.

'*Presto, presto!*' she said. 'You excite me.'

'Yesterday morning I was in Rush's,' said Georgie, 'seeing about some *crème de menthe*, which ought to have been sent the day before. Rush is very negligent sometimes – and I was just saying a sharp word about it, when suddenly I saw that Rush was not attending at all, but was looking at something behind my back, and so I looked round. Guess!'

'Don't be tantalising, *amico*,' said she. 'How can I guess? A pink elephant with blue spots!'

'No, guess again!'

'A red Indian in full war paint.'

'Certainly not! Guess again,' said Georgie, with a little sigh of relief. (It would have been awful if she had guessed.) At this moment Peppino suddenly became aware that Lucia had guessed and was up to some game.

'Give me your hand, Georgie,' she said, 'and look at me. I'm going to read your thoughts. Think of what you saw when you turned round.'

She took his hand and pressed it to her forehead, closing her eyes.

'But I do seem to see an Indian,' she said. 'Ah, not red Indian, other Indian. And – and he has slippers on and brown stockings – no, not brown stockings; it's legs. And there's a beard, and a turban.'

She gave a sigh.

'That's all I can see,' she said.

'My dear, you're marvellous,' said he. 'You're quite right.'

A slight bubbling sound came from Peppino, and Georgie began to suspect.

'I believe you've seen him!' he said. 'How tarsome you are . . . '

When they had all laughed a great deal, and Georgie had been assured that Lucia really, word of honour, had no idea what happened next, the narrative was resumed.

'So there stood the Indian, bowing and salaaming most politely and when Rush had promised me he would send my *crème de menthe* that very morning, I just looked through a wine list for a moment, and the Indian with quantities more bows came up to the counter and said, "If you will have the great goodness to give me a little brandy bottle." So Rush gave it him, and instead of paying for it, what do you think he said? Guess.'

Mrs Lucas rose with the air of Lady Macbeth and pointed her finger at Georgie.

'He said "Put it down to Mrs Quantock's account," ' she hissed.

Of course the explanation came now, and Lucia told the two men the contents of Mrs Quantock's letter. With that her cards were on the table, and though the fact of the Brahmin from Benares was news to Georgie, he had got many interesting things to tell her, for his house adjoined Mrs Quantock's and there were plenty of things which Mrs Quantock had not mentioned in her letter, so that Georgie was soon in the position of informant again. His windows overlooked Mrs Quantock's garden, and since he could not keep his eyes shut all day, it followed that the happenings there were quite common property. Indeed that was a general rule in Riseholme: anyone in an adjoining property could say, 'What an exciting game of lawn-tennis you had this afternoon!' having followed it from his bedroom. That was part of the charm of Riseholme; it was as if it contained just one happy family with common interests and pursuits. What happened in the house was a more private matter, and Mrs Quantock, for instance, would never look from the rising ground at the end of her garden into Georgie's dining-room or, if she did she would never tell anyone how many places were laid at table on that particular day when she had asked if he could give her lunch, and he had replied that to his great regret his table was full. But nobody could help seeing into gardens from back windows: the 'view' belonged to everybody.

Georgie had had wonderful views.

'That very day,' he said, 'soon after lunch, I was looking for a letter I thought I had left in my bedroom, and happening to glance out, I saw the Indian sitting under Mrs Quantock's pear tree. He was swaying a little backwards and forwards.'

'The brandy!' said Lucia excitedly. 'He has his meals in his own room.'

'No, *amica*, it was not the brandy. In fact I don't suppose the brandy had gone to Mrs Quantock's then, for he did not take it from Rush's, but asked that it should be sent . . . ' He paused a moment – 'Or did he take it away? I declare I can't remember. But anyhow when he swayed backwards and forwards, he wasn't drunk, for presently he stood on one leg, and crooked the other behind it, and remained there with his hands up, as if he was praying, for quite a long time without swaying at all. So he couldn't have been tipsy. And then he sat down again, and took off his slippers, and held his toes with one hand, while his legs were quite straight out, and put his other hand round behind his head, and grasped his other ear with it. I tried to do it on my bedroom floor, but I couldn't get near it. Then he sat up again and called "*Chela! Chela!*" and Mrs Quantock came running out.'

'Why did he say "*Chela*"?' asked Lucia.

'I wondered too. But I knew I had some clue to it, so I looked through some books by Rudyard Kipling, and found that *chela* meant "disciple". What you have told me just now about "guru" being "teacher", seems to piece the whole thing together.'

'And what did Daisy do?' asked Mrs Lucas breathlessly.

'She sat down too, and put her legs out straight in front of her like the guru, and tried to hold the toe of her shoe in her fingers, and naturally she couldn't get within yards of it. I got nearer than she did. And he said, "Beloved lady, not too far at first." '

'So you could hear too,' said Lucia.

'Naturally, for my window was open, and as you know Mrs Quantock's pear tree is quite close to the house. And then he told her to stop up one nostril with her finger and inhale through the other, and then hold her breath, while he counted six. Then she breathed it all out again, and started with the other side. She repeated that several times and he was very much pleased with her. Then she said, "It is quite wonderful; I feel so light and vigorous." '

'It would be very wonderful indeed if dear Daisy felt light,' remarked Lucia. 'What next?'

'Then they sat and swayed backwards and forwards again and muttered something that sounded like Pom!'

'That would be "Om"; and then?'

'I couldn't wait any longer for I had some letters to write.'

She smiled at him.

'I shall give you another cup of tea to reward you for your report,' she said. 'It has all been most interesting. Tell me again about the breathing in and holding your breath.'

Georgie did so, and illustrated in his own person what had happened. Next moment Lucia was imitating him, and Peppino came round in order to get a better view of what Georgie was doing. Then they all sat, inhaling through one nostril, holding their breath, and then expelling it again.

'Very interesting,' said Lucia at the end. 'Upon my word, it does give one a sort of feeling of vigour and lightness. I wonder if there is something in it.'

Chapter Three

Though The Hurst was, as befitted its *châtelaine*, the most Eliza-bethanly complete abode in Riseholme, the rest of the village, in its due degrees, fell very little short of perfection. It had but its one street some half-mile in length but that street was a gem of mediaeval domestic architecture. For the most part the houses that lined it were blocks of contiguous cottages, which had been converted either singly or by twos and threes into dwellings containing the comforts demanded by the twentieth century, but externally they preserved the antiquity which, though it might be restored or supplemented by bathrooms or other conveniences, presented a truly Elizabethan appearance. There were, of course, accretions such as old inn-signs above front doors and old bell-pulls at their sides, but the doors were uniformly of inconveniently low stature, roofs were of stone slabs or old brick, in which a suspiciously abundant crop of antirrhinums and stone crops had anchored themselves, and there was hardly a garden that did not contain a path of old paving-stones, a mulberry tree and some yews cut into shape.

Nothing in the place was more blatantly mediaeval than the village green, across which Georgie took his tripping steps after leaving the presence of his queen. Round it stood a row of great elms, and in its centre was the ducking-pond, according to Riseholme tradition, though perhaps in less classical villages it might have passed merely for a duck-pond. But in Riseholme it would have been rank heresy to dream, even in the most pessimistic moments, of its being anything but a ducking-pond. Close by it stood a pair of stocks, about which there was no doubt whatever, for Mr Lucas had purchased them from a neighbouring iconoclastic village, where they were going to be broken up, and, after having them repaired, had presented them to the village green, and chosen their site close to the ducking-pond. Round the green were grouped the shops of the village, slightly apart from the residential street, and at the far end of it was that undoubtedly Elizabethan hostelry, the Ambermere Arms, full to overflowing of ancient tables and bible-boxes, and firedogs and fire-backs, and bottles and chests and settles. These were purchased in large quantities by the American tourists who swarmed there during the summer months, at a high profit to the nimble proprietor, who thereupon purchased fresh antiquities to take their places. The Ambermere Arms in fact was the antique furniture shop of the place, and did a thriving trade, for it was much more interesting to buy objects out of a real old Elizabethan inn, than out of a shop.

Georgie had put his smart military cape over his arm for his walk, and at intervals applied his slim forefinger to one nostril, while he breathed in through the other, continuing the practice which he had observed going on in Mrs Quantock's garden. Though it made him a little dizzy, it certainly produced a sort of lightness, but soon he remembered the letter from Mrs Quantock which Lucia had read out, warning her that these exercises ought to be taken under instruction, and so desisted. He was going to deliver Lucia's answer at Mrs Quantock's house, and with a view to possibly meeting the guru, and being introduced to him, he said over to himself 'guru, guru, guru' instead of doing deep breathing, in order to accustom himself to the unusual syllables.

It would, of course, have been very strange and un-Riseholme-like to have gone to a friend's door, even though the errand was so impersonal a one as bearing somebody else's note, without enquiring whether the friend was in, and being instantly admitted if she was, and as a matter of fact, Georgie caught a glimpse, when the knocker was answered (Mrs Quantock did not have a bell at all), through the open door of the hall, of Mrs Quantock standing in the middle of the lawn on one leg. Naturally, therefore, he ran out into the garden without any further formality. She looked like a little round fat stork, whose legs had not grown, but who preserved the habits of her kind.

'Dear lady, I've brought a note for you,' he said. 'It's from Lucia.'

The other leg went down, and she turned on him the wide firm smile that she had learned in the vanished days of Christian Science.

'Om,' said Mrs Quantock, expelling the remainder of her breath. 'Thank you, my dear Georgie. It's extraordinary what Yoga has done for me already. Cold quite gone. If ever you feel out of sorts, or depressed or cross, you can cure yourself at once. I've got a visitor staying with me.'

'Have you indeed?' asked Georgie, without alluding to the thrilling excitements which had trodden so close on each other's heels since yesterday morning when he had seen the guru in Rush's shop.

'Yes; and as you've just come from dear Lucia's perhaps she may have said something to you about him, for I wrote to her about him. He's a guru of extraordinary sanctity from Benares, and he's teaching me the Way. You shall see him too, unless he's meditating. I will call to him; if he's meditating he won't hear me, so we shan't be interrupting him. He wouldn't hear a railway accident if he was meditating.'

She turned round towards the house.

'Guru, dear!' she called.

There was a moment's pause, and the Indian's face appeared at a window.

'Beloved lady!' he said.

'Guru dear, I want to introduce a friend of mine to you,' she said. 'This is Mr Pillson, and when you know him a little better you will call him Georgie.'

'Beloved lady, I know him very well indeed. I see into his clear white soul. Peace be unto you, my friend.'

'Isn't he marvellous? Fancy!' said Mrs Quantock, in an aside.

Georgie raised his hat very politely.

'How do you do?' he said. (After his quiet practice he would have said 'How do you do, Guru?' but it rhymed in a ridiculous manner and his red lips could not frame the word.)

'I am always well,' said the guru, 'I am always young and well because I follow the Way.'

'Sixty at least he tells me,' said Mrs Quantock in a hissing aside, probably audible across the channel, 'and he thinks more, but the years make no difference to him. He is like a boy. Call him "Guru".'

'Guru – ' began Georgie.

'Yes, my friend.'

'I am very glad you are well,' said Georgie wildly. He was greatly impressed, but much embarrassed. Also it was so hard to talk at a second-storey window with any sense of ease, especially when you had to address a total stranger of extraordinary sanctity from Benares.

Luckily Mrs Quantock came to the assistance of his embarrassment.

'Guru dear, are you coming down to see us?' she asked.

'Beloved lady, no!' said the level voice. 'It is laid on me to wait here. It is the time of calm and prayer when it is good to be alone. I will come down when the guides bid me. But teach our dear friend what I have taught you. Surely before long I will grasp his earthly hand, but not now. Peace! Peace! and Light!'

'Have you got some guides as well?' asked Georgie when the guru disappeared from the window. 'And are they Indians too?'

'Oh, those are his spiritual guides,' said Mrs Quantock. 'He sees them and talks to them, but they are not in the body.'

She gave a happy sigh.

'I never have felt anything like it,' she said. 'He has brought such an atmosphere into the house that even Robert feels it, and doesn't mind being turned out of his dressing-room. There, he has shut the window. Isn't it all marvellous?'

Georgie had not seen anything particularly marvellous yet, except the phenomenon of Mrs Quantock standing on one leg in the middle of the lawn, but presumably her emotion communicated itself to him by the subtle infection of the spirit.

'And what does he do?' he asked.

'My dear, it is not what he does, but what he is,' said she. 'Why, even my little bald account of him to Lucia has made her ask him to her garden-party. Of course I can't tell whether he will go or not. He seems so very much – how shall I say it? – so very much sent to me. But I shall of course ask him whether he will consent. Trances and meditation all day! And in the intervals such serenity and sweetness. You know, for instance, how tiresome Robert is about his food. Well, last night the mutton, I am bound to say, was a little underdone, and Robert was beginning to throw it about his plate in the way he has. Well, my guru got up and just said, "Show me the way to kitchen" – he leaves out little words sometimes, because they don't matter – and I took him down, and he said "Peace!" He told me to leave him there, and in ten minutes he was up again with a little plate of curry and rice and what had been underdone mutton, and you never ate anything so good. Robert had most of it and I had the rest, and my guru was so pleased at seeing Robert pleased. He said Robert had a pure white soul, just like you, only I wasn't to tell him, because for him the Way ordained that he must find it out for himself. And today before lunch again, the guru went down in the kitchen, and my cook told me he only took a pinch of pepper and a tomato and a little bit of mutton fat and a sardine and a bit of cheese, and he brought up a dish that you never saw equalled. Delicious! I shouldn't a bit wonder if Robert began breathing-exercises soon. There is one that makes you lean and young and exercises the liver.'

This sounded very entrancing.

'Can't you teach me that?' asked Georgie eagerly. He had been rather distressed about his increasing plumpness for a year past, and about his increasing age for longer than that. As for his liver he always had to be careful.

She shook her head.

'You cannot practise it except under tuition from an expert,' she said.

Georgie rapidly considered what Hermy's and Ursy's comments would be if, when they arrived tomorrow, he was found doing exercises under the tuition of a guru. Hermy, when she was not otter-hunting, could be very sarcastic, and he had a clear month of Hermy in front of him, without any otter-hunting, which, so she had informed him, was not possible in August. This was mysterious to Georgie, because it did not seem likely that all otters died in August, and a fresh brood came in like caterpillars. If Hermy was here in October, she would otter-hunt all morning and snore all afternoon, and be in the best of tempers, but the August visit required more careful steering. Yet the prospect of being lean and young and internally untroubled was wonderfully tempting.

'But couldn't he be my guru as well?' he asked.

Quite suddenly and by some demoniac possession, a desire that had been only intermittently present in Mrs Quantock's consciousness took full possession of her, a red revolutionary insurgence hoisted its banner. Why with this stupendous novelty in the shape of a guru shouldn't she lead and direct Riseholme instead of Lucia? She had long wondered why darling Lucia should be Queen of Riseholme, and had, by momentary illumination, seen herself thus equipped as far more capable of exercising supremacy. After all, everybody in Riseholme knew Lucia's old tune by now, and was in his secret consciousness quite aware that she did not play the second and third movements of the 'Moonlight Sonata', simply because they 'went faster', however much she might cloak the omission by saying that they resembled eleven o'clock in the morning and 3 p.m. And Mrs Quantock had often suspected that she did not read one quarter of the books she talked about, and that she got up subjects in the Encyclopaedia, in order to make a brave show that covered essential ignorance. Certainly she spent a good deal of money over entertaining, but Robert had lately made twenty times daily what Lucia spent annually, over Roumanian oils. As for her acting, had she not completely forgotten her words as Lady Macbeth in the middle of the sleep-walking scene?

But here was Lucia, as proved by her note, and her ADC Georgie, wildly interested in the guru. Mrs Quantock conjectured that Lucia's plan was to launch the guru at her August parties, as her own discovery. He would be a novelty, and it would be Lucia who gave Om-parties and breathing-parties and standing-on-one-leg parties, while she herself, Daisy Quantock, would be bidden to these as a humble guest, and Lucia would get all the credit, and, as likely as not, invite the discoverer, the inventress, just now and then. Mrs Quantock's guru would become Lucia's guru and all Riseholme would flock hungrily for light and leading to The Hurst. She had written to Lucia in all sincerity, hoping that she would extend the hospitality of her garden-parties to the guru, but now the very warmth of Lucia's reply caused her to suspect this ulterior motive. She had been too precipitate, too rash, too ill-advised, too sudden, as Lucia would say. She ought to have known that Lucia, with her August parties coming on, would have jumped at a guru, and withheld him for her own parties, taking the wind out of Lucia's August sails. Lucia had already suborned Georgie to leave this note, and begin to filch the guru away. Mrs Quantock saw it all now, and clearly this was not to be borne. Before she answered, she steeled herself with the triumph she had once scored in the matter of the Welsh attorney.

'Dear Georgie,' she said, 'no one would be more delighted than I if my guru consented to take you as a pupil. But you can't tell what he will do, as he said to me today, apropos of myself, "I cannot come unless I'm sent." Was not that wonderful? He knew at once he had been sent to me.'

By this time Georgie was quite determined to have the guru. The measure of his determination may be gauged from the fact that he forgot all about Lucia's garden-party.

'But he called me his friend,' he said. 'He told me I had a clean white soul.'

'Yes; but that is his attitude towards everybody,' said Mrs Quantock. 'His religion makes it impossible for him to think ill of anybody.'

'But he didn't say that to Rush,' cried Georgie, 'when he asked for some brandy, to be put down to you.'

Mrs Quantock's expression changed for a moment, but that moment was too short for Georgie to notice it. Her face instantly cleared again.

'Naturally he cannot go about saying that sort of thing,' she observed. 'Common people – he is of the highest caste – would not understand him.'

Georgie made the direct appeal.

'Please ask him to teach me,' he said.

For a moment Mrs Quantock did not answer, but cocked her head sideways in the direction of the pear tree where a thrush was singing. It fluted a couple of repeated phrases and then was silent again.

Mrs Quantock gave a great smile to the pear tree.

'Thank you, little brother,' she said.

She turned to Georgie again.

'That comes out of St Francis,' she said, 'but Yoga embraces all that is true in every religion. Well, I will ask my guru whether he will take you as a pupil, but I can't answer for what he will say.'

'What does he – what does he charge for his lesson?' asked Georgie.

The Christian Science smile illuminated her face again.

'The word "money" never passes his lips,' she said. 'I don't think he really knows what it means. He proposed to sit on the green with a beggar's bowl but of course I would not permit that, and for the present I just give him all he wants. No doubt when he goes away, which I hope will not be for many weeks yet, though no one can tell when he will have another call, I shall slip something suitably generous into his hand, but I don't think about that. Must you be going? Good-night, dear Georgie. Peace! Om!'

His last backward glance as he went out of the front door revealed her standing on one leg again, just as he had seen her first. He remembered a print of a fakir at Benares, standing in that attitude; and if the stream that flowed into the Avon could be combined with the Ganges, and the garden into the burning ghaut, and the swooping swallows into the kites, and the neat parlour-maid who showed him out, into a Brahmin, and the Chinese gong that was so prominent an object in the hall into a piece of Benares brassware, he could almost have fancied himself as standing on the brink of the sacred river. The marigolds in the garden required no transmutation . . .

Georgie had quite 'to pull himself together', as he stepped round Mrs Quantock's mulberry tree, and ten paces later round his own, before he could recapture his normal evening mood, on those occasions when he was going to dine alone. Usually these evenings were very pleasant and much occupied, for they did not occur very often in this whirl of Riseholme life, and it was not more than once a week that he spent a solitary evening, and then, if he got tired of his own company, there were half a dozen houses, easy of access, where he could betake himself in his military cloak, and spend a post-prandial hour. But oftener than not when these occasions occurred, he would be quite busy at home, dusting a little china, and rearranging ornaments on his shelves, and, after putting his rings and handkerchief in the candle-bracket of the piano, spending a serious hour (with the soft pedal down, for fear of irritating Robert) in reading his share of such duets as he would be likely to be called upon to play with Lucia during the next day or two. Though he read music much better than she did, he used to 'go over' the part alone first, and let it be understood that he had not seen it before. But then he was sure that she had done precisely the same, so they started fair. Such things whiled away very pleasantly the hours till eleven, when he went to bed, and it was seldom that he had to set out Patience-cards to tide him over the slow minutes.

But every now and then – and tonight was one of those occasions – there occurred evenings when he never went out to dinner even if he was asked, because he 'was busy indoors'. They occurred about once a month (these evenings that he was 'busy indoors') – and even an invitation from Lucia would not succeed in disturbing them. Ages ago Riseholme had decided what made Georgie 'busy indoors' once a month, and so none of his friends chatted about the nature of his engagements to anyone else, simply because everybody else knew. His business indoors, in fact, was a perfect secret, from having been public property for so long.

June had been a very busy time, not 'indoors', but with other engagements, and as Georgie went up to his bedroom, having been told by Foljambe that the hairdresser was waiting for him, and had been waiting 'this last ten minutes', he glanced at his hair in the Cromwellian mirror that hung on the stairs, and was quite aware that it was time he submitted himself to Mr Holroyd's ministrations. There was certainly an undergrowth of grey hair visible beneath his chestnut crop, that should have been attended to at least a fortnight ago. Also there was a growing thinness in the locks that crossed his head; Mr Holroyd had attended to that before, and had suggested a certain remedy, not in the least inconvenient, unless Georgie proposed to be athletic without a cap, in a high wind, and even then not necessarily so. But as he had no intention of being athletic anywhere, with or without a cap, he determined as he went up the stairs that he would follow Mr Holroyd's advice. Mr Holroyd's procedure, without this added formula, entailed sitting 'till it dried', and after that he would have dinner, and then Mr Holroyd would begin again. He was a very clever person with regard to the face and the hands and the feet. Georgie had been conscious of walking a little lamely lately; he had been even more conscious of the need of hot towels on his face and the 'tap-tap' of Mr Holroyd's fingers, and the stretchings of Mr Holroyd's thumb across rather slack surfaces of cheek and chin. In the interval between the hair and the face, Mr Holroyd should have a good supper downstairs with Foljambe and the cook. And tomorrow morning, when he met Hermy and Ursy, Georgie would be just as spick and span and young as ever, if not more so.

Georgie (happy innocent!) was completely unaware that the whole of Riseholme knew that the smooth chestnut locks which covered the top of his head, were trained like the tendrils of a grapevine from the roots, and flowed like a river over a bare head, and consequently when Mr Holroyd explained the proposed innovation, a little central wig, the edges of which would mingle in the most natural manner with his own hair, it seemed to Georgie that nobody would know the difference. In addition he would be spared those risky moments when he had to take off his hat to a friend in a high wind, for there was always the danger of his hair blowing away from the top of his head, and hanging down, like the tresses of a Rhine-maiden over one shoulder. So Mr Holroyd was commissioned to put that little affair in hand at once, and when the greyness had been attended to, and Georgie had had his dinner, there came hot towels and tappings on his face, and other ministrations. All was done about half-past ten, and when he came downstairs again for a short practice at the bass part of Beethoven's fifth symphony, ingeniously arranged for two performers on the piano, he looked with sincere satisfaction at his rosy face in the Cromwellian mirror, and his shoes felt quite comfortable again, and his nails shone like pink stars, as his hands dashed wildly about the piano in the quicker passages. But all the time the thought of the guru next door, under whose tuition he might be able to regain his youth without recourse to those expensive subterfuges (for the price of the undetectable *toupée* astonished him) rang in his head with a melody more haunting than Beethoven's. What he would have liked best of all would have been to have the guru all to himself, so that he should remain perpetually young, while all the rest of Riseholme, including Hermy and Ursy, grew old. Then, indeed, he would be king of the place, instead of serving the interests of its queen.

He rose with a little sigh, and after adjusting the strip of flannel over the keys, shut his piano and busied himself for a little with a soft duster over his cabinet of bibelots which not even Foljambe was allowed to touch. It was generally understood that he had inherited them, though the inheritance had chiefly passed to him through the medium of curiosity shops, and there were several pieces of considerable value among them. There were a gold Louis XVI snuff box, a miniature by Karl Huth, a silver toy porringer of the time of Queen Anne, a piece of Bow china, an enamelled cigarette case by Fabergé. But tonight his handling of them was not so dainty and delicate as usual, and he actually dropped the porringer on the floor as he was dusting it, for his mind still occupied itself with the guru and the practices that led to permanent youth. How quick Lucia had been to snap him up for her garden-party. Yet perhaps she would not get him, for he might say he was not sent. But surely he would be sent to Georgie, whom he knew, the moment he set eyes on him, to have a clean white soul . . .

The clock struck eleven, and, as usual on warm nights, Georgie opened the glass door into his garden and drew in a breath of the night air. There was a slip of moon in the sky which he most punctiliously saluted, wondering (though he did not seriously believe in its superstition) how Lucia could be so foolhardy as to cut the new moon. She had seen it yesterday, she told him, in London, and had taken no notice whatever of it . . . The heavens were quickly peppered with pretty stars, which Georgie after his busy interesting day enjoyed looking at, though if he had had the arrangement of them, he would certainly have put them into more definite patterns. Among them was a very red planet, and Georgie, with recollections of his classical education, easily remembered that Mars, the God of War, was symbolised in the heavens by a red star. Could that mean anything to peaceful Riseholme? Was internal warfare, were revolutionary movements possible in so serene a realm?

Chapter Four

Pink irascible Robert, prone to throw his food about his plate, if it did not commend itself to him, felt in an extremely good-natured mood that same night after dinner, for the guru had again made a visit to the kitchen with the result that instead of a slab of pale dead codfish being put before him after he had eaten some tepid soup, there appeared a delicious little fish curry. The guru had behaved with great tact; he had seen the storm gathering on poor Robert's face, as he sipped the cool effete concoction and put down his spoon again with a splash in his soup plate, and thereupon had bowed and smiled and scurried away to the kitchen to intercept the next abomination. Then returning with the little curry he explained that it was entirely for Robert, since those who sought the Way did not indulge in hot sharp foods, and so he had gobbled it up to the very last morsel.

In consequence when the guru salaamed very humbly, and said that with gracious permission of beloved lady and kind master he would go and meditate in his room, and had shambled away in his red slippers, the discussion which Robert had felt himself obliged to open with his wife, on the subject of having an unknown Indian staying with them for an indefinite period, was opened in a much more amicable key than it would have been on a slice of codfish.

'Well, now, about this Golliwog – ha-ha – I should say guru, my dear,' he began, 'what's going to happen?'

Daisy Quantock drew in her breath sharply and winced at this irreverence, but quickly remembered that she must always be sending out messages of love, north, east, south, and west. So she sent a rather spiky one in the direction of her husband who was sitting due east, so that it probably got to him at once, and smiled the particular hard firm smile which was an heirloom inherited from her last rule of life.

'No one knows,' she said brightly. 'Even the Guides can't tell where and when a guru may be called.'

'Then do you propose he should stop here till he's called somewhere else?'

She continued smiling.

'I don't propose anything,' she said. 'It's not in my hands.'

Under the calming influence of the fish curry, Robert remained still placid.

'He's a first-rate cook anyhow,' he said. 'Can't you engage him as that? Call to the kitchen, you know.'

'Darling!' said Mrs Quantock, sending out more love. But she had a quick temper, and indeed the two were outpoured together, like hot and cold taps turned on in a bath. The pellucid stream of love served to keep her temper moderately cool.

'Well, ask him,' suggested Mr Quantock, 'as you say, you never can tell where a guru may be called. Give him forty pounds a year and beer money.'

'Beer!' began Mrs Quantock, when she suddenly remembered Georgie's story about Rush and the guru and the brandy bottle, and stopped.

'Yes, dear, I said "beer",' remarked Robert a little irritably, 'and in any case I insist that you dismiss your present cook. You only took her because she was a Christian Scientist, and you've left that little sheepfold now. You used to talk about false claims I remember. Well her claim to be a cook is the falsest I ever heard of. I'd sooner take my chance with an itinerant organ grinder. But that fish curry tonight and that other thing last night, that's what I mean by good eating.'

The thought even of good food always calmed Robert's savage

breast; it blew upon him as the wind on an Aeolian harp hung in the trees, evoking faint sweet sounds.

'I'm sure, my dear,' he said, 'that I shall be willing to fall in with any pleasant arrangement about your guru, but it really isn't unreasonable in me to ask what sort of arrangement you propose. I haven't a word to say against him, especially when he goes to the kitchen; I only want to know if he is going to stop here a night or two or a year or two. Talk to him about it tomorrow with my love. I wonder if he can make bisque soup.'

Daisy Quantock carried quite a quantity of material for reflection upstairs with her, then she went to bed, pausing a moment opposite the guru's door, from inside of which came sounds of breathing so deep that it sounded almost like snoring. But she seemed to detect a timbre of spirituality about it which convinced her that he was holding high communion with the Guides. It was round him that her thoughts centred; he was the tree through the branches of which they scampered chattering.

Her first and main interest in him was sheer guruism, for she was one of those intensely happy people who pass through life in ecstatic pursuit of some idea which those who do not share it call a fad. Well might poor Robert remember the devastation of his home when Daisy, after the perusal of a little pamphlet which she picked up on a bookstall called 'The Uric Acid Monthly', came to the shattering conclusion that her buxom frame consisted almost entirely of waste-products which must be eliminated. For a greedy man the situation was frankly intolerable, for when he continued his ordinary diet (this was before the cursed advent of the Christian Science cook) she kept pointing to his well-furnished plate, and told him that every atom of that beef or mutton and potatoes, turned from the moment he swallowed it into chromogens and toxins, and that his apparent appetite was merely the result of fermentation. For herself her platter was an abominable mess of cheese and protein-powder and apples and salad-oil, while round her, like saucers of specimen seeds, were ranged little piles of nuts and pine-branches, which supplied body-building material, and which she weighed out with scrupulous accuracy, in accordance with the directions of the 'Uric Acid Monthly'. Tea and coffee were taboo, since they flooded the blood with poisons, and the kitchen boiler rumbled day and night to supply the rivers of boiling water with which (taken in sips) she inundated her system. Strange gaunt females used to come down from London, with small parcels full of tough food that tasted of travelling-bags and contained so much nutrition that a portmanteau full of it would furnish the daily rations of an army. Luckily even her iron constitution could not stand the strain of such ideal living for long, and her growing anaemia threatened to undermine a constitution seriously impaired by the precepts of perfect health. A course of beef-steaks and other substantial viands loaded with uric acid restored her to her former vigour.

Thus reinforced, she plunged with the same energy as she had devoted to repelling uric acid into the embrace of Christian Science. The inhumanity of that sect towards both herself and others took complete possession of her, and when her husband complained on a bitter January morning that his smoking-room was like an ice-house, because the housemaid had forgotten to light the fire, she had no touch of pity for him, since she knew that there was no such thing as cold or heat or pain, and therefore you could not feel cold. But now, since, according to the new creed, such things as uric acid, chromogens and poisons had no existence, she could safely indulge in decent viands again. But her unhappy husband was not a real gainer in this respect, for while he ate, she tirelessly discoursed to him on the new creed, and asked him to recite with her the True Statement of Being. And on the top of that she dismissed the admirable cook, and engaged the miscreant from whom he suffered still, though Christian Science, which had allowed her cold to make so long a false claim on her, had followed the uric-acid fad into the limbo of her discarded beliefs.

But now once more she had temporarily discovered the secret of life in the teachings of the guru, and it was, as has been mentioned, sheer guruism that constituted the main attraction of the new creed. That then being taken for granted, she turned her mind to certain side-issues, which to a true Riseholmite were of entrancing interest. She felt a strong suspicion that Lucia contemplated annexing her guru altogether, for otherwise she would not have returned so enthusiastic a response to her note, nor have sent Georgie to deliver it, nor have professed so violent an interest in the guru. What then was the correctly diabolical policy to pursue? Should Daisy Quantock refuse to take him to Mrs Lucas altogether, with a message of regret that he did not feel himself sent? Even if she did this, did she feel herself strong enough to throw down the gauntlet (in the shape of the guru) and, using him as the attraction, challenge darling Lucia to mutual combat, in order to decide who should be the leader of all that was advanced and cultured in Riseholme society? Still following that ramification of this policy, should she bribe Georgie over to her own revolutionary camp, by promising him instruction from the guru? Or following a less dashing line, should she take darling Lucia and Georgie into the charmed circle, and while retaining her own right of treasure-trove, yet share it with them in some inner ring, dispensing the guru to them, if they were good, in small doses?

Mrs Quantock's mind resembled in its workings the manoeuvres of a moth distracted by the glory of several bright lights. It dashed at one, got slightly singed, and forgetting all about that turned its attention to the second, and the third, taking headers into each in turn, without deciding which, on the whole, was the most enchanting of those luminaries. So, in order to curb the exuberance of these frenzied excursions she got a half-sheet of paper, and noted down the alternatives that she must choose from.

(i)   Shall I keep him entirely to myself?
(ii)   Shall I run him for all he is worth, and leave out L?
(iii) Shall I get G on my side?
(iv)   Shall I give L and G bits?

She paused a moment: then remembering that he had voluntarily helped her very pretty housemaid to make the beds that morning, saying that his business (like the Prince of Wales's) was to serve, she added:

(v)   Shall I ask him to be my cook?

For a few seconds the brightness of her eager interest was dimmed as the unworthy suspicion occurred to her that perhaps the prettiness of her housemaid had something to do with his usefulness in the bedrooms, but she instantly dismissed it. There was the bottle of brandy, too, which he had ordered from Rush's. When she had begged him to order anything he wanted and cause it to be put down to her account, she had not actually contemplated brandy. Then remembering that one of the most necessary conditions for progress in Yoga, was that the disciple should have complete confidence in the guru, she chased that also out of her mind. But still, even when the lines of all possible policies were written down, she could come to no decision, and putting her paper by her bed, decided to sleep over it. The rhythmical sounds of hallowed breathing came steadily from next door, and she murmured 'Om, Om,' in time with them.

*   *   *

The hours of the morning between breakfast and lunch were the time which the inhabitants of Riseholme chiefly devoted to spying on each other. They went about from shop to shop on household businesses, occasionally making purchases which they carried away with them in little paper parcels with convenient loops of string, but the real object of these excursions was to see what everybody else was doing, and learn what fresh interests had sprung up like mushrooms during the night. Georgie would be matching silks at the draper's, and very naturally he would carry them from the obscurity of the interior to the door in order to be certain about the shades, and keep his eye on the comings and goings in the street, and very naturally Mr Lucas on his way to the market gardener's to enquire whether he had yet received the bulbs from Holland, would tell him that Lucia had received the piano-arrangement of the Mozart trio. Georgie for his part would mention that Hermy and Ursy were expected that evening, and Peppino enriched by this item would 'toddle on', as his phrase went, to meet and exchange confidences with the next spy. He had noticed incidentally that Georgie carried a small oblong box with hard corners, which, perfectly correctly, he conjectured to be cigarettes for Hermy and Ursy, since Georgie never smoked.

'Well, I must be toddling on,' he said, after identifying Georgie's box of cigarettes, and being rather puzzled by a bulge in Georgie's pocket. 'You'll be looking in some time this morning, perhaps.'

Georgie had not been quite sure that he would (for he was very busy owing to the arrival of his sisters, and the necessity of going to Mr Holroyd's, in order that that artist might accurately match the shade of his hair with a view to the expensive *toupée*), but the mention of the arrival of the Mozart now decided him. He intended anyhow before he went home for lunch to stroll past The Hurst, and see if he did not hear – to adopt a mixed metaphor – the sound of the diligent practice of that classical morsel going on inside. Probably the soft pedal would be down, but he had marvellously acute hearing, and he would be very much surprised if he did not hear the recognisable chords, and even more surprised if, when they came to practise the piece together, Lucia did not give him to understand that she was reading it for the first time. He had already got a copy, and had practised his part last night, but then he was in the superior position of not having a husband who would inadvertently tell on him! Meantime it was of the first importance to get that particular shade of purple silk that had none of that 'tarsome' magenta-tint in it.

Meantime also, it was of even greater importance to observe the movements of Riseholme.

Just opposite was the village green, and as nobody was quite close to him Georgie put on his spectacles, which he could whisk off in a moment. It was these which formed that bulge in his pocket which Peppino had noticed, but the fact of his using spectacles at all was a secret that would have to be profoundly kept for several years yet. But as there was no one at all near him, he stealthily adjusted them on his small straight nose. The morning train from town had evidently come in, for there was a bustle of cabs about the door of the Ambermere Arms, and a thing that thrilled him to the marrow was the fact that Lady Ambermere's motor was undoubtedly among them. That must surely mean that Lady Ambermere herself was here, for when poor thin Miss Lyall, her companion, came in to Riseholme to do shopping, or transact such business as the majestic life at The Hall required, she always came on foot, or in very inclement weather in a small two-wheeled cart like a hip-bath. At this moment, steeped in conjecture, who should appear, walking stiffly, with her nose in the air, as if suspecting, and not choosing to verify, some faint unpleasant odour, but Lady Ambermere herself, coming from the direction of The Hurst . . . Clearly she must have got there after Peppino had left, or he would surely have mentioned the fact that Lady Ambermere had been at The Hurst, if she *had* been at The Hurst. It is true that she was only coming from the direction of The Hurst, but Georgie put into practice, in his mental processes, Darwin's principle, that in order to observe usefully, you must have a theory. Georgie's theory was that Lady Ambermere had been at The Hurst just for a minute or two, and hastily put his spectacles in his pocket. With the precision of a trained mind he also formed the theory that some business had brought Lady Ambermere into Riseholme, and that taking advantage of her presence there, she had probably returned a verbal answer to Lucia's invitation to her garden-party, which she would have received by the first post this morning. He was quite ready to put his theory to the test when Lady Ambermere had arrived at the suitable distance for his conveniently observing her, and for taking off his hat. She always treated him like a boy, which he liked. The usual salutation passed.

'I don't know where my people are,' said Lady Ambermere majestically. 'Have you seen my motor?'

'Yes, dear lady, it's in at your own arms,' said Georgie brightly. 'Happy motor!'

If Lady Ambermere unbent to anybody, she unbent to Georgie. He was of quite good family, because his mother had been a Bartlett and a second cousin of her deceased husband. Sometimes when she talked to Georgie she said 'we', implying thereby his connection with the aristocracy, and this gratified Georgie nearly as much as did her treatment of him as being quite a boy still. It was to him, as a boy still, that she answered.

'Well, the happy motor, you little rascal, must come to my arms instead of being at them,' she said with the quick wit for which Riseholme pronounced her famous. 'Fancy being able to see my motor at that distance. Young eyes!'

It was really young spectacles, but Georgie did not mind that. In fact, he would not have corrected the mistake for the world.

'Shall I run across and fetch it for you?' he asked.

'In a minute. Or whistle on your fingers like a vulgar street boy,' said Lady Ambermere. 'I'm sure you know how to.'

Georgie had not the slightest idea, but with the courage of youth, presuming, with the prudence of middle-age, that he would not really be called upon to perform so unimaginable a feat, he put two fingers up to his mouth.

'Here goes then!' he said, greatly daring. (He knew perfectly well that the dignity of Lady Ambermere would not permit rude vulgar whistling, of which he was hopelessly incapable, to summon her motor. She made a feint of stopping her ears with her hands.)

'Don't do anything of the kind,' she said. 'In a minute you shall walk with me across to the Arms, but tell me this first. I have just been to say to our good Mrs Lucas that very likely I will look in at her garden-party on Friday, if I have nothing else to do. But who is this wonderful creature she is expecting? Is it an Indian conjurer? If so, I should like to see him, because when Ambermere was in Madras I remember one coming to the Residency who had cobras and that sort of thing. I told her I didn't like snakes, and she said there shouldn't be any. In fact, it was all rather mysterious, and she didn't at present know if he was coming or not. I only said, "No snakes: I insist on no snakes." '

Georgie relieved her mind about the chance of there being snakes, and gave a short *précis* of the ascertained habits of the guru, laying special stress on his high caste.

'Yes, some of these Brahmins are of very decent family,' admitted Lady Ambermere. 'I was always against lumping all dark-skinned people together and calling them niggers. When we were at Madras I was famed for my discrimination.'

They were walking across the green as Lady Ambermere gave vent to these liberal sentiments, and Georgie even without the need of his spectacles could see Peppino, who had spied Lady Ambermere from the door of the market-gardener's, hurrying down the street, in order to get a word with her before 'her people' drove her back to The Hall.

'I came into Riseholme today to get rooms at the Arms for Olga Bracely,' she observed.

'The prima-donna?' asked Georgie, breathless with excitement.

'Yes; she is coming to stay at the Arms for two nights with Mr Shuttleworth.'

'Surely – ' began Georgie.

'No, it is all right, he is her husband, they were married last week,' said Lady Ambermere. 'I should have thought that Shuttleworth was a good enough name, as the Shuttleworths are cousins of the late lord, but she prefers to call herself Miss Bracely. I don't dispute her right to call herself what she pleases: far from it, though who the Bracelys were, I have never been able to discover. But when George Shuttleworth wrote to me saying that he and his wife were intending to stay here for a couple of days, and proposing to come over to The Hall to see me, I thought I would just look in at the Arms myself, and see that they were promised proper accommodation. They will dine with me tomorrow. I have a few people staying, and no doubt Miss Bracely will sing afterwards. My Broadwood was always considered a remarkably fine instrument. It was very proper of George Shuttleworth to say that he would be in the neighbourhood, and I dare say she is a very decent sort of woman.'

They had come to the motor by this time – the rich, the noble motor, as Mr Pepys would have described it – and there was poor Miss Lyall hung with parcels, and wearing a faint sycophantic smile. This miserable spinster, of age so obvious as to be called not the least uncertain, was Lady Ambermere's companion, and shared with her the glories of The Hall, which had been left to Lady Ambermere for life. She was provided with food and lodging and the use of the cart like a hip-bath when Lady Ambermere had errands for her to do in Riseholme, so what could a woman want more? In return for these bounties, her only duty was to devote herself body and mind to her patroness, to read the paper aloud, to set Lady Ambermere's patterns for needlework, to carry the little Chinese dog under her arm, and wash him once a week, to accompany Lady Ambermere to church, and never to have a fire in her bedroom. She had a melancholy wistful little face: her head was inclined with a backward slope on her neck, and her mouth was invariably a little open showing long front teeth, so that she looked rather like a roast hare sent up to table with its head on. Georgie always had a joke ready for Miss Lyall, of the sort that made her say, 'Oh, Mr Pillson!' and caused her to blush. She thought him remarkably pleasant.

Georgie had his joke ready on this occasion.

'Why, here's Miss Lyall!' he said. 'And what has Miss Lyall been doing while her ladyship and I have been talking? Better not ask, perhaps.'

'Oh, Mr Pillson!' said Miss Lyall, as punctually as a cuckoo clock when the hands point to the hour.

Lady Ambermere put half her weight on to the step of the motor, causing it to creak and sway.

'Call on the Shuttleworths, Georgie,' she said. 'Say I told you to. Home!'

Miss Lyall effaced herself on the front seat of the motor, like a mouse hiding in a corner, after Lady Ambermere had got in, and the footman mounted on to the box. At that moment Peppino with his bag of bulbs, a little out of breath, squeezed his way between two cabs by the side of the motor. He was just too late, and the motor moved off. It was very improbable that Lady Ambermere saw him at all.

Georgie felt very much like a dog with a bone in his mouth, who only wants to get away from all the other dogs and discuss it quietly. It is safe to say that never in twenty-four hours had so many exciting things happened to him. He had ordered a *toupée*, he had been looked on with favour by a guru, all Riseholme knew that he had had quite a long conversation with Lady Ambermere and nobody in Riseholme, except himself, knew that Olga Bracely was going to spend two nights here. Well he remembered her marvellous appearance last year at Covent Garden in the part of Brünnhilde. He had gone to town for a rejuvenating visit to his dentist, and the tarsomeness of being betwixt and between had been quite forgotten by him when he saw her awake to Siegfried's line on the mountain-top. '*Das ist keine mann*,' Siegfried had said, and, to be sure, that was very clever of him, for she looked like some slim beardless boy, and not in the least like those great fat Fraus at Baireuth, whom nobody could have mistaken for a man as they bulged and heaved even before the strings of the breastplate were uncut by his sword. And then she sat up and hailed the sun, and Georgie felt for a moment that he had quite taken the wrong turn in life, when he settled to spend his years in this boyish, maidenly manner with his embroidery and his china-dusting at Riseholme. He ought to have been Siegfried . . . He had brought a photograph of her in her cuirass and helmet, and often looked at it when he was not too busy with something else. He had even championed his goddess against Lucia, when she pronounced that Wagner was totally lacking in knowledge of dramatic effects. To be sure she had never seen any Wagner opera, but she had heard the overture to *Tristan* performed at the Queen's Hall, and if that was Wagner, well –

*   *   *

Already, though Lady Ambermere's motor had not yet completely vanished up the street, Riseholme was gently closing in round him, in order to discover by discreet questions (as in the game of Clumps) what he and she had been talking about. There was Colonel Boucher with his two snorting bulldogs closing in from one side, and Mrs Weston in her bath-chair being wheeled relentlessly towards him from another, and the two Miss Antrobuses sitting playfully in the stocks, on the third, and Peppino at close range on the fourth. Everyone knew, too, that he did not lunch till half-past one, and there was really no reason why he should not stop and chat as usual. But with the eye of the true general, he saw that he could most easily break the surrounding cordon by going off in the direction of Colonel Boucher, because Colonel Boucher always said 'Haw, hum, by Jove,' before he descended into coherent speech, and thus Georgie could forestall him with 'Good-morning, Colonel,' and pass on before he got to business. He did not like passing close to those slobbering bulldogs, but something had to be done . . . Next moment he was clear and saw that the other spies by their original impetus were still converging on each other and walked briskly down towards Lucia's house, to listen for any familiar noises out of the Mozart trio. The noises were there, and the soft pedal was down just as he expected, so, that business being off his mind, he continued his walk for a few hundred yards more, meaning to make a short circuit through fields, cross the bridge, over the happy stream that flowed into the Avon, and regain his house by the door at the bottom of the garden. Then he would sit and think . . . the guru, Olga Bracely . . . What if he asked Olga Bracely and her husband to dine, and persuaded Mrs Quantock to let the guru come? That would be three men and one woman, and Hermy and Ursy would make all square. Six for dinner was the utmost that Foljambe permitted.

He had come to the stile that led into the fields, and sat there for a moment. Lucia's tentative melodies were still faintly audible, but soon they stopped, and he guessed that she was looking out of the window. She was too great to take part in the morning spying that went on round about the green, but she often saw a good deal from her window. He wondered what Mrs Quantock was meaning to do. Apparently she had not promised the guru for the garden-party, or else Lady Ambermere would not have said that Lucia did not know whether he was coming or not. Perhaps Mrs Quantock was going to run him herself, and grant him neither to Lucia nor Georgie. In that case he would certainly ask Olga Bracely and her husband to dine, and should he or should he not ask Lucia?

The red star had risen in Riseholme: Bolshevism was treading in its peaceful air, and if Mrs Quantock was going to secrete her guru, and set up her own standard on the strength of him, Georgie felt much inclined to ask Olga Bracely to dinner, without saying anything whatever to Lucia about it, and just see what would happen next. Georgie was a Bartlett on his mother's side, and he played the piano better than Lucia, and he had twenty-four hours' leisure every day, which he could devote to being king of Riseholme . . . His nature flared up, burning with a red revolutionary flame, that was fed by his secret knowledge about Olga Bracely. Why should Lucia rule everyone with her rod of iron? Why, and again why?

Suddenly he heard his name called in the familiar alto, and there was Lucia in her Shakespeare's garden.

'*Georgino! Georgino mio!*' she cried. '*Gino!*'

Out of mere habit Georgie got down from his stile, and tripped up the road towards her. The manly seething of his soul's insurrection rebuked him, but unfortunately his legs and his voice surrendered. Habit was strong . . .

'*Amica!*' he answered. '*Buon giorno.*' ('And why do I say it in Italian?' he vainly asked himself.)

'Geordie, come and have ickle talk,' she said. 'Me want 'oo wise man to advise ickle Lucia.'

'What 'oo want?' asked Georgie, now quite quelled for the moment.

'Lots-things. Here's pwetty flower for button-holie. Now tell me about black man. Him no snakes have? Why Mrs Quantock say she thinks he no come to poo' Lucia's party-garden?'

'Oh, did she?' asked Georgie, relapsing into the vernacular.

'Yes, oh, and by the way there's a parcel come which I think must be the Mozart trio. Will you come over tomorrow morning and read it with me? Yes? About half-past eleven, then. But never mind that.'

She fixed him with her ready, birdy eye.

'Daisy asked me to ask him,' she said, 'and so to oblige poor Daisy I did. And now she says she doesn't know if he'll come. What does that mean? Is it possible that she wants to keep him to herself? She has done that sort of thing before, you know.'

This probably represented Lucia's statement of the said case about the Welsh attorney, and Georgie taking it as such felt rather embarrassed. Also that birdlike eye seemed to gimlet its way into his very soul, and divine the secret disloyalty that he had been contemplating. If she had continued to look into him, he might not only have confessed to the gloomiest suspicions about Mrs Quantock, but have let go of his secret about Olga Bracely also, and suggested the possibility of her and her husband being brought to the garden-party. But the eye at this moment unscrewed itself from him again and travelled up the road.

'There's the guru,' she said. 'Now we will see!'

Georgie, faint with emotion, peered out between the form of the peacock and the pineapple on the yew-hedge, and saw what followed. Lucia went straight up to the guru, bowed and smiled and clearly introduced herself. In another moment he was showing his white teeth and salaaming, and together they walked back to The Hurst, where Georgie palpitated behind the yew-hedge. Together they entered and Lucia's eye wore its most benignant aspect.

'I want to introduce to you, Guru,' she said without a stumble, 'a great friend of mine. This is Mr Pillson, Guru; Guru, Mr Pillson. The guru is coming to tiffin with me, Georgie. Cannot I persuade you to stop?'

'Delighted!' said Georgie. 'We met before in a sort of way, didn't we?'

'Yes, indeed. So pleased,' said the guru.

'Let us go in,' said Lucia. 'It is close on lunchtime.'

Georgie followed, after a great many bowings and politenesses from the guru. He was not sure if he had the makings of a Bolshevist. Lucia was so marvellously efficient.

Chapter Five

One of Lucia's greatnesses lay in the fact that when she found anybody out in some act of atrocious meanness, she never indulged in any idle threats of revenge: it was sufficient that she knew, and would take suitable steps on the earliest occasion. Consequently when it appeared, from the artless conversation of the guru at lunch, that the perfidious Mrs Quantock had not even asked him whether he would like to go to Lucia's garden-party or not (pending her own decision as to what she was meaning to do with him) Lucia received the information with the utmost good-humour, merely saying, 'No doubt dear Mrs Quantock forgot to tell you,' and did not announce acts of reprisal, such as striking Daisy off the list of her habitual guests for a week or two, just to give her a lesson. She even, before they sat down to lunch, telephoned over to that thwarted woman to say that she had met the guru in the street, and they had both felt that there was some wonderful bond of sympathy between them, so he had come back with her, and they were just sitting down to tiffin. She was pleased with the word 'tiffin', and also liked explaining to Daisy what it meant.

Tiffin was a great success, and there was no need for the guru to visit the kitchen in order to make something that could be eaten without struggle. He talked quite freely about his mission here, and Lucia and Georgie and Peppino, who had come in rather late, for he had been obliged to go back to the market-gardener's about the bulbs, listened entranced.

'Yes, it was when I went to my friend who keeps the bookshop,' he said, 'that I knew there was English lady who wanted guru, and I knew I was called to her. No luggage, no anything at all: as I am. Such a kind lady, too, and she will get on well, but she will find some of the postures difficult, for she is what you call globe, round.'

'Was that postures when I saw her standing on one leg in the garden?' asked Georgie, 'and when she sat down and tried to hold her toes?'

'Yes, indeed, quite so, and difficult for globe. But she has white soul.'

He looked round with a smile.

'I see many white souls here,' he said. 'It is happy place, when there are white souls, for to them I am sent.'

This was sufficient: in another minute Lucia, Georgie and Peppino were all accepted as pupils, and presently they went out into the garden, where the guru sat on the ground in a most complicated attitude which was obviously quite out of reach of Mrs Quantock.

'One foot on one thigh, other foot on other thigh,' he explained. 'And the head and back straight: it is good to meditate so.'

Lucia tried to imagine meditating so, but felt that any meditation so would certainly be on the subject of broken bones.

'Shall I be able to do that?' she asked. 'And what will be the effect?'

'You will be light and active, dear lady, and ah – here is other dear lady come to join us.'

Mrs Quantock had certainly made one of her diplomatic errors on this occasion. She had acquiesced on the telephone in her guru going to tiffin with Lucia, but about the middle of her lunch, she had been unable to resist the desire to know what was happening at The Hurst. She could not bear the thought that Lucia and her guru were together now, and her own note, saying that it was uncertain whether the guru would come to the garden-party or not filled her with the most uneasy apprehensions. She would sooner have acquiesced in her guru going to fifty garden-parties, where all was public, and she could keep an eye and a control on him, rather than that Lucia should have 'enticed him in' – that was her phrase – like this to tiffin. The only consolation was that her own lunch had been practically inedible, and Robert had languished lamentably for the guru to return, and save his stomach. She had left him glowering over a little mud and water called coffee. Robert, at any rate, would welcome the return of the guru.

She waddled across the lawn to where this harmonious party was sitting, and at that moment Lucia began to feel vindictive. The calm of victory which had permeated her when she brought the guru in to lunch, without any bother at all, was troubled and broken up, and darling Daisy's note, containing the outrageous falsity that the guru would not certainly accept an invitation which had never been permitted to reach him at all, assumed a more sinister aspect. Clearly now Daisy had intended to keep him to herself, a fact that she already suspected, and had made a hostile invasion.

'Guru, dear, you naughty thing,' said Mrs Quantock playfully, after the usual salutations had passed, 'why did you not tell your Chela you would not be home for tiffin?'

The guru had unwound his legs, and stood up.

'But see, beloved lady,' he said, 'how pleasant we all are! Take not too much thought, when it is only white souls who are together.'

Mrs Quantock patted his shoulder.

'It is all good and kind Om,' she said. 'I send out my message of love. There!'

It was necessary to descend from these high altitudes, and Lucia proceeded to do so, as in a parachute that dropped swiftly at first, and then floated in still air.

'And we're making such a lovely plan, dear Daisy,' she said. 'The guru is going to teach us all. Classes! Aren't you?'

He held his hands up to his head, palms outwards, and closed his eyes.

'I seem to feel call,' he said. 'I am sent. Surely the Guides tell me there is a sending of me. What you call classes? Yes? I teach: you learn. We all learn . . . I leave all to you. I will walk a little way off to arbour, and meditate, and then when you have arranged, you will tell guru, who is your servant. Salaam! Om!'

With the guru in her own house, and with every intention to annex him, it was no wonder that Lucia took the part of chairman in this meeting that was to settle the details of the esoteric brotherhood that was to be formed in Riseholme. Had not Mrs Quantock been actually present, Lucia in revenge for her outrageous conduct about the garden-party invitation would probably have left her out of the classes altogether, but with her sitting firm and square in a basket chair, that creaked querulously as she moved, she could not be completely ignored. But Lucia took the lead throughout, and suggested straight away that the smoking-parlour would be the most convenient place to hold the classes in.

'I should not think of invading your house, dear Daisy,' she said, 'and here is the smoking-parlour which no one ever sits in, so quiet and peaceful. Yes. Shall we consider that settled, then?'

She turned briskly to Mrs Quantock.

'And now where shall the guru stay?' she said. 'It would be too bad, dear Daisy, if we are all to profit by his classes, that you should have all the trouble and expense of entertaining him, for in your sweet little house he must be a great inconvenience, and I think you said that your husband had given up his dressing-room to him.'

Mrs Quantock made a desperate effort to retain her property.

'No inconvenience at all,' she said, 'quite the contrary in fact, dear. It is delightful having him, and Robert regards him as a most desirable inmate.'

Lucia pressed her hand feelingly.

'You and your husband are too unselfish,' she said. 'Often have I

said, "Daisy and Mr Robert are the most unselfish people I know."
Haven't I, Georgie? But we can't permit you to be so crowded.
Your only spare room, you know, *and* your husband's dressing-
room! Georgie, I know you agree with me; we must not permit dear
Daisy to be so unselfish.'

The birdlike eye produced its compelling effect on Georgie. So
short a time ago he had indulged in revolutionary ideas, and had
contemplated having the guru and Olga Bracely to dinner, without
even asking Lucia: now the faint stirrings of revolt faded like snow in
summer. He knew quite well what Lucia's next proposition would
be: he knew, too, that he would agree to it.

'No, that would never do,' he said. 'It is simply trespassing on Mrs
Quantock's good nature, if she is to board and lodge him, while he
teaches all of us. I wish I could take him in, but with Hermy and
Ursy coming tonight, I have as little room as Mrs Quantock.'

'He shall come here,' said Lucia brightly, as if she had just that
moment thought of it. 'There are Hamlet and Othello vacant' – all
her rooms were named after Shakespearian plays – 'and it will not be
the least inconvenient. Will it, Peppino? I shall really like having
him here. Shall we consider that settled, then?'

Daisy made a perfectly futile effort to send forth a message of
love to all quarters of the compass. Bitterly she repented of having
ever mentioned her guru to Lucia: it had never occurred to her that
she would annex him like this. While she was cudgelling her brains
as to how she could arrest this powerful offensive, Lucia went
sublimely on.

'Then there's the question of what we shall pay him,' she said.
'Dear Daisy tells us that he scarcely knows what money is, but I for
one could never dream of profiting by his wisdom, if I was to pay
nothing for it. The labourer is worthy of his hire, and so I suppose
the teacher is. What if we pay him five shillings each a lesson: that
will make a pound a lesson. Dear me! I shall be busy this August.
Now how many classes shall we ask him to give us? I should say six to
begin with, if everybody agrees. One every day for the next week
except Sunday. That is what you all wish? Yes? Then shall we consider
that settled?'

Mrs Quantock, still impotently rebelling, resorted to the most
dire weapon in her armoury, namely, sarcasm.

'Perhaps, darling Lucia,' she said, 'it would be well to ask my guru
if he has anything to say to your settlings. England is a free country
still, even if you happen to have come from India.'

Lucia had a deadlier weapon than sarcasm, which was the apparent unconsciousness of there having been any. For it is no use plunging a dagger into your enemy's heart, if it produces no effect whatever on him. She clapped her hands together, and gave her peal of silvery laughter.

'What a good idea!' she said. 'Then you would like me to go and tell him what we propose? Just as you like. I will trot away, shall I, and see if he agrees. Don't think of stirring, dear Daisy, I know how you feel the heat. Sit quiet in the shade. As you know, I am a real salamander, the sun is never *troppo caldo* for me.'

She tripped off to where the guru was sitting in that wonderful position. She had read the article in the Encyclopaedia about Yoga right through again this morning, and had quite made up her mind, as indeed her proceedings had just shown, that Yoga was, to put it irreverently, to be her August stunt. He was still so deep in meditation that he could only look dreamily in her direction as she approached, but then with a long sigh he got up.

'This is beautiful place,' he said. 'It is full of sweet influences and I have had high talk with Guides.'

Lucia felt thrilled.

'Ah, do tell me what they said to you,' she exclaimed.

'They told me to follow where I was led: they said they would settle everything for me in wisdom and love.'

This was most encouraging, for decidedly Lucia had been settling for him, and the opinion of the Guides was thus a direct personal testimonial. Any faint twitchings of conscience (they were of the very faintest) that she had grabbed dear Daisy's property were once and for ever quieted, and she proceeded confidently to unfold the settlements of wisdom and love, which met with the guru's entire approval. He shut his eyes a moment and breathed deeply.

'They give peace and blessing,' he said. 'It is they who ordered that it should be so. Om!'

He seemed to sink into profound depths of meditation, and Lucia hurried back to the group she had left.

'It is all too wonderful,' she said. 'The Guides have told him that they were settling everything for him in wisdom and love, so we may be sure we were right in our plans. How lovely to think that we have been guided by them! Dear Daisy, how wonderful he is! I will send across for his things, shall I, and I will have Hamlet and Othello made ready for him!'

Bitter though it was to part with her guru, it was impious to rebel against the ordinances of the Guides, but there was a trace of human resentment in Daisy's answer.

'Things!' she exclaimed. 'He hasn't got a thing in the world. Every material possession chains us down to earth. You will soon come to that, darling Lucia.'

It occurred to Georgie that the guru had certainly got a bottle of brandy, but there was no use in introducing a topic that might lead to discord, and indeed, even as Lucia went indoors to see about Hamlet and Othello, the guru himself, having emerged from meditation, joined them and sat down by Mrs Quantock.

'Beloved lady,' he said, 'all is peace and happiness. The Guides have spoken to me so lovingly of you, and they say it is best your guru should come here. Perhaps I shall return later to your kind house. They smiled when I asked that. But just now they send me here: there is more need of me here, for already you have so much light.'

Certainly the Guides were very tactful people, for nothing could have soothed Mrs Quantock so effectually as a message of that kind, which she would certainly report to Lucia when she returned from seeing about Hamlet and Othello.

'Oh, do they say I have much light already, Guru, dear?' she asked. 'That is nice of them.'

'Surely they said it, and now I shall go back to your house, and leave sweet thoughts there for you. And shall I send sweet thoughts to the home of the kind gentleman next door?'

Georgie eagerly welcomed this proposition, for with Hermy and Ursy coming that evening, he felt that he would have plenty of use for sweet thoughts. He even forbore to complete in his own mind the conjecture that was forming itself there, namely, that though the guru would be leaving sweet thoughts for Mrs Quantock, he would probably be taking away the brandy bottle for himself. But Georgie knew he was only too apt to indulge in secret cynicisms and perhaps there was no brandy to take away by this time . . . and lo and behold, he was being cynical again.

The sun was still hot when, half an hour afterwards, he got into the open cab which he had ordered to take him to the station to meet Hermy and Ursy, and he put up his umbrella with its white linen cover, to shield him from it. He did not take the motor, because either Hermy or Ursy would have insisted on driving it, and he did not choose to put himself in their charge. In all the years that he had lived at Riseholme, he never remembered a time when social events – 'work', he called it – had been so exciting and varied. There were Hermy and

Ursy coming this evening, and Olga Bracely and her husband (Olga Bracely and Mr Shuttleworth sounded vaguely improper: Georgie rather liked that) were coming tomorrow, and there was Lucia's garden-party the day after, and every day there was to be a lesson from the guru, so that God alone knew when Georgie would have a moment to himself for his embroidery or to practise the Mozart trio. But with his hair chestnut-coloured to the very roots, and his shining nails, and his comfortable boots, he felt extremely young and fit for anything. Soon, under the influence of the new creed with its postures and breathings, he would feel younger and more vigorous yet.

But he wished that it had been he who had found this pamphlet on Eastern philosophies, which had led Mrs Quantock to make the enquiries that had resulted in the epiphany of the guru. Of course when once Lucia had heard about it, she was certain to constitute herself head and leader of the movement, and it was really remarkable how completely she had done that. In that meeting in the garden just now she had just sailed through Mrs Quantock as calmly as a steamer cuts through the waters of the sea, throwing her off from her penetrating bows like a spent wave. But baffled though she was for the moment, Georgie had been aware that Mrs Quantock seethed with revolutionary ideas: she deeply resented this confiscation of what was certainly her property, though she was impotent to stop it, and Georgie knew just what she felt. It was all very well to say that Lucia's schemes were entirely in accord with the purposes of the Guides. That might be so, but Mrs Quantock would not cease to think that she had been robbed . . .

Yet nothing mattered if all the class found themselves getting young and active and loving and excellent under this tuition. It was that notion which had taken such entire command of them all, and for his part Georgie did not really care who owned the guru, so to speak, if only he got the benefit of his teachings. For social purposes Lucia had annexed him, and doubtless with him in the house she could get little instructions and hints that would not count as a lesson, but after all, Georgie had still got Olga Bracely to himself, for he had not breathed a word of her advent to Lucia. He felt rather like one who, when revolutionary ideas are in the air, had concealed a revolver in his pocket. He did not formulate to himself precisely what he was going to do with it, but it gave him a sense of power to know it was there.

The train came in, but he looked in vain for his sisters. They had distinctly said they were arriving by it, but in a couple of minutes it was perfectly clear that they had done nothing of the kind, for the only person who got out was Mrs Weston's cook, who as all the world knew went into Brinton every Wednesday to buy fish. At the rear of the train, however, was an immense quantity of luggage being taken out, which could not all be Mrs Weston's fish, and indeed, even at that distance there was something familiar to Georgie about a very large green hold-all which was dumped there. Perhaps Hermy and Ursy had travelled in the van, because 'it was such a lark', or for some other tomboy reason, and he went down the platform to investigate. There were bags of golf clubs, and a dog, and portmanteaux, and even as the conviction dawned on him that he had seen some of these objects before, the guard, to whom Georgie always gave half a crown when he travelled by this train, presented him with a note scrawled in pencil. It ran:

> DEAREST GEORGIE – It was such a lovely day that when we got to Paddington Ursy and I decided to bicycle down instead, so for a lark we sent our things on, and we may arrive tonight, but probably tomorrow. Take care of Tiptree: and give him plenty of jam. He loves it.
>
> Yours,
>
>   HERMY
>
> PS – Tipsipoozie doesn't really bite: it's only his fun.

Georgie crumpled up this odious epistle, and became aware that Tipsipoozie, a lean Irish terrier, was regarding him with peculiar disfavour, and showing all his teeth, probably in fun. In pursuance of this humorous idea, he then darted towards Georgie, and would have been extremely funny, if he had not been handicapped by the bag of golf clubs to which he was tethered. As it was, he pursued him down the platform, towing the clubs after him, till he got entangled in them and fell down.

Georgie hated dogs at any time, though he had never hated one so much as Tipsipoozie, and the problems of life became more complicated than ever. Certainly he was not going to drive back with Tipsipoozie in his cab, and it became necessary to hire another for that abominable hound and the rest of the luggage. And what on earth was to happen when he arrived home, if Tipsipoozie did not drop his fun and become serious? Foljambe, it is true, liked dogs, so perhaps dogs liked her . . . 'But it is most tarsome of Hermy!' thought Georgie bitterly. 'I wonder what the guru would do.' There ensued a very trying ten minutes, in which the station-master, the porters,

Georgie and Mrs Weston's maid all called Tipsipoozie a good dog as he lay on the ground snapping promiscuously at those who praised him. Eventually a valiant porter picked up the bag of clubs, and by holding them out in front of him at the extreme length of his arms, in the manner of a fishing rod, with Tipsipoozie on a short chain at the other end of the bag, like a savage fish, cursing and swearing, managed to propel him into the cab, and there was another half-crown gone. Georgie thereupon got into his cab and sped homewards in order to arrive there first, and consult with Foljambe. Foljambe usually thought of something.

Foljambe came out at the noise of the arriving wheels and Georgie explained the absence of his sisters and the advent of an atrocious dog.

'He's very fierce,' he said, 'but he likes jam.'

Foljambe gave that supreme smile which sometimes Georgie resented. Now he hailed it, as if it was 'an angel-face's smile'.

'I'll see to him, sir,' she said. 'I've brought up your tea.'

'But you'll take care, Foljambe, won't you?' he asked.

'I expect he'd better take care,' returned the intrepid woman.

Georgie, as he often said, trusted Foljambe completely, which must explain why he went into his drawing-room, shut the door, and looked out of the window when the second cab arrived. She opened the door, put her arms inside, and next moment emerged again with Tipsipoozie on the end of the chain, making extravagant exhibitions of delight. Then to Georgie's horror, the drawing-room door opened, and in came Tipsipoozie without any chain at all. Rapidly sending a message of love in all directions like an SOS call, Georgie put a small chair in front of him, to shield his legs. Tipsipoozie evidently thought it was a game, and hid behind the sofa to rush out again from ambush.

'Just got snappy being tied to those golf clubs,' remarked Foljambe.

But Georgie, as he put some jam into his saucer, could not help wondering whether the message of love had not done it.

He dined alone, for Hermy and Ursy did not appear, and had a great polishing of his knick-knacks afterwards, while waiting for them. No one ever felt anxious at the non-arrival of those sisters, for they always turned up from their otter-hunting or their golf sooner or later, chiefly later, in the highest spirits at the larks they had had, with amazingly dirty hands and prodigious appetites. But when twelve o'clock struck, he decided to give up all idea of their appearance that night, and having given Tipsipoozie some more jam and a comfortable bed in the woodshed, he went upstairs to his room.

Though he knew it was still possible that he might be roused by wild 'Cooees!' and showers of gravel at his window, and have to come down and minister to their gross appetites, the prospect seemed improbable and he soon went to sleep.

Georgie awoke with a start some hours later, wondering what had disturbed him. There was no gravel rattling on his window, no violent ringing of bicycle bells, nor loud genial shouts outraging the decorous calm of Riseholme, but certainly he had heard something. Next moment, the repeated noise sent his heart leaping into his throat, for quite distinctly he heard a muffled sound in the room below, which he instantly diagnosed with fatal certainty as burglars. The first emotion that mingled itself with the sheer terror was a passionate regret that Hermy and Ursy had not come. They would have thought it tremendous larks, and would have invented some wonderful offensive with fire-irons and golf clubs and dumbbells. Even Tipsipoozie, the lately-abhorred, would have been a succour in this crisis, and why, oh why, had not Georgie had him to sleep in his bedroom instead of making him cosy in the woodshed? He would have let Tipsipoozie sleep on his lovely blue quilt for the remainder of his days, if only Tipsipoozie could have been with him now, ready to have fun with the burglar below. As it was, the servants were in the attics at the top of the house, Dicky slept out, and Georgie was all alone, with the prospect of having to defend his property at risk of his life. Even at this moment, as he sat up in bed, blanched with terror, these miscreants might be putting his treasure into their pockets. The thought of the Fabergé cigarette case, and the Louis XVI snuff box, and the Queen Anne toy-porringer which he had inherited all these years, made even life seem cheap, for life would be intolerable without them, and he sprang out of bed, groped for his slippers, since until he had made a plan it was wiser not to show a light, and shuffled noiselessly towards the door.

Chapter Six

The door-handle felt icy to fingers already frozen with fright, but he stood firmly grasping it, ready to turn it noiselessly when he had quite made up his mind what to do. The first expedient that suggested itself, with an overpowering sweetness of relief, was that of locking his door, going back to bed again, and pretending that he had heard nothing. But apart from the sheer cowardice of that, which he did not mind so much, as nobody else would ever know his guilt, the thought of the burglar going off quite unmolested with his property was intolerable. Even if he could not summon up enough courage to get downstairs with his life and a poker in his hand, he must at least give them a good fright. They had frightened him, and so he would frighten them. They should not have it all their own way, and if he decided not to attack them (or him) single-handed, he could at least thump on the floor, and call out 'Burglars!' at the top of his voice, or shout 'Charles! Henry! Thomas!' as if summoning a bevy of stalwart footmen. The objection to this course, however, would be that Foljambe or somebody else might hear him, and in this case, if he did not then go downstairs to mortal combat, the knowledge of his cowardice would be the property of others beside himself . . . And all the time he hesitated, they were probably filling their pockets with his dearest possessions.

He tried to send out a message of love, but he was totally unable to do so.

Then the little clock on his mantelpiece struck two, which was a miserable hour, sundered so far from dawn.

Though he had lived through years of agony since he got out of bed, the actual passage of time, as he stood frozen to the door-handle, was but the duration of a few brief seconds, and then making a tremendous call on his courage he felt his way to his fireplace, and picked up the poker. The tongs and shovel rattled treacherously, and he hoped that had not been heard, for the essence of his plan (though he had yet no idea what that plan was) must be silence till some awful surprise broke upon them. If only he could summon the police, he could come rushing downstairs with his poker, as the professional supporters of the law gained an entrance to his house, but unfortunately the telephone was downstairs, and he could not reasonably hope to carry on a conversation with the police station without being overheard by the burglars.

He opened his door with so masterly a movement that there was no sound either from the hinges nor from the handle as he turned it, and peered out. The hall below was dark, but a long pencil of light came from the drawing-room, which showed where the reckless brutes must be, and there, too, alas! was his case of treasures. Then suddenly he heard the sound of a voice, speaking very low, and another voice answered it. At that Georgie's heart sank, for this proved that there must be at least two burglars, and the odds against him were desperate.

After that came a low, cruel laugh, the unmistakable sound of the rattle of knives and forks, and the explosive uncorking of a bottle. At that his heart sank even lower yet, for he had read that cool habitual burglars always had supper before they got to work, and therefore he was about to deal with a gang of professionals. Also that explosive uncorking clearly indicated champagne, and he knew that they were feasting on his best. And how wicked of them to take their unhallowed meal in his drawing-room, for there was no proper table there, and they would be making a dreadful mess over everything.

A current of cool night air swept up the stairs, and Georgie saw the panel of light from the open drawing-room door diminish in width, and presently the door shut with a soft thud, leaving him in the dark. At that his desperation seemed pressed and concentrated into a moment of fictitious courage, for he unerringly reasoned that they had left the drawing-room window open, and that perhaps in a few moments now they would have finished their meal and with bulging pockets would step forth unchallenged into the night. Why had he never had bolts put on his shutters, like Mrs Weston, who lived in nightly terror of burglars? But it was too late to think of that now, for it was impossible to ask them to step out till he had put bolts up, and then when he was ready begin again.

He could not let them go gorged with his champagne and laden with his treasures without reprisals of some sort, and keeping his thoughts steadily away from revolvers and clubs and sandbags, walked straight downstairs, threw open the drawing-room door, and with his poker grasped in his shaking hand, cried out in a faint, thin voice: 'If you move I shall fire.'

There was a moment of dead silence, and a little dazzled with the light he saw what faced him.

At opposite ends of his Chippendale sofa sat Hermy and Ursy. Hermy had her mouth open and held a bun in her dirty hands. Ursy had her mouth shut and her cheeks were bulging. Between them was a ham and a loaf of bread, and a pot of marmalade and a Stilton cheese, and on the floor was the bottle of champagne with two brimming bubbling tea-cups full of wine. The cork and the wire and the tinfoil they had, with some show of decency, thrown into the fireplace.

Hermy put down her bun, and gave a great shout of laughter; Ursy's mouth was disgustingly full and she exploded. Then they lay back against the arms of the sofa and howled.

Georgie was very much vexed.

'Upon my word, Hermy!' he said, and then found it was not nearly a strong enough expression. And in a moment of ungovernable irritation he said: 'Damn it all!'

Hermy showed signs of recovery first, and as Georgie came back after shutting the window, could find her voice, while Ursy collected small fragments of ham and bread which she had partially chewed.

'Lord! What a lark!' she said. 'Georgie, it's *the* most ripping lark.'

Ursy pointed to the poker.

'He'll fire if we move,' she cried. 'Or poke the fire, was it?'

'Ask another!' screamed Hermy. 'Oh, dear, he thought we were burglars, and came down with a poker, brave boy! It's positively the limit. Have a drink, Georgie.'

Suddenly her eyes grew round and awestruck, and pointing with her finger to Georgie's shoulder, she went off into another yell of laughter.

'Ursy! His hair!' she said, and buried her face in a soft cushion.

Naturally Georgie had not put his hair in order when he came downstairs, for nobody thinks about things like that when he is going to encounter burglars single-handed, and there was his bald pate and his long tresses hanging down one side.

It was most annoying, but when an irremediable annoyance has absolutely occurred, the only possible thing for a decent person to do is to take it as lightly as possible. Georgie rose gallantly to the occasion, gave a little squeal and ran from the room.

'Down again presently,' he called out, and had a heavy fall on the stairs, as he went up to his bedroom. There he had a short argument with himself. It was possible to slam his door, go to bed, and be very polite in the morning. But that would never do: Hermy and Ursy would have a joke against him for ever. It was really much better to share in the joke, identifying himself with it. So he brushed his hair in the orthodox fashion, put on a very smart dressing-gown, and came tripping downstairs again.

'My dears, what fun!' he said. 'Let's all have supper. But let's move into the dining-room, where there's a table, and I'll get another bottle of wine, and some glasses, and we'll bring Tipsipoozie in. You naughty girls, fancy arriving at a time like this. I suppose your plan was to go very quietly to bed, and come down to breakfast in the morning, and give me a fine surprise. Tell me about it now.'

So presently Tipsipoozie was having his marmalade, which did just as well as jam, and they were all eating slices off the ham, and stuffing them into split buns.

'Yes, we thought we might as well do it all in one go,' said Hermy, 'and it's a hundred and twenty miles, if it's a yard. And then it was so late when we got here, we thought we wouldn't disturb you, specially as the drawing-room window wasn't bolted.'

'Bicycles outside,' said Ursy, 'they'll just have to be out at grass till morning. Oh, Tipsi-ipsi-poozie-woozy, how is you? Hope he behaved like the good little Tiptree that he is, Georgie?'

'Oh yes, we made great friends,' said Georgie sketchily. 'He was a wee bit upset at the station, but then he had a good tea with his Uncle Georgie and played hide and seek.'

Rather rashly, Georgie made a face at Tiptree, the sort of face which amuses children. But it didn't amuse Tiptree, who made another face, in which teeth played a prominent part.

'Fool-dog,' said Hermy, carelessly smacking him across the nose. 'Always hit him if he shows his teeth, Georgie. Pass the fizz.'

'Well, so we got through the drawing-room window,' continued Ursy, 'and golly, we were hungry. So we foraged, and there we were! Jolly plucky of you, Georgie, to come down and beard us.'

'Real sport,' said Hermy. 'And how's old Fol-de-rol-de-ray? Why didn't she come down and fight us, too?'

Georgie guessed that Hermy was making a humorous allusion to Foljambe, who was the one person in Riseholme whom his two sisters seemed to hold in respect. Ursy had once set a booby-trap for Georgie, but the mixed biscuits and Brazil nuts had descended on Foljambe instead. On that occasion Foljambe, girt about in impenetrable calm, had behaved as if nothing had happened and trod on biscuits and Brazil nuts without a smile, unaware to all appearance that there was anything whatever crunching and exploding beneath her feet. That had somehow quelled the two, who, as soon as she left the room again, swept up the mess, and put the uninjured Brazil nuts back into the dessert dish . . . It would never do if Foljambe lost her prestige and was alluded to by some outrageously slangy name.

'If you mean Foljambe,' said Georgie icily, 'it was because I didn't think it worth while to disturb her.'

*   *   *

In spite of their ride, the indefatigable sisters were up early next morning, and the first thing Georgie saw out of his bathroom window was the pair of them practising lifting shots over the ducking-pond on the green till breakfast was ready. He had given a short account of last night's adventure to Foljambe when she called him, omitting the episode about his hair, and her disapproval was strongly indicated by her silence then, and the studied contempt of her manner to the sisters when they came in to breakfast.

'Hello, Foljambe,' said Hermy. 'We had a rare lark last night.'

'So I understand, miss,' said Foljambe.

'Got in through the drawing-room window,' said Hermy, hoping to make her smile.

'Indeed, miss,' said Foljambe. 'Have you any orders for the car, sir?'

'Oh, Georgie, may we run over to the links this morning?' asked Hermy. 'Mayn't Dickie-bird take us there?'

She glanced at Foljambe to see whether this brilliant wit afforded her any amusement. Apparently it didn't.

'Tell Dicky to be round at half-past ten,' said Georgie.

'Yes, sir.'

'Hurrah!' said Ursy. 'Come, too, Foljambe, and we'll have a three-ball match.'

'No, thank you, miss,' said Foljambe, and sailed from the room, looking down her nose.

'Golly, what an iceberg!' said Hermy when the door was quite shut.

*   *   *

Georgie was not sorry to have the morning to himself, for he wanted to have a little quiet practice at the Mozart trio, before he went over to Lucia's at half-past eleven, the hour when she had arranged to run through it for the first time. He would also have time to do a few posturing exercises before the first Yoga-class, which was to take place in Lucia's smoking-parlour at half-past twelve. That would make a pretty busy morning, and as for the afternoon, there would be sure to be some callers, since the arrival of his sisters had been expected, and after that he had to go to the Ambermere Arms for his visit to Olga Bracely . . . And what was he to do about her with regard to Lucia? Already he had been guilty of disloyalty, for Lady Ambermere had warned him of the prima-donna's arrival yesterday, and he had not instantly communicated that really great piece of news to Lucia. Should he make such amends as were in his power for that omission, or, greatly daring, should he keep her to himself, as Mrs Quantock so fervently wished that she had done with regard to the guru? After the adventure of last night, he felt he ought to be able to look any situation in the face, but he found himself utterly unable to conceive himself manly and erect before the birdlike eyes of the Queen, if she found out that Olga Bracely had been at Riseholme for the day of her garden-party, and that Georgie, knowing it and having gone to see her, had not informed the Court of that fact.

The spirit of Bolshevism, the desire to throw off all authority and act independently, which had assailed him yesterday returned now with redoubled force. If he had been perfectly certain that he would not be found out, there is no doubt he would have kept it from her, and yet, after all, what was the glory of going to see Olga Bracely (and perhaps even entertaining her here) if all Riseholme did not turn green with jealousy? Moreover there was every chance of being found out, for Lady Ambermere would be at the garden-party tomorrow, and she would be sure to wonder why Lucia had not asked Olga. Then it would come out that Lucia didn't know of that eminent presence, and Lady Ambermere would be astonished that Georgie had not told her. Thus he would be in the situation which his imagination was unable to face, although he had thrown the drawing-room door open in the middle of the night, and announced that he would fire with his poker.

No; he would have to tell Lucia, when he went to read the Mozart trio with her for the first time, and very likely she would call on Olga Bracely herself, though nobody had asked her to, and take all the wind out of Georgie's sails. Sickening though that would be, he could not face the alternative, and he opened his copy of the Mozart trio with a sigh. Lucia *did* push and shove, and have everything her own way. Anyhow he would *not* tell her that Olga and her husband were dining at The Hall tonight; he would not even tell her that her husband's name was Shuttleworth, and Lucia might make a dreadful mistake, and ask Mr and Mrs Bracely. That would be jam for Georgie, and he could easily imagine himself saying to Lucia, 'My dear, I thought you must have known that she had married Mr Shuttleworth and kept her maiden name! How tarsome for you! They are so touchy about that sort of thing.'

*   *   *

Georgie heard the tinkle of the treble part of the Mozart trio (Lucia always took the treble, because it had more tune in it, though she pretended that she had not Georgie's fine touch, which made the bass effective) as he let himself in to Shakespeare's garden a few minutes before the appointed time. Lucia must have seen him from the window, for the subdued noise of the piano ceased even before he had got as far as Perdita's garden round the sundial, and she opened the door to him. The faraway look was in her eyes, and the black undulations of hair had encroached a little on her forehead, but, after all, others besides Lucia had trouble with their hair, and Georgie only sympathised.

'*Georgino mio!*' she said. 'It is all being so wonderful. There seems a new atmosphere about the house since my guru came. Something holy and peaceful; do you not notice it?'

'Delicious!' said Georgie, inhaling the potpourri. 'What is he doing now?'

'Meditating, and preparing for our class. I do hope dear Daisy will not bring in discordant elements.'

'Oh, but that's not likely, is it?' said Georgie. 'I thought he said she had so much light.'

'Yes, he did. But now he is a little troubled about her, I think. She did not want him to go away from her house, and she sent over here for some silk pyjamas belonging to her husband, which he thought she had given him. But Robert didn't think so at all. The guru brought them across yesterday after he had left good thoughts for her in her house. But it was the Guides who wished him to come here; they told him so distinctly. It would have been very wrong of me not to do as they said.'

She gave a great sigh.

'Let us have an hour with Mozart,' she said, 'and repel all thought of discord. My guru says that music and flowers are good influences for those who are walkers on the Way. He says that my love for both of them which I have had all my life will help me very much.'

For one moment the mundane world obtruded itself into the calm peace.

'Any news in particular?' she asked. 'I saw you drive back from the station yesterday afternoon, for I happened to be looking out of the window, in a little moment of leisure – the guru says I work too hard, by the way – and your sisters were not with you. And yet there were two cabs, and a quantity of luggage. Did they not come?'

Georgie gave a respectably accurate account of all that had happened, omitting the fact of his terror when first he awoke, for that was not really a happening, and had had no effect on his subsequent proceedings. He also omitted the adventure about his hair, for that was quite extraneous, and said what fun they had all had over their supper at half-past two this morning.

'I think you were marvellously brave, Georgie,' said she, 'and most good-natured. You must have been sending out love, and so were full of it yourself, and that casts out fear.'

She spread the music open.

'Anything else?' she asked.

Georgie took his seat and put his rings on the candle-bracket.

'Oh yes,' he said, 'Olga Bracely, the prima-donna, you know, and her husband are arriving at the Ambermere Arms this afternoon for a couple of days.'

The old fire kindled.

'No!' exclaimed Lucia. 'Then they'll be here for my party tomorrow. Fancy if she would come and sing for us! I shall certainly leave cards today, and write later in the evening, asking her.'

'I have been asked to go and see her,' said Georgie, not proudly.

The music rest fell down with a loud slap, but Lucia paid no attention.

'Let us go together then,' she said. 'Who asked you to call on her?'

'Lady Ambermere,' said he.

'When she was in here yesterday? She never mentioned it to me. But she would certainly think it very odd of me not to call on friends of hers, and be polite to them. What time shall we go?'

Georgie made up his mind that wild horses should not drag from him the fact that Olga's husband's name was Shuttleworth, for here was Lucia grabbing at his discovery, just as she had grabbed at Daisy's discovery who was now 'her guru'. She should call him Mr Bracely then.

'Somewhere about six, do you think?' said he, inwardly raging.

He looked up and distinctly saw that sharp foxy expression cross Lucia's face, which from long knowledge of her he knew to betoken that she had thought of some new plan. But she did not choose to reveal it and re-erected the music rest.

'That will do beautifully,' she said. 'And now for our heavenly Mozart. You must be patient with me, Georgie, for you know how badly I read. *Caro!* How difficult it looks. I am frightened! Lucia never saw such a dwefful thing to read!'

And it had been those very bars which Georgie had heard through the open window just now.

'Georgie's is much more dwefful!' he said, remembering the double sharp that came in the second bar. 'Georgie fwightened too at reading it. O-o-h,' and he gave a little scream. '*Cattivo* Mozart to wite anything so dwefful diffy!'

*   *   *

It was quite clear at the class this morning that though the pupils were quite interested in the abstract messages of love which they were to shoot out in all directions, and in the atmosphere of peace with which they were to surround themselves, the branch of the subject which thrilled them to the marrow was the breathing exercises and contortions which, if persevered in, would give them youth and activity, faultless digestions and indefatigable energy. They all sat on the floor, and stopped up alternate nostrils, and held their breath till Mrs Quantock got purple in the face, and Georgie and Lucia red, and expelled their breath again with sudden puffs that set the rushes on the floor quivering, or with long quiet exhalations. Then there were certain postures to be learned, in one of which, entailing the bending of the body backwards, two of Georgie's trouser-buttons came off with a sharp snap and he felt the corresponding member of his braces, thus violently released, spring up to his shoulder. Various other embarrassing noises issued from Lucia and Daisy that sounded like the bursting of strings and tapes, but everybody pretended to hear nothing at all, or covered up the report of those explosions with coughings and clearings of the throat. But apart from these discordances, everything was fairly harmonious. Indeed, so far from Daisy introducing discords, she wore a fixed smile, which it would have been purely cynical to call superior, when Lucia asked some amazingly simple question with regard to Om. She sighed too, at intervals, but these sighs were expressive of nothing but patience and resignation, till Lucia's ignorance of the most elementary doctrines was enlightened, and though she rather pointedly looked in any direction but hers, and appeared completely unaware of her presence, she had not, after all, come here to look at Lucia, but to listen to her own (whatever Lucia might say) guru.

At the end Lucia, with her faraway look, emerged, you might say, in a dazed condition from hearing about the fastness of Thibet, where the guru had been in commune with the Guides, whose wisdom he interpreted to them.

'I feel such a difference already,' she said dreamily. 'I feel as if I could never be hasty or worried any more at all. Don't you experience that, dear Daisy?'

'Yes, dear,' said she. 'I went through all that at my first lesson. Didn't I, Guru dear?'

'I felt it too,' said Georgie, unwilling not to share in these benefits, and surreptitiously tightening his trouser-strap to compensate for the loss of buttons. 'And am I to do that swaying exercise before every meal?'

'Yes, Georgie,' said Lucia, saving her guru from the trouble of answering. 'Five times to the right and five times to the left and then five times backwards and forwards. I felt so young and light just now when we did it that I thought I was rising into the air. Didn't you, Daisy?'

Daisy smiled kindly.

'No, dear, that is levitation,' she said, 'and comes a very long way on.'

She turned briskly towards her guru.

'Will you tell them about that time when you levitated at Paddington Station?' she said. 'Or will you keep that for when Mrs Lucas gets rather further on? You must be patient, dear Lucia; we all have to go through the early stages, before we get to that.'

Mrs Quantock spoke as if she was in the habit of levitating herself, and it was but reasonable, in spite of the love that was swirling about them all, that Lucia should protest against such an attitude. Humility, after all, was the first essential to progress on the Way.

'Yes, dear,' she said. 'We will tread these early stages together, and encourage each other.'

*   *   *

Georgie went home, feeling also unusually light and hungry, for he had paid special attention to the exercise that enabled him to have his liver and digestive organs in complete control, but that did not prevent him from devoting his mind to arriving at that which had made Lucia look so sharp and foxy during their conversation about Olga Bracely. He felt sure that she was meaning to steal a march on him, and she was planning to draw first blood with the prima-donna, and, as likely as not, claim her for her own, with the same odious greed as she was already exhibiting with regard to the guru. All these years Georgie had been her faithful servant and coadjutor; now for the first time the spirit of independence had begun to seethe within him. The scales were falling from his eyes, and just as he turned into shelter of his mulberry tree, he put on his spectacles to see how Riseholme was getting on without him to assist at the morning parliament. His absence and Mrs Quantock's would be sure to evoke comment, and since the Yoga-classes were always to take place at half-past twelve, the fact that they would never be there, would soon rise to the level of a first-class mystery. It would, of course, begin to leak out that they and Lucia were having a course of Eastern philosophy that made its pupils young and light and energetic, and there was a sensation!

Like all great discoveries, the solution of Lucia's foxy look broke on him with the suddenness of a lightning-flash, and since it had been settled that she should call for him at six, he stationed himself in the window of his bathroom, which commanded a perfect view of the village green and the entrance to the Ambermere Arms at five. He had brought up with him a pair of opera-glasses, with the intention of taking them to bits, so he had informed Foljambe, and washing their lenses, but he did not at once proceed about this, merely holding them ready to hand for use. Hermy and Ursy had gone back to their golf again after lunch, and so callers would be told that they were all out. Thus he could wash the lenses, when he chose to do so, uninterrupted.

*　　*　　*

The minutes passed on pleasantly enough, for there was plenty going on. The two Miss Antrobuses frisked about the green, jumping over the stocks in their playful way, and running round the duck-pond in the eternal hope of attracting Colonel Boucher's attention to their pretty nimble movements. For many years past, they had tried to gain Georgie's serious attention, without any result, and lately they had turned to Colonel Boucher. There was Mrs Antrobus there, too, with her ham-like face and her ear-trumpet, and Mrs Weston was being pushed round and round the asphalt path below the elms in her bath-chair. She hated going slow, and her gardener and his boy took turns with her during her hour's carriage exercise, and propelled her, amid streams of perspiration, at a steady four miles an hour. As she passed Mrs Antrobus she shouted something at her, and Mrs Antrobus returned her reply, when next she came round.

Suddenly all these interesting objects vanished completely from Georgie's ken, for his dark suspicions were confirmed, and there was Lucia in her 'Hightum' hat and her 'Hightum' gown making her gracious way across the green. She had distinctly been wearing one of the 'Scrub' this morning at the class, so she must have changed after lunch, which was an unheard-of thing to do for a mere stroll on the green. Georgie knew well that this was no mere stroll; she was on her way to pay a call of the most formal and magnificent kind. She did not deviate a hair-breadth from her straight course to the door of the Arms, she just waggled her hand to Mrs Antrobus, blew a kiss to her sprightly daughters, made a gracious bow to Colonel Boucher, who stood up and took his hat off, and went on with the inexorability of the march of destiny, or of fate knocking at the door in the immortal fifth symphony. And in her hand she carried a note. Through his glasses Georgie could see it quite plainly, and it was not a little folded-up sheet, such as she commonly used, but a square thick envelope. She disappeared in the Arms and Georgie began thinking feverishly. A great deal depended on how long she stopped there.

A few little happenings beguiled the period of waiting. Mrs Weston desisted from her wild career, and came to anchor on the path just opposite the door into the Arms, while the gardener's boy sank exhausted on to the grass. It was quite easy to guess that she proposed to have a chat with Lucia when she came out. Similarly the Miss Antrobuses, who had paid no attention to her at all before, ceased from their pretty gambollings, and ran up to talk to her, so they wanted a word too. Colonel Boucher, a little less obviously, began throwing sticks into the ducking-pond for his bulldog (for Lucia would be obliged to pass the ducking-pond) and Mrs Antrobus examined the stocks very carefully, as if she had never seen them before.

And then, before a couple of minutes had elapsed Lucia came out. She had no longer the note in her hand, and Georgie began taking his opera-glasses to bits, in order to wash the lenses. For the present they had served their purpose. 'She has left a note on Olga Bracely,' said Georgie quite aloud, so powerful was the current of his thoughts. Then as a corollary came the further proposition which might be considered as proved, 'But she has not seen her.'

The justice of this conclusion was soon proved, for Lucia had hardly disengaged herself from the group of her subjects, and traversed the green on her way back to her house, when a motor passed Georgie's bathroom window, closely followed by a second; both drew up at the entrance to the Ambermere Arms. With the speed of a practised optician Georgie put his opera-glass together again, and after looking through the wrong end of it in his agitation was in time to see a man get out of the second car, and hold the carriage-door open for the occupants of the first. A lady got out first, tall and slight in figure, who stood there unwinding her motor veil, then she turned round again, and with a thump of his heart that surprised Georgie with its violence, he beheld the well-remembered features of his Brünnhilde.

Swiftly he passed into his bedroom next door, and arrayed himself in his summer Hightums; a fresh (almost pearly) suit of white duck, a mauve tie with an amethyst pin in it, socks, tightly braced up, of precisely the same colour as the tie, so that an imaginative beholder might have conjectured that on this warm day the end of his tie had melted and run down his legs; buckskin shoes with tall slim heels and a straw-hat completed this pretty Hightum. He had meant to wear it for the first time at Lucia's party tomorrow, but now, after her meanness, she deserved to be punished. All Riseholme should see it before she did.

The group round Mrs Weston's chair was still engaged in conversation when Georgie came up, and he casually let slip what a bore it was to pay calls on such a lovely day, but he had promised to visit Miss Olga Bracely, who had just arrived. So there was another nasty one for Lucia, since now all Riseholme would know of her actual arrival before Lucia did.

'And who, Mr Georgie,' asked Mrs Antrobus, presenting her trumpet to him in the manner in which an elephant presents its trunk to receive a bun, 'who was that with her?'

'Oh, her husband, Mr Shuttleworth,' said Georgie. 'They have just been married, and are on their honeymoon.' And if that was not another staggerer for Lucia, it is diffy, as Georgie would say, to know what a staggerer is. For Lucia would be last of all to know that this was not Mr Bracely.

'And will they be at Mrs Lucas's party tomorrow?' asked Mrs Weston.

'Oh, does she know them?' asked Georgie.

'Haw, haw, by Jove!' began Colonel Boucher. 'Very handsome woman. Envy you, my boy. Pity it's their honeymoon. Haw!'

Mrs Antrobus's trumpet was turned in his direction at this moment, and she heard these daring remarks.

'Naughty!' she said, and Georgie, the envied, passed on into the inn.

He sent in his card, on which he had thought it prudent to write 'From Lady Ambermere', and was presently led through into the garden behind the building. There she was, tall and lovely and welcoming, and held out a most cordial hand.

'How kind of you to come and see us,' she said. 'Georgie, this is Mr Pillson. My husband.'

'How do you do, Mr Shuttleworth,' said Georgie to show he knew, though his own Christian name had given him quite a start. For the moment he had almost thought she was speaking to him.

'And so Lady Ambermere asked you to come and see us?' Olga

went on. 'I think that was much kinder of her than to ask us to dinner. I hate going out to dinner in the country almost as much as I hate not going out to dinner in town. Besides with that great hook nose of hers, I'm always afraid that in an absent moment I might scratch her on the head and say "Pretty Polly". Is she a great friend of yours, Mr Pillson? I hope so, because everyone likes his best friends being laughed at.'

Up till that moment Georgie was prepared to indicate that Lady Ambermere was the hand and he the glove. But evidently that would not impress Olga in the least. He laughed in a most irreverent manner instead.

'Don't let us go,' she went on. 'Georgie, can't you send a telegram saying that we have just discovered a subsequent engagement and then we'll ask Mr Pillson to show us round this utterly adorable place, and dine with us afterwards. That would be so much nicer. Fancy living here! Oh, and do tell me something, Mr Pillson. I found a note when I arrived half an hour ago, from Mrs Lucas asking me and Mr Shuttleworth to go to a garden-party tomorrow. She said she didn't even hope that I should remember her, but would we come. Who is she? Really I don't think she can remember me very well, if she thinks I am Mrs Bracely. Georgie says I must have been married before, and that I have caused him to commit bigamy. That's pleasant conversation for a honeymoon, isn't it? Who is she?'

'Oh, she's quite an old friend of mine,' said Georgie, 'though I never knew she had met you before; I'm devoted to her.'

'Extremely proper. But now tell me this, and look straight in my face, so that I shall know if you're speaking the truth. Should I enjoy myself more wandering about this heavenly place than at her garden-party?'

Georgie felt that poor Lucia was really punished enough by this time.

'You will give her a great deal of pleasure if you go,' he began.

'Ah, that's not fair; it is hitting below the belt to appeal to unselfish motives. I have come here simply to enjoy myself. Go on; eyes front.'

The candour and friendliness of that beautiful face gave Georgie an impulse of courage. Besides, though no doubt in fun, she had already suggested that it would be much nicer to wander about with him and dine together than spend the evening among the splendours of The Hall.

'I've got a suggestion,' he said. 'Will you come and lunch with me first, and we'll stroll about, and then we can go to the garden-party, and if you don't like it I'll take you away again?'

'Done!' she said. 'Now don't you try to get out of it, because my husband is a witness. Georgie, give me a cigarette.'

In a moment Riseholme-Georgie had his cigarette case open.

'Do take one of mine,' he said, 'I'm Georgie too.'

'You don't say so! Let's send it to the Psychical Research, or whoever those people are who collect coincidences and say it's spooks. And a match please, one of you Georgies. Oh, how I should like never to see the inside of an Opera House again. Why mayn't I grow on the walls of a garden like this, or better still, why shouldn't I have a house and garden of my own here, and sing on the village green, and ask for halfpennies? Tell me what happens here! I've always lived in town since the time a hook-nosed Hebrew, rather like Lady Ambermere, took me out of the gutter.'

'My dear!' said Mr Shuttleworth.

'Well, out of an orphan-school at Brixton and I would much prefer the gutter. That's all about my early life just now, because I am keeping it for my memoirs which I shall write when my voice becomes a little more like a steam-whistle. But don't tell Lady Ambermere, for she would have a fit, but say you happen to know that I belong to the Surrey Bracelys. So I do; Brixton is on the Surrey side. Oh, my dear, look at the sun. It's behaving like the best sort of Claude! *Heile Sonne!*'

'I heard you do that last May,' said Georgie.

'Then you heard a most second-rate performance,' said she. 'But really being unlaced by that Thing, that great fat profligate beery Prussian, was almost too much for me. And the duet! But it was very polite of you to come, and I will do better next time. Siegfried! Brünnhilde! Siegfried! Miaou! Miaou! Bring on the next lot of cats! Darling Georgie, wasn't it awful? And you had proposed to me only the day before.'

'I was absolutely enchanted,' said Riseholme-Georgie.

'Yes, but then you didn't have that Thing breathing beer into your innocent face.' Georgie rose; the first call on a stranger in Riseholme was never supposed to last more than half an hour, however much you were enjoying it, and never less, however bored you might be, and he felt sure he had already exceeded this.

'I must be off,' he said. 'Too delightful to think that you and Mr Shuttleworth will come to lunch with me tomorrow. Half-past one, shall we say?'

'Excellent; but where do you live?'

'Just across the green. Shall I call for you?' he asked.

'Certainly not. Why should you have that bother?' she said. 'Ah, let me come with you to the inn-door, and perhaps you will show me from there.'

She passed through the hall with him, and they stood together in the sight of all Riseholme, which was strolling about the green at this as at most other hours. Instantly all faces turned round in their direction, like so many sunflowers following the sun, while Georgie pointed out his particular mulberry tree. When everybody had had a good look, he raised his hat.

'*A domani* then,' she said. 'So many thanks.'

And quite distinctly she kissed her hand to him as he turned away . . .

'So she talks Italian too,' thought Georgie, as he dropped little crumbs of information to his friends on his way to his house. '*Domani*, that means tomorrow. Oh yes; she was meaning lunch.'

It is hardly necessary to add that on the table in his hall there was one of Lucia's commoner kinds of note, merely a half-sheet folded together in her own manner. Georgie felt that it was scarcely more necessary to read it, for he felt quite sure that it contained some excuse for not coming to his house at six in order to call on Mr and Mrs Bracely. But he gave a glance at it before he rolled it up in a ball for Tipsipoozie to play with, and found its contents to be precisely what he expected, the excuse being that she had not done her practising. But the postscript was interesting, for it told him that she had asked Foljambe to give her his copy of *Siegfried* . . .

Georgie strolled down past The Hurst before dinner. Mozart was silent now, but there came out of the open windows the most amazing hash of sound, which he could just recognise as being the piano arrangement of the duet between Brünnhilde and Siegfried at the end. He would have been dull indeed if he had not instantly guessed what *that* signified.

Chapter Seven

A fresh thrill went through an atmosphere already super-saturated with excitement, when next morning all Lucia's friends who had been bidden to the garden-party (Tightum) were rung up on the telephone and informed that the party was Hightum. That caused a good deal of extra work, because the Tightum robes had to be put away again, and the Hightums aired and brushed and valetted. But it was well worth it, for Riseholme had not the slightest difficulty in conjecturing that Olga Bracely was to be among the guests. For a cultured and artistic centre the presence of a star that blazed so regally in the very zenith of the firmament of art absolutely demanded the Hightum which the presence of poor Lady Ambermere (though she would not have liked that) had been powerless to bring out of their cupboards. And these delightful anticipations concentrated themselves into one rose-coloured point of joy, when no less than two independent observers, without collusion, saw the piano-tuner either entering or leaving The Hurst, while a third, an ear-witness, unmistakably heard the tuning of the piano actually going on. It was thus clear to all penetrating minds that Olga Bracely was going to sing. It was further known that something was going on between her and Georgie, for she had been heard by one Miss Antrobus to ask for Georgie's number at the telephone in the Ambermere Arms. Etiquette forbade her actually to listen to what passed, but she could not help hearing Olga laugh at something (presumably) that Georgie said. He himself took no part in the green-parliament that morning, but had been seen to dash into the fruiterer's and out again, before he went in a great hurry to The Hurst, shortly after twelve-thirty. Classes on Eastern philosophy under the tuition of Mrs Quantock's Indian were already beginning to be hinted at, but today in the breathless excitement about the prima-donna nobody cared about that; they might all have been taking lessons in cannibalism, and nobody would have been interested. Finally about one o'clock one of the motors in which the party had arrived yesterday drew up at the door of the Ambermere Arms, and presently Mr Bracely – no, dear, Mr Shuttleworth – got in and drove off alone. That was very odd conduct in a lately married bridegroom, and it was hoped that there had been no quarrel.

Olga had, of course, been given no directions as to Hightum or Tightum, and when she walked across to Georgie's house shortly after half-past one only Mrs Weston who was going back home to lunch at top speed was aware that she was dressed in a very simple dark blue morning frock, that would almost have passed for Scrub. It is true that it was exceedingly well cut, and had not the look of having been rolled up in a ball and hastily ironed out again that usually distinguished Scrub, and she also wore a string of particularly fine pearls round her neck, the sort of ornament that in Riseholme would only be seen in an evening Hightum, even if anybody in Riseholme had owned such things. Lucia, not long ago, had expressed the opinion that jewels were vulgar except at night, and for her part she wore none at all, preferring one Greek cameo of uncertain authenticity.

Georgie received Olga alone, for Hermy and Ursy were not yet back from their golf.

'It is good of you to let me come without my husband,' she said. 'His excuse is toothache and he has driven into Brinton – '

'I'm very sorry,' said Georgie.

'You needn't be, for now I'll tell you his real reason. He thought that if he lunched with you he would have to come on to the garden-party, and that he was absolutely determined not to do. You were the thin edge of the wedge, in fact. My dear, what a delicious house. All panelled, with that lovely garden behind. And croquet – may we play croquet after lunch? I always try to cheat, and if I'm found out I lose my temper. Georgie won't play with me, so I play with my maid.'

'This Georgie will,' said he.

'How nice of him! And do you know what we did this morning, before the toothache didn't begin? We went all over that house three doors away, which is being done up. It belongs to the proprietor of the Ambermere Arms. And – oh, I wonder if you can keep a secret?'

'Yes,' said Georgie. He probably had never kept one yet, but there was no reason why he shouldn't begin now.

'Well, I'm absolutely determined to buy it, only I daren't tell my husband until I've done it. He has an odd nature. When a thing is done, settled, and there's no help for it, he finds it adorable, but he also finds fatal objections to doing it at all, if he is consulted about it before it is done. So not a word! I shall buy it, make the garden, furnish it, down to the minutest detail, and engage the servants, and then he'll give it me for a birthday present. I had to tell somebody or I should burst.'

Georgie nearly swooned with fervour and admiration.

'But what a perfect plan!' he said. 'You really like our little Riseholme?'

'It's not a question of liking; it's a mere detail of not being able to do without it. I don't like breathing, but I should die if I didn't. I want some delicious, hole-in-the-corner, lazy backwater sort of place, where nothing ever happens, and nobody ever does anything. I've been observing all the morning, and your habits are adorable.

Nothing ever happens here, and that will precisely suit me, when I get away from my work.'

Georgie was nearer swooning than ever at this. He could hardly believe his ears when she talked of Riseholme being a lazy backwater, and almost thought she must have been speaking of London, where, as Lucia had acutely observed, people sat in the Park all morning and talked of each other's affairs, and spent the afternoon at picture-galleries, and danced all night. There was a flippant, lazy existence.

But she was far too much absorbed in her project to notice his stupefaction.

'But if you breathe a word,' she said, 'everything will be spoilt. It has to burst on Georgie. Oh, and there's another mulberry tree in your garden as well as the one in front. It's too much.'

Her eyes followed Foljambe out of the door.

'And I know your parlour-maid is called Paravicini or Grosvenor,' she said.

'No, she is Foljambe,' said Georgie.

She laughed.

'I knew I was right,' she said. 'It's practically the same thing. Oh, and last night! I never had such an awful evening. Why didn't you warn me, and my husband should have had toothache then instead of this morning.'

'What happened?' asked he.

'But the woman's insane, that Ambermere parrot, I mean. Georgie and I were ten minutes late, and she had a jet tiara on, and why did she ask us to dine at a quarter to eight, if she meant a quarter to eight, instead of saying half-past seven? They were actually going into dinner when we came, a mournful procession of three moth-eaten men and three whiskered women. Upon which the procession broke up, as if we had been the riot act, and was arranged again, as a funeral procession, and Georgie with Lady Ambermere was the hearse. We dined in the family vault and talked about Lady Ambermere's pug. She talked about you, too, and said you were of county family, and that Mrs Lucas was a very decent sort of woman, and that she herself was going to look in on her garden-party today. Then she looked at my pearls, and asked if they were genuine. So I looked at her teeth, and there was no need to ask about them.'

'Don't miss out a moment,' said Georgie greedily.

'Whenever Lady Ambermere spoke, everybody else was silent. I didn't grasp that at first, for no one had explained the rules. So she stopped in the middle of a sentence and waited till I had finished.

Then she went on again, precisely where she had left off. Then when we came into the drawing-room, the whiskered ladies and I, there was a little woman like a mouse sitting there, and nobody introduced her. So naturally I went to talk to her, before which the great parrot said, "Will you kindly fetch my wool-work, Miss Lyall?" and Miss Lyall took a sack out of the corner, and inside was the sacred carpet. And then I waited for some coffee and cigarettes, and I waited, and I waited, and I am waiting still. The Parrot said that coffee always kept her awake, and that was why. And then Georgie came in with the others, and I could see by his face that he hadn't had a cigarette either. It was then half-past nine. And then each man sat down between two women, and Pug sat in the middle and looked for fleas. Then Lady Ambermere got up, and came across the charmed circle to me. She said: "I hope you have brought your music, Mrs Shuttle-worth. Kindly open the piano, Miss Lyall. It was always considered a remarkably fine instrument." '

Olga waved the fork on which was impaled a piece of the pineapple which Georgie had purchased that morning at the fruiterer's.

'The stupendous cheek!' she said. 'I thought it must be a joke, and laughed with the greatest politeness. But it wasn't! You'll hardly believe it, but it wasn't! One of the whiskered ones said, "That will be a great treat," and another put on the face that everyone wears at concerts. And I was so stunned that I sang, and Lady Ambermere beat time, and Pug barked.'

She pointed a finger at Georgie.

'Never till the Day of Judgement,' she said, 'when Lady Ambermere gnashes her beautiful teeth for ever and ever, will I set foot in that house again. Nor she in my house. I will set fire to it sooner. There! My dear, what a good lunch you have given me. May we play croquet at once?'

Lucia's garden-parties were scheduled from four to seven and half an hour before the earliest guest might be expected, she was casting an eagle eye over the preparations which today were on a very sumptuous scale. The bowls were laid out in the bowling-alley, not because anybody in Hightums dresses was the least likely to risk the stooping down and the strong movements that the game entailed, but because bowls were Elizabethan. Between the alley and the lawn nearer to the house was a large marquee, where the commoner crowd – though no crowd could be really common in Riseholme – would refresh itself. But even where none are common there may still be degrees in rarity, and by the side of this general refreshment room was a smaller tent carpeted with Oriental rugs, and having inside it some half-dozen chairs, and two seats which can only be described as thrones, for Lady Ambermere or Olga Bracely, while Lucia's guru, though throneworthy, would very kindly sit in one of his most interesting attitudes on the floor. This tent was designed only for high converse, and common guests (if they were good) would be led into it and introduced to the great presences, while for the refreshment of the presences, in intervals of audience, a more elaborate meal, with peaches and four sorts of sandwiches, was laid in the smoking-parlour. Thus those guests for whom audiences were not provided, could have the felicity of seeing the great ones pass across the lawn on their excursions for food, and possibly trip over the croquet hoops, which had been left up to give an air of naturalness to the lawn. In the smoking-parlour an Elzevir or two were left negligently open, as if Mr and Mrs Lucas had been reading the works of Persius and Juvenal when the first guests arrived. In the music-room, finally, which was not usually open on these occasions, there were fresh flowers: the piano, too, was open, and if you had not seen the Elzevirs in the smoking-parlour, it would have been reasonable for the early guests, if they penetrated here, to imagine that Mrs Lucas had been running over the last act of *Siegfried* a minute before.

In this visit of final inspection Lucia was accompanied by her guru, for he was part of the domestic *dramatis personae*, and she wanted him to be 'discovered' in the special tent. She pointed out the site of his proposed 'discovery' to him.

'Probably the first person I shall bring in here,' she said, 'will be Lady Ambermere, for she is noted for her punctuality. She is so anxious to see you, and would it not be exciting if you found you had met before? Her husband was Governor of Madras, and she spent many years in India.'

'Madras, gracious lady?' asked the guru. 'I, too, know Madras: there are many dark spirits in Madras. And she was at English Residency?'

'Yes. She says Mr Kipling knows nothing about India. You and she will have much to talk about. I wish I could sit on the floor, too, and listen to what you say to each other.'

'It will be great treat,' said the guru thoughtfully, 'I love all who love my wonderful country.'

Suddenly he stopped, and put his hands up to his head, palms outward.

'There are wonderful vibrations today,' he said. 'All day I feel that some word is on way from the Guides, some great message of light.'

'Oh, wouldn't it be wonderful if it came to you in the middle of my garden-party?' said Lucia enthusiastically.

'Ah, gracious lady, the great word comes not so. It comes always in solitude and quiet. Gracious lady knows that as well as Guru.'

Pure guruism and social pre-eminence struggled together in Lucia. Guruism told her that she ought to be ecstatic at the idea of a great message coming and should instantly smile on his desire for solitude and quiet, while social pre-eminence whispered to her that she had already dangled the presence of a high-caste mystic from Benares before the eyes of Lady Ambermere, who only came from Madras. On the other hand Olga Bracely was to be an even more resplendent guest than either Lady Ambermere or the guru; surely Olga Bracely was enough to set this particular garden-party on the giddiest of pinnacles. And an awful consequence lurked as a possibility if she attempted to force her guru not to immure himself in solitude and quiet, which was that conceivably he might choose to go back to the pit whence he was digged, namely the house of poor Daisy Quantock. The thought was intolerable, for with him in her house, she had seen herself as dispenser of Eastern Mysteries, and Mistress of Omism to Riseholme. In fact the guru was her August stunt; it would never do to lose him before the end of July, and rage to see all Riseholme making pilgrimages to Daisy. There was a thin-lipped firmness, too, about him at this moment: she felt that under provocation he might easily defy or desert her. She felt she had to yield, and so decided to do so in the most complete manner.

'Ah, yes,' she said. 'I know how true that is. Dear Guru, go up to Hamlet: no one will disturb you there. But if the message comes through before Lady Ambermere goes away, promise me you will come back.'

He went back to the house, where the front door was already open to admit Lady Ambermere, who was telling 'her people' when to come back for her, and fled with the heels of his slippers tapping on the oak stairs up to Hamlet. Softly he shut out the dark spirits from Madras, and made himself even more secure by turning the key in his door. It would never do to appear as a high-caste Brahmin from Benares before anyone who knew India with such fatal intimacy, for he might not entirely correspond with her preconceived notions of such a person.

Lady Ambermere's arrival was soon followed by that of other guests, and instead of going into the special tent reserved for the lions, she took up a commanding position in the middle of the lawn, where she could examine everybody through her tortoiseshell-handled lorgnette. She kept Peppino by her, who darted forward to shake hands with his wife's guests, and then darted back again to her. Poor Miss Lyall stood behind her chair, and from time to time as ordered, gave her a cape, or put up her parasol, or adjusted her footstool for her, or took up Pug or put him down as her patroness required. Most of the time Lady Ambermere kept up a majestic monologue.

'You have a pretty little garden here, Mr Lucas,' she said, 'though perhaps inconveniently small. Your croquet lawn does not look to me the full size, and then there is no tennis-court. But I think you have a little strip of grass somewhere, which you use for bowls, have you not? Presently I will walk around with you and see your domain. Put Pug down again, please, Miss Lyall, and let him run about. See, he wants to play with one of those croquet balls. Put it in motion for him, and he will run with it. Bless me, who is that coming up the path at such a tremendous speed in a bath-chair? Oh, I see, it is Mrs Weston. She should not go as fast as that. If Pug was to stray on to the path he would be run over. Better pick up Pug again, Miss Lyall, till she has gone by. And here is Colonel Boucher. If he had brought his bulldogs, I should have asked him to take them away again. I should like a cup of tea, Miss Lyall, with plenty of milk in it, and not too strong. You know how I like my tea. And a biscuit or something for Pug, with a little cream in a saucer or anything that's handy.'

'Won't you come into the smoking-parlour, and have tea there, Lady Ambermere?' asked Peppino.

'The smoking-parlour?' asked she. 'How very strange to lay tea in a smoking-room.'

Peppino explained that nobody had in all probability used the smoking-parlour to smoke in for five or six years.

'Oh, if that is so, I will come,' said she. 'Better bring Pug along, too, Miss Lyall. There is a croquet-hoop. I am glad I saw it or I should have stumbled over it perhaps. Oh, this is the smoking-parlour, is it? Why do you have rushes on the floor? Put Pug in a chair, Miss Lyall, or he may prick his paws. Books, too, I see. That one lying open is an old one. It is Latin poetry. The library at The Hall is very famous for its classical literature. The first Viscount collected it, and it numbers many thousands of volumes.'

'Indeed, it is the most wonderful library,' said Peppino. 'I can never tear myself away from it, when I am at The Hall.'

'I do not wonder. I am a great student myself and often spend a morning there, do I not, Miss Lyall? You should have some new glass put in those windows, Mr Lucas. On a dark day it must be very difficult to see here. By the way, your good wife told me that there would probably be a very remarkable Indian at her party, a Brahmin from Benares, she said. I should like to have a talk with him while I am having my tea. Kindly prepare a peach for me, Miss Lyall.'

Peppino had heard about the retirement of the guru, in consequence of a message from the Guides being expected, and proceeded to explain this to Lady Ambermere, who did not take the slightest notice, as she was looking at the peaches through her lorgnette.

'That one nearest me looks eatable,' she said. 'And then I do not see Miss Olga Bracely, though I distinctly told her I should be here this afternoon, and she said Mrs Lucas had asked her. She sang to us yesterday evening at The Hall, and very creditably indeed. Her husband, Mr Shuttleworth, is a cousin of the late lord's.'

Lucia had come into the smoking-parlour during this speech, and heard these fatal words. At the moment she would gladly have recalled her invitation to Olga Bracely altogether, sooner than have alluded therein to Mr Bracely. But that was one of the irremediable things of life, and since it was no use wasting regret on that, she was only the more eager for Olga to come, whatever her husband's name was. She braced herself up to the situation.

'Peppino, are you looking after Lady Ambermere?' she said. 'Dear Lady Ambermere, I hope they are all taking care of you.'

'A very decent peach,' said Lady Ambermere. 'The south wall of my garden is covered with them, and they are always of a peculiarly delicious flavour. The Hall is famed for its peaches. I understood that Miss Bracely was going to be here, Mrs Lucas. I cannot imagine what makes her so late. I was always famed for my punctuality myself. I have finished my tea.'

The lawn outside was now growing thick with people all in their Hightums, and Lady Ambermere as she emerged from the smoking-parlour again viewed the scene with marked disfavour. The two Miss Antrobuses had just arrived, and skipped up to their hostess with pretty cries.

'We are dreadfully late,' said the eldest, 'but it was all Piggy's fault.'

'No, Goosie, it was yours,' said the other. 'How can you be so naughty as to say it was mine? Dear Mrs Lucas, what a lovely party it's being, and may we go and play bowls?'

Lady Ambermere regarded their retreating backs, as they raced off with arms intertwined to the bowling-green.

'And who are those young ladies?' she asked. 'And why Piggy and Goosie? Miss Lyall, do not let Pug go to the bowls. They are very heavy.'

Elsewhere Mrs Antrobus was slowly advancing from group to group, with her trumpet violently engaged in receiving refreshment. But conversation was not quite so varied as usual, for there was an attitude of intense expectation about with regard to the appearance of Miss Bracely, that made talk rather jerky and unconsecutive. Then also it had gone about that the mysterious Indian, who had been seen now and then during the last week, was actually staying with Mrs Lucas, and why was he not here? More unconjecturable yet, though not so thrillingly interesting, was the absence of Mr Georgie. What could have happened to him, that he was not flitting about on his hostess's errands, and being the life and soul of the party? It was in vain that Mrs Antrobus plodded on her methodical course, seeking answers to all these riddles, and that Mrs Weston in her swifter progression dashed about in her bath-chair from group to group, wherever people seemed to be talking in an animated manner. She could learn nothing, and Mrs Antrobus could learn nothing, in fact the only information to be had on the subject was what Mrs Weston herself supplied. She had a very high-coloured handsome face, and an extremely impressive manner, as if she was imparting information of the very highest importance. She naturally spoke in a loud, clear voice, so that she had not got to raise it much even when she addressed Mrs Antrobus. Her wealth of discursive detail was absolutely unrivalled, and she was quite the best observer in Riseholme.

'The last I saw of Miss Bracely,' she said, exactly as if she had been told to describe something on oath in the witness-box, 'was a little after half-past one today. It must have been after half-past because when I got home it was close on a quarter to two, and I wasn't a hundred yards from my house when I saw her. As soon as I saw her I said to my gardener boy, Henry Luton, who was pushing me – he's the son of old Mrs Luton who kept the fish shop, and when she died last year, I began to get my fish from Brinton, for I didn't fancy the look of the new person who took on the business, and Henry went to live with his aunt. That was his father's sister, not his mother's, for Mrs Luton never had a sister, and no brothers either. Well, I said to Henry, "You can go a bit slower, Henry, as we're late, we're late, and a minute or two more doesn't make any difference." "No, ma'am," said Henry, touching his cap, so we went slower. Miss Bracely was just opposite the ducking-pond then, and presently she came out between the elms. She had just an ordinary morning frock on; it was dark blue, about the same shade as your cape, Mrs Antrobus, or perhaps a little darker, for the sunshine brightened it up. Quite simple it was, nothing grand. And she looked at the watch on her wrist, and she seemed to me to walk a little quicker after that, as if she was a bit late, just as I was. But slower than I was going, I could not go, for I was crawling along, and before she got off the grass, I had come to the corner of Church Lane, and though I turned my head round sharp, like that, at the very last moment, so as to catch the last of her, she hadn't more than stepped off the grass on to the road before the laurestinus at the corner of Colonel Boucher's garden – no, of the Vicar's garden – hid her from me. And if you ask me – '

Mrs Weston stopped for a moment, nodding her head up and down, to emphasise the importance of what she had said, and to raise the expectations of Mrs Antrobus to the highest pitch, as to what was coming.

'And if you ask me where I think she was going and what she was going to do,' she said, 'I believe she was going out to lunch and that she was going to one of those houses there, just across the road, for she made a beeline across the green towards them. Well, there are three houses there: there's Mrs Quantock's, and it couldn't have been that, or else Mrs Quantock would have had some news of her, or Colonel Boucher's, and it wouldn't have been that, for the Colonel would have had news of her, and we all know whose the third house just there is.'

Mrs Antrobus had not completely followed this powerful reasoning.

'But Colonel Boucher and Mrs Quantock are both here, eh?' said she.

Mrs Weston raised her voice a little.

'That's what I'm saying,' she announced, 'but who isn't here whom we should expect to see, and where's his house?'

It was generally felt that Mrs Weston had hit the nail on the head. What that nail precisely was no one knew, because she had not explained why both Olga Bracely and Georgie were absentees. But now came the climax, bang on the top of the nail, a shrewd straight stroke.

'So there she was having her lunch with Mr Georgie,' said Mrs Weston, now introducing this name for the first time, with the highest dramatic art, 'and they would be seeing round his house afterwards.

And then when it was time to come here, Mr Georgie would have remembered that the party was Hightum not Tightum, and there was Miss Bracely not in Hightum at all, nor even Tightum, in my opinion, but Scrub. No doubt she said to him, "Is it a very grand sort of party, Mr Pillson?" and he couldn't do other than reply, for we all received notice that it was Hightum – mine came about twelve – he couldn't do other than reply, "Yes, Miss Bracely, it is." "Good gracious me," she would say, "and I've only got this old rag on. I must go back to the Ambermere Arms, and tell my maid – for she brought a maid in that second motor – and tell my maid to put me out something tidy." "But that will be a great bother for you," he would say, or something of that sort, for I don't pretend to know what he actually did say, and she would reply, "Oh Mr Pillson, but I must put on something tidy, and it would be so kind of you, if you would wait for me, while I do that, and let us go together." That's what *she* said.'

Mrs Weston made a sign to her gardener to proceed, wishing to leave the stage at the moment of climax.

'And that's why they're both late,' she said, and was whirled away in the direction of the bowling-green.

The minutes went on, and still nobody appeared who could possibly have accounted for the three-lined whip of Hightums, but by degrees Lucia, who had utterly failed to decoy Lady Ambermere into the place of thrones, began to notice a certain thinning on her lawns. Her guests, it would seem, were not in process of dispersal, for it was a long way off seven o'clock yet, and also none would be so ill-mannered as to leave without shaking hands and saying what a delicious afternoon they had spent. But certainly the lawns grew emptier, and she was utterly unable to explain this extraordinary phenomenon, until she happened to go close to the windows of her music-room. Then, looking in, she saw that not only was every chair there occupied, but people were standing about in expectant groups. For a moment, her heart beat high ... Could Olga have arrived and by some mistake have gone straight in there? It was a dreamlike possibility, but it burst like a ray of sunshine on the party that was rapidly becoming a nightmare to her – for everyone, not Lady Ambermere alone, was audibly wondering when the guru was coming, and when Miss Bracely was going to sing.

At the moment as she paused, a window in the music-room was opened, and Piggy's odious head looked out.

'Oh, Mrs Lucas,' she said. 'Goosie and I have got beautiful seats, and Mamma is quite close to the piano where she will hear excellently.

Has she promised to sing *Siegfried*? Is Mr Georgie going to play for her? It's *the* most delicious surprise; how could you be so sly and clever as not to tell anybody?'

Lucia cloaked her rage under the most playful manner, as she ran into the music-room through the hall.

'You naughty things!' she said. 'Do all come into the garden! It's a garden-party, and I couldn't guess where you had all gone. What's all this about singing and playing? I know nothing of it.'

She herded the incredulous crowd out into the garden again, all in their Hightums, every one of them, only to meet Lady Ambermere with Pug and Miss Lyall coming in.

'Better be going, Miss Lyall,' she said. 'Kindly run out and find my people. Oh, here's Mrs Lucas. Been very pleasant indeed, thank you, goodbye. Your charming garden. Yes.'

'Oh, but it's very early,' said Lucia. 'It's hardly six yet.'

'Indeed!' said Lady Ambermere. 'Been so charming,' and she marched out after Miss Lyall into Shakespeare's garden.

It was soon terribly evident that other people were sharing Lady Ambermere's conclusion about the delights of the afternoon, and the necessity of getting home. Colonel Boucher had to take his bulldogs for a run and walk off the excitement of the party; Piggy and Goosie explained to their mother that nobody was going to sing, and by silvery laughter tried to drown her just indignation, and presently Lucia had the agony of seeing Mrs Quantock seated on one of the thrones, that had been designed for much worthier ends, and Peppino sitting in the other, while a few guests drifted about the lawn with all the purposelessness of autumn leaves. What with the guru, presumably meditating upstairs still, and with Olga Bracely most conspicuously absent, she had hardly nervous energy left to wonder what could have become of Georgie. Never in all the years of his ministry had he failed to be at her elbow through the entire duration of her garden-parties, flying about on her errands like a tripping Hermes, herding her flocks if she wanted them in one part of the garden rather than another, like a sagacious sheepdog, and coming back to heel again ready for further tasks. But today Georgie was mysteriously away, for he had neither applied for leave nor given any explanation, however improbable, of his absence. He at least would have prevented Lady Ambermere, the only cornerstone of the party, from going away in what must be called a huff, and have continued to tell Lucia how marvellous she was, and what a beautiful party they were having. With the prospect of two other much more magnificent cornerstones,

Lucia had not provided any further entertainment for her guests: there was not the conjurer from Brinton, nor the three young ladies who played banjo-trios, nor even the mild performing doves which cooed so prettily, and walked up their mistress's outstretched fingers according to order, if they felt disposed. There was nothing to justify Hightums, there was scarcely even sufficient to warrant Tightums. Scrub was written all over 'the desert's dusty face'.

It was about half-past six when the miracles began, and without warning the guru walked out into the garden. Probably he had watched the departure of the great motor with its chauffeur and footman, and Miss Lyall and Lady Ambermere and Pug, and with his intuitive sagacity had conjectured that the danger from Madras was over. He wore his new red slippers, a wonderful turban and an ecstatic smile. Lucia and Daisy met him with cries of joy, and the remaining guests, those drifting autumn leaves, were swept up, as it were, by some compelling broom and clustered in a heap in front of him. There had been a Great Message, a Word of Might, full of Love and Peace. Never had there been such a Word . . .

And then, even before they had all felt the full thrill of that, once more the door from the house opened, and out came Olga Bracely and Georgie. It is true that she had still her blue morning frock, which Mrs Weston had designated as Scrub, but it was a perfectly new Scrub, and if it had been completely covered with Paris labels, they would not have made its *provenance* one whit clearer. 'Dear Mrs Lucas,' she said, 'Mr Georgie and I are terribly late, and it was quite my fault. There was a game of croquet that wouldn't come to an end, and my life has been guided by only one principle, and that is to finish a game of croquet whatever happens. I missed six trains once by finishing a game of croquet. And Mr Georgie was so unkind: he wouldn't give me a cup of tea, or let me change my frock, but dragged me off to see you. And I won!'

The autumn leaves turned green and vigorous again, while Georgie went to get refreshment for his conqueror, and they were all introduced. She allowed herself to be taken with the utmost docility – how unlike Somebody – into the tent with the thrones: she confessed to having stood on tiptoe and looked into Mrs Quantock's garden and wanted to see it so much from the other side of the wall. And this garden, too – might she go and wander all over this garden when she had finished the most delicious peach that the world held? She was so glad she had not had tea with Mr Georgie: he would never have given her such a good peach . . .

Now the departing guests in their Hightums, lingering on the village green a little, and being rather sarcastic about the utter failure of Lucia's party, could hardly help seeing Georgie and Olga emerge from his house and proceed swiftly in the direction of The Hurst, and Mrs Antrobus, who retained marvellous eyesight as compensation for her defective hearing, saw them go in, and simultaneously thought that she had left her parasol at The Hurst. Next moment she was walking thoughtfully away in that direction. Mrs Weston had been the next to realise what had happened, and though she had to go round by the road in her bath-chair, she passed Mrs Antrobus a hundred yards from the house, her pretext for going back being that Lucia had promised to lend her the book by Antonio Caporelli (or was it Caporetto?).

So once more the door into the garden opened, and out shot Mrs Weston. Olga by this time had made her tour of the garden, and might she see the house? She might. There was a pretty music-room. At this stage, just as Mrs Weston was poured out in the garden, as with the floodgates being opened, the crowd that followed her came surging into Shakespeare's garden, and never had the mermaid's tail, behind which was secreted the electric bell, experienced such feverish usage. Pressure after pressure invoked its aid, and the pretexts for readmission were soon not made at all, or simply disregarded by the parlour-maid. Colonel Boucher might have left a bulldog, and Mrs Antrobus an ear trumpet, or Miss Antrobus (Piggy) a shoelace, and the other Miss Antrobus (Goosie) a shoehorn: but in brisk succession the guests who had been so sarcastic about the party on the village green jostled each other in order to revisit the scenes of their irony. Miss Olga Bracely had been known to enter the portals, and as many of them who entered after her, found a guru as well.

Olga was in the music-room when the crowd had congested the hall. People were introduced to her, and sank down into the nearest chairs. Mrs Antrobus took up her old place by the keyboard of the piano. Everybody seemed to be expecting something, and by degrees the import of their longing was borne in upon Olga. They waited, and waited and waited, much as she had waited for a cigarette the evening before. She looked at the piano, and there was a comfortable murmur from her audience. She looked at Lucia, who gave a great gasp, and said nothing at all. She was the only person present who was standing now except her hostess, and Mrs Weston's gardener, who had wheeled his mistress's chair into an admirable position for hearing. She was not too well pleased, but after all . . .

'Would you like me to sing?' she asked Lucia. 'Yes? Ah, there's a copy of *Siegfried*. Do you play?'

Lucia could not smile any more than she was smiling already.

'Is it very diffy?' she asked. 'Could I read it, Georgie? Shall I try?' She slid on to the music-stool.

'Me to begin?' she asked, finding that Olga had opened the book at the salutation of Brünnhilde, which Lucia had practised so diligently all the morning.

She got no answer. Olga, standing by her, had assumed a perfectly different aspect. For her gaiety, her lightness, was substituted some air of intense concentrated seriousness which Lucia did not understand at all. She was looking straight in front of her, gathering herself in, and paying not the smallest attention to Lucia or anybody else.

'One, two,' said Lucia. 'Three. Now,' and she plunged wildly into a sea of demi-semi-quavers. Olga had just opened her mouth, but shut it again.

'No,' she said. 'Once more,' and she whistled the *motif*.

'Oh! it's so diffy!' said Lucia, beginning again. 'Georgie! Turn over!'

Georgie turned over, and Lucia, counting audibly to herself, made an incomparable mess all over the piano.

Olga turned to her accompanist.

'Shall I try?' she said.

She sat down at the piano, and made some sort of sketch of the accompaniment, simplifying, and yet retaining the essence. And then she sang.

Chapter Eight

Throughout August, guruism reigned supreme over the cultured life of Riseholme, and the priestess and dispenser of its mysteries was Lucia. Never before had she ruled from so elate a pinnacle, nor wielded so secure a supremacy. None had access to the guru but through her: all his classes were held in the smoking-parlour and he meditated only in Hamlet or in the sequestered arbour at the end of the laburnum walk. Once he had meditated on the village green, but Lucia did not approve of that and had led him, still rapt, home by the hand.

The classes had swelled prodigiously, for practically all Riseholmites now were at some stage of instruction, with the exception of Hermy and Ursy, who pronounced the whole thing 'piffle', and, as gentle chaff for Georgie, sometimes stood on one leg in the middle of the lawn and held their breath. Then Hermy would say 'One, two, three!' and they shouted 'Om!' at the tops of their discordant voices. Now that the guru was practically interned in The Hurst, they had actually never set eyes on him, for they had not chosen to come to the Hightum garden-party, preferring to have a second round of golf, and meeting Lucia next day had been distinctly irreverent on the subject of Eastern philosophy. Since then she had not been aware of their existence.

Lucia now received special instruction from the guru in a class all by herself, so prodigious was her advance in Yoga, for she could hold her breath much longer than anybody else, and had mastered six postures, while the next class which she attended also consisted of the other original members, namely Daisy Quantock, Georgie and Peppino. They had got on very well, too, but Lucia had quite shot away from them, and now if the guru had other urgent spiritual claims on him, she gave instruction to a less advanced class herself. For this purpose she habited herself in a peculiarly becoming dress of white linen, which reached to her feet and had full flowing sleeves like a surplice. It was girdled with a silver cord with long tassels, and had mother-of-pearl buttons and a hood at the back lined with white satin which came over her head. Below its hem as she sat and taught in a really rather advanced posture showed the toes of her white morocco slippers, and she called it her 'Teacher's Robe'. The class which she taught consisted of Colonel Boucher, Piggy Antrobus and Mrs Weston: sometimes the Colonel brought his bulldogs with him, who lay and snorted precisely as if they were doing breathing exercises, too. A general air of joyful mystery and spiritual endeavour blew balmily round them all, and without any doubt the exercises and the deep breathing were extremely good for them.

One evening, towards the end of the month, Georgie was sitting in his garden, for the half-hour before dressing-time, thinking how busy he was, and yet how extraordinarily young and fresh he felt. Usually this month when Hermy and Ursy were with him was very fatiguing, and in ordinary years he would have driven away with Foljambe and Dicky on the day after their departure, and had a quiet week by the seaside. But now, though his sisters were going away tomorrow morning, he had no intention of taking a well-earned rest, in spite of the fact that not only had he been their host all this time, but had done an amazing quantity of other things as well. There had

been the daily classes to begin with, which entailed much work in the
way of meditation and exercises, as well as the actual learning, and
also he had had another job which might easily have taxed his energies
to the utmost any other year. For Olga Bracely had definitely bought
that house without which she had felt that life was not worth living,
and Georgie all this month had at her request been exercising a
semi-independent supervision over its decoration and furnishing.
She had ordered the general scheme herself and had sent down
from London the greater part of the furniture, but Georgie was
commissioned to report on any likely pieces of old stuff that he could
find, and if expedition was necessary to act on his own responsibility
and buy them. But above all secrecy was still necessary till the house
was so complete that her Georgie might be told, and by the end of
the month Riseholme generally was in a state of prostration following
on the violent and feverish curiosity as to who had taken the house.
Georgie had gone so far as to confess that he knew, but the most
pathetic appeals as to the owner's identity had fallen on obdurate, if
not deaf, ears. Not the smallest hint would he give on the subject,
and though those incessant visits to the house, those searchings for
furniture, the bestowal of it in suitable places, the superintendence
of the making of the garden, the interviewings of paperhangers,
plumbers, upholsterers, painters, carpenters and so forth occupied a
great deal of time, the delicious mystery about it all, and the fact that
he was doing it for so adorable a creature, rendered his exertions a
positive refreshment. Another thing which, in conjunction with this
and his youth-giving studies, made him feel younger than ever was
the discreet arrival and perfect success of his *toupée*. No longer was
there any need to fear the dislocation of his espaliered locks. He felt
so secure and undetectable in that regard that he had taken to wearing
no hat, and was soon about to say that his hair was growing more
thickly than ever in consequence. But it was not quite time for that
yet: it would be inartistic to suggest that just a couple of weeks of
hatlessness had produced so desirable a result.

*   *   *

As he sat at ease after the labours of the day he wondered how the
coming of Olga Bracely to Riseholme would affect the economy of
the place. It was impossible to think of her with her beauty, her
charm, her fame, her personality as taking any second place in its
life. Unless she was really meaning to use Riseholme as a retreat, to
take no part in its life at all, it was hard to see what part she would

take except the first part. One who by her arrival at Lucia's ever-memorable party had converted it in a moment from the most dire of Scrubs (in a psychical sense) to the Hightumest gathering ever known could not lay aside her distinction and pre-eminence. Never had Lucia 'scored' so amazingly as over Olga's late appearance, which had the effect of bringing back all her departed guests with the compulsion of a magnet over iron-filings, and sending up the whole party like a rocket into the zenith of social success. All Riseholme knew that Olga had come (after playing croquet with Georgie the entire afternoon) and had given them free, gratis and for nothing, such a treat as only the wealthiest could obtain with the most staggering fees. Lady Ambermere alone, driving back to The Hall with Pug and poor Miss Lyall, was the only person who had not shared in that, and she knew all about it next day, for Georgie had driven out on purpose to tell her, and met Lucia coming away. How, then, would the advent of Olga affect Riseholme's social working generally, and how would it affect Lucia in particular? And what would Lucia say when she knew on whose behalf Georgie was so busy with plumbers and painters, and with buying so many of the desirable treasures in the Ambermere Arms?

Frankly he could not answer these conundrums: they presupposed inconceivable situations, which yet, though inconceivable, were shortly coming to pass, for Olga's advent might be expected before October, that season of tea-parties that ushered in the multifarious gaieties of the winter. Would Olga form part of the moonlit circle to whom Lucia played the first movement of the 'Moonlight Sonata', and give a long sigh at the end like the rest of them? And would Lucia when they had all recovered a little from the invariable emotion go to her and say, 'Olga *mia*, just a little bit out of the *Valkyrie*? It would be so pleasant.' Somehow Georgie, with all his imagination, could not picture such a scene. And would Olga take the part of second citizenness or something of the sort when Lucia played Portia? Would Olga join the elementary class of Yoga, and be instructed by Lucia in her Teacher's Robe? Would she sing treble in the Christmas Carols, while Lucia beat time, and said in syllables dictated by the rhythm, 'Trebles a little flat! My poor ears!'? Georgie could not imagine any of these things, and yet, unless Olga took no part in the social life of Riseholme at all (and that was equally inconceivable) what was the alternative? True, she had said that she was coming here because it was so ideally lazy a backwater, but Georgie did not take that seriously. She would soon see what Riseholme was when its life poured down in spate, whirling her punt along with it.

And finally, what would happen to him, when Olga was set as a shining star in this firmament? Already he revolved about her, he was aware, like some eager delighted little moon, drawn away from the orbit where it had encircled so contentedly by the more potent planet. And the measure of his detachment from that old orbit might be judged precisely by the fact that the process of detachment which was already taking place was marked by no sense of the pull of opposing forces at all. The great new star sailing into the heavens had just picked him up by force of its superior power of attraction, even as by its momentary conjunction with Lucia at the garden-party it had raised her to a magnitude she had never possessed before. That magnitude was still Lucia's, and no doubt would be until the great star appeared again. Then without effort its shining must surely eclipse every other illumination, just as without effort it must surely attract all the little moons to itself. Or would Lucia manage somehow or other, either by sheer force of will, by desperate and hostile endeavour, or, on the other hand, by some supreme tact and cleverness, to harness the great star to her own chariot? He thought the desperate and hostile endeavour was more in keeping with Lucia's methods, and this quiet evening hour represented itself to him as the lull before the storm.

The actual quiet of the moment was suddenly broken into. His front door banged, and the house was filled with running footsteps and screams of laughter. But it was not uncommon for Hermy and Ursy to make this sort of entrance, and at the moment Georgie had not the slightest idea of how much further-reaching was the disturbance of the tranquillity. He but drew a couple of long breaths, said 'Om' once or twice, and was quite prepared to find his deeper calm unshattered.

Hermy and Ursy ran down the steps into the garden where he sat still yelling with laughter, and still Georgie's imagination went no further than to suppose that one of them had laid a stymie for the other at their golf, or driven a ball out of bounds or done some other of these things that appeared to make the game so diverting to them.

'Georgie, you'll never guess!' cried Hermy.

'The guru: the Om, of high caste and extraordinary sanctity,' cried Ursy.

'The Brahmin from Benares,' shrieked Hermy.

'The great Teacher! Who do you think he is?' said Ursy. 'We'd never seen him before – '

'But we recognised him at once – '

'He recognised us, too, and didn't he run? – '

'Into The Hurst and shut the door – '

Georgie's deeper calm suddenly quivered like a jelly.

'My dears, you needn't howl so, or talk quite so loud,' he said. 'All Riseholme will hear you. Tell me without shouting who it was you thought you recognised.'

'There's no think about it,' said Hermy. 'It was one of the cooks from the Calcutta Restaurant in Bedford Street – '

'Where we often have lunch,' said Ursy. 'He makes the most delicious curries.'

'Especially when he's a little tipsy,' said Hermy.

'And is about as much a Brahmin as I am.'

'And always said he came from Madras.'

'We always tip him to make the curry himself, so he isn't quite ignorant about money.'

'O Lord!' said Hermy, wiping her eyes. 'If it isn't the limit!'

'And to think of Mrs Lucas and Colonel Boucher and you and Mrs Quantock, and Piggy and all the rest of them sitting round a cook,' said Ursy, 'and drinking in his wisdom. Mr Quantock was on the right track after all when he wanted to engage him.'

Georgie with a fallen heart had first to satisfy himself that this was not one of his sisters' jokes, and then tried to raise his fallen heart by remembering that the guru had often spoken of the dignity of simple manual work, but somehow it was a blow, if Hermy and Ursy were right, to know that this was a tipsy contriver of curry. There was nothing in the simple manual office of curry-making that could possibly tarnish sanctity, but the amazing tissue of falsehoods with which the guru had modestly masked his innocent calling was not so markedly in the spirit of the Guides, as retailed by him. It was of the first importance, however, to be assured that his sisters had not at present communicated their upsetting discovery to anybody but himself, and after that to get their promise that they would not do so.

This was not quite so easy, for Hermy and Ursy had projected a round of visits after dinner to every member of the classes with the exception of Lucia, who should wake up next morning to find herself the only illusioned person in the place.

'She wouldn't like that, you know,' said Hermy with brisk malice. 'We thought it would serve her out for never asking us to her house again after her foolish old garden-party.'

'My dear, you never wanted to go,' said Georgie.

'I know we didn't, but we rather wanted to tell her we didn't want to go. She wasn't nice. Oh, I don't think we can give up telling everybody. It has made such sillies of you all. I think he's a real sport.'

'So do I,' said Ursy. 'We shall soon have him back at his curry-oven again. What a laugh we shall have with him.'

They subsided for just as long as it took Foljambe to come out of the house, inform them that it was a quarter of an hour to dinner-time, and return again. They all rose obediently.

'Well, we'll talk about it at dinner-time,' said Georgie diplomatically. 'And I'll just go down to the cellar first to see if I can find something you like.'

'Good old Georgie,' said Hermy. 'But if you're going to bribe us, you must bribe us well.'

'We'll see,' said he.

Georgie was quite right to be careful over his Veuve Clicquot, especially since it was a bottle of that admirable beverage that Hermy and Ursy had looted from his cellar on the night of their burglarious entry. He remembered that well, though he had – chiefly from the desire to keep things pleasant about his hair – joined in 'the fun', and had even produced another half-bottle. But tonight, even more than then, there was need for the abolition of all petty economies, for the situation would be absolutely intolerable if Hermy and Ursy spread about Riseholme the fact that the introducers and innermost circle of Yoga philosophers had sat at the feet of no Gamaliel at all, but at those of a curry-cook from some low restaurant. Indeed he brought up a second bottle tonight with a view, if Hermy and Ursy were not softened by the first, to administer that also. They would then hardly be in a condition to be taken seriously if they still insisted on making a house-to-house visit in Riseholme, and tearing the veil from off the features of the guru. Georgie was far too upright of purpose to dream of making his sisters drunk, but he was willing to make great sacrifices in order to render them kind. What the inner circle would do about this cook he had no idea; he must talk to Lucia about it, before the advanced class tomorrow morning. But anything was better than letting Hermy and Ursy loose in Riseholme with their rude laughs and discreditable exposures. This evening safely over, he could discuss with Lucia what was to be done, for Hermy and Ursy would have vanished at cockcrow, as they were going in for some golf-competition at a safe distance. Lucia might recommend doing nothing at all, and wish to continue enlightening studies as if nothing had happened. But Georgie felt that the romance would have evaporated from the classes as regards himself. Or again they might have to get rid of the guru somehow. He only felt quite sure that Lucia would agree with him that Daisy Quantock must not be told. She with her thwarted ambitions of being the prime dispenser of guruism to Riseholme might easily 'turn nasty' and let it be widely known that she and Robert had seen through that fraud long ago, and had considered whether they should not offer the guru the situation of cook in their household, for which he was so much better qualified. She might even add that his leanings towards her pretty housemaid had alone dissuaded her.

The evening went off with a success more brilliant than Georgie had anticipated, and it was quite unnecessary to open the second bottle of champagne. Hermy and Ursy, perhaps under the influence of the first, perhaps from innate good nature, perhaps because they were starting so very early next morning, and wanted to be driven into Brinton, instead of taking a slower and earlier train at Riseholme, readily gave up their project of informing the whole of Riseholme of their discovery, and went to bed as soon as they had rooked their brother of eleven shillings at cutthroat bridge. They continued to say, 'I'll play the guru,' whenever they had to play a knave, but Georgie found it quite easy to laugh at that, so long as the humour of it did not spread. He even himself said, 'I'll guru you, then,' when he took a trick with the Knave of Trumps.

The agitation and uncertainty caused him not to sleep very well, and in addition there was a good deal of disturbance in the house, for his sisters had still all their packing in front of them when they went to bed and the doze that preceded sleep was often broken by the sound of the banging of luggage, the clash of golf clubs and steps on the stairs as they made ready for their departure.

But after a while these disturbances ceased, and it was out of a deep sleep that he awoke with the sense that some noise had awakened him. Apparently they had not finished yet, for there was surely some faint stir of movement somewhere. Anyhow they respected his legitimate desire for quiet, for the noise, whatever it was, was extremely stealthy and subdued. He thought of his absurd lark about burglars on the night of their arrival, and smiled at the notion. His *toupée* was in a drawer close to his bed, but he had no substantial impulse to put it on, and make sure that the noise was not anything other than his sisters' preparations for their early start. For himself, he would have had everything packed and corded long before dinner, if he was to start next day, except just a suitcase that would hold the apparatus of immediate necessities, but then dear Hermy and Ursy were so ramshackle in their ways. Some time he would have bells put on all the shutters as he had determined to do a month ago, and then no sort of noise would disturb him any more . . .

The Yoga-class next morning was (unusually) to assemble at ten, since Peppino, who would not miss it for anything, was going to have a day's fishing in the happy stream that flowed into the Avon, and he wanted to be off by eleven. Peppino had made great progress lately and had certain curious dizzy symptoms when he meditated which were highly satisfactory.

Georgie breakfasted with his sisters at eight (they had enticed the motor out of him to convey them to Brinton) and when they were gone, Foljambe informed him that the housemaid had a sore throat, and had not 'done' the drawing-room. Foljambe herself would 'do' it, when she had cleaned the 'young ladies'' rooms (there was a hint of scorn in this) upstairs, and so Georgie sat on the window seat of the dining-room, and thought how pleasant peace and quietness were. But just when it was time to start for The Hurst in order to talk over the disclosures of the night before with Lucia before the class, and perhaps to frame some secretive policy which would obviate further exposure, he remembered that he had left his cigarette case (the pretty straw one with the turquoise in the corner) in the drawing-room and went to find it. The window was open, and apparently Foljambe *had* just come in to let fresh air into the atmosphere which Hermy and Ursy had so uninterruptedly contaminated last night with their 'fags', as they called them, but his cigarette case was not on the table where he thought he had left it. He looked round, and then stood rooted to the spot.

His glass case of treasures was not only open but empty. Gone was the Louis XVI snuff box, gone was the miniature of Karl Huth, gone the piece of Bow china, and gone the Fabergé cigarette case. Only the Queen Anne toy-porringer was there, and in the absence of the others, it looked to him, as no doubt it had looked to the burglar, indescribably insignificant.

Georgie gave a little low wailing cry, but did not tear his hair for obvious reasons. Then he rang the bell three times in swift succession, which was the signal to Foljambe that even if she was in her bath, she must come at once. In she came with one of Hermy's horrid woollen jerseys that had been left behind, in her hand.

'Yes, sir, what is it?' she asked, in an agitated manner, for never could she remember Georgie having rung the bell three times except once when a fish-bone had stuck in his throat, and once again when a note had announced to him that Piggy was going to call and hoped to find him alone. For answer Georgie pointed to the rifled treasure-case. 'Gone! Burgled!' he said. 'Oh, my God!'

At that supreme moment the telephone bell sounded.

'See what it is,' he said to Foljambe, and put the Queen Anne toy-porringer in his pocket.

She came hurrying back.

'Mrs Lucas wants you to come around at once,' she said.

'I can't,' said Georgie. 'I must stop here and send for the police. Nothing must be moved,' and he hastily replaced the toy-porringer on the exact circle of pressed velvet where it had stood before.

'Yes, sir,' said Foljambe, but in another moment she returned.

'She would be very much obliged if you would come at once,' she said. 'There's been a robbery in the house.'

'Well, tell her there's been one in mine,' said Georgie irritably. Then good nature mixed with furious curiosity came to his aid.

'Wait here, then, Foljambe, on this very spot,' he said, 'and see that nobody touches anything. I shall probably ring up the police from The Hurst. Admit them.'

In his agitation he put on his hat, instead of going bareheaded, and was received by Lucia, who had clearly been looking out of the music-room window, at the door. She wore her Teacher's Robe.

'Georgie,' she said, quite forgetting to speak Italian in her greeting, 'someone broke into Philip's safe last night, and took a hundred pounds in bank-notes. He had put them there only yesterday in order to pay in cash for that cob. And my Roman pearls.'

Georgie felt a certain pride of achievement.

'I've been burgled, too,' he said. 'My Louis XVI snuff box is worth more than that, and there's the piece of Bow china, and the cigarette case, and the Karl Huth as well.'

'My dear! Come inside,' said she. 'It's a gang. And I was feeling so peaceful and exalted. It will make a terrible atmosphere in the house. My guru will be profoundly affected. An atmosphere where thieves have been will stifle him. He has often told me how he cannot stop in a house where there have been wicked emotions at play. I must keep it from him. I cannot lose him.'

Lucia had sunk down on a spacious Elizabethan settle in the hall. The humorous spider mocked them from the window, the humorous stone fruit from the plate beside the potpourri bowl. Even as she repeated, 'I cannot lose him,' again, a tremendous rap came on the front door, and Georgie, at a sign from his queen, admitted Mrs Quantock.

'Robert and I have been burgled,' she said. 'Four silver spoons – thank God, most of our things are plate – eight silver forks and a Georgian tankard. I could have spared all but the last.'

A faint sign of relief escaped Lucia. If the foul atmosphere of thieves permeated Daisy's house, too, there was no great danger that her guru would go back there. She instantly became sublime.

'Peace!' she said. 'Let us have our class first, for it is ten already, and not let any thought of revenge or evil spoil that for us. If I sent for the police now I could not concentrate. I will not tell my guru what has happened to any of us, but for poor Peppino's sake I will ask him to give us rather a short lesson. I feel completely calm. Om.'

Vague nightmare images began to take shape in Georgie's mind, unworthy suspicions based on his sisters' information the evening before. But with Foljambe keeping guard over the Queen Anne porringer, there was nothing more to fear, and he followed Lucia, her silver cord with tassels gently swinging as she moved, to the smoking-parlour, where Peppino was already sitting on the floor, and breathing in a rather more agitated manner than was usual with the advanced class. There were fresh flowers on the table, and the scented morning breeze blew in from the garden. According to custom they all sat down and waited, getting calmer and more peaceful every moment. Soon there would be the tapping of slippered heels on the walk of broken paving-stones outside, and for the time they would forget all these disturbances. But they were all rather glad that Lucia was to ask the guru to give them a shorter lesson than usual.

They waited. Presently the hands of the Cromwellian timepiece which was the nearest approach to an Elizabethan clock that Lucia had been able at present to obtain, pointed to a quarter past ten.

'My guru is a little late,' said she.

Two minutes afterwards, Peppino sneezed. Two minutes after that Daisy spoke, using irony.

'Would it not be well to see what has happened to your guru, dear?' she asked. 'Have you seen your guru this morning?'

'No, dear,' said Lucia, not opening her eyes, for she was 'concentrating', 'he always meditates before a class.'

'So do I,' said Daisy, 'but I have meditated long enough.'

'Hush!' said Lucia. 'He is coming.'

That proved to be a false alarm, for it was nothing but Lucia's Persian cat, who had a quarrel with some dead laurel leaves. Lucia rose.

'I don't like to interrupt him,' she said, 'but time is getting on.'

She left the smoking-parlour with the slow supple walk that she adopted when she wore her Teacher's Robes. Before many seconds had passed, she came back more quickly and with no suppleness.

'His door is locked,' she said; 'and yet there's no key in it.'

'Did you look through the keyhole, Lucia *mia*?' asked Mrs Quantock, with irrepressible irony.

Naturally Lucia disregarded this.

'I knocked,' she said, 'and there was no reply. I said, "Master, we are waiting," and he didn't answer.'

Suddenly Georgie spoke, as with the report of a cork flying out of a bottle.

'My sisters told me last night that he was the curry-cook at the Calcutta Restaurant,' he said. 'They recognised him, and they thought he recognised them. He comes from Madras, and is no more a Brahmin than Foljambe.'

Peppino bounded to his feet.

'What?' he said. 'Let's get a poker and break in the door! I believe he's gone and I believe he's the burglar. Ring for the police.'

'Curry-cook, is he?' said Daisy. 'Robert and I were right after all. We knew what your guru was best fitted for, dear Lucia, but then of course you always know best, and you and he have been fooling us finely. But you didn't fool me. I knew when you took him away from me, what sort of a bargain you had made. Guru, indeed! He's the same class as Mrs Eddy, and I saw through her fast enough. And now what are we to do? For my part, I shall just get home, and ring up for the police, and say that the Indian who has been living with you all these weeks has stolen my spoons and forks and my Georgian tankard. Guru, indeed! Burglaroo, I call him! There!'

Her passion, like Hyperion's, had lifted her upon her feet, and she stood there defying the whole of the advanced class, short and stout and wholly ridiculous, but with some revolutionary menace about her. She was not exactly 'terrible as an army with banners', but she was terrible as an elderly lady with a long-standing grievance that had been accentuated by the loss of a Georgian tankard, and that was terrible enough to make Lucia adopt a conciliatory attitude. Bitterly she repented having stolen Daisy's guru at all, if the suspicions now thickening in the air proved to be true, but after all they were not proved yet. The guru might still walk in from the arbour on the laburnum alley which they had not yet searched, or he might be levitating with the door key in his pocket. It was not probable but it was possible, and at this crisis possibilities were things that must be clung to, for otherwise you would simply have to submerge, like those U-boats.

They searched all the garden, but found no trace of the curry-cook: they made guarded enquiries of the servants as to whether he had been seen, but nothing whatever could be learned about him. So when Peppino took a ponderous hammer and a stout chisel from his tool chest and led the way upstairs, they all knew that the decisive moment had come. Perhaps he might be meditating (for indeed it was likely that he had a good deal to meditate about), but perhaps – Peppino called to him in his most sonorous tones, and said that he would be obliged to break his lock if no answer came, and presently the house resounded with knockings as terrible as those in Macbeth, and much louder. Then suddenly the lock gave, and the door was open.

The room was empty, and as they had all conjectured by now, the bed was unslept in. They opened the drawers of the wardrobe and they were as empty as the room. Finally, Peppino unlocked the door of a large cupboard that stood in the corner, and with a clinking and crashing of glass there poured out a cataract of empty brandy bottles. Emptiness: that was the keynote of the whole scene, and blank consternation its effect.

'My brandy!' said Mrs Quantock in a strangled voice. 'There are fourteen or fifteen bottles. That accounts for the glazed look in his eyes which you, dear Lucia, thought was concentration. I call it distillation.'

'Did he take it from your cellar?' asked Lucia, too shattered to feel resentment, but still capable of intense curiosity.

'No: he had a standing order from me to order any little things he might want from my tradesmen. I wish I had my bills sent in every week.'

'Yes, dear,' said Lucia.

Georgie's eyes sought hers.

'I saw him buy the first bottle,' he said. 'I remember telling you about it. It was at Rush's'

Peppino gathered up his hammer and chisel.

'Well, it's no use sitting here and thinking of old times,' he observed. 'I shall ring up the police station and put the whole matter into their hands, as far as I am concerned. They'll soon lay hands on him, and he can do his postures in prison for the next few years.'

'But we don't know that it was he who committed all these burglaries yet,' said Lucia.

No one felt it was worth answering this, for the others had all tried and convicted him already.

'I shall do the same,' said Georgie.

'My tankard,' said Mrs Quantock.

Lucia got up. '*Peppino mio,*' she said, 'and you, Georgie, and you, Daisy, I want you before you do anything at all to listen to me for five minutes. Just consider this. What sort of figure shall we all cut if we put the matter into the hands of the police? They will probably catch him, and it will all come out that we have been the dupes of a curry-cook. Think what we have all been doing for this last month, think of our classes, our exercises, our – everything. We have been made fools of, but for my part, I simply couldn't bear that everybody should know I had been made a fool of. Anything but that. What's a hundred pounds compared to that, or a tankard – '

'My Louis XVI snuff box was worth at least that without the other things,' said Georgie, still with a secret satisfaction in being the greatest sufferer.

'And it was my hundred pounds, not yours, *carissima,*' said Peppino. But it was clear that Lucia's words were working within him like leaven.

'I'll go halves with you,' she said. 'I'll give you a cheque for fifty pounds.'

'And who would like to go halves in my tankard?' said Daisy with bitter irony. 'I want my tankard.'

Georgie said nothing, but his mind was extremely busy. There was Olga soon coming to Riseholme, and it would be awful if she found it ringing with the tale of the guru, and glancing across to Peppino, he saw a thoughtful and sympathetic look in his eyes, that seemed to indicate that his mind was working on parallel lines. Certainly Lucia had given them all something to meditate upon. He tried to imagine the whole story being shouted into Mrs Antrobus's ear-trumpet on the village green, and could not endure the idea. He tried to imagine Mrs Weston ever ceasing to talk about it, and could not picture her silence. No doubt they had all been taken in, too, but here in this empty bedroom were the original dupes, who encouraged the rest.

After Mrs Quantock's enquiry a dead silence fell.

'What do you propose, then?' asked Peppino, showing signs of surrender.

Lucia exerted her utmost wiles.

'*Caro!*' she said. 'I want 'oo to propose. Daisy and me, we silly women, we want 'oo and Georgie to tell us what to do. But if Lucia must speak, I fink – '

She paused a moment, and observing strong disgust at her playfulness on Mrs Quantock's face, reverted to ordinary English again.

'I should do something of this sort,' she said. 'I should say that dear Daisy's guru had left us quite suddenly, and that he has had a call somewhere else. His work here was done; he had established our classes, and set all our feet upon the Way. He always said that something of the sort might happen to him – '

'I believe he had planned it all along,' said Georgie. 'He knew the thing couldn't last for ever, and when my sisters recognised him, he concluded it was time to bolt.'

'With all the available property he could lay hands on,' said Mrs Quantock.

Lucia fingered her tassel.

'Now about the burglaries,' she said. 'It won't do to let it be known that three burglaries were committed in one night, and that simultaneously Daisy's guru was called away – '

'My guru, indeed!' said Mrs Quantock, fizzing with indignation at the repetition of this insult.

'That might give rise to suspicion,' continued Lucia calmly, disregarding the interruption, 'and we must stop the news from spreading. Now with regard to our burglary . . . let me think a moment.'

She had got such complete control of them all now that no one spoke.

'I have it,' she said. 'Only Boaler knows, for Peppino told her not to say a word till the police had been sent for. You must tell her, *carissimo*, that you have found the hundred pounds. That settles that. Now you, Georgie.'

'Foljambe knows,' said Georgie.

'Then tell her not to say a word about it. Put some more things out in your lovely treasure-case, no one will notice. And you, Daisy.'

'Robert is away,' said she, quite meekly, for she had been thinking things over. 'My maid knows.'

'And when he comes back, will he notice the loss of the tankard? Did you often use it?'

'About once in ten years.'

'Chance it, then,' said Lucia. 'Just tell your maid to say nothing about it.'

She became deliciously modest again.

'There!' she said. 'That's just a little rough idea of mine and now Peppino and Georgie will put their wise heads together, and tell us what to do.'

That was easily done: they repeated what she had said, and she corrected them if they went wrong. Then once again she stood fingering the tassels of her Teacher's Robe.

'About our studies,' she said. 'I for one should be very sorry to drop them altogether, because they made such a wonderful difference to me, and I think you all felt the same. Look at Georgie now: he looks ten years younger than he did a month ago, and as for Daisy, I wish I could trip about as she does. And it wouldn't do, would it, to drop everything just because Daisy's guru – I mean our guru – had been called away. It would look as if we weren't really interested in what he taught us, as if it was only the novelty of having a – a Brahmin among us that had attracted us.'

Lucia smiled benignly at them all.

'Perhaps we shall find, by and by, that we can't progress much all by ourselves,' she said, 'and it will all drop quietly. But don't let us drop it with a bang. I shall certainly take my elementary class as usual this afternoon.'

She paused.

'In my Robe, just as usual,' she said.

Chapter Nine

The fish for which Mrs Weston sent to Brinton every week since she did not like the look of the successor to Tommy Luton's mother lay disregarded on the dish, while with fork and fish-slice in her hand, as aids to gesticulation, she was recounting to Colonel Boucher the complete steps that had led up to her remarkable discovery.

'It was the day of Mrs Lucas's garden-party,' she said, 'when first I began to have my ideas, and you may be sure I kept them to myself, for I'm not one to speak before I'm pretty sure, but now if the King and Queen came to me on their bended knee and said it wasn't so, I shouldn't believe them. Well – as you may remember, we all went back to Mrs Lucas's party again about half-past six, and it was an umbrella that one had left behind, and a stick that another had forgotten, and what not, for me it was a book all about Venice, that I wanted to borrow, most interesting I am sure, but I haven't had time to glance at it yet, and there was Miss Bracely just come!'

Mrs Weston had to pause a moment for her maid, Elizabeth Luton (cousin of Tommy), jogged her elbow with the dish-cover in a manner that could not fail to remind her that Colonel Boucher was still waiting for his piece of brill. As she carved it for him, he rapidly ran over in his mind what seemed to be the main points so far, for as yet there was no certain clue as to the purpose of this preliminary matter. He guessed either Guru or Miss Bracely. Then he received his piece of brill, and Mrs Weston laid down her carving implements again.

'You'd better help yourself, ma'am,' said Elizabeth discreetly.

'So I had, and I'll give you a piece of advice too, Elizabeth, and that is to give the Colonel a glass of wine. Burgundy! I was only wondering this afternoon when it began to turn chilly, if there was a bottle or two of the old Burgundy left, which Mr Weston used to be so fond of, and there was. He bought it on the very spot where it was made, and he said there wasn't a headache in it, not if you drank it all night. He never did, for a couple of glasses and one more was all he ever took, so I don't know how he knew about drinking it all night, but he was a very fine judge of wine. So I said to Elizabeth, "A bottle of the old Burgundy, Elizabeth." Well, on that evening I stopped behind a bit, to have another look at the guru, and get my book, and when I came up the street again, what should I see but Miss Bracely walking in to the little front garden at "Old Place". It was getting dark, I know, and my eyes aren't like Mrs Antrobus's, which I call gimlets, but I saw her plain enough. And if it wasn't the next day, it was the day after that, that they began mending the roof, and since then, there have been plumbers and painters and upholsterers and furniture vans at the door day and night.'

'Haw, hum,' said the Colonel, 'then do you mean that it's Miss Bracely who has taken it?'

Mrs Weston nodded her head up and down.

'I shall ask you what you think when I've told you all,' she said. 'Well! There came a day, and if today's Friday it would be last Tuesday fortnight, and if today's Thursday, for I get mixed about it this morning, and then I never get it straight till next Sunday, but if today's Thursday, then it would be last Monday fortnight, when the guru went away very suddenly, and I'm sure I wasn't very sorry, because those breathings made me feel very giddy and yet I didn't like to be out of it all. Mr Georgie's sisters went away the same day, and I've often wondered whether there was any connection between the two events, for it was odd their happening together like that, and I'm not sure we've heard the last of it yet.'

Colonel Boucher began to wonder whether this was going to be about the guru after all and helped himself to half a partridge. This had the effect of diverting Mrs Weston's attention.

'No,' she said. 'I insist on your taking the whole bird. They are quite small, and I was disappointed when I saw them plucked, and a bit of cold ham and a savoury is all the rest of your dinner. Mary asked me if I wouldn't have an apple tart as well, but I said, "No; the Colonel never touches sweets, but he'll have a partridge, a whole partridge," I said, "and he won't complain of his dinner." Well! On the day that they all went away, whatever the explanation of that was, I was sitting in my chair opposite the Arms, when out came the landlord followed by two men carrying the settle that stood on the right of the fireplace in the hall. So I said, "Well, landlord, who has ordered that handsome piece?" For handsome it was with its carved arms. And he said, "Good-morning, ma'am" – no, "Good-afternoon, ma'am," it would be – "It's for Miss" – and then he stopped dead and corrected himself, "It's for Mr Pillson." '

Mrs Weston rapidly took a great quantity of mouthfuls of partridge. As soon as possible she went on.

'So perhaps you can tell me where it is now, if it was for Mr Georgie,' she said. 'I was there only two days ago, and it wasn't in his hall, or in his dining-room, or in his drawing-room, for though there are changes there, that settle isn't one of them. It's his treasure-case that's so altered. The snuff box is gone, and the cigarette case and the piece of Bow china, and instead there's a rat-tail spoon which he used to have on his dinner-table, and made a great fuss with, and a bit of Worcester china that used to stand on the mantelpiece, and a different cigarette case, and a bead-bag. I don't know where that came from, but if he inherited it, he didn't inherit much that time, I priced it at five shillings. But there's no settle in the treasure-case or out of it, and if you want to know where that settle is, it's in Old Place, because I saw it there myself, when the door was open, as I passed. He bought it – Mr Georgie – on behalf of Miss Bracely, unless you suppose that Mr Georgie is going to live in Old Place one day and his own house the next. No; it's Miss Bracely who is going to live at Old Place and that explains the landlord saying "Miss" and then stopping. For some reason, and I dare say that won't puzzle me long, now I can give my mind to it, she's making a secret about it, and only Mr Georgie and the landlord of the Arms know. Of course he had to, for Old Place is his, and I wish I had bought it myself now, for he got it for an old song.'

'Well, by Jove, you have pieced it together finely,' said Colonel Boucher.

'Wait a bit,' said Mrs Weston, rising to her climax. 'This very day, when Mary, that's my cook as you know, was coming back from Brinton with that bit of brill we've been eating, for they hadn't got an ounce of turbot, which I wanted, a luggage-train was standing at Riseholme station, and they had just taken out of it a case that could have held nothing but a grand piano. And if that's not enough for you, Colonel, there were two big dress-baskets as well, which I think must have contained linen, for they were corded, and it took two men to move each of them, so Mary said, and there's nothing so heavy as linen properly packed, unless it's plate, and there printed on them in black – no, it would be white, because the dress-baskets are black, were two initials, O. B. And if you can point to another O. B. in Riseholme I shall think I've lost my memory.'

At this moment of supreme climax, the telephone bell rang in the hall, shrill through the noise of cracking walnuts, and in came Elizabeth with the news that Mr Georgie wanted to know if he might come in for half an hour and chat. If it had been Olga Bracely herself, she could hardly have been more welcome; virtue (the virtue of observation and inference) was receiving its immediate reward.

'Delighted; say I'm delighted, Elizabeth,' said Mrs Weston, 'and now, Colonel, why should you sit all alone here, and I all alone in the drawing-room? Bring your decanter and your glass with you, and you shall spare me half a glass for myself, and if you can't guess what one of the questions that I shall ask Mr Georgie is: well – '

Georgie made haste to avail himself of this hospitality for he was bursting with the most important news that had been his since the night of the burglaries. Today he had received permission to let it be known that Olga was coming to Old Place, for Mr Shuttleworth had been informed of the purchase and furnishing of the house, and had, as expected, presented his wife with it, a really magnificent gift. So now Riseholme might know, too, and Georgie, as eager as Hermes, if not quite so swift, tripped across to Mrs Weston's, on his delightful errand. It was, too, of the nature of just such a punitive expedition as Georgie thoroughly enjoyed, for Lucia all this week had been rather haughty and cold with him for his firm refusal to tell her who the purchaser of Old Place was. He had admitted that he knew, but had said that he was under promise not to reveal that, until permitted, and Lucia had been haughty in consequence. She had, in fact, been so haughty that when Georgie rang her up just now, before ringing Mrs Weston up, to ask if he might spend an hour after dinner there, fully intending to tell her the great news, she had replied through her parlour-maid that she was very busy at the piano. Very well, if she preferred the second and third movements of the 'Moonlight Sonata', which she had seriously taken in hand, to Georgie's company, why, he would offer himself and his great news elsewhere. But he determined not to bring it out at once; that sort of thing must be kept till he said it was time to go away. Then he would bring it out, and depart in the blaze of Success.

He had brought a pretty piece of embroidery with him to occupy himself with, for his work had fallen into sad arrears during August, and he settled himself comfortably down close to the light, so that at the cost of very little eyestrain, he need not put on his spectacles.

'Any news?' he asked, according to the invariable formula. Mrs Weston caught the Colonel's eye. She was not proposing to bring out her tremendous interrogation just yet.

'Poor Mrs Antrobus. Toothache!' she said. 'I was in the chemist's this morning and who should come in but Miss Piggy, and she wanted a drop of laudanum and had to say what it was for, and even then she had to sign a paper. Very unpleasant, I call it, to be obliged to let a chemist know that your mother has a toothache. But there it was, tell him she had to, or go away without any laudanum. I don't know whether Mr Doubleday wasn't asking more than he should, just out of inquisitiveness, for I don't see what business it is of his. I know what I should have said: "Oh, Mr Doubleday, I want it to make laudanum tartlets, we are all so fond of laudanum tartlets." Something sharp and sarcastic like that, to show him his place. But I expect it did Mrs Antrobus good, for there she was on the green in the afternoon, and her face wasn't swollen for I had a good look at her. Oh, and there was something I wanted to ask you, Mr Georgie, and I had it on the tip of my tongue a moment ago. We talked about it at dinner, the Colonel and I, while we were eating our bit of partridge, and I thought "Mr Georgie will be sure to be able to tell us," and if you didn't ring up on the telephone immediately afterwards! That seemed just Providential, but what's the use of that, if I can't remember what it was that I wanted to ask you.'

This seemed a good opening for his startling news, but Georgie rejected it, as it was too early yet. 'I wonder what it could have been,' he said.

'Well, it will come back to me presently, and here's our coffee, and I see Elizabeth hasn't forgotten to bring a drop of something good for you two gentlemen. And I don't say that I won't join you, if Elizabeth will bring another glass. What with a glass of Burgundy at my dinner, and a drop of brandy now, I shall be quite tipsy unless I take care. The guru now, Mr Georgie, no, that's not what I wanted to ask you about – but has there been any news of the guru?'

For a moment in this juxtaposition of the topics of brandy and guru, Georgie was afraid that something might have leaked out about the contents of the cupboard in Othello. But it was evidently a chance combination, for Mrs Weston went straight on without waiting for an answer.

'What a day that was,' she said, 'when he and Miss Olga Bracely were both at Mrs Lucas's garden-party. Ah, now I've got it; now I know what I wanted to ask. When will Miss Olga Bracely come to live at Old Place? Quite soon now, I suppose.'

If Georgie had not put down his embroidery with great expedition, he would undoubtedly have pricked his finger.

'But how on earth did you know she was coming at all?' he said. 'I was just going to tell you that she was coming, as a great bit of news. How tarsome! It's spoiled all my pleasure.'

'Haw, hum, not a very gallant speech, when you're talking to Mrs Weston,' said the Colonel, who hated Georgie's embroidery.

Luckily the pleasure in the punitive part of the expedition remained and Georgie recovered himself. He had some news too; he could answer Mrs Weston's question.

'But it was to have been such a secret until the whole thing was ready,' he said. 'I knew all along; I have known since the day of the garden-party. No one but me, not even her husband.'

He was well rewarded for the recovery of his temper. Mrs Weston put down her glass of something good untasted.

'What?' she said. 'Is she going to live here alone in hiding from him? Have they quarrelled so soon?'

Georgie had to disappoint her about this, and gave the authentic version.

'And she's coming next week, Monday probably,' he said.

They were all now extremely happy, for Mrs Weston felt convinced that nobody else had put two and two together with the same brilliant result as herself, and Georgie was in the even superior position of having known the result without having to do any addition at all, and Colonel Boucher enjoyed the first fruits of it all. When they parted, having thoroughly discussed it, the chief preoccupation in the minds of all was the number of Riseholmites that each of them would be the first to pass on the news to. Mrs Weston could tell Elizabeth that night, and Colonel Boucher his bulldogs, but the first blood was really drawn by Georgie, who seeing a light in Mrs Quantock's drawing-room when he returned, dropped in for a moment and scored a right and left by telling Robert who let him in, before going upstairs, and Mrs Quantock when he got there. It was impossible to do any more that night.

*   *   *

Lucia was always very busy of a morning in polishing the sword and shield of Art, in order to present herself daily to her subjects in shining armour, and keep a little ahead of them all in culture, and thus did not as a rule take part in the parliament on the green. Moreover Georgie usually dropped in before lunch, and her casual interrogation 'Any news?' as they sat down to the piano, elicited from him, as in a neat little jug, the cream of the morning's milkings. Today she was attired in her Teacher's Robe, for the elementary class, though not always now in full conclave, gathered at her house on Tuesdays and Fridays. There had been signs of late that the interest of her pupils was on the wane, for Colonel Boucher had not appeared for two meetings, nor had Mrs Weston come to the last, but it was part of Lucia's policy to let guruism die a natural death without herself facilitating its happy release, and she meant to be ready for her class at the appointed times as long as anybody turned up. Besides the Teacher's Robe was singularly becoming and she often wore it when there was no question of teaching at all.

But today, though she would not have been surprised at the complete absence of pupils, she was still in consultation with her cook over the commissariat of the day, when a succession of tinklings from the mermaid's tail announced that a full meeting was assembling. Her maid in fact had announced to her without pause except to go to the door and back, though it still wanted a few minutes to eleven, that Colonel Boucher, Mrs Weston, Mrs Antrobus and Piggy were all assembled in the smoking-parlour. Even as she passed through the hall on her way there, Georgie came hurrying across Shakespeare's garden, his figure distorted through the wavy glass of the windows, and she opened the door to him herself.

'*Georgino mio*,' she said, 'oo not angry with Lucia for saying she was busy last night? And now I'm just going to take my Yoga-class. They all came rather early and I haven't seen any of them yet. Any news?'

Georgie heaved a sigh; all Riseholme knew by this time, and he was going to score one more by telling Lucia.

'My dear, haven't you heard yet?' he asked. 'I was going to tell you last night.'

'The tenant of Old Place?' asked Lucia unerringly.

'Yes. Guess!' said Georgie tantalisingly. This was his last revelation and he wanted to spin it out.

Lucia decided on a great stroke, involving risks but magnificent if it came off. In a flash she guessed why all the Yoga-class had come so super-punctually; each of them she felt convinced wanted to have the joy of telling her, after everybody else knew, who the new tenant was. On the top of this bitterness was the added acrimony of Georgie, whose clear duty it was to have informed her the moment he knew, wanting to make the same revelation to her, last of all Riseholme. She had already had her suspicions, for she had not forgotten the fact that Olga Bracely and Georgie had played croquet all afternoon when they should have been at her garden-party, and she determined to risk all for the sake of spoiling Georgie's pleasure in telling her. She gave her silvery laugh, that started, so she had ascertained, on A flat above the treble clef.

'*Georgino*, did all my questions as to who it was really take you in?' she asked. 'Just as if I hadn't known all along! Why, Miss Olga Bracely, of course!'

Georgie's fallen face showed her how completely she had spoiled his pleasure.

'Who told you?' he asked.

She rattled her tassels.

'Little bird!' she said. 'I must run away to my class, or they will scold me.'

Once again before they settled down to high philosophies, Lucia had the pleasure of disappointing the ambitions of her class to surprise, inform and astonish her.

'Good-morning to you all,' she said, 'and before we settle down I'll give you a little bit of news now that at last I'm allowed to. Dear Miss Olga Bracely, whom I think you all met here, is coming to live at Old Place. Will she not be a great addition to our musical parties? Now, please.'

But this splendid bravado was but a scintillation, on a hard and highly polished surface, and had Georgie been able to penetrate into Lucia's heart he would have found complete healing for his recent severe mortification. He did not really believe that Lucia had known all along, like himself, who the new tenant was, for her enquiries had seemed to be pointed with the most piercing curiosity, but, after all, Lucia (when she did not forget her part) was a fine actress, and perhaps all the time he thought he had been punishing her, she had been fooling him. And, in any case, he certainly had not had the joy of telling her; whether she had guessed or really knew, it was she who had told him, and there was no getting over it. He went back straight home and drew a caricature of her.

But if Georgie was sitting with a clouded brow, Lucia was troubled by nothing less than a raging tornado of agitated thought. Though Olga would undoubtedly be a great addition to the musical talent of Riseholme, would she fall into line, and, for instance, 'bring her music' and sing after dinner when Lucia asked her? As regards music, it was possible that she might be almost too great an addition, and cause the rest of the gifted amateurs to sink into comparative insignificance. At present Lucia was high-priestess at every altar of Art, and she could not think with equanimity of seeing anybody in charge of the ritual at any. Again to so eminent an opera-singer there must be conceded a certain dramatic knowledge, and indeed Georgie had often spoken to Lucia of that superb moment when Brünnhilde woke and hailed the sun. Must Lucia give up the direction of dramatic art as well as of music?

Point by point pricked themselves out of the general gloom, and hoisted danger signals; then suddenly the whole was in blaze together. What if Olga took the lead, not in this particular or in that, but attempted to constitute herself supreme in the affairs of Riseholme? It was all very well for her to be a brilliant bird of passage just for a couple of days, and drop, so to speak, 'a moulted feather, an eagle's feather' on Lucia's party, thereby causing it to shine out from all previous festivities, making it the Hightumest affair that had ever happened, but it was a totally different matter to contemplate her permanent residence here. It seemed possible that then she might keep her feathers to line her own eyrie. She thought of Belshazzar's feast, and the writing of doom on the wall which she was Daniel enough to interpret herself. 'Thy kingdom is divided,' it said, 'and given to the Bracelys or the Shuttleworths.'

She rallied her forces. If Olga meant to show herself that sort of

woman, she should soon know with whom she had to deal. Not but
what Lucia would give her the chance first of behaving with suitable
loyalty and obedience; she would even condescend to cooperate with
her so long as it was perfectly clear that she aimed at no supremacy.
But there was only one lawgiver in Riseholme, one court of appeal,
one dispenser of destiny.

Her own firmness of soul calmed and invigorated her, and changing
her Teacher's Robe for a walking dress, she went out up the road
that led by Old Place, to see what could be observed of the interior
from outside.

Chapter Ten

One morning about the middle of October, Lucia was seated at
breakfast and frowning over a note she had just received. It began
without any formality and was written in pencil.

> Do look in about half-past nine on Saturday and be silly for an
> hour or two. We'll play games and dance, shall we? Bring your
> husband of course, and don't bother to reply.
>
>   O. B.

'An invitation,' she said icily, as she passed it to her husband.
'Rather short notice.'

'We're not doing anything, are we?' he asked.

Peppino was a little imperceptive sometimes.

'No, it wasn't that I meant,' she said. 'But there's a little more
informality about it than one would expect.'

'Probably it's an informal party,' said he.

'It certainly seems most informal. I am not accustomed to be asked
quite like that.'

Peppino began to be aware of the true nature of the situation.

'I see what you mean, *cara*,' he said. 'So don't let us go. Then she
will take the hint perhaps.'

Lucia thought this over for a moment and found that she rather
wanted to go. But a certain resentment that had been slowly accumu-
lating in her mind for some days past began to leak out first, before
she consented to overlook Olga's informality.

'It is a fortnight since I called on her,' she said, 'and she has not
even returned the call. I dare say they behave like that in London in
certain circles, but I don't know that London is any better for it.'

'She has been away twice since she came,' said Peppino. 'She has hardly been here for a couple of days together yet.'

'I may be wrong,' said Lucia. 'No doubt I am wrong. But I should have thought that she might have spared half an hour out of these days in returning my call. However, she thought not.'

Peppino suddenly recollected a thrilling piece of news which most unaccountably he had forgotten to tell Lucia.

'Dear me, something slipped my memory,' he said. 'I met Mrs Weston yesterday afternoon, who told me that half an hour ago Miss Bracely had seen her in her bath-chair and had taken the handles from Tommy Luton, and pushed her twice round the green, positively running.'

'That does not seem to me of very prime importance,' said Lucia, though she was thrilled to the marrow. 'I do not wonder it slipped your memory, *caro*.'

'*Carissima*, wait a minute. That is not all. She told Mrs Weston that she would have returned her call, but that she hadn't got any calling cards.'

'Impossible!' cried Lucia. 'They could have printed them at Ye Olde Booke Shop in an afternoon.'

'That may be so, indeed, if you say so, it is,' said Peppino. 'Anyhow she said she hadn't got any calling cards, and I don't see why she should lie about it.'

'No, it is not the confession one would be likely to make,' said she, 'unless it was true. Or even if it was,' she added.

'Anyhow it explains why she has not been here,' said Peppino. 'She would naturally like to do everything in order, when she called on you, *carissima*. It would have been embarrassing if you were out, and she could not hand in her card.'

'And about Mr Shuttleworth?' asked she in an absent voice, as if she had no real interest in her question.

'He has not been seen yet at all, as far as I can gather.'

'Then shall we have no host, if we drop in tomorrow night?'

'Let us go and see, *cara*,' said he gaily.

Apart from this matter of her call not being returned, Lucia had not as yet had any reason to suspect Olga of revolutionary designs on the throne. She had done odd things – pushing Mrs Weston's chair round the green was one of them, smoking a cigarette as she came back from church on Sunday was another – but these she set down to the Bohemianism and want of polish which might be expected from her upbringing, if you could call an orphan school at

Brixton an upbringing at all. This terrific fact Georgie had let slip in his stern determination to know twice as much about Olga as anybody else, and Lucia had treasured it. She had in the last fortnight labelled Olga as 'rather common', retaining, however, a certain respect for her professional career, given that that professional career was to be thrown down as a carpet for her own feet. But, after all, if Olga was a bit Bohemian in her way of life, as exhibited by the absence of calling cards, Lucia was perfectly ready to overlook that (confident in the refining influence of Riseholme), and to go to the informal party next day, if she felt so disposed, for no direct answer was asked for.

There was a considerable illumination in the windows of Old Place when she and Peppino set out after dinner next night to go to the 'silly' party, kindly overlooking the informality and the absence of a return visit to her call. It had been a sloppy day of rain, and, as was natural, Lucia carried some very smart indoor shoes in a paper parcel and Peppino had his Russian goloshes on. These were immense snow-boots, in which his evening shoes were completely encased, but Lucia preferred not to disfigure her feet to that extent, and was clad in neat walking-boots which she could exchange for her smart satin footwear in the cloakroom. The resumption of walking-boots when the evening was over was rather a feature among the ladies and was called 'the cobbler's at-home'. The two started rather late, for it was fitting that Lucia should be the last to arrive.

They had come to the door of Old Place, and Peppino was fumbling in the dark for the bell, when Lucia gave a little cry of agony and put her hands over her ears, just as if she had been seized with a double-earache of peculiar intensity.

'Gramophone,' she said faintly.

There could be no doubt about that. From the window close at hand came out the excruciating strains of a very lusty instrument, and the record was that of a vulgar 'catchy' waltz-tune, taken down from a brass-band. All Riseholme knew what her opinion about gramophones was; to the lover of Beethoven they were like indecent and profane language loudly used in a public place. Only one, so far as was known, had ever come to Riseholme, and that was introduced by the misguided Robert Quantock. Once he had turned it on in her presence, but the look of agony which crossed her face was such that he had to stop it immediately. Then the door was opened, and the abominable noise poured out in increased volume.

Lucia paused for a moment in indecision. Would it be the great, the magnificent thing to go home without coming in, trusting to Peppino to let it be widely known what had turned her back from the door? There was a good deal to be said for that, for it would be living up to her own high and immutable standards. On the other hand she particularly wanted to see what standard of entertaining Olga was initiating. The 'silly evening' was quite a new type of party, for since she had directed and controlled the social side of things there had been no 'silly evenings' of any kind in Riseholme, and it might be a good thing to ensure the failure of this (in case she did not like it) by setting the example of a bored and frosty face. But if she went in, the gramophone must be stopped. She would sit and wince, and Peppino must explain her feeling about gramophones. That would be a suitable exhibition of authority. Or she might tell Olga.

Lucia put on her satin shoes, leaving her boots till the hour of the cobbler's at-home came, and composing her face to a suitable wince was led by a footman on tiptoe to the door of the big music-room which Georgie had spoken of.

'If you'll please to step in very quietly, ma'am,' he said.

The room was full of people; all Riseholme was there, and since there were not nearly enough chairs (Lucia saw *that* at once) a large number were sitting on the floor on cushions. At the far end of the room was a slightly raised dais, to the corner of which the grand piano had been pushed, on the top of which, with its braying trumpet pointing straight at Lucia, was an immense gramophone. On the dais was Olga dancing. She was dressed in some white soft fabric shimmering with silver, which left her beautiful arms bare to the shoulder. It was cut squarely and simply about the neck, and hung in straight folds down to just above her ankles. She held in her hands some long shimmering scarf of brilliant red, that floated and undulated as she moved, as if inspired by some life of its own that it drew out of her slim superb vitality. From the cloud of shifting crimson, with the slow billows of silver moving rhythmically round her body, that beautiful face looked out deliciously smiling and brimming with life . . .

Lucia had hardly entered when with a final bray the gramophone came to the end of its record, and Olga swept a great curtsey, threw down her scarf, and stepped off the dais. Georgie was sitting on the floor close to it, and jumped up, leading the applause. For a moment, though several heads had been turned at Lucia's entrance, nobody took the slightest notice of her, indeed, the first apparently to recognise her presence was her hostess, who just kissed her hand to her, and then continued talking to Georgie. Then Olga threaded her way through the besprinkled floor, and came up to her.

'How wise you were to miss that very poor performance,' she said. 'But Mr Georgie insisted that I should make a fool of myself.'

'Indeed, I am sorry not to have been here for it,' said Lucia in her most stately manner. 'It seemed to me very far from being a poor performance, very far indeed. *Caro mio*, you remember Miss Bracely.'

'*Si, si molto bene*,' said Peppino, shaking hands.

'Ah, and you talk Italian,' said Olga. '*Che bella lingua!* I wish I knew it.'

'You have a very good pronunciation,' said Lucia.

'*Tante grazie.* You know everyone here of course. Now, what shall we do next? Clumps or charades or what? Ah, there are some cigarettes. Won't you have one?'

Lucia gave a little scream of dismay.

'A cigarette for me? That would be a very odd thing,' she said. Then relenting, as she remembered that Olga must be excused for her ignorance, she added: 'You see I never smoke. Never.'

'Oh, you should learn,' said Olga. 'Now let's play clumps. Does everyone know clumps? If they don't they will find out. Or shall we dance? There's the gramophone to dance to.'

Lucia put up her hands in playful petition.

'Oh please, no gramophone!' she said.

'Oh, don't you like it?' said Olga. 'It's so horrible that I adore it, as I adore dreadful creatures in an aquarium. But I think we won't dance till after supper. We'll have supper extremely soon, partly because I am dying of famine, and partly because people are sillier afterwards. But just one game of clumps first. Let's see; there are but enough for four clumps. Please make four clumps, everybody, and – and will you and two more go out with Mr Georgie, Mrs Lucas? We will be as quick as we can, and we won't think of anything that will make Mr Georgie blush. Oh, there he is! He heard!'

Olga's intense enjoyment of her own party was rapidly galvanising everybody into a much keener gaiety than was at all usual in Rise-holme, where as a rule, the hostess was somewhat anxious and watchful, fearing that her guests were not amusing themselves, and that the sandwiches would give out. There was a sit-down supper when the clumps were over (Mrs Quantock had been the first to guess Beethoven's little toe on his right foot, which made Lucia wince) and there were not enough men and maids to wait, and so people foraged for themselves, and Olga paraded up and down the room with a bottle of champagne in one hand, and a dish of lobster-salad in the other. She sat for a minute or two first at one table and then at another, and asked silly riddles, and sent to the kitchen for a ham, and put out all the electric light by mistake, when she meant to turn on some more. Then when supper was over they all took their seats back into the music-room and played musical chairs, at the end of which Mrs Quantock was left in with Olga, and it was believed that she said 'Damn', when Mrs Quantock won. Georgie was in charge of the gramophone which supplied deadly music, quite forgetting that this was agony to Lucia, and not even being aware when she made a sign to Peppino, and went away having a cobbler's at-home all to herself. Nobody noticed when Saturday ended and Sunday began, for Georgie and Colonel Boucher were cockfighting on the floor, Georgie screaming out 'How tarsome' when he was upset, and Colonel Boucher very red in the face saying 'Haw, hum. Never thought I should romp again like this. By Jove, most amusing!' Georgie was the last to leave and did not notice till he was halfway home that he had a ham-frill adorning his shirt front. He hoped that it had been Olga who put it there, when he had to walk blindfold across the floor and try to keep in a straight line.

Riseholme got up rather late next morning, and had to hurry over its breakfast in order to be in time for church. There was a slight feeling of reaction abroad, and a sense of having been young and amused, and of waking now to the fact of church-bells and middle-age. Colonel Boucher, singing the bass of 'A few more years shall roll', felt his mind instinctively wandering to the cockfight the evening before, and depressedly recollecting that a considerable number of years had rolled already. Mrs Weston, with her bath-chair in the aisle and Tommy Luton to hand her hymn-book and prayer-book as she required, looked sideways at Mrs Quantock, and thought how strange it was that Daisy, so few hours ago, had been racing round a solitary chair with Georgie's finger on the gramo-phone, while Georgie, singing tenor by Colonel Boucher's ample side, saw with keen annoyance that there was a stain of tarnished silver on his forefinger, accounted for by the fact that after breakfast he had been cleaning the frame which held the photograph of Olga Bracely and had been astonished to hear the church-bells beginning. Another conducement to depression on his part was the fact that he was lunching with Lucia, and he could not imagine what Lucia's attitude would be towards the party last night. She had come to church rather late, having no use for the General Confession, and sang with stony fervour. She wore her usual church-face, from which nothing whatever could be gathered. A great many stealthy glances right and left from everybody failed to reveal the presence of their hostess of last night. Georgie, in particular, was sorry for this; he would have liked her to show that capacity for respectable seriousness which her presence at church that morning would have implied; while Lucia, in particular, was glad of this, for it confirmed her view that Miss Bracely was not, nor could ever be, a true Riseholmite. She had thought as much last night, and had said so to Peppino. She proposed to say the same to Georgie today.

Then came a stupefying surprise as Mr Rumbold walked from his stall to the pulpit for the sermon. Generally he gave out the number of the short anthem which accompanied this manoeuvre, but today he made no such announcement. A discreet curtain hid the organist from the congregation, and veiled his gymnastics with the stops and his antic dancing on the pedals, and now when Mr Rumbold moved from his stall, there came from the organ the short introduction to Bach's 'Mein gläubiges Herze', which even Lucia had allowed to be nearly 'equal' to Beethoven. And then came the voice . . .

The reaction after the romp last night went out like a snuffed candle at this divine singing, which was charged with the joyfulness of some heavenly child. It grew low and soft, it rang out again, it lingered and tarried, it quickened into the ultimate triumph. No singing could have been simpler, but that simplicity could only have sprung from the highest art. But now the art was wholly unconscious; it was part of the singer who but praised God as the thrushes do. She who had made gaiety last night, made worship this morning.

As they sat down for the discourse, Colonel Boucher discreetly whispered to Georgie 'By Jove.' And Georgie rather more audibly answered 'Adorable.' Mrs Weston drew a half a crown from her purse instead of her usual shilling, to be ready for the offertory, and Mrs Quantock wondered if she was too old to learn to sing.

* * *

Georgie found Lucia very full of talk that day at luncheon, and markedly more Italian than usual. Indeed she put down an Italian grammar when he entered the drawing-room, and covered it up with the essays of Antonio Caporelli. This possibly had some connection with the fact that she had encouraged Olga last night with regard to her pronunciation.

'*Ben arrivato, Georgio,*' she said. '*Ho finito il libro di Antonio Caporelli quanta memento. E magnifico!*'

Georgie thought she had finished it long ago, but perhaps he was mistaken. The sentence flew off Lucia's tongue as if it was perched there all quite ready.

'*Sono un poco fatigata dopo il* – dear me how rusty I am getting in Italian for I can't remember the word,' she went on. 'Anyhow I am a little tired after last night. A delightful little party, was it not? It was clever of Miss Bracely to get so many people together at so short a notice. Once in a while that sort of romp is very well.'

'I enjoyed it quite enormously,' said Georgie.

'I saw you did, *cattivo ragazzo*,' said she. 'You quite forgot about your poor Lucia and her horror of that dreadful gramophone. I had to exert all the calmness that Yoga has given me not to scream. But you were naughty with the gramophone over those musical chairs – unmusical chairs, as I said to Peppino, didn't I, *caro*? – taking it off and putting it on again so suddenly. Each time I thought it was the end. *E pronta la colazione. Andiamo.*'

Presently they were seated; the menu, an unusual thing in itself at luncheon, was written in Italian, the scribe being clearly Lucia.

'I shall want a lot of Georgino's *tempo* this week,' she said, 'for Peppino and I have quite settled we must give a little after-dinner party next Saturday, and I want you to help me to arrange some impromptu tableaux. Everything impromptu must just be sketched out first, and I dare say Miss Bracely worked a great deal at her dance last night and I wish I had seen more of it. She was a little awkward in the management of her draperies I thought, but I dare say she does not know much about dancing. Still it was very graceful and effective for an amateur, and she carried it off very well.'

'Oh, but she is not quite an amateur,' said Georgie. 'She has played in *Salome*.'

Lucia pursed her lips.

'Indeed, I am sorry she played in that,' she said. 'With her un-doubtedly great gifts I should have thought she might have found a worthier object. Naturally I have not heard it. I should be very much ashamed to be seen there. But about our tableaux now. Peppino thought we might open with the Execution of Mary Queen of Scots. It is a dreadful thing that I have lost my pearls. He would be the executioner and you the priest. Then I should like to have the awakening of Brünnhilde.'

'That would be lovely,' said Georgie. 'Have you asked Miss Olga if she will?'

'*Georgino mio*, you don't quite understand,' said Lucia. 'This

party is to be for Miss Bracely. I was her guest last night in spite of
the gramophone, and indeed I hope she will find nothing in my
house that jars on her as much as her gramophone jarred on me. I
had a dreadful nightmare last night – didn't I, Peppino? – in consequence. About the Brünnhilde tableau, I thought Peppino would
be Siegfried – and perhaps you could learn just fifteen or twenty
bars of the music and play it while the curtain was up. You can play
the same over again if it is encored. Then how about King Cophetua
and the beggar-maid? I should be with my back to the audience,
and should not turn round at all; it would be quite your tableau.
We will just sketch them out, as I said, and have a grouping or two
to make sure we don't get in each other's way, and I will see that
there are some dresses of some kind which we can just throw on.
The tableaux with a little music, serious music, would be quite
sufficient to keep everybody interested.'

By this time Georgie had got a tolerable inkling of the import of
all this. It was not at present to be war; it was to be magnificent
rivalry, a throwing down perhaps of a gauntlet, which none would
venture to pick up. To confirm this view, Lucia went on with
gathering animation.

'I do not propose to have games, romps shall I call them?' she said,
'for as far as I know Riseholme, and perhaps I know it a little better
than dear Miss Bracely, Riseholme does not care for that sort of thing.
It is not quite in our line; we may be right or wrong, I am sure I do not
know, but as a matter of fact, we *don't* care for that sort of thing. Dear
Miss Bracely did her very best last night; I am sure she was prompted
only by the most hospitable motives, but how should she know? The
supper too. Peppino counted nineteen empty champagne bottles.'

'Eighteen, *carissima*,' said Peppino.

'I think you told me nineteen, *caro*, but it makes very little
difference. Eighteen empty champagne bottles standing on the
sideboard, and no end to the caviare sandwiches which were left
over. It was all too much, though there were not nearly enough
chairs, and indeed I never got one at all except just at supper.'

Lucia leaned forward over the table, with her hands clasped.

'There was display about it, *Georgino*, and you know how I hate
display,' she said. 'Shakespeare was content with the most modest
scenery for his masterpieces, and it would be a great mistake if we
allowed ourselves to be carried away by mere wasteful opulence. In
all the years I have lived here, and contributed in my humble way to
the life of the place, I have heard no complaints about my suppers or

teas, nor about the quality of entertainment which I offer my guests when they are so good as to say "*Si*," to *le mie invitazione*. Art is not advanced by romping, and we are able to enjoy ourselves without two hundred caviare sandwiches being left over. And such wasteful cutting of the ham; I had to slice the chunk she gave me over and over again before I could eat it.'

Georgie felt he could not quite let this pass.

'Well, I had an excellent supper,' he said, 'and I enjoyed it very much. Besides, I saw Peppino tucking in like anything. Ask him what he thought of it.'

Lucia gave her silvery laugh.

'*Georgino*, you are a boy,' she said artfully, 'and "tuck in" as you so vulgarly call it without thinking. I'm saying nothing against the supper, but I'm sure that Peppino and Colonel Boucher would have felt better this morning if they had been wiser last night. But that's not the real point. I want to show Miss Bracely, and I'm sure she will be grateful for it, the sort of entertainment that has contented us at Riseholme for so long. I will frame it on her lines; I will ask all and sundry to drop in with just a few hours' notice, as she did. Everything shall be good, and there shall be about it all something that I seemed to miss last night. There was a little bit – how shall I say it? – a little bit of the footlights about it all. And the footlights didn't seem to me to have been extinguished at church-time this morning. The singing of that very fine aria was theatrical, I can't call it less than theatrical.'

She fixed Georgie with her black beady eye, and smoothed her undulated hair.

'Theatrical,' she said again. 'Now let us have our coffee in the music-room. Shall Lucia play a little bit of Beethoven to take out any nasty taste of gramophone? Me no likey gramophone at all. Nebber!'

*   *   *

Georgie now began to feel himself able to sympathise with that surfeited swain who thought how happy he could be with either, were t'other dear charmer away. Certainly he had been very happy with Lucia all these years, before t'other dear charmer alighted in Riseholme, and now he felt that should Lucia decide, as she had often so nearly decided, to spend the winter on the Riviera, Riseholme would still be a very pleasant place of residence. He never was quite sure how seriously she had contemplated a winter on the Riviera, for the mere mention of it had always been enough to make him protest that Riseholme could not possibly exist without her, but today, as he sat and heard (rather than listened to) a series of slow movements, with a brief and hazardous attempt at the scherzo of the 'Moonlight', he felt that if any talk of the Riviera came up, he would not be quite so insistent as to the impossibility of Riseholme continuing to exist without her. He could, for instance, have existed perfectly well this Sunday afternoon if Lucia had been even at Timbuctoo or the Antipodes, for as he went away last night, Olga had thrown a casual intimation to him that she would be at home, if he had nothing better to do, and cared to drop in. Certainly he had nothing better to do but he had something worse to do . . .

Peppino was sitting in the window seat, with eyes closed, because he listened to music better so, and with head that nodded occasionally, presumably for the same reason. But the cessation of the slow movement naturally made him cease to listen, and he stirred and gave the sigh with which Riseholme always acknowledged the end of a slow movement. Georgie sighed too, and Lucia sighed; they all sighed, and then Lucia began again. So Peppino closed his eyes again, and Georgie continued his mental analysis of the situation.

At present, so he concluded, Lucia did not mean war. She meant, as by some great armed demonstration, to exhibit the Riseholme spirit in its full panoply, and then crush into dazzled submission any potential rivalry. She meant also to exert an educational influence, for she allowed that Olga had great gifts, and she meant to train and refine those gifts so that they might, when exercised under benign but autocratic supervision, conduce to the strength and splendour of Riseholme. Naturally she must be loyally and ably assisted, and Georgie realised that the tableau of King Cophetua (his tableau as she had said) partook of the nature of a bribe, and, if that word was invidious, of a raising of his pay. It was equally certain that this prolonged recital of slow movements was intended to produce in his mind a vivid consciousness of the contrast between the romp last night and the present tranquil hour, and it did not fail in this respect.

Lucia shut the piano-lid, and almost before they had given their sighs, spoke.

'I think I will have a little dinner party first,' she said. 'I will ask Lady Ambermere. That will make us four, with you Georgie, and Miss Bracely and Mr Shuttleworth will make six. The rest I shall ask to come in at nine, for I know Lady Ambermere does not like late hours. And now shall we talk over our tableaux?'

So even Lucia's mind had not been wholly absorbed in Beethoven, though Georgie, as usual, told her she had never played so divinely.

Chapter Eleven

The manoeuvres of the next week became so bewilderingly complicated that by Wednesday Georgie was almost thinking of going away to the seaside with Foljambe and Dicky in sheer despair, and in after years he could not without great mental effort succeed in straightening it all out, and the effort caused quite a buzzing in his head . . . That Sunday evening Lucia sent an invitation to Lady Ambermere for 'dinner and tableaux', to which Lady Ambermere's 'people' replied by telephone on Monday afternoon that her ladyship was sorry to be unable. Lucia therefore gave up the idea of a dinner party, and reverted to her original scheme of an evening party like Olga's got up on the spur of the moment, with great care and most anxious preparation. The rehearsals for the impromptu tableaux meantime went steadily forward behind closed doors, and Georgie wrestled with twenty bars of the music of the 'Awakening of Brünnhilde'. Lucia intended to ask nobody until Friday evening, and Olga should see what sort of party Riseholme could raise at a moment's notice.

Early on Tuesday morning the devil entered into Daisy Quantock, probably by means of subconscious telepathy, and she proceeded to go round the green at the morning parliament, and ask everybody to come in for a good romp on Saturday evening, and they all accepted. Georgie, Lucia and Olga were absentees, and so, making a house-to-house visitation she went first to Georgie. He with secret knowledge of the tableaux (indeed he was stitching himself a robe to be worn by King Cophetua at the time and hastily bundled it under the table) regretted that he was already engaged. This was rather mysterious, but he might have planned, for all Mrs Quantock knew, an evening when he would be 'busy indoors', and since those evenings were never to be pried upon, she asked no questions, but went off to Lucia's to give her invitation there. There again she was met with a similarly mysterious refusal. Lucia much regretted that she and Peppino were unable to come, and she hoped Daisy would have a lovely party. Even as she spoke, she heard her telephone bell ringing, and hurried off to find that Georgie, faithful lieutenant, was acquainting her with the fact that Mrs Quantock was planning a party for Saturday; he did not know how far she had got. At that moment she had got just halfway to Old Place, walking at unusual speed. Lucia grasped the situation with amazing quickness, and cutting off Georgie with a snap, she abandoned all idea of her party being impromptu, and rang up Olga. She would secure her anyhow . . .

The telephone was in the hall, and Olga, with her hat on, was just preparing to go out, when the bell sounded. The words of grateful acceptance were on her very lips when her front-door bell rang too, very long and insistently, and had hardly left off when it began again. Olga opened the door herself and there was Mrs Quantock on the doorstep with her invitation for Saturday night. She was obliged to refuse, but promised to look in, if she was not very late in getting away from Mrs Lucas's (and pop went the cat out of the bag). Another romp would be lovely.

Already the evils of decentralisation and overlapping were becoming manifest. Lucia rang up house after house, only to find that its inhabitants were already engaged. She had got Olga and Georgie, and could begin the good work of education and the crushing of rivalry, not by force but by pure and refined example, but Mrs Quantock had got everybody else. In the old days this could never have happened, for everything revolved round one central body. Now with the appearance of this other great star, all the known laws of gravity and attraction were upset.

Georgie, again summoned to the telephone, recommended an appeal to Mrs Quantock's better nature, which Lucia rejected, doubting whether she had one.

'But what about the tableaux?' asked Georgie. 'We three can't very well do tableaux for Miss Olga to look at.'

Then Lucia showed herself truly great.

'The merit of the tableaux does not consist in the number of the audience,' she said.

She paused a moment.

'Have you got the Cophetua-robe to set properly?' she asked.

'Oh, it'll do,' said Georgie dejectedly.

*   *   *

On Tuesday afternoon Olga rang up Lucia again to say that her husband was arriving that day, so might she bring him on Saturday? To this Lucia cordially assented, but she felt that a husband and wife sitting together and looking at another husband and wife doing tableaux would be an unusual entertainment, and not characteristic of Riseholme's best. She began to waver about the tableaux and to consider dinner instead. She also wondered whether she had been wronging dear Daisy, and whether she had a better nature after all. Perhaps Georgie might ascertain.

Georgie was roused from a little fatigued nap by the telephone, for he had fallen asleep over King Cophetua's robe. Lucia explained the situation and delicately suggested that it would be so easy for him to 'pop in' to dear Daisy's, and be very diplomatic. There was nobody like Georgie for tact. So with a heavy yawn he popped in.

'You've come about this business on Saturday,' said Daisy unerringly. 'Haven't you?'

Georgie remembered his character for tact.

'How wonderful of you to guess that!' he said. 'I thought we might see if we couldn't arrange something, if we put our heads together. It's such a pity to split up. We – I mean Lucia has got Miss Olga and her husband coming, and – '

'And I've got everybody else,' said Daisy brightly. 'And Miss Bracely is coming over here, if she gets away early. Probably with such a small party she will.'

'Oh, I shouldn't count on that,' said he. 'We are having some tableaux, and they always take longer than you think. Dear me, I shouldn't have said that, as they were to be impromptu, but I really believe my head is going. You know how thorough Lucia is; she is taking a great deal of trouble about them.'

'I hadn't heard about that,' said Mrs Quantock.

She thought a moment.

'Well; I don't want to spoil Lucia's evening,' she said, 'for I'm sure nothing could be so ridiculous as three people doing tableaux for two others. And on the other hand, I don't want her to spoil mine, for what's to prevent her going on with the tableaux till church-time next morning if she wishes to keep Miss Bracely away from my house? I'm sure after the way she behaved about my guru – Well, never mind that. How would it be if we had the tableaux first at Lucia's, and then came on here? If Lucia cares to suggest that to me, and my guests consent, I don't mind doing that.'

By six o'clock on Tuesday evening therefore all the telephone bells of Riseholme were merrily ringing again. Mrs Quantock stipulated that Lucia's party should end at 10.45 precisely, if it didn't end before, and that everyone should then be free to flock across to her house. She proposed a romp that should even outshine Olga's, and was deep in the study of a manual of 'Round Games', which included 'Hunt the Slipper' . . .

*   *   *

Georgie and Peppino took turns at the telephone, ringing up all Mrs Quantock's guests, and informing them of the double pleasure which awaited them on Saturday. Since Georgie had let out the secret of the impromptu tableaux to Mrs Quantock there was no reason why the rest of Riseholme should not learn of this first-hand from The Hurst, instead of second-hand (with promises not to repeat it) from Mrs Quantock. It appeared that she had a better nature than Lucia credited her with, but to expect her not to tell everybody about the tableaux would be putting virtue to an unfair test.

'So that's all settled,' said Georgie, as he returned with the last acceptance, 'and how fortunately it has happened after all. But what a day it has been. Nothing but telephoning from morning till night. If we go on like this the company will pay a dividend this year, and return us some of our own pennies.'

Lucia had got a quantity of pearl beads and was stringing them for the tableau of Mary Queen of Scots.

'Now that everyone knows,' she said, 'we might allow ourselves a little more elaboration in our preparations. There is an Elizabethan axe at the Ambermere Arms which I might borrow for Peppino. Then about the Brünnhilde tableau. It is dawn, is it not? We might have the stage quite dark when the curtain goes up, and turn up a lamp very slowly behind the scene, so that it shines on my face. A lamp being turned up very slowly is wonderfully effective. It produces a perfect illusion. Could you manage that with one hand and play the music of the awakening with the other, Georgino?'

'I'm quite sure I couldn't,' said he.

'Well then Peppino must do it before he comes on. We will have movement in this tableau; I think that will be quite a new idea. Peppino shall come in – just two steps – when he has turned the lamp up, and he will take off my shield and armour –'

'But the music will never last out,' cried Georgie. 'I shall have to start earlier.'

'Yes, perhaps that would be better,' said Lucia calmly. 'That real piece of chain-armour too, I am glad I remembered Peppino had that. Marshall is cleaning it now, and it will give a far finer effect than the tawdry stuff they use in opera. Then I sit up very slowly, and wave first my right arm and then my left, and then both. I should like to practise that now on the sofa!'

Lucia had just lain down, when the telephone sounded again and Georgie got up.

'That's to announce a dividend,' he said, and tripped into the hall.

'Is that Mrs Lucas's?' said a voice he knew.

'Yes, Miss Olga,' he said, 'and this is me.'

'Oh, Mr Georgie, how fortunate,' she said. 'You can give my message now to Mrs Lucas, can't you? I'm a perfect fool, you know, and horribly forgetful.'

'What's the matter?' asked Georgie faintly.

'It's about Saturday. I've just remembered that Georgie and I – not you, you know – are going away for the weekend. Will you tell Mrs Lucas how sorry I am?'

Georgie went back to the music-room, where Lucia had just got both her arms waving. But at the sight of his face she dropped them and took a firm hold of herself.

'Well, what is it?' she said.

Georgie gave the message, and she got off the sofa, rising to her feet, while her mind rose to the occasion.

'I am sorry that Miss Bracely will not see our tableaux,' she said. 'But as she was not acting in them I do not know that it makes much difference.'

A deadly flatness, although Olga's absence made no difference, descended on the three. Lucia did not resume her arm-work, for after all these years her acting might be supposed to be good enough for Riseholme without further practice, and nothing more was heard of the borrowing of the axe from the Ambermere Arms. But having begun to thread her pearl beads, she finished them; Georgie, however, cared no longer whether the gold border of King Cophetua's mantle went quite round the back or not, and having tacked on the piece he was working at, rolled it up. It was just going to be an ordinary party, after all. His cup was empty.

But Lucia's was not yet quite full, for at this moment Miss Lyall's pony hip-bath stopped at the gate, and a small stableboy presented a note, which required an answer. In spite of all Lucia's self-control, the immediate answer it got was a flush of heightened colour.

'Mere impertinence,' she said. 'I will read it aloud.'

'DEAR MRS LUCAS – I was in Riseholme this morning, and learn from Mrs Weston that Miss Bracely will be at your house on Saturday night. So I shall be enchanted to come to dinner after all. You must know that I make a rule of not going out in the evening, except for some special reason, but it would be a great pleasure to hear her sing again. I wonder if you would have dinner at 7:30 instead of 8, as I do not like being out very late.'

There was a short pause.

'*Caro*,' said Lucia, trembling violently, 'perhaps you would kindly tell Miss Lyall that I do not expect Miss Bracely on Saturday, and that I do not expect Lady Ambermere either.'

'My dear – ' he began.

'I will do it myself then,' she said.

*   *   *

It was as Georgie walked home after the delivery of this message that he wanted to fly away and be at rest with Foljambe and Dicky. He had been frantically excited ever since Sunday at the idea of doing tableaux before Olga, and today in especial had been a mere feverish hash of telephoning and sewing which all ended in nothing at all, for neither tableaux nor romps seemed to hold the least attraction for him now that Olga was not going to be there. And then all at once it dawned on him that he must be in love with Olga, for why else should her presence or absence make such an astounding difference to him? He stopped dead opposite Mrs Quantock's mulberry tree.

'More misery! More unhappiness!' he said to himself. Really if life at Riseholme was to become a series of agitated days ending in devastating discoveries, the sooner he went away with Foljambe and Dicky the better. He did not quite know what it was like to be in love, for the nearest he had previously ever got to it was when he saw Olga awake on the mountain-top and felt that he had missed his vocation in not being Siegfried, but from that he guessed. This time, too, it was about Olga, not about her as framed in the romance of legend and song, but of her as she appeared at Riseholme, taking as she did now, an ecstatic interest in the affairs of the place. So short a time ago, when she contemplated coming here first, she had spoken of it as a lazy backwater. Now she knew better than that, for she could listen to Mrs Weston far longer than anybody else, and ask for more histories when even she had run dry. And yet Lucia seemed hardly to interest her at all. Georgie wondered why that was.

He raised his eyes as he muttered these desolated syllables and there was Olga just letting herself out of the front garden of Old Place. Georgie's first impulse was to affect not to see her, and turn into his bachelor house, but she had certainly seen him, and made so shrill and piercing a whistle on her fingers that, pretend as he would not to have seen her, it was ludicrous to appear not to have heard her. She beckoned to him.

'Georgie, the most awful thing has happened,' she said, as they came within speaking distance. 'Oh, I called you Georgie by mistake then. When one once does that, one must go on doing it on purpose. Guess!' she said in the best Riseholme manner.

'You can come to Lucia's party after all,' said he.

'No, I can't. Well, you'll never guess because you move in such high circles, so I'll tell you. Mrs Weston's Elizabeth is going to be married to Colonel Boucher's Atkinson. I don't know his Christian name, nor her surname, but they're the ones!'

'You don't say so!' said Georgie, stung for a moment out of his own troubles. 'But will they both leave? What will either of the others do? Mrs Weston can't have a manservant, and how on earth is she to get on without Elizabeth? Besides – '

A faint flush mounted to his cheek.

'I know. You meant babies,' said Olga ruthlessly. 'Didn't you?'

'Yes,' said Georgie.

'Then why not say so? You and I were babies once, though no one is old enough to remember that, and we shouldn't have liked our parents and friends to have blushed when they mentioned us. Georgie, you are a prude.'

'No, I'm not,' said Georgie, remembering he was probably in love with a married woman.

'It doesn't matter whether you are or not. Now there's only one thing that can happen to Mrs Weston and the Colonel. They must marry each other too. Then Atkinson can continue to be Colonel Boucher's man and Elizabeth the parlour-maid, unless she is busy with what made you blush. Then they can get help in; you will lend them Foljambe, for instance. It's time you began to be of some good in your wicked selfish life. So that's settled. It only remains for us to make them marry each other.'

'Aren't you getting on rather fast?' asked Georgie.

'I'm not getting on at all at present, I'm only talking. Come into my house instantly, and we'll drink vermouth. Vermouth always makes me brilliant unless it makes me idiotic, but we'll hope for the best.'

Presently they were seated in Olga's music-room, with a bottle of vermouth between them.

'Now drink fair, Georgie,' she said, 'and as you drink tell me all about the young people's emotional history.'

'Atkinson and Elizabeth?' asked Georgie.

'No, my dear; Colonel Boucher and Mrs Weston. They have an emotional history. I am sure you all thought they were going to marry each other once. And they constantly dine together tête-à-tête. Now that's a very good start. Are you quite sure he hasn't got a wife and family in Egypt, or she a husband and family somewhere else? I don't want to rake up family skeletons.'

'I've never heard of them,' said Georgie.

'Then we'll take them as non-existent. You certainly would have heard of them if there were any, and very likely if there weren't. And they both like eating, drinking and the latest intelligence. Don't they?'

'Yes. But – '

'But what? What more do you or they want? Isn't that a better start for married life than many people get?'

'But aren't they rather old?' asked Georgie.

'Not much older than you and me, and if it wasn't that I've got my own Georgie, I would soon have somebody else's. Do you know who I mean?'

'No!' said Georgie firmly. Though all this came at the end of a most harrowing day, it or the vermouth exhilarated him.

'Then I'll tell you just what Mrs Weston told me. "He's always been devoted to Lucia," said Mrs Weston, "and he has never looked at anybody else. There was Piggy Antrobus – " Now do you know who I mean?'

Georgie suddenly giggled.

'Yes,' he said.

'Then don't talk about yourself so much, my dear, and let us get to the point. Now this afternoon I dropped in to see Mrs Weston and as she was telling me about the tragedy, she said by accident (just as I called you Georgie just now by accident) "And I don't know what Jacob will do without Atkinson." Now is or is not Colonel Boucher's name Jacob? There you are then! That's one side of the question. She called him Jacob by accident and so she'll call him Jacob on purpose before very long.'

Olga nodded her head up and down in precise reproduction of Mrs Weston.

'I'd hardly got out of the house,' she said in exact imitation of Mrs Weston's voice, 'before I met Colonel Boucher. It would have been about three o'clock – no it couldn't have been three, because I had got back home and was standing in the hall when it struck three, and my clock's a shade fast if anything. Well; Colonel Boucher said to me, "Haw, hum, quite a domestic crisis, by Jove." And so I pretended I didn't know, and he told me all about it. So I said, "Well, it is a domestic crisis, and you'll lose Atkinson." "Haw, hum," said he, "and poor Jane, I should say, Mrs Weston, will lose Elizabeth." There!'

She got up and lit a cigarette.

'Oh, Georgie, do you grasp the inwardness of that?' she said. 'Their dear old hearts were laid bare by the trouble that had come upon them, and each of them spoke of the other, as each felt for the other. Probably neither of them had said Jacob or Jane in the whole course of their lives. But the Angel of the Lord descended and troubled the waters. If you think that's profane, have some more vermouth. It's making me brilliant, though you wouldn't have thought it. Now listen!'

She sat down again close to him, her face brimming with a humorous enthusiasm. Humour in Riseholme was apt to be a little unkind; if you mentioned the absurdities of your friends, there was just a speck of malice in your wit. But with her there was none of that; she gave an imitation of Mrs Weston with the most ruthless fidelity, and yet it was kindly to the bottom. She liked her for talking in that emphatic voice and being so particular as to what time it was. 'Now first of all you are coming to dine with me tonight,' said Olga.

'Oh, I'm afraid that tonight – ' began Georgie, shrinking from any further complications. He really must have a quiet evening, and go to bed very early.

'What are you afraid of tonight?' she asked. 'You're only going to wash your hair. You can do that tomorrow. So you and I, that's two, and Mrs Weston and Colonel Jacob, that's four, which is enough, and I don't believe there's anything to eat in the house. But there's something to drink, which is my point. Not for you and me, mind; we've got to keep our heads and be clever. Don't have any more vermouth. But Jane and Jacob are going to have quantities of champagne. Not tipsy, you understand, but at their best, and unguardedly appreciative of each other and us. And when they go away, they will exchange a chaste kiss at Mrs Weston's door, and she will ask him in. No! I think she'll ask him in first. And when they wake up tomorrow morning, they will both wonder how they could possibly, and jointly ask themselves what everybody else will say. And then they'll thank God and Olga and Georgie that they did, and live happily for an extraordinary number of years. My dear, how infinitely happier they will be together than they are being now. Funny old dears! Each at its own fireside, saying that it's too old, bless them! And you and I will sing "Voice that breathed o'er Eden" and in the middle our angel-voices will crack, and we will sob into our handkerchief, and Eden will be left breathing deeply all by itself like the guru. Why did you never tell me about the guru? Mrs Weston's a better friend to me than you are, and I must ring for my cook – no I'll telephone first to Jacob and Jane – and see what there is to eat afterwards. You will sit here quietly, and when I have finished I will tell you what your part is.'

During dinner, according to Olga's plan of campaign, the conversation was to be general, because she hated to have two conversations going on when only four people were present, since she found that she always wanted to join in the other one. This was the main principle she inculcated on Georgie, stamping it on his memory by a simile of peculiar vividness. 'Imagine there is an Elizabethan spittoon in the middle of the table,' she said, 'and keep on firmly spitting into it. I want you when there's any pause to spit about two things, one, how dreadfully unhappy both Jacob and Jane will be without their paragons, the other, how pleasant is conversation and companionship. I shall be chaffing you, mind, all the time and saying *you* must get married. After dinner I shall probably stroll in the garden with Jacob. Don't come. Keep him after dinner for some little time, for then's my opportunity of talking to Jane, and give him at least three glasses of port. Gracious, it's time to dress, and the Lord prosper us.'

Georgie found himself the last to arrive, when he got back to Olga's, and all three of them shook hands rather as people shake hands before a funeral. They went into dinner at once and Olga instantly began. 'How many years did you say your admirable Atkinson had been with you?' she asked Colonel Boucher.

'Twenty; getting on for twenty-one,' said he. 'Great nuisance; 'pon my word it's worse than a nuisance.'

Georgie had a bright idea.

'But what's a nuisance, Colonel?' he asked.

'Eh, haven't you heard? I thought it would have been all over the place by now. Atkinson's going to be married.'

'No!' said Georgie. 'Whom to?'

Mrs Weston could not bear not to announce this herself. 'To my Elizabeth,' she said. 'Elizabeth came to me this morning. "May I speak to you a minute, ma'am?" she asked, and I thought nothing more than that perhaps she had broken a tea-cup. "Yes," said I quite cheerfully, "and what have you come to tell me?" '

It was getting almost too tragic and Olga broke in.

'Let's try to forget all about it, for an hour or two,' she said. 'It was nice of you all to take pity on me and come and have dinner, otherwise I should have been quite alone. If there's one thing I cannot bear it's being alone in the evening. And to think that anybody chooses to be alone when he needn't! Look at that wretch there,' and she pointed to Georgie, 'who lives all by himself instead of marrying. Liking to be alone is the worst habit I know; much worse than drink.'

'Now do leave me alone,' said Georgie.

'I won't, my dear, and when dinner is over Mrs Weston and I are going to put our heads together, and when you come out we shall announce to you the name of your bride. I should put a tax of twenty shillings on the pound on all bachelors; they should all marry or starve.'

Suddenly she turned to Colonel Boucher.

'Oh, Colonel,' she said. 'What have I been saying? How dreadfully stupid of me not to remember that you were a bachelor too. But I wouldn't have you starve for anything. Have some more fish instantly to show you forgive me. Georgie, change the subject – you're always talking about yourself.'

Georgie turned with admirable docility to Mrs Weston.

'It's too miserable for you,' he said. 'How will you get on without Elizabeth? How long has she been with you?'

Mrs Weston went straight back to where she had left off.

'So I said, "What have you come to tell me?" quite cheerfully, thinking it was a tea-cup. And she said, "I'm going to be married, ma'am," and she blushed so prettily that you'd have thought she was a girl of twenty, though she was seventeen when she came to me – no, she was just eighteen, and that's fifteen years ago, and that makes her thirty-three. "Well, Elizabeth," I said, "you haven't told me yet who it is, but whether it's the Archbishop of Canterbury or the Prince of Wales – for I felt I had to make a little joke like that – I hope you'll make him as happy as you've made me all these years." '

'You old darling,' said Olga. 'I should have gone into hysterics, and forbade the banns.'

'No, Miss Bracely, you wouldn't,' said Mrs Weston, 'you'd have been just as thankful as me, that she'd got a good husband to take care of and to be taken care of by, because then she said, "Lor ma'am, it's none of they – not them great folks. It's the Colonel's

Atkinson." You ask the Colonel for Atkinson's character, Miss Bracely, and then you'd be just as thankful as I was.'

'The Colonel's Atkinson is a slow coach, just like Georgie,' said Olga. 'He and Elizabeth have been living side by side all these years, and why couldn't the man make up his mind before? The only redeeming circumstance is that he has done it now. Our poor Georgie now –'

'Now you're going to be rude to Colonel Boucher again,' said Georgie. 'Colonel, we've been asked here to be insulted.'

Colonel Boucher had nothing stronger than a mild tolerance for Georgie and rather enjoyed snubbing him.

'Well, if you call a glass of wine and a dinner like this an insult,' he said, ' 'pon my word I don't know what you'd call a compliment.'

'I know what I call a compliment,' said Olga, 'and that's your all coming to dine with me at such short notice. About Georgie's approaching nuptials now –'

'You're too tarsome,' said he. 'If you go on like that, I shan't ask you to the wedding. Let's talk about Elizabeth's. When are they going to get married, Mrs Weston?'

'That's what I said to Elizabeth. "Get an almanack, Elizabeth," said I, "so that you won't choose a Sunday. Don't say the twentieth of next month without looking it out. But if the twentieth isn't a Sunday or a Friday mind, for though I don't believe in such things, still you never know – " There was Mrs Antrobus now,' said Mrs Weston suddenly, putting in a footnote to her speech to Elizabeth, 'it was on a Friday she married, and within a year she got as deaf as you see her now. Then Mr Weston's uncle, his uncle by marriage I should say, he was another Friday marriage and they missed their train when going off on their honeymoon, and had to stay all night where they were without a sponge or a toothbrush between them, for all their luggage was in the train being whirled away to Torquay. "So make it the twentieth, Elizabeth," I said, "if it isn't a Friday or a Sunday, and I shall have time to look round me, and so will the Colonel, though I don't expect that either of us will find your equals! And don't cry, Elizabeth," I said, for she was getting quite watery, "for if you cry about a marriage, what'll be left for a funeral?" '

'Ha! Upon my word, I call that splendid of you,' said the Colonel. 'I told Atkinson I wished I had never set eyes on him, before I wished him joy.'

Olga got up.

'Look after Colonel Boucher, Georgie,' she said, 'and ring for anything you want. Look at the moon! Isn't it heavenly. How Atkinson and Elizabeth must be enjoying it.'

The two men spent a half-hour of only moderately enjoyable conversation, for Georgie kept the grindstone of the misery of his lot without Atkinson, and the pleasure of companionship, firmly to the Colonel's nose. It was no use for him to attempt to change the subject to the approaching tableaux, to a vague rumour that Piggy had fallen face downwards in the ducking-pond, that Mrs Quantock and her husband had turned a table this afternoon with remarkable results, for it had tapped out that his name was Robert and hers Daisy. Whichever way he turned, Georgie herded him back on to the stony path that he had been bidden to take, with the result that when Georgie finally permitted him to go into the music-room, he was a-thirst for the more genial companionship of the ladies. Olga got up as they entered.

'Georgie's so lazy,' she said, 'that it's no use asking him. But do let you and me have a turn up and down my garden, Colonel. There's a divine moon and it's quite warm.'

They stepped out into the windless night.

'Fancy its being October,' she said. 'I don't believe there is any winter in Riseholme, nor autumn either, for that matter. You are all so young, so deliciously young. Look at Georgie in there: he's like a boy still, and as for Mrs Weston, she's twenty-five: not a day older.'

'Yes, wonderful woman,' said he. 'Always agreeable and lively. Handsome, too: I consider Mrs Weston a very handsome woman. Hasn't altered an atom since I knew her.'

'That's the wonderful thing about you all!' said she. 'You are all just as brisk and young as you were ten years ago. It's ridiculous. As for you, I'm not sure that you're not the most ridiculous of the lot. I feel as if I had been having dinner with three delightful cousins a little younger – not much, but just a little – than myself. Gracious! How you all made me romp the other night here. What a pace you go, Colonel! What's your walking like if you call this a stroll?'

Colonel Boucher moderated his pace. He thought Olga had been walking so quickly.

'I'm very sorry,' he said. 'Certainly Riseholme is a healthy bracing place. Perhaps we do keep our youth pretty well. God bless me, but the days go by without one's noticing them. To think that I came here with Atkinson close on ten years ago.'

This did very well for Olga: she swiftly switched off on to it.

'It's quite horrid for you losing your servant,' she said. 'Servants do become friends, don't they, especially to anyone living alone. Georgie and Foljambe, now! But I shouldn't be a bit surprised if Foljambe had a mistress before very long.'

'No, really? I thought you were just chaffing him at dinner. Georgie marrying, is he? His wife'll take some of his needlework off his hands. May I – ah – may I enquire the lady's name?'

Olga decided to play a great card. She had just found it, so to speak, in her hand, and it was most tempting. She stopped.

'But can't you guess?' she said. 'Surely I'm not absolutely on the wrong track?'

'Ah, Miss Antrobus,' said he. 'The one I think they call Piggy. No, I should say there was nothing in that.'

'Oh, that had never occurred to me,' said she. 'I dare say I'm quite wrong. I only judged from what I thought I noticed in poor Georgie. I dare say it's only what he should have done ten years ago, but I fancy there's a spark alive still. Let us talk about something else, though we won't go in quite yet, shall we?' She felt quite safe in her apparent reluctance to tell him; the Riseholme gluttony for news made it imperative for him to ask more.

'Really, I must be very dull,' he said. 'I dare say an eye new to the place sees more. Who is it, Miss Bracely?'

She laughed.

'Ah, how bad a man is at observing a man!' she said. 'Didn't you see Georgie at dinner? He hardly took his eyes off her.'

She had a great and glorious reward. Colonel Boucher's face grew absolutely blank in the moonlight with sheer astonishment.

'Well, you surprise me,' he said. 'Surely a fine woman, though lame, wouldn't look at a needle-woman – well, leave it at that.'

He stamped his feet and put his hands in his pockets.

'It's growing a bit chilly,' he said. 'You'll be catching cold, Miss Bracely, and what will your husband say if he finds out I've been strolling about with you out of doors after dinner?'

'Yes, we'll go in,' she said. 'It is chilly. How thoughtful you are for me.'

Georgie, little knowing the cat's paw that had been made of him, found himself being detached from Mrs Weston by the Colonel, and this suited him very well, for presently Olga said she would sing, unless anybody minded, and called on him to accompany her. She stood just behind him, leaning over him sometimes with a hand on his shoulder, and sang three ruthless simple English songs, appropriate to the matter in hand. She sang, 'I Attempt from Love's

Sickness to Fly', and 'Sally in Our Alley', and 'Come Live with Me', and sometimes beneath the rustle of leaves turned over she whispered to him. 'Georgie, I'm cleverer than anybody ever was, and I shall die in the night,' she said once. Again more enigmatically she said, 'I've been a cad, but I'll tell you about it when they've gone. Stop behind.' And then some whisky came in, and she insisted on the 'young people' having some of that; finally she saw them off at the door, and came running back to Georgie. 'I've been a cad,' she said, 'because I hinted that you were in love with Mrs Weston. My dear, it was simply perfect! I believe it to have been the last straw, and if you don't forgive me you needn't. Wasn't it clever? He simply couldn't stand that, for it came on the top of your being so young.'

'Well, really – ' said Georgie.

'I know. And I must be a cad again. I'm going up to my bedroom; you may come, too, if you like, because it commands a view of Church Road. I shouldn't sleep a wink unless I knew that he had gone in with her. It'll be precisely like Faust and Marguerite going into the house, and you and I are Mephistopheles and Martha. Come quick!'

From the dark of the window they watched Mrs Weston's bath-chair being pushed up the lit road.

'It's the Colonel pushing it,' whispered Olga, squeezing him into a corner of the window. 'Look! There's Tommy Luton on the path. Now they've stopped at her gate . . . I can't bear the suspense . . . Oh, Georgie, they've gone in! And Atkinson will stop, and so will Elizabeth, and you've promised to lend them Foljambe. Which house will they live at, do you think? Aren't you happy?'

Chapter Twelve

The miserable Lucia started a run of extreme bad luck about this time, of which the adventure or misadventure of the guru seemed to be the prelude, or perhaps the news of her want of recognition of the August moon, which Georgie had so carefully saluted, may have arrived at that satellite by October. For she had simply 'cut' the August moon . . .

There was the fiasco about Olga coming to the tableaux, which was the cause of her sending that very tart reply, via Miss Lyall, to Lady Ambermere's impertinence, and the very next morning, Lady

Ambermere, coming again into Riseholme, perhaps for that very purpose, had behaved to Lucia as Lucia had behaved to the moon, and cut her. That was irritating, but the counter-irritant to it had been that Lady Ambermere had then gone to Olga's, and been told that she was not at home, though she was very audibly practising in her music-room at the time. Upon which Lady Ambermere had said 'Home' to her people, and got in with such unconcern of the material world that she sat down on Pug.

Mrs Quantock had heard both 'Home' and Pug, and told the cut Lucia, who was a hundred yards away, about it. She also told her about the engagement of Atkinson and Elizabeth, which was all she knew about events in those houses. On which Lucia with a kind smile had said, 'Dear Daisy, what slaves some people are to their servants. I am sure Mrs Weston and Colonel Boucher will be quite miserable, poor things. Now I must run home. How I wish I could stop and chat on the green!' And she gave her silvery laugh, for she felt much better now that she knew Olga had said she was out to Lady Ambermere, when she was so audibly in.

Then came a second piece of bad luck. Lucia had not gone more than a hundred yards past Georgie's house, when he came out in a tremendous hurry. He rapidly measured the distance between himself and Lucia, and himself and Mrs Quantock, and made a beeline for Mrs Quantock, since she was the nearest. Olga had just telephoned to him . . .

'Good-morning,' he said breathlessly, determined to cap anything she said. 'Any news?'

'Yes, indeed,' she said. 'Haven't you heard?'

Georgie had one moment of heart-sink.

'What?' he said.

'Atkinson and Eliz – ' she began.

'Oh, that,' said he scornfully. 'And talking of them, of course you've heard the rest. *Haven't* you? Why, Mrs Weston and Colonel Boucher are going to follow their example, unless they set it themselves, and get married first.'

'No!' said Mrs Quantock in the loudest possible Riseholme voice of surprise.

'Oh, yes. I really knew it last night. I was dining at Old Place and they were there. Olga and I both settled there would be something to talk in the morning. Shall we stroll on the green a few minutes?'

Georgie had a lovely time. He hurried from person to person, leaving Mrs Quantock to pick up a few further gleanings. Everyone

was there except Lucia, and she, but for the accident of her being
further off than Mrs Quantock, would have been the first to know.

When this tour was finished Georgie sat to enjoy the warm comforting glow of envy that surrounded him. Nowadays the meeting
place at the green had insensibly transferred itself to just opposite
Old Place, and it was extremely interesting to hear Olga practising
as she always did in the morning. Interesting though it was, Riseholme
had at first been a little disappointed about it, for everyone had
thought that she would sing Brünnhilde's part or Salome's part
through every day, or some trifle of that kind. Instead she would
perform an upwards scale in gradual *crescendo*, and on the highest
most magnificent note would enunciate at the top of her voice,
'Yawning York!' Then starting soft again she would descend in
crescendo to a superb low note and enunciate 'Love's Lilies Lonely'.
Then after a dozen repetitions of this, she would start off with full
voice, and get softer and softer until she just whispered that York
was yawning, and do the same with Love's Lilies. But you never
could tell what she might not sing, and some mornings there would
be long trills and leapings on to high notes, long notes and leaping
on to trills, and occasionally she sang a real song. That was worth
waiting for, and Georgie did not hesitate to let drop that she had
sung four last night to his accompaniment. And hardly had he
repeated that the third time, when she appeared at her window, and
before all Riseholme called out 'Georgie!' with a trill at the end, like
a bird shaking its wings. Before all Riseholme!

So in he went. Had Lucia known that, it would quite have wiped
the gilt off Lady Ambermere's being refused admittance. In point of
fact it did wipe the gilt off when, about an hour afterwards, Georgie
went to lunch, because he told her. And if there had been any gilt left
about anywhere, that would have vanished, too, when in answer to
some rather damaging remark she made about poor Daisy's interests
in the love-affairs of other people's servants, she learned that it was
of the love-affairs of their superiors that all Riseholme had been
talking for at least an hour by now.

Again there was ill-luck about the tableaux on Saturday, for in
the Brünnhilde scene, Peppino in his agitation turned the lamp
that was to be a sunrise completely out, and Brünnhilde had to hail
the midnight, or at any rate a very obscure twilight. Georgie, it is
true, with wonderful presence of mind, turned on an electric light
when he had finished playing, but it was more like a flash of lightning
than a slow, wonderful dawn. The tableaux were over well before

10.45, and though Lucia, in answer to the usual pressings, said she would 'see about' doing them again, she felt that Mrs Weston and Colonel Boucher, who made their first public appearance as the happy pair, attracted more than their proper share of attention. The only consolation was that the romps that followed at poor Daisy's were a complete fiasco. It was in vain, too, at supper, that she went from table to table, and helped people to lobster salad and champagne, and had not enough chairs, and generally imitated all that had apparently made Olga's party so supreme a success. But on this occasion the recipe for the dish and not the dish itself was served up, and the hunting of the slipper produced no exhilaration in the chase . . .

But far more untoward events followed. Olga came back on the next Monday, and immediately after Lucia received a card for an evening 'At Home', with 'Music' in the bottom left-hand corner. It happened to be wet that afternoon, and seeing Olga's shut motor coming from the station with four men inside, she leaped to the conclusion that these were four musicians for the music. A second motor followed with luggage, and she quite distinctly saw the un-mistakable shape of a 'cello against the window. After that no more guessing was necessary, for it was clear that poor Olga had hired the awful string-quartet from Brinton, that played in the lounge at the Royal Hotel after dinner. The Brinton string-quartet! She had heard them once at a distance and that was quite enough. Lucia shuddered as she thought of those doleful fiddlers. It was indeed strange that Olga, with all the opportunities she had had for hearing good music, should hire the Brinton string-quartet, but, after all, that was entirely of a piece with her views about the gramophone. Perhaps the gramophone would have its share in this musical evening. But she had said she would go: it would be very unkind to Olga to stop away now, for Olga must know by this time her passion for music, so she went. She sincerely hoped that she would not be conducted to the seat of honour, and be obliged to say a few encouraging words to the string-quartet afterwards.

Once again she came rather late, for the music had begun. It had only just begun, for she recognised – who should recognise if not she? – the early bars of a Beethoven quartet. She laid her hand on Peppino's arm.

'Brinton: Beethoven,' she said limply.

She slipped into a chair next to Daisy Quantock, and sat in her well-known position when listening to music, with her head forward, her chin resting on her hand, and the faraway look in her eyes. Nothing of course could wholly take away the splendour of that glorious composition, and she was pleased that there was no applause between the movements, for she had rather expected that Olga would clap, and interrupt the unity of it all. Occasionally, too, she was agreeably surprised by the Brinton string-quartet: they seemed to have some inklings, though not many. Once she winced very much when a string broke.

Olga (she was rather a restless hostess) came up to her when it was over.

'So glad you could come,' she said. 'Aren't they divine?'

Lucia gave her most indulgent smile.

'Perfect music! Glorious!' she said. 'And they really played it very creditably. But I am a little spoiled, you know, for the last time I heard that it was performed by the Spanish Quartet. I know one ought never to compare, but have you ever heard the Spanish Quartet, Miss Bracely?'

Olga looked at her in surprise.

'But they are the Spanish Quartet!' she said, pointing to the players.

Lucia had raised her voice rather as she spoke, for when she spoke on music she spoke for everybody to hear. And a great many people undoubtedly did hear, among whom, of course, was Daisy Quantock. She gave one shrill squeal of laughter, like a slate-pencil, and from that moment granted plenary absolution to *poor dear* Lucia for all her greed and grabbing with regard to the guru.

But instantly all Olga's good nature awoke: unwittingly (for her remark that this *was* the Spanish Quartet had been a mere surprised exclamation), she had made a guest of hers uncomfortable, and must at once do all she could to remedy that.

'It's a shocking room for echoes, this,' she said. 'Do all of you come up a little nearer, and you will be able to hear the playing so much better. You lose all shade, all fineness here. I came here on purpose to ask you to move up, Mrs Lucas: there are half a dozen chairs unoccupied near the platform.'

It was a kindly intention that prompted the speech, but for all real Riseholme practical purposes, quite barren, for many people had heard Lucia's remarks, and Peppino also had already been wincing at the Brinton quartet. In that fell moment the Bolshevists laid bony fingers on the sceptre of her musical autocracy . . . But who would have guessed that Olga would get the Spanish Quartet from London to come down to Riseholme?

Staggering from these blows, she had to undergo an even shrewder stroke yet. Already, in the intelligence department, she had been sadly behind-hand in news, her tableaux-party had been anything but a success, this one little remark of Olga's had shaken her musically, but at any rate up till this moment she had shown herself mistress of the Italian tongue, while to strengthen that she was being very diligent with her dictionary, grammar and Dante's *Paradiso*. Then as by a bolt out of a clear sky that temple, too, was completely demolished, in the most tragic fashion.

*   *   *

A few days after the disaster of the Spanish-Brinton Quartet, Olga received a letter from Signor Cortese, the eminent Italian composer, to herald the completion of his opera, *Lucretia*. Might he come down to Riseholme for a couple of nights, and, figuratively, lay it at her feet, in the hope that she would raise it up, and usher it into the world? All the time he had been writing it, as she knew, he had thought of her in the name part and he would come down today, tomorrow, at a moment's notice by day or night to submit it to her. Olga was delighted and sent an effusive telegram of many sheets, full of congratulation and welcome, for she wanted above all things to 'create' the part. So would Signor Cortese come down that very day?

She ran upstairs with the news to her husband.

'My dear, *Lucretia* is finished,' she said, 'and that angel practically offers it me. Now what are we to do about dinner tonight? Jacob and Jane are coming, and neither you nor they, I suppose, speak one word of Italian, and you know what mine is, firm and intelligible and operatic but not conversational. What are we to do? He hates talking English . . . Oh, I know, if I can only get Mrs Lucas. They always talk Italian, I believe, at home. I wonder if she can come. She's musical, too, and I shall ask her husband, I think: that'll be a man over, but it will be another *Italiano* – '

Olga wrote at once to Lucia, mentioning that Cortese was staying with them, but, quite naturally, saying nothing about the usefulness of Peppino and her being able to engage the musician in his own tongue, for that she took for granted. An eager affirmative (such a great pleasure) came back to her, and for the rest of the day, Lucia and Peppino made up neat little sentences to let off to the dazzled Cortese, at the moment when they said 'good-night', to show that they could have talked Italian all the time, had there been any occasion for doing so.

Mrs Weston and Colonel Boucher had already arrived when Lucia and her husband entered, and Lucia had quite a shock to see on what intimate terms they were with their hostess. They actually called each other Olga and Jacob and Jane, which was most surprising and almost painful. Lucia (perhaps because she had not known about it soon enough) had been a little satirical about the engagement, rather as if it was a slight on her that Jacob had not been content with celibacy and Jane with her friendship, but she was sure she wished them both 'nothing but well'. Indeed the moment she got over the shock of seeing them so intimate with Olga, she could not have been surpassed in cordiality.

'We see but little of our old friends now,' she said to Olga and Jane jointly, 'but we must excuse their desire for solitude in their first glow of their happiness. Peppino and I remember that sweet time, oh, ever so long ago.'

This might have been tact, or it might have been cat. That Peppino and she sympathised as they remembered their beautiful time was tact, that it was so long ago was cat. Altogether it might be described as a cat chewing tact. But there was a slight air of patronage about it, and if there was one thing Mrs Weston would not, and could not and did not even intend to stand, it was that. Besides it had reached her ears that Mrs Lucas had said something about there being no difficulty in finding bridesmaids younger than the bride.

'Fancy! How clever of you to remember so long ago,' she said. 'But, then, you have the most marvellous memory, dear, and keep it wonderfully!'

Olga intervened.

'How kind of you and Mr Lucas to come at such short notice,' she said. 'Cortese hates talking English, so I shall put him between you and me, and you'll talk to him all the time, won't you? And you won't laugh at me, will you, when I join in with my atrocious attempts? And I shall buttress myself on the other side with your husband, who will firmly talk across me to him.'

Lucia had to say something. A further exposure was at hand, quite inevitably. It was no use for her and Peppino to recollect a previous engagement.

'Oh, my Italian is terribly rusty,' she said, knowing that Mrs Weston's eye was on her . . . Why had she not sent Mrs Weston a handsome wedding-present that morning?

'Rusty? We will ask Cortese about that when you've had a good talk to him. Ah, here he is!'

Cortese came into the room, florid and loquacious, pouring out a stream of apology for his lateness to Olga, none of which was the least intelligible to Lucia. She guessed what he was saying, and next moment Olga, who apparently understood him perfectly, and told him with an enviable fluency that he was not late at all, was introducing him to her, and explaining that '*la Signora*' (Lucia understood this) and her husband talked Italian. She did not need to reply to some torrent of amiable words from him, addressed to her, for he was taken on and introduced to Mrs Weston, and the Colonel. But he instantly whirled round to her again, and asked her something. Not knowing the least what he meant, she replied:

'*Si; tante grazie.*'

He looked puzzled for a moment and then repeated his question in English.

'In what deestrict of Italy 'ave you voyaged most?'

Lucia understood that: so did Mrs Weston, and Lucia pulled herself together.

'*In Roma,*' she said. '*Che bella città! Adoro Roma, ed il mio marito. Non e vero, Peppino?*'

Peppino cordially assented: the familiar ring of this fine intelligible Italian restored his confidence, and he asked Cortese whether he was not very fond of music . . .

Dinner seemed interminable to Lucia. She kept a watchful eye on Cortese, and if she saw he was about to speak to her, she turned hastily to Colonel Boucher, who sat on her other side, and asked him something about his *cari cani*, which she translated to him. While he answered she made up another sentence in Italian about the blue sky or Venice, or very meanly said her husband had been there, hoping to direct the torrent of Italian eloquence to him. But she knew that, as an Italian conversationalist, neither she nor Peppino had a rag of reputation left them, and she dismally regretted that they had not chosen French, of which they both knew about as much, instead of Italian, for the vehicle of their linguistic distinction.

Olga meantime continued to understand all that Cortese said, and to reply to it with odious fluency, and at the last, Cortese having said something to her which made her laugh, he turned to Lucia.

'I've said to Meesis Shottlewort' . . . and he proceeded to explain his joke in English.

'*Molto bene,*' said Lucia with a dying flicker. '*Molto divertente. Non e vero, Peppino?*'

'*Si, si,*' said Peppino miserably.

And then the final disgrace came, and it was something of a relief to have it over. Cortese, in excellent spirits with his dinner and his wine and the prospect of Olga taking the part of Lucretia, turned beamingly to Lucia again.

'Now we will all spick English,' he said. 'This is one very pleasant evening. I enjoy me very much. *Ecco!*'

Just once more Lucia shot up into flame.

'*Parlate Inglese molto bene,*' she said, and except when Cortese spoke to Olga, there was no more Italian that night.

Even the unique excitement of hearing Olga 'try over' the great scene in the last act could not quite absorb Lucia's attention after this awful fiasco, and though she sat leaning forward with her chin in her hand, and the faraway look in her eyes, her mind was furiously busy as to how to make anything whatever out of so bad a job. Everyone present knew that her Italian, as a medium for conversation, had suffered a complete breakdown, and it was no longer any real use, when Olga did not quite catch the rhythm of a passage, to murmur '*Uno, due, tre*' unconsciously to herself; she might just as well have said 'one, two, three' for any effect it had on Mrs Weston. The story would be all over Riseholme next day, and she felt sure that Mrs Weston, that excellent observer and superb reporter, had not failed to take it all in, and would not fail to do justice to it. Blow after blow had been rained upon her palace door; it was little wonder that the whole building was a-quiver. She had thought of starting a Dante-class this winter, for printed Italian, if you had a dictionary and a translation in order to prepare for the class, could be easily interpreted: it was the spoken word which you had to understand without any preparation at all, and not in the least knowing what was coming, that had presented such insurmountable difficulties. And yet who, when the story of this evening was known, would seek instruction from a teacher of that sort? Would Mrs Weston come to her Dante-class? Would she? Would she? No, she would not.

*   *   *

Lucia lay long awake that night, tossing and turning in her bed in that delightful apartment in 'Midsummer Night's Dream', and reviewing the fell array of these unlucky affairs. As she eyed them, black shapes against the glow of her firelight, it struck her that the same malevolent influence inspired them all. For what had caused the failure and flatness of her tableaux (omitting the unfortunate incident about the lamp) but the absence of Olga? Who was it who had occasioned her unfortunate remark about the Spanish Quartet but Olga, whose clear duty it had been, when she sent the invitation for the musical party, to state (so that there could be no mistake about it) that those eminent performers were to entrance them? Who could have guessed that she would have gone to the staggering expense of having them down from London? The Brinton Quartet was the utmost that any sane imagination could have pictured, and Lucia's extremely sane imagination had pictured just that, with such extreme vividness that it had never occurred to her that it could be anybody else. Certainly Olga should have put 'Spanish Quartet' in the bottom left-hand corner instead of 'Music' and then Lucia would have known all about it, and have been speechless with emotion when they had finished the Beethoven, and wiped her eyes, and pulled herself together again. It really looked as if Olga had laid a trap for her . . .

Even more like a trap were the horrid events of this evening. Trap was not at all too strong a word for them. To ask her to the house, and then suddenly spring upon her the fact that she was expected to talk Italian . . . Was that an open, an honourable proceeding? What if Lucia had actually told Olga (and she seemed to recollect it) that she and Peppino often talked Italian at home? That was no reason why she should be expected, offhand like that, to talk Italian any-where else. She should have been told what was expected of her, so as to give her the chance of having a previous engagement. Lucia hated underhand ways, and they were particularly odious in one whom she had been willing to educate and refine up to the highest standards of Riseholme. Indeed it looked as if Olga's nature was actually incapable of receiving cultivation. She went on her own rough independent lines, giving a romp one night, and not coming to the tableaux on another, and getting the Spanish Quartet without consultation on a third, and springing this dreadful Pentecostal party on them on a fourth. Olga clearly meant mischief: she wanted to set herself up as leader of Art and Culture in Riseholme. Her conduct admitted of no other explanation.

Lucia's benevolent scheme of educating and refining vanished like morning mists, and through her drooping eyelids, the firelight seemed strangely red . . . She had been too kind, too encouraging: now she must collect her forces round her and be stern. As she dozed off to sleep, she reminded herself to ask Georgie to lunch next day. He and Peppino and she must have a serious talk. She had seen Georgie comparatively little just lately, and she drowsily and uneasily wondered how that was.

*   *   *

Georgie by this time had quite got over the desolation of the moment when standing in the road opposite Mrs Quantock's mulberry tree he had given vent to that bitter cry of 'More misery! more unhappiness!' His nerves on that occasion had been worn to fiddlestrings with all the fuss and fiasco of planning the tableaux, and thus fancying himself in love had been just the last straw. But the fact that he had been Olga's chosen confidant in her wonderful scheme of causing Mrs Weston and the Colonel to get engaged, and the distinction of being singled out by Olga to this friendly intimacy, had proved a great tonic. It was quite clear that the existence of Mr Shuttleworth constituted a hopeless bar to the fruition of his passion, and, if he was completely honest with himself, he was aware that he did not really hate Mr Shuttleworth for standing in his path. Georgie was gentle in all his ways, and his manner of falling in love was very gentle, too. He admired Olga immensely, he found her stimulating and amusing, and since it was out of the question really to be her lover, he would have enjoyed, next best to that, being her brother, and such little pangs of jealousy as he might experience from time to time, were rather in the nature of small electric shocks voluntarily received. He was devoted to her with a warmth that his supposed devotion to Lucia had never kindled in him; he even went so far as to dream about her in an agitated though respectful manner. Without being conscious of any unreality about his sentiments, he really wanted to dress up as a lover rather than to be one, for he could form no notion at present of what it felt to be absorbed in anyone else. Life was so full as it was: there really was no room for anything else, especially if that something else must be of the quality which rendered everything else colourless.

This state of mind, this quality of emotion was wholly pleasurable and quite exciting, and instead of crying out 'More misery! more unhappiness!' he could now, as he passed the mulberry, say to himself 'More pleasures! more happiness!'

Yet as he ran down the road to lunch with Lucia he was conscious that she was likely to stand, an angel perhaps, but certainly one with a flaming sword, between him and all the interests of the new life which was undoubtedly beginning to bubble in Riseholme, and to which Georgie found it so pleasant to take his little mug, and have it filled with exhilarating liquid. And if Lucia proved to be standing in his path, forbidding his approach, he, too, was armed for combat, with a revolutionary weapon, consisting of a rolled-up copy of some of Debussy's music for the piano – Olga had lent it him a few days ago – and he had been very busy over 'Poissons d'or'. He was further armed by the complete knowledge of the Italian débâcle of last night, which, from his knowledge of Lucia, he judged must constitute a crisis. Something would have to happen . . . Several times lately Olga had, so to speak, run full-tilt into Lucia, and had passed on leaving a staggering form behind her. And in each case, so Georgie clearly perceived, Olga had not intended to butt into or stagger anybody. Each time, she had knocked Lucia down purely by accident, but if these accidents occurred with such awful frequency, it was to be expected that Lucia would find another name for them: they would have to be re-christened. With all his Riseholme appetite for complications and events Georgie guessed that he was not likely to go empty away from this lunch. In addition there were other topics of extraordinary interest, for really there had been very odd experiences at Mrs Quantock's last night, when the Italian débâcle was going on, a little way up the road. But he was not going to bring that out at once.

Lucia hailed him with her most cordial manner, and with a superb effrontery began to talk Italian just as usual, though she must have guessed that Georgie knew all about last night.

'*Bon arrivato, amico mio*,' she said. 'Why, it must be three days since we met. *Che ha fatto il signorino?* And what have you got there?'

Georgie, having escaped being caught over Italian, had made up his mind not to talk any more ever.

'Oh, they are some little things by Debussy,' he said. 'I want to play one of them to you afterwards. I've just been glancing through it.'

'*Bene, molto bene!*' said she. 'Come in to lunch. But I can't promise to like it, Georgino. Isn't Debussy the man who always makes me want to howl like a dog at the sound of the gong? Where did you get these from?'

'Olga lent me them,' said Georgie negligently. He really did call her Olga to her face now, by request.

Lucia's bugles began to sound.

'Yes, I should think Miss Bracely would admire that sort of music,' she said. 'I suppose I am too old-fashioned, though I will not condemn your little pieces of Debussy before I have heard them. Old-fashioned! Yes! I was certainly too old-fashioned for the music she gave us last night. *Dio mio!*'

'Oh, didn't you enjoy it?' asked he.

Lucia sat down, without waiting for Peppino.

'Poor Miss Bracely!' she said. 'It was very kind of her in intention to ask me, but she would have been kinder to have asked Mrs Antrobus instead, and have told her not to bring her ear-trumpet. To hear that lovely voice, for I do her justice, and there are lovely notes in her voice, *lovely*, to hear that voice shrieking and screaming away, in what she called the great scene, was simply pitiful. There was no melody, and above all there was no form. A musical composition is like an architectural building; it must be built up and constructed. How often have I said that! You must have colour, and you must have line, otherwise I cannot concede you the right to say you have music.'

Lucia finished her egg in a hurry, and put her elbows on the table.

'I hope I am not hidebound and limited,' she said, 'and I think you will acknowledge, Georgie, that I am not. Even in the divinest music of all, I am not blind to defects, if there are defects. The "Moonlight Sonata", for instance. You have often heard me say that the two last movements do not approach the first in perfection of form. And if I am permitted to criticise Beethoven, I hope I may be allowed to suggest that Mr Cortese has not produced an opera which will render *Fidelio* ridiculous. But really I am chiefly sorry for Miss Bracely. I should have thought it worth her while to render herself not unworthy to interpret *Fidelio*, whatever time and trouble that cost her, rather than to seek notoriety by helping to foist on to the world a fresh combination of engine-whistles and grunts. *Non e vero*, Peppino? How late you are.'

Lucia had not determined on this declaration of war without anxious consideration. But it was quite obvious to her that the enemy was daily gaining strength, and therefore the sooner she came to open hostilities the better, for it was equally obvious to her mind that Olga was a pretender to the throne she had occupied for so long. It was time to mobilise, and she had first to state her views and her plan of campaign to the chief of her staff.

'No, we did not quite like our evening, Peppino and I, did we, *caro*?' she went on. 'And Mr Cortese! His appearance! He is like a huge hairdresser. His touch on the piano: if you can imagine a wild bull butting at the keys, you will have some idea of it. And above all, his Italian! I gathered that he was a Neapolitan, and we all know what Neapolitan dialect is like. Tuscans and Romans, who between them, I believe – *lingua Toscano in bocca Romana*, you remember – know how to speak their own tongue, find Neapolitans totally unintelligible. For myself, and I speak for *mio sposo* as well, I do not want to understand what Romans do not understand. *La bella lingua* is sufficient for me.'

'I hear that Olga could understand him quite well,' said Georgie, betraying his complete knowledge of all that had happened.

'That may be so,' said Lucia. 'I hope she understood his English too, and his music. He had not an "h" when he spoke English, and I have not the slightest doubt in my own mind that his Italian was equally illiterate. It does not matter; I do not see that Mr Cortese's linguistic accomplishments concern us. But his music does, if poor Miss Bracely, with her lovely notes, is going to study it, and appear as Lucretia. I am sorry if that is so. Any news?'

Really it was rather magnificent, and it was war as well; of that there could not be the slightest doubt. All Riseholme, by this time, knew that Lucia and Peppino had not been able to understand a word of what Cortese had said, and here was the answer to the backbiting suggestion, vividly put forward by Mrs Weston on the green that morning, that the explanation was that Lucia and Peppino did not know Italian. They could not reasonably be expected to know Neapolitan dialect; the language of Dante satisfied their humble needs. They found it difficult to understand Cortese when he spoke English, but that did not imply that they did not know English. Dante's tongue and Shakespeare's tongue sufficed them . . .

'And what were the words of the libretto like?' asked Georgie.

Lucia fixed him with her beady eyes, ready and eager to show how delighted she was to bestow approbation wherever it was deserved.

'Wonderful!' she said. 'I felt, and so did Peppino, that the words were as utterly wasted on that formless music as was poor Miss Bracely's voice. How did it go, Peppino? Let me think!'

Lucia raised her head again with the faraway look.

'*Amore misterio!*' she said. '*Amore profondo! Amore profondo del vasto mar.*' Ah, there was our poor *bella lingua* again. I wonder who wrote the libretto.'

'Mr Cortese wrote the libretto,' said Georgie.

Lucia did not hesitate for a moment, but gave her silvery laugh.

'Oh, dear me, no,' she said. 'If you had heard him talk you would know he could not have. Well, have we not had enough of Mr Cortese and his works? Any news? What did you do last night, when Peppino and I were in our *purgatorio*?'

Georgie was almost equally glad to get off the subject of Italian. The less said in or of Italian the better.

'I was dining with Mrs Quantock,' he said. 'She had a very interesting Russian woman staying with her, Princess Popoffski.'

Lucia laughed again.

'Dear Daisy!' she said. 'Tell me about the Russian princess. Was she a guru? Dear me, how easily some people are taken in! The guru! Well, we were all in the same boat there. We took the guru on poor Daisy's valuation, and I still believe he had very remarkable gifts, curry-cook or not. But Princess Popoffski now – '

'We had a séance,' said Georgie.

'Indeed! And Princess Popoffski was the medium?'

Georgie grew a little dignified.

'It is no use adopting that tone, *cara*,' he said, relapsing into Italian. 'You were not there; you were having your purgatory at Olga's. It was very remarkable. We touched hands all round the table; there was no possibility of fraud.'

Lucia's views on psychic phenomena were clearly known to Rise-holme; those who produced them were fraudulent, those who were taken in by them were dupes. Consequently there was irony in the baby-talk of her reply.

'Me dood!' she said. 'Me very dood, and listen carefully. Tell Lucia!'

Georgie recounted the experiences. The table had rocked and tapped out names. The table had whirled round, though it was a very heavy table. Georgie had been told that he had two sisters, one of whom in Latin was a bear.

'How did the table know that?' he asked. 'Ursa, a bear, you know. And then, while we were sitting there, the Princess went off into a trance. She said there was a beautiful spirit present, who blessed us all. She called Mrs Quantock Margarita, which, as you may know, is the Italian for Daisy.'

Lucia smiled.

'Thank you for explaining, Georgino,' she said.

There was no mistaking the irony of that, and Georgie thought he would be ironical too.

'I didn't know if you knew,' he said. 'I thought it might be Neapolitan dialect.'

'Pray, go on!' said Lucia, breathing through her nose.

'And she said I was Georgie,' said Georgie, 'but that there was another Georgie not far off. That was odd, because Olga's house, with Mr Shuttleworth, were so close. And then the Princess went into very deep trance, and the spirit that was there took possession of her.'

'And who was that?' asked Lucia.

'His name was Amadeo. She spoke in Amadeo's voice; indeed it was Amadeo who was speaking. He was a Florentine and knew Dante quite well. He materialised; I saw him.'

A bright glorious vision flashed upon Lucia. The Dante-class might not, even though it was clearly understood that Cortese spoke un-intelligible Neapolitan, be a complete success, if the only attraction was that she herself taught Dante, but it would be quite a different proposition if Princess Popoffski, controlled by Amadeo, Dante's friend, was present. They might read a Canto first, and then hold a séance of which Amadeo – via Princess Popoffski – would take charge. While this was simmering in her mind, it was important to drop all irony and be extremely sympathetic.

'Georgino! How wonderful!' she said. 'As you know, I am sceptical by nature, and want all evidence carefully sifted. I dare say I am too critical, and that is a fault. But fancy getting in touch with a friend of Dante's! What would one not give? Tell me: what is this Princess like? Is she the sort of person one could ask to dinner?'

Georgie was still sore over the irony to which he had been treated. He had, moreover, the solid fact behind him that Daisy Quantock (Margarita) had declared that in no circumstances would she permit Lucia to annex her Princess. She had forgiven Lucia for annexing the guru (and considering that she had only annexed a curry-cook, it was not so difficult) but she was quite determined to run her Princess herself.

'Yes, you might ask her,' he said. If irony was going about, there was no reason why he should not have a share.

Lucia bounced from her seat, as if it had been a spring cushion.

'We will have a little party,' she said. 'We three, and dear Daisy and her husband and the Princess. I think that will be enough; psychics hate a crowd, because it disturbs the influences. Mind! I do not say I believe in her power yet, but I am quite open-minded; I should like to be convinced. Let me see! We are doing nothing tomorrow. Let us have our little dinner tomorrow. I will send a line to dear Daisy at once, and say how enormously your account of the séance has interested me. I should like dear Daisy to have something to console her for that terrible fiasco about her guru. And then, Georgino *mio*, I will listen to your Debussy. Do not expect anything; if it seems to me formless, I shall say so. But if it seems to me promising, I shall be equally frank. Perhaps it is great; I cannot tell you about that till I have heard it. Let me write my note first.'

That was soon done, and Lucia, having sent it by hand, came into the music-room, and drew down the blinds over the window through which the autumn sun was streaming. Very little art, as she had once said, would 'stand' daylight; only Shakespeare or Dante or Beethoven and perhaps Bach, could complete with the sun.

Georgie, for his part, would have liked rather more light, but after all Debussy wrote such very odd chords and sequences that it was not necessary to wear his spectacles.

Lucia sat in a high chair near the piano, with her chin in her hand, tremendously erect.

Georgie took off his rings and laid them on the candle-bracket, and ran his hands nimbly over the piano.

'Poissons d'or,' he said. 'Goldfish!'

'Yes; pesci d'oro,' said Lucia, explaining it to Peppino.

Lucia's face changed as the elusive music proceeded. The faraway look died away, and became puzzled; her chin came out of her hand, and the hand it came out of covered her eyes.

Before Georgie had got to the end the answer to her note came, and she sat with it in her hand, which, released from covering her eyes, tried to beat time. On the last note she got up with a regretful sigh.

'Is it finished?' she asked. 'And yet I feel inclined to say "When is it going to begin?" I haven't been fed; I haven't drunk in anything. Yes, I warned you I should be quite candid. And there's my verdict. I am sorry. Me vewy sowwy! But you played it, I am sure, beautifully, Georgino; you were a buono avvocato: you said all that could be said for your client. Shall I open this note before we discuss it more fully? Give Georgino a cigarette, Peppino! I am sure he deserves one, after all those accidentals.'

She pulled up the blind again in order to read her note and as she read her face clouded.

'Ah! I am sorry for that,' she said. 'Peppino, the Princess does not go out in the evening; they always have a séance there. I dare say Daisy means to ask us some evening soon. We will keep an evening or two open. It is a long time since I have seen dear Daisy; I will pop round this afternoon.'

Chapter Thirteen

Spiritualism, and all things pertaining to it, swept over Riseholme like the amazing growth of some tropical forest, germinating and shooting out its surprising vegetation, and rearing into huge fantastic shapes. In the centre of this wonderful jungle was a temple, so to speak, and that temple was the house of Mrs Quantock . . .

A strange Providence was the origin of it all. Mrs Quantock, a week before, had the toothache, and being no longer in the fold of Christian Science, found that it was no good at all to tell herself that it was a false claim. False claim it might be, but it was so plausible at once that it quite deceived her, and she went up to London to have its falsity demonstrated by a dentist. Since the collapse of Yoga and the flight of the curry-cook, she had embarked on no mystical adventure, and she starved for some new fad. Then when her first visit to the dentist was over (the tooth required three treatments) and she went to a vegetarian restaurant to see if there was anything enlightening to be got out of that, she was delighted to find herself sitting at a very small table with a very communicative lady who ate cabbages in perfectly incredible quantities. She had a round pale face like the moon behind the clouds, enormous eyebrows that almost met over her nose, and a strange low voice, of husky tone, and a pronunciation quite as foreign as Signor Cortese's. She wore some very curious rings with large engraved amethysts and turquoises in them, and since in the first moments of their conversation she had volunteered the information that vegetarianism was the only possible diet for any who were cultivating their psychical powers, Mrs Quantock asked her if these weird finger-ornaments had any mystical signification. They had; one was Gnostic, one was Rosicrucian, and the other was Cabalistic . . . It is easy to picture Mrs Quantock's delight; adventure had met her with smiling mouth and mysterious eyes. In the course of an animated conversation of half an hour, the lady explained that if Mrs Quantock was, like her, a searcher after psychical truths, and cared to come to her flat at half-past four that afternoon, she would try to help her. She added with some little diffidence that the fee for a séance was a guinea, and, as she left, took a card out of a case, encrusted with glowing rubies, and gave it her. That was the Princess Popoffski.

Now here was a curious thing. For the last few evenings at
Riseholme, Mrs Quantock had been experimenting with a table, and
found that it creaked and tilted and tapped in the most encouraging
way when she and Robert laid their hands on it. Then something –
whatever it was that moved the table – had indicated by raps that her
name was Daisy and his Robert, as well as giving them other
information, which could not so easily be verified. Robert had grown
quite excited about it, and was vexed that the séances were interrupted
by his wife's expedition to London. But now how providential that
was. She had walked straight from the dentist into the arms of Princess
Popoffski.

It was barely half-past four when Mrs Quantock arrived at the
Princess's flat, in a pleasant quiet side street off Charing Cross Road.
A small dapper little gentleman received her, who explained that he
was the Princess's secretary, and conducted her through several small
rooms into the presence of the Sybil. These rooms, so Mrs Quantock
thrillingly noticed, were dimly lit by oil lamps that stood in front of
shrines containing images of the great spiritual guides from Moses
down to Madame Blavatski, a smell of incense hung about, there
were vases of flowers on the tables, and strange caskets set with
winking stones. In the last of these rooms the Princess was seated,
and for the moment Mrs Quantock hardly recognised her, for she
wore a blue robe, which left her massive arms bare, and up them
writhed serpent-shaped bracelets of many coils. She fixed her eyes
on Mrs Quantock, as if she had never seen her before, and made no
sign of recognition.

'The Princess has been meditating,' said the secretary in a whisper.
'She'll come to herself presently.'

For a moment meditation unpleasantly reminded Mrs Quantock
of the guru, but nothing could have been less like that ill-starred
curry-cook than this majestic creature. Eventually she gave a great
sigh and came out of her meditation.

'Ah, it is my friend,' she said. 'Do you know that you have a purple
halo?'

This was very gratifying, especially when it was explained that
only the most elect had purple halos, and soon other elect souls
assembled for the séance. In the centre of the table was placed a
musical box and a violin, and hardly had the circle been made, and
the lights turned down, when the most extraordinary things began to
happen. A perfect storm of rappings issued from the table, which
began to rock violently, and presently there came peals of laughter

in a high voice, and those who had been here before said that it was Pocky. He was a dear naughty boy, so Mrs Quantock's neighbour explained to her, so full of fun, and when on earth had been a Hungarian violinist. Still invisible, Pocky wished them all much laughter and joy, and then suddenly said ' 'Ullo, 'ullo, 'ere's a new friend. I like her,' and Mrs Quantock's neighbour, with a touch of envy in her voice, told her that Pocky clearly meant her. Then Pocky said that they had been having heavenly music on the other side that day, and that if the new friend would say 'Please' he would play them some of it.

So Mrs Quantock, trembling with emotion, said, 'Please, Pocky,' and instantly he began to play on the violin the spirit tune which he had just been playing on the other side. After that, the violin clattered back on to the middle of the table again, and Pocky, blowing showers of kisses to them all, went away amid peals of happy laughter.

Silence fell, and then a deep bass voice said, 'I am coming, Amadeo!' and out of the middle of the table appeared a faint luminousness. It grew upwards and began to take form. Swathes of white muslin shaped themselves in the darkness, and there appeared a white face, in among the topmost folds of the muslin, with a Roman nose and a melancholy expression. He was not gay like Pocky, but he was intensely impressive, and spoke some lines in Italian, when asked to repeat a piece of Dante. Mrs Quantock knew they were Italian, because she recognised '*notte*' and '*uno*' and '*caro*', familiar words on Lucia's lips.

The séance came to an end, and Mrs Quantock having placed a guinea with the utmost alacrity in a sort of offertory plate which the Princess's secretary negligently but prominently put down on a table in one of the other rooms, waited to arrange for another séance. But most unfortunately the Princess was leaving town next day on a much-needed holiday, for she had been giving three séances a day for the last two months and required rest.

'Yes, we're off tomorrow, the Princess and I,' said he, 'for a week at the Royal Hotel at Brinton. Pleasant bracing air, always sets her up. But after that she'll be back in town. Do you know that part of the country?'

Daisy could hardly believe her ears.

'Brinton?' she said. 'I live close to Brinton.'

Her whole scheme flashed completely upon her, even as Athene sprang full-grown from the brain of Zeus.

'Do you think that she might be induced to spend a few days with me at Riseholme?' she said. 'My husband and I are so much interested in psychical things. You would be our guest, too, I hope. If she rested for a few days at Brinton first? If she came on to me afterwards? And then if she was thoroughly rested, perhaps she would give us a séance or two. I don't know – '

Mrs Quantock felt a great diffidence in speaking of guineas in the same sentence with Princesses, and had to make another start.

'If she were thoroughly rested,' she said, 'and if a little circle perhaps of four, at the usual price, would be worth her while. Just after dinner, you know, and nothing else to do all day but rest. There are pretty drives and beautiful air. All very quiet, and I think I may say more comfortable than the hotel. It would be such a pleasure.'

Mrs Quantock heard the clinking of bracelets from the room where the Princess was still reposing, and there she stood in the door, looking unspeakably majestic, but very gracious. So Mrs Quantock put her proposition before her, the secretary coming to the rescue on the subject of the usual fees, and when two days afterwards Mrs Quantock returned to Riseholme, it was to get ready the spare room and Robert's room next to it for these thrilling visitors, whose first séance Georgie and Piggy had attended, on the evening of the Italian *débâcle* . . .

*   *   *

The Quantocks had taken a high and magnificent line about the 'usual fees' for the séances, an expensive line, but then Roumanian oils had been extremely prosperous lately. No mention whatever of these fees was made to their guests, no offertory-plate was put in a prominent position in the hall, there was no fumbling for change or the discreet pressure of coins into the secretary's hand; the entire cost was borne by Roumanian oils. The Princess and Mrs Quantock, apparently, were old friends; they spoke to each other at dinner as 'dear friend', and the Princess declared in the most gratifying way that they had been most intimate in a previous incarnation, without any allusion to the fact that in this incarnation they had met for the first time last week at a vegetarian restaurant. She was kind enough, it was left to be understood, to give a little séance after dinner at the house of her 'dear friend', and so, publicly, the question of money never came up.

Now the Princess was to stay three nights, and therefore, as soon as Mrs Quantock had made sure of that, she proceeded to fill up each of the séances without asking Lucia to any of them. It was not that she had not fully forgiven her for her odious grabbing of the guru, for she had done that on the night of the Spanish Quartet; it was rather that she meant to make sure that there would by no possibility be anything to forgive concerning her conduct with regard to the Princess. Lucia could not grab her and so call Daisy's powers of forgiveness into play again, if she never came near her, and Daisy meant to take proper precautions that she should not come near her. Accordingly Georgie and Piggy were asked to the first séance (if it did not go very well, it would not particularly matter with them), Olga and Mr Shuttleworth were bidden to the second, and Lady Ambermere with Georgie again to the third. This – quite apart from the immense interest of psychic phenomena – was deadly work, for it would be bitter indeed to Lucia to know, as she most undoubtedly would, that Lady Ambermere, who had cut her so firmly, was dining twice and coming to a séance. Daisy, it must again be repeated, had quite forgiven Lucia about the guru, but Lucia must take the consequences of what she had done.

It was after the first séance that the frenzy for spiritualism seized Riseholme. The Princess, with great good nature, gave some further exhibitions of her psychical power in addition to the séances, and even as Georgie the next afternoon was receiving Lucia's cruel verdict about Debussy, the Sybil was looking at the hands of Colonel Boucher and Mrs Weston, and unerringly probing into their past, and lifting the corner of the veil, giving them both glimpses into the future. She knew that the two were engaged, for that she had learned from Mrs Quantock in her morning's drive, and did not attempt to conceal the fact, but how could it be accounted for that, looking impressively from the one to the other, she said that a woman no longer young but tall, and with fair hair, had crossed their lives and had been connected with one of them for years past? It was impossible to describe Elizabeth more accurately than that, and Mrs Weston in high excitement confessed that her maid who had been with her for fifteen years entirely corresponded with what the Princess had seen in her hand. After that it took only a moment's further scrutiny for the Princess to discover that Elizabeth was going to be happy too. Then she found that there was a man connected with Elizabeth, and Colonel Boucher's hand, to which she transferred her gaze, trembled with delightful anticipation. She seemed to see a man there; she was not quite sure, but was there a man who perhaps had been known to him for a long time? There was. And then by degrees the affairs of Elizabeth and Atkinson were unerringly unravelled. It was little wonder that the Colonel pushed Mrs Weston's bath-chair with record speed to Ye Signe of Ye Daffodil, and by the greatest good luck obtained a copy of *The Palmist's Manual*.

At another of these informal séances attended by Goosie and Mrs Antrobus, even stranger things had happened, for the Princess's hands, as they held a little preliminary conversation, began to tremble and twitch even more strongly than Colonel Boucher's, and Mrs Quantock hastily supplied her with a pencil and a quantity of sheets of foolscap paper, for this trembling and twitching implied that Reschia, an ancient Egyptian priestess, was longing to use the Princess's hand for automatic writing. After a few wild scrawls and plunges with the pencil, the Princess, though she still continued to talk to them, covered sheet after sheet in large flowing handwriting. This, when it was finished and the Princess sunk back in her chair, proved to be the most wonderful spiritual discourse, describing the happiness and harmony which pervaded the whole universe, and was only temporarily obscured by the mists of materiality. These mists were wholly withdrawn from the vision of those who had passed over. They lived in the midst of song and flowers and light and love . . . Towards the end there was a less intelligible passage about fire from the clouds. It was rendered completely intelligible the very next day when there was a thunderstorm, surely an unusual occurrence in November. If that had not happened Mrs Quantock's interpretation of it, as referring to Zeppelins, would have been found equally satisfactory. It was no wonder after that, that Mrs Antrobus, Piggy and Goosie spent long evenings with pencils and paper, for the Princess said that everybody had the gift of automatic writing, if they would only take pains and patience to develop it. Everybody had his own particular guide, and it was the very next day that Piggy obtained a script clearly signed Annabel Nicostratus and Jamifleg followed very soon after for her mother and sister, and so there was no jealousy.

But the crown and apex of these manifestations was undoubtedly the three regular séances which took place to the three select circles after dinner. Musical boxes resounded, violins gave forth ravishing airs, the sitters were touched by unseen fingers when everybody's hands were touching all around the table, and from the middle of it materialisations swathed in muslin were built up. Pocky came, visible to the eye, and played spirit music. Amadeo, melancholy and impressive, recited Dante, and Cardinal Newman, not visible to the eye but audible to the ear, joined in singing 'Lead, Kindly Light', which the secretary requested them to encourage him with, and blessed them profusely at the conclusion. Lady Ambermere was so much impressed, and so nervous of driving home alone, that she insisted on Georgie's going back to The Hall with her, and consigning her person to Pug and Miss Lyall, and for the three days of the Princess's visit, there was practically no subject discussed at the parliaments on the green, except the latest manifestations. Olga went to town for a crystal, and Georgie for a planchette, and Riseholme temporarily became a spiritualistic republic, with the Princess as priestess and Mrs Quantock as President.

Lucia, all this time, was almost insane with pique and jealousy, for she sat in vain waiting for an invitation to come to a séance, and would, long before the three days were over, have welcomed with enthusiasm a place at one of the inferior and informal exhibitions. Since she could not procure the Princess for dinner, she asked Daisy to bring her to lunch or tea or at any hour day or night which was convenient. She made Peppino hang about opposite Daisy's house, with orders to drop his stick, or let his hat blow off, if he saw even the secretary coming out of the gate, so as possibly to enter into conversation with him, while she positively forced herself one morning into Daisy's hall, and cried 'Margarita' in silvery tones. On this occasion Margarita came out of the drawing-room with a most determined expression on her face, and shut the door carefully behind her.

'Dearest Lucia,' she said, 'how nice to see you! What is it?'

'I just popped in for a chat,' said she. 'I haven't set eyes on you since the evening of the Spanish Quartet.'

'No! So long ago as that, is it? Well, you must come in again sometime very soon, won't you? The day after tomorrow I shall be much less busy. Promise to look in then.'

'You have a visitor with you, have you not?' asked Lucia desperately.

'Yes! Two, indeed, dear friends of mine. But I am afraid you would not like them. I know your opinion about anything connected with spiritualism, and – isn't it silly of us? – we've been dabbling in that.'

'Oh, but how interesting,' said Lucia. 'I – I am always ready to learn, and alter my opinions if I am wrong.'

Mrs Quantock did not move from in front of the drawing-room door.

'Yes?' she said. 'Then we will have a great talk about it, when you come to see me the day after tomorrow. But I know I shall find you hard to convince.'

She kissed the tips of her fingers in a manner so hopelessly final that there was nothing to do but go away.

Then with poor generalship, Lucia altered her tactics, and went up to the village green where Piggy was telling Georgie about the script signed Annabel. This was repeated again for Lucia's benefit.

'Wasn't it too lovely?' said Piggy. 'So Annabel's my guide, and she writes a hand quite unlike mine.'

Lucia gave a little scream, and put her fingers to her ears.

'Gracious me!' she said. 'What has come over Riseholme? Wherever I go I hear nothing but talk of séances, and spirits, and automatic writing. Such a pack of nonsense, my dear Piggy. I wonder at a sensible girl like you.'

Mrs Weston, propelled by the Colonel, whirled up in her bath-chair.

'*The Palmist's Manual* is too wonderful,' she said, 'and Jacob and I sat up over it till I don't know what hour. There's a break in his line of life, just at the right place, when he was so ill in Egypt, which is most remarkable, and when Tommy Luton brought round my bath-chair this morning – I had it at the garden door, because the gravel's just laid at my front door, and the wheels sink so far into it – "Tommy," I said, "let me look at your hand a moment," and there on his line of fate, was the little cross that means bereavement. It came just right didn't it, Jacob? when he was thirteen, for he's fourteen this year, and Mrs Luton died just a year ago. Of course I didn't tell Tommy that, for I only told him to wash his hands, but it was most curious. And has your planchette come yet, Mr Georgie? I shall be most anxious to know what it writes, so if you've got an evening free any night soon just come round for a bit of dinner, and we'll make an evening of it, with table turning and planchette and palmistry. Now tell me all about the séance the first night. I wish I could have been present at a real séance, but of course Mrs Quantock can't find room for everybody, and I'm sure it was most kind of her to let the Colonel and me come in yesterday afternoon. We were thrilled with it, and who knows but that the Princess didn't write *The Palmist's Manual*, for on the title page it says it's by P. and that might be Popoffski as easily as not, or perhaps Princess.'

This allusion to there not being room for everybody was agony to Lucia. She laughed in her most silvery manner.

'Or, perhaps Peppino,' she said. 'I must ask *mio caro* if he wrote it. Or does it stand for Pillson? Georgino, are you the author of *The Palmist's Manual*? *Ecco!* I believe it was you.'

This was not quite wise, for no one detested irony more than Mrs Weston, or was sharper to detect it. Lucia should never have been ironical just then, nor indeed have dropped into Italian.

'No,' she said. 'I'm sure it was neither *il Signor Peppino* nor *il Signor Pillson* who wrote it. I believe it was the *Principessa*. So, *ecco*! And did we not have a delicious evening at Miss Bracely's the other night? Such lovely singing, and so interesting to learn that Signor Cortese made it all up. And those lovely words, for though I didn't understand much of them, they sounded so exquisite. And fancy Miss Bracely talking Italian so beautifully when we none of us knew she talked it at all.'

Mrs Weston's amiable face was crimson with suppressed emotion, of which these few words were only the most insignificant leakage, and a very awkward pause succeeded which was luckily broken by everybody beginning to talk again very fast and brightly. Then Mrs Weston's chair scudded away; Piggy skipped away to the stocks where Goosie was sitting with a large sheet of foolscap, in case her hand twitched for automatic script, and Lucia turned to Georgie, who alone was left.

'Poor Daisy!' she said. 'I dropped in just now, and really I found her very odd and strange. What with her crazes for Christian Science, and uric acid and gurus and mediums, one wonders if she is quite sane. So sad! I should be dreadfully sorry if she had some mental collapse; that sort of thing is always so painful. But I know of a first-rate place for rest-cures; I think it would be wise if I just casually dropped the name of it to Mr Robert, in case. And this last craze seems so terribly infectious. Fancy Mrs Weston dabbling in palmistry! It is too comical, but I hope I did not hurt her feelings by suggesting that Peppino or you wrote the *Manual*. It is dangerous to make little jokes to poor Mrs Weston.'

Georgie quite agreed with that, but did not think it necessary to say in what sense he agreed with it. Every day now Lucia was pouring floods of light on a quite new side of her character, which had been undeveloped, like the print from some photographic plate lying in the dark so long as she was undisputed mistress of Rise-holme. But, so it struck him now, since the advent of Olga, she had taken up a critical ironical standpoint, which previously she had reserved for Londoners. At every turn she had to criticise and condemn where once she would only have praised. So few months ago, there had been that marvellous Hightum garden-party, when Olga had sung long after Lady Ambermere had gone away. That was her garden-party; the splendour and success of it had been hers, and no one had been allowed to forget that until Olga came back again. But the moment that happened, and Olga began to sing on her own account (which after all, so Georgie thought, she had a perfect right to do), the whole aspect of affairs was changed. She romped, and Riseholme did not like romps; she sang in church, and that was theatrical; she gave a party with the Spanish Quartet, and Brinton was publicly credited with the performance. Then had come Mrs Quantock and her Princess, and, lo, it would be kind to remember the name of an establishment for rest-cures, in the hope of saving poor Daisy's sanity. Again Colonel Boucher and Mrs Weston were intending to get married, and consulted a *Palmist's Manual*, so they too helped to develop as with acid the print that had lain so long in the dark.

'Poor thing!' said Lucia, 'it is dreadful to have no sense of humour, and I'm sure I hope that Colonel Boucher will thoroughly understand that she has none before he speaks the fatal words. But then he has none either, and I have often noticed that two people without any sense of humour find each other most witty and amusing. A sense of humour, I expect, is not a very common gift; Miss Bracely has none at all, for I do not call romping humour. As for poor Daisy, what can rival her solemnity in sitting night after night round a table with someone who may or may not be a Russian princess – Russia of course is a very large place, and one does not know how many princesses there may be there – and thrilling over a pot of luminous paint and a false nose and calling it Amadeo the friend of Dante.'

This was too much for Georgie.

'But you asked Mrs Quantock and the Princess to dine with you,' he said, 'and hoped there would be a séance afterwards. You wouldn't have done that, if you thought it was only a false nose and a pot of luminous paint.'

'I may have been impulsive,' said Lucia, speaking very rapidly. 'I dare say I'm impulsive, and if my impulses lie in the direction of extending such poor hospitality as I can offer to my friends, and their friends, I am not ashamed of them. Far otherwise. But when I see and observe the awful effect of this so-called spiritualism on people whom I should have thought sensible and well-balanced – I do not include poor dear Daisy among them – then I am only thankful that my impulses did not happen to lead me into countenancing such piffle, as your sister so truly observed about poor Daisy's guru.'

They had come opposite Georgie's house, and suddenly his drawing-room window was thrown up. Olga's head looked out.

'Don't have a fit, Georgie, to find me here,' she said. 'Good-morning, Mrs Lucas; you were behind the mulberry, and I didn't see you. But something's happened to my kitchen range, and I can't have lunch at home. Do give me some. I've brought my crystal, and we'll gaze and gaze. I can see nothing at present except my own nose and the window. Are you psychical, Mrs Lucas?'

This was the last straw; all Lucia's grievances had been flocking together like swallows for their flight, and to crown all came this open annexation of Georgie. There was Olga, sitting in his window, all unasked, and demanding lunch, with her silly ridiculous crystal in her hand, wondering if Lucia was psychical.

Her silvery laugh was a little shrill. It started a full tone above its normal pitch.

'No, dear Miss Bracely,' she said. 'I am afraid I am much too commonplace and matter-of-fact to care about such things. It is a great loss I know, and deprives me of the pleasant society of Russian princesses. But we are all made differently; that is very lucky. I must get home, Georgie.'

It certainly seemed very lucky that everyone was not precisely like Lucia at that moment, or there would have been quarrelling.

She walked quickly off, and Georgie entered his house. Lucia had really been remarkably rude, and, if allusion was made to it, he was ready to confess that she seemed a little worried. Friendship would allow that, and candour demanded it. But no allusion of any sort was made. There was a certain flush on Olga's face, and she explained that she had been sitting over the fire.

The Princess's visit came to an end next day, and all the world knew that she was going back to London by the 11.00 a.m. express. Lady Ambermere was quite aware of it, and drove in with Pug and Miss Lyall, meaning to give her a lift to the station, leaving Mrs Quantock, if she wanted to see her guest off, to follow with the Princess's luggage in the fly which, no doubt, had been ordered. But Daisy had no intention of permitting this sort of thing, and drove calmly away with her dear friend in Georgie's motor, leaving the baffled Lady Ambermere to follow or not as she liked. She did like, though not much, and found herself on the platform among a perfect crowd of Riseholmites who had strolled down to the station on this lovely morning to see if parcels had come. Lady Ambermere took very little notice of them, but managed that Pug should give his paw to the Princess as she took her seat, and waved her hand to Mrs Quantock's dear friend, as the train slid out of the station.

'The late lord had some Russian relations,' she said majestically. 'How did you get to know her?'

'I met her at Tsarskoe Selo,' was on the tip of Mrs Quantock's tongue, but she was afraid that Lady Ambermere might not understand, and ask her when she had been to Tsarskoe Selo. It was grievous work making jokes for Lady Ambermere.

*　　*　　*

The train sped on to London, and the Princess opened the envelope which her hostess had discreetly put in her hand, and found that *that* was all right. Her hostess had also provided her with an admirable lunch, which her secretary took out of a Gladstone bag. When that was finished, she wanted her cigarettes, and as she looked for these, and even after she had found them, she continued to search for something else. There was the musical box there, and some curious pieces of elastic, and the violin was in its case, and there was a white mask. But she still continued to search . . .

*　　*　　*

About the same time as she gave up the search, Mrs Quantock wandered upstairs to the Princess's room. A less highly vitalised nature than hers would have been in a stupor of content, but she was more in a frenzy of content than in a stupor. How fine that frenzy was may be judged from the fact that perhaps the smallest ingredient in it was her utter defeat of Lucia. She cared comparatively little for that glorious achievement, and she was not sure that when the Princess came back again, as she had arranged to do on her next holiday, she would not ask Lucia to come to a séance. Indeed she had little but pity for the vanquished, so great were the spoils. Never had Riseholme risen to such a pitch of enthusiasm, and with good cause had it done so now, for of all the wonderful and exciting things that had ever happened there, these séances were the most delirious. And better even than the excitement of Riseholme was the cause of its excitement, for spiritualism and the truth of inexplicable psychic phenomena had flashed upon them all. Tableaux, romps, Yoga, the 'Moonlight Sonata', Shakespeare, Christian Science, Olga herself, uric acid, Elizabethan furniture, the engagement of Colonel Boucher and Mrs Weston, all these tremendous topics had paled like fire in the sunlight before the revelation that had now dawned. By practice and patience, by zealous concentration on crystals and palms, by the waiting for automatic script to develop, you attained to the highest mysteries, and could evoke Cardinal Newman, or Pocky . . .

There was the bed in which the Sybil had slept; there was the fresh vase of flowers, difficult to procure in November, but still obtainable, which she loved to have standing near her. There was the chest of drawers in which she had put her clothes, and Mrs Quantock pulled them open one by one, finding fresh emanations and vibrations everywhere. The lowest one stuck a little, and she had to use force to it . . .

The smile was struck from her face, as it flew open. Inside it were billows and billows of the finest possible muslin. Fold after fold of it she drew out, and with it there came a pair of false eyebrows. She recognised them at once as being Amadeo's. The muslin belonged to Pocky as well.

She needed but a moment's concentrated thought, and in swift succession rejected two courses of action that suggested themselves. The first was to use the muslin herself; it would make summer garments for years. The chief reason against that was that she was a little old for muslin. The second course was to send the whole paraphernalia back to her dear friend, with or without a comment. But that would be tantamount to a direct accusation of fraud. Never any more, if she did that, could she dispense her dear friend to Riseholme like an expensive drug. She would not so utterly burn her boats. There remained only one other judicious course of action, and she got to work.

It had been a cold morning, clear and frosty, and she had caused a good fire to be lit in the Princess's bedroom, for her to dress by. It still prospered in the grate, and Mrs Quantock, having shut the door and locked it, put on to it the false eyebrows, which, as they turned to ash, flew up the chimney. Then she fed it with muslin; yards and yards of muslin she poured on to it; never had there been so much muslin nor that so exquisitely fine. It went to her heart to burn it, but there was no time for minor considerations; every atom of that evidence must be purged by fire. The Princess would certainly not write and say that she had left some eyebrows and a hundred yards of muslin behind her, for, knowing what she did, it would be to her interests as well as Mrs Quantock's that those properties should vanish, as if they never had been.

Up the chimney in sheets of flame went this delightful fabric; sometimes it roared there, as if it had set the chimney on fire, and she had to pause, shielding her scorched face, until the hollow rumbling had died down. But at last the holocaust was over, and she unlocked the door again. No one knew but she, and no one should ever know. The guru had turned out to be a curry-cook, but no intruding Hermy had been here this time. As long as crystals fascinated and automatic writing flourished, the secret of the muslin and the eyebrows should repose in one bosom alone. Riseholme had been electrified by spiritualism, and, even now, the séances had been cheap at the price, and in spite of this discovery, she felt by no means sure that she would not ask the Princess to come again and minister to their spiritual needs.

She had hardly got downstairs when Robert came in from the green, where he had been recounting the experiences of the last séance.

'Looked as if there was a chimney on fire,' he said. 'I wish it was the kitchen chimney. Then perhaps the beef mightn't be so raw as it was yesterday.'

Thus is comedy intertwined with tragedy!

Chapter Fourteen

Georgie was very busily engaged during the first weeks of December on a watercolour sketch of Olga sitting at her piano and singing. The difficulty of it was such that at times he almost despaired of accomplishing it, for the problem of how to draw her face and her mouth wide open and yet retain the likeness seemed almost insoluble. Often he sat in front of his own looking-glass with his mouth open, and diligently drew his own face, in order to arrive at the principles of the changes of line which took place. Certainly the shape of a person's face, when his mouth was wide open, altered so completely that you would have thought him quite unrecognisable, however skilfully the artist reproduced his elongated countenance, and yet Georgie could easily recognise that face in the glass as his. Forehead, eyes and cheekbones alone retained their wonted aspect; even the nose seemed to lengthen if you opened your mouth very wide . . . Then how again was he to indicate that she was singing and not yawning, or preparing for a sneeze? His most successful sketch at present looked precisely as if she was yawning, and made Georgie's jaws long to yawn too. Perhaps the shape of the mouth in the two positions was really the same, and it was only the sound that led you to suppose that an open-mouthed person was singing. But perhaps the piano would supply the necessary suggestion; Olga would not sit down at the piano merely to yawn or sneeze, for she could do that anywhere.

Then a brilliant idea struck him: he would introduce a shaded lamp standing on the piano, and then her face would be in red shadow. Naturally this entailed fresh problems with regard to light, but light seemed to present less difficulty than likeness. Besides he could make her dress, and the keys of the piano very like indeed. But when he came to painting again he despaired. There must be red shadow on her face and yellow light on her hands, and on her green dress, and presently the whole thing looked not so much like Olga singing by lamplight, as a lobster-salad spread out in the sunlight. The more he painted, the more vividly did the lettuce leaves and the dressing and the lobster emerge from the paper. So he took away the lamp, and shut Olga's mouth, and there she would be at her piano just going to sing.

These artistic agonies had rewards which more than compensated for them, for regularly now he took his drawing-board and his paintbox across to her house, and sat with her while she practised. There were none of love's lilies low or yawning York now, for she was very busy learning her part in *Lucretia*, spending a solid two hours at it every morning, and Georgie began to perceive what sort of work it implied to produce the spontaneous ease with which Brünnhilde hailed the sun. More astounding even was the fact that this mere learning of notes was but the preliminary to what she called 'real work'. And when she had got through the mere mechanical part of it, she would have to study. Then when her practice was over, she would indulgently sit with her head in profile against a dark background, and Georgie would suck one end of his brush and bite the other, and wonder whether he would ever produce anything which he could dare to offer her. By daily poring on her face, he grew not to admire only but to adore its youth and beauty, by daily contact with her he began to see how fresh and how lovely was the mind that illuminated it.

'Georgie, I'm going to scold you,' she said one day, as she took up her place against the black panel. 'You're a selfish little brute. You think of nothing but your own amusement. Did that ever strike you?'

Georgie gasped with surprise. Here was he spending the whole of every morning trying to do something which would be a worthy Christmas present for her (to say nothing of the hours he had spent with his mouth open in front of his glass, and the cost of the beautiful frame which he had ordered) and yet he was supposed to be only thinking about himself. Of course Olga did not know that the picture was to be hers . . .

'How tarsome you are!' he said. 'You're always finding fault with me. Explain.'

'Well, you're neglecting your old friends for your new one,' she said. 'My dear, you should never drop an old friend. For instance, when did you last play duets with Mrs Lucas?'

'Oh, not so very long ago,' said Georgie.

'Quite long enough, I am sure. But I don't actually mean sitting down and thumping the piano with her. When did you last think about her and make plans for her and talk baby-language?'

'Who told you I ever did?' asked Georgie.

'Gracious! How can I possibly remember that sort of thing? I should say at a guess that everybody told me. Now poor Mrs Lucas is feeling out of it, and neglected and dethroned. It's all on my mind rather, and I'm talking to you about it, because it's largely your fault. Now we're talking quite frankly, so don't fence, and say it's mine. I know exactly what you mean, but you are perfectly wrong. Primarily, it's Mrs Lucas's fault, because she's quite the stupidest woman I ever saw, but it's partly your fault too.'

She turned round.

'Come, Georgie, let's have it out,' she said. 'I'm perfectly powerless to do anything, because she detests me, and you've got to help her and help me, and drop your selfishness. Before I came here, she used to run you all, and give you treats like going to her tableaux and listening to her stupid old "Moonlight Sonata", and talking seven words of Italian. And then I came along with no earthly intention except to enjoy my holidays, and she got it into her head that I was trying to run the place instead of her. Isn't that so? Just say "yes".'

'Yes,' said Georgie.

'Well, that puts me in an odious position and a helpless position. I did my best to be nice to her; I went to her house until she ceased to ask me, and asked her here for everything that I thought would amuse her, until she ceased to come. I took no notice of her rudeness, which was remarkable, or of her absurd patronising airs, which didn't hurt me in the smallest degree. But Georgie, she would continue to make such a dreadful ass of herself, and think it was my fault. Was it my fault that she didn't know the Spanish Quartet when she heard it, or that she didn't know a word of Italian, when she pretended she did, or that the other day (it was the last time I saw her, when you played your Debussy to us at Aunt Jane's) she talked to me about inverted fifths?'

Olga suddenly burst out laughing, and Georgie assumed the Rise-holme face of intense curiosity.

'You must tell me all about that,' he said, 'and I'll tell you the rest which you don't know.'

Olga succumbed too, and began to talk in Aunt Jane's voice, for she had adopted her as an aunt.

'Well, it was last Monday week,' she said, 'or was it Sunday? No it couldn't have been Sunday because I don't have anybody to tea that day, as Elizabeth goes over to Jacob's and spends the afternoon with Atkinson, or the other way about, which doesn't signify, as the point is that Elizabeth should be free. So it was Monday, and Aunt Jane – it's me talking again – had the tea-party at which you played "Poisson d'Or". And when it was finished, Mrs Lucas gave a great sigh, and said, "Poor Georgino! Wasting his time over that rubbish," though she knew quite well that I had given it to you. And so I said, "Would you call it rubbish, do you think?" and she said, "Quite. Every rule of music is violated. Don't those inverted fifths make you wince, Miss Bracely?" '

Olga laughed again, and spoke in her own voice.

'Oh, Georgie, she is an ass,' she said. 'What she meant I suppose was consecutive fifths; you can't invert a fifth. So I said (I really meant it as a joke), "Of course there is that, but you must forgive Debussy that for the sake of that wonderful passage of submerged tenths!" And she took it quite gravely and shook her head, and said she was afraid she was a purist. What happened next? That's all I know.'

'Directly afterwards,' said Georgie, 'she brought the music to me, and asked me to show her where the passage of tenths came. I didn't know, but I found some tenths, and she brightened up and said, "Yes, it is true; those submerged tenths are very impressive." Then I suggested that the submerged tenth was not a musical expression, but referred to a section of the population. On which she said no more, but when she went away she asked me to send her some book on harmony. I dare say she is looking for the submerged tenth still.'

Olga lit a cigarette and became grave again.

'Well, it can't go on,' she said. 'We can't have the poor thing feeling angry and out of it. Then there was Mrs Quantock absolutely refusing to let her see the Princess.'

'That was her own fault,' said Georgie. 'It was because she was so greedy about the guru.'

'That makes it all the bitterer. And I can't do anything, because she blames me for it all. I would ask her and her Peppino here every night, and listen to her dreary tunes every evening, and let her have it all her own way, if it would do any good. But things have gone too far; she wouldn't come. It has all happened without my noticing it. I never added it all up as it went along, and I hate it.'

Georgie thought of the spiritualistic truths.

'If you're an incarnation,' he said in a sudden glow of admiration, 'you're the incarnation of an angel. How you can forgive her odious manners to you – '

'My dear, shut up,' said Olga. 'We've got to do something. Now how would it be if you gave a nice party on Christmas night, and asked her at once? Ask her to help you in getting it up; make it clear she's going to run it.'

'All right. You'll come, won't you?'

'Certainly I will not. Perhaps I will come in after dinner with Goosie or someone of that sort. Don't you see it would spoil it all if I were at dinner? You must rather pointedly leave me out. Give her a nice expensive refined Christmas present too. You might give her that picture you're doing of me – No, I suppose she wouldn't like that. But just comfort her and make her feel you can't get on without her. You've been her right hand all these years. Make her give her tableaux again. And then I think you must ask me in afterwards. I long to see her and Peppino as Brünnhilde and Siegfried. Just attend to her, Georgie, and buck her up. Promise me you will. And do it as if your heart was in it, otherwise it's no good.'

Georgie began packing up his paintbox. This was not the plan he had hoped for on Christmas Day, but if Olga wished this, it had got to be done.

'Well, I'll do my best,' he said.

'Thanks ever so much. You're a darling. And how is your planchette getting on? I've been lazy about my crystal, but I get so tired of my own nose.'

'Planchette would write nothing but a few names,' said Georgie, omitting the fact that Olga's was the most frequent. 'I think I shall drop it.'

This was but reasonable, for since Riseholme had some new and absorbing excitement every few weeks, to say nothing of the current excitement of daily life, it followed that even the most thrilling pursuits could not hold the stage for very long. Still, the interest in spiritualism had died down with the rapidity of the seed on stony ground.

'Even Mrs Quantock seems to have cooled,' said Olga. 'She and her husband were here last night, and they looked rather bored when I suggested table-turning. I wonder if anything has happened to put her off it?'

'What do you think could have?' asked Georgie with Riseholme alacrity.

'Georgie, do you really believe in the Princess and Pocky?' she asked.

Georgie looked round to see that there was no one within hearing.

'I did at the time,' he said, 'at least I think I did. But it seems less likely now. Who was the Princess anyway? Why didn't we ever hear of her before? I believe Mrs Quantock met her in the train or something.'

'So do I,' said Olga. 'But not a word. It makes Aunt Jane and Uncle Jacob completely happy to believe in it all. Their lines of life are enormous, and they won't die till they're over a hundred. Now go and see Mrs Lucas, and if she doesn't ask you to lunch you can come back here.'

Georgie put down his picture and painting-apparatus at his house, and went on to Lucia's, definitely conscious that though he did not want to have her to dinner on Christmas Day, or go back to his duets and his ADC duties, there was a spice and savour in so doing that came entirely from the fact that Olga wished him to, that by this service he was pleasing her. In itself it was distasteful, in itself it tended to cut him off from her, if he had to devote his time to Lucia, but he still delighted in doing it.

'I believe I am falling in love with her this time,' said Georgie to himself . . . 'She's wonderful; she's big; she's – '

At that moment his thoughts were violently diverted, for Robert Quantock came out of his house in a tremendous hurry, merely scowling at Georgie, and positively trotted across the green in the direction of the newsagents. Instantly Georgie recollected that he had seen him there already this morning before his visit to Olga, buying a new twopenny paper in a yellow cover called *Todd's News*. They had had a few words of genial conversation, and what could have happened in the last two hours that made Robert merely gnash his teeth at Georgie now, and make a second visit to the paper-shop?

It was impossible not to linger a moment and see what Robert did

when he got to the paper-shop, and with the aid of his spectacles
Georgie perceived that he presently loaded himself with a whole
packet of papers in yellow covers, presumably *Todd's News*. Flesh and
blood could not resist the cravings of curiosity, and making a detour,
so as to avoid being gnashed at again by Robert, who was coming
rapidly back in his direction, he strolled round to the paper-shop and
asked for a copy of *Todd's News*. Instantly the bright December
morning grew dark with mystery, for the proprietor told him that
Mr Quantock had bought every copy he possessed of it. No further
information could be obtained, except that he had bought a copy of
every other daily paper as well.

Georgie could make nothing of it whatever, and having observed
Robert hurry into his house again, went on his errand to Lucia. Had
he seen what Robert did when he got home, it is doubtful if he could
have avoided breaking into the house and snatching a copy of *Todd's
News* from him . . .

Robert went to his study, and locked the door. He drew out from
under his blotting-pad the first copy of *Todd's News* that he had
bought earlier in the morning, and put it with the rest. Then with a
furrowed brow he turned to the police-reports in *The Times* and
after looking at them laid the paper down. He did the same to the
Daily Telegraph, the *Daily Mail*, the *Morning Post*, the *Daily Chronicle*.
Finally (this was the last of the daily papers) he perused the *Daily
Mirror*, tore it in shreds, and said, 'Damn.'

He sat for a while in thought, trying to recollect if anybody in
Riseholme except Colonel Boucher took in the *Daily Mirror*. But he
felt morally certain that no one did, and letting himself out of his
study, and again locking the door after him, he went into the street,
and saw at a glance that the Colonel was employed in whirling Mrs
Weston round the green. Instead of joining them he hurried to the
Colonel's house and, for there was no time for half-measures, fixed
Atkinson with his eye, and said he would like to write a note to
Colonel Boucher. He was shown into his sitting-room, and saw the
Daily Mirror lying open on the table. As soon as he was left alone, he
stuffed it into his pocket, told Atkinson he would speak to the Colonel
instead, and intercepted the path of the bath-chair. He was nearly
run over, but stood his ground, and in a perfectly firm voice asked
the Colonel if there was any news in the morning papers. With the
Colonel's decided negative ringing joyfully in his ears, he went home
again, and locked himself for the second time into his study.

There is a luxury, when some fell danger has been averted by promptness and presence of mind, in living through the moments of that danger again, and Robert opened *Todd's News*, for that gave the fuller account, and read over the paragraph in the police news headed 'Bogus Russian Princess'. But now he gloated over the lines which had made him shudder before when he read how Marie Lowenstein, of 15 Gerald Street, Charing Cross Road, calling herself Princess Popoffski, had been brought up at the Bow Street Police Court for fraudulently professing to tell fortunes and produce materialised spirits at a séance in her flat. Sordid details followed: a detective who had been there seized an apparition by the throat, and turned on the electric light. It was the woman Popoffski's throat that he held, and her secretary, Hezekiah Schwarz, was discovered under the table detaching an electric hammer. A fine was inflicted . . .

A moment's mental debate was sufficient to determine Robert not to tell his wife. It was true that she had produced Popoffski, but then he had praised and applauded her for that; he, no less than she, had been convinced of Popoffski's integrity, high rank and marvellous psychic powers, and together they had soared to a pinnacle of unexampled greatness in the Riseholme world. Besides, poor Daisy would be simply flattened out if she knew that Popoffski was no better than the guru. He glanced at the pile of papers, and at the fireplace . . .

It had been a cold morning, clear and frosty, and a good blaze prospered in the grate. Out of each copy of *Todd's News* he tore the page on which were printed the police reports, and fed the fire with them. Page after page he put upon it; never had so much paper been devoted to one grate. Up the chimney they flew in sheets of flame; sometimes he was afraid he had set it on fire, and he had to pause, shielding his scorched face, until the hollow rumbling had died down. With the page from two copies of the *Daily Mirror* the holocaust was over, and he unlocked the door again. No one in Riseholme knew but he, and no one should ever know. Riseholme had been electrified by spiritualism, and even now the séances had been cheap at the price.

The debris of all these papers he caused to be removed by the housemaid, and this was hardly done when his wife came in from the green.

'I thought there was a chimney on fire, Robert,' she said. 'You would have liked it to be the kitchen chimney as you said the other day.'

'Stuff and nonsense, my dear,' said he. 'Lunchtime, isn't it?'

'Yes. Ah, there's the post. None for me, and two for you.'

She looked at him narrowly as he took his letters. Perhaps their subconscious minds (according to her dear friend's theory) held communication, but only the faintest unintelligible ripple of that appeared on the surface.

'I haven't heard from my Princess since she went away,' she remarked.

Robert gave a slight start; he was a little off his guard from the reaction after his anxiety.

'Indeed!' he said. 'Have you written to her?'

She appeared to try to remember.

'Well, I really don't believe I have,' she said. 'That is remiss of me. I must send her a long budget one of these days.'

This time he looked narrowly at her. Had she a secret, he wondered, as well as he? What could it be? . . .

*   *   *

Georgie found his mission none too easy, and it was only the thought that it was a labour of love, or something very like it, that enabled him to persevere. Even then for the first few minutes he thought it might prove love's labour's lost, so bright and unreal was Lucia.

He had half crossed Shakespeare's garden, and had clearly seen her standing at the window of the music-room, when she stole away, and next moment the strains of some slow movement, played very loud, drowned the bell on the mermaid's tail so completely that he wondered whether it had rung at all. As a matter of fact, Lucia and Peppino were in the midst of a most serious conversation when Georgie came through the gate, which was concerned with deciding what was to be done. A party at The Hurst sometime during Christmas week was as regular as the festival itself, but this year everything was so unusual. Who were to be asked in the first place? Certainly not Mrs Weston, for she had talked Italian to Lucia in a manner impossible to misinterpret, and probably, so said Lucia with great acidity, she would be playing children's games with her *promesso*. It was equally impossible to ask Miss Bracely and her husband, for relations were already severed on account of the Spanish Quartet and Signor Cortese, and as for the Quantocks, did Peppino expect Lucia to ask Mrs Quantock again ever? Then there was Georgie, who had become so different and strange, and . . . Well here was Georgie. Hastily she sat down at the piano, and Peppino closed his eyes for the slow movement.

The opening of the door was lost on Lucia, and Peppino's eyes were closed. Consequently Georgie sat down on the nearest chair, and waited. At the end Peppino sighed, and he sighed too.

'Who is that?' said Lucia sharply. 'Why, is it you, Georgie? What a stranger. Aren't you? Any news?'

This was all delivered in the coldest of tones, and Lucia snatched a morsel of wax off E flat.

'I've heard none,' said Georgie in great discomfort. 'I just dropped in.'

Lucia fixed Peppino with a glance. If she had shouted at the top of her voice she could not have conveyed more unmistakably that she was going to manage this situation.

'Ah, that is very pleasant,' she said. 'Peppino and I have been so busy lately that we have seen nobody. We are quite country-cousins, and so the town-mouse must spare us a little cheese. How is dear Miss Bracely now?'

'Very well,' said Georgie. 'I saw her this morning.'

Lucia gave a sigh of relief. 'That is good,' she said. 'Peppino, do you hear? Miss Bracely is quite well. Not overtired with practising that new opera? *Lucy Greecia*, was it? Oh, how silly I am! *Lucretia*; that was it, by that extraordinary Neapolitan. Yes. And what next? Our good Mrs Weston, now! Still thinking about her nice young man? Making orange-flower wreaths, and choosing bridesmaids? How naughty I am! Yes. And then dear Daisy? How is she? Still entertaining princesses? I look in the Court Circular every morning to see if Princess Pop – Pop – Popoff isn't it? if Princess Popoff has popped off to see her cousin the Czar again. Dear me!'

The amount of malice, envy and all uncharitableness which Lucia managed to put into this quite unrehearsed speech was positively amazing. She had not thought it over beforehand for a moment; it came out with the august spontaneity of lightning leaping from a cloud. Not till that moment had Georgie guessed at a tithe of all that Olga had felt so certain about, and a double emotion took hold of him. He was immensely sorry for Lucia, never having conjectured how she must have suffered before she attained to so superb a sourness, and he adored the intuition that had guessed it and wanted to sweeten it.

The outburst was not quite over yet, though Lucia felt distinctly better.

'And you, Georgie,' she said, 'though I'm sure we are such strangers that I ought to call you Mr Pillson, what have you been doing?

Playing Miss Bracely's accompaniments, and sewing wedding-dresses all day, and raising spooks all night? Yes.'

Lucia had caught this 'Yes' from Lady Ambermere, having found it peculiarly obnoxious. You laid down a proposition, or asked a question, and then confirmed it yourself.

'And Mr Cortese,' she said, 'is he still roaring out his marvellous English and Italian? Yes. What a full life you lead, Georgie. I suppose you have no time for your painting now.'

This was not a bow drawn at a venture, for she had seen Georgie come out of Old Place with his paintbox and drawing-board, but this direct attack on him did not lessen the power of the 'sweet charity' which had sent him here. He blew the bugle to rally all the good nature for which he was capable.

'No, I have been painting lately,' he said, 'at least I have been trying to. I'm doing a little sketch of Miss Bracely at her piano, which I want to give her on Christmas Day. But it's so difficult. I wish I had brought it round to ask your advice, but you would only have screamed with laughter at it. It's a dreadful failure: much worse than those I gave you for your birthdays. Fancy your keeping them still in your lovely music-room. Send them to the pantry, and I'll do something better for you next.'

Lucia, try as she might, could not help being rather touched by that. There they all were: 'Golden Autumn Woodland', 'Bleak December', 'Yellow Daffodils', and 'Roses of Summer' . . .

'Or have them blacked over by the boot-boy,' she said. 'Take them down, Georgie, and let me send them to be blacked.'

This was much better: there was playfulness behind the sarcasm now, which peeped out from it. He made the most of that.

'We'll do that presently,' he said. 'Just now I want to engage you and Peppino to dine with me on Christmas Day. Now don't be tarsome and say you're engaged. But one can never tell with you.'

'A party?' asked Lucia suspiciously.

'Well, I thought we would have just one of our old evenings together again,' said Georgie, feeling himself remarkably clever. 'We'll have the Quantocks, shan't we, and Colonel and Mrs Colonel, and you and Peppino, and me, and Mrs Rumbold? That'll make eight, which is more than Foljambe likes, but she must lump it. Mr Rumbold is always singing carols all Christmas evening with the choir, and she will be alone.'

'Ah, those carols,' said Lucia, wincing.

'I know: I will provide you with little wads of cotton-wool. Do come and we'll have just a party of eight. I've asked no one yet and perhaps nobody will come. I want you and Peppino, and the rest may come or stop away. Do say you approve.'

Lucia could not yield at once. She had to press her fingers to her forehead.

'So kind of you, Georgie,' she said, 'but I must think. Are we doing anything on Christmas night, *carrissimo*? Where's your engagement-book? Go and consult it.'

This was a grand manoeuvre, for hardly had Peppino left the room when she started up with a little scream and ran after him.

'Me so stupid,' she cried. 'Me put it in smoking-room, and poor *caro* will look for it ever so long. Back in minute, Georgino.'

Naturally this was perfectly clear to Georgie. She wanted to have a short private consultation with Peppino, and he waited rather hopefully for their return, for Peppino, he felt sure, was bored with this Achilles-attitude of sitting sulking in the tent. They came back wreathed in smiles, and instantly embarked on the question of what to do after dinner. No romps: certainly not, but why not the tableaux again? The question was still under debate when they went in to lunch. It was settled affirmatively during the macaroni, and Lucia said that they all wanted to work her to death, and so get rid of her. They had thought – she and Peppino – of having a little holiday on the Riviera, but anyhow they would put it off till after Christmas. Georgie's mouth was full of crashing toast at the moment, and he could only shake his head. But as soon as the toast could be swallowed, he made the usual reply with great fervour.

Georgie was hardly at all complacent when he walked home afterwards, and thought how extremely good-natured he had been, for he could not but feel that this marvellous forbearance was a sort of mistletoe growth on him, quite foreign really to his nature. Never before had Lucia showed so shrewish and venomous a temper; he had not thought her capable of it. For the gracious queen, there was substituted a snarling fishwife, but then as Georgie calmly pursued the pacific mission of comfort to which Olga had ordained him, how the fishwife's wrinkles had been smoothed out, and the asps withered from her tongue. Had his imagination ever pictured Lucia saying such things to him, it would have supplied him with no sequel but a complete severance of relations between them. Instead of that he had consulted her and truckled to her: truckled, yes, he had truckled, and he was astonished at himself. Why had he truckled? And the beautiful mouth and kindly eyes of Olga supplied the answer.

Certainly he must drop in at once, and tell her the result of the mission. Perhaps she would reward him by calling him a darling again. Really he deserved that she should say something nice to him.

It was a day of surprises for Georgie. He found Olga at home, and recounted, without losing any of the substance, the sarcasms of Lucia, and his own amazing tact and forbearance. He did not comment, he just narrated the facts in the vivid Riseholme manner, and waited for his reward.

Olga looked at him a moment in silence: then she deliberately wiped her eyes.

'Oh, poor Mrs Lucas,' she said. 'She must have been miserable to have behaved like that! I am so sorry. Now what else can you do, Georgie, to make her feel better?'

'I think I've done everything that could have been required of *me*,' said Georgie. 'It was all I could do to keep my temper at all. I will give my party at Christmas, because I promised you I would.'

'Oh, but it's ten days to Christmas yet,' said Olga. 'Can't you paint her portrait, and give it her for a present? Oh, I think you could, playing the "Moonlight Sonata".'

Georgie felt terribly inclined to be offended and tell Olga that she was tired of him; or to be dignified and say he was unusually busy. Never had he shown such forbearance towards downright rudeness as he had shown to Lucia, and though he had shown that for Olga's sake, she seemed to be without a single spark of gratitude, but continued to urge her request.

'Do paint a little picture of her,' she repeated. 'She would love it, and make it young and interesting. Think over it, anyhow: perhaps you'll think of something better than that. And now won't you go and secure all your guests for Christmas at once?'

Georgie turned to leave the room, but just as he got to the door she spoke again:

'I think you're a brick,' she said.

Somehow this undemonstrative expression of approval began to glow in Georgie's heart as he walked home. Apparently she took it for granted that he was going to behave with all the perfect tact and good-temper that he had shown. It did not surprise her in the least; she had almost forgotten to indicate that she had noticed it at all. And that, as he thought about it, seemed a far deeper compliment than if she had told him how wonderful he was. She took it for granted, no more nor less, that he would be kind and pleasant, whatever Lucia said. He had not fallen short of her standard . . .

Chapter Fifteen

Georgie's Christmas party had just taken its seats at his round rosewood table without a cloth, and he hoped that Foljambe would be quick with the champagne, because there had been rather a long wait before dinner, owing to Lucia and Peppino being late, and conversation had been a little jerky. Lucia, as usual, had sailed into the room, without a word of apology, for she was accustomed to come last when she went out to dinner, and on her arrival dinner was always announced immediately. The few seconds that intervened were employed by her in saying just one kind word to everybody. Tonight, however, these gratifying utterances had not been received with the gratified responses to which she was accustomed: there was a different atmosphere abroad, and it was as if she were no more than one-eighth of the entire party . . . But it would never do to hurry Foljambe, who was a little upset already by the fact of there being eight to dinner, which was two more than she approved of.

Lucia was on Georgie's right, Mrs Colonel, as she had decided to call herself, on his left. Next her was Peppino, then Mrs Quantock, then the Colonel, then Mrs Rumbold (who resembled a grey hungry mouse), and Mr Quantock completed the circle round to Lucia again. Everyone had a small bunch of violets in the napkin, but Lucia had the largest. She had also a footstool.

'Capital good soup,' remarked Mr Quantock. 'Can't get soup like this at home.'

There was dead silence. Why was there never a silence when Olga was there, wondered Georgie. It wasn't because she talked, she somehow caused other people to talk.

'Tommy Luton hasn't got measles,' said Mrs Weston. 'I always said he hadn't, though there are measles about. He came to walk as usual this morning, and is going to sing in the carols tonight.'

She suddenly stopped.

Georgie gave an imploring glance at Foljambe, and looked at the champagne glasses. She took no notice. Lucia turned to Georgie, with an elbow on the table between her and Mr Quantock.

'And what news, Georgie?' she said. 'Peppino and I have been so busy that we haven't seen a soul all day. What have you been doing? Any planchette?'

She looked brightly at Mrs Quantock.

'Yes, dear Daisy, I needn't ask you what you've been doing. Table-turning, I expect. I know how interested you are in psychical matters. I should be, too, if only I could be certain that I was not dealing with fraudulent people.'

Georgie felt inclined to give a hollow groan and sink under the table when this awful polemical rhetoric began. To his unbounded surprise Mrs Quantock answered most cordially.

'You are quite right, dear Lucia,' she said. 'Would it not be terrible to find that a medium, some dear friend perhaps, whom one implicitly trusted, was exposed as fraudulent? One sees such exposures in the paper sometimes. I should be miserable if I thought I had ever sat with a medium who was not honest. They fine the wretches well, though, if they are caught, and they deserve it.'

Georgie observed, and couldn't the least understand, a sudden blank expression cross Robert's face. For the moment he looked as if he were dead but had been beautifully stuffed. But Georgie gave but a cursory thought to that, for the amazing supposition dawned on him that Lucia had not been polemical at all, but was burying instead of chopping with the hatchet. It was instantly confirmed, for Lucia took her elbow off the table, and turned to Robert.

'You and dear Daisy have been very lucky in your spiritualistic experiences,' she said. 'I hear on all sides what a charming medium you had. Georgie quite lost his heart to her.'

' 'Pon my word; she was delightful,' said Robert. 'Of course she was a dear friend of Daisy's, but one has to be very careful when one hears of the dreadful exposures, as my wife said, that occur sometimes. Fancy finding that a medium whom you believed to be perfectly honest had yards and yards of muslin and a false nose or two concealed about her. It would sicken me of the whole business.'

A loud pop announced that Foljambe had allowed them all some champagne at last, but Georgie hardly heard it, for glancing up at Daisy Quantock, he observed that the same dead and stuffed look had come over her face which he had just now noticed on her husband's countenance. Then they both looked up at each other with a glance that to him bristled with significance. An agonised questioning, an imploring petition for silence seemed to inspire it; it was as if each had made unwittingly some hopeless *faux pas*. Then they instantly looked away from each other again; their necks seemed to crack with the rapidity with which they turned them right and left, and they burst into torrents of speech to the grey hungry mouse and the Colonel respectively.

Georgie was utterly mystified: his Riseholme instinct told him that there was something below all this, but his Riseholme instinct could not supply the faintest clue as to what it was. Both of the Quantocks, it seemed clear, knew something perilous about the Princess, but surely if Daisy had read in the paper that the Princess had been exposed and fined, she would not have touched on so dangerous a subject. Then the curious incident about *Todd's News* inevitably occurred to him, but that would not fit the case, since it was Robert and not Daisy who had bought that inexplicable number of the yellow print. And then Robert had hinted at the discovery of yards and yards of muslin and a false nose. Why had he done that unless he had discovered them, or unless . . . Georgie's eyes grew round with the excitement of the chase . . . unless Robert had some other reason to suspect the integrity of the dear friend, and had said this at haphazard. In that case what was Robert's reason for suspicion? Had *he*, not Daisy, read in the paper of some damaging disclosures, and had Daisy (also having reason to suspect the Princess) alluded to the damaging exposures in the paper by pure haphazard? Anyhow they had both looked dead and stuffed when the other alluded to mediumistic frauds, and both had said how lucky their own experiences had been. 'Oh!' – Georgie almost said it aloud – What if Robert had seen a damaging exposure in *Todd's News*, and therefore bought up every copy that was to be had? Then, indeed, he would look dead and stuffed, when Daisy alluded to damaging exposures in the paper. Had a stray copy escaped him, and did Daisy know? What did Robert know? Had they exquisite secrets from each other?

Lucia was being talked to across him by Mrs Weston, who had also pinned down the attention of Peppino on the other side of her. At that precise moment the flood of Mrs Quantock's spate of conversation to the Colonel dried up, and Robert could find nothing more to say to the hungry mouse. Georgie in this backwater of his own thoughts was whirled into the current again. But before he sank he caught Mrs Quantock's eye and put a question that arose from his exciting backwater.

'Have you heard from the Princess lately?' he asked.

Robert's head went round with the same alacrity as he had turned it away.

'Oh, yes,' said she. 'Two days ago was it, Robert?'

'I heard yesterday,' said Robert firmly.

Mrs Quantock looked at her husband with an eager encouraging earnestness.

'So you did!' she said. 'I'm getting jealous. Interesting, dear?'

'Yes, dear, haw, haw,' said Robert, and again their eyes met.

This time Georgie had no doubts at all. They were playing the same game now: they smiled and smirked at each other. They had not been playing the same game before. Now they recognised that there was a conspiracy between them . . . But he was host; his business for the moment was to make his guests comfortable, and not pry into their inmost bosoms. So before Mrs Weston realised that she had the whole table attending to her, he said:

'I shall get it out of Robert after dinner. And I'll tell you, Mrs Quantock.'

'Before Atkinson came to the Colonel,' said Mrs Weston, going on precisely where she had left off, 'and that was five years before Elizabeth came to me – let me see – was it five or was it four and a half? – four and a half we'll say, he had another servant whose name was Ahab Crowe.'

'No!' said Georgie.

'Yes!' said Mrs Weston, hastily finishing her champagne, for she saw Foljambe coming near – 'Yes, Ahab Crowe. He married, too, just like Atkinson is going to, and that's an odd coincidence in itself. I tell the Colonel that if Ahab Crowe hadn't married, he would be with him still, and who can say that he'd have fancied Elizabeth? And if he hadn't, I don't believe that the Colonel and I would ever have – well, I'll leave that alone, and spare my blushes. But that's not what I was saying. Whom do you think Ahab Crowe married? You can have ten guesses each, and you would never come right, for it can't be a common name. It was Miss Jackdaw. Crowe, Jackdaw. I never heard anything like that, and if you ask the Colonel about it, he'll confirm every word I've said. Boucher, Weston: why that's quite commonplace in comparison, and I'm sure that's an event enough for me.'

Lucia gave her silvery laugh.

'Dear Mrs Weston,' she said, 'you must really tell me at once when the happy day will be. Peppino and I are thinking of going to the Riviera – '

Georgie broke in.

'You shan't do anything of the kind,' he said. 'What's to happen to us? 'Oo very selfish, Lucia.'

The conversation broke up again into duets and trios, and Lucia could have a private conversation with her host. But half an hour ago, so Georgie reflected, they had all been walking round each other like dogs going on tiptoe with their tails very tightly curled, and growling gently to themselves, aware that a hasty snap, or the breach of the smallest observance of etiquette, might lead to a general quarrel. But now they all had the reward of their icy politenesses: there was no more ice, except on their plates, and the politeness was not a matter of etiquette. At present, they might be considered a republic, but no one knew what was going to happen after dinner. Not a word had been said about the tableaux.

Lucia dropped her voice as she spoke to him, and put in a good deal of Italian for fear she might be overheard.

'*Non cognosce* anybody?' she asked. '*I tablini*, I mean. And are we all to sit in the *aula*, while the *salone* is being got ready?'

'*Si*,' said Georgie. 'There's a fire. When you go out, keep them there. *I domestichi* are making *salone* ready.'

'*Molto bene*. Then Peppino and you and I just steal away. *La lampa* is acting beautifully. We tried it over several times.'

'Everybody's tummin',' said Georgie, varying the cipher.

'Me so *nervosa*!' said Lucia. 'Fancy me doing Brünnhilde before opera-Brünnhilde. Me can't bear it.'

Georgie knew that Lucia had been thrilled and delighted to know that Olga so much wanted to come in after dinner and see the tableaux, so he found it quite easy to induce Lucia to nerve herself up to an ordeal so passionately desired. Indeed he himself was hardly less excited at the thought of being King Cophetua.

At that moment, even as the crackers were being handed round, the sound of the carol-singers was heard from outside, and Lucia had to wince, as 'Good King Wenceslas' looked out. When the Page and the King sang their speeches, the other voices grew *piano*, so that the effect was of a solo voice accompanied. When the Page sang, Lucia shuddered.

'That's the small red-haired boy who nearly deafens me in church,' she whispered to Georgie. 'Don't you hope his voice will crack soon?'

She said this very discreetly, so as not to hurt Mrs Rumbold's feelings, for she trained the choir. Everyone knew that the King was Mr Rumbold, and said 'Charming' to each other, after he had sung.

'I liked that boy's voice, too,' said Mrs Weston. 'Tommy Luton used to have a lovely voice, but this one's struck me as better-trained even than Tommy Luton's. Great credit to you, Mrs Rumbold.'

The grey hungry mouse suddenly gave a shrill cackle of a laugh, quite inexplicable. Then Georgie guessed.

He got up.

'Now nobody must move,' he said, 'because we haven't drunk

"absent friends" yet. I'm just going out to see that they have a bit of supper in the kitchen before they go on.'

His trembling legs would scarcely carry him to the door, and he ran out. There were half a dozen little choirboys, four men and one tall cloaked woman . . .

'Divine!' he said to Olga. 'Aunt Jane thought your voice very well trained. Come in soon, won't you?'

'Yes: all flourishing?'

'Swimming,' said Georgie. 'Lucia hoped your voice would crack soon. But it's all being lovely.'

He explained about food in the kitchen and hurried back to his guests. There was the riddle of the Quantocks to solve: there were the *tableaux vivants* imminent: there was the little red-haired boy coming in soon. What a Christmas night!

*   *   *

Soon after Georgie's hall began to fill up with guests, and yet not a word was said about tableaux. It grew so full that nobody could have said for certain whether Lucia and Peppino were there or not. Olga certainly was: there was no mistaking that fact. And then Foljambe opened the drawing-room door and sounded a gong.

The lamp behaved perfectly and an hour later one Brünnhilde was being extremely kind to the other, as they sat together. 'If you really want to know my view, dear Miss Bracely,' said Lucia, 'it's just that. You must be Brünnhilde for the time being. Singing, of course, as you say, helps it out: you can express so much by singing. You are so lucky there. I am bound to say I had qualms when Peppino – or was it Georgie – suggested we should do Brünnhilde and Siegfried. I said it would be so terribly difficult. Slow: it has to be slow, and to keep gestures slow when you cannot make them mere illustrations of what you are singing – well, I am sure, it is very kind of you to be so flattering about it – but it is difficult to do that.'

'And you thought them all out for yourself?' said Olga. 'Marvellous!'

'Ah, if I had ever seen you do it,' said Lucia, 'I am sure I should have picked up some hints! And King Cophetua! Won't you give me a little word for our dear King Cophetua? I was so glad after the strain of Brünnhilde to have my back to the audience. Even then there is the difficulty of keeping quite still, but I am sure you know that quite as well as I do, from having played Brünnhilde yourself. Georgie was very much impressed by your performance of it. And

Mary Queen of Scots now! The shrinking of the flesh, and the resignation of the spirit! That is what I tried to express. You must come and help me next time I attempt this sort of thing again. That will not be quite soon, I am afraid, for Peppino and I are thinking of going to the Riviera for a little holiday.'

'Oh, but how selfish!' said Olga. 'You mustn't do that.'

Lucia gave the silvery laugh.

'You are all very tiresome about my going to the Riviera,' she said. 'But I don't promise that I shall give it up yet. We shall see! Gracious! How late it is. We must have sat very late over dinner. Why were you not asked to dinner, I wonder! I shall scold Georgie for not asking you. Ah, there is dear Mrs Weston going away. I must say good-night to her. She would think it very strange if I did not. Colonel Boucher, too! Oh, they are coming this way to save us the trouble of moving.'

A general move was certainly taking place, not in the direction of the door, but to where Olga and Lucia were sitting.

'It's snowing,' said Piggy excitedly to Olga. 'Will you mark my footsteps well, my page?'

'Piggy, you – you Goosie,' said Olga hurriedly. 'Goosie, weren't the tableaux lovely?'

'And the carols,' said Goosie. 'I adored the carols. I guessed. Did you guess, Mrs Lucas?'

Olga resorted to the mean trick of treading on Goosie's foot and apologising. That was cowardly because it was sure to come out sometime. And Goosie again trod on dangerous ground by saying that if the Page had trod like that, there was no need for any footsteps to be marked for him.

*   *   *

It was snowing fast, and Mrs Weston's wheels left a deep track, but in spite of that, Daisy and Robert had not gone fifty yards from the door when they came to a full stop.

'Now, what is it?' said Daisy. 'Out with it. Why did you talk about the discovery of muslin?'

'I only said that we were fortunate in a medium whom after all you picked up at a vegetarian restaurant,' said he. 'I suppose I may indulge in general conversation. If it comes to that, why did you talk about exposure in the papers?'

'General conversation,' said Mrs Quantock all in one word. 'So that's all, is it?'

'Yes,' said Robert, 'you may know something, and – '

'Now don't put it all on me,' said Daisy. 'If you want to know what I think, it is that you've got some secret.'

'And if you want to know what I think,' he retorted, 'it is that I know you have.'

Daisy hesitated a moment; the snow was white on her shoulder and she shook her cloak.

'I hate concealment,' she said. 'I found yards and yards of muslin and a pair of Amadeo's eyebrows in that woman's bedroom the very day she went away.'

'And she was fined last Thursday for holding a séance at which a detective was present,' said Robert. 'Fifteen, Gerard Street. He seized Amadeo or Cardinal Newman by the throat, and it was that woman.'

She looked hastily round.

'When you thought that the chimney was on fire, I was burning muslin,' she said.

'When you thought the chimney was on fire, I was burning every copy of *Todd's News*,' said he. 'Also a copy of the *Daily Mirror*, which contained the case. It belonged to the Colonel. I stole it.'

She put her hand through his arm.

'Let's get home,' she said. 'We must talk it over. No one knows one word except you and me?'

'Not one, my dear,' said Robert cordially. 'But there are suspicions. Georgie suspects, for instance. He saw me buy all the copies of *Todd's News*, at least he was hanging about. Tonight he was clearly on the track of something, though he gave us a very tolerable dinner.'

They went into Robert's study: it was cold, but neither felt it, for they glowed with excitement and enterprise.

'That was a wonderful stroke of yours, Robert,' said she. 'It was masterly: it saved the situation. The *Daily Mirror*, too: how right you were to steal it. A horrid paper I always thought. Yes, Georgie suspects something, but luckily he doesn't know what he suspects.'

'That's why we both said we had just heard from that woman,' said Robert.

'Of course. You haven't got a copy of *Todd's News*, have you?'

'No: at least I burned every page of the police reports,' said he. 'It was safer.'

'Quite so. I cannot show you Amadeo's eyebrows for the same reason. Nor the muslin. Lovely muslin, my dear: yards of it. Now what we must do is this: we must continue to be interested in psychical things; we mustn't drop them, or seem to be put off them. I wish now I had taken you into my confidence at the beginning and told you about Amadeo's eyebrows.'

'My dear, you acted for the best,' said he. 'So did I when I didn't tell you about *Todd's News*. Secrecy even from each other was more prudent, until it became impossible. And I think we should be wise to let it be understood that we hear from the Princess now and then. Perhaps in a few months she might even visit us again. It – it would be humorous to be behind the scenes, so to speak, and observe the credulity of the others.'

Daisy broke into a broad grin.

'I will certainly ask dear Lucia to a séance, if we do,' she said. 'Dear me! How late it is: there was such a long wait between the tableaux. But we must keep our eyes on Georgie, and be careful how we answer his impertinent questions. He is sure to ask some. About getting that woman down again, Robert. It might be foolhardy, for we've had an escape, and shouldn't put our heads into the same noose again. On the other hand, it would disarm suspicion for ever, if, after a few months, I asked her to spend a few days of holiday here. You said it was a fine only, not imprisonment?'

The week was a busy one: Georgie in particular never had a moment to himself. The Hurst, so lately a desert, suddenly began to rejoice with joy and singing and broke out into all manner of edifying gaieties. Lucia, capricious queen, quite forgot all the vitriolic things she had said to him, and gave him to understand that he was just as high in favour as ever before, and he was as busy with his duties as ever he had been. Whether he would have fallen into his old place so readily if he had been a free agent, was a question that did not arise, for though it was Lucia who employed him, it was Olga who drove him there. But he had his consolation, for Lucia's noble forgiveness of all the disloyalties against her, included Olga's as well, and out of all the dinners and music parties, and recitations from Peppino's new book of prose-poems which was already in proof, and was read to select audiences from end to end, there was none to which Olga was not bidden, and none at which she failed to appear. Lucia even overlooked the fact that she had sung in the carols on Christmas night, though she had herself declared that it was the voice of the red-haired boy which was so peculiarly painful to her. Georgie's picture of her (she never knew that Olga had really commissioned it) hung at the side of the piano in the music-room, where the print of Beethoven had hung before, and it gave her the acutest gratification. It represented her sitting, with eyes cast down at her piano, and was indeed much on the same scheme as the yet unfinished one of Olga, which had been postponed in its favour, but there was no time for Georgie to think out another position, and his hand was in with regard to the perspective of pianos. So there it hung with its title, 'The Moonlight Sonata', painted in gilt letters on its frame, and Lucia, though she continued to say that he had made her far, far too young, could not but consider that he had caught her expression exactly . . .

So Riseholme flocked back to The Hurst like sheep that have been astray, for it was certain to find Olga there, even as it had turned there, deeply breathing, to the classes of the guru. It had to sit through the prose-poems of Peppino, it had to listen to the old, old tunes and sigh at the end, but Olga mingled her sighs with theirs, and often after a suitable pause Lucia would say winningly to Olga: 'One little song, Miss Bracely. Just a stanza? Or am I trespassing too much on your good nature? Where is your accompanist? I declare I am jealous of him: I shall pop into his place someday! Georgino, Miss Bracely is going to sing us something. Is not that a treat? Sh-sh, please, ladies and gentlemen.'

And she rustled to her place, and sat with the farthest-away expression ever seen on mortal face, while she trespassed on Miss Bracely's good nature.

*   *   *

Then Georgie had the other picture to finish, which he hoped to get ready in time to be a New Year's present, since Olga had insisted on Lucia's being done first. He had certainly secured an admirable likeness of her, and there was in it just all that his stippled, fussy representation of Lucia lacked. 'Bleak December' and 'Yellow Daffodils' and the rest of the series lacked it, too: for once he had done something in the doing of which he had forgotten himself. It was by no means a work of genius, for Georgie was not possessed of one grain of that, and the talent it displayed was by no means of a high order, but it had something of the naturalness of a flower that grew from the earth which nourished it.

On the last day of the year he was putting a few final touches to it, little high reflected lights on the black keys, little blacknesses of shadow in the moulding of the panel behind his hand. He had finished with her altogether, and now she sat in the window seat, looking out, and playing with the blind-tassel. He had been so much absorbed in his work that he had scarcely noticed that she had been rather unusually silent.

'I've got a piece of news for you,' she said at length.

Georgie held his breath, as he drew a very thin line of body-colour along the edge of A flat.

'No! What is it?' he said. 'Is it about the Princess?'

Olga seemed to hail this as a diversion.

'Ah, let's talk about that for a minute,' she said. 'What you ought to have done was to order another copy of *Todd's News* at once.'

'I know I ought, but I couldn't get one when I thought of it afterwards. That was tarsome. But I feel sure there was something about her in it.'

'And you can't get anything out of the Quantocks?'

'No, though I've laid plenty of traps for them. There's an understanding between them now. They both know something. When I lay a trap, it isn't any use: they look at the trap, and then they look at each other afterwards.'

'What sort of traps?'

'Oh, anything. I say suddenly, "What a bore it is that there are so many frauds among mediums, especially paid ones." You see, I don't believe for a moment that these séances were held for nothing, though we didn't pay for going to them. And then Robert says that he would never trust a paid medium, and she looks at him approvingly, and says "Dear Princess!" The other day – it was a very good trap – I said, "Is it true that the Princess is coming to stay with Lady Ambermere?" It wasn't a lie: I only asked.'

'And then?' said Olga.

'Robert gave an awful twitch, not a jump exactly, but a twitch. But she was on the spot and said, "Ah, that would be nice. I wonder if it's true. The Princess didn't mention it in her last letter." And then he looked at her approvingly. There is something there, no one shall convince me otherwise.'

Olga suddenly burst out laughing.

'What's the matter?' asked Georgie.

'Oh, it's all so delicious!' she said. 'I never knew before how terribly interesting little things were. It's all wildly exciting, and there are fifty things going on just as exciting. Is it all of you who take such a tremendous interest in them that makes them so absorbing, or is it that they are absorbing in themselves, and ordinary dull people, not Riseholmites, don't see how exciting they are? Tommy Luton's measles: the Quantocks' secret: Elizabeth's lover! And to think that I believed I was coming to a backwater.'

Georgie held up his picture and half closed his eyes. 'I believe it's finished,' he said. 'I shall have it framed, and put it in my drawing-room.'

This was a trap, and Olga fell into it.

'Yes, it will look nice there,' she said. 'Really, Georgie, it is very clever of you.'

He began washing his brushes.

'And what was your news?' he said.

She got up from her seat.

'I forgot all about it, with talking of the Quantocks' secret,' she said. 'That just shows you: I completely forgot, Georgie. I've just accepted an offer to sing in America, a four months' engagement, at fifty thousand million pounds a night. A penny less, and I wouldn't have gone. But I really can't refuse. It's all been very sudden, but they want to produce *Lucretia* there before it appears in England. Then I come back, and sing in London all the summer. Oh, me!'

There was dead silence, while Georgie dried his brushes.

'When do you go?' he asked.

'In about a fortnight.'

'Oh,' said he.

She moved down the room to the piano and shut it without speaking, while he folded the paper round his finished picture.

'Why don't you come, too?' she said at length. 'It would do you no end of good, for you would get out of this darling twopenny place which will all go inside a nutshell. There are big things in the world, Georgie: seas, continents, people, movements, emotions. I told my Georgie I was going to ask you, and he thoroughly approves. We both like you, you know. It would be lovely if you would come. Come for a couple of months, anyhow: of course you'll be our guest, please.'

The world, at that moment, had grown absolutely black to him, and it was by that that he knew who, for him, was the light of it. He shook his head.

'Why can't you come?' she said.

He looked at her straight in the face.

'Because I adore you,' he said.

Epilogue or Preface

The glad word went round Riseholme one March morning that the earliest flower in Perdita's garden was in bloom. The day was one of those glories of the English springtime, with large white clouds blown across wide spaces of blue sky by the south-west wind, and with swift shadows that bowled across the green below them. Parliament was in full conclave that day, and in the elms the rooks were busy.

An awful flatness had succeeded Olga's departure. Riseholme naturally took a good deal of credit for the tremendous success which had attended the production of *Lucretia*, since it so rightly considered that the real cradle of the opera was here, where she had tried it over for the first time. Lucia seemed to remember it better than anybody, for she remembered all sorts of things which no one else had the faintest recollection of: how she had discussed music with Signor Cortese, and he had asked her where she had her musical training. Such a treat to talk Italian with a Roman – *lingua Toscana in bocca Romana* – and what a wonderful evening it was. Poor Mrs Colonel recollected very little of this, but Lucia had long been aware that her memory was going sadly. After producing *Lucretia* in New York, Olga had appeared in some of her old roles, notably in the part of Brünnhilde, and Lucia was very reminiscent of that charming party of Christmas Day at dear Georgino's, when they had the tableaux. Dear Olga was so simple and unspoiled: she had come to Lucia afterwards, and asked her to tell her how she had worked out her scheme of gestures in the awakening, and Lucia had been very glad, very glad indeed to give her a few hints. In fact, Lucia was quite herself: it was only her subjects whom it had been a little hard to stir up. Georgie in particular had been very listless and dull, and Lucia, for all her ingenuity, was at a complete loss to find a reason for it.

But today the warm inflowing tide of spring seemed to renovate the muddy flats, setting the weeds, that had lain dank and dispirited, a-floating again on the return of the water. No one could quite resist the magic of the season, and Georgie, who had intended out of mere politeness to go to see the earliest of Perdita's stupid flowers (having been warned of its epiphany by telephone from The Hurst) found, when he set foot outside his house on that warm windy morning, that it would be interesting to stroll across the green first, and see if there was any news. All the news he had really cared about for the last two months was news from America, of which he had a small packet done up in a pink riband.

After getting rid of Piggy, he went to the newspaper-shop, to get his *Times*, which most unaccountably had not arrived, and the sight of *Todd's News* in its yellow cover stirred his drowsy interest. Not one atom of light had ever been thrown on that extraordinary occurrence when Robert bought the whole issue, and though Olga never failed to enquire, he had not been able to give her the slightest additional information. Occasionally he set a languid trap for one of the Quantocks, but they never by any chance fell into it. The whole affair must be classed with problems like the origin of evil, among the insoluble mysteries of life.

It was possible to get letters by the second post an hour earlier than the house-to-house delivery by calling at the office, and as Georgie was waiting for his *Times*, Mrs Quantock came hurrying out of the post-office with a small packet in her hands, which she was opening as she walked. She was so much absorbed by this that she did not see Georgie at all, though she passed quite close to him, and soon after shed a registered envelope. At that the 'old familiar glamour' began to steal over him again, and he found himself wondering with intensity what it contained.

She was now some hundred yards in front of him, walking in the direction of The Hurst, and there could be no doubt that she, too, was on her way to see Perdita's first flower. He followed her going more briskly than she and began to catch her up. Soon (this time by accident, not in the manner in which, through eagerness, she had untidily cast the registered envelope away) she dropped a small paper, and Georgie picked it up, meaning to give it her. It had printed matter on the front of it, and was clearly a small pamphlet. He could not possibly help seeing what that printed matter was, for it was in capital letters:

INCREASE YOUR HEIGHT

Georgie quickened his step, and the old familiar glamour brightened round him. As soon as he got within speaking distance, he called to her, and turning round, 'like a guilty thing surprised', a little box flew out of her hand. As it fell the lid came off, and there was scattered on the green grass a multitude of red lozenges. She gave a cry of dismay.

'Oh! Mr Georgie, how you startled me,' she said. 'Do help me to pick them up. Do you think the damp will have hurt them? Any news? I was so wrapped up in what I was doing that I've spoken to nobody.'

Georgie assisted in the recovery of the red lozenges.

'You dropped this as you walked,' he said. 'I picked it up in order to give it you.'

'Ah, that is kind, and did you see what it was?'

'I couldn't help seeing the outside,' said Georgie.

She looked at him a moment, wondering what was the most prudent course. If she said nothing more, he would probably tell everybody . . .

'Well, then, I shall let you into the whole secret,' she said. 'It's the most wonderful invention, and increases your height, whatever your age is, from two to six inches. Fancy! There are some exercises you have to do, rather like those Yoga ones, every morning, and you eat three lozenges a day. Quite harmless they are, and then you soon begin to shoot up. It sounds incredible, doesn't it? but there are so many testimonials that I can't doubt it is genuine. Here's one of a man who grew six inches. I saw it advertised in some paper, and sent for it. Only a guinea! What fun when Robert begins to see that I am taller than he is! But now not a word! Don't tell dear Lucia whatever you do. She is half a head taller than I, and it would be no fun if everybody grew from two to six inches. You may write for them, and I'll give you the address, but you must tell nobody.'

'Too wonderful,' said Georgie. 'I shall watch you. Here we are. Look, there's Perdita's flower. What a beauty!'

It was not necessary to press the mermaid's tail, for Lucia had seen them from the music-room, and they heard her high heels clacking over the polished floor of the hall.

'Listen! No more need of high heels!' said Mrs Quantock. 'And I've got something else to tell you. Lucia may hear that. Ah, dear Lucia, what a wonderful Perdita-blossom!'

'Is it not?' said Lucia, blowing kisses to Georgie, and giving them to Daisy. 'That shows spring is here. *Primavera!* And Peppino's *piccolo libro* comes out today. I should not be a bit surprised if you each of you found a copy of it arrived before evening. Glorious! It's glorious!'

Surely it was no wonder that Georgie's blood began to canter along his arteries again. There had been very pleasant exciting years before now, requiring for their fuel no more than was ready at this moment to keep up the fire. Mrs Quantock was on tiptoe, so to speak, to increase her height, Peppino was just delivered of a second of these vellum volumes with seals and tapes outside, Mrs Weston was going to become Mrs Colonel at the end of the week, and at the same hour and church Elizabeth was going to become Mrs Atkinson. Had these things no savour, because –

'How is 'oo?' said Georgie, with a sudden flush of the springtime through him. 'Me vewy well, sank 'oo and me so want to read Peppino's bookie-bookie.'

' 'Oo come in,' said Lucia. 'Evewybody come in. Now, who's got ickle bit news?'

Mrs Quantock had been walking on her toes all across the hall, in anticipation of the happy time when she would be from two to six inches taller. As the animated pamphlet said, the world assumed a totally different aspect when you were even two inches taller. She was quite sorry to sit down.

'Is next week very full with you, dear Lucia?' she asked.

Lucia pressed her finger to her forehead.

'Monday, Tuesday, Wednesday,' she began. 'No, not Tuesday, I am doing nothing on Tuesday. You want to be the death of me between you. Why?'

'I hope that my dear friend, Princess Popoffski, will be staying with me,' said Mrs Quantock. 'Do get over your prejudice against spiritualism, and give it a chance. Come to a séance on Tuesday. You, too, of course, Georgie: I know better than to invite Lucia without you.'

Lucia put on the faraway look which she reserved for the master-pieces of music, and for Georgie's hopeless devotion.

'Lovely! That will be lovely!' she said. 'Most interesting! I shall come with a perfectly open mind.'

Georgie scarcely lamented the annihilation of a mystery. He must surely have imagined the mystery, for it all collapsed like a card-house, if the Princess was coming back. The séances had been most remarkable, too; and he would have to get out his planchette again.

'And what's going to happen on Wednesday?' he asked Lucia. 'All I know is that I've not been asked. Me's offended.'

'Ickle surprise,' said Lucia. 'You're not engaged that evening, are you? Nor you, dear Daisy? That's lovely. Eight o'clock? No, I think a quarter to. That will give us more time. I shan't tell you what it is.'

Mrs Quantock, grasping her lozenges, wondered how much taller she would be by then. As Lucia played to them, she drew a lozenge out of the box and put it into her mouth, in order to begin growing at once. It tasted rather bitter, but not unpleasantly so.

MISS MAPP

Preface

I lingered at the window of the garden-room from which Miss Mapp so often and so ominously looked forth. To the left was the front of her house, straight ahead the steep cobbled way, with a glimpse of the High Street at the end, to the right the crooked chimney and the church.

The street was populous with passengers, but search as I might, I could see none who ever so remotely resembled the objects of her vigilance.

E. F. BENSON
Lamb House, Rye

Chapter One

MISS ELIZABETH MAPP might have been forty, and she had taken advantage of this opportunity by being just a year or two older. Her face was of high vivid colour and was corrugated by chronic rage and curiosity; but these vivifying emotions had preserved to her an astonishing activity of mind and body, which fully accounted for the comparative adolescence with which she would have been credited anywhere except in the charming little town which she had inhabited so long. Anger and the gravest suspicions about everybody had kept her young and on the boil.

She sat, on this hot July morning, like a large bird of prey at the very convenient window of her garden-room, the ample bow of which formed a strategical point of high value. This garden-room, solid and spacious, was built at right angles to the front of her house, and looked straight down the very interesting street which debouched at its lower end into the High Street of Tilling. Exactly opposite her front door the road turned sharply, so that as she looked out from this projecting window, her own house was at right angles on her left, the street in question plunged steeply downwards in front of her, and to her right she commanded an uninterrupted view of its further course which terminated in the disused graveyard surrounding the big Norman church. Anything of interest about the church, however, could be gleaned from a guidebook, and Miss Mapp did not occupy herself much with such coldly venerable topics. Far more to her mind was the fact that between the church and her strategic window was the cottage in which her gardener lived, and she could thus see, when not otherwise engaged, whether he went home before twelve, or failed to get back to her garden again by one, for he had to cross the street in front of her very eyes. Similarly she could observe whether any of his abandoned family ever came out from her garden door weighted with suspicious baskets, which might contain smuggled vegetables. Only yesterday morning she had hurried forth with a dangerous smile to intercept a laden urchin, with enquiries as to what was in 'that nice basket'. On that occasion that nice basket had proved to contain a strawberry net which was being sent for repair to the gardener's wife; so there was nothing more to be done except verify its return. This she did from a side window of the garden-room which commanded the strawberry beds; she could sit quite close to that, for it was screened by the large-leaved branches of a fig tree and she could spy unseen.

Otherwise this road to the right leading up to the church was of no great importance (except on Sunday morning, when she could get a practically complete list of those who attended Divine Service), for no one of real interest lived in the humble dwellings which lined it. To the left was the front of her own house at right angles to the strategic window, and with regard to that a good many useful observations might be, and were, made. She could, from behind a curtain negligently half-drawn across the side of the window nearest the house, have an eye on her housemaid at work, and notice if she leaned out of a window, or made remarks to a friend passing in the street, or waved salutations with a duster. Swift upon such discoveries, she would execute a flank march across the few steps of garden and steal into the house, noiselessly ascend the stairs, and catch the offender red-handed at this public dalliance. But all such domestic espionage to right and left was flavourless and insipid compared to the tremendous discoveries which daily and hourly awaited the trained observer of the street that lay directly in front of her window.

There was little that concerned the social movements of Tilling that could not be proved, or at least reasonably conjectured, from Miss Mapp's eyrie. Just below her house on the left stood Major Flint's residence, of Georgian red brick like her own, and opposite was that of Captain Puffin. They were both bachelors, though Major Flint was generally supposed to have been the hero of some amazingly amorous adventures in early life, and always turned the subject with great abruptness when anything connected with duelling was mentioned. It was not, therefore, unreasonable to infer that he had had experiences of a bloody sort, and colour was added to this romantic conjecture by the fact that in damp, rheumatic weather his left arm was very stiff, and he had been known to say that his wound troubled him. What wound that was no one exactly knew (it might have been anything from a vaccination mark to a sabre-cut), for having said that his wound troubled him, he would invariably add: 'Pshaw! that's enough about an old campaigner'; and though he might subsequently talk of nothing else except the old campaigner, he drew a veil over his old campaigns. That he had seen service in India was, indeed, probable by his referring to lunch as tiffin, and calling to his parlour-maid with the ejaculation of '*Quai-hai*'. As her name was Sarah, this was clearly a reminiscence of days in bungalows. When not in a rage, his manner to his own sex was bluff and hearty; but whether in a rage or not, his manner to the fairies, or lovely woman, was gallant and pompous in the extreme. He certainly had a lock of hair in a small gold specimen case on his watch-chain, and had been seen to kiss it when, rather carelessly, he thought that he was unobserved.

Miss Mapp's eye, as she took her seat in her window on this sunny July morning, lingered for a moment on the Major's house, before she proceeded to give a disgusted glance at the pictures on the back page of her morning illustrated paper, which chiefly represented young women dancing in rings in the surf, or lying on the beach in attitudes which Miss Mapp would have scorned to adjust herself to. Neither the Major nor Captain Puffin were very early risers, but it was about time that the first signals of animation might be expected. Indeed, at this moment, she quite distinctly heard that muffled roar which to her experienced ear was easily interpreted to be '*Quai-hai!*'

'So the Major has just come down to breakfast,' she mechanically inferred, 'and it's close on ten o'clock. Let me see: Tuesday, Thursday, Saturday – Porridge morning.'

Her penetrating glance shifted to the house exactly opposite to that in which it was porridge morning, and even as she looked a hand was thrust out of a small upper window and deposited a sponge on the sill. Then from the inside the lower sash was thrust firmly down, so as to prevent the sponge from blowing away and falling into the street. Captain Puffin, it was therefore clear, was a little later than the Major that morning. But he always shaved and brushed his teeth before his bath, so that there was but a few minutes between them.

General manoeuvres in Tilling, the gradual burstings of fluttering life from the chrysalis of the night, the emergence of the ladies of the town with their wicker baskets in their hands for housekeeping purchases, the exodus of men to catch the 11.20 a.m. steam-tram out to the golf links, and other first steps in the duties and diversions of the day, did not get into full swing till half-past ten, and Miss Mapp had ample time to skim the headlines of her paper and indulge in chaste meditations about the occupants of these two houses, before she need really make herself alert to miss nothing. Of the two, Major Flint, without doubt, was the more attractive to the feminine sense; for years Miss Mapp had tried to cajole him into marrying her, and had not nearly finished yet. With his record of adventure, with the romantic reek of India (and camphor) in the tiger-skin of the rugs

that strewed his hall and surged like a rising tide up the wall, with his
haughty and gallant manner, with his loud pshawings and sniffs at
'nonsense and balderdash', his thumpings on the table to emphasise
an argument, with his wound and his prodigious swipes at golf, his
intolerance of any who believed in ghosts, microbes or vegetarianism,
there was something dashing and risky about him; you felt that you
were in the presence of some hot coal straight from the furnace of
creation. Captain Puffin, on the other hand, was of clay so different
that he could hardly be considered to be made of clay at all. He was
lame and short and meagre, with strings of peaceful beads and Papuan
aprons in his hall instead of wild tiger-skins, and had a jerky, in-
attentive manner and a high-pitched voice. Yet to Miss Mapp's
mind there was something behind his unimpressiveness that had a
mysterious quality – all the more so, because nothing of it appeared
on the surface. Nobody could call Major Flint, with his bawlings and
his sniffings, the least mysterious. He laid all his loud cards on the
table, great hulking kings and aces. But Miss Mapp felt far from sure
that Captain Puffin did not hold a joker which would some time
come to light. The idea of being Mrs Puffin was not so attractive as
the other, but she occasionally gave it her remote consideration.

Yet there was mystery about them both, in spite of the fact that
most of their movements were so amply accounted for. As a rule,
they played golf together in the morning, reposed in the afternoon,
as could easily be verified by anyone standing on a still day in the
road between their houses and listening to the loud and rhythmical
breathings that fanned the tranquil air, certainly went out to tea-
parties afterwards and played bridge till dinner-time; or if no such
entertainment was proffered them, occupied armchairs at the county
club, or laboriously amassed a hundred at billiards. Though tea-
parties were profuse, dining out was very rare at Tilling; Patience or
a jig-saw puzzle occupied the hour or two that intervened between
domestic supper and bedtime; but again and again, Miss Mapp had
seen lights burning in the sitting-room of those two neighbours at
an hour when such lights as were still in evidence at Tilling were
strictly confined to bedrooms, and should, indeed, have been extinguished there. And only last week, being plucked from slumber by
some unaccountable indigestion (for which she blamed a small green
apple), she had seen at no less than twelve-thirty in the morning the
lights in Captain Puffin's sitting-room still shining through the blind.
This had excited her so much that at risk of toppling into the street,
she had craned her neck from her window, and observed a similar

illumination in the house of Major Flint. They were not together then, for in that case any prudent householder (and God knew that they both of them scraped and saved enough, or, if He didn't know, Miss Mapp did) would have quenched his own lights, if he were talking to his friend in his friend's house. The next night, the pangs of indigestion having completely vanished, she set her alarum clock at the same timeless hour, and had observed exactly the same phenomenon. Such late hours, of course, amply accounted for these late breakfasts; but why, so Miss Mapp pithily asked herself, why these late hours? Of course they both kept summertime, whereas most of Tilling utterly refused (except when going by train) to alter their watches because Mr Lloyd George told them to; but even allowing for that . . . then she perceived that summertime made it later than ever for its adherents, so that was no excuse.

Miss Mapp had a mind that was incapable of believing the improbable, and the current explanation of these late hours was very improbable, indeed. Major Flint often told the world in general that he was revising his diaries, and that the only uninterrupted time which he could find in this pleasant whirl of life at Tilling was when he was alone in the evening. Captain Puffin, on his part, confessed to a student's curiosity about the ancient history of Tilling, with regard to which he was preparing a monograph. He could talk, when permitted, by the hour about the reclamation from the sea of the marsh land south of the town, and about the old Roman road which was built on a raised causeway, of which traces remained; but it argued, so thought Miss Mapp, an unprecedented egoism on the part of Major Flint, and an equally unprecedented love of antiquities on the part of Captain Puffin, that they should prosecute their studies (with gas at the present price) till such hours. No; Miss Mapp knew better than that, but she had not made up her mind exactly what it was that she knew. She mentally rejected the idea that egoism (even in these days of diaries and autobiographies) and antiquities accounted for so much study, with the same healthy intolerance with which a vigorous stomach rejects unwholesome food, and did not allow herself to be insidiously poisoned by its retention. But as she took up her light aluminium opera-glasses to make sure whether it was Isabel Poppit or not who was now stepping with that high, prancing tread into the stationer's in the High Street, she exclaimed to herself, for the three hundred and sixty-fifth time after breakfast: 'It's very baffling'; for it was precisely a year today since she had first seen those mysterious midnight squares of illuminated blind. 'Baffling', in fact, was a word that constantly made short appearances in Miss Mapp's vocabulary, though its retention for a whole year over one subject was unprecedented. But never yet had 'baffled' sullied her wells of pure undefiled English.

Movement had begun; Mrs Plaistow, carrying her wicker basket, came round the corner by the church, in the direction of Miss Mapp's window, and as there was a temporary coolness between them (following violent heat) with regard to some worsted of brilliant rose-madder hue, which a forgetful draper had sold to Mrs Plaistow, having definitely promised it to Miss Mapp . . . but Miss Mapp's large-mindedness scorned to recall the sordid details of this paltry appropriation. The heat had quite subsided, and Miss Mapp was, for her part, quite prepared to let the coolness regain the normal temperature of cordiality the moment that Mrs Plaistow returned that worsted. Outwardly and publicly friendly relationships had been resumed, and as the coolness had lasted six weeks or so, it was probable that the worsted had already been incorporated into the ornamental border of Mrs Plaistow's jumper or winter scarf, and a proper expression of regret would have to do instead. So the nearer Mrs Plaistow approached, the more invisible she became to Miss Mapp's eye, and when she was within saluting distance had vanished altogether. Simultaneously Miss Poppit came out of the stationer's in the High Street.

Mrs Plaistow turned the corner below Miss Mapp's window, and went bobbing along down the steep hill. She walked with the motion of those mechanical dolls sold in the street, which have three legs set as spokes to a circle, so that their feet emerge from their dress with Dutch and rigid regularity, and her figure had a certain squat rotundity that suited her gait. She distinctly looked into Captain Puffin's dining-room window as she passed, and with the misplaced juvenility so characteristic of her waggled her plump little hand at it. At the corner beyond Major Flint's house she hesitated a moment, and turned off down the entry into the side street where Mr Wyse lived. The dentist lived there, too, and as Mr Wyse was away on the continent of Europe, Mrs Plaistow was almost certain to be visiting the other. Rapidly Miss Mapp remembered that at Mrs Bartlett's bridge party yesterday Mrs Plaistow had selected soft chocolates for consumption instead of those stuffed with nougat or almonds. That furnished additional evidence for the dentist, for generally you could not get a nougat chocolate at all if Godiva Plaistow had been in the room for more than a minute or two . . . As she crossed the narrow cobbled roadway, with the grass growing luxuriantly between the rounded pebbles, she stumbled and recovered herself with a swift little forward run, and the circular feet twinkled with the rapidity of those of a thrush scudding over the lawn.

By this time Isabel Poppit had advanced as far as the fish shop three doors below the turning down which Mrs Plaistow had vanished. Her prancing progress paused there for a moment, and she waited with one knee highly elevated, like a statue of a curveting horse, before she finally decided to pass on. But she passed no further than the fruit shop next door, and took the three steps that elevated it from the street in a single prance, with her Roman nose high in the air. Presently she emerged, but with no obvious rotundity like that of a melon projecting from her basket, so that Miss Mapp could see exactly what she had purchased, and went back to the fish shop again. Surely she would not put fish on the top of fruit, and even as Miss Mapp's lucid intelligence rejected this supposition, the true solution struck her. 'Ice,' she said to herself, and, sure enough, projecting from the top of Miss Poppit's basket when she came out was an angular peak, wrapped up in paper already wet.

Miss Poppit came up the street and Miss Mapp put up her illustrated paper again, with the revolting picture of the Brighton sea-nymphs turned towards the window. Peeping out behind it, she observed that Miss Poppit's basket was apparently oozing with bright venous blood, and felt certain that she had bought redcurrants. That, coupled with the ice, made conjecture complete. She had bought redcurrants slightly damaged (or they would not have oozed so speedily), in order to make that iced redcurrant fool of which she had so freely partaken at Miss Mapp's last bridge party. That was a very scurvy trick, for iced redcurrant fool was an invention of Miss Mapp's, who, when it was praised, said that she inherited the recipe from her grandmother. But Miss Poppit had evidently entered the lists against Grandmamma Mapp, and she had as evidently guessed that quite inferior fruit – fruit that was distinctly 'off' – was undetectable when severely iced. Miss Mapp could only hope that the fruit in the basket now bobbing past her window was so much 'off' that it had begun to ferment. Fermented redcurrant fool was nasty to the taste, and, if persevered in, disastrous in its effects. General unpopularity might be needed to teach Miss Poppit not to trespass on Grandmamma Mapp's preserves.

Isabel Poppit lived with a flashy and condescending mother just round the corner beyond the gardener's cottage, and opposite the west end of the church. They were comparatively new inhabitants of Tilling, having settled here only two or three years ago, and Tilling had not yet quite ceased to regard them as rather suspicious characters. Suspicion smouldered, though it blazed no longer. They were certainly rich, and Miss Mapp suspected them of being profiteers. They kept a butler, of whom they were both in considerable awe, who used almost to shrug his shoulders when Mrs Poppit gave him an order: they kept a motor car to which Mrs Poppit was apt to allude more frequently than would have been natural if she had always been accustomed to one, and they went to Switzerland for a month every winter and to Scotland 'for the shooting-season', as Mrs Poppit terribly remarked, every summer. This all looked very black, and though Isabel conformed to the manners of Tilling in doing household shopping every morning with her wicker basket, and buying damaged fruit for fool, and in dressing in the original home-made manner indicated by good breeding and narrow incomes, Miss Mapp was sadly afraid that these habits were not the outcome of chaste and instinctive simplicity, but of the ambition to be received by the old families of Tilling as one of them. But what did a true Tillingite want with a butler and a motor car? And if these were not sufficient to cast grave doubts on the sincerity of the inhabitants of Ye Smalle House, there was still very vivid in Miss Mapp's mind that dreadful moment, undimmed by the years that had passed over it, when Mrs Poppit broke the silence at an altogether too sumptuous lunch by asking Mrs Plaistow if she did not find the supertax a grievous burden on 'our little incomes' . . . Miss Mapp had drawn in her breath sharply, as if in pain, and after a few gasps turned the conversation . . . Worst of all, perhaps, because more recent, was the fact that Mrs Poppit had just received the dignity of the MBE, or Member of the Order of the British Empire, and put it on her cards too, as if to keep the scandal alive. Her services in connection with the Tilling hospital had been entirely confined to putting her motor car at its disposal when she did not want it herself, and not a single member of the Tilling Working Club, which had knitted its fingers to the bone and made enough seven-tailed bandages to reach to the moon, had been offered a similar decoration. If anyone had she would have known what to do: a stinging letter to the Prime Minister saying that she worked not with hope of distinction, but from pure patriotism, would have certainly been Miss Mapp's rejoinder. She actually drafted the letter, when Mrs Poppit's name appeared, and diligently waded through column after column of subsequent lists, to make sure that she, the originator of the Tilling Working Club, had not been the victim of a similar insult.

Mrs Poppit was a climber: that was what she was, and Miss Mapp was obliged to confess that very nimble she had been. The butler and the motor car (so frequently at the disposal of Mrs Poppit's friends) and the incessant lunches and teas had done their work; she had fed rather than starved Tilling into submission, and Miss Mapp felt that she alone upheld the dignity of the old families. She was positively the only old family (and a solitary spinster at that) who had not surrendered to the Poppits. Naturally she did not carry her staunchness to the extent, so to speak, of a hunger-strike, for that would be singular conduct, only worthy of suffragettes, and she partook of the Poppits' hospitality to the fullest extent possible, but (here her principles came in) she never returned the hospitality of the Member of the British Empire, though she occasionally asked Isabel to her house, and abused her soundly on all possible occasions . . .

This spiteful retrospect passed swiftly and smoothly through Miss Mapp's mind, and did not in the least take off from the acuteness with which she observed the tide in the affairs of Tilling which, after the ebb of the night, was now flowing again, nor did it, a few minutes after Isabel's disappearance round the corner, prevent her from hearing the faint tinkle of the telephone in her own house. At that she started to her feet, but paused again at the door. She had shrewd suspicions about her servants with regard to the telephone: she was convinced (though at present she had not been able to get any evidence on the point) that both her cook and her parlour-maid used it for their own base purposes at her expense, and that their friends habitually employed it for conversation with them. And perhaps – who knows? – her housemaid was the worst of the lot, for she affected an almost incredible stupidity with regard to the instrument, and pretended not to be able either to speak through it or to understand its cacklings. All that might very well be assumed in order to divert suspicion, so Miss Mapp paused by the door to let any of these delinquents get deep in conversation with her friend: a soft and stealthy advance towards the room called the morning-room (a small apartment opening out of the hall, and used chiefly for the bestowal of hats and cloaks and umbrellas) would then enable her to catch one of them red-mouthed, or at any rate to overhear fragments of conversation which would supply equally direct evidence.

She had got no further than the garden door into her house when Withers, her parlour-maid, came out. Miss Mapp thereupon began to smile and hum a tune. Then the smile widened and the tune stopped.

'Yes, Withers?' she said. 'Were you looking for me?'

'Yes, Miss,' said Withers. 'Miss Poppit has just rung you up – '

Miss Mapp looked much surprised.

'And to think that the telephone should have rung without my hearing it,' she said. 'I must be growing deaf, Withers, in my old age. What does Miss Poppit want?'

'She hopes you will be able to go to tea this afternoon and play bridge. She expects that a few friends may look in at a quarter to four.'

A flood of lurid light poured into Miss Mapp's mind. To expect that a few friends may look in was the orthodox way of announcing a regular party to which she had not been asked, and Miss Mapp knew as if by a special revelation that if she went, she would find that she made the eighth to complete two tables of bridge. When the butler opened the door, he would undoubtedly have in his hand a half-sheet of paper on which were written the names of the expected friends, and if the caller's name was not on that list, he would tell her with brazen impudence that neither Mrs Poppit nor Miss Poppit were at home, while, before the baffled visitor had turned her back, he would admit another caller who duly appeared on his reference paper . . . So then the Poppits were giving a bridge party to which she had only been bidden at the last moment, clearly to take the place of some expected friend who had developed influenza, lost an aunt or been obliged to go to London: here, too, was the explanation of why (as she had overheard yesterday) Major Flint and Captain Puffin were only intending to play one round of golf today, and to come back by the two-twenty train. And why seek any further for the explanation of the lump of ice and the redcurrants (probably damaged) which she had observed Isabel purchase? And anyone could see (at least Miss Mapp could) why she had gone to the stationer's in the High Street just before. Packs of cards.

Who the expected friend was who had disappointed Mrs Poppit could be thought out later: at present, as Miss Mapp smiled at Withers and hummed her tune again, she had to settle whether she was going to be delighted to accept, or obliged to decline. The argument in favour of being obliged to decline was obvious: Mrs Poppit deserved to be 'served out' for not including her among the original guests, and if she declined it was quite probable that at this late hour her hostess might not be able to get anyone else, and so one of her tables would be completely spoiled. In favour of accepting was the fact that she would get a rubber of bridge and a good tea, and would be able to say something disagreeable about the redcurrant fool, which would serve Miss Poppit out for attempting to crib her ancestral dishes ...

A bright, a joyous, a diabolical idea struck her, and she went herself to the telephone, and genteelly wiped the place where Withers had probably breathed on it.

'So kind of you, Isabel,' she said, 'but I am very busy today, and you didn't give me much notice, did you? So I'll try to look in if I can, shall I? I might be able to squeeze it in.'

There was a pause, and Miss Mapp knew that she had put Isabel in a hole. If she successfully tried to get somebody else, Miss Mapp might find she could squeeze it in, and there would be nine. If she failed to get someone else, and Miss Mapp couldn't squeeze it in, then there would be seven ... Isabel wouldn't have a tranquil moment all day.

'Ah, do squeeze it in,' she said in those horrid wheedling tones which for some reason Major Flint found so attractive. That was one of the weak points about him, and there were many, many others. But that was among those which Miss Mapp found it difficult to condone.

'If I possibly can,' said Miss Mapp. 'But at this late hour – Goodbye, dear, or only *au reservoir*, we hope.'

She heard Isabel's polite laugh at this nearly new and delicious malaprop before she rang off. Isabel collected malaprops and wrote them out in a notebook. If you reversed the notebook and began at the other end, you would find the collection of Spoonerisms, which were very amusing, too.

Tea, followed by a bridge party, was, in summer, the chief manifestation of the spirit of hospitality in Tilling. Mrs Poppit, it is true, had attempted to do something in the way of dinner parties, but though she was at liberty to give as many dinner parties as she pleased, nobody else had followed her ostentatious example. Dinner parties entailed a higher scale of living; Miss Mapp, for one, had accurately counted the cost of having three hungry people to dinner, and found that one such dinner party was not nearly compensated for, in the way of expense, by being invited to three subsequent dinner parties by your guests. Voluptuous teas were the rule, after which you really wanted no more than little bits of things, a cup of soup, a slice of cold tart, or a dished-up piece of fish and some toasted cheese. Then, after the excitement of bridge (and bridge was very exciting in

Tilling), a jig-saw puzzle or Patience cooled your brain and composed your nerves. In winter, however, with its scarcity of daylight, Tilling commonly gave evening bridge parties, and asked the requisite number of friends to drop in after dinner, though everybody knew that everybody else had only partaken of bits of things. Probably the ruinous price of coal had something to do with these evening bridge parties, for the fire that warmed your room when you were alone would warm all your guests as well, and then, when your hospitality was returned, you could let your sitting-room fire go out. But though Miss Mapp was already planning something in connection with winter bridge, winter was a long way off yet . . .

Before Miss Mapp got back to her window in the garden-room Mrs Poppit's great offensive motor car, which she always alluded to as 'the Royce', had come round the corner and, stopping opposite Major Flint's house, was entirely extinguishing all survey of the street beyond. It was clear enough then that she had sent the Royce to take the two out to the golf links, so that they should have time to play their round and catch the two-twenty back to Tilling again, so as to be in good time for the bridge party. Even as she looked, Major Flint came out of his house on one side of the Royce and Captain Puffin on the other. The Royce obstructed their view of each other, and simultaneously each of them shouted across to the house of the other. Captain Puffin emitted a loud 'Coo-ee, Major' (an Australian ejaculation, learned on his voyages), while Major Flint bellowed, '*Quai-hai*, Captain,' which, all the world knew, was of Oriental origin. The noise each of them made prevented him from hearing the other, and presently one in a fuming hurry to start ran round in front of the car at the precise moment that the other ran round behind it, and they both banged loudly on each other's knockers. These knocks were not so precisely simultaneous as the shouts had been, and this led to mutual discovery, hailed with peals of falsetto laughter on the part of Captain Puffin and the more manly guffaws of the Major . . . After that the Royce lumbered down the grass-grown cobbles of the street, and after a great deal of reversing managed to turn the corner.

Miss Mapp set off with her basket to do her shopping. She carried in it the weekly books, which she would leave, with payment but not without argument, at the tradesmen's shops. There was an item for suet which she intended to resist to the last breath in her body, though her butcher would probably surrender long before that. There was an item for eggs at the dairy which she might have to pay, though it was a monstrous overcharge. She had made up her mind about the laundry, she intended to pay that bill with an icy countenance and say 'Good-morning for ever,' or words to that effect, unless the proprietor instantly produced the – the article of clothing which had been lost in the wash (like King John's treasures), or refunded an ample sum for the replacing of it. All these quarrelsome errands were meat and drink to Miss Mapp: Tuesday morning, the day on which she paid and disputed her weekly bills, was as enjoyable as Sunday mornings when, sitting close under the pulpit, she noted the glaring inconsistencies and grammatical errors in the discourse. After the bills were paid and business was done, there was pleasure to follow, for there was a fitting-on at the dressmakers, the fitting-on of a tea-gown, to be worn at winter-evening bridge parties, which, unless Miss Mapp was sadly mistaken, would astound and agonise by its magnificence all who set eyes on it. She had found the description of it, as worn by Mrs Titus W. Trout, in an American fashion paper; it was of what was described as kingfisher blue, and had lumps and wedges of lace round the edge of the skirt, and orange chiffon round the neck. As she set off with her basket full of tradesmen's books, she pictured to herself with watering mouth the fury, the jealousy, the madness of envy which it would raise in all properly constituted breasts.

In spite of her malignant curiosity and her cancerous suspicions about all her friends, in spite, too, of her restless activities, Miss Mapp was not, as might have been expected, a lady of lean and emaciated appearance. She was tall and portly, with plump hands, a broad, benignant face and dimpled, well-nourished cheeks. An acute observer might have detected a danger warning in the sidelong glances of her rather bulgy eyes, and in a certain tightness at the corners of her expansive mouth, which boded ill for any who came within snapping distance, but to a more superficial view she was a rollicking, good-natured figure of a woman. Her mode of address, too, bore out this misleading impression: nothing, for instance, could have been more genial just now than her telephone voice to Isabel Poppit, or her smile to Withers, even while she so strongly suspected her of using the telephone for her own base purposes, and as she passed along the High Street, she showered little smiles and bows on acquaintances and friends. She markedly drew back her lips in speaking, being in no way ashamed of her long white teeth, and wore a practically perpetual smile when there was the least chance of being under observation. Though at sermon time on Sunday, as has been already remarked, she greedily noted the weaknesses and errors of which those twenty minutes was so rewardingly full, she sat all the time with down-dropped eyes and a pretty sacred smile on her lips, and now, when she spied on the other side of the street the figure of the vicar, she tripped slantingly across the road to him, as if by the move of a knight at chess, looking everywhere else, and only perceiving him with glad surprise at the very last moment. He was a great frequenter of tea-parties and except in Lent an assiduous player of bridge, for a clergyman's duties, so he very properly held, were not confined to visiting the poor and exhorting the sinner. He should be a man of the world, and enter into the pleasures of his prosperous parishioners, as well as into the trials of the troubled. Being an accomplished card-player he entered not only into their pleasures but their pockets, and there was no lady of Tilling who was not pleased to have Mr Bartlett for a partner. His winnings, so he said, he gave annually to charitable objects, though whether the charities he selected began at home was a point on which Miss Mapp had quite made up her mind. 'Not a penny of that will the poor ever see,' was the gist of her reflections when on disastrous days she paid him seven-and-ninepence. She always called him 'padre', and had never actually caught him looking over his adversaries' hands.

'Good-morning, Padre,' she said as soon as she perceived him. 'What a lovely day! The white butterflies were enjoying themselves so in the sunshine in my garden. And the swallows!'

Miss Mapp, as every reader will have perceived, wanted to know whether he was playing bridge this afternoon at the Poppits. Major Flint and Captain Puffin certainly were, and it might be taken for granted that Godiva Plaistow was. With the Poppits and herself that made six . . .

Mr Bartlett was humorously archaic in speech. He interlarded archaisms with Highland expressions, and his face was knobby, like a chest of drawers.

'Ha, good-morrow, fair dame,' he said. 'And prithee, art not thou even as ye white butterflies?'

'Oh, Mr Bartlett,' said the fair dame with a provocative glance. 'Naughty! Comparing me to a delicious butterfly!'

'Nay, prithee, why naughty?' said he. 'Yea, indeed, it's a day to make ye little fowles rejoice! Ha! I perceive you are on the errands of the guid wife Martha.' And he pointed to the basket.

'Yes; Tuesday morning,' said Miss Mapp. 'I pay all my household books on Tuesday. Poor but honest, dear Padre. What a rush life is today! I hardly know which way to turn. Little duties in all directions! And you; you're always busy! Such a busy bee!'

'Busy B? Busy Bartlett, quo' she! Yes, I'm a busy B today, Mistress Mapp. Sermon all morning: choir practice at three, a baptism at six. No time for a walk today, let alone a bit turn at the gowf.'

Miss Mapp saw her opening, and made a busy beeline for it.

'Oh, but you should get regular exercise, Padre,' said she. 'You take no care of yourself. After the choir practice now, and before the baptism, you could have a brisk walk. To please me!'

'Yes. I had meant to get a breath of air then,' said he. 'But ye guid Dame Poppit has insisted that I take a wee hand at the cartes with them, the wifey and I. Prithee, shall we meet there?'

('That makes seven without me,' thought Miss Mapp in parenthesis.) Aloud she said:

'If I can squeeze it in, Padre. I have promised dear Isabel to do my best.'

'Well, and a lassie can do no mair,' said he. '*Au reservoir* then.'

Miss Mapp was partly pleased, partly annoyed by the agility with which the Padre brought out her own particular joke. It was she who had brought it down to Tilling, and she felt she had an option on it at the end of every interview, if she meant (as she had done on this occasion) to bring it out. On the other hand it was gratifying to see how popular it had become. She had heard it last month when on a visit to a friend at that sweet and refined village called Riseholme. It was rather looked down on there, as not being sufficiently intellectual. But within a week of Miss Mapp's return, Tilling rang with it, and she let it be understood that she was the original humorist.

Godiva Plaistow came whizzing along the pavement, a short, stout, breathless body who might, so thought Miss Mapp, have acted up to the full and fell associations of her Christian name without exciting the smallest curiosity on the part of the lewd. (Miss Mapp had much the same sort of figure, but her height, so she was perfectly satisfied to imagine, converted corpulence into majesty.) The swift alternation of those Dutch-looking feet gave the impression that Mrs Plaistow was going at a prodigious speed, but they could stop revolving without any warning, and then she stood still. Just when a collision with Miss Mapp seemed imminent, she came to a dead halt.

It was as well to be quite certain that she was going to the Poppits, and Miss Mapp forgave and forgot about the worsted until she had found out. She could never quite manage the indelicacy of saying

'Godiva', whatever Mrs Plaistow's figure and age might happen to be, but always addressed her as 'Diva', very affectionately, whenever they were on speaking terms.

'What a lovely morning, Diva darling,' she said; and noticing that Mr Bartlett was well out of earshot, 'The white butterflies were enjoying themselves so in the sunshine in my garden. And the swallows.'

Godiva was telegraphic in speech.

'Lucky birds,' she said. 'No teeth. Beaks.'

Miss Mapp remembered her disappearance round the dentist's corner half an hour ago, and her own firm inference on the problem.

'Toothache, darling?' she said. 'So sorry.'

'Wisdom,' said Godiva. 'Out at one o'clock. Gas. Ready for bridge this afternoon. Playing? Poppits.'

'If I can squeeze it in, dear,' said Miss Mapp. 'Such a hustle today.'

Diva put her hand to her face as 'wisdom' gave her an awful twinge. Of course she did not believe in the 'hustle', but her pangs prevented her from caring much.

'Meet you then,' she said. 'Shall be all comfortable then. *Au* – '

This was more than could be borne, and Miss Mapp hastily interrupted.

'*Au reservoir*, Diva dear,' she said with extreme acerbity, and Diva's feet began swiftly revolving again.

The problem about the bridge party thus seemed to be solved. The two Poppits, the two Bartletts, the Major and the Captain with Diva darling and herself made eight, and Miss Mapp with a sudden recrudescence of indignation against Isabel with regard to the redcurrant fool and the belated invitation, made up her mind that she would not be able to squeeze it in, thus leaving the party one short. Even apart from the redcurrant fool it served the Poppits right for not asking her originally, but only when, as seemed now perfectly clear, somebody else had disappointed them. But just as she emerged from the butcher's shop, having gained a complete victory in the matter of that suet, without expending the last breath in her body or anything like it, the whole of the seemingly solid structure came toppling to the ground. For on emerging, flushed with triumph, leaving the baffled butcher to try his tricks on somebody else if he chose but not on Miss Mapp, she ran straight into the Disgrace of Tilling and her sex, the suffragette, post-impressionist artist (who painted from the nude, both male and female), the socialist and the Germanophil, all incarnate in one frame. In spite of these execrable antecedents, it was quite in vain that Miss Mapp had tried to poison the collective mind of Tilling against this Creature. If she hated anybody, and she undoubtedly did, she hated Irene Coles. The bitterest part of it all was that if Miss Coles was amused at anybody, and she undoubtedly was, she was amused at Miss Mapp.

Miss Coles was strolling along in the attire to which Tilling generally had got accustomed, but Miss Mapp never. She had an old wide-awake hat jammed down on her head, a tall collar and stock, a large loose coat, knickerbockers and grey stockings. In her mouth was a cigarette, in her hand she swung the orthodox wicker basket. She had certainly been to the other fishmonger's at the end of the High Street, for a lobster, revived perhaps after a sojourn on the ice, by this warm sun, which the butterflies and the swallows had been rejoicing in, was climbing with claws and waving legs over the edge of it.

Irene removed her cigarette from her mouth and did something in the gutter which is usually associated with the floor of third-class smoking carriages. Then her handsome, boyish face, more boyish because her hair was closely clipped, broke into a broad grin.

'Hello, Mapp!' she said. 'Been giving the tradesmen what for on Tuesday morning?'

Miss Mapp found it extremely difficult to bear this obviously insolent form of address without a spasm of rage. Irene called her Mapp because she chose to, and Mapp (more bitterness) felt it wiser not to provoke Coles. She had a dreadful, humorous tongue, an indecent disregard of public or private opinion, and her gift of mimicry was as appalling as her opinion about the Germans. Sometimes Miss Mapp alluded to her as 'quaint Irene', but that was as far as she got in the way of reprisals.

'Oh, you sweet thing!' she said. 'Treasure!'

Irene, in some ghastly way, seemed to take note of this. Why men like Captain Puffin and Major Flint found Irene 'fetching' and 'killing' was more than Miss Mapp could understand, or wanted to understand.

Quaint Irene looked down at her basket. 'Why, there's my lunch going over the top like those beastly British Tommies,' she said, 'Get back, love.'

Miss Mapp could not quite determine whether 'love' was a sarcastic echo of 'Treasure'. It seemed probable.

'Oh, what a dear little lobster,' she said. 'Look at his sweet claws.'

'I shall do more than look at them soon,' said Irene, poking it into her basket again. 'Come and have tiffin, *quai-hai*, I've got to look after myself today.'

'What has happened to your devoted Lucy?' asked Miss Mapp. Irene lived in a very queer way with one gigantic maid, who, but for her sex, might have been in the Guards.

'Ill. I suspect scarlet-fever,' said Irene. 'Very infectious, isn't it? I was up nursing her all last night.'

Miss Mapp recoiled. She did not share Major Flint's robust views about microbes.

'But I hope, dear, you've thoroughly disinfected – '

'Oh, yes. Soap and water,' said Irene. 'By the way, are you Poppiting this afternoon?'

'If I can squeeze it in,' said Miss Mapp.

'We'll meet again, then. Oh – '

'*Au reservoir*,' said Miss Mapp instantly.

'No; not that silly old chestnut!' said Irene. 'I wasn't going to say that. I was only going to say: "Oh, do come to tiffin." You and me and the lobster. Then you and me. But it's a bore about Lucy. I was painting her. Fine figure, gorgeous legs. You wouldn't like to sit for me till she's well again?'

Miss Mapp gave a little squeal and bolted into her dressmaker's. She always felt battered after a conversation with Irene, and needed kingfisher blue to restore her.

Chapter Two

There is not in all England a town so blatantly picturesque as Tilling, nor one, for the lover of level marsh land, of tall reedy dykes, of enormous sunsets and rims of blue sea on the horizon, with so fortunate an environment. The hill on which it is built rises steeply from the level land, and, crowned by the great grave church so conveniently close to Miss Mapp's residence, positively consists of quaint corners, rough-cast and timber cottages, and mellow Georgian fronts. Corners and quaintnesses, gems, glimpses and bits are an obsession to the artist, and in consequence, during the summer months, not only did the majority of its inhabitants turn out into the cobbled ways with sketching-blocks, canvases and paintboxes, but every morning brought into the town charabancs from neighbouring places loaded with passengers, many of whom joined the artistic residents, and you would have thought (until an inspection of their

productions convinced you of the contrary) that some tremendous
outburst of Art was rivalling the Italian Renaissance. For those who
were capable of tackling straight lines and the intricacies of perspective there were the steep cobbled streets of charming and
irregular architecture, while for those who rightly felt themselves
colourists rather than architectural draughtsmen, there was the view
from the top of the hill over the marshes. There, but for one straight
line to mark the horizon (and that could easily be misty) there were
no petty conventionalities in the way of perspective, and the eager
practitioner could almost instantly plunge into vivid greens and
celestial blues, or, at sunset, into pinks and chromes and rose-madder.

Tourists who had no pictorial gifts would pick their way among
the sketchers, and search the shops for cracked china and bits of
brass. Few if any of them left without purchasing one of the famous
Tilling money-boxes, made in the shape of a pottery pig, who bore
on his back that remarkable legend of his authenticity which ran:

> I won't be druv,
> Though I am willing.
> Good-morning, my love,
> Said the Pig of Tilling.

Miss Mapp had a long shelf full of these in every colour to adorn
her dining-room. The one which completed her collection, of a
pleasant magenta colour, had only just been acquired. She called
them 'my sweet rainbow of piggies', and often when she came down
to breakfast, especially if Withers was in the room, she said: 'Good-
morning, quaint little piggies.' When Withers had left the room she
counted them.

The corner where the street took a turn towards the church, just
below the window of her garden-room, was easily the most popular
stance for sketchers. You were bewildered and bowled over by 'bits'.
For the most accomplished of all there was that rarely attempted
feat, the view of the steep downward street, which, in spite of all the
efforts of the artist, insisted, in the sketch, on going up hill instead.
Then, next in difficulty, was the street after it had turned, running
by the gardener's cottage up to the churchyard and the church. This,
in spite of its difficulty, was a very favourite subject, for it included,
on the right of the street, just beyond Miss Mapp's garden wall, the
famous crooked chimney, which was continually copied from every
point of view. The expert artist would draw it rather more crooked
than it really was, in order that there might be no question that he

had not drawn it crooked by accident. This sketch was usually negotiated from the three steps in front of Miss Mapp's front door. Opposite the church-and-chimney-artists would sit others, drawing the front door itself (difficult), and moistening their pencils at their cherry lips, while a little further down the street was another battalion hard at work at the gabled front of the garden-room and its picturesque bow. It was a favourite occupation of Miss Mapp's, when there was a decent gathering of artists outside, to pull a table right into the window of the garden-room, in full view of them, and, quite unconscious of their presence, to arrange flowers there with a smiling and pensive countenance. She had other little playful public pastimes: she would get her kitten from the house, and induce it to sit on the table while she diverted it with the tassel of the blind, and she would kiss it on its sweet little sooty head, or she would write letters in the window, or play Patience there, and then suddenly become aware that there was no end of ladies and gentlemen looking at her. Sometimes she would come out of the house, if the steps were very full, with her own sketching paraphernalia in her hands and say, ever so coyly: 'May I scriggle through?' or ask the squatters on her own steps if they could find a little corner for her. That was so interesting for them: they would remember afterwards that just while they were engaged on their sketches, the lady of that beautiful house at the corner, who had been playing with her kitten in the window, came out to sketch too. She addressed gracious and yet humble remarks to them: 'I see you are painting my sweet little home. May I look? Oh, what a lovely little sketch!' Once, on a never-to-be-forgotten day, she observed one of them take a camera from his pocket and rapidly focus her as she stood on the top step. She turned full-faced and smiling to the camera just in time to catch the click of the shutter, but then it was too late to hide her face, and perhaps the picture might appear in the *Graphic* or the *Sketch*, or among the posturing nymphs of a neighbouring watering-place . . .

This afternoon she was content to 'scriggle' through the sketchers, and humming a little tune, she passed up to the churchyard. ('Scriggle' was one of her own words, highly popular; it connoted squeezing and wriggling.) There she carefully concealed herself under the boughs of the weeping ash tree directly opposite the famous south porch of the church. She had already drawn in the lines of this south porch on her sketching-block, transferring them there by means of a tracing from a photograph, so that formed a very promising beginning to her sketch. But she was nicely placed not only with regard to her sketch, for, by peeping through the pretty foliage of the tree, she could command the front door of Mrs Poppit's (MBE) house.

Miss Mapp's plans for the bridge party had, of course, been completely upset by the encounter with Irene in the High Street. Up till that moment she had imagined that, with the two ladies of the house and the Bartletts and the Major and the Captain and Godiva and herself, two complete tables of bridge would be formed, and she had, therefore, determined that she would not be able to squeeze the party into her numerous engagements, thereby spoiling the second table. But now everything was changed: there were eight without her, and unless, at a quarter to four, she saw reason to suppose, by noting the arrivals at the house, that three bridge tables were in contemplation, she had made up her mind to 'squeeze it in', so that there would be nine gamblers, and Isabel or her mother, if they had any sense of hospitality to their guests, would be compelled to sit out for ever and ever. Miss Mapp had been urgently invited: sweet Isabel had made a great point of her squeezing it in, and if sweet Isabel, in order to be certain of a company of eight, had asked quaint Irene as well, it would serve her right. An additional reason, besides this piece of good nature in managing to squeeze it in, for the sake of sweet Isabel, lay in the fact that she would be able to take some redcurrant fool, and after one spoonful exclaim 'Delicious,' and leave the rest uneaten.

The white butterflies and the swallows were still enjoying themselves in the sunshine, and so, too, were the gnats, about whose pleasure, especially when they settled on her face, Miss Mapp did not care so much. But soon she quite ceased to regard them, for, before the quaint little gilded boys on each side of the clock above the north porch had hammered out the three-quarters after three on their bells, visitors began to arrive at the Poppits' door, and Miss Mapp was very active looking through the boughs of the weeping ash and sitting down again to smile and ponder over her sketch with her head a little on one side, if anybody approached. One by one the expected guests presented themselves and were admitted: Major Flint and Captain Puffin, the Padre and his wife, darling Diva with her head muffled in a 'cloud', and finally Irene, still dressed as she had been in the morning, and probably reeking with scarlet-fever. With the two Poppits these made eight players, so as soon as Irene had gone in, Miss Mapp hastily put her sketching things away, and holding her admirably accurate drawing with its wash of sky not quite dry, in her hand, hurried to the door, for it would never do to arrive after the two tables had started, since in that case it would be she who would have to sit out.

Boon opened the door to her three staccato little knocks, and sulkily consulted his list. She duly appeared on it and was admitted. Having banged the door behind her he crushed the list up in his hand and threw it into the fireplace: all those whose presence was desired had arrived, and Boon would turn his bovine eye on any subsequent caller, and say that his mistress was out.

'And may I put my sketching things down here, please, Boon,' said Miss Mapp ingratiatingly. 'And will no one touch my drawing? It's a little wet still. The church porch.'

Boon made a grunting noise like the Tilling pig, and slouched away in front of her down the passage leading to the garden, sniffing. There they were, with the two bridge-tables set out in a shady corner of the lawn, and a buffet vulgarly heaped with all sorts of dainty confections which made Miss Mapp's mouth water, obliging her to swallow rapidly once or twice before she could manage a wide, dry smile: Isabel advanced.

'De-do, dear,' said Miss Mapp. 'Such a rush! But managed to squeeze it in, as you wouldn't let me off.'

'Oh, that was nice of you, Miss Mapp,' said Isabel.

A wild and awful surmise seized Miss Mapp.

'And your dear mother?' she said. 'Where is Mrs Poppit?'

'Mamma had to go to town this morning. She won't be back till close on dinner-time.'

Miss Mapp's smile closed up like a furled umbrella. The trap had snapped behind her: it was impossible now to scriggle away. She had completed, instead of spoiling, the second table.

'So we're just eight,' said Isabel, poking at her, so to speak, through the wires. 'Shall we have a rubber first and then some tea? Or tea first. What says everybody?'

Restless and hungry murmurs, like those heard at the sea-lions' enclosure in the Zoological Gardens when feeding-time approaches, seemed to indicate tea first, and with gallant greetings from the Major, and archaistic welcomes from the Padre, Miss Mapp headed the general drifting movement towards the buffet. There may have been tea there, but there was certainly iced coffee and lager beer and large jugs with dew on the outside and vegetables floating in a bubbling liquid in the inside, and it was all so vulgar and opulent that with one accord everyone set to work in earnest, in order that the garden should present a less gross and greedy appearance. But there was no sign at present of the redcurrant fool, which was baffling . . .

'And have you had a good game of golf, Major?' asked Miss Mapp, making the best of these miserable circumstances. 'Such a lovely day! The white butterflies were enjoying – '

She became aware that Diva and the Padre, who had already heard about the white butterflies, were in her immediate neighbourhood, and broke off.

'Which of you beat? Or should I say "won"!' she asked.

Major Flint's long moustache was dripping with lager beer, and he made a dexterous, sucking movement.

'Well, the Army and the Navy had it out,' he said. 'And if for once Britain's Navy was not invincible, eh, Puffin?'

Captain Puffin limped away pretending not to hear, and took his heaped plate and brimming glass in the direction of Irene.

'But I'm sure Captain Puffin played quite beautifully too,' said Miss Mapp in the vain attempt to detain him. She liked to collect all the men round her, and then scold them for not talking to the other ladies.

'Well, a game's a game,' said the Major. 'It gets through the hours, Miss Mapp. Yes: we finished at the fourteenth hole, and hurried back to more congenial society. And what have you done today? Fairy-errands, I'll be bound. Titania! Ha!'

Suet errands and errands about a missing article of underclothing were really the most important things that Miss Mapp had done today, now that her bridge party scheme had so miscarried, but naturally she would not allude to these.

'A little gardening,' she said. 'A little sketching. A little singing. Not time to change my frock and put on something less shabby. But I wouldn't have kept sweet Isabel's bridge party waiting for anything, and so I came straight from my painting here. Padre, I've been trying to draw the lovely south porch. But so difficult! I shall give up trying to draw, and just enjoy myself with looking. And there's your dear Evie! How de do, Evie love?'

Godiva Plaistow had taken off her cloud for purposes of mastication, but wound it tightly round her head again as soon as she had eaten as much as she could manage. This had to be done on one side of her mouth, or with the front teeth in the nibbling manner of a rabbit. Everybody, of course, by now knew that she had had a wisdom tooth out at one o'clock with gas, and she could allude to it without explanation.

'Dreamed I was playing bridge,' she said, 'and had a hand of aces.

As I played the first it went off in my hand. All over. Blood. Hope it'll come true. Bar the blood.'

Miss Mapp found herself soon afterwards partnered with Major Flint and opposed by Irene and the Padre. They had hardly begun to consider their first hands when Boon staggered out into the garden under the weight of a large wooden bucket, packed with ice, that surrounded an interior cylinder.

'Redcurrant fool at last,' thought Miss Mapp, adding aloud: 'Oh poor little me, is it, to declare? Shall I say "no trumps"?'

'Mustn't consult your partner, Mapp,' said Irene, puffing the end of her cigarette out of its holder. Irene was painfully literal.

'I don't, darling,' said Miss Mapp, beginning to fizz a little. 'No trumps. Not a trump. Not any sort of trump. There! What are we playing for, by the way?'

'Bob a hundred,' said the Padre, forgetting to be either Scotch or archaic.

'Oh, gambler! You want the poor-box to be the rich box, Padre,' said Miss Mapp, surveying her magnificent hand with the greatest satisfaction. If it had not contained so many court-cards, she would have proposed playing for sixpence, not a shilling a hundred.

All semblance of manners was invariably thrown to the winds by the ladies of Tilling when once bridge began; primeval hatred took their place. The winners of any hand were exasperatingly condescending to the losers, and the losers correspondingly bitter and tremulous. Miss Mapp failed to get her contract, as her partner's contribution to success consisted of more twos and threes than were ever seen together before, and when quaint Irene at the end said, 'Bad luck, Mapp,' Miss Mapp's hands trembled so much with passion that she with difficulty marked the score. But she could command her voice sufficiently to say, 'Lovely of you to be sympathetic, dear.' Irene in answer gave a short, hoarse laugh and dealt.

By this time Boon had deposited at the left hand of each player a cup containing a red creamy fluid, on the surface of which bubbles intermittently appeared. Isabel, at this moment being dummy, had strolled across from the other table to see that everybody was comfortable and provided with sustenance in times of stress, and here was clearly the proper opportunity for Miss Mapp to take a spoonful of this attempt at redcurrant fool, and with a wry face, hastily (but not too hastily) smothered in smiles, to push the revolting compound away from her. But the one spoonful that she took was so delicious and exhilarating, that she was positively unable to be good for Isabel. Instead, she drank her cup to the dregs in an absent manner, while considering how many trumps were out. The redcurrant fool made a similarly agreeable impression on Major Flint.

' 'Pon my word,' he said. 'That's amazingly good. Cooling on a hot day like this. Full of champagne.'

Miss Mapp, seeing that it was so popular, had, of course, to claim it again as a family invention.

'No, dear Major,' she said. 'There's no champagne in it. It's my Grandmamma Mapp's famous redcurrant fool, with little additions perhaps by me. No champagne: yolk of egg and a little cream. Dear Isabel has got it very nearly right.'

The Padre had promised to take more tricks in diamonds than he had the slightest chance of doing. His mental worry communicated itself to his voice.

'And why should there be nary a wee drappie o' champagne in it?' he said, 'though your Grandmamma Mapp did invent it. Weel, let's see your hand, partner. Eh, that's a sair sight.'

'And there'll be a sair wee score agin us when ye're through with the playin' o' it,' said Irene, in tones that could not be acquitted of a mocking intent. 'Why the hell – hallelujah did you go on when I didn't support you?'

Even that one glass of redcurrant fool, though there was no champagne in it, had produced, together with the certainty that her opponent had overbidden his hand, a pleasant exhilaration in Miss Mapp; but yolk of egg, as everybody knew, was a strong stimulant. Suddenly the name redcurrant fool seemed very amusing to her.

'Redcurrant fool!' she said. 'What a quaint, old-fashioned name! I shall invent some others. I shall tell my cook to make some gooseberry-idiot, or strawberry-donkey . . . My play, I think. A ducky little ace of spades.'

'Haw! haw! gooseberry-idiot!' said her partner. 'Capital! You won't beat that in a hurry! And a two of spades on the top of it.'

'You wouldn't expect to find a two of spades at the bottom of it,' said the Padre with singular acidity.

The Major was quick to resent this kind of comment from a man, cloth or no cloth.

'Well, by your leave, Bartlett, by your leave, I repeat,' he said, 'I shall expect to find twos of spades precisely where I please, and when I want your criticism – '

Miss Mapp hastily intervened.

'And after my wee ace, a little king-piece,' she said. 'And if my partner doesn't play the queen to it! Delicious! And I play just one more . . . Yes . . . lovely, partner puts wee trumpy on it! I'm not surprised; it takes more than that to surprise me; and then Padre's got another spade, I ken fine!'

'Hoots!' said the Padre with temperate disgust.

The hand proceeded for a round or two in silence, during which, by winks and gestures to Boon, the Major got hold of another cupful of redcurrant fool. There was already a heavy penalty of tricks against Miss Mapp's opponents, and after a moment's refreshment, the Major led a club, of which, at this period, Miss Mapp seemed to have none. She felt happier than she had been ever since, trying to spoil Isabel's second table, she had only succeeded in completing it.

'Little trumpy again,' she said, putting it on with the lightness of one of the white butterflies and turning the trick. 'Useful little trumpy – '

She broke off suddenly from the chant of victory which ladies of Tilling were accustomed to indulge in during cross-roughs, for she discovered in her hand another more than useless little clubby . . . The silence that succeeded became tense in quality. Miss Mapp knew she had revoked and squeezed her brains to think how she could possibly dispose of the card, while there was a certain calmness about the Padre, which but too clearly indicated that he was quite content to wait for the inevitable disclosure. This came at the last trick, and though Miss Mapp made one forlorn attempt to thrust the horrible little clubby underneath the other cards and gather them up, the Padre pounced on it.

'What ho, fair lady!' he said, now completely restored. 'Methinks thou art forsworn! Let me have a keek at the last trick but three! Verily I wis that thou didst trump ye club aforetime. I said so; there it is. Eh, that's bonny for us, partner!'

Miss Mapp, of course, denied it all, and a ruthless reconstruction of the tricks took place. The Major, still busy with redcurrant fool, was the last to grasp the disaster, and then instantly deplored the unsportsmanlike greed of his adversaries.

'Well, I should have thought in a friendly game like this – ' he said. 'Of course, you're within your right, Bartlett: might is right, hey? but upon my word, a pound of flesh, you know . . . Can't think what made you do it, partner.'

'You never asked me if I had any more clubs,' said Miss Mapp shrilly, giving up for the moment the contention that she had not revoked. 'I always ask if my partner has no more of a suit, and I always maintain that a revoke is more the partner's fault than the player's. Of course, if our adversaries claim it – '

'Naturally we do, Mapp,' said Irene. 'You were down on me sharp enough the other day.'

Miss Mapp wrinkled her face up into the sweetest and extremest smile of which her mobile features were capable.

'Darling, you won't mind my telling you that just at this moment you are being dummy,' she said, 'and so you mustn't speak a single word. Otherwise there is no revoke, even if there was at all, which I consider far from proved yet.'

There was no further proof possible beyond the clear and final evidence of the cards, and since everybody, including Miss Mapp herself, was perfectly well aware that she had revoked, their opponents merely marked up the penalty and the game proceeded. Miss Mapp, of course, following the rule of correct behaviour after revoking, stiffened into a state of offended dignity, and was extremely polite and distant with partner and adversaries alike. This demeanour became even more majestic when in the next hand the Major led out of turn. The moment he had done it, Miss Mapp hurriedly threw a random card out of her hand on to the table, in the hope that Irene, by some strange aberration, would think she had led first.

'Wait a second,' said she. 'I call a lead. Give me a trump, please.'

Suddenly the awful expression as of some outraged empress faded from Miss Mapp's face, and she gave a little shriek of laughter which sounded like a squeaking slate pencil.

'Haven't got one, dear,' she said. 'Now may I have your permission to lead what I think best? Thank you.'

There now existed between the four players that state of violent animosity which was the usual atmosphere towards the end of a rubber. But it would have been a capital mistake to suppose that they were not all enjoying themselves immensely. Emotion is the salt of life, and here was no end of salt. Everyone was overbidding his hand, and the penalty tricks were a glorious cause of vituperation, scarcely veiled, between the partners who had failed to make good, and caused epidemics of condescending sympathy from the adversaries which produced a passion in the losers far keener than their fury at having lost. What made the concluding stages of this contest the more exciting was that an evening breeze suddenly arising just as a deal was ended, made the cards rise in the air like a covey of partridges. They were recaptured, and all the hands were found to be complete with

the exception of Miss Mapp's, which had a card missing. This, an ace
of hearts, was discovered by the Padre, face upwards, in a bed of
mignonette, and he was vehement in claiming a fresh deal, on the
grounds that the card was exposed. Miss Mapp could not speak at all
in answer to this preposterous claim: she could only smile at him, and
proceed to declare trumps as if nothing had happened . . . The Major
alone failed to come up to the full measure of these enjoyments, for
though all the rest of them were as angry with him as they were with
each other, he remained in a most indecorous state of good-humour,
drinking thirstily of the redcurrant fool, and when he was dummy,
quite failing to mind whether Miss Mapp got her contract or not.
Captain Puffin, at the other table, seemed to be behaving with the
same impropriety, for the sound of his shrill, falsetto laugh was as
regular as his visits to the bucket of redcurrant fool. What if there
was champagne in it after all, so Miss Mapp luridly conjectured!
What if this unseemly good-humour was due to incipient intoxication?
She took a little more of that delicious decoction herself.

It was unanimously determined, when the two rubbers came to an
end almost simultaneously, that, as everything was so pleasant and
agreeable, there should be no fresh sorting of the players. Besides,
the second table was only playing stakes of sixpence a hundred, and
it would be very awkward and unsettling that anyone should play
these moderate points in one rubber and those high ones the next.
But at this point Miss Mapp's table was obliged to endure a pause,
for the Padre had to hurry away just before six to administer the rite
of baptism in the church which was so conveniently close. The Major
afforded a good deal of amusement, as soon as he was out of hearing,
by hoping that he would not baptise the child the Knave of Hearts if
it was a boy, or, if a girl, the Queen of Spades; but in order to spare
the susceptibilities of Mrs Bartlett, this admirable joke was not
communicated to the next table, but enjoyed privately. The author
of it, however, made a note in his mind to tell it to Captain Puffin, in
the hopes that it would cause him to forget his ruinous half-crown
defeat at golf this morning. Quite as agreeable was the arrival of a
fresh supply of redcurrant fool, and as this had been heralded a few
minutes before by a loud pop from the butler's pantry, which looked
on to the lawn, Miss Mapp began to waver in her belief that there
was no champagne in it, particularly as it would not have suited the
theory by which she accounted for the Major's unwonted good-
humour, and her suggestion that the pop they had all heard so clearly
was the opening of a bottle of stone ginger-beer was not delivered

with conviction. To make sure, however, she took one more sip of the new supply, and, irradiated with smiles, made a great concession.

'I believe I was wrong,' she said. 'There is something in it beyond yolk of egg and cream. Oh, there's Boon; he will tell us.'

She made a seductive face at Boon, and beckoned to him.

'Boon, will you think it very inquisitive of me,' she asked archly, 'if I ask you whether you have put a teeny drop of champagne into this delicious redcurrant fool?'

'A bottle and a half, Miss,' said Boon morosely, 'and half a pint of old brandy. Will you have some more, Miss?'

Miss Mapp curbed her indignation at this vulgar squandering of precious liquids, so characteristic of Poppits. She gave a shrill little laugh.

'Oh, no, thank you, Boon!' she said. 'I mustn't have any more. Delicious, though.'

Major Flint let Boon fill up his cup while he was not looking.

'And we owe this to your grandmother, Miss Mapp?' he asked gallantly. 'That's a second debt.'

Miss Mapp acknowledged this polite subtlety with a reservation.

'But not the champagne in it, Major,' she said. 'Grandmamma Nap –'

The Major beat his thigh in ecstasy.

'Ha! That's a good Spoonerism for Miss Isabel's book,' he said. 'Miss Isabel, we've got a new –'

Miss Mapp was very much puzzled at this slight confusion in her speech, for her utterance was usually remarkably distinct. There might be some little joke made at her expense on the effect of Grandmamma Mapp's invention if this lovely Spoonerism was published. But if she who had only just tasted the redcurrant fool tripped in her speech, how amply were Major Flint's good nature and Captain Puffin's incessant laugh accounted for. She herself felt very good-natured, too. How pleasant it all was!

'Oh, naughty!' she said to the Major. 'Pray, hush! you're disturbing them at their rubber. And here's the Padre back again!'

The new rubber had only just begun (indeed, it was lucky that they cut their cards without any delay) when Mrs Poppit appeared on her return from her expedition to London. Miss Mapp begged her to take her hand, and instantly began playing.

'It would really be a kindness to me, Mrs Poppit,' she said; '(No diamonds at all, partner?) but of course, if you won't – You've been missing such a lovely party. So much enjoyment!'

Suddenly she saw that Mrs Poppit was wearing on her ample breast a small piece of riband with a little cross attached to it. Her entire stock of good-humour vanished, and she smiled her widest.

'We needn't ask what took you to London,' she said. 'Congratulations! How was the dear King?'

This rubber was soon over, and even as they were adding up the score, there arose a shrill outcry from the next table, where Mrs Plaistow, as usual, had made the tale of her winnings sixpence in excess of what anybody else considered was due to her. The sound of that was so familiar that nobody looked up or asked what was going on.

'Darling Diva and her bawbees, Padre,' said Miss Mapp in an aside. 'So modest in her demands. Oh, she's stopped! Somebody has given her sixpence. Not another rubber? Well, perhaps it is rather late, and I must say good-night to my flowers before they close up for the night. All those shillings mine? Fancy!'

Miss Mapp was seething with excitement, curiosity and rage, as with Major Flint on one side of her and Captain Puffin on the other, she was escorted home. The excitement was due to her winnings, the rage to Mrs Poppit's Order, the curiosity to the clue she believed she had found to those inexplicable lights that burned so late in the houses of her companions. Certainly it seemed that Major Flint was trying not to step on the joints of the paving-stones, and succeeding very imperfectly, while Captain Puffin, on her left, was walking very unevenly on the cobbles. Even making due allowance for the difficulty of walking evenly there at any time, Miss Mapp could not help thinking that a teetotaller would have made a better job of it than that. Both gentlemen talked at once, very agreeably but rather carefully, Major Flint promising himself a studious evening over some very interesting entries in his Indian Diary, while Captain Puffin anticipated the speedy solution of that problem about the Roman road which had puzzled him so long. As they said their '*Au reservoirs*' to her on her doorstep, they took off their hats more often than politeness really demanded.

Once in her house Miss Mapp postponed her good-nights to her sweet flowers, and hurried with the utmost speed of which she was capable to her garden-room, in order to see what her companions were doing. They were standing in the middle of the street, and Major Flint, with gesticulating forefinger, was being very impressive over something . . .

*   *   *

Interesting as was Miss Mapp's walk home, and painful as was the light which it had conceivably thrown on the problem that had baffled her for so long, she might have been even more acutely disgusted had she lingered on with the rest of the bridge party in Mrs Poppit's garden, so revolting was the sycophantic loyalty of the newly decorated Member of the British Empire . . . She described minutely her arrival at the Palace, her momentary nervousness as she entered the Throne-room, the instantaneousness with which that all vanished when she came face to face with her Sovereign.

'I assure you, he gave the most gracious smile,' she said, 'just as if we had known each other all our lives, and I felt at home at once. And he said a few words to me – such a beautiful voice he has. Dear Isabel, I wish you had been there to hear it, and then – '

'Oh, Mamma, what did he say?' asked Isabel, to the great relief of Mrs Plaistow and the Bartletts, for while they were bursting with eagerness to know with the utmost detail all that had taken place, the correct attitude in Tilling was profound indifference to anybody of whatever degree who did not live at Tilling, and to anything that did not happen there. In particular, any manifestation of interest in kings or other distinguished people was held to be a very miserable failing . . . So they all pretended to look about them, and take no notice of what Mrs Poppit was saying, and you might have heard a pin drop. Diva silently and hastily unwound her cloud from over her ears, risking catching cold in the hole where her tooth had been, so terrified was she of missing a single syllable.

'Well, it was very gratifying,' said Mrs Poppit; 'he whispered to some gentleman standing near him, who I think was the Lord Chamberlain, and then told me how interested he had been in the good work of the Tilling hospital, and how especially glad he was to be able – and just then he began to pin my Order on – to be able to recognise it. Now I call that wonderful to know all about the Tilling hospital! And such neat, quick fingers he has: I am sure it would take me double the time to make a safety-pin hold, and then he gave me another smile, and passed me on, so to speak, to the Queen, who stood next him, and who had been listening to all he had said.'

'And did she speak to you too?' asked Diva, quite unable to maintain the right indifference.

'Indeed she did: she said, "So pleased," and what she put into those two words I'm sure I can never convey to you. I could hear how sincere they were: it was no set form of words, as if she meant nothing by it. She *was* pleased: she was just as interested in what I had done for the Tilling hospital as the King was. And the crowds outside: they lined the Mall for at least fifty yards. I was bowing and smiling on this side and that till I felt quite dizzy.'

'And was the Prince of Wales there?' asked Diva, beginning to wind her head up again. She did not care about the crowds.

'No, he wasn't there,' said Mrs Poppit, determined to have no embroidery in her story, however much other people, especially Miss Mapp, decorated remarkable incidents till you hardly recognised them. 'He wasn't there. I dare say something had unexpectedly detained him, though I shouldn't wonder if before long we all saw him. For I noticed in the evening paper which I was reading on the way down here, after I had seen the King, that he was going to stay with Lord Ardingly for this very next weekend. And what's the station for Ardingly Park if it isn't Tilling? Though it's quite a private visit, I feel convinced that the right and proper thing for me to do is to be at the station, or, at any rate, just outside, with my Order on. I shall not claim acquaintance with him, or anything of that kind,' said Mrs Poppit, fingering her Order; 'but after my reception today at the Palace, nothing can be more likely than that His Majesty might mention – quite casually, of course – to the Prince that he had just given a decoration to Mrs Poppit of Tilling. And it would make me feel very awkward to think that that had happened, and I was not somewhere about to make my curtsey.'

'Oh, Mamma, may I stand by you, or behind you?' asked Isabel, completely dazzled by the splendour of this prospect and prancing about the lawn ...

This was quite awful: it was as bad as, if not worse than, the historically disastrous remark about supertax, and a general rigidity, as of some partial cataleptic seizure, froze Mrs Poppit's guests, rendering them, like incomplete Marconi installations, capable of receiving, but not of transmitting. They received these impressions, they also continued (mechanically) to receive more chocolates and sandwiches, and such refreshments as remained on the buffet; but no one could intervene and stop Mrs Poppit from exposing herself further. One reason for this, of course, as already indicated, was that they all longed for her to expose herself as much as she possibly could, for if there was a quality – and, indeed, there were many – on which Tilling prided itself, it was on its immunity from snobbishness: there were, no doubt, in the great world with which Tilling concerned itself so little kings and queens and dukes and Members of the Order of the British Empire; but every Tillingite knew that he or she (particularly she) was just as good as any of them, and indeed better, being more fortunate than they in living in Tilling . . . And if there was a process in the world which Tilling detested, it was being patronised, and there was this woman telling them all what she felt it right and proper for her, as Mrs Poppit of Tilling (MBE), to do, when the Heir Apparent should pass through the town on Saturday. The rest of them, Mrs Poppit implied, might do what they liked, for they did not matter; but she – she must put on her Order and make her curtsey. And Isabel, by her expressed desire to stand beside, or even behind, her mother for this degrading moment had showed of what stock she came.

Mrs Poppit had nothing more to say on this subject; indeed, as Diva reflected, there was really nothing more that could be said, unless she suggested that they should all bow and curtsey to her for the future, and their hostess proceeded, as they all took their leave, to hope that they had enjoyed the bridge party which she had been unavoidably prevented from attending.

'But my absence made it possible to include Miss Mapp,' she said. 'I should not have liked poor Miss Mapp to feel left out; I am always glad to give Miss Mapp pleasure. I hope she won her rubber; she does not like losing. Will no one have a little more redcurrant fool? Boon has made it very tolerably today. A Scotch recipe of my great-grandmother's.'

Diva gave a little cackle of laughter as she enfolded herself in her cloud again. She had heard Miss Mapp's ironical enquiry as to how the dear King was, and had thought at the time that it was probably a pity that Miss Mapp had said that.

*   *   *

Though abhorrence of snobbery and immunity from any taint of it was so fine a characteristic of public social life at Tilling, the expected passage of this distinguished visitor through the town on Saturday next became very speedily known, and before the wicker-baskets of the ladies in their morning marketings next day were half full, there was no quarter which the news had failed to reach. Major Flint had it from Mrs Plaistow, as he went down to the eleven-twenty tram out to the golf links, and though he had not much time to spare (for his work last night on his old diaries had caused him to breakfast unusually late that morning to the accompaniment of a dismal headache from over-application), he had stopped to converse with Miss Mapp immediately afterwards, with one eye on the time, for naturally he could not fire off that sort of news point-blank at her, as if it was a matter of any interest or importance.

'Good-morning, dear lady,' he said. 'By Jove! what a picture of health and freshness you are!'

Miss Mapp cast one glance at her basket to see that the paper quite concealed that article of clothing which the perfidious laundry had found. (Probably the laundry knew where it was all the time, and – in a figurative sense, of course – was 'trying it on'.)

'Early to bed and early to rise, Major,' she said. 'I saw my sweet flowers open their eyes this morning! Such a beautiful dew!'

'Well, my diaries kept me up late last night,' he said. 'When all you fascinating ladies have withdrawn is the only time at which I can bring myself to sit down to them.'

'Let me recommend six to eight in the morning, Major,' said Miss Mapp earnestly. 'Such a freshness of brain then.'

That seemed to be a cul-de-sac in the way of leading up to the important subject, and the Major tried another turning.

'Good, well-fought game of bridge we had yesterday,' he said. 'Just met Mrs Plaistow; she stopped on for a chat after we had gone.'

'Dear Diva; she loves a good gossip,' said Miss Mapp effusively. 'Such an interest she has in other people's affairs. So human and sympathetic. I'm sure our dear hostess told her all about her adventures at the Palace.'

There was only seven minutes left before the tram started, and though this was not a perfect opening, it would have to do. Besides, the Major saw Mrs Plaistow coming energetically along the High Street with whirling feet.

'Yes, and we haven't finished with – ha – royalty yet,' he said, getting the odious word out with difficulty. 'The Prince of Wales will be passing through the town on Saturday, on his way to Ardingly Park, where he is spending the Sunday.'

Miss Mapp was not betrayed into the smallest expression of interest.

'That will be nice for him,' she said. 'He will catch a glimpse of our beautiful Tilling.'

'So he will! Well, I'm off for my game of golf. Perhaps the Navy will be a bit more efficient today.'

'I'm sure you will both play perfectly!' said Miss Mapp.

Diva had 'popped' into the grocer's. She always popped everywhere just now; she popped across to see a friend, and she popped home again; she popped into church on Sunday, and occasionally popped up to town, and Miss Mapp was beginning to feel that somebody ought to let her know, directly or by insinuation, that she popped too much. So, thinking that an opportunity might present itself now, Miss Mapp read the news-board outside the stationer's till Diva popped out of the grocer's again. The headlines of news, even the largest of them, hardly reached her brain, because it was entirely absorbed in another subject. Of course, the first thing was to find out by what train . . .

Diva trundled swiftly across the street.

'Good-morning, Elizabeth,' she said. 'You left the party too early yesterday. Missed a lot. How the King smiled! How the Queen said "So pleased."'

'Our dear hostess would like that,' said Miss Mapp pensively. 'She would be so pleased, too. She and the Queen would both be pleased. Quite a pair of them.'

'By the way, on Saturday next – ' began Diva.

'I know, dear,' said Miss Mapp. 'Major Flint told me. It seemed quite to interest him. Now I must pop into the stationer's – '

Diva was really very obtuse.

'I'm popping in there, too,' she said. 'Want a timetable of the trains.'

Wild horses would not have dragged from Miss Mapp that this was precisely what she wanted.

'I only wanted a little ruled paper,' she said. 'Why, here's dear Evie popping out just as we pop in! Good-morning, sweet Evie. Lovely day again.'

Mrs Bartlett thrust something into her basket which very much resembled a railway timetable. She spoke in a low, quick voice, as if afraid of being overheard, and was otherwise rather like a mouse. When she was excited she squeaked.

'So good for the harvest,' she said. 'Such an important thing to have a good harvest. I hope next Saturday will be fine; it would be a pity if he had a wet day. We were wondering, Kenneth and I, what would be the proper thing to do, if he came over for service – oh, here is Kenneth!'

She stopped abruptly, as if afraid that she had betrayed too much interest in next Saturday and Sunday. Kenneth would manage it much better.

'Ha! lady fair,' he exclaimed. 'Having a bit crack with wee wifey? Any news this bright morning?'

'No, dear Padre,' said Miss Mapp, showing her gums. 'At least, I've heard nothing of any interest. I can only give you the news of my garden. Such lovely new roses in bloom today, bless them!'

Mrs Plaistow had popped into the stationer's, so this perjury was undetected.

The Padre was noted for his diplomacy. Just now he wanted to convey the impression that nothing which could happen next Saturday or Sunday could be of the smallest interest to him; whereas he had spent an almost sleepless night in wondering whether it would, in certain circumstances, be proper to make a bow at the beginning of his sermon and another at the end; whether he ought to meet the visitor at the west door; whether the mayor ought to be told, and whether there ought to be special psalms . . .

'Well, lady fair,' he said. 'Gossip will have it that ye Prince of Wales is staying at Ardingly for the Sunday; indeed, he will, I suppose, pass through Tilling on Saturday afternoon – '

Miss Mapp put her forefinger to her forehead, as if trying to recollect something.

'Yes, now somebody did tell me that,' she said. 'Major Flint, I believe. But when you asked for news I thought you meant something that really interested me. Yes, Padre?'

'Aweel, if he comes to service on Sunday – ?'

'Dear Padre, I'm sure he'll hear a very good sermon. Oh, I see what you mean! Whether you ought to have any special hymn? Don't ask poor little me! Mrs Poppit, I'm sure, would tell you. She knows all about courts and etiquette.'

Diva popped out of the stationer's at this moment.

'Sold out,' she announced. 'Everybody wanted timetables this morning. Evie got the last. Have to go to the station.'

'I'll walk with you, Diva, dear,' said Miss Mapp. 'There's a parcel that – Goodbye, dear Evie, *au reservoir*.'

She kissed her hand to Mrs Bartlett, leaving a smile behind it, as it fluttered away from her face, for the Padre.

Miss Mapp was so impenetrably wrapped in thought as she worked among her sweet flowers that afternoon, that she merely stared at a 'love-in-a-mist', which she had absently rooted up instead of a piece of groundsel, without any bleeding of the heart for one of her sweet flowers. There were two trains by which He might arrive – one at quarter-past four, which would get him to Ardingly for tea, the other at quarter-to seven. She was quite determined to see him, but more inflexible than that resolve was the Euclidean postulate that no one in Tilling should think that she had taken any deliberate step to do so. For the present she had disarmed suspicion by the blankness of her indifference as to what might happen on Saturday or Sunday; but she herself strongly suspected that everybody else, in spite of the public attitude of Tilling to such subjects, was determined to see him too. How to see and not be seen was the question which engrossed her, and though she might possibly happen to be at that sharp corner outside the station where every motor had to go slow, on the arrival of the 4.15, it would never do to risk being seen there again precisely at 6.45. Mrs Poppit, shameless in her snobbery, would no doubt be at the station with her Order on at both these hours, if the arrival did not take place by the first train, and Isabel would be prancing by or behind her, and, in fact, dreadful though it was to contemplate, all Tilling, she reluctantly believed, would be hanging about . . . Then an idea struck her, so glorious, that she put the uprooted love-in-a-mist in the weed-basket, instead of planting it again, and went quickly indoors, up to the attics, and from there popped – really popped, so tight was the fit – through a trap-door on to the roof. Yes: the station was plainly visible, and if the quarter-past four was the favoured train, there would certainly be a motor from Ardingly Park waiting there in good time for its arrival. From the house-roof she could ascertain that, and she would then have time to trip down the hill and get to her coal merchant's at that sharp corner outside the station, and ask, rather peremptorily, when the coke for her central heating might be expected. It was due now, and though it would be unfortunate if it arrived before Saturday, it was quite easy to smile away her peremptory manner, and say that Withers had not told her. Miss Mapp hated prevarication, but a major force sometimes came along . . . But if no motors from Ardingly Park were in waiting for the quarter-past four (as spied from her house-roof), she need not risk being seen in the neighbourhood of the station, but would again make observations some few minutes before the quarter-to seven was due. There was positively no other train by which He could come . . .

The next day or two saw no traceable developments in the situation, but Miss Mapp's trained sense told her that there was underground work of some kind going on: she seemed to hear faint hollow taps and muffled knockings, and, so to speak, the silence of some unusual pregnancy. Up and down the High Street she observed short whispered conversations going on between her friends, which broke off on her approach. This only confirmed her view that these secret colloquies were connected with Saturday afternoon, for it was not to be expected that, after her freezing reception of the news, any

projected snobbishness should be confided to her, and though she
would have liked to know what Diva and Irene and darling Evie were
meaning to do, the fact that they none of them told her, showed that
they were aware that she, at any rate, was utterly indifferent to and
above that sort of thing. She suspected, too, that Major Flint had
fallen victim to this un-Tillinglike mania, for on Friday afternoon,
when passing his door, which happened to be standing open, she
quite distinctly saw him in front of his glass in the hall (standing on
the head of one of the tigers to secure a better view of himself),
trying on a silk top-hat. Her own errand at this moment was to the
draper's, where she bought a quantity of pretty pale blue braid, for a
little domestic dressmaking which was in arrears, and some riband of
the same tint. At this clever and unusual hour for shopping, the High
Street was naturally empty, and after a little hesitation and many
anxious glances to right and left, she plunged into the toyshop and
bought a pleasant little Union Jack with a short stick attached to it.
She told Mr Dabnet very distinctly that it was a present for her
nephew, and concealed it inside her parasol, where it lay quite flat
and made no perceptible bulge . . .

At four o'clock on Saturday afternoon, she remembered that the
damp had come in through her bedroom ceiling in a storm last winter,
and told Withers she was going to have a look to see if any tiles were
loose. In order to ascertain this for certain, she took up through the
trap-door a pair of binocular glasses, through which it was also easy
to identify anybody who might be in the open yard outside the station.
Even as she looked, Mrs Poppit and Isabel crossed the yard into the
waiting-room and ticket-office. It was a little surprising that there
were not more friends in the station-yard, but at the moment she
heard a loud *Quai-hai* in the street below, and cautiously peering
over the parapet, she got an admirable view of the Major in a frock-
coat and tall hat. A 'Coo-ee' answered him, and Captain Puffin, in a
new suit (Miss Mapp was certain of it) and a Panama hat, joined him.
They went down the street and turned the corner . . . Across the
opening to the High Street there shot the figure of darling Diva.

While waiting for them to appear again in the station-yard, Miss
Mapp looked to see what vehicles were standing there. It was already
ten minutes past four, and the Ardingly motors must have been there
by this time, if there was anything 'doing' by the 4.15. But positively
the only vehicle there was an open trolley laden with a piano in a
sack. Apart from knowing all about that piano, for Mrs Poppit had
talked about little else than her new upright Blüthner before her visit

to Buckingham Palace, a moment's reflection convinced Miss Mapp that this was a very unlikely mode of conveyance for any guest . . . She watched for a few moments more, but as no other friends appeared in the station-yard, she concluded that they were hanging about the street somewhere, poor things, and decided not to make enquiries about her coke just yet.

She had tea while she arranged flowers, in the very front of the window in her garden-room, and presently had the satisfaction of seeing many of the baffled loyalists trudging home. There was no need to do more than smile and tap the window and kiss her hand: they all knew that she had been busy with her flowers, and that she knew what they had been busy about . . . Out again they all came towards half-past six, and when she had watched the last of them down the hill, she hurried back to the roof again, to make a final inspection of the loose tiles through her binoculars. Brief but exciting was that inspection, for opposite the entrance to the station was drawn up a motor. So clear was the air and so serviceable her binoculars that she could distinguish the vulgar coronet on the panels, and as she looked Mrs Poppit and Isabel hurried across the station-yard. It was then but the work of a moment to slip on the dust-cloak trimmed with blue braid, adjust the hat with the blue riband, and take up the parasol with its furled Union Jack inside it. The stick of the flag was uppermost; she could whip it out in a moment.

*   *   *

Miss Mapp had calculated her appearance to a nicety. Just as she got to the sharp corner opposite the station, where all cars slowed down and her coal-merchant's office was situated, the train drew up. By the gates into the yard were standing the Major in his top-hat, the Captain in his Panama, Irene in a civilised skirt; Diva in a brand-new walking dress, and the Padre and wee wifey. They were all looking in the direction of the station, and Miss Mapp stepped into the coal-merchant's unobserved. Oddly enough the coke had been sent three days before, and there was no need for peremptoriness.

'So good of you, Mr Wootten!' she said; 'and why is everyone standing about this afternoon?'

Mr Wootten explained the reason of this, and Miss Mapp, grasping her parasol, went out again as the car left the station. There were too many dear friends about, she decided, to use the Union Jack, and having seen what she wanted to she determined to slip quietly away again. Already the Major's hat was in his hand, and he was bowing low, so too were Captain Puffin and the Padre, while Irene, Diva and Evie were making little ducking movements . . . Miss Mapp was determined, when it came to her turn, to show them, as she happened to be on the spot, what a proper curtsey was.

The car came opposite her, and she curtseyed so low that recovery was impossible, and she sat down in the road. Her parasol flew out of her hand and out of her parasol flew the Union Jack. She saw a young man looking out of the window, dressed in khaki, grinning broadly, but not, so she thought, graciously, and it suddenly struck her that there was something, beside her own part in the affair, which was not as it should be. As he put his head in again there was loud laughter from the inside of the car.

Mr Wootten helped her up and the entire assembly of her friends crowded round her, hoping she was not hurt.

'No, dear Major, dear Padre, not at all, thanks,' she said. 'So stupid: my ankle turned. Oh, yes, the Union Jack I bought for my nephew, it's his birthday tomorrow. Thank you. I just came to see about my coke: of course I thought the Prince had arrived when you all went down to meet the quarter-past four. Fancy my running straight into it all! How well he looked.'

This was all rather lame, and Miss Mapp hailed Mrs Poppit's appearance from the station as a welcome diversion . . . Mrs Poppit was looking vexed.

'I hope you saw him well, Mrs Poppit,' said Miss Mapp, 'after meeting two trains, and taking all that trouble.'

'Saw who?' said Mrs Poppit with a deplorable lack both of manner and grammar. 'Why' – light seemed to break on her odious countenance. 'Why, you don't think that was the Prince, do you, Miss Mapp? He arrived here at one, so the station-master has just told me, and has been playing golf all afternoon.'

The Major looked at the Captain, and the Captain at the Major. It was months and months since they had missed their Saturday afternoon's golf.

'It was the Prince of Wales who looked out of that car-window,' said Miss Mapp firmly. 'Such a pleasant smile. I should know it anywhere.'

'The young man who got into the car at the station was no more the Prince of Wales than you are,' said Mrs Poppit shrilly. 'I was close to him as he came out: I curtseyed to him before I saw.'

Miss Mapp instantly changed her attack: she could hardly hold her smile on to her face for rage.

'How very awkward for you,' she said. 'What a laugh they will all have over it this evening! Delicious!'

Mrs Poppit's face suddenly took on an expression of the tenderest solicitude.

'I hope, Miss Mapp, you didn't jar yourself when you sat down in the road just now,' she said.

'Not at all, thank you so much,' said Miss Mapp, hearing her heart beat in her throat . . . If she had had a naval fifteen-inch gun handy, and had known how to fire it, she would, with a sense of duty accomplished, have discharged it point-blank at the Order of the Member of the British Empire, and at anybody else who might be within range . . .

*   *   *

Sunday, of course, with all the opportunities of that day, still remained, and the seats of the auxiliary choir, which were advantageously situated, had never been so full, but as it was all no use, the Major and Captain Puffin left during the sermon to catch the twelve-twenty tram out to the links. On this delightful day it was but natural that the pleasant walk there across the marsh was very popular, and golfers that afternoon had a very trying and nervous time, for the ladies of Tilling kept bobbing up from behind sand-dunes and bunkers, as, regardless of the players, they executed swift flank marches in all directions. Miss Mapp returned exhausted about teatime to hear from Withers that the Prince had spent an hour or more rambling about the town, and had stopped quite five minutes at the corner by the garden-room. He had actually sat down on Miss Mapp's steps and smoked a cigarette. She wondered if the end of the cigarette was there still: it was hateful to have cigarette-ends defiling the steps to her front door, and often before now, when sketchers were numerous, she had sent her housemaid out to remove these untidy relics. She searched for it, but was obliged to come to the reluctant conclusion that there was nothing to remove . . .

Chapter Three

Diva was sitting at the open drawing-room window of her house in the High Street, cutting with a pair of sharp nail scissors into the old chintz curtains which her maid had told her no longer 'paid for the mending'. So, since they refused to pay for their mending any more, she was preparing to make them pay, pretty smartly too, in other ways. The pattern was of little bunches of pink roses peeping out through trellis work, and it was these which she had just begun to cut out. Though Tilling was noted for the ingenuity with which its more fashionable ladies devised novel and quaint effects in their dress in an economical manner, Diva felt sure, ransack her memory though she might, that nobody had thought of *this* before.

The hot weather had continued late into September and showed no signs of breaking yet, and it would be agreeable to her and acutely painful to others that just at the end of the summer she should appear in a perfectly new costume, before the days of jumpers and heavy skirts and large woollen scarves came in. She was preparing, therefore, to take the light white jacket which she wore over her blouse, and cover the broad collar and cuffs of it with these pretty roses. The belt of the skirt would be similarly decorated, and so would the edge of it, if there were enough clean ones. The jacket and skirt had already gone to the dyer's, and would be back in a day or two, white no longer, but of a rich purple hue, and by that time she would have hundreds of these little pink roses ready to be tacked on. Perhaps a piece of the chintz, trellis and all, could be sewn over the belt, but she was determined to have single little bunches of roses peppered all over the collar and cuffs of the jacket and, if possible, round the edge of the skirt. She had already tried the effect, and was of the opinion that nobody could possibly guess what the origin of these roses was. When carefully sewn on they looked as if they were a design in the stuff.

She let the circumcised roses fall on to the window seat, and from time to time, when they grew numerous, swept them into a cardboard box. Though she worked with zealous diligence, she had an eye to the movements in the street outside, for it was shopping-hour, and there were many observations to be made. She had not anything like Miss Mapp's genius for conjecture, but her memory was appallingly good, and this was the third morning running on which Elizabeth had gone into the grocer's. It was odd to go to your grocer's every day like that; groceries twice a week was sufficient for most people. From here on the floor above the street she could easily look into Elizabeth's basket, and she certainly was carrying nothing away with her from the grocer's, for the only thing there was a small bottle done up in white paper with sealing wax, which, Diva had no need to be told, certainly came from the chemist's, and was no doubt connected with too many plums.

Miss Mapp crossed the street to the pavement below Diva's house, and precisely as she reached it, Diva's maid opened the door into the drawing-room, bringing in the second post, or rather not bringing in the second post, but the announcement that there wasn't any second post. This opening of the door caused a draught, and the bunches of roses which littered the window seat rose brightly in the air. Diva managed to beat most of them down again, but two fluttered out of the window. Precisely then, and at no other time, Miss Mapp looked up, and one settled on her face, the other fell into her basket. Her trained faculties were all on the alert, and she thrust them both inside her glove for future consideration, without stopping to examine them just then. She only knew that they were little pink roses, and that they had fluttered out of Diva's window . . .

She paused on the pavement, and remembered that Diva had not yet expressed regret about the worsted, and that she still 'popped' as much as ever. Thus Diva deserved a punishment of some sort, and happily, at that very moment she thought of a subject on which she might be able to make her uncomfortable. The street was full, and it would be pretty to call up to her, instead of ringing her bell, in order to save trouble to poor overworked Janet. (Diva only kept two servants, though of course poverty was no crime.)

'Diva darling!' she cooed.

Diva's head looked out like a cuckoo in a clock preparing to chime the hour.

'Hello!' she said. 'Want me?'

'May I pop up for a moment, dear?' said Miss Mapp. 'That's to say if you're not very busy.'

'Pop away,' said Diva. She was quite aware that Miss Mapp said 'pop' in crude inverted commas, so to speak, for purposes of mockery, and so she said it herself more than ever. 'I'll tell my maid to pop down and open the door.'

While this was being done, Diva bundled her chintz curtains together and stored them and the roses she had cut out into her work-cupboard, for secrecy was an essential to the construction of these decorations. But in order to appear naturally employed, she pulled out the woollen scarf she was knitting for the autumn and winter, forgetting for the moment that the rose-madder stripe at the end on which she was now engaged was made of that fatal worsted which Miss Mapp considered to have been feloniously appropriated. That was the sort of thing Miss Mapp never forgot. Even among her sweet flowers. Her eye fell on it the moment she entered the room, and she tucked the two chintz roses more securely into her glove.

'I thought I would just pop across from the grocer's,' she said. 'What a pretty scarf, dear! That's a lovely shade of rose-madder. Where can I have seen something like it before?'

This was clearly ironical, and had best be answered by irony. Diva was no coward.

'Couldn't say, I'm sure,' she said.

Miss Mapp appeared to recollect, and smiled as far back as her wisdom-teeth. (Diva couldn't do that.)

'I have it,' she said. 'It was the wool I ordered at Heynes's, and then he sold it you, and I couldn't get any more.'

'So it was,' said Diva. 'Upset you a bit. There was the wool in the shop. I bought it.'

'Yes, dear; I see you did. But that wasn't what I popped in about. This coal-strike, you know.'

'Got a cellar full,' said Diva.

'Diva, you've not been hoarding, have you?' asked Miss Mapp with great anxiety. 'They can take away every atom of coal you've got, if so, and fine you I don't know what for every hundredweight of it.'

'Pooh!' said Diva, rather forcing the indifference of this rude interjection.

'Yes, love, pooh by all means, if you like poohing!' said Miss Mapp. 'But I should have felt very unfriendly if one morning I found you were fined – found you were fined – quite a play upon words – and I hadn't warned you.'

Diva felt a little less poohish.

'But how much do they allow you to have?' she asked.

'Oh, quite a little: enough to go on with. But I dare say they won't discover you. I just took the trouble to come and warn you.'

Diva did remember something about hoarding; there had surely been dreadful exposures of prudent housekeepers in the papers which were very uncomfortable reading.

'But all these orders were only for the period of the war,' she said.

'No doubt you're right, dear,' said Miss Mapp brightly. 'I'm sure I hope you are. Only if the coal-strike comes on, I think you'll find that the regulations against hoarding are quite as severe as they ever were. Food hoarding, too. Twemlow – such a civil man – tells me that he thinks we shall have plenty of food, or anyhow sufficient for everybody for quite a long time, provided that there's no hoarding. Not been hoarding food, too, dear Diva? You naughty thing: I believe that great cupboard is full of sardines and biscuits and Bovril.'

'Nothing of the kind,' said Diva indignantly. 'You shall see for yourself' – and then she suddenly remembered that the cupboard was full of chintz curtains and little bunches of pink roses, neatly cut out of them, and a pair of nail scissors.

There was a perfectly perceptible pause, during which Miss Mapp noticed that there were no curtains over the window. There certainly used to be, and they matched with the chintz cover of the window seat, which was decorated with little bunches of pink roses peeping through trellis. This was in the nature of a bonus: she had not up till then connected the chintz curtains with the little things that had fluttered down upon her and were now safe in her glove; her only real object in this call had been to instil a general uneasiness into Diva's mind about the coal-strike and the danger of being well provided with fuel. That she humbly hoped that she had accomplished. She got up.

'Must be going,' she said. 'Such a lovely little chat! But what has happened to your pretty curtains?'

'Gone to the wash,' said Diva firmly.

'Liar,' thought Miss Mapp, as she tripped downstairs. 'Diva would have sent the cover of the window seat too, if that was the case. Liar,' she thought again as she kissed her hand to Diva, who was looking gloomily out of the window.

* * *

As soon as Miss Mapp had gained her garden-room, she examined the mysterious treasures in her left-hand glove. Without the smallest doubt Diva had taken down her curtains (and high time too, for they were sadly shabby), and was cutting the roses out of them. But what on earth was she doing that for? For what garish purpose could she want to use bunches of roses cut out of chintz curtains?

Miss Mapp had put the two specimens of which she had providentially become possessed in her lap, and they looked very pretty against the navy-blue of her skirt. Diva was very ingenious: she used up all sorts of odds and ends in a way that did credit to her undoubtedly parsimonious qualities. She could trim a hat with a toothbrush and a banana in such a way that it looked quite Parisian till you firmly analysed its component parts, and most of her ingenuity was devoted to dress: the more was the pity that she had such a roundabout figure that her waistband always reminded you of the equator . . .

'Eureka!' said Miss Mapp aloud, and, though the telephone bell was ringing, and the postulant might be one of the servants' friends ringing them up at an hour when their mistress was usually in the High Street, she glided swiftly to the large cupboard underneath the stairs which was full of the things which no right-minded person could bear to throw away: broken basket chairs, pieces of brown paper, cardboard boxes without lids, and cardboard lids without boxes, old bags with holes in them, keys without locks and locks without keys and worn chintz covers. There was one – it had once adorned the sofa in the garden-room – covered with red poppies (very easy to cut out), and Miss Mapp dragged it dustily from its corner, setting in motion a perfect cascade of cardboard lids and some door-handles.

Withers had answered the telephone, and came to announce that Twemlow the grocer regretted he had only two large tins of corned beef, but –

'Then say I will have the tongue as well, Withers,' said Miss Mapp. 'Just a tongue – and then I shall want you and Mary to do some cutting out for me.'

The three went to work with feverish energy, for Diva had got a start, and by four o'clock that afternoon there were enough poppies cut out to furnish, when in seed, a whole street of opium dens. The dress selected for decoration was, apart from a few mildew-spots, the colour of ripe corn, which was superbly appropriate for September. 'Poppies in the corn,' said Miss Mapp over and over to herself, remembering some sweet verses she had once read by Bernard Shaw or Clement Shorter or somebody like that about a garden of sleep somewhere in Norfolk . . .

'No one can work as neatly as you, Withers,' she said gaily, 'and I shall ask you to do the most difficult part. I want you to sew my lovely poppies over the collar and facings of the jacket, just spacing them a little and making a dainty irregularity. And then Mary – won't you, Mary? – will do the same with the waistband while I put a border of them round the skirt, and my dear old dress will look quite new and lovely. I shall be at home to nobody, Withers, this afternoon, even if the Prince of Wales came and sat on my doorstep again. We'll all work together in the garden, shall we, and you and Mary must scold me if you think I'm not working hard enough. It will be delicious in the garden.'

Thanks to this pleasant plan, there was not much opportunity for Withers and Mary to be idle . . .

*   *   *

Just about the time that this harmonious party began their work, a far from harmonious couple were being just as industrious in the grand spacious bunker in front of the tee to the last hole on the golf links. It was a beautiful bunker, consisting of a great slope of loose, steep sand against the face of the hill, and solidly shored up with timber. The Navy had been in better form today, and after a decisive victory over the Army in the morning and an indemnity of half a crown, its match in the afternoon, with just the last hole to play, was all square. So Captain Puffin, having the honour, hit a low, nervous drive that tapped loudly at the timbered wall of the bunker, and cuddled down below it, well protected from any future assault.

'Phew! That about settles it,' said Major Flint boisterously. 'Bad place to top a ball! Give me the hole?'

This insolent question needed no answer, and Major Flint drove, skying the ball to a prodigious height. But it had to come to earth sometime, and it fell like Lucifer, son of the morning, in the middle of the same bunker . . . So the Army played three more, and, sweating profusely, got out. Then it was the Navy's turn, and the Navy had to lie on its keel above the boards of the bunker, in order to reach its ball at all, and missed it twice.

'Better give it up, old chap,' said Major Flint. 'Unplayable.'

'Then see me play it,' said Captain Puffin, with a chewing motion of his jaws.

'We shall miss the tram,' said the Major, and, with the intention of giving annoyance, he sat down in the bunker with his back to Captain Puffin, and lit a cigarette. At his third attempt nothing happened; at the fourth the ball flew against the boards, rebounded briskly again into the bunker, trickled down the steep, sandy slope and hit the Major's boot.

'Hit you, I think,' said Captain Puffin. 'Ha! So it's my hole, Major!'

Major Flint had a short fit of aphasia. He opened and shut his mouth and foamed. Then he took a half-crown from his pocket.

'Give that to the Captain,' he said to his caddie, and without looking round, walked away in the direction of the tram. He had not gone a hundred yards when the whistle sounded, and it puffed away homewards with ever-increasing velocity.

Weak and trembling from passion, Major Flint found that after a few tottering steps in the direction of Tilling he would be totally unable to get there unless fortified by some strong stimulant, and turned back to the clubhouse to obtain it. He always went dead-lame when beaten at golf, while Captain Puffin was lame in any circumstances, and the two, no longer on speaking terms, hobbled into the clubhouse, one after the other, each unconscious of the other's presence. Summoning his last remaining strength Major Flint roared for whisky, and was told that, according to regulation, he could not be served until six. There was lemonade and stone ginger-beer . . . You might as well have offered a man-eating tiger bread and milk. Even the threat that he would instantly resign his membership unless provided with drink produced no effect on a polite steward, and he sat down to recover as best he might with an old volume of *Punch*. This seemed to do him little good. His forced abstemiousness was rendered the more intolerable by the fact that Captain Puffin, hobbling in immediately afterwards, fetched from his locker a large flask full of the required elixir, and proceeded to mix himself a long, strong tumblerful. After the Major's rudeness in the matter of the half-crown, it was impossible for any sailor of spirit to take the first step towards reconciliation.

Thirst is a great leveller. By the time the refreshed Puffin had penetrated halfway down his glass, the Major found it impossible to be proud and proper any longer. He hated saying he was sorry (no man more) and wouldn't have been sorry if he had been able to get a drink. He twirled his moustache a great many times and cleared his throat – it wanted more than that to clear it – and capitulated.

'Upon my word, Puffin, I'm ashamed of myself for – ha! – for not taking my defeat better,' he said. 'A man's no business to let a game ruffle him.'

Puffin gave his alto cackling laugh.

'Oh, that's all right, Major,' he said. 'I know it's awfully hard to lose like a gentleman.'

He let this sink in, then added:

'Have a drink, old chap?'

Major Flint flew to his feet.

'Well, thank ye, thank ye,' he said. 'Now where's that soda water you offered me just now?' he shouted to the steward.

The speed and completeness of the reconciliation was in no way remarkable, for when two men quarrel whenever they meet, it follows that they make it up again with corresponding frequency, else there could be no fresh quarrels at all. This one had been a shade more acute than most, and the drop into amity again was a shade more precipitous.

Major Flint in his eagerness had put most of his moustache into the life-giving tumbler, and dried it on his handkerchief.

'After all, it was a most amusing incident,' he said. 'There was I with my back turned, waiting for you to give it up, when your bl – wretched little ball hit my foot. I must remember that. I'll serve you with the same spoon someday, at least I would if I thought it sportsmanlike. Well, well, enough said. Astonishing good whisky, that of yours.'

Captain Puffin helped himself to rather more than half of what now remained in the flask.

'Help yourself, Major,' he said.

'Well, thank ye, I don't mind if I do,' he said, reversing the flask over the tumbler. 'There's a good tramp in front of us now that the last tram has gone. Tram and tramp! Upon my word, I've half a mind to telephone for a taxi.'

This, of course, was a direct hint. Puffin ought clearly to pay for a taxi, having won two half-crowns today. This casual drink did not constitute the usual drink stood by the winner, and paid for with cash over the counter. A drink (or two) from a flask was not the same thing . . . Puffin naturally saw it in another light. He had paid for the whisky which Major Flint had drunk (or owed for it) in his wine-merchant's bill. That was money just as much as a florin pushed across the counter. But he was so excessively pleased with himself over the adroitness with which he had claimed the last hole, that he quite overstepped the bounds of his habitual parsimony.

'Well, you trot along to the telephone and order a taxi,' he said, 'and I'll pay for it.'

'Done with you,' said the other.

Their comradeship was now on its most felicitous level again, and they sat on the bench outside the clubhouse till the arrival of their unusual conveyance.

'Lunching at the Poppits' tomorrow?' asked Major Flint.

'Yes. Meet you there? Good. Bridge afterwards, I suppose.'

'Sure to be. Wish there was a chance of more redcurrant fool. That was a decent tipple, all but the redcurrants. If I had had all the old brandy that was served for my ration in one glass, and all the champagne in another, I should have been better content.'

Captain Puffin was a great cynic in his own misogynistic way.

'Camouflage for the fair sex,' he said. 'A woman will lick up half a bottle of brandy if it's called plum-pudding, and ask for more, whereas if you offered her a small brandy and soda, she would think you were insulting her.'

'Bless them, the funny little fairies,' said the Major.

'Well, what I tell you is true, Major,' said Puffin. 'There's old Mapp. Teetotaller she calls herself, but she played a bo'sun's part in that redcurrant fool. Bit rosy, I thought her, as we escorted her home.'

'So she was,' said the Major. 'So she was. Said goodbye to us on her doorstep as if she thought she was a perfect Venus Ana – Ana something.'

'*Anno Domini*,' giggled Puffin.

'Well, well, we all get long in the tooth in time,' said Major Flint charitably. 'Fine figure of a woman, though.'

'Eh?' said Puffin archly.

'Now none of your sailor-talk ashore, Captain,' said the Major, in high good humour. 'I'm not a marrying man any more than you are. Better if I had been perhaps, more years ago than I care to think about. Dear me, my wound's going to trouble me tonight.'

'What do you do for it, Major?' asked Puffin.

'Do for it? Think of old times a bit over my diaries.'

'Going to let the world have a look at them someday?' asked Puffin.

'No, sir, I am not,' said Major Flint. 'Perhaps a hundred years hence – the date I have named in my will for their publication – someone may think them not so uninteresting. But all this toasting and buttering and grilling and frying your friends, and serving them up hot for all the old cats at a tea-table to mew over – Pah!'

Puffin was silent a moment in appreciation of these noble sentiments.

'But you put in a lot of work over them,' he said at length. 'Often when I'm going up to bed, I see the light still burning in your sitting-room window.'

'And if it comes to that,' rejoined the Major, 'I'm sure I've often dozed off when I'm in bed and woken again, and pulled up my blind, and what not, and there's your light still burning. Powerful long roads those old Romans must have made, Captain.'

The ice was not broken, but it was cracking in all directions under this unexampled thaw. The two had clearly indicated a mutual suspicion of each other's industrious habits after dinner . . . They had never got quite so far as this before: some quarrel had congealed the surface again. But now, with a desperate disagreement just behind them, and the unusual luxury of a taxi just in front, the vernal airs continued blowing in the most springlike manner.

'Yes, that's true enough,' said Puffin. 'Long roads they were, and dry roads at that, and if I stuck to them from after my supper every evening till midnight or more, I should be smothered in dust.'

'Unless you washed the dust down just once in a while,' said Major Flint.

'Just so. Brain-work's an exhausting process; requires a little stimulant now and again,' said Puffin. 'I sit in my chair, you under- stand, and perhaps doze for a bit after my supper, and then I'll get my maps out, and have them handy beside me. And then, if there's something interesting in the evening paper, perhaps I'll have a look at it, and bless me, if by that time it isn't already half-past ten or eleven, and it seems useless to tackle archaeology then. And I just – just while away the time till I'm sleepy. But there seems to be a sort of legend among the ladies here, that I'm a great student of local topography and Roman roads, and all sorts of truck, and I find it better to leave it at that. Tiresome to go into long explanations. In fact,' added Puffin in a burst of confidence, 'the study I've done on Roman roads these last six months wouldn't cover a threepenny piece.'

Major Flint gave a loud, choking guffaw and beat his fat leg.

'Well, if that's not the best joke I've heard for many a long day,' he said. 'There I've been in the house opposite you these last two years, seeing your light burning late night after night, and thinking to myself, "There's my friend Puffin still at it! Fine thing to be an enthusiastic archaeologist like that. That makes short work of a lonely evening for him if he's so buried in his books or his maps – Mapps, ha! ha! – that he doesn't seem to notice whether it's twelve o'clock or one or two, maybe!" And all the time you've been sitting snoozing and boozing in your chair, with your glass handy to wash the dust down.'

Puffin added his falsetto cackle to this merriment.

'And, often I've thought to myself,' he said, ' "There's my friend the Major in his study opposite, with all his diaries round him, making a note here, and copying an extract there, and conferring with the Viceroy one day, and reprimanding the Maharajah of Bom-be-boo another. He's spending the evening on India's coral strand, he is, having tiffin and shooting tigers and Gawd knows what – " '

The Major's laughter boomed out again.

'And I never kept a diary in my life!' he cried. 'Why there's enough cream in this situation to make a dishful of meringues. You and I, you know, the students of Tilling! The serious-minded students who do a hard day's work when all the pretty ladies have gone to bed. Often and often has old – I mean has that fine woman, Miss Mapp, told me that I work too hard at night! Recommended me to get earlier to bed, and do my work between six and eight in the morning! Six and eight in the morning! That's a queer time of day to recommend an old campaigner to be awake at! Often she's talked to you, too, I bet my hat, about sitting up late and exhausting the nervous faculties.'

Major Flint choked and laughed and inhaled tobacco smoke till he got purple in the face.

'And you sitting up one side of the street,' he gasped, 'pretending to be interested in Roman roads, and me on the other pulling a long face over my diaries, and neither of us with a Roman road or a diary to our names. Let's have an end to such unsociable arrangements, old friend; you bring your Roman roads and the bottle to lay the dust over to me one night, and I'll bring my diaries and my peg over to you the next. Never drink alone – one of my maxims in life – if you can find someone to drink with you. And there were you within a few yards of me all the time sitting by your old solitary self, and there was I sitting by my old solitary self, and we each thought the other a serious-minded old buffer, busy on his life-work. I'm blessed if I heard of two such pompous old frauds as you and I, Captain! What a sight of hypocrisy there is in the world, to be sure! No offence – mind: I'm as bad as you, and you're as bad as me, and we're both as bad as each other. But no more solitary confinement of an evening for Benjamin Flint, as long as you're agreeable.'

The advent of the taxi was announced, and arm in arm they limped down the steep path together to the road. A little way off to the left was the great bunker which, primarily, was the cause of their present amity. As they drove by it, the Major waggled his red hand at it.

'*Au reservoir*,' he said. 'Back again soon!'

*   *   *

It was late that night when Miss Mapp felt that she was physically incapable of tacking on a single poppy more to the edge of her skirt, and went to the window of the garden-room where she had been working, to close it. She glanced up at the top storey of her own house, and saw that the lights in the servants' rooms were out: she glanced to the right and concluded that her gardener had gone to bed: finally, she glanced down the street and saw with a pang of pleasure that the windows of the Major's house showed no sign of midnight labour. This was intensely gratifying: it indicated that her influence was at work in him, for in response to her wish, so often and so tactfully urged on him, that he would go to bed earlier and not work so hard at night, here was the darkened window, and she dismissed as unworthy the suspicion which had been aroused by the redcurrant fool. The window of his bedroom was dark too: he must have already put out his light, and Miss Mapp made haste over her little tidyings so that she might not be found a transgressor to her own precepts. But there was a light in Captain Puffin's house: he had a less impressionable nature than the Major and was in so many ways far inferior. And did he really find Roman roads so wonderfully exhilarating? Miss Mapp sincerely hoped that he did, and that it was nothing else of less pure and innocent allurement that kept him up . . . As she closed the window very gently, it did just seem to her that there had been something equally baffling in Major Flint's egoistical vigils over his diaries; that she had wondered whether there was not something else (she had hardly formulated what) which kept his lights burning so late. But she would now cross him – dear man – and his late habits, out of the list of riddles about Tilling which awaited solution. Whatever it had been (diaries or what not) that used to keep him up, he had broken the habit now, whereas Captain Puffin had not. She took her poppy-bordered skirt over her arm, and smiled her thankful way to bed. She could allow herself to wonder with a little more definiteness, now that the Major's lights were out and he was abed, what it could be which rendered Captain Puffin so oblivious to the passage of time, when he was investigating Roman roads. How glad she was that the Major was not with him . . . 'Benjamin Flint!' she said to herself as, having put her window open, she trod softly (so as not to disturb the slumberer next door) across her room on her fat white feet to her big white bed. 'Good-night, Major Benjy,' she whispered, as she put her light out.

*   *   *

It was not to be supposed that Diva would act on Miss Mapp's alarming hints that morning as to the fate of coal-hoarders, and give, say, a ton of fuel to the hospital at once, in lieu of her usual smaller

MAPP AND LUCIA: VOLUME ONE

Christmas contribution, without making further enquiries in the
proper quarters as to the legal liabilities of having, so she ascertained,
three tons in her cellar, and as soon as her visitor had left her this
morning, she popped out to see Mr Wootten, her coal-merchant.
She returned in a state of fury, for there were no regulations whatever
in existence with regard to the amount of coal that any householder
might choose to amass, and Mr Wootten complimented her on her
prudence in having got in a reasonable supply, for he thought it
quite probable that, if the coal-strike took place, there would be
some difficulty in a month's time from now in replenishing cellars.
'But we've had a good supply all the summer,' added agreeable Mr
Wootten, 'and all my customers have got their cellars well stocked.'

Diva rapidly recollected that the perfidious Elizabeth was among
them.

'Oh but, Mr Wootten,' she said, 'Miss Mapp popped – dropped in
to see me just now. Told me she had hardly got any.'

Mr Wootten turned up his ledger. It was not etiquette to disclose
the affairs of one client to another, but if there was a cantankerous
customer, one who was never satisfied with prices and quality, that
client was Miss Mapp . . . He allowed a broad grin to overspread his
agreeable face.

'Well, ma'am, if in a month's time I'm short of coal, there are
friends of yours in Tilling who can let you have plenty,' he permitted
himself to say . . .

It was idle to attempt to cut out bunches of roses while her hand
was so feverish, and she trundled up and down the High Street to
cool off. Had she not been so prudent as to make enquiries, as likely
as not she would have sent a ton of coal that very day to the hospital,
so strongly had Elizabeth's perfidious warning inflamed her
imagination as to the fate of hoarders, and all the time Elizabeth's
own cellars were glutted, though she had asserted that she was almost
fuelless. Why, she must have in her possession more coal than Diva
herself, since Mr Wootten had clearly implied that it was Elizabeth
who could be borrowed from! And all because of a wretched piece of
rose-madder worsted . . .

By degrees she calmed down, for it was no use attempting to plan
revenge with a brain at fever-heat. She must be calm and icily
ingenious. As the cooling-process went on she began to wonder
whether it was worsted alone that had prompted her friend's diabolical
suggestion. It seemed more likely that another motive (one strangely
Elizabethan) was the cause of it. Elizabeth might be taken for certain

as being a coal-hoarder herself, and it was ever so like her to divert suspicion by pretending her cellar was next to empty. She had been equally severe on any who might happen to be hoarding food, in case transport was disarranged and supplies fell short, and with a sudden flare of authentic intuition, Diva's mind blazed with the conjecture that Elizabeth was hoarding food as well.

Luck ever attends the bold and constructive thinker: the apple, for instance, fell from the tree precisely when Newton's mind was groping after the law of gravity, and as Diva stepped into her grocer's to begin her morning's shopping (for she had been occupied with roses ever since breakfast) the attendant was at the telephone at the back of the shop. He spoke in a lucid telephone-voice.

'We've only two of the big tins of corned beef,' he said; and there was a pause, during which, to a psychic, Diva's ears might have seemed to grow as pointed with attention as a satyr's. But she could only hear little hollow quacks from the other end.

'Tongue as well. Very good. I'll send them up at once,' he added, and came forward into the shop.

'Good-morning,' said Diva. Her voice was tremulous with anxiety and investigation. 'Got any big tins of corned beef? The ones that contain six pounds.'

'Very sorry, ma'am. We've only got two, and they've just been ordered.'

'A small pot of ginger then, please,' said Diva recklessly. 'Will you send it round immediately?'

'Yes, ma'am. The boy's just going out.'

That was luck. Diva hurried into the street, and was absorbed by the headlines of the news outside the stationer's. This was a favourite place for observation, for you appeared to be quite taken up by the topics of the day, and kept an oblique eye on the true object of your scrutiny . . . She had not got to wait long, for almost immediately the grocer's boy came out of the shop with a heavy basket on his arm, delivered the small pot of ginger at her own door, and proceeded along the street. He was, unfortunately, a popular and a conversational youth, who had a great deal to say to his friends, and the period of waiting to see if he would turn up the steep street that led to Miss Mapp's house was very protracted. At the corner he deliberately put down the basket altogether and lit a cigarette, and never had Diva so acutely deplored the spread of the tobacco-habit among the juvenile population.

Having refreshed himself he turned up the steep street.

He passed the fishmonger's and the fruiterer's; he did not take the turn down to the dentist's and Mr Wyse's. He had no errand to the Major's house or to the Captain's. Then, oh then, he rang the bell at Miss Mapp's back door. All the time Diva had been following him, keeping her head well down so as to avert the possibility of observation from the window of the garden-room, and walking so slowly that the motion of her feet seemed not circular at all . . . Then the bell was answered, and he delivered into Withers's hands one, two tins of corned beef and a round ox tongue. He put the basket on his head and came down the street again, shrilly whistling. If Diva had had any reasonably small change in her pocket, she would assuredly have given him some small share in it. Lacking this, she trundled home with all speed, and began cutting out roses with swift and certain strokes of the nail scissors.

Now she had already noticed that Elizabeth had paid visits to the grocer's on three consecutive days (three consecutive days: think of it!), and given that her purchases on other occasions had been on the same substantial scale as today, it became a matter of thrilling interest as to where she kept these stores. She could not keep them in the coal cellar, for that was already bursting with coal, and Diva, who had assisted her (the base one) in making a prodigious quantity of jam that year from her well-stocked garden, was aware that the kitchen cupboards were like to be as replete as the coal cellar, before those hoardings of dead oxen began. Then there was the big cupboard under the stairs, but that could scarcely be the site of this prodigious cache, for it was full of cardboard and curtains and carpets and all the rubbishy accumulations which Elizabeth could not bear to part with. Then she had large cupboards in her bedroom and spare rooms full to overflowing of mouldy clothes, but there was positively not another cupboard in the house that Diva knew of, and she crushed her temples in her hands in the attempt to locate the hiding-place of the hoard.

Diva suddenly jumped up with a happy squeal of discovery, and in her excitement snapped her scissors with so random a stroke that she completely cut in half the bunch of roses that she was engaged on. There was another cupboard, the best and biggest of all and the most secret and the most discreet. It lay embedded in the wall of the garden-room, cloaked and concealed behind the shelves of a false bookcase, which contained no more than the simulacra of books, just books with titles that had never yet appeared on any honest book. There were twelve volumes of 'The Beauties of Nature', a shelf full of 'Elegant Extracts', there were volumes simply called 'Poems', there were 'Commentaries', there were 'Travels' and 'Astronomy' and the lowest and tallest shelf was full of 'Music'. A card-table habitually stood in front of this false repository of learning, and it was only last week that Diva, prying casually round the room while Elizabeth had gone to take off her gardening-gloves, had noticed a modest catch let into the woodwork. Without doubt, then, the bookcase was the door of the cupboard, and with a stroke of intuition, too sure to be called a guess, Diva was aware that she had correctly inferred the storage of this nefarious hoard. It only remained to verify her conclusion, and, if possible, expose it with every circumstance of public ignominy. She was in no hurry: she could bide her time, aware that, in all probability, every day that passed would see an addition to its damning contents. Someday, when she was playing bridge and the card-table had been moved out, in some rubber when she herself was dummy and Elizabeth greedily playing the hand, she would secretly and accidentally press the catch which her acute vision had so providentially revealed to her . . .

She attacked her chintz curtains again with her appetite for the pink roses agreeably whetted. Another hour's work would give her sufficient bunches for her purpose, and unless the dyer was as perfidious as Elizabeth, her now purple jacket and skirt would arrive that afternoon. Two days' hard work would be sufficient for so accomplished a needlewoman as herself to make these original decorations.

In the meantime, for Diva was never idle, and was chiefly occupied with dress, she got out a certain American fashion paper. There was in it the description of a tea-gown worn by Mrs Titus W. Trout which she believed was within her dressmaking capacity. She would attempt it, anyhow, and if it proved to be beyond her, she could entrust the more difficult parts to that little dressmaker whom Elizabeth employed, and who was certainly very capable. But the costume was of so daring and splendid a nature that she feared to take anyone into her confidence about it, lest some hint or gossip – for Tilling was a gossipy place – might leak out. Kingfisher blue! It made her mouth water to dwell on the sumptuous syllables!

*　　*　　*

Miss Mapp was so feverishly occupied all next morning with the application of poppies to the corn-coloured skirt that she paid very little attention to the opening gambits of the day, either as regards the world in general, or, more particularly, Major Benjy. After his early retirement last night he was probably up with the lark this morning, and when between half-past ten and eleven his sonorous 'Quai-hai!' sounded through her open window, the shock she experienced interrupted for a moment her floral industry. It was certainly very odd that, having gone to bed at so respectable an hour last night, he should be calling for his porridge only now, but with an impulse of unusual optimism, she figured him as having been at work on his diaries before breakfast, and in that absorbing occupation having forgotten how late it was growing. That, no doubt, was the explanation, though it would be nice to know for certain, if the information positively forced itself on her notice . . . As she worked, (framing her lips with elaborate motions to the syllables) she dumbly practised the phrase 'Major Benjy'. Sometimes in moments of gallantry he called her 'Miss Elizabeth', and she meant, when she had got accustomed to it by practice, to say 'Major Benjy' to him by accident, and he would, no doubt, beg her to make a habit of that friendly slip of the tongue . . . 'Tongue' led to a new train of thought, and presently she paused in her work, and pulling the card-table away from the deceptive bookcase, she pressed the concealed catch of the door, and peeped in.

There was still room for further small precautions against starvation owing to the impending coal-strike, and she took stock of her provisions. Even if the strike lasted quite a long time, there would now be no immediate lack of the necessaries of life, for the cupboard glistened with tinned meats, and the flour-merchant had sent a very sensible sack. This with considerable exertion she transferred to a high shelf in the cupboard, instead of allowing it to remain standing on the floor, for Withers had informed her of an unpleasant rumour about a mouse, which Mary had observed, lost in thought in front of the cupboard. 'So mousie shall only find tins on the floor now,' thought Miss Mapp. 'Mousie shall try his teeth on tins.' . . . There was tea and coffee in abundance, jars of jam filled the kitchen shelves, and if this morning she laid in a moderate supply of dried fruits, there was no reason to face the future with anything but fortitude. She would see about that now, for, busy though she was, she could not miss the shopping-parade. Would Diva, she wondered, be at her window, snipping roses out of chintz curtains? The careful, thrifty soul. Perhaps this time tomorrow, Diva, looking out of her window, would see that somebody else had been quicker about being thrifty than she. That would be fun!

The Major's dining-room window was open, and as Miss Mapp

passed it, she could not help hearing loud, angry remarks about eggs coming from inside. That made it clear that he was still at breakfast, and that if he had been working at his diaries in the fresh morning hours and forgetting the time, early rising, in spite of his early retirement last night, could not be supposed to suit his Oriental temper. But a change of habits was invariably known to be upsetting, and Miss Mapp was hopeful that in a day or two he would feel quite a different man. Further down the street was quaint Irene lounging at the door of her new studio (a converted coach-house), smoking a cigarette and dressed like a jockey.

'Hello, Mapp,' she said. 'Come and have a look round my new studio. You haven't seen it yet. I shall give a house-warming next week. Bridge party!'

Miss Mapp tried to steel herself for the hundredth time to appear quite unconscious that she was being addressed when Irene said 'Mapp' in that odious manner. But she never could summon up sufficient nerve to be rude to so awful a mimic . . .

'Good-morning, dear one,' she said sycophantically. 'Shall I peep in for a moment?'

The decoration of the studio was even more appalling than might have been expected. There was a German stove in the corner made of pink porcelain, the rafters and roof were painted scarlet, the walls were of magenta distemper and the floor was blue. In the corner was a very large orange-coloured screen. The walls were hung with specimens of Irene's art, there was a stout female with no clothes on at all, whom it was impossible not to recognise as being Lucy; there were studies of fat legs and ample bosoms, and on the easel was a picture, evidently in process of completion, which represented a man. From this Miss Mapp instantly averted her eyes.

'Eve,' said Irene, pointing to Lucy.

Miss Mapp naturally guessed that the gentleman who was almost in the same costume was Adam, and turned completely away from him.

'And what a lovely idea to have a blue floor, dear,' she said. 'How original you are. And that pretty scarlet ceiling. But don't you find when you're painting that all these bright colours disturb you?'

'Not a bit: they stimulate your sense of colour.'

Miss Mapp moved towards the screen.

'What a delicious big screen,' she said.

'Yes, but don't go behind it, Mapp,' said Irene, 'or you'll see my model undressing.'

Miss Mapp retreated from it precipitately, as from a wasps' nest, and examined some of the studies on the wall, for it was more than probable from the unfinished picture on the easel that Adam lurked behind the delicious screen. Terrible though it all was, she was conscious of an unbridled curiosity to know who Adam was. It was dreadful to think that there could be any man in Tilling so depraved as to stand to be looked at with so little on . . .

Irene strolled round the walls with her.

'Studies of Lucy,' she said.

'I see, dear,' said Miss Mapp. 'How clever! Legs and things! But when you have your bridge party, won't you perhaps cover some of them up, or turn them to the wall? We should all be looking at your pictures instead of attending to our cards. And if you were thinking of asking the Padre, you know . . . '

They were approaching the corner of the room where the screen stood, when a movement there as if Adam had hit it with his elbow made Miss Mapp turn round. The screen fell flat on the ground and within a yard of her stood Mr Hopkins, the proprietor of the fish-shop just up the street. Often and often had Miss Mapp had pleasant little conversations with him, with a view to bringing down the price of flounders. He had little bathing-drawers on . . .

'Hello, Hopkins, are you ready?' said Irene. 'You know Miss Mapp, don't you?'

Miss Mapp had not imagined that Time and Eternity combined could hold so embarrassing a moment. She did not know where to look, but wherever she looked, it should not be at Hopkins. But (wherever she looked) she could not be unaware that Hopkins raised his large bare arm and touched the place where his cap would have been, if he had had one.

'Good-morning, Hopkins,' she said. 'Well, Irene darling, I must be trotting, and leave you to your – ' she hardly knew what to call it – 'to your work.'

She tripped from the room, which seemed to be entirely full of unclothed limbs, and redder than one of Mr Hopkins's boiled lobsters hurried down the street. She felt that she could never face him again, but would be obliged to go to the establishment in the High Street where Irene dealt, when it was fish she wanted from a fish-shop . . . Her head was in a whirl at the brazenness of mankind, especially womankind. How had Irene started the overtures that led to this? Had she just said to Hopkins one morning: 'Will you come to my studio and take off all your clothes?' If Irene had not been such a wonderful mimic, she would certainly have felt it her duty to go straight to the Padre, and, pulling down her veil, confide to him the whole sad story. But as that was out of the question, she went into Twemlow's and ordered four pounds of dried apricots.

Chapter Four

The dyer, as Diva had feared, proved perfidious, and it was not till the next morning that her maid brought her the parcel containing the coat and skirt of the projected costume. Diva had already done her marketing, so that she might have no other calls on her time to interfere with the tacking on of the bunches of pink roses, and she hoped to have the dress finished in time for Elizabeth's afternoon bridge party next day, an invitation to which had just reached her. She had also settled to have a cold lunch today, so that her cook as well as her parlour-maid could devote themselves to the job.

She herself had taken the jacket for decoration, and was just tacking the first rose on to the collar, when she looked out of the window, and what she saw caused her needle to fall from her nerveless hand. Tripping along the opposite pavement was Elizabeth. She had on a dress, the material of which, after a moment's gaze, Diva identified: it was that corn-coloured coat and skirt which she had worn so much last spring. But the collar, the cuffs, the waistband and the hem of the skirt were covered with staring red poppies. Next moment, she called to remembrance the chintz that had once covered Elizabeth's sofa in the garden-room.

Diva wasted no time, but rang the bell. She had to make certain.

'Janet,' she said, 'go straight out into the High Street, and walk close behind Miss Mapp. Look very carefully at her dress; see if the poppies on it are of chintz.'

Janet's face fell.

'Why, ma'am, she's never gone and – ' she began.

'Quick!' said Diva in a strangled voice.

Diva watched from her window. Janet went out, looked this way and that, spied the quarry, and skimmed up the High Street on feet that twinkled as fast as her mistress's. She came back much out of breath with speed and indignation.

'Yes, ma'am,' she said. 'They're chintz sure enough. Tacked on, too, just as you were meaning to do. Oh, ma'am – '

Janet quite appreciated the magnitude of the calamity and her voice failed.

'What are we to do, ma'am?' she added.

Diva did not reply for a moment, but sat with eyes closed in profound and concentrated thought. It required no reflection to decide how impossible it was to appear herself tomorrow in a dress which seemed to ape the costume which all Tilling had seen Elizabeth wearing today, and at first it looked as if there was nothing to be done with all those laboriously acquired bunches of rosebuds; for it was clearly out of the question to use them as the decoration for any costume, and idle to think of sewing them back into the snipped and gashed curtains. She looked at the purple skirt and coat that hungered for their flowers, and then she looked at Janet. Janet was a short, roundabout person; it was ill-naturedly supposed that she had much the same figure as her mistress . . .

Then the light broke, dazzling and diabolical, and Diva bounced to her feet, blinded by its splendour.

'My coat and skirt are yours, Janet,' she said. 'Get with the work both of you. Bustle. Cover it with roses. Have it finished tonight. Wear it tomorrow. Wear it always.'

She gave a loud cackle of laughter and threaded her needle.

'Lor, ma'am!' said Janet, admiringly. 'That's a teaser! And thank you, ma'am!'

'It was roses, roses all the way.' Diva had quite miscalculated the number required, and there were sufficient not only to cover collar, cuffs and border of the skirt with them but to make another line of them six inches above the hem. Original and gorgeous as the dress would be, it was yet a sort of parody of Elizabeth's costume which was attracting so much interest and attention as she popped in and out of shops today. Tomorrow that would be worn by Janet, and Janet (or Diva was much mistaken) should encourage her friends to get permission to use up old bits of chintz. Very likely chintz decoration would become quite a vogue among the servant maids of Tilling . . . How Elizabeth had got hold of the idea mattered nothing, but anyhow she would be surfeited with the idea before Diva had finished with her. It was possible, of course (anything was possible), that it had occurred to her independently, but Diva was loath to give so innocent an ancestry to her adoption of it. It was far more sensible to take for granted that she had got wind of Diva's invention by some odious, underhand piece of spying. What that might be must be investigated (and probably determined) later, but at present the business of Janet's roses eclipsed every other interest.

Miss Mapp's shopping that morning was unusually prolonged, for

it was important that every woman in Tilling should see the poppies
on the corn-coloured ground, and know that she had worn that dress
before Diva appeared in some mean adaptation of it. Though the
total cost of her entire purchases hardly amounted to a shilling, she
went in and out of an amazing number of shops, and made a prodigious
series of enquiries into the price of commodities that ranged from
motor cars to sealing wax, and often entered a shop twice because
(wreathed in smiling apologies for her stupidity) she had forgotten
what she was told the first time. By twelve o'clock she was satisfied
that practically everybody, with one exception, had seen her, and
that her costume had aroused a deep sense of jealousy and angry
admiration. So cunning was the handiwork of herself, Withers and
Mary that she felt fairly sure that no one had the slightest notion of
how this decoration of poppies was accomplished, for Evie had run
round her in small mouse-like circles, murmuring to herself: 'Very
effective idea; is it woven into the cloth, Elizabeth? Dear me, I wonder
where I could get some like it,' and Mrs Poppit had followed her all
up the street, with eyes glued to the hem of her skirt, and a completely
puzzled face: 'But then,' so thought Elizabeth sweetly, 'even members
of the Order of the British Empire can't have everything their own
way.' As for the Major, he had simply come to a dead stop when he
bounced out of his house as she passed, and said something very
gallant and appropriate. Even the absence of that one inhabitant of
Tilling, dear Diva, did not strike a jarring note in this paean of
triumph, for Miss Mapp was quite satisfied that Diva was busy indoors,
working her fingers to the bone over the application of bunches of
roses, and, as usual, she was perfectly correct in her conjecture. But
dear Diva would have to see the new frock tomorrow afternoon, at the
latest, when she came to the bridge party. Perhaps she would then, for
the first time, be wearing the roses herself, and everybody would very
pleasantly pity her. This was so rapturous a thought, that when Miss
Mapp, after her prolonged shopping and with her almost empty basket,
passed Mr Hopkins standing outside his shop on her return home
again, she gave him her usual smile, though without meeting his eye,
and tried to forget how much of him she had seen yesterday. Perhaps
she might speak to him tomorrow and gradually resume ordinary
relations, for the prices at the other fish- shop were as high as the
quality of the fish was low . . . She told herself that there was nothing
actually immoral in the human skin, however embarrassing it was.

*   *   *

Miss Mapp had experienced a cruel disappointment last night, though the triumph of this morning had done something to soothe it, for Major Benjy's window had certainly been lit up to a very late hour, and so it was clear that he had not been able, twice in succession, to tear himself away from his diaries, or whatever else detained him, and go to bed at a proper time. Captain Puffin, however, had not sat up late; indeed he must have gone to bed quite unusually early, for his window was dark by half-past nine. Tonight, again the position was reversed, and it seemed that Major Benjy was 'good' and Captain Puffin was 'bad'. On the whole, then, there was cause for thankfulness, and as she added a tin of biscuits and two jars of Bovril to her prudent stores, she found herself a conscious sceptic about those Roman roads. Diaries (perhaps) were a little different, for egoism was a more potent force than archaeology, and for her part she now definitely believed that Roman roads spelt some form of drink. She was sorry to believe it, but it was her duty to believe something of the kind, and she really did not know what else to believe. She did not go so far as mentally to accuse him of drunkenness, but considering the way he absorbed redcurrant fool, it was clear that he was no foe to alcohol and probably watered the Roman roads with it. With her vivid imagination she pictured him –

Miss Mapp recalled herself from this melancholy reflection and put up her hand just in time to save a bottle of Bovril which she had put on the top shelf in front of the sack of flour from tumbling to the ground. With the latest additions she had made to her larder, it required considerable ingenuity to fit all the tins and packages in, and for a while she diverted her mind from Captain Puffin's drinking to her own eating. But by careful packing and balancing she managed to stow everything away with sufficient economy of space to allow her to shut the door, and then put the card-table in place again. It was then late, and with a fond look at her sweet flowers sleeping in the moonlight, she went to bed. Captain Puffin's sitting-room was still alight, and even as she deplored this, his shadow in profile crossed the blind. Shadows were queer things – she could make a beautiful shadow-rabbit on the wall by a dexterous interlacement of fingers and thumbs – and certainly this shadow, in the momentary glance she had of it, appeared to have a large moustache. She could make nothing whatever out of that, except to suppose that just as fingers and thumbs became a rabbit, so his nose became a moustache, for he could not have grown one since he came back from golf . . .

*   *   *

She was out early for her shopping next morning, for there were some delicacies to be purchased for her bridge party, more particularly some little chocolate cakes she had lately discovered which looked very small and innocent, but were in reality of so cloying and substantial a nature, that the partaker thereof would probably not feel capable of making any serious inroads into other provisions. Naturally she was much on the alert today, for it was more than possible that Diva's dress was finished and in evidence. What colour it would be she did not know, but a large quantity of rosebuds would, even at a distance, make identification easy. Diva was certainly not at her window this morning, so it seemed more than probable that they would soon meet.

Far away, just crossing the High Street at the further end, she caught sight of a bright patch of purple, very much of the required shape. There was surely a pink border round the skirt and a pink panel on the collar, and just as surely Mrs Bartlett, recognisable for her gliding mouse-like walk, was moving in its fascinating wake. Then the purple patch vanished into a shop, and Miss Mapp, all smiles and poppies, went with her basket up the street. Presently she encountered Evie, who, also all smiles, seemed to have some communication to make, but only got as far as 'Have you seen' – when she gave a little squeal of laughter, quite inexplicable, and glided into some dark entry. A minute afterwards, the purple patch suddenly appeared from a shop and almost collided with her. It was not Diva at all, but Diva's Janet.

The shock was so indescribably severe that Miss Mapp's smile was frozen, so to speak, as by some sudden congealment on to her face, and did not thaw off it till she had reached the sharp turn at the end of the street, where she leaned heavily on the railing and breathed through her nose. A light autumnal mist overlay the miles of marsh, but the sun was already drinking it up, promising the Tillingites another golden day. The tidal river was at the flood, and the bright water lapped the bases of the turf-covered banks that kept it within its course. Beyond that was the tram-station towards which presently Major Benjy and Captain Puffin would be hurrying to catch the tram that would take them out to the golf links. The straight road across the marsh was visible, and the railway bridge. All these things were pitilessly unchanged, and Miss Mapp noted them blankly, until rage began to restore the numbed current of her mental processes.

*   *   *

If the records of history contained any similar instance of such treachery and low cunning as was involved in this plot of Diva's to dress Janet in the rosebud chintz, Miss Mapp would have liked to be told clearly and distinctly what it was. She could trace the workings of Diva's base mind with absolute accuracy, and if all the archangels in the hierarchy of heaven had assured her that Diva had originally intended the rosebuds for Janet, she would have scorned them for their clumsy perjury. Diva had designed and executed that dress for herself, and just because Miss Mapp's ingenuity (inspired by the two rosebuds that had fluttered out of the window) had forestalled her, she had taken this fiendish revenge. It was impossible to pervade the High Street covered with chintz poppies when a parlour-maid was being equally pervasive in chintz rosebuds, and what was to be done with this frock executed with such mirth and malice by Withers, Mary and herself she had no idea. She might just as well give it Withers, for she could no longer wear it herself, or tear the poppies from the hem and bestrew the High Street with them . . . Miss Mapp's face froze into immobility again, for here, trundling swiftly towards her, was Diva herself.

Diva appeared not to see her till she got quite close.

'Morning, Elizabeth,' she said. 'Seen my Janet anywhere?'

'No,' said Miss Mapp.

Janet (no doubt according to instructions received) popped out of a shop, and came towards her mistress.

'Here she is,' said Diva. 'All right, Janet. You go home. I'll see to the other things.'

'It's a lovely day,' said Miss Mapp, beginning to lash her tail. 'So bright.'

'Yes. Pretty trimming of poppies,' said Diva. 'Janet's got rosebuds.'

This was too much.

'Diva, I didn't think it of you,' said Miss Mapp in a shaking voice. 'You saw my new frock yesterday, and you were filled with malice and envy, Diva, just because I had thought of using flowers off an old chintz as well as you, and came out first with it. You had meant to wear that purple frock yourself – though I must say it fits Janet perfectly – and just because I was first in the field you did this. You gave Janet that frock, so that I should be dressed in the same style as your parlour-maid, and you've got a black heart, Diva!'

'That's nonsense,' said Diva firmly. 'Heart's as red as anybody's, and talking of black hearts doesn't become *you*, Elizabeth. You knew I was cutting out roses from my curtains – '

Miss Mapp laughed shrilly.

'Well, if I happen to notice that you've taken your chintz curtains down,' she said with an awful distinctness that showed the wisdom-teeth of which Diva had got three at the most, 'and pink bunches of roses come flying out of your window into the High Street, even my poor wits, small as they are, are equal to drawing the conclusion that you are cutting roses out of curtains. Your well-known fondness for dress did the rest. With your permission, Diva, I intend to draw exactly what conclusions I please on every occasion, including this one.'

'Ho! That's how you got the idea then,' said Diva. 'I knew you had cribbed it from me.'

'Cribbed?' asked Miss Mapp, in ironical ignorance of what so vulgar and slangy an expression meant.

'Cribbed means taking what isn't yours,' said Diva. 'Even then, if you had only acted in a straightforward manner – '

Miss Mapp, shaken as with palsy, regretted that she had let slip, out of pure childlike joy, in irony, the manner in which she had obtained the poppy-notion, but in a quarrel regrets are useless, and she went on again.

'And would you very kindly explain how or when I have acted in a manner that was not straightforward,' she asked with laborious politeness. 'Or do I understand that a monopoly of cutting up chintz curtains for personal adornment has been bestowed on you by Act of Parliament?'

'You knew I was meaning to make a frock with chintz roses on it,' said Diva. 'You stole my idea. Worked night and day to be first. Just like you. Mean behaviour.'

'It was meaner to give that frock to Janet,' said Miss Mapp.

'You can give yours to Withers,' snapped Diva.

'Much obliged, Mrs Plaistow,' said Miss Mapp.

*   *   *

Diva had been watching Janet's retreating figure, and feeling that though revenge was sweet, revenge was also strangely expensive, for she had sacrificed one of the most strikingly successful frocks she had ever made on that smoking altar. Now her revenge was gratified, and deeply she regretted the frock. Miss Mapp's heart was similarly wrung by torture: revenge too had been hers (general revenge on Diva for existing), but this dreadful counter-stroke had made it quite impossible for her to enjoy the use of this frock any more, for she could not habit herself like a housemaid. Each, in fact, had, as matters at present stood, completely wrecked the other, like two express trains meeting in top-speed collision, and, since the quarrel had clearly risen to its utmost height, there was no farther joy of battle to be anticipated, but only the melancholy task of counting the corpses. So they paused, breathing very quickly and trembling, while both sought for some way out. Besides Miss Mapp had a bridge party this afternoon, and if they parted now in this extreme state of tension, Diva might conceivably not come, thereby robbing herself of her bridge and spoiling her hostess's table. Naturally any permanent quarrel was not contemplated by either of them, for if quarrels were permanent in Tilling, nobody would be on speaking terms any more with anyone else in a day or two, and (hardly less disastrous) there could be no fresh quarrels with anybody, since you could not quarrel without words. There might be songs without words, as Mendelssohn had proved, but not rows without words. By what formula could this deadly antagonism be bridged without delay?

Diva gazed out over the marsh. She wanted desperately to regain her rosebud-frock, and she knew that Elizabeth was starving for further wearing of her poppies. Perhaps the wide, serene plain below inspired her with a hatred of littleness. There would be no loss of dignity in making a proposal that her enemy, she felt sure, would accept: it merely showed a Christian spirit, and set an example to Elizabeth, to make the first move. Janet she did not consider.

'If you are in a fit state to listen to reason, Elizabeth,' she began.

Miss Mapp heaved a sigh of relief. Diva had thought of something. She swallowed the insult at a gulp.

'Yes, dear,' she said.

'Got an idea. Take away Janet's frock, and wear it myself. Then you can wear yours. Too pretty for parlour-maids. Eh?'

A heavenly brightness spread over Miss Mapp's face.

'Oh, how wonderful of you to have thought of that, Diva,' she said. 'But how shall we explain it all to everybody?'

Diva clung to her rights. Though clearly Christian, she was human.

'Say I thought of tacking chintz on and told you,' she said.

'Yes, darling,' said Elizabeth. 'That's beautiful, I agree. But poor Janet!'

'I'll give her some other old thing,' said Diva. 'Good sort, Janet. Wants me to win.'

'And about her having been seen wearing it?'

'Say she hasn't ever worn it. Say they're mad,' said Diva.

Miss Mapp felt it better to tear herself away before she began distilling all sorts of acidities that welled up in her fruitful mind. She could, for instance, easily have agreed that nothing was more probable than that Janet had been mistaken for her mistress . . .

'*Au reservoir* then, dear,' she said tenderly. 'See you at about four? And will you wear your pretty rosebud frock?'

This was agreed to, and Diva went home to take it away from Janet.

*   *   *

The reconciliation of course was strictly confined to matters relating to chintz and did not include such extraneous subjects as coal strike or food-hoarding, and even in the first glowing moments of restored friendliness, Diva began wondering whether she would have the opportunity that afternoon of testing the truth of her conjecture about the cupboard in the garden-room. Cudgel her brains as she might she could think of no other cache that could contain the immense amount of provisions that Elizabeth had probably accumulated, and she was all on fire to get to practical grips with the problem. As far as tins of corned beef and tongues went, Elizabeth might possibly have buried them in her garden in the manner of a dog, but it was not likely that a hoarder would limit herself to things in tins. No: there was a cupboard somewhere ready to burst with strong supporting foods . . .

Diva intentionally arrived a full quarter of an hour on the hither side of punctuality, and was taken by Withers out into the garden-room, where tea was laid, and two card-tables were in readiness. She was, of course, the first of the guests, and the moment Withers withdrew to tell her mistress that she had come, Diva stealthily glided to the cupboard, from in front of which the bridge-table had been removed, feeling the shrill joy of some romantic treasure hunter. She found the catch, she pressed it, she pulled open the door and the whole of the damning profusion of provisions burst upon her delighted eyes. Shelf after shelf was crowded with eatables; there were tins of corned beef and tongues (that she knew already), there was a sack of flour, there were tubes of Bath Oliver biscuits, bottles of Bovril, the yield of a thousand condensed Swiss cows, jars of prunes . . . All these were in the front row, flush with the door, and who knew to what depth the cupboard extended? Even as she feasted her eyes on this incredible store, some package on the top shelf wavered and toppled, and she had only just time to shut the door again, in order to prevent it falling out on to the floor. But this displacement prevented the door from wholly closing, and push and shove as Diva might, she could not get the catch to click home, and the only result of her energy and efforts was to give rise to a muffled explosion from within, just precisely as if something made of cardboard had burst. That mental image was so vivid that to her fevered imagination it seemed to be real. This was followed by certain faint taps from within against 'Elegant Extracts' and 'Astronomy'.

Diva grew very red in the face, and said 'Drat it' under her breath. She did not dare open the door again in order to push things back, for fear of an uncontrollable stream of 'things' pouring out. Some nicely balanced equilibrium had clearly been upset in those capacious shelves, and it was impossible to tell, without looking, how deep and how extensive the disturbance was. And in order to look, she had to open the bookcase again . . . Luckily the pressure against the door was not sufficiently heavy to cause it to swing wide, so the best she could do was to leave it just ajar with temporary quiescence inside. Simultaneously she heard Miss Mapp's step, and had no more than time to trundle at the utmost speed of her whirling feet across to the window, where she stood looking out, and appeared quite unconscious of her hostess's entry.

'Diva darling, how sweet of you to come so early!' she said. 'A little cosy chat before the others arrive.'

Diva turned round, much startled.

'Hello!' she said. 'Didn't hear you. Got Janet's frock you see.'

('What makes Diva's face so red?' thought Miss Mapp.)

'So I see, darling,' she said. 'Lovely rose-garden. How well it suits you, dear! Did Janet mind?'

'No. Promised her a new frock at Christmas.'

'That will be nice for Janet,' said Elizabeth enthusiastically. 'Shall we pop into the garden, dear, till my guests come?'

Diva was glad to pop into the garden and get away from the immediate vicinity of the cupboard, for though she had planned and looked forward to the exposure of Elizabeth's hoarding, she had not meant it to come, as it now probably would, in crashes of tins and bursting of Bovril bottles. Again she had intended to have opened that door quite casually and innocently while she was being dummy, so that everyone could see how accidental the exposure was, and to have gone poking about the cupboard in Elizabeth's absence was a shade too professional, so to speak, for the usual detective work of Tilling. But the fuse was set now. Sooner or later the explosion must come. She wondered as they went out to commune with Elizabeth's sweet flowers till the other guests arrived how great a torrent would be let loose. She did not repent her exploration – far from it – but her pleasurable anticipations were strongly diluted with suspense.

Miss Mapp had found such difficulty in getting eight players together today, that she had transgressed her principles and asked Mrs Poppit as well as Isabel, and they, with Diva, the two Bartletts, and the Major and the Captain, formed the party. The moment Mrs Poppit appeared, Elizabeth hated her more than ever, for she put up her glasses, and began to give her patronising advice about her garden, which she had not been allowed to see before.

'You have quite a pretty little piece of garden, Miss Mapp,' she said, 'though, to be sure, I fancied from what you said that it was more extensive. Dear me, your roses do not seem to be doing very well. Probably they are old plants and want renewing. You must send your gardener round – you keep a gardener? – and I will let you have a dozen vigorous young bushes.'

Miss Mapp licked her dry lips. She kept a kind of gardener: two days a week.

'Too good of you,' she said, 'but that rose-bed is quite sacred, dear Mrs Poppit. Not all the vigorous young bushes in the world would tempt me. It's my "Friendship's Border": some dear friend gave me each of my rose trees.'

Mrs Poppit transferred her gaze to the wistaria that grew over the steps up to the garden-room. Some of the dear friends she thought must be centenarians.

'Your wistaria wants pruning sadly,' she said. 'Your gardener does not understand wistarias. That corner there was made, I may say, for fuchsias. You should get a dozen choice fuchsias.'

Miss Mapp laughed.

'Oh, you must excuse me,' she said with a glance at Mrs Poppit's brocaded silk. 'I can't bear fuchsias. They always remind me of overdressed women. Ah, there's Mr Bartlett. How-de-do, Padre. And dear Evie!'

Dear Evie appeared fascinated by Diva's dress.

'Such beautiful rosebuds,' she murmured, 'and what a lovely shade of purple. And Elizabeth's poppies too, quite a pair of you. But surely this morning, Diva, didn't I see your good Janet in just such another dress, and I thought at the time how odd it was that – '

'If you saw Janet this morning,' said Diva quite firmly, 'you saw her in her print dress.'

'And here's Major Benjy,' said Miss Mapp, who had made her slip about his Christian name yesterday, and had been duly entreated to continue slipping. 'And Captain Puffin. Well, that is nice! Shall we go into my little garden shed, dear Mrs Poppit, and have our tea?'

Major Flint was still a little lame, for his golf today had been of the nature of gardening, and he hobbled up the steps behind the ladies, with that little cock-sparrow sailor following him and telling the Padre how badly and yet how successfully he himself had played.

'Pleasantest room in Tilling, I always say, Miss Elizabeth,' said he, diverting his mind from a mere game to the fairies.

'My dear little room,' said Miss Mapp, knowing that it was much larger than anything in Mrs Poppit's house. 'So tiny!'

'Oh, not a bad-sized little room,' said Mrs Poppit encouragingly. 'Much the same proportions, on a very small scale, as the Throne-room at Buckingham Palace.'

'That beautiful Throne-room!' exclaimed Miss Mapp. 'A cup of tea, dear Mrs Poppit? None of that naughty redcurrant fool, I am afraid. And a little chocolate cake?'

These substantial chocolate cakes soon did their fell work of producing the sense of surfeit, and presently Elizabeth's guests dropped off gorged from the tea-table. Diva fortunately remembered their consistency in time, and nearly cleared a plate of jumbles instead, which the hostess had hoped would form a pleasant accompaniment to her dessert at her supper this evening, and was still crashingly engaged on them when the general drifting movement towards the two bridge-tables set in. Mrs Poppit, with her glasses up, followed by Isabel, was employed in making a tour of the room, in case, as Miss Mapp had already determined, she never saw it again, examining the quality of the carpet, the curtains, the chair-backs with the air of a doubtful purchaser.

'And quite a quantity of books, I see,' she announced as she came opposite the fatal cupboard. 'Look, Isabel, what a quantity of books. There is something strange about them, though; I do not believe they are real.'

She put out her hand and pulled at the back of one of the volumes of 'Elegant Extracts'. The door swung open, and from behind it came a noise of rattling, bumping and clattering. Something soft and heavy thumped on to the floor, and a cloud of floury dust arose. A bottle of Bovril embedded itself quietly there without damage, and a tin of Bath Oliver biscuits beat a fierce tattoo on one of corned beef.

Innumerable dried apricots from the burst package flew about like shrapnel, and tapped at the tins. A jar of prunes, breaking its fall on the flour, rolled merrily out into the middle of the floor.

The din was succeeded by complete silence. The Padre had said 'What ho, i' fegs?' during the tumult, but his voice had been drowned by the rattling of the dried apricots. The Member of the Order of the British Empire stepped free of the provisions that bumped round her, and examined them through her glasses. Diva crammed the last jumble into her mouth and disposed of it with the utmost rapidity. The birthday of her life had come, as Miss Rossetti said.

'Dear Elizabeth!' she exclaimed. 'What a disaster! All your little stores in case of the coal-strike. Let me help to pick them up. I do not think anything is broken. Isn't that lucky?'

Evie hurried to the spot.

'Such a quantity of good things,' she said rapidly under her breath. 'Tinned meats and Bovril and prunes, and ever so many apricots. Let me pick them all up, and with a little dusting . . . Why, what a big cupboard, and such a quantity of good things.'

Miss Mapp had certainly struck a streak of embarrassments. What with naked Mr Hopkins, and Janet's frock and this unveiling of her hoard, life seemed at the moment really to consist of nothing else than beastly situations. How on earth that catch of the door had come undone, she had no idea, but much as she would have liked to suspect foul play from somebody, she was bound to conclude that Mrs Poppit with her prying hands had accidentally pressed it. It was like Diva, of course, to break the silence with odious allusions to hoarding, and bitterly she wished that she had not started the topic the other day, but had been content to lay in her stores without so pointedly affirming that she was doing nothing of the kind. But this was no time for vain laments, and restraining a natural impulse to scratch and beat Mrs Poppit, she exhibited an admirable inventiveness and composure. Though she knew it would deceive nobody, everybody had to pretend he was deceived.

'Oh, my poor little Christmas presents for your needy parishioners, Padre,' she said. 'You've seen them before you were meant to, and you must forget all about them. And so little harm done, just an apricot or two. Withers will pick them all up, so let us get to our bridge.'

Withers entered the room at this moment to clear away tea, and Miss Mapp explained it all over again.

'All our little Christmas presents have come tumbling out, Withers,' she said. 'Will you put as many as you can back in the cupboard and take the rest indoors? Don't tread on the apricots.'

It was difficult to avoid doing this, as the apricots were everywhere, and their colour on the brown carpet was wonderfully protective. Miss Mapp herself had already stepped on two, and their adhesive stickiness was hard to get rid of. In fact, for the next few minutes the coal-shovel was in strong request for their removal from the soles of shoes, and the fender was littered with their squashed remains . . . The party generally was distinctly thoughtful as it sorted itself out into two tables, for every single member of it was trying to assimilate the amazing proposition that Miss Mapp had, halfway through September, loaded her cupboard with Christmas presents on a scale that staggered belief. The feat required thought: it required a faith so childlike as to verge on the imbecile. Conversation during deals had an awkward tendency towards discussion of the coal-strike. As often as it drifted there the subject was changed very abruptly, just as if there was some occult reason for not speaking of so natural a topic. It concerned everybody, but it was rightly felt to concern Miss Mapp the most . . .

Chapter Five

It was the Major's turn to entertain his friend, and by half-past nine, on a certain squally October evening, he and Puffin were seated by the fire in the diary-room, while the rain volleyed at the windows and occasional puffs of stinging smoke were driven down the chimney by the gale that squealed and buffeted round the house. Puffin, by way of keeping up the comedy of Roman roads, had brought a map of the district across from his house, but the more essential part of his equipment for this studious evening was a bottle of whisky. Originally the host had provided whisky for himself and his guest at these pleasant chats, but there were undeniable objections to this plan, because the guest always proved unusually thirsty, which tempted his host to keep pace with him, while if they both drank at their own expense, the causes of economy and abstemiousness had a better chance. Also, while the Major took his drinks short and strong in a small tumbler, Puffin enriched his with lemons and sugar in a large one, so that nobody could really tell if equality as well as fraternity was realised. But if each brought his own bottle . . .

It had been a trying day, and the Major was very lame. A drenching storm had come up during their golf, while they were far from the clubhouse, and Puffin, being three up, had very naturally refused to accede to his opponent's suggestion to call the match off. He was perfectly willing to be paid his half-crown and go home, but Major Flint, remembering that Puffin's game usually went to pieces if it rained, had rejected this proposal with the scorn that it deserved. There had been other disagreeable incidents as well. His driver, slippery from rain, had flown out of the Major's hands on the twelfth tee, and had 'shot like a streamer of the northern morn', and landed in a pool of brackish water left by an unusually high tide. The ball had gone into another pool nearer the tee. The ground was greasy with moisture, and three holes further on Puffin had fallen flat on his face instead of lashing his fifth shot home on to the green, as he had intended. They had given each other stymies, and each had holed his opponent's ball by mistake; they had wrangled over the correct procedure if you lay in a rabbit-scrape or on the tram lines; the Major had lost a new ball; there was a mushroom on one of the greens between Puffin's ball and the hole . . . All these untoward incidents had come crowding in together, and from the Major's point of view, the worst of them all had been the collective incident that Puffin, so far from being put off by the rain, had, in spite of mushroom and falling down, played with a steadiness of which he was usually quite incapable. Consequently Major Flint was lame and his wound troubled him, while Puffin, in spite of his obvious reasons for complacency, was growing irritated with his companion's ill-temper, and was half blinded by wood-smoke.

He wiped his streaming eyes.

'You should get your chimney swept,' he observed.

Major Flint had put his handkerchief over his face to keep the wood-smoke out of his eyes. He blew it off with a loud, indignant puff.

'Oh! Ah! Indeed!' he said.

Puffin was rather taken aback by the violence of these interjections; they dripped with angry sarcasm.

'Oh, well! No offence,' he said.

'A man,' said the Major impersonally, 'makes an offensive remark, and says "No offence." If your own fireside suits you better than mine, Captain Puffin, all I can say is that you're at liberty to enjoy it!'

This was all rather irregular: they had indulged in a good stiff breeze this afternoon, and it was too early to ruffle the calm again. Puffin plucked and proffered an olive-branch.

'There's your handkerchief,' he said, picking it up. 'Now let's have one of our comfortable talks. Hot glass of grog and a chat over the fire: that's the best thing after such a wetting as we got this afternoon. I'll take a slice of lemon, if you'll be so good as to give it me, and a lump of sugar.'

The Major got up and limped to his cupboard. It struck him precisely at that moment that Puffin scored considerably over lemons and sugar, because he was supplied with them gratis every other night; whereas he himself, when Puffin's guest, took nothing off his host but hot water. He determined to ask for some biscuits, anyhow, tomorrow . . .

'I hardly know whether there's a lemon left,' he grumbled. 'I must lay in a store of lemons. As for sugar – '

Puffin chose to disregard this suggestion.

'Amusing incident the other day,' he said brightly, 'when Miss Mapp's cupboard door flew open. The old lady didn't like it. Don't suppose the poor of the parish will see much of that corned beef.'

The Major became dignified.

'Pardon me,' he said. 'When an esteemed friend like Miss Elizabeth tells me that certain provisions are destined for the poor of the parish, I take it that her statement is correct. I expect others of my friends, while they are in my presence, to do the same. I have the honour to give you a lemon, Captain Puffin, and a slice of sugar. I should say a lump of sugar. Pray make yourself comfortable.'

This dignified and lofty mood was often one of the after-effects of an unsuccessful game of golf. It generally yielded quite quickly to a little stimulant. Puffin filled his glass from the bottle and the kettle, while his friend put his handkerchief again over his face.

'Well, I shall just have my grog before I turn in,' he observed, according to custom. 'Aren't you going to join me, Major?'

'Presently, sir,' said the Major.

Puffin knocked out the consumed cinders in his pipe against the edge of the fender. Major Flint apparently was waiting for this, for he withdrew his handkerchief and closely watched the process. A minute piece of ash fell from Puffin's pipe on to the hearthrug, and he jumped to his feet and removed it very carefully with the shovel.

'I have your permission, I hope?' he said witheringly.

'Certainly, certainly,' said Puffin. 'Now get your glass, Major. You'll feel better in a minute or two.'

Major Flint would have liked to have kept up this magnificent attitude, but the smell of Puffin's steaming glass beat dignity down, and after glaring at him, he limped back to the cupboard for his whisky bottle. He gave a lamentable cry when he beheld it.

'But I got that bottle in only the day before yesterday,' he shouted, 'and there's hardly a drink left in it.'

'Well, you did yourself pretty well last night,' said Puffin. 'Those small glasses of yours, if frequently filled up, empty a bottle quicker than you seem to realise.'

Motives of policy prevented the Major from receiving this with the resentment that was proper to it, and his face cleared. He would get quits over these incessant lemons and lumps of sugar.

'Well, you'll have to let me borrow from you tonight,' he said genially, as he poured the rest of the contents of his bottle into the glass. 'Ah, that's more the ticket! A glass of whisky a day keeps the doctor away.'

The prospect of sponging on Puffin was most exhilarating, and he put his large slippered feet on to the fender.

'Yes, indeed, that was a highly amusing incident about Miss Mapp's cupboard,' he said. 'And wasn't Mrs Plaistow down on her like a knife about it? Our fair friends, you know, have a pretty sharp eye for each other's little failings. They've no sooner finished one squabble than they begin another, the pert little fairies. They can't sit and enjoy themselves like two old cronies I could tell you of, and feel at peace with all the world.'

He finished his glass at a gulp, and seemed much surprised to find it empty.

'I'll be borrowing a drop from you, old friend,' he said.

'Help yourself, Major,' said Puffin, with a keen eye as to how much he took.

'Very obliging of you. I feel as if I caught a bit of a chill this afternoon. My wound.'

'Be careful not to inflame it,' said Puffin.

'Thank ye for the warning. It's this beastly climate that touches it up. A winter in England adds years on to a man's life unless he takes care of himself. Take care of yourself, old boy. Have some more sugar.'

Before long the Major's hand was moving slowly and instinctively towards Puffin's whisky bottle again.

'I reckon that big glass of yours, Puffin,' he said, 'holds between three and a half times to four times what my little tumbler holds. Between three and a half and four I should reckon. I may be wrong.'

'Reckoning the water in, I dare say you're not far out, Major,' said he. 'And according to my estimate you mix your drink somewhere about three and a half times to four stronger than I mix mine.'

'Oh, come, come!' said the Major.

'Three and a half to four times, *I* should say,' repeated Puffin. 'You won't find I'm far out.'

He replenished his big tumbler, and instead of putting the bottle back on the table, absently deposited it on the floor on the far side of his chair. This second tumbler usually marked the most convivial period of the evening, for the first would have healed whatever unhappy discords had marred the harmony of the day, and, those being disposed of, they very contentedly talked through their hats about past prowesses, and took a rosy view of the youth and energy which still beat in their vigorous pulses. They would begin, perhaps, by extolling each other: Puffin, when informed that his friend would be fifty-four next birthday, flatly refused (without offence) to believe it, and, indeed, he was quite right in so doing, because the Major was in reality fifty-six. In turn, Major Flint would say that his friend had the figure of a boy of twenty, which caused Puffin presently to feel a little cramped and to wander negligently in front of the big looking-glass between the windows, and find this compliment much easier to swallow than the Major's age. For the next half-hour they would chiefly talk about themselves in a pleasant glow of self-satisfaction. Major Flint, looking at the various implements and trophies that adorned the room, would suggest putting a sporting challenge in *The Times*.

' 'Pon my word, Puffin,' he would say, 'I've half a mind to do it. Retired Major of His Majesty's Forces – the King, God bless him!' (and he took a substantial sip); ' "Retired Major, aged fifty-four, challenges any gentleman of fifty years or over." '

'Forty,' said Puffin sycophantically, as he thought over what he would say about himself when the old man had finished.

'Well, we'll halve it, we'll say forty-five, to please you, Puffin – let's see, where had I got to? – "Retired Major challenges any gentleman of forty-five years or over to – to a shooting match in the morning, followed by half a dozen rounds with four-ounce gloves, a game of golf, eighteen holes, in the afternoon, and a billiard match of two hundred up after tea." Ha! ha! I shouldn't feel much anxiety as to the result.'

'My confounded leg!' said Puffin. 'But I know a retired captain from His Majesty's merchant service – the King, God bless him! – aged fifty – '

'Ho! ho! Fifty, indeed!' said the Major, thinking to himself that a dried-up little man like Puffin might be as old as an Egyptian mummy. Who can tell the age of a kipper? . . .

'Not a day less, Major. "Retired Captain, aged fifty, who'll take on all comers of forty-two and over, at a steeplechase, round of golf, billiard match, hopping match, gymnastic competition, swinging Indian clubs – " No objection, gentlemen? Then carried *nem. con.*'

This gaseous mood, athletic, amatory or otherwise (the amatory ones were the worst), usually faded slowly, like the light from the setting sun or an exhausted coal in the grate, about the end of Puffin's second tumbler, and the gentlemen after that were usually somnolent, but occasionally laid the foundation for some disagreement next day, which they were too sleepy to go into now. Major Flint by this time would have had some five small glasses of whisky (equivalent, as he bitterly observed, to one in pre-war days), and as he measured his next with extreme care and a slightly jerky movement, would announce it as being his nightcap, though you would have thought he had plenty of nightcaps on already. Puffin correspondingly took a thimbleful more (the thimble apparently belonging to some housewife of Anak), and after another half-hour of sudden single snores and startings awake again, of pipes frequently lit and immediately going out, the guest, still perfectly capable of coherent speech and voluntary motion in the required direction, would stumble across the dark cobbles to his house, and doors would be very carefully closed for fear of attracting the attention of the lady who at this period of the evening was usually known as 'Old Mappy'. The two were perfectly well aware of the sympathetic interest that Old Mappy took in all that concerned them, and that she had an eye on their evening séances was evidenced by the frequency with which the corner of her blind in the window of the garden-room was raised between, say, half-past nine and eleven at night. They had often watched with giggles the pencil of light that escaped, obscured at the lower end by the outline of Old Mappy's head, and occasionally drank to the 'Guardian Angel'. Guardian Angel, in answer to direct enquiries, had been told by Major Benjy during the last month that he worked at his diaries on three nights in the week and went to bed early on the others, to the vast improvement of his mental grasp.

'And on Sunday night, dear Major Benjy?' asked Old Mappy in the character of Guardian Angel.

'I don't think you knew my beloved, my revered mother, Miss

Elizabeth,' said Major Benjy. 'I spend Sunday evening as – Well, well.'

The very next Sunday evening Guardian Angel had heard the sound of singing. She could not catch the words, and only fragments of the tune, which reminded her of 'The roseate morn hath passed away'. Brimming with emotion, she sang it softly to herself as she undressed, and blamed herself very much for ever having thought that dear Major Benjy – She peeped out of her window when she had extinguished her light, but fortunately the singing had ceased.

*   *   *

Tonight, however, the epoch of Puffin's second big tumbler was not accompanied by harmonious developments. Major Benjy was determined to make the most of this unique opportunity of drinking his friend's whisky, and whether Puffin put the bottle on the further side of him, or under his chair, or under the table, he came padding round in his slippers and standing near the ambush while he tried to interest his friend in tales of love or tiger-shooting so as to distract his attention. When he mistakenly thought he had done so, he hastily refilled his glass, taking unusually stiff doses for fear of not getting another opportunity, and altogether omitting to ask Puffin's leave for these maraudings. When this had happened four or five times, Puffin, acting on the instinct of the polar bear who eats her babies for fear that anybody else should get them, surreptitiously poured the rest of his bottle into his glass, and filled it up to the top with hot water, making a mixture of extraordinary power.

Soon after this Major Flint came rambling round the table again. He was not sure whether Puffin had put the bottle by his chair or behind the coal-scuttle, and was quite ignorant of the fact that wherever it was, it was empty. Amorous reminiscences tonight had been the accompaniment to Puffin's second tumbler.

'Devilish fine woman she was,' he said, 'and that was the last that Benjamin Flint ever saw of her. She went up to the hills next morning – '

'But the last you saw of her just now was on the deck of the P&O at Bombay,' objected Puffin. 'Or did she go up to the hills on the deck of the P&O? Wonderful line!'

'No, sir,' said Benjamin Flint, 'that was Helen, *la belle Hélène*. It was *la belle Hélène* whom I saw off at the Apollo Bunder. I don't know if I told you – By Gad, I've kicked the bottle over. No idea you'd put it there. Hope the cork's in.'

'No harm if it isn't,' said Puffin, beginning on his third most fiery glass. The strength of it rather astonished him.

'You don't mean to say it's empty?' asked Major Flint. 'Why just now there was close on a quarter of a bottle left.'

'As much as that?' asked Puffin. 'Glad to hear it.'

'Not a drop less. You don't mean to say – Well, if you can drink that and can say hippopotamus afterwards, I should put that among your challenges, to men of four hundred and two: I should say forty-two. It's a fine thing to have a strong head, though if I drank what you've got in your glass, I should be tipsy, sir.'

Puffin laughed in his irritating falsetto manner.

'Good thing that it's in my glass then, and not your glass,' he said. 'And lemme tell you, Major, in case you don't know it, that when I've drunk every drop of this and sucked the lemon, you'll have had far more out of my bottle this evening than I have. My usual twice and – and my usual nightcap, as you say, is what's my ration, and I've had no more than my ration. Eight Bells.'

'And a pretty good ration you've got there,' said the baffled Major. 'Without your usual twice.'

Puffin was beginning to be aware of that as he swallowed the fiery mixture, but nothing in the world would now have prevented his drinking every single drop of it. It was clear to him, among so much that was dim owing to the wood-smoke, that the Major would miss a good many drives tomorrow morning.

'And whose whisky is it?' he said, gulping down the fiery stuff.

'I know whose it's going to be,' said the other.

'And I know whose it is now,' retorted Puffin, 'and I know whose whisky it is that's filled you up ti' as a drum. Tight as a drum,' he repeated very carefully.

Major Flint was conscious of an unusual activity of brain, and, when he spoke, of a sort of congestion and entanglement of words. It pleased him to think that he had drunk so much of somebody else's whisky, but he felt that he ought to be angry.

'That's a very unmentionable sor' of thing to say,' he remarked. 'An' if it wasn't for the sacred claims of hospitality, I'd make you explain just what you mean by that, and make you eat your words. Pologise, in fact.'

Puffin finished his glass at a gulp, and rose to his feet.

'Pologies be blowed,' he said. 'Hittopopamus!'

'And were you addressing that to me?' asked Major Flint with deadly calm.

'Of course, I was. Hippot – same animal as before. Pleasant old boy. And as for the lemon you lent me, well, I don't want it any more. Have a suck at it, ole fellow! I don't want it any more.'

The Major turned purple in the face, made a course for the door like a knight's move at chess (a long step in one direction and a short one at right angles to the first) and opened it. The door thus served as an aperture from the room and a support to himself. He spoke no word of any sort or kind: his silence spoke for him in a far more dignified manner than he could have managed for himself.

Captain Puffin stood for a moment wreathed in smiles, and fingering the slice of lemon, which he had meant playfully to throw at his friend. But his smile faded, and by some sort of telepathic perception he realised how much more decorous it was to say (or, better, to indicate) good-night in a dignified manner than to throw lemons about. He walked in dots and dashes like a Morse code out of the room, bestowing a naval salute on the Major as he passed. The latter returned it with a military salute and a suppressed hiccup. Not a word passed.

Then Captain Puffin found his hat and coat without much difficulty, and marched out of the house, slamming the door behind him with a bang that echoed down the street and made Miss Mapp dream about a thunderstorm. He let himself into his own house, and bent down before his expired fire, which he tried to blow into life again. This was unsuccessful, and he breathed in a quantity of wood-ash.

He sat down by his table and began to think things out. He told himself that he was not drunk at all, but that he had taken an unusual quantity of whisky, which seemed to produce much the same effect as intoxication. Allowing for that, he was conscious that he was extremely angry about something, and had a firm idea that the Major was very angry too.

'But woz'it all been about?' he vainly asked himself. 'Woz'it all been about?'

He was roused from his puzzling over this unanswerable conundrum by the clink of the flap in his letter-box. Either this was the first post in the morning, in which case it was much later than he thought, and wonderfully dark still, or it was the last post at night, in which case it was much earlier than he thought. But, whichever it was, a letter had been slipped into his box, and he brought it in. The gum on the envelope was still wet, which saved trouble in opening it. Inside was a half-sheet containing but a few words. This curt epistle ran as follows:

Sir – My seconds will wait on you in the course of tomorrow morning.

Your faithful obedient servant,

BENJAMIN FLINT

Captain Puffin.

Puffin felt as calm as a tropic night, and as courageous as a captain. Somewhere below his courage and his calm was an appalling sense of misgiving. That he successfully stifled.

'Very proper,' he said aloud. 'Qui' proper. Insults. Blood. Seconds won't have to wait a second. Better get a good sleep.'

He went up to his room, fell on to his bed and instantly began to snore.

*   *   *

It was still dark when he awoke, but the square of his window was visible against the blackness, and he concluded that though it was not morning yet, it was getting on for morning, which seemed a pity. As he turned over on to his side his hand came in contact with his coat, instead of a sheet, and he became aware that he had all his clothes on. Then, as with a crash of cymbals and the beating of a drum in his brain, the events of the evening before leaped into reality and significance. In a few hours now arrangements would have been made for a deadly encounter. His anger was gone, his whisky was gone, and in particular his courage was gone. He expressed all this compendiously by moaning 'Oh, God!'

He struggled to a sitting position, and lit a match at which he kindled his candle. He looked for his watch beside it, but it was not there. What could have happened – then he remembered that it was in its accustomed place in his waistcoat pocket. A consultation of it followed by holding it to his ear only revealed the fact that it had stopped at half-past five. With the lucidity that was growing brighter in his brain, he concluded that this stoppage was due to the fact that he had not wound it up . . . It was after half-past five then, but how much later only the Lords of Time knew – Time which bordered so closely on Eternity.

He felt that he had no use whatever for Eternity but that he must not waste Time. Just now, that was far more precious.

From somewhere in the Cosmic Consciousness there came to him a thought, namely, that the first train to London started at half-past six in the morning. It was a slow train, but it got there, and in any case it went away from Tilling. He did not trouble to consider how that thought came to him: the important point was that it had come. Coupled with that was the knowledge that it was now an undiscoverable number of minutes after half-past five.

There was a Gladstone bag under his bed. He had brought it back from the clubhouse only yesterday, after that game of golf which had been so full of disturbances and wet stockings, but which now wore the shimmering security of peaceful, tranquil days long past. How little, so he thought to himself, as he began swiftly storing shirts, ties, collars and other useful things into his bag, had he appreciated the sweet amenities of life, its pleasant conversations and companionships, its topped drives, and mushrooms and incalculable incidents. Now they wore a glamour and a preciousness that was bound up with life itself. He starved for more of them, not knowing while they were his how sweet they were.

The house was not yet astir, when ten minutes later he came downstairs with his bag. He left on his sitting-room table, where it would catch the eye of his housemaid, a sheet of paper on which he wrote 'Called away' (he shuddered as he traced the words). 'Forward no letters. Will communicate . . . ' (Somehow the telegraphic form seemed best to suit the urgency of the situation.) Then very quietly he let himself out of his house.

He could not help casting an apprehensive glance at the windows of his quondam friend and prospective murderer. To his horror he observed that there was a light behind the blind of the Major's bedroom, and pictured him writing to his seconds – he wondered who the 'seconds' were going to be – or polishing up his pistols. All the rumours and hints of the Major's duels and affairs of honour, which he had rather scorned before, not wholly believing them, poured like a red torrent into his mind, and he found that now he believed them with a passionate sincerity. Why had he ever attempted (and with such small success) to call this fire-eater a hippopotamus?

The gale of the night before had abated, and thick chilly rain was falling from a sullen sky as he tiptoed down the hill. Once round the corner and out of sight of the duellist's house, he broke into a limping run, which was accelerated by the sound of an engine-whistle from the station. It was mental suspense of the most agonising kind not to know how long it was after his watch had stopped that he had awoke, and the sound of that whistle, followed by several short puffs of steam, might prove to be the six-thirty bearing away to London, on business or pleasure, its secure and careless pilgrims. Splashing through puddles, lopsidedly weighted by his bag, with his mackintosh flapping against his legs, he gained the sanctuary of the waiting-room and booking-office, which was lighted by a dim expiring lamp, and scrutinised the face of the murky clock . . .

With a sob of relief he saw that he was in time. He was, indeed, in exceptionally good time, for he had a quarter of an hour to wait. An anxious internal debate followed as to whether or not he should take a return ticket. Optimism, that is to say, the hope that he would return to Tilling in peace and safety before the six months for which the ticket was available inclined him to the larger expense, but in these disquieting circumstances, it was difficult to be optimistic and he purchased a first-class single, for on such a morning, and on such a journey, he must get what comfort he could from looking-glasses, padded seats and coloured photographs of places of interest on the line. He formed no vision at all of the future: that was a dark well into which it was dangerous to peer. There was no bright speck in its unplumbable depths: unless Major Flint died suddenly without revealing the challenge he had sent last night, and the promptitude with which its recipient had disappeared rather than face his pistol, he could not frame any grouping of events which would make it possible for him to come back to Tilling again, for he would either have to fight (and this he was quite determined not to do) or be pointed at by the finger of scorn as the man who had refused to do so, and this was nearly as unthinkable as the other. Bitterly he blamed himself for having made a friend (and worse than that, an enemy) of one so obsolete and old-fashioned as to bring duelling into modern life . . . As far as he could be glad of anything he was glad that he had taken a single, not a return ticket.

He turned his eyes away from the blackness of the future and let his mind dwell on the hardly less murky past. Then, throwing up his hands, he buried his face in them with a hollow groan. By some miserable forgetfulness he had left the challenge on his chimney-piece, where his housemaid would undoubtedly find and read it. That would explain his absence far better than the telegraphic instructions he had left on his table. There was no time to go back for it now, even if he could have faced the risk of being seen by the Major, and in an hour or two the whole story, via Withers, Janet, etc., would be all over Tilling.

It was no use then thinking of the future nor of the past, and in order to anchor himself to the world at all and preserve his sanity he had to confine himself to the present. The minutes, long though each tarried, were slipping away and provided his train was punctual, the passage of five more of these laggards would see him safe. The newsboy took down the shutters of his stall, a porter quenched the expiring lamp, and Puffin began to listen for the rumble of the approaching train. It stayed three minutes here: if up to time it would be in before a couple more minutes had passed.

There came from the station-yard outside the sound of heavy footsteps running. Some early traveller like himself was afraid of missing the train. The door burst open, and, streaming with rain and panting for breath, Major Flint stood at the entry. Puffin looked wildly round to see whether he could escape, still perhaps unobserved, on to the platform, but it was too late, for their eyes met.

In that instant of abject terror, two things struck Puffin. One was that the Major looked at the open door behind him as if meditating retreat, the second that he carried a Gladstone bag. Simultaneously Major Flint spoke, if indeed that reverberating thunder of scornful indignation can be called speech.

'Ha! I guessed right then,' he roared. 'I guessed, sir, that you might be meditating flight, and I – in fact, I came down to see whether you were running away. I was right. You are a coward, Captain Puffin! But relieve your mind, sir. Major Flint will not demean himself to fight with a coward.'

Puffin gave one long sigh of relief, and then, standing in front of his own Gladstone bag, in order to conceal it, burst into a cackling laugh.

'Indeed!' he said. 'And why, Major, was it necessary for you to pack a Gladstone bag in order to stop me from running away? I'll tell you what has happened. You were running away, and you know it. I guessed you would. I came to stop you, you, you quaking runaway. Your wound troubled you, hey? Didn't want another, hey?'

There was an awful pause, broken by the entry from behind the Major of the outside porter, panting under the weight of a large portmanteau.

'You had to take your portmanteau, too,' observed Puffin witheringly, 'in order to stop me. That's a curious way of stopping me. You're a coward, sir! But go home. You're safe enough. This will be a fine story for tea-parties.'

Puffin turned from him in scorn, still concealing his own bag. Unfortunately the flap of his coat caught it, precariously perched on the bench, and it bumped to the ground.

'What's that?' said Major Flint.

They stared at each other for a moment and then simultaneously
burst into peals of laughter. The train rumbled slowly into the station,
but neither took the least notice of it, and only shook their heads and
broke out again when the station-master urged them to take their
seats. The only thing that had power to restore Captain Puffin to
gravity was the difficulty of getting the money for his ticket refunded,
while the departure of the train with his portmanteau in it did the
same for the Major.

*   *   *

The events of that night and morning, as may easily be imagined,
soon supplied Tilling with one of the most remarkable conundrums
that had ever been forced upon its notice. Puffin's housemaid, during
his absence at the station, found and read not only the notice intended
for her eyes, but the challenge which he had left on the chimney-
piece. She conceived it to be her duty to take it down to Mrs Gashly,
his cook, and while they were putting the bloodiest construction on
these inscriptions, their conference was interrupted by the return of
Captain Puffin in the highest spirits, who, after a vain search for the
challenge, was quite content, as its purport was no longer fraught
with danger and death, to suppose that he had torn it up. Mrs Gashly,
therefore, after preparing breakfast at this unusually early hour, went
across to the back door of the Major's house, with the challenge in
her hand, to borrow a nutmeg grater, and gleaned the information
that Mrs Dominic's employer (for master he could not be called) had
gone off in a great hurry to the station early that morning with a
Gladstone bag and a portmanteau, the latter of which had been seen
no more, though the Major had returned. So Mrs Gashly produced
the challenge, and having watched Miss Mapp off to the High Street
at half-past ten, Dominic and Gashly went together to her house, to
see if Withers could supply anything of importance, or, if not, a
nutmeg grater. They were forced to be content with the grater, but
pored over the challenge with Withers, and she having an errand to
Diva's house, told Janet, who without further ceremony bounded
upstairs to tell her mistress. Hardly had Diva heard, than she plunged
into the High Street, and, with suitable additions, told Miss Mapp,
Evie, Irene and the Padre under promise, in each case, of the strictest
secrecy. Ten minutes later Irene had asked the defenceless Mr
Hopkins, who was being Adam again, what he knew about it, and
Evie, with her mouse-like gait that looked so rapid and was so
deliberate, had the mortification of seeing Miss Mapp outdistance

her and be admitted into the Poppits' house, just as she came in view of the front door. She rightly conjectured that, after the affair of the store-cupboard in the garden-room, there could be nothing of lesser importance than 'the duel' which could take that lady through those abhorred portals. Finally, at ten minutes past eleven, Major Flint and Captain Puffin were seen by one or two fortunate people (the morning having cleared up) walking together to the tram, and, without exception, everybody knew that they were on their way to fight their duel in some remote hollow of the sand-dunes.

Miss Mapp had gone straight home from her visit to the Poppits just about eleven, and stationed herself in the window where she could keep an eye on the houses of the duellists. In her anxiety to outstrip Evie and be the first to tell the Poppits, she had not waited to hear that they had both come back and knew only of the challenge and that they had gone to the station. She had already formed a glorious idea of her own as to what the history of the duel (past or future) was, and intoxicated with emotion had retired from the wordy fray to think about it, and, as already mentioned, to keep an eye on the two houses just below. Then there appeared in sight the Padre, walking swiftly up the hill, and she had barely time under cover of the curtain to regain the table where her sweet chrysanthemums were pining for water when Withers announced him. He wore a furrowed brow and quite forgot to speak either Scotch or Elizabethan English. A few rapid words made it clear that they both had heard the main outlines.

'A terrible situation,' said the Padre. 'Duelling is in direct contra-vention of all Christian principles, and, I believe, of the civil law. The discharge of a pistol, in unskilful hands, may lead to deplorable results. And Major Flint, so one has heard, is an experienced duellist . . . That, of course, makes it even more dangerous.'

It was at this identical moment that Major Flint came out of his house and *quai-hai*ed cheerily to Puffin. Miss Mapp and the Padre, deep in these bloody possibilities, neither saw nor heard them. They passed together down the road and into the High Street, unconscious that their every look and action was being more commented on than the Epistle to the Hebrews. Inside the garden-room Miss Mapp sighed, and bent her eyes on her chrysanthemums.

'Quite terrible!' she said. 'And in our peaceful, tranquil Tilling!'

'Perhaps the duel has already taken place, and – and they've missed,' said the Padre. 'They were both seen to return to their houses early this morning.'

'By whom?' asked Miss Mapp jealously. She had not heard that.

'By Hopkins,' said he. 'Hopkins saw them both return.'

'I shouldn't trust that man too much,' said Miss Mapp. 'Hopkins may not be telling the truth. I have no great opinion of his moral standard.'

'Why is that?'

This was no time to discuss the nudity of Hopkins and Miss Mapp put the question aside.

'That does not matter now, dear Padre,' she said. 'I only wish I thought the duel had taken place without accident. But Major Benjy's – I mean Major Flint's – portmanteau has not come back to his house. Of that I'm sure. What if they have sent it away to some place where they are unknown, full of pistols and things?'

'Possible – terribly possible,' said the Padre. 'I wish I could see my duty clear. I should not hesitate to – well, to do the best I could to induce them to abandon this murderous project. And what do you imagine was the root of the quarrel?'

'I couldn't say, I'm sure,' said Miss Mapp. She bent her head over the chrysanthemums.

'Your distracting sex,' said he with a moment's gallantry, 'is usually the cause of quarrel. I've noticed that they both seemed to admire Miss Irene very much.'

Miss Mapp raised her head and spoke with great animation.

'Dear, quaint Irene, I'm sure, has nothing whatever to do with it,' she said with perfect truth. 'Nothing whatever!'

There was no mistaking the sincerity of this, and the Padre, Tillingite to the marrow, instantly concluded that Miss Mapp knew what (or who) was the cause of all this unique disturbance. And as she bent her head again over the chrysanthemums, and quite distinctly grew brick-red in the face, he felt that delicacy prevented his enquiring any further.

'What are you going to do, dear Padre?' she asked in a low voice, choking with emotion. 'Whatever you decide will be wise and Christian. Oh, these violent men! Such babies, too!'

The Padre was bursting with curiosity, but since his delicacy forbade him to ask any of the questions which effervesced like sherbet round his tongue, he propounded another plan.

'I think my duty is to go straight to the Major,' he said, 'who seems to be the principal in the affair, and tell him that I know all – and guess the rest,' he added.

'Nothing that I have said,' declared Miss Mapp in great confusion, 'must have anything to do with your guesses. Promise me that, Padre.'

This intimate and fruitful conversation was interrupted by the sound of two pairs of steps just outside, and before Withers had had time to say 'Mrs Plaistow,' Diva burst in.

'They have both taken the eleven-twenty tram,' she said, and sank into the nearest chair.

'Together?' asked Miss Mapp, feeling a sudden chill of disappointment at the thought of a duel with pistols trailing off into one with golf clubs.

'Yes, but that's a blind,' panted Diva. 'They were talking and laughing together. Sheer blind! Duel among the sand-dunes!'

'Padre, it is your duty to stop it,' said Miss Mapp faintly.

'But if the pistols are in a portmanteau – ' he began.

'What portmanteau?' screamed Diva, who hadn't heard about that.

'Darling, I'll tell you presently,' said Miss Mapp. 'That was only a guess of mine, Padre. But there's no time to lose.'

'But there's no tram to catch,' said the Padre. 'It has gone by this time.'

'A taxi then, Padre! Oh, lose no time!'

'Are you coming with me?' he said in a low voice. 'Your presence – '

'Better not,' she said. 'It might – Better not,' she repeated.

He skipped down the steps and was observed running down the street.

'What about the portmanteau?' asked the greedy Diva.

*   *   *

It was with strong misgivings that the Padre started on his Christian errand, and had not the sense of adventure spiced it, he would probably have returned to his sermon instead, which was Christian, too. To begin with, there was the ruinous expense of taking a taxi out to the golf links, but by no other means could he hope to arrive in time to avert an encounter that might be fatal. It must be said to his credit that, though this was an errand distinctly due to his position as the spiritual head of Tilling, he rejected, as soon as it occurred to him, the idea of charging the hire of the taxi to Church Expenses, and as he whirled along the flat road across the marsh, the thing that chiefly buoyed up his drooping spirits and annealed his courage was the romantic nature of his mission. He no longer, thanks to what Miss Mapp had so clearly refrained from saying, had the slightest doubt that she, in some manner that scarcely needed conjecture, was the cause of the duel he was attempting to avert. For years it had been a matter of unwearied and confidential discussion as to whether and when she would marry either Major Flint or Captain Puffin, and it was superfluous to look for any other explanation. It was true that she, in popular parlance, was 'getting on', but so, too, and at exactly the same rate, were the representatives of the United Services, and the sooner that two out of the three of them 'got on' permanently, the better. No doubt some crisis had arisen, and inflamed with love . . . He intended to confide all this to his wife on his return.

On his return! The unspoken words made his heart sink. What if he never did return? For he was about to place himself in a position of no common danger. His plan was to drive past the clubhouse, and then on foot, after discharging the taxi, to strike directly into the line of tumbled sand-dunes which, remote and undisturbed and full of large convenient hollows, stretched along the coast above the flat beach. Any of those hollows, he knew, might prove to contain the duellists in the very act of firing, and over the rim of each he had to pop his unprotected head. He (if in time) would have to separate the combatants, and who knew whether, in their very natural chagrin at being interrupted, they might not turn their combined pistols on him first, and settle with each other afterwards? One murder the more made little difference to desperate men. Other shocks, less deadly but extremely unnerving, might await him. He might be too late, and pop his head over the edge of one of these craters, only to discover it full of bleeding if not mangled bodies. Or there might be only one mangled body, and the other, unmangled, would pursue him through the sand-dunes and offer him life at the price of silence. That, he painfully reflected, would be a very difficult decision to make. Luckily, Captain Puffin (if he proved to be the survivor) was lame . . .

With drawn face and agonised prayers on his lips, he began a systematic search of the sand-dunes. Often his nerve nearly failed him, and he would sink panting among the prickly bents before he dared to peer into the hollow up the sides of which he had climbed. His ears shuddered at the anticipation of hearing from near at hand the report of pistols, and once a backfire from a motor passing along the road caused him to leap high in the air. The sides of these dunes were steep, and his shoes got so full of sand, that from time to time, in spite of the urgency of his errand, he was forced to pause in order to empty them out. He stumbled in rabbit holes, he caught his foot and once his trousers in strands of barbed wire, the remnant of coast defences in the Great War, he crashed among potsherds and abandoned kettles; but with a thoroughness that did equal credit to his wind and his Christian spirit, he searched a mile of perilous dunes from end to end, and peered into every important hollow. Two hours later, jaded and torn and streaming with perspiration, he came, in the vicinity of the clubhouse, to the end of his fruitless search.

He staggered round the corner of it and came in view of the eighteenth green. Two figures were occupying it, and one of these was in the act of putting. He missed. Then he saw who the figures were: it was Captain Puffin who had just missed his putt, it was Major Flint who now expressed elated sympathy.

'Bad luck, old boy,' he said. 'Well, a jolly good match and we halve it. Why, there's the Padre. Been for a walk? Join us in a round this afternoon, Padre! Blow your sermon!'

Chapter Six

The same delightful prospect at the end of the High Street, over the marsh, which had witnessed not so long ago the final encounter in the Wars of the Roses and the subsequent armistice, was, of course, found to be peculiarly attractive that morning to those who knew (and who did not?) that the combatants had left by the eleven-twenty steam-tram to fight among the sand-dunes, and that the intrepid Padre had rushed after them in a taxi. The Padre's taxi had returned empty, and the driver seemed to know nothing whatever about anything, so the only thing for everybody to do was to put off lunch and wait for the arrival of the next tram, which occurred at one thirty-seven. In consequence, all the doors in Tilling flew open like those of cuckoo clocks at ten minutes before that hour, and this pleasant promenade was full of those who so keenly admired autumn tints.

From here the progress of the tram across the plain was in full view; so, too, was the shed-like station across the river, which was the terminus of the line, and expectation, when the two-waggoned little train approached the end of its journey, was so tense that it was almost disagreeable. A couple of hours had elapsed since, like the fishers who sailed away into the West and were seen no more till the corpses lay out on the shining sand, the three had left for the sand-dunes, and a couple of hours, so reasoned the Cosmic

Consciousness of Tilling, gave ample time for a duel to be fought, if the Padre was not in time to stop it, and for him to stop it if he was. No surgical assistance, as far as was known, had been summoned, but the reason for that might easily be that a surgeon's skill was no longer, alas! of any avail for one, if not both, of the combatants. But if such was the case, it was nice to hope that the Padre had been in time to supply spiritual aid to anyone whom first-aid and probes were powerless to succour.

The variety of *dénouements* which the approaching tram, that had now cut off steam, was capable of providing was positively bewildering. They whirled through Miss Mapp's head like the autumn leaves which she admired so much, and she tried in vain to catch them all, and, when caught, to tick them off on her fingers. Each, moreover, furnished diverse and legitimate conclusions. For instance (taking the thumb).

I   If nobody of the slightest importance arrived by the tram, that might be because
    (a) Nothing had happened, and they were all playing golf.
    (b) The worst had happened, and, as the Padre had feared, the duellists had first shot him and then each other.
    (c) The next worst had happened, and the Padre was arranging for the reverent removal of the corpse of
        (i)   Major Benjy, or
        (ii) Captain Puffin, or those of
        (iii) Both.

Miss Mapp let go of her thumb and lightly touched her forefinger.

II The Padre might arrive alone.
    In that case anything or nothing might have happened to either or both of the others, and the various contingencies hanging on this arrival were so numerous that there was not time to sort them out.
III The Padre might arrive with two limping figures whom he assisted.
    Here it must not be forgotten that Captain Puffin always limped, and the Major occasionally. Miss Mapp did not forget it.
IV The Padre might arrive with a stretcher. Query – Whose?
V   The Padre might arrive with two stretchers.
VI Three stretchers might arrive from the shining sands, at the town where the women were weeping and wringing their hands.

In that case Miss Mapp saw herself busily employed in strengthening poor Evie, who now was running about like a mouse from group to group picking up crumbs of Cosmic Consciousness.

Miss Mapp had got as far as sixthly, though she was aware she had not exhausted the possibilities, when the tram stopped. She furtively took out from her pocket (she had focused them before she put them in) the opera-glasses through which she had watched the station-yard on a day which had been very much less exciting than this. After one glance she put them back again, feeling vexed and disappointed with herself, for the *dénouement* which they had so unerringly disclosed was one that had not entered her mind at all. In that moment she had seen that out of the tram there stepped three figures and no stretcher. One figure, it is true, limped, but in a manner so natural, that she scorned to draw any deductions from that halting gait. They proceeded, side by side, across the bridge over the river towards the town.

It is no use denying that the Cosmic Consciousness of the ladies of Tilling was aware of a disagreeable anticlimax to so many hopes and fears. It had, of course, hoped for the best, but it had not expected that the best would be quite as bad as this. The best, to put it frankly, would have been a bandaged arm, or something of that kind. There was still room for the more hardened optimist to hope that something of some sort had occurred, or that something of some sort had been averted, and that the whole affair was not, in the delicious new slang phrase of the Padre's, which was spreading like wildfire through Tilling, a 'washout'. Pistols might have been innocuously discharged for all that was known to the contrary. But it looked bad.

Miss Mapp was the first to recover from the blow, and took Diva's podgy hand.

'Diva, darling,' she said, 'I feel so deeply thankful. What a wonderful and beautiful end to all our anxiety!'

There was a subconscious regret with regard to the anxiety. The anxiety was, so to speak, a dear and beloved departed . . . And Diva did not feel so sure that the end was so beautiful and wonderful. Her grandfather, Miss Mapp had reason to know, had been a butcher, and probably some inherited indifference to slaughter lurked in her tainted blood.

'There's the portmanteau still,' she said hopefully. 'Pistols in the portmanteau. Your idea, Elizabeth.'

'Yes, dear,' said Elizabeth; 'but thank God I must have been very wrong about the portmanteau. The outside porter told me that he

brought it up from the station to Major Benjy's house half an hour
ago. Fancy your not knowing that! I feel sure he is a truthful man,
for he attends the Padre's confirmation class. If there had been pistols
in it, Major Benjy and Captain Puffin would have gone away too. I
am quite happy about that now. It went away and it has come back.
That's all about the portmanteau.'

She paused a moment.

'But what does it contain, then?' she said quickly, more as if she
was thinking aloud than talking to Diva. 'Why did Major Benjy pack
it and send it to the station this morning? Where has it come back
from? Why did it go there?'

She felt that she was saying too much, and pressed her hand to her
head.

'Has all this happened this morning?' she said. 'What a full
morning, dear! Lovely autumn leaves! I shall go home and have my
lunch and rest. *Au reservoir*, Diva.'

Miss Mapp's eternal *reservoirs* had begun to get on Diva's nerves,
and as she lingered here a moment more a great idea occurred to
her, which temporarily banished the disappointment about the
duellists. Elizabeth, as all the world knew, had accumulated a great
reservoir of provisions in the false bookcase in her garden-room, and
Diva determined that, if she could think of a neat phrase, the very
next time Elizabeth said *au reservoir* to her, she would work in an
allusion to Elizabeth's own reservoir of corned beef, tongue, flour,
Bovril, dried apricots and condensed milk. She would have to frame
some stinging rejoinder which would 'escape her' when next Elizabeth
used that stale old phrase: it would have to be short, swift and
spontaneous, and therefore required careful thought. It would be
good to bring 'pop' into it also. 'Your reservoir in the garden-room
hasn't gone "pop" again, I hope, darling?' was the first draft that
occurred to her, but that was not sufficiently condensed. 'Pop goes
the reservoir,' on the analogy of the weasel, was better. And, better
than either, was there not some sort of corn called popcorn, which
Americans ate? . . . 'Have you any popcorn in your reservoir?' That
would be a nasty one . . .

But it all required thinking over, and the sight of the Padre and the
duellists crossing the field below, as she still lingered on this escarp-
ment of the hill, brought the duel back to her mind. It would have
been considered inquisitive even at Tilling to put direct questions to
the combatants, and (still hoping for the best) ask them point-blank
'Who won?' or something of that sort; but until she arrived at some

sort of information, the excruciating pangs of curiosity that must be endured could be likened only to some acute toothache of the mind with no dentist to stop or remove the source of the trouble. Elizabeth had already succumbed to these pangs of surmise and excitement, and had frankly gone home to rest, and her absence, the fact that for the next hour or two she could not, except by some extraordinary feat on the telephone, get hold of anything which would throw light on the whole prodigious situation, inflamed Diva's brain to the highest pitch of inventiveness. She knew that she was Elizabeth's inferior in point of reconstructive imagination, and the present moment, while the other was recuperating her energies for fresh assaults on the unknown, was Diva's opportunity. The one person who might be presumed to know more than anybody else was the Padre, but while he was with the duellists, it was as impossible to ask him what had happened as to ask the duellists who had won. She must, while Miss Mapp rested, get hold of the Padre without the duellists.

Even as Athene sprang full grown and panoplied from the brain of Zeus, so from Diva's brain there sprang her plan complete. She even resisted the temptation to go on admiring autumn tints, in order to see how the interesting trio 'looked' when, as they must presently do, they passed close to where she stood, and hurried home, pausing only to purchase, pay for, and carry away with her from the provision shop a large and expensively dressed crab, a dainty of which the Padre was inordinately fond. Ruinous as this was, there was a note of triumph in her voice when, on arrival, she called loudly for Janet, and told her to lay another place at the luncheon table. Then putting a strong constraint on herself, she waited three minutes by her watch, in order to give the Padre time to get home, and then rang him up and reminded him that he had promised to lunch with her that day. It was no use asking him to lunch in such a way that he might refuse: she employed without remorse this pitiless *force majeure*.

The engagement was short and brisk. He pleaded that not even now could he remember even having been asked (which was not surprising), and said that he and wee wifie had begun lunch. On which Diva unmasked her last gun, and told him that she had ordered a crab on purpose. That silenced further argument, and he said that he and wee wifie would be round in a jiffy, and rang off. She did not particularly want wee wifie, but there was enough crab.

Diva felt that she had never laid out four shillings to better purpose, when, a quarter of an hour later, the Padre gave her the full account of his fruitless search among the sand-dunes, so deeply impressive was his sense of being buoyed up to that incredibly fatiguing and perilous excursion by some Power outside himself. It never even occurred to her to think that it was an elaborate practical joke on the part of the Power outside himself, to spur him on to such immense exertions to no purpose at all. He had only got as far as this over his interrupted lunch with wee wifie, and though she, too, was in agonised suspense as to what happened next, she bore the repetition with great equanimity, only making small mouse-like noises of impatience which nobody heard. He was quite forgetting to speak either Scotch or Elizabethan English, so obvious was the absorption of his hearers, without these added aids to command attention.

'And then I came round the corner of the clubhouse,' he said, 'and there were Captain Puffin and the Major finishing their match on the eighteenth hole.'

'Then there's been no duel at all,' said Diva, scraping the shell of the crab.

'I feel sure of it. There wouldn't have been time for a duel and a round of golf, in addition to the impossibility of playing golf immediately after a duel. No nerves could stand it. Besides, I asked one of their caddies. They had come straight from the tram to the clubhouse, and from the clubhouse to the first tee. They had not been alone for a moment.'

'Washout,' said Diva, wondering whether this had been worth four shillings, so tame was the conclusion.

Mrs Bartlett gave a little squeak which was her preliminary to speech.

'But I do not see why there may not be a duel yet, Kenneth,' she said. 'Because they did not fight this morning – excellent crab, dear Diva, so good of you to ask us – there's no reason why there shouldn't be a duel this afternoon. Oh dear me, and cold beef as well: I shall be quite stuffed. Depend upon it a man doesn't take the trouble to write a challenge and all that, unless he means business.'

The Padre held up his hand. He felt that he was gradually growing to be the hero of the whole affair. He had certainly looked over the edge of numberless hollows in the sand-dunes with vivid anticipations of having a bullet whizz by him on each separate occasion. It behoved him to take a sublime line.

'My dear,' he said, 'business is hardly a word to apply to murder. That within the last twenty-four hours there was the intention of fighting a duel, I don't deny. But something has decidedly happened which has averted that deplorable calamity. Peace and reconciliation is the result of it, and I have never seen two men so unaffectedly friendly.'

Diva got up and whirled round the table to get the port for the Padre, so pleased was she at a fresh idea coming to her while still dear Elizabeth was resting. She attributed it to the crab.

'We've all been on a false scent,' she said. 'Peace and reconciliation happened before they went out to the sand-dunes at all. It happened at the station. They met at the station, you know. It is proved that Major Flint went there. Major wouldn't send portmanteau off alone. And it's proved that Captain Puffin went there too, because the note which his housemaid found on the table before she saw the challenge from the Major, which was on the chimney-piece, said that he had been called away very suddenly. No: they both went to catch the early train in order to go away before they could be stopped, and kill each other. But why didn't they go? What happened? Don't suppose the outside porter showed them how wicked they were, confirmation class or no confirmation class. Stumps me. Almost wish Elizabeth was here. She's good at guessing.'

The Padre's eye brightened. Reaction after the perils of the morning, crab and port combined to make a man of him.

'Eh, 'tis a bonny wee drappie of port whatever, Mistress Plaistow,' he said. 'And I dinna ken that ye're far wrang in jaloosing that Mistress Mapp might have a wee bitty word to say aboot it a', 'gin she had the mind.'

'She was wrong about the portmanteau,' said Diva. 'Confessed she was wrong.'

'Hoots! I'm not mindin' the bit pochmantie,' said the Padre.

'What else does she know?' asked Diva feverishly.

There was no doubt that the Padre had the fullest attention of the two ladies again, and there was no need to talk Scotch any more.

'Begin at the beginning,' he said. 'What do we suppose was the cause of the quarrel?'

'Anything,' said Diva. 'Golf, tiger-skins, coal-strike, summertime.'

He shook his head.

'I grant you words may pass on such subjects,' he said. 'We feel keenly, I know, about summertime in Tilling, though we shall all be reconciled over that next Sunday, when real time, God's time, as I am venturing to call it in my sermon, comes in again.'

Diva had to bite her tongue to prevent herself bolting off on this new scent. After all, she had invested in crab to learn about duelling, not about summertime.

'Well?' she said.

'We may have had words on that subject,' said the Padre, booming as if he was in the pulpit already, 'but we should, I hope, none of us go so far as to catch the earliest train with pistols, in defence of our conviction about summertime. No, Mrs Plaistow, if you are right, and there is something to be said for your view, in thinking that they both went to such lengths as to be in time for the early train, in order to fight a duel undisturbed, you must look for a more solid cause than that.'

Diva vainly racked her brains to think of anything more worthy of the highest pitches of emotion than this. If it had been she and Miss Mapp who had been embroiled, hoarding and dress would have occurred to her. But as it was, no one in his senses could dream that the Captain and the Major were sartorial rivals, unless they had quarrelled over the question as to which of them wore the snuffiest old clothes.

'Give it up,' she said. 'What did they quarrel about?'

'Passion!' said the Padre, in those full, deep tones in which next Sunday he would allude to God's time. 'I do not mean anger, but the flame that exalts man to heaven or – or does exactly the opposite!'

'But whomever for?' asked Diva, quite thrown off her bearings. Such a thing had never occurred to her, for, as far as she was aware, passion, except in the sense of temper, did not exist in Tilling. Tilling was far too respectable.

The Padre considered this a moment.

'I am betraying no confidence,' he said, 'because no one has confided in me. But there certainly is a lady in this town – I do not allude to Miss Irene – who has long enjoyed the Major's particular esteem. May not some deprecating remark – '

Wee wifie gave a much louder squeal than usual.

'He means poor Elizabeth,' she said in a high, tremulous voice. 'Fancy, Kenneth!'

Diva, a few seconds before, had seen no reason why the Padre should drink the rest of her port, and was now in the act of drinking some of that unusual beverage herself. She tried to swallow it, but it was too late, and next moment all the openings in her face were fountains of that delicious wine. She choked and she gurgled, until the last drop had left her windpipe – under the persuasion of pattings on the back from the others – and then she gave herself up to loud, hoarse laughter, through which there shrilled the staccato squeaks of wee wifie. Nothing, even if you are being laughed at yourself, is so infectious as prolonged laughter, and the Padre felt himself forced to join it. When one of them got a little better, a relapse ensued by reason of infection from the others, and it was not till exhaustion set in, that this triple volcano became quiescent again.

'Only fancy!' said Evie faintly. 'How did such an idea get into your head, Kenneth?'

His voice shook as he answered.

'Well, we were all a little worked up this morning,' he said. 'The idea – really, I don't know what we have all been laughing at – '

'I do,' said Diva. 'Go on. About the idea – '

A feminine, a diabolical inspiration flared within wee wifie's mind.

'Elizabeth suggested it herself,' she squealed.

Naturally Diva could not help remembering that she had found Miss Mapp and the Padre in earnest conversation together when she forced her way in that morning with the news that the duellists had left by the 11.20 tram. Nobody could be expected to have so short a memory as to have forgotten *that*. Just now she forgave Elizabeth for anything she had ever done. That might have to be reconsidered afterwards, but at present it was valid enough.

'Did she suggest it?' she asked.

The Padre behaved like a man, and lied like Ananias.

'Most emphatically she did not,' he said.

The disappointment would have been severe, had the two ladies believed this confident assertion, and Diva pictured a delightful interview with Elizabeth, in which she would suddenly tell her the wild surmise the Padre had made with regard to the cause of the duel, and see how she looked then. Just see how she looked then: that was all – self-consciousness and guilt would fly their colours . . .

*   *   *

Miss Mapp had been tempted when she went home that morning, after enjoying the autumn tints, to ask Diva to lunch with her, but remembered in time that she had told her cook to broach one of the tins of corned beef which no human wizard could coax into the store-cupboard again, if he shut the door after it. Diva would have been sure to say something acid and allusive, to remark on its excellence being happily not wasted on the poor people in the hospital, or, if she had not said anything at all about it, her silence as she ate a great deal would have had a sharp flavour. But Miss Mapp would have liked, especially when she went to take her rest afterwards on the big sofa in the garden-room, to have had somebody to talk to, for her brain seethed with conjectures as to what had happened, was happening and would happen, and discussion was the best method of simplifying a problem, of narrowing it down to the limits of probability, whereas when she was alone now with her own imaginings, the most fantastic of them seemed plausible. She had, however, handed a glorious suggestion to the Padre, the one, that is, which concerned the cause of the duel, and it had been highly satisfactory to observe the sympathy and respect with which he had imbibed it. She had, too, been so discreet about it; she had not come within measurable distance of asserting that the challenge had been in any way connected with her. She had only been very emphatic on the point of its not being connected with poor dear Irene, and then occupied herself with her sweet flowers. That had been sufficient, and she felt in her bones and marrow that he inferred what she had meant him to infer . . .

The vulture of surmise ceased to peck at her for a few moments as she considered this, and followed up a thread of gold . . . Though the Padre would surely be discreet, she hoped that he would 'let slip' to dear Evie in the course of the vivid conversation they would be sure to have over lunch, that he had a good guess as to the cause which had led to that savage challenge. Upon which dear Evie would be certain to ply him with direct squeaks and questions, and when she 'got hot' (as in animal, vegetable and mineral) his reticence would lead her to make a good guess too. She might be incredulous, but there the idea would be in her mind, while if she felt that these stirring days were no time for scepticism, she could hardly fail to be interested and touched. Before long (how soon Miss Mapp was happily not aware) she would 'pop in' to see Diva, or Diva would 'pop in' to see her, and, Evie observing a discretion similar to that of the Padre and herself, would soon enable dear Diva to make a good guess too. After that, all would be well, for dear Diva ('such a gossiping darling') would undoubtedly tell everybody in Tilling, under vows of secrecy (so that she should have the pleasure of telling everybody herself) just what her good guess was. Thus, very presently, all Tilling would know exactly that which Miss Mapp had not said to the dear Padre, namely, that the duel which had been fought (or which hadn't been fought) was 'all about' her. And the best of it was, that though everybody knew, it would still be a great and beautiful secret, reposing inviolably in every breast or chest, as the case might be. She had no anxiety about anybody asking direct questions of the duellists, for if duelling, for years past, had been a subject which no delicately minded

person alluded to purposely in Major Benjy's presence, how much
more now after this critical morning would that subject be taboo?
That certainly was a good thing, for the duellists if closely questioned
might have a different explanation, and it would be highly
inconvenient to have two contradictory stories going about. But, as
it was, nothing could be nicer: the whole of the rest of Tilling, under
promise of secrecy, would know, and even if under further promises
of secrecy they communicated their secret to each other, there would
be no harm done . . .

After this excursion into Elysian fields, poor Miss Mapp had to get
back to her vulture again, and the hour's rest that she had felt was
due to herself as the heroine of a duel became a period of extraordinary cerebral activity. Puzzle as she might, she could make
nothing whatever of the portmanteau and the excursion to the early
train, and she got up long before her hour was over, since she found
that the more she thought, the more invincible were the objections
to any conclusion that she drowningly grasped at. Whatever attack
she made on this mystery, the garrison failed to march out and
surrender but kept their flag flying, and her conjectures were woefully
blasted by the forces of the most elementary reasons. But as the
agony of suspense, if no fresh topic of interest intervened, would be
frankly unendurable, she determined to concentrate no more on it,
but rather to commit it to the ice-house or safe of her subconscious
mind, from which at will, when she felt refreshed and reinvigorated,
she could unlock it and examine it again. The whole problem was
more superlatively baffling than any that she could remember having
encountered in all these inquisitive years, just as the subject of it was
more majestic than any, for it concerned not hoarding, nor visits of
the Prince of Wales, nor poppy-trimmed gowns, but life and death
and firing of deadly pistols. And should love be added to this august
list? Certainly not by her, though Tilling might do what it liked. In
fact Tilling always did.

She walked across to the bow-window from which she had conducted so many exciting and successful investigations. But today the
view seemed as stale and unprofitable as the world appeared to
Hamlet, even though Mrs Poppit at that moment went waddling
down the street and disappeared round the corner where the dentist
and Mr Wyse lived. With a sense of fatigue Miss Mapp recalled the
fact that she had seen the housemaid cleaning Mr Wyse's windows
yesterday – ('Children dear, was it yesterday?') – and had noted her
industry, and drawn from it the irresistible conclusion that Mr Wyse

was probably expected home. He usually came back about mid-October, and let slip allusions to his enjoyable visits in Scotland and his *villeggiatura* (so he was pleased to express it) with his sister the Contessa di Faraglione at Capri. That Contessa Faraglione was rather a mythical personage to Miss Mapp's mind: she was certainly not in a mediaeval copy of *Who's Who?* which was the only accessible handbook in matters relating to noble and notable personages, and though Miss Mapp would not have taken an oath that she did not exist, she saw no strong reason for supposing that she did. Certainly she had never been to Tilling, which was strange as her brother lived there, and there was nothing but her brother's allusions to certify her. About Mrs Poppit now: had she gone to see Mr Wyse or had she gone to the dentist? One or other it must be, for apart from them that particular street contained nobody who counted, and at the bottom it simply conducted you out into the uneventful country. Mrs Poppit was all dressed up, and she would never walk in the country in such a costume. It would do either for Mr Wyse or the dentist, for she was the sort of woman who would like to appear grand in the dentist's chair, so that he might be shy of hurting such a fine lady. Then again, Mrs Poppit had wonderful teeth, almost too good to be true, and before now she had asked who lived at that pretty little house just round the corner, as if to show that she didn't know where the dentist lived! Or had she found out by some underhand means that Mr Wyse had come back, and had gone to call on him and give him the first news of the duel, and talk to him about Scotland? Very likely they had neither of them been to Scotland at all: they conspired to say that they had been to Scotland and stayed at shooting-lodges (keepers' lodges more likely) in order to impress Tilling with their magnificence . . .

Miss Mapp sat down on the central-heating pipes in her window, and fell into one of her reconstructive musings. Partly, if Mr Wyse was back, it was well just to run over his record; partly she wanted to divert her mind from the two houses just below, that of Major Benjy on the one side and that of Captain Puffin on the other, which contained the key to the great, insoluble mystery, from conjecture as to which she wanted to obtain relief. Mr Wyse, anyhow, would serve as a mild opiate, for she had never lost an angry interest in him. Though he was for eight months of the year, or thereabouts, in Tilling, he was never, for a single hour, *of* Tilling. He did not exactly invest himself with an air of condescension and superiority – Miss Mapp did him that justice – but he made other people invest him with it, so that it came to the same thing: he was invested. He did not drag the fact of his sister being the Contessa Faraglione into conversation, but if talk turned on sisters, and he was asked about his, he confessed to her nobility. The same phenomenon appeared when the innocent county of Hampshire was mentioned, for it turned out that he knew the county well, being one of the Wyses of Whitchurch. You couldn't say he talked about it, but he made other people talk about it . . . He was quite impervious to satire on such points, for when, goaded to madness, Miss Mapp had once said that she was one of the Mapps of Maidstone, he had merely bowed and said: 'A very old family, I believe,' and when the conversation branched off on to old families he had rather pointedly said 'we' to Miss Mapp. So poor Miss Mapp was sorry she had been satirical . . . But for some reason, Tilling never ceased to play up to Mr Wyse, and there was not a tea-party or a bridge party given during the whole period of his residence there to which he was not invited. Hostesses always started with him, sending him round a note with 'To await answer', written in the top left-hand corner, since he had clearly stated that he considered the telephone an undignified instrument only fit to be used for household purposes, and had installed his in the kitchen, in the manner of the Wyses of Whitchurch. That alone, apart from Mr Wyse's old-fashioned notions on the subject, made telephoning impossible, for your summons was usually answered by his cook, who instantly began scolding the butcher irrespective and disrespectful of whom you were. When her mistake was made known to her, she never apologised, but grudgingly said she would call Mr Figgis, who was Mr Wyse's valet. Mr Figgis always took a long time in coming, and when he came he sneezed or did something disagreeable and said: 'Yes, yes; what is it?' in a very testy manner. After explanations he would consent to tell his master, which took another long time, and even then Mr Wyse did not come himself, and usually refused the proffered invitation. Miss Mapp had tried the expedient of sending Withers to the telephone when she wanted to get at Mr Wyse, but this had not succeeded, for Withers and Mr Wyse's cook quarrelled so violently before they got to business that Mr Figgis had to calm the cook and Withers to complain to Miss Mapp . . . This, in brief, was the general reason why Tilling sent notes to Mr Wyse. As for chatting through the telephone, which was the main use of telephones, the thing was quite out of the question.

Miss Mapp revived a little as she made this piercing analysis of Mr Wyse, and the warmth of the central-heating pipes, on this baffling

day of autumn tints, was comforting . . . No one could say that Mr
Wyse was not punctilious in matters of social etiquette, for though
he refused three-quarters of the invitations which were showered on
him, he invariably returned the compliment by an autograph note
hoping that he might have the pleasure of entertaining you at lunch
on Thursday next, for he always gave a small luncheon-party on
Thursday. These invitations were couched in Chesterfield-terms:
Mr Wyse said that he had met a mutual friend just now who had
informed him that you were in residence, and had encouraged him
to hope that you might give him the pleasure of your company, etc.
This was alluring diction: it presented the image of Mr Wyse stepping
briskly home again, quite heartened up by this chance encounter,
and no longer the prey to melancholy at the thought that you might
not give him the joy. He was encouraged to hope . . . These polite
expressions were traced in a neat upright hand on paper which, when
he had just come back from Italy, often bore a coronet on the top
with 'Villa Faraglione, Capri' printed on the right-hand top corner
and 'Amelia' (the name of his putative sister) in sprawling gilt on the
left, the whole being lightly erased. Of course he was quite right to
filch a few sheets, but it threw rather a lurid light on his character
that they should be such grand ones.

Last year only, in a fit of passion at Mr Wyse having refused six
invitations running on the plea of other engagements, Miss Mapp
had headed a movement, the object of which was that Tilling should
not accept any of Mr Wyse's invitations unless he accepted its. This
had met with theoretical sympathy; the Bartletts, Diva, Irene, the
Poppits had all agreed – rather absently – that it would be a very
proper thing to do, but the very next Thursday they had all, including
the originator, met on Mr Wyse's doorstep for a luncheon-party, and
the movement then and there collapsed. Though they all protested
and rebelled against such a notion, the horrid fact remained that
everybody basked in Mr Wyse's effulgence whenever it was disposed
to shed itself on them. Much as they distrusted the information they
dragged out of him, they adored hearing about the Villa Faraglione,
and dressed themselves in their very best clothes to do so. Then
again there was the quality of the lunch itself: often there was caviare,
and it was impossible (though the interrogator who asked whether it
came from Twemlow's feared the worst) not to be mildly excited to
know, when Mr Wyse referred the question to Figgis, that the caviare
had arrived from Odessa that morning. The haunch of roe-deer came
from Perthshire; the wine, on the subject of which the Major could

not be silent, and which often made him extremely talkative, was
from 'my brother-in-law's vineyard'. And Mr Wyse would taste it
with the air of a connoisseur and say: 'Not quite as good as last year:
I must tell the Cont – I mean my sister.'

Again when Mr Wyse did condescend to honour a tea-party or
a bridge party, Tilling writhed under the consciousness that their
general deportment was quite different from that which they ordinarily
practised among themselves. There was never any squabbling at Mr
Wyse's table, and such squabbling as took place at the other tables
was conducted in low hissings and whispers, so that Mr Wyse should
not hear. Diva never haggled over her gains or losses when he was
there, the Padre never talked Scotch or Elizabethan English. Evie
never squeaked like a mouse, no shrill recriminations or stately
sarcasms took place between partners, and if there happened to be a
little disagreement about the rules, Mr Wyse's decision, though he
was not a better player than any of them, was accepted without a
murmur. At intervals for refreshment, in the same way, Diva no longer
filled her mouth and both hands with nougat chocolate; there was no
scrambling or jostling, but the ladies were waited on by the gentlemen,
who then refreshed themselves. And yet Mr Wyse in no way asserted
himself, or reduced them all to politeness by talking about the polished
manners of Italians; it was Tilling itself which chose to behave in this
unusual manner in his presence. Sometimes Diva might forget herself
for a moment, and address something withering to her partner, but
the partner never replied in suitable terms, and Diva became honey-
mouthed again. It was, indeed, if Mr Wyse had appeared at two or
three parties, rather a relief not to find him at the next, and breathe
freely in less rarefied air. But whether he came or not he always
returned the invitation by one to a Thursday luncheon-party, and
thus the high circles of Tilling met every week at his house.

Miss Mapp came to the end of this brief retrospect, and determined,
when once it was proved that Mr Wyse had arrived, to ask him to tea
on Tuesday. That would mean lunch with him on Thursday, and it
was unnecessary to ask anybody else unless Mr Wyse accepted. If he
refused, there would be no tea-party . . . But, after the events of the
last twenty-four hours, there was no vividness in these plans and
reminiscences, and her eye turned to the profile of the Colonel's
house.

'The portmanteau,' she said to herself . . . No: she must take her
mind off that subject. She would go for a walk, not into the High
Street, but into the quiet level country, away from the turmoil of

passion (in the Padre's sense) and quarrels (in her own), where she could cool her curiosity and her soul with contemplation of the swallows and the white butterflies (if they had not all been killed by the touch of frost last night) and the autumn tints of which there were none whatever in the treeless marsh . . . Decidedly the shortest way out of the town was that which led past Mr Wyse's house. But before leaving the garden-room she practised several faces at the looking-glass opposite the door, which should suitably express, if she met anybody to whom the cause of the challenge was likely to have spread, the bewildering emotion which the unwilling cause of it must feel. There must be a wistful wonder, there must be a certain pride, there must be the remains of romantic excitement, and there must be deep womanly anxiety. The carriage of the head 'did' the pride, the wide-open eyes 'did' the wistful wonder and the romance, the deep womanly anxiety lurked in the tremulous smile, and a violent rubbing of the cheeks produced the colour of excitement. In answer to any impertinent questions, if she encountered such, she meant to give an absent answer, as if she had not understood. Thus equipped she set forth.

It was rather disappointing to meet nobody, but as she passed Mr Wyse's bow-window she adjusted the chrysanthemums she wore, and she had a good sight of his profile and the back of Mrs Poppit's head. They appeared deep in conversation, and Miss Mapp felt that the tiresome woman was probably giving him a very incomplete account of what had happened. She returned late for tea, and broke off her apologies to Withers for being such a trouble because she saw a note on the hall table. There was a coronet on the back of the envelope, and it was addressed in the neat, punctilious hand which so well expressed its writer. Villa Faraglione, Capri, a coronet and Amelia all lightly crossed out headed the page, and she read:

DEAR MISS MAPP – It is such a pleasure to find myself in our little Tilling again, and our mutual friend Mrs Poppit, MBE, tells me you are in residence, and encourages me to hope that I may induce you to take *déjeuner* with me on Thursday, at one o'clock. May I assure you, with all delicacy, that you will not meet here anyone whose presence could cause you the slightest embarrassment?

Pray excuse this hasty note. Figgis will wait for your answer if you are in.

Yours very sincerely,

ALGERNON WYSE

Had not Withers been present, who might have misconstrued her action, Miss Mapp would have kissed the note; failing that, she forgave Mrs Poppit for being an MBE.

'The dear woman!' she said. 'She has heard, and has told him.'

Of course she need not ask Mr Wyse to tea now . . .

Chapter Seven

A white frost on three nights running and a terrible blackening of dahlias, whose reputation was quite gone by morning, would probably have convinced the ladies of Tilling that it was time to put summer clothing in camphor and winter clothing in the back-yard to get aired, even if the Padre had not preached that remarkable sermon on Sunday. It was so remarkable that Miss Mapp quite forgot to note grammatical lapses and listened entranced.

The text was, 'He made summer and winter', and after repeating the words very impressively, so that there might be no mistake about the origin of the seasons, the Padre began to talk about something quite different – namely, the unhappy divisions which exist in Christian communities. That did not deceive Miss Mapp for a moment: she saw precisely what he was getting at over his oratorical fences. He got at it . . .

Ever since summertime had been inaugurated a few years before, it had been one of the chronic dissensions of Tilling. Miss Mapp, Diva and the Padre flatly refused to recognise it, except when they were going by train or tram, when principle must necessarily go to the wall, or they would never have succeeded in getting anywhere, while Miss Mapp, with the halo of martyrdom round her head, had once arrived at a summertime party an hour late, in order to bear witness to the truth, and, in consequence, had got only dregs of tea and the last faint strawberry. But the Major and Captain Puffin used the tram so often, that they had fallen into the degrading habit of dislocating their clocks and watches on the first of May, and dislocating them again in the autumn, when they were forced into uniformity with properly minded people. Irene was flippant on the subject, and said that any old time would do for her. The Poppits followed convention, and Mrs Poppit, in naming the hour for a party to the stalwarts, wrote '4.30 (your 3.30)'. The King, after all, had invited her to be decorated at a particular hour, summertime, and what was good enough for the King was good enough for Mrs Poppit.

The sermon was quite uncompromising. There was summer and winter, by Divine ordinance, but there was nothing said about summertime and wintertime. There was but one Time, and even as Life only stained the white radiance of eternity, as the gifted but, alas! infidel poet remarked, so, too, did Time. But ephemeral as Time was, noon in the Bible clearly meant twelve o'clock, and not one o'clock: towards even, meant towards even, and not the middle of a broiling afternoon. The sixth hour similarly was the Roman way of saying twelve. Wintertime, in fact, was God's time, and though there was nothing wicked (far from it) in adopting strange measures, yet the simple, the childlike, clung to the sacred tradition, which they had received from their fathers and forefathers at their mother's knee. Then followed a long and eloquent passage, which recapitulated the opening about unhappy divisions, and contained several phrases, regarding the lengths to which such divisions might go, which were strikingly applicable to duelling. The peroration recapitulated the recapitulation, in case anyone had missed it, and the coda, the close itself, in the full noon of the winter sun, was full of joy at the healing of all such unhappy divisions. And now . . . The rain rattling against the windows drowned the Doxology.

The doctrine was so much to her mind that Miss Mapp gave a shilling to the offertory instead of her usual sixpence, to be devoted to the organist and choir fund. The Padre, it is true, had changed the hour of services to suit the heresy of the majority, and this for a moment made her hand falter. But the hope, after this convincing sermon, that next year morning service would be at the hour falsely called twelve decided her not to withdraw this handsome contribution.

Frosts and dead dahlias and sermons then were together overwhelmingly convincing, and when Miss Mapp went out on Monday morning to do her shopping, she wore a tweed skirt and jacket, and round her neck a long woollen scarf to mark the end of the summer. Mrs Poppit, alone in her disgusting ostentation, had seemed to think two days ago that it was cold enough for furs, and she presented a truly ridiculous aspect in an enormous sable coat, under the weight of which she could hardly stagger, and stood rooted to the spot when she stepped out of the Royce. Brisk walking and large woollen scarves saved the others from feeling the cold and from being unable to move, and this morning the High Street was dazzling with the shifting play of bright colours. There was quite a group of scarves at the corner, where Miss Mapp's street debouched into the High Street: Irene was there (for it was probably too cold for Mr Hopkins that morning), looking quainter than ever in corduroys and mauve stockings with an immense orange scarf bordered with pink. Diva was there, wound up in so delicious a combination of rose-madder and Cambridge blue, that Miss Mapp, remembering the history of the rose-madder, had to remind herself how many things there were in the world more important than worsted. Evie was there in vivid green with a purple border, the Padre had a knitted magenta waist-coat, and Mrs Poppit that great sable coat which almost prevented movement. They were all talking together in a very animated manner when first Miss Mapp came in sight, and if, on her approach, con-versation seemed to wither, they all wore, besides their scarves, very broad, pleasant smiles. Miss Mapp had a smile, too, as good as anybody's.

'Good-morning, all you dear things,' she said. 'How lovely you all look – just like a bed of delicious flowers! Such nice colours! My poor dahlias are all dead.'

Quaint Irene uttered a hoarse laugh, and, swinging her basket, went quickly away. She often did abrupt things like that. Miss Mapp turned to the Padre.

'Dear Padre, what a delicious sermon!' she said. 'So glad you preached it! Such a warning against all sorts of divisions!'

The Padre had to compose his face before he responded to these compliments.

'I'm reecht glad, fair lady,' he replied, 'that my bit discourse was to your mind. Come, wee wifie, we must be stepping.'

Quite suddenly all the group, with the exception of Mrs Poppit, melted away. Wee wifie gave a loud squeal, as if to say something, but her husband led her firmly off, while Diva, with rapidly revolving feet, sped like an arrow up the centre of the High Street.

'Such a lovely morning!' said Miss Mapp to Mrs Poppit, when there was no one else to talk to. 'And everyone looks so pleased and happy, and all in such a hurry, busy as bees, to do their little businesses. Yes.'

Mrs Poppit began to move quietly away with the deliberate, tortoise-like progression necessitated by the fur coat. It struck Miss Mapp that she, too, had intended to take part in the general breaking up of the group, but had merely been unable to get under way as fast as the others.

'Such a lovely fur coat,' said Miss Mapp sycophantically. 'Such beautiful long fur! And what is the news this morning? Has a little bird been whispering anything?'

'Nothing,' said Mrs Poppit very decidedly, and having now sufficient way on to turn, she went up the street down which Miss Mapp had just come. The latter was thus left all alone with her shopping basket and her scarf.

With the unerring divination which was the natural fruit of so many years of ceaseless conjecture, she instantly suspected the worst. All that busy conversation which her appearance had interrupted, all those smiles which her presence had seemed but to render broader and more hilarious, certainly concerned her. They could not still have been talking about that fatal explosion from the cupboard in the garden-room, because the duel had completely silenced the last echoes of that, and she instantly put her finger on the spot. Somebody had been gossiping (and how she hated gossip); somebody had given voice to what she had been so studiously careful not to say. Until that moment, when she had seen the rapid breaking up of the group of her friends all radiant with merriment, she had longed to be aware that somebody had given voice to it, and that everybody (under seal of secrecy) knew the unique queenliness of her position, the overwhelmingly interesting role that the violent passions of men had cast her for. She had not believed in the truth of it herself, when that irresistible seizure of coquetry took possession of her as she bent over her sweet chrysanthemums; but the Padre's respectful reception of it had caused her to hope that everybody else might believe in it. The character of the smiles, however, that wreathed the faces of her friends did not quite seem to give fruition to that hope. There were smiles and smiles, respectful smiles, sympathetic smiles, envious and admiring smiles, but there were also smiles of hilarious and mocking incredulity. She concluded that she had to deal with the latter variety.

'Something,' thought Miss Mapp, as she stood quite alone in the High Street, with Mrs Poppit labouring up the hill, and Diva already a rose-madder speck in the distance, 'has got to be done,' and it only remained to settle what. Fury with the dear Padre for having hinted precisely what she meant, intended and designed that he should hint, was perhaps the paramount emotion in her mind; fury with everybody else for not respectfully believing what she did not believe herself made an important pendant.

'What am I to do?' said Miss Mapp aloud, and had to explain to Mr Hopkins, who had all his clothes on, that she had not spoken to him. Then she caught sight again of Mrs Poppit's sable coat hardly further off than it had been when first this thunderclap of an intuition deafened her, and still reeling from the shock, she remembered that it was almost certainly Mrs Poppit who was the cause of Mr Wyse writing her that exquisitely delicate note with regard to Thursday. It was a herculean task, no doubt, to plug up all the fountains of talk in Tilling which were spouting so merrily at her expense, but a beginning must be made before she could arrive at the end. A short scurry of nimble steps brought her up to the sables.

'Dear Mrs Poppit,' she said, 'if you are walking by my little house, would you give me two minutes' talk? And – so stupid of me to forget just now – will you come in after dinner on Wednesday for a little rubber? The days are closing in now; one wants to make the most of the daylight, and I think it is time to begin our pleasant little winter evenings.'

This was a bribe, and Mrs Poppit instantly pocketed it, with the effect that two minutes later she was in the garden-room, and had deposited her sable coat on the sofa ('Quite shook the room with the weight of it,' said Miss Mapp to herself while she arranged her plan).

She stood looking out of the window for a moment, writhing with humiliation at having to be suppliant to the Member of the British Empire. She tried to remember Mrs Poppit's Christian name, and was even prepared to use that, but this crowning ignominy was saved her, as she could not recollect it.

'Such an annoying thing has happened,' she said, though the words seemed to blister her lips. 'And you, dear Mrs Poppit, as a woman of the world, can advise me what to do. The fact is that somehow or other, and I can't think how, people are saying that the duel last week, which was so happily averted, had something to do with poor little me. So absurd! But you know what gossips we have in our dear little Tilling.'

Mrs Poppit turned on her a fallen and disappointed face.

'But hadn't it?' she said. 'Why, when they were all laughing about it just now' ('I was right, then,' thought Miss Mapp, 'and what a tactless woman!'), 'I said I believed it. And I told Mr Wyse.'

Miss Mapp cursed herself for her frankness. But she could obliterate that again, and not lose a rare (goodness knew how rare!) believer.

'I am in such a difficult position,' she said. 'I think I ought to let it be understood that there is no truth whatever in such an idea, however much truth there may be. And did dear Mr Wyse believe – in fact, I know he must have, for he wrote me, oh, such a delicate, understanding note. He, at any rate, takes no notice of all that is being said and hinted.'

Miss Mapp was momentarily conscious that she meant precisely the opposite of this. Dear Mr Wyse *did* take notice, most respectful notice, of all that was being said and hinted, thank goodness! But a glance at Mrs Poppit's fat and interested face showed her that the verbal discrepancy had gone unnoticed, and that the luscious flavour of romance drowned the perception of anything else. She drew a handkerchief out, and buried her thoughtful eyes in it a moment, rubbing them with a stealthy motion, which Mrs Poppit did not perceive, though Diva would have.

'My lips are sealed,' she continued, opening them very wide, 'and I can say nothing, except that I want this rumour to be contradicted. I dare say those who started it thought it was true, but, true or false, I must say nothing. I have always led a very quiet life in my little house, with my sweet flowers for my companions, and if there is one thing more than another that I dislike, it is that my private affairs should be made matters of public interest. I do no harm to anybody, I wish everybody well, and nothing – nothing will induce me to open my lips upon this subject. I will not,' cried Miss Mapp, 'say a word to defend or justify myself. What is true will prevail. It comes in the Bible.'

Mrs Poppit was too much interested in what she said to mind where it came from.

'What can I do?' she asked.

'Contradict, dear, the rumour that I have had anything to do with the terrible thing which might have happened last week. Say on my authority that it is so. I tremble to think' – here she trembled very much – 'what might happen if the report reached Major Benjy's ears, and he found out who had started it. We must have no more duels in Tilling. I thought I should never survive that morning.'

'I will go and tell Mr Wyse instantly – dear,' said Mrs Poppit.

That would never do. True believers were so scarce that it was wicked to think of unsettling their faith.

'Poor Mr Wyse!' said Miss Mapp with a magnanimous smile. 'Do not think, dear, of troubling him with these little trumpery affairs. He will not take part in these little tittle-tattles. But if you could let dear Diva and quaint Irene and sweet Evie and the good Padre know that I laugh at all such nonsense – '

'But they laugh at it, too,' said Mrs Poppit.

That would have been baffling for anyone who allowed herself to be baffled, but that was not Miss Mapp's way.

'Oh, that bitter laughter!' she said. 'It hurt me to hear it. It was envious laughter, dear, scoffing, bitter laughter. I heard! I cannot bear that the dear things should feel like that. Tell them that I say how silly they are to believe anything of the sort. Trust me, I am right about it. I wash my hands of such nonsense.'

She made a vivid dumb-show of this, and after drying them on an imaginary towel, let a sunny smile peep out the eyes which she had rubbed.

'All gone!' she said; 'and we will have a dear little party on Wednesday to show we are all friends again. And we meet for lunch at dear Mr Wyse's the next day? Yes? He will get tired of poor little me if he sees me two days running, so I shall not ask him. I will just try to get two tables together, and nobody shall contradict dear Diva, however many shillings she says she has won. I would sooner pay them all myself than have any more of our unhappy divisions. You will have talked to them all before Wednesday, will you not, dear?'

As there were only four to talk to, Mrs Poppit thought that she could manage it, and spent a most interesting afternoon. For two years now she had tried to unfreeze Miss Mapp, who, when all was said and done, was the centre of the Tilling circle, and who, if any attempt was made to shove her out towards the circumference, always gravitated back again. And now, on these important errands she was Miss Mapp's accredited ambassador, and all the terrible business of the opening of the store-cupboard and her decoration as MBE was quite forgiven and forgotten. There would be so much walking to be done from house to house, that it was impossible to wear her sable coat unless she had the Royce to take her about . . .

The effect of her communications would have surprised anybody who did not know Tilling. A less subtle society, when assured from a first-hand, authoritative source that a report which it had entirely refused to believe was false, would have prided itself on its perspicacity, and said that it had laughed at such an idea, as soon as ever it heard it, as being palpably (look at Miss Mapp!) untrue. Not so Tilling. The very fact that, by the mouth of her ambassador, she so uncompromisingly denied it, was precisely why Tilling began to wonder if there was not something in it, and from wondering if there was not something in it, surged to the conclusion that there certainly was. Diva, for instance, the moment she was told that Elizabeth (for Mrs Poppit remembered her Christian name perfectly) utterly and scornfully denied the truth of the report, became intensely thoughtful.

'Say there's nothing in it?' she observed. 'Can't understand that.'

At that moment Diva's telephone bell rang, and she hurried out and in.

'Party at Elizabeth's on Wednesday,' she said. 'She saw me laughing. Why ask me?'

Mrs Poppit was full of her sacred mission.

'To show how little she minds your laughing,' she suggested.

'As if it wasn't true, then. Seems like that. Wants us to think it's not true.'

'She was very earnest about it,' said the ambassador.

Diva got up, and tripped over the outlying skirts of Mrs Poppit's fur coat as she went to ring the bell.

'Sorry,' she said. 'Take it off and have a chat. Tea's coming. Muffins!'

'Oh, no, thanks!' said Mrs Poppit. 'I've so many calls to make.'

'What? Similar calls?' asked Diva. 'Wait ten minutes. Tea, Janet. Quickly.'

She whirled round the room once or twice, all corrugated with perplexity, beginning telegraphic sentences, and not finishing them: 'Says it's not true – laughs at notion of – And Mr Wyse believes – The Padre believed. After all, the Major – Little cock-sparrow Captain Puffin – Or t'other way round, do you think? – No other explanation, you know – Might have been blood – '

She buried her teeth in a muffin.

'Believe there's something in it,' she summed up.

She observed her guest had neither tea nor muffin.

'Help yourself,' she said. 'Want to worry this out.'

'Elizabeth absolutely denies it,' said Mrs Poppit. 'Her eyes were full of – '

'Oh, anything,' said Diva. 'Rubbed them. Or pepper if it was at lunch. That's no evidence.'

'But her solemn assertion – ' began Mrs Poppit, thinking that she was being a complete failure as an ambassador. She was carrying no conviction at all.

'Saccharine!' observed Diva, handing her a small phial. 'Haven't got more than enough sugar for myself. I expect Elizabeth's got plenty – well, never mind that. Don't you see? If it wasn't true she would try to convince us that it was. Seemed absurd on the face of it. But if she tries to convince us that it isn't true – well, something in it.'

There was the gist of the matter, and Mrs Poppit proceeding next to the Padre's house, found more muffins and incredulity. Nobody

seemed to believe Elizabeth's assertion that there was 'nothing in it'.
Evie ran round the room with excited squeaks, the Padre nodded his
head, in confirmation of the opinion which, when he first delivered
it, had been received with mocking incredulity over the crab. Quaint
Irene, intent on Mr Hopkins's left knee in the absence of the model,
said, 'Good old Mapp: better late than never.' Utter incredulity, in
fact, was the ambassador's welcome . . . and all the incredulous were
going to Elizabeth's party on Wednesday.

Mrs Poppit had sent the Royce home for the last of her calls, and
staggered up the hill past Elizabeth's house. Oddly enough, just as
she passed the garden-room, the window was thrown up.

'Cup of tea, dear Susan?' said Elizabeth. She had found an old note
of Mrs Poppit's among the waste paper for the firing of the kitchen
oven fully signed.

'Just two minutes' talk, Elizabeth,' she promptly responded.

*   *   *

The news that nobody in Tilling believed her left Miss Mapp more
than calm, on the bright side of calm, that is to say. She had a few
indulgent phrases that tripped readily off her tongue for the dear
things who hated to be deprived of their gossip, but Susan certainly
did not receive the impression that this playful magnanimity was
attained with an effort. Elizabeth did not seem really to mind: she
was very gay. Then, skilfully changing the subject, she mourned over
her dead dahlias.

Though Tilling with all its perspicacity could not have known it,
the intuitive reader will certainly have perceived that Miss Mapp's
party for Wednesday night had, so to speak, further irons in its fire.
It had originally been a bribe to Susan Poppit, in order to induce
her to spread broadcast that that ridiculous rumour (whoever had
launched it) had been promptly denied by the person whom it most
immediately concerned. It served a second purpose in showing that
Miss Mapp was too high above the mire of scandal, however
interesting, to know or care who might happen to be wallowing in
it, and for this reason she asked everybody who had done so. Such
loftiness of soul had earned her an amazing bonus, for it had induced
those who sat in the seat of the scoffers before to come hastily off,
and join the thin but unwavering ranks of the true believers, who
up till then had consisted only of Susan and Mr Wyse. Frankly, so
blest a conclusion had never occurred to Miss Mapp: it was one of
those unexpected rewards that fall like ripe plums into the lap of

the upright. By denying a rumour she had got everybody to believe it, and when on Wednesday morning she went out to get the chocolate cakes which were so useful in allaying the appetites of guests, she encountered no broken conversations and gleeful smiles, but sidelong glances of respectful envy.

But what Tilling did not and could not know was that this, the first of the autumn after-dinner bridge parties, was destined to look on the famous tea-gown of kingfisher-blue, as designed for Mrs Trout. No doubt other ladies would have hurried up their new gowns, or at least have camouflaged their old ones, in honour of the annual inauguration of evening bridge, but Miss Mapp had no misgivings about being outshone. And once again here she felt that luck waited on merit, for though when she dressed that evening she found she had not anticipated that artificial light would cast a somewhat pale (though not ghastly) reflection from the vibrant blue on to her features, similar in effect to (but not so marked as) the light that shines on the faces of those who lean over the burning brandy and raisins of 'snapdragon', this interesting pallor seemed very aptly to bear witness to all that she had gone through. She did not look ill – she was satisfied as to that – she looked gorgeous and a little wan.

The bridge-tables were not set out in the garden-room, which entailed a scurry over damp gravel on a black, windy night, but in the little square parlour above her dining-room, where Withers, in the intervals of admitting her guests, was laying out plates of sandwiches and the chocolate cakes, reinforced when the interval for refreshments came with hot soup, whisky and syphons, and a jug of 'cup' prepared according to an ancestral and economical recipe, which Miss Mapp had taken a great deal of trouble about. A single bottle of white wine, with suitable additions of ginger, nutmeg, herbs and soda water, was the mother of a gallon of a drink that seemed aflame with fiery and probably spirituous ingredients. Guests were very careful how they partook of it, so stimulating it seemed.

Miss Mapp was reading a book on gardening upside down (she had taken it up rather hurriedly) when the Poppits arrived, and sprang to her feet with a pretty cry at being so unexpectedly but delightfully disturbed.

'Susan! Isabel!' she said. 'Lovely of you to have come! I was reading about flowers, making plans for next year.'

She saw the four eyes riveted to her dress. Susan looked quite shabby in comparison, and Isabel did not look anything at all.

'My dear, too lovely!' said Mrs Poppit slowly.

Miss Mapp looked brightly about, as if wondering what was too lovely: at last she guessed.

'Oh, my new frock?' she said. 'Do you like it, dear? How sweet of you. It's just a little nothing that I talked over with that nice Miss Greele in the High Street. We put our heads together, and invented something quite cheap and simple. And here's Evie and the dear Padre. So kind of you to look in.'

Four more eyes were riveted on it.

'Enticed you out just once, Padre,' went on Miss Mapp. 'So sweet of you to spare an evening. And here's Major Benjy and Captain Puffin. Well, that is nice!'

This was really tremendous of Miss Mapp. Here was she meeting without embarrassment or awkwardness the two, who if the duel had not been averted, would have risked their very lives over some dispute concerning her. Everybody else, naturally, was rather taken aback for the moment at this situation, so deeply dyed in the dramatic. Should either of the gladiators have heard that it was the Padre who undoubtedly had spread the rumour concerning their hostess, Mrs Poppit was afraid that even his cloth might not protect him. But no such deplorable calamity occurred, and only four more eyes were riveted to the kingfisher-blue.

'Upon my word,' said the Major, 'I never saw anything more beautiful than that gown, Miss Elizabeth. Straight from Paris, eh? Paris in every line of it.'

'Oh, Major Benjy,' said Elizabeth. 'You're all making fun of me and my simple little frock. I'm getting quite shy. Just a bit of old stuff that I had. But so nice of you to like it. I wonder where Diva is. We shall have to scold her for being late. Ah – she shan't be scolded. Diva, darl – '

The endearing word froze on Miss Mapp's lips and she turned deadly white. In the doorway, in equal fury and dismay, stood Diva, dressed in precisely the same staggeringly lovely costume as her hostess. Had Diva and Miss Greele put their heads together too? Had Diva got a bit of old stuff . . . ?

Miss Mapp pulled herself together first and moistened her dry lips.

'So sweet of you to look in, dear,' she said. 'Shall we cut?'

Naturally the malice of cards decreed that Miss Mapp and Diva should sit next each other as adversaries at the same table, and the combined effect of two lots of kingfisher-blue was blinding. Complete silence on every subject connected, however remotely, with dress was, of course, the only line for correct diplomacy to pursue, but then Major Benjy was not diplomatic, only gallant.

'Never saw such stunning gowns, eh, Padre?' he said. 'Dear me, they are very much alike too, aren't they? Pair of exquisite sisters.'

It would be hard to say which of the two found this speech the more provocative of rage, for while Diva was four years younger than Miss Mapp, Miss Mapp was four inches taller than Diva. She cut the cards to her sister with a hand that trembled so much that she had to do it again, and Diva could scarcely deal.

*   *   *

Mr Wyse frankly confessed the next day when, at one o'clock, Elizabeth found herself the first arrival at his house, that he had been very self-indulgent.

'I have given myself a treat, dear Miss Mapp,' he said. 'I have asked three entrancing ladies to share my humble meal with me, and have provided – is it not shocking of me? – nobody else to meet them. Your pardon, dear lady, for my greediness.'

Now this was admirably done. Elizabeth knew very well why two out of the three men in Tilling had not been asked (very gratifying, that reason was), and with the true refinement of which Mr Wyse was so amply possessed, here he was taking all the blame on himself, and putting it so prettily. She bestowed her widest smile on him.

'Oh, Mr Wyse,' she said. 'We shall all quarrel over you.'

Not until Miss Mapp had spoken did she perceive how subtle her words were. They seemed to bracket herself and Mr Wyse together: all the men (two out of the three, at any rate) had been quarrelling over her, and now there seemed a very fair prospect of three of the women quarrelling over Mr Wyse . . .

Without being in the least effeminate, Mr Wyse this morning looked rather like a modern Troubadour. He had a velveteen coat on, a soft, fluffy, mushy tie which looked as if made of Shirley poppies, very neat knickerbockers, brown stockings with blobs, like the fruit of plane trees, dependent from elaborate 'tops', and shoes with a cascade of leather frilling covering the laces. He might almost equally well be about to play golf over putting-holes on the lawn as the guitar. He made a gesture of polished, polite dissent, not contradicting, yet hardly accepting this tribute, remitting it perhaps, just as the King when he enters the City of London touches the sword of the Lord Mayor and tells him to keep it . . .

'So pleasant to be in Tilling again,' he said. 'We shall have a cosy, busy winter, I hope. You, I know, Miss Mapp, are always busy.'

'The day is never long enough for me,' said Elizabeth enthusiastically. 'What with my household duties in the morning, and my garden, and our pleasant little gatherings, it is always bedtime too soon. I want to read a great deal this winter, too.'

Diva (at the sight of whom Elizabeth had to make a strong effort of self-control) here came in, together with Mrs Poppit, and the party was complete. Elizabeth would have been willing to bet that, in spite of the warmness of the morning, Susan would have on her sable coat, and though, technically, she would have lost, she more than won morally, for Mr Wyse's repeated speeches about his greediness were hardly out of his mouth when she discovered that she had left her handkerchief in the pocket of her sable coat, which she had put over the back of a conspicuous chair in the hall. Figgis, however, came in at the moment to say that lunch was ready, and she delayed them all very much by a long, ineffectual search for it, during which Figgis, with a visible effort, held up the sable coat, so that it was displayed to the utmost advantage. And then, only fancy, Susan discovered that it was in her sable muff all the time!

All three ladies were on tenterhooks of anxiety as to who was to be placed on Mr Wyse's right, who on his left, and who would be given only the place between two other women. But his tact was equal to anything.

'Miss Mapp,' he said, 'will you honour me by taking the head of my table and be hostess for me? Only I must have that vase of flowers removed, Figgis; I can look at my flowers when Miss Mapp is not here. Now, what have we got for breakfast – lunch, I should say?'

The macaroni which Mr Wyse had brought back with him from Naples naturally led on to Italian subjects, and the general scepticism about the Contessa di Faraglione had a staggering blow dealt it.

'My sister,' began Mr Wyse (and by a swift sucking motion, Diva drew into her mouth several serpents of dependent macaroni in order to be able to listen better without this agitating distraction), 'my sister, I hope, will come to England this winter, and spend several weeks with me.' (Sensation.)

'And the Count?' asked Diva, having swallowed the serpents.

'I fear not; Cecco – Francesco, you know – is a great stay-at-home. Amelia is looking forward very much to seeing Tilling. I shall insist on her making a long stay here, before she visits our relations at Whitchurch.'

Elizabeth found herself reserving judgement. She would believe in the Contessa Faraglione – no one more firmly – when she saw her, and had reasonable proofs of her identity.

'Delightful!' she said, abandoning with regret the fruitless pursuit with a fork of the few last serpents that writhed on her plate. 'What an addition to our society! We shall all do our best to spoil her, Mr Wyse. When do you expect her?'

'Early in December. You must be very kind to her, dear ladies. She is an insatiable bridge-player. She has heard much of the great players she will meet here.'

That decided Mrs Poppit. She would join the correspondence class conducted by 'Little Slam', in 'Cosy Corner'. Little Slam, for the sum of two guineas, payable in advance, engaged to make first-class players of anyone with normal intelligence. Diva's mind flew off to the subject of dress, and the thought of the awful tragedy concerning the tea-gown of kingfisher-blue, combined with the endive salad, gave a wry twist to her mouth for a moment.

'I, as you know,' continued Mr Wyse, 'am no hand at bridge.'

'Oh, Mr Wyse, you play beautifully,' interpolated Elizabeth.

'Too flattering of you, Miss Mapp. But Amelia and Cecco do not agree with you. I am never allowed to play when I am at the Villa Faraglione, unless a table cannot be made up without me. But I shall look forward to seeing many well-contested games.'

The quails and the figs had come from Capri, and Miss Mapp, greedily devouring each in turn, was so much incensed by the information that she had elicited about them, that, though she joined in the general Lobgesang, she was tempted to enquire whether the ice had not been brought from the South Pole by some Antarctic expedition. Her mind was not, like poor Diva's, taken up with obstinate questionings about the kingfisher-blue tea-gown, for she had already determined what she was going to do about it. Naturally it was impossible to contemplate fresh encounters like that of last night, but another gown, crimson-lake, the colour of Mrs Trout's toilet for the second evening of the Duke of Hampshire's visit, as *Vogue* informed her, had completely annihilated Newport with its splendour. She had already consulted Miss Greele about it, who said that if the kingfisher-blue was bleached first the dye of crimson-lake would be brilliant and pure . . . The thought of that, and the fact that Miss Greele's lips were professionally sealed, made her able to take Diva's arm as they strolled about the garden afterwards. The way in which both Diva and Susan had made up to Mr Wyse during lunch was really very shocking, though it did not surprise Miss Mapp, but she supposed their heads had been turned by the prospect of playing bridge with a countess. Luckily she expected nothing better of either of them, so their conduct was in no way a blow or a disappointment to her.

This companionship with Diva was rather prolonged, for the adhesive Susan, staggering about in her sables, clung close to their host and simulated a clumsy interest in chrysanthemums; and whatever the other two did, manoeuvred herself into a strong position between them and Mr Wyse, from which, operating on interior lines, she could cut off either assailant. More depressing yet (and throwing a sad new light on his character), Mr Wyse seemed to appreciate rather than resent the appropriation of himself, and instead of making a sortie through the beleaguering sables, would beg Diva and Elizabeth, who were so fond of fuchsias and knew about them so well, to put their heads together over an afflicted bed of these flowers in quite another part of the garden, and tell him what was the best treatment for their anaemic condition. Pleasant and proper though it was to each of them that Mr Wyse should pay so little attention to the other, it was bitter as the endive salad to both that he should tolerate, if not enjoy, the companionship which the forwardness of Susan forced on him, and while they absently stared at the fuchsias, the fire kindled, and Elizabeth spake with her tongue.

'How very plain poor Susan looks today,' she said. 'Such a colour, though to be sure I attribute that more to what she ate and drank than to anything else. Crimson. Oh, those poor fuchsias! I think I should throw them away.'

The common antagonism, Diva felt, had drawn her and Elizabeth into the most cordial of understandings. For the moment she felt nothing but enthusiastic sympathy with Elizabeth, in spite of her kingfisher-blue gown . . . What on earth, in parenthesis, was she to do with hers? She could not give it to Janet: it was impossible to contemplate the idea of Janet walking about the High Street in a teagown of kingfisher-blue just in order to thwart Elizabeth . . .

'Mr Wyse seems taken with her,' said Diva. 'How he can! Rather a snob. MBE. She's always popping in here. Saw her yesterday going round the corner of the street.'

'What time, dear?' asked Elizabeth, nosing the scent.

'Middle of the morning.'

'And I saw her in the afternoon,' said Elizabeth. 'That great lumbering Rolls-Royce went tacking and skidding round the corner below my garden-room.'

'Was she in it?' asked Diva.

This appeared rather a slur on Elizabeth's reliability in observation.

'No, darling, she was sitting on the top,' she said, taking the edge off the sarcasm, in case Diva had not intended to be critical, by a little laugh. Diva drew the conclusion that Elizabeth had actually seen her inside.

'Think it's serious?' she said. 'Think he'll marry her?'

The idea of course, repellent and odious as it was, had occurred to Elizabeth, so she instantly denied it.

'Oh, you busy little matchmaker,' she said brightly. 'Such an idea never entered my head. You shouldn't make such fun of dear Susan. Come, dear, I can't look at fuchsias any more. I must be getting home and must say goodbye – *au reservoir*, rather – to Mr Wyse, if Susan will allow me to get a word in edgeways.'

Susan seemed delighted to let Miss Mapp get this particular word in edgewise, and after a little speech from Mr Wyse, in which he said that he would not dream of allowing them to go yet, and immediately afterwards shook hands warmly with them both, hoping that the reservoir would be a very small one, the two were forced to leave the artful Susan in possession of the field . . .

It all looked rather black. Miss Mapp's vivid imagination altogether failed to picture what Tilling would be like if Susan succeeded in becoming Mrs Wyse and the sister-in-law of a countess, and she sat down in her garden-room and closed her eyes for a moment, in order to concentrate her power of figuring the situation. What dreadful people these climbers were! How swiftly they swarmed up the social ladder with their Rolls-Royces and their redcurrant fool, and their sables! A few weeks ago she herself had never asked Susan into her house, while the very first time she came she unloosed the sluices of the store-cupboard, and now, owing to the necessity of getting her aid in stopping that mischievous rumour, which she herself had been so careful to set on foot, regarding the cause of the duel, Miss Mapp had been positively obliged to flatter and to 'Susan' her. And if Diva's awful surmise proved to be well-founded, Susan would be in a position to patronise them all, and talk about counts and countesses with the same air of unconcern as Mr Wyse. She would be bidden to the Villa Faraglione, she would play bridge with Cecco and Amelia, she would visit the Wyses of Whitchurch . . .

What was to be done? She might head another movement to put Mr Wyse in his proper place; this, if successful, would have the agreeable result of pulling down Susan a rung or two should she carry out her design. But the failure of the last attempt and Mr Wyse's eminence did not argue well for any further manoeuvre of the kind. Or should she poison Mr Wyse's mind with regard to Susan? . . . Or was she herself causelessly agitated?

Or –

Curiosity rushed like a devastating tornado across Miss Mapp's mind, rooting up all other growths, buffeting her with the necessity of knowing what the two whom she had been forced to leave in the garden were doing now, and snatching up her opera-glasses she glided upstairs, and let herself out through the trap-door on to the roof. She did not remember if it was possible to see Mr Wyse's garden or any part of it from that watchtower, but there was a chance . . .

Not a glimpse of it was visible. It lay quite hidden behind the red-brick wall which bounded it, and not a chrysanthemum or a fuchsia could she see. But her blood froze as, without putting the glasses down, she ran her eye over such part of the house-wall as rose above the obstruction. In his drawing-room window on the first floor were seated two figures. Susan had taken her sables off: it was as if she intended remaining there for ever, or at least for tea . . .

Chapter Eight

The hippopotamus quarrel over their whisky between Major Flint and Captain Puffin, which culminated in the challenge and all the shining sequel, had had the excellent effect of making the United Services more united than ever. They both knew that, had they not severally run away from the encounter, and, so providentially, met at the station, very serious consequences might have ensued. Had not both but only one of them been averse from taking or risking life, the other would surely have remained in Tilling, and spread disastrous reports about the bravery of the refugee; while if neither of them had had scruples on the sacredness of human existence there might have been one if not two corpses lying on the shining sands. Naturally the fact that they both had taken the very earliest opportunity of averting an encounter by flight, made it improbable that any future quarrel would be proceeded with to violent extremes, but it was much safer to run no risks, and not let verbal disagreements rise to hippo-potamus-pitch again. Consequently when there was any real danger of such savagery as was implied in sending challenges, they hastened, by mutual concessions, to climb down from these perilous places, where loss of balance might possibly occur. For which of them could be absolutely certain that next time the other of them might not be more courageous? . . .

They were coming up from the tram-station one November evening, both fizzing and fuming a good deal, and the Major was extremely lame, lamer than Puffin. The rattle of the tram had made argument impossible during the transit from the links, but they had both in this enforced silence thought of several smart repartees, supposing that the other made the requisite remarks to call them out, and on arrival at the Tilling station they went on at precisely the same point at which they had broken off on starting from the station by the links.

'Well, I hope I can take a beating in as English a spirit as anybody,' said the Major.

This was lucky for Captain Puffin: he had thought it likely that he would say just that, and had got a stinger for him.

'And it worries you to find that your hopes are doomed to disappointment,' he swiftly said.

Major Flint stepped in a puddle which cooled his foot but not his temper.

'Most offensive remark,' he said. 'I wasn't called Sporting Benjy in the regiment for nothing. But never mind that. A worm-cast – '

'It wasn't a worm-cast,' said Puffin. 'It was sheep's dung!'

Luck had veered here: the Major had felt sure that Puffin would reiterate that utterly untrue contention.

'I can't pretend to be such a specialist as you in those matters,' he said, 'but you must allow me sufficient power of observation to know a worm-cast when I see it. It was a worm-cast, sir, a cast of a worm, and you had no right to remove it. If you will do me the favour to consult the rules of golf – ?'

'Oh, I grant you that you are more a specialist in the rules of golf, Major, than in the practice of it,' said Puffin brightly.

Suddenly it struck Sporting Benjy that the red signals of danger danced before his eyes, and though the odious Puffin had scored twice to his once, he called up all his powers of self-control, for if his friend was anything like as exasperated as himself, the breeze of disagreement might develop into a hurricane. At the moment he was passing through a swing-gate which led to a short cut back to the town, but before he could take hold of himself he had slammed it back in his fury, hitting Puffin, who was following him, on the knee.

Then he remembered he was a sporting Christian gentleman, and no duellist.

'I'm sure I beg your pardon, my dear fellow,' he said, with the utmost solicitude. 'Uncommonly stupid of me. The gate flew out of my hand. I hope I didn't hurt you.'

Puffin had just come to the same conclusion as Major Flint: magnanimity was better than early trains, and ever so much better than bullets. Indeed there was no comparison . . .

'Not hurt a bit, thank you, Major,' he said, wincing with the shrewdness of the blow, silently cursing his friend for what he felt sure was no accident, and limping with both legs. 'It didn't touch me. Ha! What a brilliant sunset. The town looks amazingly picturesque.'

'It does indeed,' said the Major. 'Fine subject for Miss Mapp.'

Puffin shuffled alongside.

'There's still a lot of talk going on in the town,' he said, 'about that duel of ours. Those fairies of yours are all agog to know what it was about. I am sure they all think that there was a lady in the case. Just like the vanity of the sex. If two men have a quarrel, they think it must be because of their silly faces.'

Ordinarily the Major's gallantry would have resented this view, but the reconciliation with Puffin was too recent to risk just at present.

'Poor little devils,' he said. 'It makes an excitement for them. I wonder who they think it is. It would puzzle me to name a woman in Tilling worth catching an early train for.'

'There are several who'd be surprised to hear you say that, Major,' said Puffin archly.

'Well, well,' said the other, strutting and swelling, and walking without a sign of lameness . . .

They had come to where their houses stood opposite each other on the steep cobbled street, fronted at its top end by Miss Mapp's garden-room. She happened to be standing in the window, and the Major made a great flourish of his cap, and laid his hand on his heart.

'And there's one of them,' said Puffin, as Miss Mapp acknowledged these florid salutations with a wave of her hand, and tripped away from the window.

'Poking your fun at me,' said the Major. 'Perhaps she was the cause of our quarrel, hey? Well, I'll step across, shall I, about half-past nine, and bring my diaries with me?'

'I'll expect you. You'll find me at my Roman roads.'

The humour of this joke never staled, and they parted with hoots and guffaws of laughter.

It must not be supposed that duelling, puzzles over the portmanteau, or the machinations of Susan had put out of Miss Mapp's head her amiable interest in the hour at which Major Benjy went to bed. For some time she had been content to believe, on direct information from him, that he went to bed early and worked at his diaries on alternate evenings, but maturer consideration had led her to wonder whether he was being quite as truthful as a gallant soldier should be. For though (on alternate evenings) his house would be quite dark by half-past nine, it was not for twelve hours or more afterwards that he could be heard *quai-hai*ing for his breakfast, and unless he was in some incipient stage of sleeping-sickness, such hours provided more than ample slumber for a growing child, and might be considered excessive for a middle-aged man. She had a mass of evidence to show that on the other set of alternate nights his diaries (which must, in parenthesis, be of extraordinary fullness) occupied him into the small hours, and to go to bed at half-past nine on one night and after one o'clock on the next implied a complicated kind of regularity which cried aloud for elucidation. If he had only breakfasted early on the mornings after he had gone to bed early, she might have allowed herself to be weakly credulous, but he never *quai-hai*ed earlier than half-past nine, and she could not but think that to believe blindly in such habits would be a triumph not for faith but for foolishness. 'People,' said Miss Mapp to herself, as her attention refused to concentrate on the evening paper, 'don't do it. I never heard of a similar case.'

She had been spending the evening alone, and even the conviction that her cold apple tart had suffered diminution by at least a slice, since she had so much enjoyed it hot at lunch, failed to occupy her mind for long, for this matter had presented itself with a clamouring insistence that drowned all other voices. She had tried, when, at the conclusion of her supper, she had gone back to the garden-room, to immerse herself in a book, in an evening paper, in the portmanteau problem, in a jig-saw puzzle, and in Patience, but none of these supplied the stimulus to lead her mind away from Major Benjy's evenings, or the narcotic to dull her unslumbering desire to solve a problem that was rapidly becoming one of the greater mysteries.

Her radiator made a seat in the window agreeably warm, and a chink in the curtains gave her a view of the Major's lighted window. Even as she looked, the illumination was extinguished. She had expected this, as he had been at his diaries late – quite naughtily late – the evening before, so this would be a night of infant slumber for twelve hours or so.

Even as she looked, a chink of light came from his front door, which immediately enlarged itself into a full oblong. Then it went completely out. 'He has opened the door, and has put out the hall-light,' whispered Miss Mapp to herself . . . 'He has gone out and shut the door . . . (Perhaps he is going to post a letter.) . . . He has gone into Captain Puffin's house without knocking. So he is expected.'

Miss Mapp did not at once guess that she held in her hand the key to the mystery. It was certainly Major Benjy's night for going to bed early . . . Then a fierce illumination beat on her brain. Had she not, so providentially, actually observed the Major cross the road, unmistakable in the lamplight, and had she only looked out of her window after the light in his was quenched, she would surely have told herself that good Major Benjy had gone to bed. But good Major Benjy, on ocular evidence, she now knew to have done nothing of the kind: he had gone across to see Captain Puffin . . . He was not good.

She grasped the situation in its hideous entirety. She had been deceived and hoodwinked. Major Benjy never went to bed early at all: on alternate nights he went and sat with Captain Puffin. And Captain Puffin, she could not but tell herself, sat up on the other set of alternate nights with the Major, for it had not escaped her observation that when the Major seemed to be sitting up, the Captain seemed to have gone to bed. Instantly, with strong conviction, she suspected orgies. It remained to be seen (and she would remain to see it) to what hour these orgies were kept up.

About eleven o'clock a little mist had begun to form in the street, obscuring the complete clarity of her view, but through it there still shone the light from behind Captain Puffin's red blind, and the mist was not so thick as to be able wholly to obscure the figure of Major Flint when he should pass below the gas lamp again into his house. But no such figure passed. Did he then work at his diaries every evening? And what price, to put it vulgarly, Roman roads?

Every moment her sense of being deceived grew blacker, and every moment her curiosity as to what they were doing became more unbearable. After a spasm of tactical thought she glided back into her house from the garden-room, and, taking an envelope in her hand, so that she might, if detected, say that she was going down to the letter-box at the corner to catch the early post, she unbolted her door and let herself out. She crossed the street and tiptoed along the pavement to where the red light from Captain Puffin's window shone like a blurred danger-signal through the mist.

From inside came a loud duet of familiar voices: sometimes they spoke singly, sometimes together. But she could not catch the words: they sounded blurred and indistinct, and she told herself that she was very glad that she could not hear what they said, for that would have seemed like eavesdropping. The voices sounded angry. Was there another duel pending? And what was it about this time?

Quite suddenly, from so close at hand that she positively leaped off the pavement into the middle of the road, the door was thrown open and the duet, louder than ever, streamed out into the street. Major Benjy bounced out on to the threshold, and stumbled down the two steps that led from the door.

'Tell you it was a worm-cast,' he bellowed. 'Think I don't know a worm-cast when I see a worm-cast?'

Suddenly his tone changed: this was getting too near a quarrel.

'Well, good-night, old fellow,' he said. 'Jolly evening.'

He turned and saw, veiled and indistinct in the mist, the female figure in the roadway. Undying coquetry, as Mr Stevenson so finely remarked, awoke, for the topic preceding the worm-cast had been 'the sex'.

'Bless me,' he crowed, 'if there isn't an unprotected lady all 'lone here in the dark, and lost in the fog. 'Llow me to 'scort you home, madam. Lemme introduce myself and friend – Major Flint, that's me, and my friend Captain Puffin.'

He put up his hand and whispered an aside to Miss Mapp: 'Revolutionised the theory of navigation.'

Major Benjy was certainly rather gay and rather indistinct, but his polite gallantry could not fail to be attractive. It was naughty of him to have said that he went to bed early on alternate nights, but really . . . Still, it might be better to slip away unrecognised, and, thinking it would be nice to scriggle by him and disappear in the mist, she made a tactical error in her scriggling, for she scriggled full into the light that streamed from the open door where Captain Puffin was standing.

He gave a shrill laugh.

'Why, it's Miss Mapp,' he said in his high falsetto. 'Blow me, if it isn't our mutual friend Miss Mapp. What a 'strordinary coincidence.'

Miss Mapp put on her most winning smile. To be dignified and at the same time pleasant was the proper way to deal with this situation. Gentlemen often had a glass of grog when they thought the ladies had gone upstairs. That was how, for the moment, she summed things up.

'Good-evening,' she said. 'I was just going down to the pillar-box to post a letter,' and she exhibited her envelope. But it dropped out of her hand, and the Major picked it up for her.

'I'll post it for you,' he said very pleasantly. 'Save you the trouble. Insist on it. Why, there's no stamp on it! Why, there's no address on it! I say, Puffie, here's a letter with no address on it. Forgotten the address, Miss Mapp? Think they'll remember it at the post-office? Well, that's one of the mos' comic things I ever came across. An, an anonymous letter, eh?'

The night air began to have a most unfortunate effect on Puffin. When he came out it would have been quite unfair to have described him as drunk. He was no more than gay and ready to go to bed. Now he became portentously solemn, as the cold mist began to do its deadly work.

'A letter,' he said impressively, 'without an address is an uncommonly dangerous thing. Hic! Can't tell into whose hands it may fall. I would sooner go 'bout with a loaded pistol than with a letter without any address. Send it to the bank for safety. Send for the police. Follow my advice and send for the p'lice. Police!'

Miss Mapp's penetrating mind instantly perceived that that dreadful Captain Puffin was drunk, and she promised herself that Tilling should ring with the tale of his excesses tomorrow. But Major Benjy, whom, if she mistook not, Captain Puffin had been trying, with perhaps some small success, to lead astray, was a gallant gentleman still, and she conceived the brilliant but madly mistaken idea of throwing herself on his protection.

'Major Benjy,' she said, 'I will ask you to take me home. Captain Puffin has had too much to drink – '

'Woz that?' asked Captain Puffin, with an air of great interest.

Miss Mapp abandoned dignity and pleasantness, and lost her temper.

'I said you were drunk,' she said with great distinctness. 'Major Benjy, will you – '

Captain Puffin came carefully down the two steps from the door on to the pavement.

'Look here,' he said, 'this all needs 'splanation. You say I'm drunk, do you? Well, I say you're drunk, going out like this in mill' of the night to post letter with no 'dress on it. Shamed of yourself, mill'aged woman going out in the mill' of the night in the mill' of Tilling. Very shocking thing. What do you say, Major?'

Major Benjy drew himself up to his full height, and put on his hat in order to take it off to Miss Mapp.

'My fren' Cap'n Puffin,' he said, 'is a man of strictly 'stemious habits. Boys together. Very serious thing to call a man of my fren's character drunk. If you call him drunk, why shouldn't he call you drunk? Can't take away man's character like that.'

'Abso –' began Captain Puffin. Then he stopped and pulled himself together.

'Absolooly,' he said without a hitch.

'Tilling shall hear of this tomorrow,' said Miss Mapp, shivering with rage and sea-mist.

Captain Puffin came a step closer.

'Now I'll tell you what it is, Miss Mapp,' he said. 'If you dare to say that I was drunk, Major and I, my fren' the Major and I will say you were drunk. Perhaps you think my fren' the Major's drunk too. But sure's I live, I'll say we were taking lil' walk in the moonlight and found you trying to post a letter with no 'dress on it, and couldn't find the slit to put it in. But 'slong as you say nothing, I say nothing. Can't say fairer than that. Liberal terms. Mutual Protection Society. Your lips sealed, our lips sealed. Strictly private. All trespassers will be prosecuted. By order. Hic!'

Miss Mapp felt that Major Benjy ought instantly to have challenged his ignoble friend to another duel for this insolent suggestion, but he did nothing of the kind, and his silence, which had some awful quality of consent about it, chilled her mind, even as the sea-mist, now thick and cold, made her certain that her nose was turning red. She still boiled with rage, but her mind grew cold with odious apprehensions: she was like an ice-pudding with scalding sauce . . . There they all stood, veiled in vapours, and outlined by the red light that streamed from the still-open door of the intoxicated Puffin, getting colder every moment.

'Yessorno,' said Puffin, with chattering teeth.

Bitter as it was to accept those outrageous terms, there really seemed, without the Major's support, to be no way out of it.

'Yes,' said Miss Mapp.

Puffin gave a loud crow.

'The ayes have it, Major,' he said. 'So we're all frens again. Goonight everybody.'

*   *   *

Miss Mapp let herself into her house in an agony of mortification. She could scarcely realise that her little expedition, undertaken with so much ardent and earnest curiosity only a quarter of an hour ago,

had ended in so deplorable a surfeit of sensation. She had gone out
in obedience to an innocent and, indeed, laudable desire to ascertain
how Major Benjy spent those evenings on which he had deceived her
into imagining that, owing to her influence, he had gone ever so
early to bed, only to find that he sat up ever so late and that she was
fettered by a promise not to breathe to a soul a single word about the
depravity of Captain Puffin, on pain of being herself accused out of
the mouth of two witnesses of being equally depraved herself. More
wounding yet was the part played by her Major Benjy in these odious
transactions, and it was only possible to conclude that he put a higher
value on his fellowship with his degraded friend than on chivalry
itself . . . And what did his silence imply? Probably it was a defensive
one; he imagined that he, too, would be included in the stories that
Miss Mapp proposed to sow broadcast upon the fruitful fields of
Tilling, and, indeed, when she called to mind his bellowing about
worm-casts, his general instability of speech and equilibrium, she
told herself that he had ample cause for such a supposition. He,
when his lights were out, was abetting, assisting and perhaps joining
Captain Puffin. When his window was alight on alternate nights she
made no doubt now that Captain Puffin was performing a similar
role. This had been going on for weeks under her very nose, without
her having the smallest suspicion of it.

Humiliated by all that had happened, and flattened in her own
estimation by the sense of her blindness, she penetrated to the
kitchen and lit a gas-ring to make herself some hot cocoa, which
would at least comfort her physical chatterings. There was a letter
for Withers, slipped sideways into its envelope, on the kitchen table,
and mechanically she opened and read it by the bluish flame of the
burner. She had always suspected Withers of having a young man,
and here was proof of it. But that he should be Mr Hopkins of the
fish-shop!

There is known to medical science a pleasant device known as a
counter-irritant. If the patient has an aching and rheumatic joint he
is counselled to put some hot burning application on the skin, which
smarts so agonisingly that the ache is quite extinguished. Meta-
phorically, Mr Hopkins was thermogene to Miss Mapp's outraged
and aching consciousness, and the smart occasioned by the knowledge
that Withers must have encouraged Mr Hopkins (else he could
scarcely have written a letter so familiar and amorous), and thus be
contemplating matrimony, relieved the aching humiliation of all that
had happened in the sea-mist. It shed a new and lurid light on

Withers, it made her mistress feel that she had nourished a serpent in her bosom, to think that Withers was contemplating so odious an act of selfishness as matrimony. It would be necessary to find a new parlour-maid, and all the trouble connected with that would not nearly be compensated for by being able to buy fish at a lower rate. That was the least that Withers could do for her, to insist that Mr Hopkins should let her have dabs and plaice exceptionally cheap. And ought she to tell Withers that she had seen Mr Hopkins . . . no, that was impossible: she must write it, if she decided (for Withers's sake) to make this fell communication.

Miss Mapp turned and tossed on her uneasy bed, and her mind went back to the Major and the Captain and that fiasco in the fog. Of course she was perfectly at liberty (having made her promise under practical compulsion) to tell everybody in Tilling what had occurred, trusting to the chivalry of the men not to carry out their counter-threat, but looking at the matter quite dispassionately, she did not think it would be wise to trust too much to chivalry. Still, even if they did carry out their unmanly menace, nobody would seriously believe that she had been drunk. But they might make a very disagreeable joke of pretending to do so, and, in a word, the prospect frightened her. Whatever Tilling did or did not believe, a residuum of ridicule would assuredly cling to her, and her reputation of having perhaps been the cause of the quarrel which, so happily, did not end in a duel, would be lost for ever. Evie would squeak, quaint Irene would certainly burst into hoarse laughter when she heard the story. It was very inconvenient that honesty should be the best policy.

Her brain still violently active switched off for a moment on to the eternal problem of the portmanteau. Why, so she asked herself for the hundredth time, if the portmanteau contained the fatal apparatus of duelling, did not the combatants accompany it? And if (the only other alternative) it did not – ?

An idea so luminous flashed across her brain that she almost thought the room had leaped into light. The challenge distinctly said that Major Benjy's seconds would wait upon Captain Puffin in the course of the morning. With what object then could the former have gone down to the station to catch the early train? There could be but one object, namely to get away as quickly as possible from the dangerous vicinity of the challenged Captain. And why did Captain Puffin leave that note on his table to say that he was suddenly called away, except in order to escape from the ferocious neighbourhood of his challenger?

'The cowards!' ejaculated Miss Mapp. 'They both ran away from each other! How blind I've been!'

The veil was rent. She perceived how, carried away with the notion that a duel was to be fought among the sand-dunes, Tilling had quite overlooked the significance of the early train. She felt sure that she had solved everything now, and gave herself up to a rapturous consideration of what use she would make of the precious solution. All regrets for the impossibility of ruining the character of Captain Puffin with regard to intoxicants were gone, for she had an even deadlier blacking to hand. No faintest hesitation at ruining the reputation of Major Benjy as well crossed her mind; she gloried in it, for he had not only caused her to deceive herself about the early hours on alternate nights, but by his infamous willingness to back up Captain Puffin's bargain, he had shown himself imperviously water-proof to all chivalrous impulses. For weeks now the sorry pair of them had enjoyed the spurious splendours of being men of blood and valour, when all the time they had put themselves to all sorts of inconvenience in catching early trains and packing bags by candlelight in order to escape the hot impulses of quarrel that, as she saw now, were probably derived from drained whisky bottles. That mysterious holloaing about worm-casts was just such another disagreement. And, crowning rapture of all, her own position as cause of the projected duel was quite unassailed. Owing to her silence about drink, no one would suspect a mere drunken brawl: she would still figure as heroine, though the heroes were terribly dismantled. To be sure, it would have been better if their ardour about her had been such that one of them, at the least, had been prepared to face the ordeal, that they had not both preferred flight, but even without that she had much to be thankful for. 'It will serve them both,' said Miss Mapp (interrupted by a sneeze, for she had been sitting up in bed for quite a considerable time), 'right.'

To one of Miss Mapp's experience, the first step of her new and delightful strategic campaign was obvious, and she spent hardly any time at all in the window of her garden-room after breakfast next morning, but set out with her shopping basket at an unusually early hour. She shuddered as she passed between the front doors of her miscreant neighbours, for the chill of last night's mist and its dreadful memories still lingered there, but her present errand warmed her soul even as the tepid November day comforted her body. No sign of life was at present evident in those bibulous abodes, no *quai-hais* had indicated breakfast, and she put her utmost irony into the reflection that the United Services slept late after their protracted industry last night over diaries and Roman roads. By a natural revulsion, violent in proportion to the depth of her previous regard for Major Benjy, she hugged herself more closely on the prospect of exposing him than on that of exposing the other. She had had daydreams about Major Benjy and the conversion of these into nightmares annealed her softness into the semblance of some red-hot stone, giving vengeance a concentrated sweetness as of saccharine contrasted with ordinary lump sugar. This sweetness was of so powerful a quality that she momentarily forgot all about the contents of Withers's letter on the kitchen table, and tripped across to Mr Hopkins's with an oblivious smile for him.

'Good-morning, Mr Hopkins,' she said. 'I wonder if you've got a nice little dab for my dinner today? Yes? Will you send it up then, please? What a mild morning, like May!'

The opening move, of course, was to tell Diva about the revelation that had burst on her the night before. Diva was incomparably the best disseminator of news: she walked so fast, and her telegraphic style was so brisk and lucid. Her terse tongue, her revolving feet! Such a gossip!

'Diva darling, I had to look in a moment,' said Elizabeth, pecking her affectionately on both cheeks. 'Such a bit of news!'

'Oh, Contessa di Faradidleony,' said Diva sarcastically. 'I heard yesterday. Journey put off.'

Miss Mapp just managed to stifle the excitement which would have betrayed that this was news to her.

'No, dear, not that,' she said. 'I didn't suspect you of not knowing that. Unfortunate though, isn't it, just when we were all beginning to believe that there was a Contessa di Faradidleony! What a sweet name! For my part I shall believe in her when I see her. Poor Mr Wyse!'

'What's the news then?' asked Diva.

'My dear, it all came upon me in a flash,' said Elizabeth. 'It explains the portmanteau and the early train and the duel.'

Diva looked disappointed. She thought this was to be some solid piece of news, not one of Elizabeth's ideas only.

'Drive ahead,' she said.

'They ran away from each other,' said Elizabeth, mouthing her words as if speaking to a totally deaf person who understood lip-reading. 'Never mind the cause of the duel: that's another affair. But whatever the cause,' here she dropped her eyes, 'the Major having sent the challenge packed his portmanteau. He ran away, dear Diva, and met Captain Puffin at the station running away too.'

'But did – ' began Diva.

'Yes, dear, the note on Captain Puffin's table to his housekeeper said he was called away suddenly. What called him away? Cowardice, dear! How ignoble it all is. And we've all been thinking how brave and wonderful they were. They fled from each other, and came back together and played golf. I never thought it was a game for men. The sand-dunes where they were supposed to be fighting! They might lose a ball there, but that would be the utmost. Not a life. Poor Padre! Going out there to stop a duel, and only finding a game of golf. But I understand the nature of men better now. What an eye-opener!'

Diva by this time was trundling away round the room, and longing to be off in order to tell everybody. She could find no hole in Elizabeth's arguments; it was founded as solidly as a Euclidean proposition.

'Ever occurred to you that they drink?' she asked. 'Believe in Roman roads and diaries? I don't.'

Miss Mapp bounded from her chair. Danger flags flapped and crimsoned in her face. What if Diva went flying round Tilling, suggesting that in addition to being cowards those two men were drunkards? They would, as soon as any hint of the further exposure reached them, conclude that she had set the idea on foot, and then –

'No, Diva darling,' she said, 'don't dream of imagining such a thing. So dangerous to hint anything of the sort. Cowards they may be, and indeed are, but never have I seen anything that leads me to suppose that they drink. We must give them their due, and stick to what we know; we must not launch accusations wildly about other matters, just because we know they are cowards. A coward need not be a drunkard, thank God! It is all miserable enough, as it is!'

Having averted this danger, Miss Mapp, with her radiant, excited face, seemed to be bearing all the misery very courageously, and as Diva could no longer be restrained from starting on her morning round they plunged together into the maelstrom of the High Street, riding and whirling in its waters with the solution of the portmanteau and the early train for life-buoy. Very little shopping was done that morning, for every permutation and combination of Tilling society (with the exception, of course, of the cowards) had to be formed on the pavement with a view to the amplest possible discussion. Diva, as might have been expected, gave proof of her accustomed perfidy

before long, for she certainly gave the Padre to understand that the
chain of inductive reasoning was of her own welding and Elizabeth
had to hurry after him to correct this grabbing impression; but the
discovery in itself was so great, that small false notes like these could
not spoil the glorious harmony. Even Mr Wyse abandoned his usual
neutrality with regard to social politics and left his tall malacca cane
in the chemist's, so keen was his gusto, on seeing Miss Mapp on the
pavement outside, to glean any fresh detail of evidence.

By eleven o'clock that morning, the two duellists were universally
known as 'the cowards', the Padre alone demurring, and being
swampingly outvoted. He held (sticking up for his sex) that the Major
had been brave enough to send a challenge (on whatever subject) to
his friend, and had, though he subsequently failed to maintain that
high level, shown courage of a high order, since, for all he knew,
Captain Puffin might have accepted it. Miss Mapp was spokesman
for the mind of Tilling on this too indulgent judgement.

'Dear Padre,' she said, 'you are too generous altogether. They
both ran away: you can't get over that. Besides you must remember
that, when the Major sent the challenge, he knew Captain Puffin, oh
so well, and quite expected he would run away – '

'Then why did he run away himself?' asked the Padre.

This was rather puzzling for a moment, but Miss Mapp soon
thought of the explanation.

'Oh, just to make sure,' she said, and Tilling applauded her ready
irony.

And then came the climax of sensationalism, when at about ten
minutes past eleven the two cowards emerged into the High Street
on their way to catch the eleven-twenty tram out to the links. The
day threatened rain, and they both carried bags which contained a
change of clothes. Just round the corner of the High Street was the
group which had applauded Miss Mapp's quickness, and the cowards
were among the breakers. They glanced at each other, seeing that
Miss Mapp was the most towering of the breakers, but it was too late
to retreat, and they made the usual salutations.

'Good-morning,' said Diva, with her voice trembling. 'Off to catch
the early train together – I mean the tram.'

'Good-morning, Captain Puffin,' said Miss Mapp with extreme
sweetness. 'What a nice little travelling bag! Oh, and the Major's got
one too! H'm!'

A certain dismay looked from Major Flint's eyes, Captain Puffin's
mouth fell open, and he forgot to shut it.

'Yes; change of clothes,' said the Major. 'It looks a threatening morning.'

'Very threatening,' said Miss Mapp. 'I hope you will do nothing rash or dangerous.'

There was a moment's silence, and the two looked from one face to another of this fell group. They all wore fixed, inexplicable smiles.

'It will be pleasant among the sand-dunes,' said the Padre, and his wife gave a loud squeak.

'Well, we shall be missing our tram,' said the Major. '*Au – au reservoir*, ladies.'

Nobody responded at all, and they hurried off down the street, their bags bumping together very inconveniently.

'Something's up, Major,' said Puffin, with true Tilling perspicacity, as soon as they had got out of hearing . . .

*   *   *

Precisely at the same moment Miss Mapp gave a little cooing laugh.

'Now I must run and do my bittie shopping, Padre,' she said, and kissed her hand all round . . . The curtain had to come down for a little while on so dramatic a situation. Any discussion, just then, would be an anticlimax.

Chapter Nine

Captain Puffin found but a sombre diarist when he came over to study his Roman roads with Major Flint that evening, and indeed he was a sombre antiquarian himself. They had pondered a good deal during the day over their strange reception in the High Street that morning and the recondite allusions to bags, sand-dunes and early trains, and the more they pondered the more probable it became that not only was something up, but, as regards the duel, everything was up. For weeks now they had been regarded by the ladies of Tilling with something approaching veneration, but there seemed singularly little veneration at the back of the comments this morning. Following so closely on the encounter with Miss Mapp last night, this irreverent attitude was probably due to some atheistical manoeuvre of hers. Such, at least, was the Major's view, and when he held a view he usually stated it, did Sporting Benjy.

'We've got you to thank for this, Puffin,' he said. 'Upon my soul, I was ashamed of you for saying what you did to Miss Mapp last night. Utter absence of any chivalrous feeling hinting that if she said you were drunk you would say she was. She was as sober and lucid last night as she was this morning. And she was devilish lucid, to my mind, this morning.'

'Pity you didn't take her part last night,' said Puffin. 'You thought that was a very ingenious idea of mine to make her hold her tongue.'

'There are finer things in this world, sir, than ingenuity,' said the Major. 'What your ingenuity has led to is this public ridicule. You may not mind that yourself – you may be used to it – but a man should regard the consequences of his act on others ... My status in Tilling is completely changed. Changed for the worse, sir.'

Puffin emitted his fluty, disagreeable laugh.

'If your status in Tilling depended on a reputation for bloodthirsty bravery,' he said, 'the sooner it was changed the better. We're in the same boat: I don't say I like the boat, but there we are. Have a drink, and you'll feel better. Never mind your status.'

'I've a good mind never to have a drink again,' said the Major, pouring himself out one of his stiff little glasses, 'if a drink leads to this sort of thing.'

'But it didn't,' said Puffin. 'How it all got out, I can't say, nor for that matter can you. If it hadn't been for me last night, it would have been all over Tilling that you and I were tipsy as well. That wouldn't have improved our status that I can see.'

'It was in consequence of what you said to Mapp – ' began the Major.

'But, good Lord, where's the connection?' asked Puffin. 'Produce the connection! Let's have a look at the connection! There ain't any connection! Duelling wasn't as much as mentioned last night.'

Major Flint pondered this in gloomy, sipping silence.

'Bridge party at Mrs Poppit's the day after tomorrow,' he said. 'I don't feel as if I could face it. Suppose they all go on making allusions to duelling and early trains and that? I shan't be able to keep my mind on the cards for fear of it. More than a sensitive man ought to be asked to bear.'

Puffin made a noise that sounded rather like 'Fudge!'

'Your pardon?' said the Major haughtily.

'Granted by all means,' said Puffin. 'But I don't see what you're in such a taking about. We're no worse off than we were before we got a reputation for being such fire-eaters. Being fire-eaters is a washout, that's all. Pleasant while it lasted, and now we're as we were.'

'But we're not,' said the Major. 'We're detected frauds! That's not the same as being a fraud; far from it. And who's going to rub it in, my friend? Who's been rubbing away for all she's worth? Miss Mapp, to whom, if I may say so without offence, you behaved like a cur last night.'

'And another cur stood by and wagged his tail,' retorted Puffin.

This was about as far as it was safe to go, and Puffin hastened to say something pleasant about the hearthrug, to which his friend had a suitable rejoinder. But after the affair last night, and the dark sayings in the High Street this morning, there was little content or cosiness about the session. Puffin's brazen optimism was but a tinkling cymbal, and the Major did not feel like tinkling at all. He but snorted and glowered, revolving in his mind how to square Miss Mapp. Allied with her, if she could but be won over, he felt he could face the rest of Tilling with indifference, for hers would be the most penetrating shafts, the most stinging pleasantries. He had more too, so he reflected, to lose than Puffin, for till the affair of the duel the other had never been credited with deeds of bloodthirsty gallantry, whereas he had enjoyed no end of a reputation in amorous and honourable affairs. Marriage no doubt would settle it satisfactorily, but this bachelor life, with plenty of golf and diaries, was not to be lightly exchanged for the unknown. Short of that . . .

A light broke, and he got to his feet, following the gleam and walking very lame out of general discomfiture.

'Tell you what it is, Puffin,' he said. 'You and I, particularly you, owe that estimable lady a very profound apology for what happened last night. You ought to withdraw every word you said, and I every word that I didn't say.'

'Can't be done,' said Puffin. 'That would be giving up my hold over your lady friend. We should be known as drunkards all over the shop before you could say winkie. Worse off than before.'

'Not a bit of it. If it's Miss Mapp, and I'm sure it is, who has been spreading these – these damaging rumours about our duel, it's because she's outraged and offended, quite rightly, at your conduct to her last night. Mine, too, if you like. Ample apology, sir, that's the ticket.'

'Dog-ticket,' said Puffin. 'No thanks.'

'Very objectionable expression,' said Major Flint. 'But you shall do as you like. And so, with your permission, shall I. I shall apologise for my share in that sorry performance, in which, thank God, I only played a minor role. That's my view, and if you don't like it, you may dislike it.'

Puffin yawned.

'Mapp's a cat,' he said. 'Stroke a cat and you'll get scratched. Shy a brick at a cat, and she'll spit at you and skedaddle. You're poor company tonight, Major, with all these qualms.'

'Then, sir, you can relieve yourself of my company,' said the Major, 'by going home.'

'Just what I was about to do. Good-night, old boy. Same time tomorrow for the tram, if you're not too badly mauled.'

Miss Mapp, sitting by the hot-water pipes in the garden-room, looked out not long after to see what the night was like. Though it was not yet half-past ten the cowards' sitting-rooms were both dark, and she wondered what precisely that meant. There was no bridge party anywhere that night, and apparently there were no diaries or Roman roads either. Why this sober and chastened darkness? . . .

The Major *quai-hai*ed for his breakfast at an unusually early hour next morning, for the courage of this resolve to placate, if possible, the hostility of Miss Mapp had not, like that of the challenge, oozed out during the night. He had dressed himself in his frock-coat, seen last on the occasion when the Prince of Wales proved not to have come by the six thirty-seven, and no female breast however furious could fail to recognise the compliment of such a formality. Dressed thus, with top-hat and patent-leather boots, he was clearly observed from the garden-room to emerge into the street just when Captain Puffin's hand thrust the sponge on to the window sill of his bathroom. Probably he too had observed this apparition, for his fingers prematurely loosed hold of the sponge, and it bounded into the street. Wild surmises flashed into Miss Mapp's active brain, the most likely of which was that Major Benjy was going to propose to Mrs Poppit, for if he had been going up to London for some ceremonial occasion, he would be walking down the street instead of up it. And then she saw his agitated finger press the electric bell of her own door. So he was not on his way to propose to Mrs Poppit . . .

She slid from the room and hurried across the few steps of garden to the house just in time to intercept Withers, though not with any idea of saying that she was out. Then Withers, according to instructions, waited till Miss Mapp had tiptoed upstairs, and conducted the Major to the garden-room, promising that she would 'tell' her mistress. This was unnecessary, as her mistress knew. The Major pressed a half-crown into her astonished hand, thinking it was a florin. He couldn't precisely account for that impulse, but general propitiation was at the bottom of it.

Miss Mapp meantime had sat down on her bed, and firmly rejected the idea that his call had anything to do with marriage. During all these years of friendliness he had not got so far as that, and, whatever the future might hold, it was not likely that he would begin now at this moment when she was so properly punishing him for his un-chivalrous behaviour. But what could the frock-coat mean? (There was Captain Puffin's servant picking up the sponge. She hoped it was covered with mud.) It would be a very just continuation of his punishment to tell Withers she would not see him, but the punishment which that would entail on herself would be more than she could bear, for she would not know a moment's peace while she was ignorant of the nature of his errand. Could he be on his way to the Padre's to challenge him for that very stinging allusion to sand-dunes yesterday, and was he come to give her fair warning, so that she might stop a duel? It did not seem likely. Unable to bear the suspense any longer, she adjusted her face in the glass to an expression of frozen dignity and threw over her shoulders the cloak trimmed with blue in which, on the occasion of the Prince's visit, she had sat down in the middle of the road. That matched the Major's frock-coat.

She hummed a little song as she mounted the few steps to the garden-room, and stopped just after she had opened the door. She did not offer to shake hands.

'You wish to see me, Major Flint?' she said, in such a voice as icebergs might be supposed to use when passing each other by night in the Arctic seas.

Major Flint certainly looked as if he hated seeing her, instead of wishing it, for he backed into a corner of the room and dropped his hat.

'Good-morning, Miss Mapp,' he said. 'Very good of you. I – I called.'

He clearly had a difficulty in saying what he had come to say, but if he thought that she was proposing to give him the smallest assistance, he was in error.

'Yes, you called,' said she. 'Pray be seated.'

He did so; she stood; he got up again.

'I called,' said the Major, 'I called to express my very deep regret at my share, or, rather, that I did not take a more active share – I allowed, in fact, a friend of mine to speak to you in a manner that did equal discredit – '

Miss Mapp put her head on one side, as if trying to recollect some trivial and unimportant occurrence.

'Yes?' she said. 'What was that?'

'Captain Puffin,' began the Major.

Then Miss Mapp remembered it all.

'I hope, Major Flint,' she said, 'that you will not find it necessary to mention Captain Puffin's name to me. I wish him nothing but well, but he and his are no concern of mine. I have the charity to suppose that he was quite drunk on the occasion to which I imagine you allude. Intoxication alone could excuse what he said. Let us leave Captain Puffin out of whatever you have come to say to me.'

This was adroit; it compelled the Major to begin all over again.

'I come entirely on my own account,' he began.

'I understand,' said Miss Mapp, instantly bringing Captain Puffin in again. 'Captain Puffin, now I presume sober, has no regret for what he said when drunk. I quite see, and I expected no more and no less from him. Yes. I am afraid I interrupted you.'

Major Flint threw his friend overboard like ballast from a bumping balloon.

'I speak for myself,' he said. 'I behaved, Miss Mapp, like a – ha – worm. Defenceless lady, insolent fellow drunk – I allude to Captain P—. I'm very sorry for my part in it.'

Up till this moment Miss Mapp had not made up her mind whether she intended to forgive him or not; but here she saw how crushing a penalty she might be able to inflict on Puffin if she forgave the erring and possibly truly repentant Major. He had already spoken strongly about his friend's offence, and she could render life supremely nasty for them both – particularly Puffin – if she made the Major agree that he could not, if truly sorry, hold further intercourse with him. There would be no more golf, no more diaries. Besides, if she was observed to be friendly with the Major again and to cut Captain Puffin, a very natural interpretation would be that she had learned that in the original quarrel the Major had been defending her from some odious tongue to the extent of a challenge, even though he subsequently ran away. Tilling was quite clever enough to make that inference without any suggestion from her . . . But if she forgave neither of them, they would probably go on boozing and golfing together, and saying quite dreadful things about her, and not care very much whether she forgave them or not. Her mind was made up, and she gave a wan smile.

'Oh, Major Flint,' she said, 'it hurt me so dreadfully that you should have stood by and heard that man – if he is a man – say those awful things to me and not take my side. It made me feel so lonely. I had always been such good friends with you, and then you turned your back on me like that. I didn't know what I had done to deserve it. I lay awake ever so long.'

This was affecting, and he violently rubbed the nap of his hat the wrong way . . . Then Miss Mapp broke into her sunniest smile.

'Oh, I'm so glad you came to say you were sorry!' she said. 'Dear Major Benjy, we're quite friends again.'

She dabbed her handkerchief on her eyes.

'So foolish of me!' she said. 'Now sit down in my most comfortable chair and have a cigarette.'

Major Flint made a peck at the hand she extended to him, and cleared his throat to indicate emotion. It really was a great relief to think that she would not make awful allusions to duels in the middle of bridge parties.

'And since you feel as you do about Captain Puffin,' she said, 'of course, you won't see anything more of him. You and I are quite one, aren't we, about that? You have dissociated yourself from him completely. The fact of your being sorry does that.'

It was quite clear to the Major that this condition was involved in his forgiveness, though that fact, so obvious to Miss Mapp, had not occurred to him before. Still, he had to accept it, or go unhouseled again. He could explain to Puffin, under cover of night, or perhaps in deaf-and-dumb alphabet from his window . . .

'Infamous, unforgivable behaviour!' he said. 'Pah!'

'So glad you feel that,' said Miss Mapp, smiling till he saw the entire row of her fine teeth. 'And oh, may I say one little thing more? I feel this: I feel that the dreadful shock to me of being insulted like that was quite a lovely little blessing in disguise, now that the effect has been to put an end to your intimacy with him. I never liked it, and I liked it less than ever the other night. He's not a fit friend for you. Oh, I'm so thankful!'

Major Flint saw that for the present he was irrevocably committed to this clause in the treaty of peace. He could not face seeing it torn up again, as it certainly would be, if he failed to accept it in its entirety, nor could he imagine himself leaving the room with a renewal of hostilities. He would lose his game of golf today as it was, for apart from the fact that he would scarcely have time to change his clothes (the idea of playing golf in a frock-coat and top-hat was inconceivable) and catch the 11.20 tram, he could not be seen in Puffin's company at all. And, indeed, in the future, unless Puffin could be induced to apologise and Miss Mapp to forgive, he saw, if he was to play golf at all with his friend, that endless deceptions and subterfuges were necessary in order to escape detection. One of them would have to set out ten minutes before the other, and walk to the tram by some unusual and circuitous route; they would have to play in a clandestine and furtive manner, parting company before they got to the clubhouse; disguises might be needful; there was a peck of difficulties ahead. But he would have to go into these later; at present he must be immersed in the rapture of his forgiveness.

'Most generous of you, Miss Elizabeth,' he said. 'As for that – well, I won't allude to him again.'

Miss Mapp gave a happy little laugh, and having made a further plan, switched away from the subject of captains and insults with alacrity.

'Look!' she said. 'I found these little rosebuds in flower still, though it is the end of November. Such brave little darlings, aren't they? One for your buttonhole, Major Benjy? And then I must do my little shoppings or Withers will scold me – Withers is so severe with me, keeps me in such order! If you are going into the town, will you take me with you? I will put on my hat.'

Requests for the present were certainly commands, and two minutes later they set forth. Luck, as usual, befriended ability, for there was Puffin at his door, itching for the Major's return (else they would miss the tram); and lo! there came stepping along Miss Mapp in her blue-trimmed cloak, and the Major attired as for marriage – top-hat, frock-coat and buttonhole. She did not look at Puffin and cut him; she did not seem (with the deceptiveness of appearances) to see him at all, so eager and agreeable was her conversation with her companion. The Major, so Puffin thought, attempted to give him some sort of dazed and hunted glance; but he could not be certain even of that, so swiftly had it to be transformed into a genial interest in what Miss Mapp was saying, and Puffin stared open-mouthed after them, for they were terrible as an army with banners. Then Diva, trundling swiftly out of the fish-shop, came, as well she might, to a dead halt, observing this absolutely inexplicable phenomenon.

'Good-morning, Diva darling,' said Miss Mapp. 'Major Benjy and I are doing our little shopping together. So kind of him, isn't it? and very naughty of me to take up his time. I told him he ought to be playing golf. Such a lovely day! *Au reservoir*, sweet! Oh, and there's the Padre, Major Benjy! How quickly he walks! Yes, he sees us! And there's Mrs Poppit; everybody is enjoying the sunshine. What a beautiful fur coat, though I should think she found it very heavy and warm. Good-morning, dear Susan! You shopping, too, like Major Benjy and me? How is your dear Isabel?'

Miss Mapp made the most of that morning; the magnanimity of her forgiveness earned her incredible dividends. Up and down the High Street she went, with Major Benjy in attendance, buying grocery, stationery, gloves, eau-de-Cologne, bootlaces, the 'Literary Supplement' of *The Times*, dried camomile flowers, and every conceivable thing that she might possibly need in the next week, so that her shopping might be as protracted as possible. She allowed him (such was her firmness in 'spoiling' him) to carry her shopping basket, and when that was full, she decked him like a sacrificial ram with little parcels hung by loops of string. Sometimes she took him into a shop in case there might be someone there who had not seen him yet on her leash; sometimes she left him on the pavement in a prominent position, marking, all the time, just as if she had been a clinical thermometer, the feverish curiosity that was burning in Tilling's veins. Only yesterday she had spread the news of his cowardice broadcast; today their comradeship was of the chattiest and most genial kind. There he was, carrying her basket, and wearing frock-coat and top-hat and hung with parcels like a Christmas tree, spending the entire morning with her instead of golfing with Puffin. Miss Mapp positively shuddered as she tried to realise what her state of mind would have been, if she had seen him thus coupled with Diva. She would have suspected (rightly in all probability) some loathsome intrigue against herself. And the cream of it was that until she chose, nobody could possibly find out what had caused this metamorphosis so paralysing to enquiring intellects, for Major Benjy would assuredly never tell anyone that there was a reconciliation, due to his apology for his rudeness, when he had stood by and permitted an intoxicated Puffin to suggest disgraceful bargains. Tilling – poor Tilling – would go crazy with suspense as to what it all meant.

Never had there been such a shopping! It was nearly lunchtime when, at her front door, Major Flint finally stripped himself of her parcels and her companionship and hobbled home, profusely perspiring, and lame from so much walking on pavements in tight patent-leather shoes. He was weary and footsore; he had had no golf, and, though forgiven, was but a wreck. She had made him ridiculous all the morning with his frock-coat and top-hat and his porterages, and if forgiveness entailed any more of these nightmare sacraments of friendliness, he felt that he would be unable to endure the fatiguing accessories of the regenerate state. He hung up his top-hat and wiped his wet and throbbing head; he kicked off his shoes and shed his frock-coat, and furiously *quai-hai*ed for a whisky and soda and lunch.

His physical restoration was accompanied by a quickening of dismay at the general prospect. What (to put it succinctly) was life worth, even when unharassed by allusions to duels, without the solace of golf, quarrels and diaries in the companionship of Puffin? He hated Puffin – no one more so – but he could not possibly get on without him, and it was entirely due to Puffin that he had spent so outrageous a morning, for Puffin, seeking to silence Miss Mapp by his intoxicated bargain, had been the prime cause of all this misery. He could not even, for fear of that all-seeing eye in Miss Mapp's garden-room, go across to the house of the unforgiven sea-captain, and by a judicious recital of his woes induce him to beg Miss Mapp's forgiveness instantly. He would have to wait till the kindly darkness fell . . . 'Mere slavery!' he exclaimed with passion.

A tap at his sitting-room door interrupted the chain of these melancholy reflections, and his permission to enter was responded to by Puffin himself. The Major bounced from his seat.

'You mustn't stop here,' he said in a low voice, as if afraid that he might be overheard. 'Miss Mapp may have seen you come in.'

Puffin laughed shrilly.

'Why, of course she did,' he gaily assented. 'She was at her window all right. Ancient lights, I shall call her. What's this all about now?'

'You must go back,' said Major Flint agitatedly. 'She must see you go back. I can't explain now. But I'll come across after dinner when it's dark. Go; don't wait.'

He positively hustled the mystified Puffin out of the house, and Miss Mapp's face, which had grown sharp and pointed with doubts and suspicions when she observed him enter Major Benjy's house, dimpled, as she saw him return, into her sunniest smiles. 'Dear Major Benjy,' she said, 'he has refused to see him,' and she cut the string of the large cardboard box which had just arrived from the dyer's with the most pleasurable anticipations . . .

Well, it was certainly very magnificent, and Miss Greele was quite right, for there was not the faintest tinge to show that it had originally been kingfisher-blue. She had not quite realised how brilliant crimson-lake was in the piece; it seemed almost to cast a ruddy glow on the very ceiling, and the fact that she had caused the orange chiffon with which the neck and sleeves were trimmed to be dyed black (following the exquisite taste of Mrs Titus Trout) only threw the splendour of the rest into more dazzling radiance. Kingfisher-blue would appear quite ghostly and corpse-like in its neighbourhood; and painful though that would be for Diva, it would, as all her well-wishers must hope, be a lesson to her not to indulge in such garishness. She should be taught her lesson (D.V.), thought Miss Mapp, at Susan's bridge party tomorrow evening. Captain Puffin was being taught a lesson, too, for we are never too old to learn, or, for that matter, to teach.

Though the night was dark and moonless, there was an inconveniently brilliant gas lamp close to the Major's door, and that strategist, carrying his round roll of diaries, much the shape of a bottle, under his coat, went about half-past nine that evening to look at the rain-gutter which had been weeping into his yard, and let himself out of the back door round the corner. From there he went down past the fishmonger's, crossed the road, and doubled back again up Puffin's side of the street, which was not so vividly illuminated, though he took the precaution of making himself little with bent knees, and of limping. Puffin was already warming himself over the fire and imbibing Roman roads, and was disposed to be hilarious over the Major's shopping.

'But why top-hat and frock-coat, Major?' he asked. 'Another visit of the Prince of Wales, I asked myself, or the Voice that breathed o'er Eden? Have a drink – one of mine, I mean? I owe you a drink for the good laugh you gave me.'

Had it not been for this generosity and the need of getting on the right side of Puffin, Major Flint would certainly have resented such clumsy levity, but this double consideration caused him to take it with unwonted good-humour. His attempt to laugh, indeed, sounded a little hollow, but that is the habit of self-directed merriment.

'Well, I allow it must have seemed amusing,' he said. 'The fact was that I thought she would appreciate my putting a little ceremony into my errand of apology, and then she whisked me off shopping before I could go and change.'

'Kiss and friends again, then?' asked Puffin.

The Major grew a little stately over this.

'No such familiarity passed,' he said. 'But she accepted my regrets with – ha – the most gracious generosity. A fine-spirited woman, sir; you'll find the same.'

'I might if I looked for it,' said Puffin. 'But why should I want to make it up? You've done that, and that prevents her talking about duelling and early trains. She can't mock at me because of you. You might pass me back my bottle, if you've taken your drink.'

The Major reluctantly did so.

'You must please yourself, old boy,' he said. 'It's your business, and no one's ever said that Benjy Flint interfered in another man's affairs. But I trust you will do what good feeling indicates. I hope you value our jolly games of golf and our pleasant evenings sufficiently highly.'

'Eh! how's that?' asked Puffin. 'You going to cut me too?'

The Major sat down and put his large feet on the fender. 'Tact and diplomacy, Benjy, my boy,' he reminded himself.

'Ha! That's what I like,' he said, 'a good fire and a friend, and the rest of the world may go hang. There's no question of cutting, old man; I needn't tell you that – but we must have one of our good talks. For instance, I very unceremoniously turned you out of my house this afternoon, and I owe you an explanation of that. I'll give it you in one word: Miss Mapp saw you come in. She didn't see me come in here this evening – ha! ha! – and that's why I can sit at my ease. But if she knew – '

Puffin guessed.

'What has happened, Major, is that you've thrown me over for Miss Mapp,' he observed.

'No, sir, I have not,' said the Major with emphasis. 'Should I be sitting here and drinking your whisky if I had? But this morning, after that lady had accepted my regret for my share in what occurred the other night, she assumed that since I condemned my own conduct unreservedly, I must equally condemn yours. It really was like a conjuring trick; the thing was done before I knew anything about it. And before I'd had time to say, "Hold on a bit," I was being led up and down the High Street, carrying as much merchandise as a drove of camels. God, sir, I suffered this morning; you don't seem to realise that I suffered; I couldn't stand any more mornings like that: I haven't the stamina.'

'A powerful woman,' said Puffin reflectively.

'You may well say that,' observed Major Flint. 'That is finely said. A powerful woman she is, with a powerful tongue, and able to be powerful nasty, and if she sees you and me on friendly terms again, she'll turn the full hose on to us both unless you make it up with her.'

'H'm, yes. But as likely as not she'll tell me and my apologies to go hang.'

'Have a try, old man,' said the Major encouragingly.

Puffin looked at his whisky bottle.

'Help yourself, Major,' he said. 'I think you'll have to help me out, you know. Go and interview her: see if there's a chance of my favourable reception.'

'No, sir,' said the Major firmly, 'I will not run the risk of another morning's shopping in the High Street.'

'You needn't. Watch till she comes back from her shopping tomorrow.'

Major Benjy clearly did not like the prospect at all, but Puffin grew firmer and firmer in his absolute refusal to lay himself open to rebuff, and presently, they came to an agreement that the Major was to go on his ambassadorial errand next morning. That being settled, the still undecided point about the worm-cast gave rise to a good deal of heat, until, it being discovered that the window was open, and that their voices might easily carry as far as the garden-room, they made malignant rejoinders to each other in whispers. But it was impossible to go on quarrelling for long in so confidential a manner, and the disagreement was deferred to a more convenient occasion. It was late when the Major left, and after putting out the light in Puffin's hall, so that he should not be silhouetted against it, he slid into the darkness, and reached his own door by a subtle detour.

Miss Mapp had a good deal of division of her swift mind, when, next morning, she learned the nature of Major Benjy's second errand. If she, like Mr Wyse, was to encourage Puffin to hope that she would accept his apologies, she would be obliged to remit all further punishment of him, and allow him to consort with his friend again. It was difficult to forgo the pleasure of his chastisement, but, on the other hand, it was just possible that the Major might break away, and, whether she liked it or not (and she would not), refuse permanently to give up Puffin's society. That would be awkward since she had publicly paraded her reconciliation with him. What further inclined her to clemency, was that this very evening the crimson-lake tea-gown would shed its effulgence over Mrs Poppit's bridge party, and Diva would never want to hear the word 'kingfisher' again. That was enough to put anybody in a good temper. So the diplomatist returned to the miscreant with the glad tidings that Miss Mapp would hear his supplication with a favourable ear, and she took up a stately position in the garden-room, which she selected as audience chamber, near the bell so that she could ring for Withers if necessary.

*   *   *

Miss Mapp's mercy was largely tempered with justice, and she proposed, in spite of the leniency which she would eventually exhibit, to give Puffin 'what for', first. She had not for him, as for Major Benjy, that feminine weakness which had made it a positive luxury to forgive him: she never even thought of Puffin as Captain Dicky, far less let the pretty endearment slip off her tongue accidentally, and the luxury which she anticipated from the interview was that of administering a quantity of hard slaps. She had appointed half-past twelve as the hour for his suffering, so that he must go without his golf again.

She put down the book she was reading when he appeared, and gazed at him stonily without speech. He limped into the middle of the room. This might be forgiveness, but it did not look like it, and he wondered whether she had got him here on false pretences.

'Good-morning,' said he.

Miss Mapp inclined her head. Silence was gold.

'I understood from Major Flint – ' began Puffin.

Speech could be gold too.

'If,' said Miss Mapp, 'you have come to speak about Major Flint you have wasted your time. And mine!'

(How different from Major Benjy, she thought. What a shrimp!)

The shrimp gave a slight gasp. The thing had got to be done, and the sooner he was out of range of this powerful woman the better.

'I am extremely sorry for what I said to you the other night,' he said.

'I am glad you are sorry,' said Miss Mapp.

'I offer you my apologies for what I said,' continued Puffin.

The whip whistled.

'When you spoke to me on the occasion to which you refer,' said Miss Mapp, 'I saw of course at once that you were not in a condition to speak to anybody. I instantly did you that justice, for I am just to everybody. I paid no more attention to what you said than I should have paid to any tipsy vagabond in the slums. I dare say you hardly remember what you said, so that before I hear your expression of regret, I will remind you of it. You threatened, unless I promised to tell nobody in what a disgusting condition you were, to say that I was tipsy. Elizabeth Mapp tipsy! That was what you said, Captain Puffin.'

Captain Puffin turned extremely red. ('Now the shrimp's being boiled,' thought Miss Mapp.)

'I can't do more than apologise,' said he. He did not know whether he was angrier with his ambassador or her.

'Did you say you couldn't do "more"?' said Miss Mapp with an air of great interest. 'How curious! I should have thought you couldn't have done less.'

'Well, what more can I do?' asked he.

'If you think,' said Miss Mapp, 'that you hurt me by your conduct that night, you are vastly mistaken. And if you think you can do no more than apologise, I will teach you better. You can make an effort, Captain Puffin, to break with your deplorable habits, to try to get back a little of the self-respect, if you ever had any, which you have lost. You can cease trying, oh, so unsuccessfully, to drag Major Benjy down to your level. That's what you can do.'

She let these withering observations blight him.

'I accept your apologies,' she said. 'I hope you will do better in the future, Captain Puffin, and I shall look anxiously for signs of improvement. We will meet with politeness and friendliness when we are brought together and I will do my best to wipe all remembrance of your tipsy impertinence from my mind. And you must do your best too. You are not young, and engrained habits are difficult to get rid of. But do not despair, Captain Puffin. And now I will ring for Withers and she will show you out.'

She rang the bell, and gave a sample of her generous oblivion.

'And we meet, do we not, this evening at Mrs Poppit's?' she said, looking not at him, but about a foot above his head. 'Such pleasant evenings one always has there, I hope it will not be a wet evening, but the glass is sadly down. Oh, Withers, Captain Puffin is going. Good-morning, Captain Puffin. Such a pleasure!'

Miss Mapp hummed a rollicking little tune as she observed him totter down the street.

'There!' she said, and had a glass of Burgundy for lunch as a treat.

Chapter Ten

The news that Mr Wyse was to be of the party that evening at Mrs Poppit's and was to dine there first, *en famille* (as he casually let slip in order to air his French), created a disagreeable impression that afternoon in Tilling. It was not usual to do anything more than 'have a tray' for your evening meal, if one of these winter bridge parties followed, and there was, to Miss Mapp's mind, a deplorable tendency to ostentation in this dinner-giving before a party. Still, if Susan was determined to be extravagant, she might have asked Miss Mapp as well, who resented this want of hospitality. She did not

like, either, this hole-and-corner *en famille* work with Mr Wyse; it
indicated a pushing familiarity to which, it was hoped, Mr Wyse's
eyes were open.

There was another point: the party, it had been ascertained, would
in all number ten, and if, as was certain, there would be two bridge-
tables, that seemed to imply that two people would have to cut out.
There were often nine at Mrs Poppit's bridge parties (she appeared
to be unable to count), but on those occasions Isabel was generally
told by her mother that she did not care for bridge, and so there was
no cutting out, but only a pleasant book for Isabel. But what would
be done with ten? It was idle to hope that Susan would sit out: as
hostess she always considered it part of her duties to play solidly the
entire evening. Still, if the cutting of cards malignantly ordained that
Miss Mapp was ejected, it was only reasonable to expect that after
her magnanimity to the United Services, either Major Benjy or
Captain Puffin would be so obdurate in his insistence that she must
play instead of him, that it would be only ladylike to yield.

She did not, therefore, allow this possibility to dim the pleasure
she anticipated from the discomfiture of darling Diva, who would be
certain to appear in the kingfisher-blue tea-gown, and find herself
ghastly and outshone by the crimson-lake which was the colour of
Mrs Trout's second toilet, and Miss Mapp, after prolonged thought
as to her most dramatic moment of entrance in the crimson-lake,
determined to arrive when she might expect the rest of the guests to
have already assembled. She would risk, it is true, being out of a
rubber for a little, since bridge might have already begun, but play
would have to stop for a minute of greetings when she came in, and
she would beg everybody not to stir, and would seat herself quite,
quite close to Diva, and openly admire her pretty frock, 'like one I
used to have . . . !'

It was, therefore, not much lacking of ten o'clock when, after she
had waited a considerable time on Mrs Poppit's threshold, Boon
sulkily allowed her to enter, but gave no answer to her timid enquiry
of: 'Am I very late, Boon?' The drawing-room door was a little ajar,
and as she took off the cloak that masked the splendour of the
crimson-lake, her acute ears heard the murmur of talk going on,
which indicated that bridge had not yet begun, while her acute nostrils
detected the faint but certain smell of roast grouse, which showed
what Susan had given Mr Wyse for dinner, probably telling him that
the birds were a present to her from the shooting-lodge where she
had stayed in the summer. Then, after she had thrown herself a

glance in the mirror, and put on her smile, Boon preceded her, slightly shrugging his shoulders, to the drawing-room door, which he pushed open, and grunted loudly, which was his manner of announcing a guest. Miss Mapp went tripping in, almost at a run, to indicate how vexed she was with herself for being late, and there, just in front of her, stood Diva, dressed not in kingfisher-blue at all, but in the crimson-lake of Mrs Trout's second toilet. Perfidious Diva had had her dress dyed too . . .

Miss Mapp's courage rose to the occasion. Other people, majors and tipsy captains, might be cowards, but not she. Twice now (omitting the matter of the Wars of the Roses) had Diva by some cunning, which it was impossible not to suspect of a diabolical origin, clad her odious little roundabout form in splendours identical with Miss Mapp's, but now, without faltering even when she heard Evie's loud squeak, she turned to her hostess, who wore the Order of MBE on her ample breast, and made her salutations in a perfectly calm voice.

'Dear Susan, don't scold me for being so late,' she said, 'though I know I deserve it. So sweet of you! Isabel darling and dear Evie! Oh, and Mr Wyse! Sweet Irene! Major Benjy and Captain Puffin! Had a nice game of golf? And the Padre! . . . '

She hesitated a moment wondering, if she could, without screaming or scratching, seem aware of Diva's presence. Then she soared, lambent as flame.

'Diva darling!' she said, and bent and kissed her, even as St Stephen in the moment of martyrdom prayed for those who stoned him. Flesh and blood could not manage more, and she turned to Mr Wyse, remembering that Diva had told her that the Contessa Faradiddleony's arrival was postponed.

'And your dear sister has put off her journey, I understand,' she said. 'Such a disappointment! Shall we see her at Tilling at all, do you think?'

Mr Wyse looked surprised.

'Dear lady,' he said, 'you're the second person who has said that to me. Mrs Plaistow asked me just now – '

'Yes; it was she who told me,' said Miss Mapp in case there was a mistake. 'Isn't it true?'

'Certainly not. I told my housekeeper that the Contessa's maid was ill, and would follow her, but that's the only foundation I know of for this rumour. Amelia encourages me to hope that she will be here early next week.'

'Oh, no doubt that's it!' said Miss Mapp in an aside so that Diva could hear. 'Darling Diva's always getting hold of the most erroneous information. She must have been listening to servants' gossip. So glad she's wrong about it.'

Mr Wyse made one of his stately inclinations of the head.

'Amelia will regret very much not being here tonight,' he said, 'for I see all the great bridge-players are present.'

'Oh, Mr Wyse!' said she. 'We shall all be humble learners compared with the Contessa, I expect.'

'Not at all!' said Mr Wyse. 'But what a delightful idea of yours and Mrs Plaistow's to dress alike in such lovely gowns. Quite like sisters.'

Miss Mapp could not trust herself to speak on this subject, and showed all her teeth, not snarling but amazingly smiling. She had no occasion to reply, however, for Captain Puffin joined them, eagerly deferential.

'What a charming surprise you and Mrs Plaistow have given us, Miss Mapp,' he said, 'in appearing again in the same beautiful dresses. Quite like – '

Miss Mapp could not bear to hear what she and Diva were like, and wheeled about, passionately regretting that she had forgiven Puffin. This manoeuvre brought her face to face with the Major.

'Upon my word, Miss Elizabeth,' he said, 'you look magnificent tonight.'

He saw the light of fury in her eyes, and guessed, mere man as he was, what it was about. He bent to her and spoke low.

'But, by Jove!' he said with supreme diplomacy, 'somebody ought to tell our good Mrs Plaistow that some women can wear a wonderful gown and others – ha!'

'Dear Major Benjy,' said she. 'Cruel of you to poor Diva.'

But instantly her happiness was clouded again, for the Padre had a very ill-inspired notion.

'What ho! fair Madam Plaistow,' he humorously observed to Miss Mapp. 'Ah! *Peccavi!* I am in error. It is Mistress Mapp. But let us to the cards! Our hostess craves thy presence at yon table.'

Contrary to custom Mrs Poppit did not sit firmly down at a table, nor was Isabel told that she had an invincible objection to playing bridge. Instead she bade everybody else take their seats, and said that she and Mr Wyse had settled at dinner that they much preferred looking on and learning to playing. With a view to enjoying this incredible treat as fully as possible, they at once seated themselves on a low sofa at the far end of the room where they could not look or learn at all, and engaged in conversation. Diva and Elizabeth, as might have been expected from the malignant influence which watched over their attire, cut in at the same table and were partners, so that they had, in spite of the deadly antagonism of identical tea-gowns, a financial interest in common, while a further bond between them was the eagerness with which they strained their ears to overhear anything that their hostess and Mr Wyse were saying to each other.

Miss Mapp and Diva alike were perhaps busier when they were being dummy than when they were playing the cards. Over the background of each mind was spread a hatred of the other, red as their tea-gowns, and shot with black despair as to what on earth they should do now with those ill-fated pieces of pride. Miss Mapp was prepared to make a perfect chameleon of hers, if only she could get away from Diva's hue, but what if, having changed, say, to purple, Diva became purple too? She could not stand a third coincidence, and besides, she much doubted whether any gown that had once been of so pronounced a crimson-lake, could successfully attempt to appear of any other hue except perhaps black. If Diva died, she might perhaps consult Miss Greele as to whether black would be possible, but then if Diva died, there was no reason for not wearing crimson-lake for ever, since it would be an insincerity of which Miss Mapp humbly hoped she was incapable, to go into mourning for Diva just because she died.

In front of this lurid background of despair moved the figures which would have commanded all her attention, have aroused all the feelings of disgust and pity of which she was capable, had only Diva stuck to kingfisher-blue. There they sat on the sofa, talking in voices which it was impossible to overhear, and if ever a woman made up to a man, and if ever a man was taken in by shallow artifices, 'they', thought Miss Mapp, 'are the ones'. There was no longer any question that Susan was doing her utmost to inveigle Mr Wyse into matrimony, for no other motive, not politeness, not the charm of conversation, not the low, comfortable seat by the fire could possibly have had force enough to keep her for a whole evening from the bridge-table. That dinner *en famille*, so Miss Mapp sarcastically reflected – what if it was the first of hundreds of similar dinners *en famille*? Perhaps, when safely married, Susan would ask her to one of the family dinners, with a glassful of foam which she called champagne, and the leg of a crow which she called game from the shooting-lodge . . . There was no use in denying that Mr Wyse

seemed to be swallowing flattery and any other form of bait as fast
as they were supplied him; never had he been so made up to since
the day, now two years ago, when Miss Mapp herself wrote him
down as uncapturable. But now, on this awful evening of crimson-
lake, it seemed only prudent to face the prospect of his falling into
the nets which were spread for him . . . Susan the sister-in-law of a
Contessa. Susan the wife of the man whose urbanity made all Tilling
polite to each other, Susan a Wyse of Whitchurch! It made Miss
Mapp feel positively weary of earth . . .

Nor was this the sum of Miss Mapp's mental activities, as she sat
being dummy to Diva, for, in addition to the rage, despair and disgust
with which these various topics filled her, she had narrowly to watch
Diva's play, in order, at the end, to point out to her with lucid
firmness all the mistakes she had made, while with snorts and sniffs
and muttered exclamations and jerks of the head and pullings-out of
cards and puttings of them back with amazing assertions that she had
not quitted them, she wrestled with the task she had set herself of
getting two no-trumps. It was impossible to count the tricks that
Diva made, for she had a habit of putting her elbow on them after
she had raked them in, as if in fear that her adversaries would filch
them when she was not looking, and Miss Mapp, distracted with
other interests, forgot that no-trumps had been declared and thought
it was hearts, of which Diva played several after their adversaries'
hands were quite denuded of them. She often did that 'to make sure'.

'Three tricks,' she said triumphantly at the conclusion, counting
the cards in the cache below her elbow.

Miss Mapp gave a long sigh, but remembered that Mr Wyse was
present.

'You could have got two more,' she said, 'if you hadn't played
those hearts, dear. You would have been able to trump Major Benjy's
club and the Padre's diamond, and we should have gone out. Never
mind, you played it beautifully otherwise.'

'Can't trump when it's no-trumps,' said Diva, forgetting that Mr
Wyse was there. 'That's nonsense. Got three tricks. Did go out. Did
you think it was hearts? Wasn't.'

Miss Mapp naturally could not demean herself to take any notice
of this.

'Your deal, is it, Major Benjy?' she asked. 'Me to cut?'

Diva had remembered just after her sharp speech to her partner
that Mr Wyse was present, and looked towards the sofa to see if
there were any indications of pained surprise on his face which

might indicate that he had heard. But what she saw there – or, to be more accurate, what she failed to see there – forced her to give an exclamation which caused Miss Mapp to look round in the direction where Diva's bulging eyes were glued . . . There was no doubt whatever about it: Mrs Poppit and Mr Wyse were no longer there. Unless they were under the sofa they had certainly left the room together and altogether. Had she gone to put on her sable coat on this hot night? Was Mr Wyse staggering under its weight as he fitted her into it? Miss Mapp rejected the supposition; they had gone to another room to converse more privately. This looked very black indeed, and she noted the time on the clock in order to ascertain, when they came back, how long they had been absent.

The rubber went on its wild way, relieved from the restraining influence of Mr Wyse, and when, thirty-nine minutes afterwards, it came to its conclusion and neither the hostess nor Mr Wyse had returned, Miss Mapp was content to let Diva muddle herself madly, adding up the score with the assistance of her fingers, and went across to the other table till she should be called back to check her partner's figures. They would be certain to need checking.

'Has Mr Wyse gone away already, dear Isabel?' she said. 'How early!'

('And four makes nine,' muttered Diva, getting to her little finger.)

Isabel was dummy, and had time for conversation.

'I think he has only gone with Mamma into the conservatory,' she said – 'no more diamonds, partner? – to advise her about the orchids.'

Now the conservatory was what Miss Mapp considered a potting-shed with a glass roof, and the orchids were one anaemic odonto-glossum, and there would scarcely be room besides that for Mrs Poppit and Mr Wyse. The potting-shed was visible from the drawing-room window, over which curtains were drawn.

'Such a lovely night,' said Miss Mapp. 'And while Diva is checking the score may I have a peep at the stars, dear? So fond of the sweet stars.'

She glided to the window (conscious that Diva was longing to glide too, but was preparing to quarrel with the Major's score) and took her peep at the sweet stars. The light from the hall shone full into the potting-shed, but there was nobody there. She made quite sure of that.

Diva had heard about the sweet stars, and for the first time in her life made no objection to her adversaries' total.

'You're right, Major Flint, eighteen-pence,' she said. 'Stupid of me: I've left my handkerchief in the pocket of my cloak. I'll pop out and get it. Back in a minute. Cut again for partners.'

She trundled to the door and popped out of it before Miss Mapp had the slightest chance of intercepting her progress. This was bitter, because the dining-room opened out of the hall, and so did the book-cupboard with a window which dear Susan called her boudoir. Diva was quite capable of popping into both of these apartments. In fact, if the truants were there, it was no use bothering about the sweet stars any more, and Diva would already have won . . .

There was a sweet moon as well, and just as baffled Miss Mapp was turning away from the window, she saw that which made her positively glue her nose to the cold window-pane, and tuck the curtain in, so that her silhouette should not be visible from outside. Down the middle of the garden path came the two truants, Susan in her sables and Mr Wyse close beside her with his coat-collar turned up. Her ample form with the small round head on the top looked like a short-funnelled locomotive engine, and he like the driver on the footplate. The perfidious things had said they were going to consult over the orchid. Did orchids grow on the lawn? It was news to Miss Mapp if they did.

They stopped, and Mr Wyse quite clearly pointed to some celestial object, moon or star, and they both gazed at it. The sight of two such middle-aged people behaving like this made Miss Mapp feel quite sick, but she heroically continued a moment more at her post. Her heroism was rewarded, for immediately after the inspection of the celestial object, they turned and inspected each other. And Mr Wyse kissed her.

Miss Mapp 'scriggled' from behind the curtain into the room again.

'Aldebaran!' she said. 'So lovely!'

Simultaneously Diva re-entered with her handkerchief, thwarted and disappointed, for she had certainly found nobody either in the boudoir or in the dining-room. But there was going to be a sit-down supper, and as Boon was not there, she had taken a *marron glacé*.

Miss Mapp was flushed with excitement and disgust, and almost forgot about Diva's gown.

'Found your hanky, dear?' she said. 'Then shall we cut for partners again? You and me, Major Benjy. Don't scold me if I play wrong.'

She managed to get a seat that commanded a full-face view of the door, for the next thing was to see how 'the young couple' (as she had already labelled them in her sarcastic mind) 'looked' when they returned from their amorous excursion to the orchid that grew on the lawn. They entered, most unfortunately, while she was in the middle of playing a complicated hand, and her brain was so switched off from the play by their entrance that she completely lost the thread of what she was doing, and threw away two tricks that simply required to be gathered up by her, but now lurked below Diva's elbow. What made it worse was that no trace of emotion, no heightened colour, no coy and downcast eye betrayed a hint of what had happened on the lawn. With brazen effrontery Susan informed her daughter that Mr Wyse thought a little leaf-mould . . .

'What a liar!' thought Miss Mapp, and triumphantly put her remaining trump on to her dummy's best card. Then she prepared to make the best of it.

'We've lost three, I'm afraid, Major Benjy,' she said. 'Don't you think you overbid your hand just a little wee bit?'

'I don't know about that, Miss Elizabeth,' said the Major. 'If you hadn't let those two spades go, and hadn't trumped my best heart – '

Miss Mapp interrupted with her famous patter.

'Oh, but if I had taken the spades,' she said quickly, 'I should have had to lead up to Diva's clubs, and then they would have got the rough in diamonds, and I should have never been able to get back into your hand again. Then at the end if I hadn't trumped your heart, I should have had to lead the losing spade and Diva would have over-trumped; and brought in her club, and we should have gone down two more. If you follow me, I think you'll agree that I was right to do that. But all good players overbid their hands some-times, Major Benjy. Such fun!'

The supper was unusually ostentatious, but Miss Mapp saw the reason for that; it was clear that Susan wanted to impress poor Mr Wyse with her wealth, and probably when it came to settlements, he would learn some very unpleasant news. But there were agreeable little circumstances to temper her dislike of this extravagant display, for she was hungry, and Diva, always a gross feeder, spilt some hot chocolate sauce on the crimson-lake, which, if indelible, might supply a solution to the problem of what was to be done now about her own frock. She kept an eye, too, on Captain Puffin, to see if he showed any signs of improvement in the direction she had indicated to him in her interview, and was rejoiced to see that one of these glances was clearly the cause of his refusing a second glass of port. He had already taken the stopper out of the decanter when their eyes met . . . and then he put it back again. Improvement already!

Everything else (pending the discovery as to whether chocolate on crimson-lake spelt ruin) now faded into a middle distance, while the affairs of Susan and poor Mr Wyse occupied the entire foreground of Miss Mapp's consciousness. Mean and cunning as Susan's conduct must have been in entrapping Mr Wyse when others had failed to gain his affection, Miss Mapp felt that it would be only prudent to continue on the most amicable of terms with her, for as future sister-in-law to a countess, and wife to the man who by the mere exercise of his presence could make Tilling sit up and behave, she would doubtless not hesitate about giving Miss Mapp some nasty ones back if retaliation demanded. It was dreadful to think that this audacious climber was so soon to belong to the Wyses of Whitchurch, but since the moonlight had revealed that such was Mr Wyse's intention, it was best to be friends with the Mammon of the British Empire. Poppit-cum-Wyse was likely to be a very important centre of social life in Tilling, when not in Scotland or Whitchurch or Capri, and Miss Mapp wisely determined that even the announcement of the engagement should not induce her to give voice to the very proper sentiments which it could not help inspiring.

After all she had done for Susan, in letting the door of high-life in Tilling swing open for her when she could not possibly keep it shut any longer, it seemed only natural that, if she only kept on good terms with her now, Susan would insist that her dear Elizabeth must be the first to be told of the engagement. This made her pause before adopting the obvious course of setting off immediately after breakfast next morning, and telling all her friends, under promise of secrecy, just what she had seen in the moonlight last night. Thrilling to the narrator as such an announcement would be, it would be even more thrilling, provided only that Susan had sufficient sense of decency to tell her of the engagement before anybody else, to hurry off to all the others and inform them that she had known of it ever since the night of the bridge party.

It was important, therefore, to be at home whenever there was the slightest chance of Susan coming round with her news, and Miss Mapp sat at her window the whole of that first morning, so as not to miss her, and hardly attended at all to the rest of the pageant of life that moved within the radius of her observation. Her heart beat fast when, about the middle of the morning, Mr Wyse came round the dentist's corner, for it might be that the bashful Susan had sent him to make the announcement, but, if so, he was bashful too, for he walked by her house without pause. He looked rather worried, she thought (as well he might), and passing on he disappeared round the church corner, clearly on his way to his betrothed. He carried a square parcel in his hand, about as big as some jewel-case that might contain a tiara. Half an hour afterwards, however, he came back, still carrying the tiara. It occurred to her that the engagement might have been broken off . . . A little later, again with a quickened pulse, Miss Mapp saw the Royce lumber down from the church corner. It stopped at her house, and she caught a glimpse of sables within. This time she felt certain that Susan had come with her interesting news, and waited till Withers, having answered the door, came to enquire, no doubt, whether she would see Mrs Poppit. But, alas, a minute later the Royce lumbered on, carrying the additional weight of the Christmas number of *Punch*, which Miss Mapp had borrowed last night and had not, of course, had time to glance at yet.

Anticipation is supposed to be pleasanter than any fulfilment, however agreeable, and if that is the case, Miss Mapp during the next day or two had more enjoyment than the announcement of fifty engagements could have given her, so constantly (when from the garden-room she heard the sound of the knocker on her front door) did she spring up in certainty that this was Susan, which it never was. But however enjoyable it all might be, she appeared to herself at least to be suffering tortures of suspense, through which by degrees an idea, painful and revolting in the extreme, yet strangely exhilarating, began to insinuate itself into her mind. There seemed a deadly probability of the correctness of the conjecture, as the week went by without further confirmation of that kiss, for, after all, who knew anything about the character and antecedents of Susan? As for Mr Wyse, was he not a constant visitor to the fierce and fickle South, where, as everyone knew, morality was wholly extinct? And how, if it was all too true, should Tilling treat this hitherto unprecedented situation? It was terrible to contemplate this moral upheaval, which might prove to be a social upheaval also. Time and again, as Miss Mapp vainly waited for news, she was within an ace of communicating her suspicions to the Padre. He ought to know, for Christmas (as was usual in December) was daily drawing nearer . . .

There came some halfway through that month a dark and ominous afternoon, the rain falling sad and thick, and so unusual a density of cloud dwelling in the upper air that by three o'clock Miss Mapp was quite unable, until the street lamp at the corner was lit, to carry out the minor duty of keeping an eye on the houses of Captain Puffin and Major Benjy. The Royce had already lumbered by her door since lunchtime, but so dark was it that, peer as she might, it was lost in the gloom before it came to the dentist's corner, and Miss Mapp had to face the fact that she really did not know whether it had turned into the street where Susan's lover lived or had gone straight on. It was easier to imagine the worst, and she had already pictured to herself a clandestine meeting between those passionate ones, who under cover of this darkness were imperviously concealed from any observation (beneath an umbrella) from her house-roof. Nothing but a powerful searchlight could reveal what was going on in the drawing-room window of Mr Wyse's house, and apart from the fact that she had not got a powerful searchlight, it was strongly improbable that anything of a very intimate nature was going on there . . . it was not likely that they would choose the drawing-room window. She thought of calling on Mr Wyse and asking for the loan of a book, so that she would see whether the sables were in the hall, but even then she would not really be much further on. Even as she considered this a sea-mist began to creep through the street outside, and in a few minutes it was blotted from view. Nothing was visible, and nothing audible but the hissing of the shrouded rain.

Suddenly from close outside came the sound of a door-knocker imperiously plied, which could be no other than her own. Only a telegram or some urgent errand could bring anyone out on such a day, and unable to bear the suspense of waiting till Withers had answered it, she hurried into the house to open the door herself. Was the news of the engagement coming to her at last? Late though it was, she would welcome it even now, for it would atone, in part at any rate . . . It was Diva.

'Diva dear!' said Miss Mapp enthusiastically, for Withers was already in the hall. 'How sweet of you to come round. Anything special?'

'Yes,' said Diva, opening her eyes very wide, and spreading a shower of moisture as she whisked off her mackintosh. 'She's come.'

This could not refer to Susan . . .

'Who?' asked Miss Mapp.

'Faradiddleony,' said Diva.

'No!' said Miss Mapp very loud, so much interested that she quite forgot to resent Diva's being the first to have the news. 'Let's have a comfortable cup of tea in the garden-room. Tea, Withers.'

Miss Mapp lit the candles there, for, lost in meditation, she had been sitting in the dark, and with reckless hospitality poked the fire to make it blaze.

'Tell me all about it,' she said. That would be a treat for Diva, who was such a gossip.

'Went to the station just now,' said Diva. 'Wanted a new timetable. Besides the Royce had just gone down. Mr Wyse and Susan on the platform.'

'Sables?' asked Miss Mapp parenthetically, to complete the picture.

'Swaddled. Talked to them. Train came in. Woman got out. Kissed Mr Wyse. Shook hands with Susan. Both hands. While luggage was got out.'

'Much?' asked Miss Mapp quickly.

'Hundreds. Covered with coronets and Fs. Two cabs.'

Miss Mapp's mind, on a hot scent, went back to the previous telegraphic utterance.

'Both hands did you say, dear?' she asked. 'Perhaps that's the Italian fashion.'

'Maybe. Then what else do you think? Faradiddleony kissed Susan! Mr Wyse and she must be engaged. I can't account for it any other way. He must have written to tell his sister. Couldn't have told her then at the station. Must have been engaged some days and we never knew. They went to look at the orchid. Remember? That was when.'

It was bitter, no doubt, but the bitterness could be transmuted into an amazing sweetness.

'Then now I can speak,' said Miss Mapp with a sigh of great relief. 'Oh, it has been so hard keeping silence, but I felt I ought to. I knew all along, Diva dear, all, all along.'

'How?' asked Diva with a fallen crest.

Miss Mapp laughed merrily.

'I looked out of the window, dear, while you went for your hanky and peeped into dining-room and boudoir, didn't you? There they were on the lawn, and they kissed each other. So I said to myself: "Dear Susan has got him! Perseverance rewarded!" '

'H'm. Only a guess of yours. Or did Susan tell you?'

'No, dear, she said nothing. But Susan was always secretive.'

'But they might not have been engaged at all,' said Diva with a brightened eye. 'Man doesn't always marry a woman he kisses!'

Diva had betrayed the lowness of her mind now by hazarding that which had for days dwelt in Miss Mapp's mind as almost certain. She drew in her breath with a hissing noise as if in pain.

'Darling, what a dreadful suggestion,' she said. 'No such idea ever occurred to me. Secretive I thought Susan might be, but immoral, never. I must forget you ever thought that. Let's talk about something less painful. Perhaps you would like to tell me more about the Contessa.'

Diva had the grace to look ashamed of herself, and to take refuge in the new topic so thoughtfully suggested.

'Couldn't see clearly,' she said. 'So dark. But tall and lean. Sneezed.'

'That might happen to anybody, dear,' said Miss Mapp, 'whether tall or short. Nothing more?'

'An eyeglass,' said Diva after thought.

'A single one?' asked Miss Mapp. 'On a string? How strange for a woman.'

That seemed positively the last atom of Diva's knowledge, and though Miss Mapp tried on the principles of psychoanalysis to disinter something she had forgotten, the catechism led to no results whatever. But Diva had evidently something else to say, for after finishing her tea she whizzed backwards and forwards from window to fireplace with little grunts and whistles, as was her habit when she was struggling with utterance. Long before it came out, Miss Mapp had, of course, guessed what it was. No wonder Diva found difficulty in speaking of a matter in which she had behaved so deplorably . . .

'About that wretched dress,' she said at length. 'Got it stained with chocolate first time I wore it, and neither I nor Janet can get it out.'

('Hurrah,' thought Miss Mapp.)

'Must have it dyed again,' continued Diva. 'Thought I'd better tell you. Else you might have yours dyed the same colour as mine again. Kingfisher-blue to crimson-lake. All came out of *Vogue* and Mrs Trout. Rather funny, you know, but expensive. You should have seen your face, Elizabeth, when you came in to Susan's the other night.'

'Should I, dearest?' said Miss Mapp, trembling violently.

'Yes. Wouldn't have gone home with you in the dark for anything. Murder.'

'Diva dear,' said Miss Mapp anxiously, 'you've got a mind which likes to put the worst construction on everything. If Mr Wyse kisses his intended you think things too terrible for words; if I look surprised you think I'm full of hatred and malice. Be more generous, dear. Don't put evil constructions on all you see.'

'Ho!' said Diva with a world of meaning.

'I don't know what you intend to convey by ho,' said Miss Mapp, 'and I shan't try to guess. But be kinder, darling, and it will make you happier. Thinketh no evil, you know! Charity!'

Diva felt that the limit of what was tolerable was reached when Elizabeth lectured her on the need of charity, and she would no doubt have explained tersely and unmistakably exactly what she meant by 'Ho!' had not Withers opportunely entered to clear away tea. She brought a note with her, which Miss Mapp opened. 'Encourage me to hope,' were the first words that met her eye: Mrs Poppit had been encouraging him to hope again.

'To dine at Mr Wyse's tomorrow,' she said. 'No doubt the announcement will be made then. He probably wrote it before he went to the station. Yes, a few friends. You going, dear?'

Diva instantly got up.

'Think I'll run home and see,' she said. 'By the by, Elizabeth, what about the – the tea-gown, if I go? You or I?'

'If yours is all covered with chocolate, I shouldn't think you'd like to wear it,' said Miss Mapp.

'Could tuck it away,' said Diva, 'just for once. Put flowers. Then send it to dyer's. You won't see it again. Not crimson-lake, I mean.'

Miss Mapp summoned the whole of her magnanimity. It had been put to a great strain already and was tired out, but it was capable of one more effort.

'Wear it then,' she said. 'It'll be a treat to you. But let me know if you're not asked. I dare say Mr Wyse will want to keep it very small. Goodbye, dear; I'm afraid you'll get very wet going home.'

Chapter Eleven

The sea-mist and the rain continued without intermission next morning, but shopping with umbrellas and mackintoshes was unusually brisk, for there was naturally a universally felt desire to catch sight of a Contessa with as little delay as possible. The foggy conditions perhaps added to the excitement, for it was not possible to see more than a few yards, and thus at any moment anybody might almost run into her. Diva's impressions, meagre though they were, had been thoroughly circulated, but the morning passed, and the ladies of Tilling went home to change their wet things and take a little ammoniated quinine as a precaution after so long and chilly an exposure, without a single one of them having caught sight of the single eyeglass. It was disappointing, but the disappointment was bearable since Mr Wyse, so far from wanting his party to be very small, had been encouraged by Mrs Poppit to hope that it would include all his world of Tilling with one exception. He had hopes with regard to the Major and the Captain, and the Padre and wee

wifie, and Irene and Miss Mapp, and of course Isabel. But apparently
he despaired of Diva.

She alone therefore was absent from this long, wet shopping, for
she waited indoors, almost pen in hand, to answer in the affirmative
the invitation which had at present not arrived. Owing to the thick-
ness of the fog, her absence from the street passed unnoticed, for
everybody supposed that everybody else had seen her, while she,
biting her nails at home, waited and waited and waited. Then she
waited. About a quarter past one she gave it up, and duly telephoned,
according to promise, via Janet and Withers, to Miss Mapp to say
that Mr Wyse had not yet hoped. It was very unpleasant to let them
know, but if she had herself rung up and been answered by Elizabeth,
who usually rushed to the telephone, she felt that she would sooner
have choked than have delivered this message. So Janet telephoned
and Withers said she would tell her mistress. And did.

Miss Mapp was steeped in pleasant conjectures. The most likely of
all was that the Contessa had seen that roundabout little busybody in
the station, and taken an instant dislike to her through her single
eyeglass. Or she might have seen poor Diva inquisitively inspecting
the luggage with the coronets and the Fs on it, and have learned with
pain that this was one of the ladies of Tilling. 'Algernon,' she would
have said (so said Miss Mapp to herself), 'who is that queer little
woman? Is she going to steal some of my luggage?' And then Algernon
would have told her that this was poor Diva, quite a decent sort of
little body. But when it came to Algernon asking his guests for the
dinner party in honour of his betrothal and her arrival at Tilling, no
doubt the Contessa would have said, 'Algernon, I beg . . . ' Or if
Diva – poor Diva – was right in her conjectures that the notes had
been written before the arrival of the train, it was evident that
Algernon had torn up the one addressed to Diva, when the Contessa
heard whom she was to meet the next evening . . . Or Susan might
easily have insinuated that they would have two very pleasant tables
of bridge after dinner without including Diva, who was so wrong and
quarrelsome over the score. Any of these explanations were quite
satisfactory, and since Diva would not be present, Miss Mapp would
naturally don the crimson-lake. They would all see what crimson-
lake looked like when it decked a suitable wearer and was not parodied
on the other side of a card-table. How true, as dear Major Benjy had
said, that one woman could wear what another could not . . . And if
there was a woman who could not wear crimson-lake it was Diva . . .
Or was Mr Wyse really ashamed to let his sister see Diva in the

crimson-lake? It would be just like him to be considerate of Diva, and
not permit her to make a guy of herself before the Italian aristocracy.
No doubt he would ask her to lunch someday, quite quietly. Or
had ... Miss Mapp bloomed with pretty conjectures, like some Alpine
meadow when smitten into flower by the spring, and enjoyed her
lunch very much indeed.

The anxiety and suspense of the morning, which, instead of being
relieved, had ended in utter gloom, gave Diva a headache, and she
adopted her usual strenuous methods of getting rid of it. So, instead
of lying down and taking aspirin and dozing, she set out after lunch
to walk it off. She sprinted and splashed along the miry roads,
indifferent as to whether she stepped in puddles or not, and careless
how wet she got. She bit on the bullet of her omission from the
dinner party this evening, determining not to mind one atom about
it, but to look forward to a pleasant evening at home instead of
going out (like this) in the wet. And never – never under any
circumstances would she ask any of the guests what sort of an
evening had been spent, how Mr Wyse announced the news, and
how the Faradiddleony played bridge. (She said that satirical word
aloud, mouthing it to the puddles and the dripping hedgerows.)
She would not evince the slightest interest in it all; she would cover
it with spadefuls of oblivion, and when next she met Mr Wyse she
would, whatever she might feel, behave exactly as usual. She plumed
herself on this dignified resolution, and walked so fast that the
hedgerows became quite transparent. That was the proper thing to
do; she had been grossly slighted, and, like a true lady, would
be unaware of that slight; whereas poor Elizabeth, under such
circumstances, would have devised a hundred petty schemes for
rendering Mr Wyse's life a burden to him. But if – if (she only said
'if') she found any reason to believe that Susan was at the bottom
of this, then probably she would think of something worthy not so
much of a true lady but of a true woman. Without asking any
questions, she might easily arrive at information which would enable
her to identify Susan as the culprit, and she would then act in some
way which would astonish Susan. What that way was she need not
think yet, and so she devoted her entire mind to the question all the
way home.

Feeling better and with her headache quite gone, she arrived in
Tilling again drenched to the skin. It was already after teatime, and
she abandoned tea altogether, and prepared to console herself for
her exclusion from gaiety with a 'good blow-out' in the shape of

regular dinner, instead of the usual muffin now and a tray later. To add dignity to her feast, she put on the crimson-lake tea-gown for the last time that it would be crimson-lake (though the same tea-gown still), since tomorrow it would be sent to the dyer's to go into perpetual mourning for its vanished glories. She had meant to send it today, but all this misery and anxiety had put it out of her head.

Having dressed thus, to the great astonishment of Janet, she sat down to divert her mind from trouble by Patience. As if to reward her for her stubborn fortitude, the malignity of the cards relented, and she brought out an intricate matter three times running. The clock on her mantelpiece chiming a quarter to eight, surprised her with the lateness of the hour, and recalled to her with a stab of pain that it was dinner-time at Mr Wyse's, and at this moment some seven pairs of eager feet were approaching the door. Well, she was dining at a quarter to eight, too; Janet would enter presently to tell her that her own banquet was ready, and gathering up her cards, she spent a pleasant though regretful minute in looking at herself and the crimson-lake for the last time in her long glass. The tremendous walk in the rain had given her an almost equally high colour. Janet's foot was heard on the stairs, and she turned away from the glass. Janet entered.

'Dinner?' said Diva.

'No, ma'am, the telephone,' said Janet. 'Mr Wyse is on the telephone, and wants to speak to you very particularly.'

'Mr Wyse himself?' asked Diva, hardly believing her ears, for she knew Mr Wyse's opinion of the telephone.

'Yes, ma'am.'

Diva walked slowly, but reflected rapidly. What must have happened was that somebody had been taken ill at the last moment – was it Elizabeth? – and that he now wanted her to fill the gap . . . She was torn in two. Passionately as she longed to dine at Mr Wyse's, she did not see how such a course was compatible with dignity. He had only asked her to suit his own convenience; it was not out of encouragement to hope that he invited her now. No; Mr Wyse should want. She would say that she had friends dining with her; that was what the true lady would do.

She took up the earpiece and said, 'Hello!'

It was certainly Mr Wyse's voice that spoke to her, and it seemed to tremble with anxiety.

'Dear lady,' he began, 'a most terrible thing has happened – '

(Wonder if Elizabeth's very ill, thought Diva.)

'Quite terrible,' said Mr Wyse. 'Can you hear?'

'Yes,' said Diva, hardening her heart.

'By the most calamitous mistake the note which I wrote you yesterday was never delivered. Figgis has just found it in the pocket of his overcoat. I shall certainly dismiss him unless you plead for him. Can you hear?'

'Yes,' said Diva excitedly.

'In it I told you that I had been encouraged to hope that you would dine with me tonight. There was such a gratifying response to my other invitations that I most culpably and carelessly, dear lady, thought that everybody had accepted. Can you hear?'

'Of course I can!' shouted Diva.

'Well, I come on my knees to you. Can you possibly forgive the joint stupidity of Figgis and me, and honour me after all? We will put dinner off, of course. At what time, in case you are ever so kind and indulgent as to come, shall we have it? Do not break my heart by refusing. Su – Mrs Poppit will send her car for you.'

'I have already dressed for dinner,' said Diva proudly. 'Very pleased to come at once.'

'You are too kind; you are angelic,' said Mr Wyse. 'The car shall start at once; it is at my door now.'

'Right,' said Diva.

'Too good – too kind,' murmured Mr Wyse. 'Figgis, what do I do next?'

Diva clapped the instrument into place.

'Powder,' she said to herself, remembering what she had seen in the glass, and whizzed upstairs. Her fish would have to be degraded into kedgeree, though plaice would have done just as well as sole for that; the cutlets could be heated up again, and perhaps the whisking for the apple-meringue had not begun yet, and could still be stopped.

'Janet!' she shouted. 'Going out to dinner! Stop the meringue.'

She dashed an interesting pallor on to her face as she heard the hooting of the Royce, and coming downstairs, stepped into its warm luxuriousness, for the electric lamp was burning. There were Susan's sables there – it was thoughtful of Susan to put them in, but ostentatious – and there was a carriage rug, which she was convinced was new, and was very likely a present from Mr Wyse. And soon there was the light streaming out from Mr Wyse's open door, and Mr Wyse himself in the hall to meet and greet and thank and bless her. She pleaded for the contrite Figgis, and was conducted in a blaze of triumph into the drawing-room, where all Tilling was awaiting her. She was led up to the Contessa, with whom Miss Mapp, wreathed in sycophantic smiles, was eagerly conversing.

The crimson-lakes . . .

*   *   *

There were embarrassing moments during dinner; the Contessa, confused by having so many people introduced to her in a lump, got all their names wrong, and addressed her neighbours as Captain Flint and Major Puffin, and thought that Diva was Mrs Mapp. She seemed vivacious and good-humoured, dropped her eyeglass into her soup, talked with her mouth full, and drank a good deal of wine, which was a very bad example for Major Puffin. Then there were many sudden and complete pauses in the talk, for Diva's news of the kissing of Mrs Poppit by the Contessa had spread like wildfire through the fog this morning, owing to Miss Mapp's dissemination of it, and now, whenever Mr Wyse raised his voice ever so little, everybody else stopped talking, in the expectation that the news was about to be announced. Occasionally, also, the Contessa addressed some remark to her brother in shrill and voluble Italian, which rather confirmed the gloomy estimate of her table-manners in the matter of talking with her mouth full, for to speak in Italian was equivalent to whispering, since the purport of what she said could not be understood by anybody except him . . . Then also, the sensation of dining with a countess produced a slight feeling of strain, which, in addition to the correct behaviour which Mr Wyse's presence always induced, almost congealed correctness into stiffness. But as dinner went on her evident enjoyment of herself made itself felt, and her eccentricities, though carefully observed and noted by Miss Mapp, were not succeeded by silences and hurried bursts of conversation.

'And is your ladyship making a long stay in Tilling?' asked the (real) Major, to cover the pause which had been caused by Mr Wyse saying something across the table to Isabel.

She dropped her eyeglass with quite a splash into her gravy, pulled it out again by the string as if landing a fish and sucked it.

'That depends on you gentlemen,' she said with greater audacity than was usual in Tilling. 'If you and Major Puffin and that sweet little Scotch clergyman all fall in love with me, and fight duels about me, I will stop for ever . . . '

The Major recovered himself before anybody else.

'Your ladyship may take that for granted,' he said gallantly, and a perfect hubbub of conversation rose to cover this awful topic.

She laid her hand on his arm.

'You must not call me ladyship, Captain Flint,' she said. 'Only servants say that. Contessa, if you like. And you must blow away this fog for me. I have seen nothing but bales of cotton-wool out of the window. Tell me this, too: why are those ladies dressed alike? Are they sisters? Mrs Mapp, the little round one, and her sister, the big round one?'

The Major cast an apprehensive eye on Miss Mapp seated just opposite, whose acuteness of hearing was one of the terrors of Tilling . . . His apprehensions were perfectly well founded, and Miss Mapp hated and despised the Contessa from that hour.

'No, not sisters,' said he, 'and your la – you've made a little error about the names. The one opposite is Miss Mapp, the other Mrs Plaistow.'

The Contessa moderated her voice.

'I see; she looks vexed, your Miss Mapp. I think she must have heard, and I will be very nice to her afterwards. Why does not one of you gentlemen marry her? I see I shall have to arrange that. The sweet little Scotch clergyman now; little men like big wives. Ah! Married already is he to the mouse? Then it must be you, Captain Flint. We must have more marriages in Tilling.'

Miss Mapp could not help glancing at the Contessa, as she made this remarkable observation. It must be the cue, she thought, for the announcement of that which she had known so long . . . In the space of a wink the clever Contessa saw that she had her attention, and spoke rather loudly to the Major.

'I have lost my heart to your Miss Mapp,' she said. 'I am jealous of you, Captain Flint. She will be my great friend in Tilling, and if you marry her, I shall hate you, for that will mean that she likes you best.'

Miss Mapp hated nobody at that moment, not even Diva, off whose face the hastily applied powder was crumbling, leaving little red marks peeping out like the stars on a fine evening. Dinner came to an end with roasted chestnuts brought by the Contessa from Capri.

'I always scold Amelia for the luggage she takes with her,' said Mr Wyse to Diva. 'Amelia dear, you are my hostess tonight' – everybody saw him look at Mrs Poppit – 'you must catch somebody's eye.'

'I will catch Miss Mapp's,' said Amelia, and all the ladies rose as if connected with some hidden mechanism which moved them simultaneously . . . There was a great deal of pretty diffidence at the door, but the Contessa put an end to that.

'Eldest first,' she said, and marched out, making Miss Mapp, Diva and the mouse feel remarkably young. She might drop her eyeglass and talk with her mouth full, but really such tact . . . They all determined to adopt this pleasing device in the future. The disappointment about the announcement of the engagement was sensibly assuaged, and Miss Mapp and Susan, in their eagerness to be younger than the Contessa, and yet take precedence of all the rest, almost stuck in the doorway. They rebounded from each other, and Diva whizzed out between them. Quaint Irene went in her right place – last. However quaint Irene was, there was no use in pretending that she was not the youngest.

However hopelessly Amelia had lost her heart to Miss Mapp, she did not devote her undivided attention to her in the drawing-room, but swiftly established herself at the card-table, where she proceeded, with a most complicated sort of Patience and a series of cigarettes, to while away the time till the gentlemen joined them. Though the ladies of Tilling had plenty to say to each other, it was all about her, and such comments could not conveniently be made in her presence. Unless, like her, they talked some language unknown to the subject of their conversation, they could not talk at all, and so they gathered round her table, and watched the lightning rapidity with which she piled black knaves on red queens in some packs and red knaves on black queens in others. She had taken off all her rings in order to procure a greater freedom of finger, and her eyeglass continued to crash on to a glittering mass of magnificent gems. The rapidity of her motions was only equalled by the swift and surprising monologue that poured from her mouth.

'There, that odious king gets in my way,' she said. 'So like a man to poke himself in where he isn't wanted. *Bacco!* No, not that: I have a cigarette. I hear all you ladies are terrific bridge-players: we will have a game presently, and I shall sink into the earth with terror at your Camorra! *Dio!* there's another king, and that's his own queen whom he doesn't want at all. He is *amoroso* for that black queen, who is quite covered up, and he would like to be covered up with her. Susan, my dear' (that was interesting, but they all knew it already), 'kindly ring the bell for coffee. I expire if I do not get my coffee at once, and a toothpick. Tell me all the scandal of Tilling, Miss Mapp, while I play – all the dreadful histories of that Major and that Captain. Such a grand air has the Captain – no, it is the Major, the one who

does not limp. Which of all you ladies do they love most? It is Miss
Mapp, I believe: that is why she does not answer me. Ah! here is the
coffee, and the other king: three lumps of sugar, dear Susan, and
then stir it up well, and hold it to my mouth, so that I can drink
without interruption. Ah, the ace! He is the intervener, or is it the
King's Proctor? It would be nice to have a proctor who told you all
the love-affairs that were going on. Susan, you must get me a proctor:
you shall be my proctor. And here are the men – the wretches, they
have been preferring wine to women, and we will have our bridge,
and if anybody scolds me, I shall cry, Miss Mapp, and Captain Flint
will hold my hand and comfort me.'

She gathered up a heap of cards and rings, dropped them on the
floor, and cut with the remainder.

Miss Mapp was very lenient with the Contessa, who was her
partner, and pointed out the mistakes of her and their adversaries
with the most winning smile and eagerness to explain things clearly.
Then she revoked heavily herself, and the Contessa, so far from
being angry with her, burst into peals of unquenchable merriment.
This way of taking a revoke was new to Tilling, for the right thing
was for the revoker's partner to sulk and be sarcastic for at least
twenty minutes after. The Contessa's laughter continued to spurt
out at intervals during the rest of the rubber, and it was all very
pleasant; but at the end she said she was not up to Tilling standards
at all, and refused to play any more. Miss Mapp, in the highest good-
humour, urged her not to despair.

'Indeed, dear Contessa,' she said, 'you play very well. A little
overbidding of your hand, perhaps, do you think? but that is a
tendency we are all subject to: I often overbid my hand myself. Not
a little wee rubber more? I'm sure I should like to be your partner
again. You must come and play at my house some afternoon. We
will have tea early, and get a good two hours. Nothing like practice.'

The evening came to an end without the great announcement
being made, but Miss Mapp, as she reviewed the events of the
party, sitting next morning in her observation-window, found the
whole evidence so overwhelming that it was no longer worth while
to form conjectures, however fruitful, on the subject, and she
diverted her mind to pleasing reminiscences and projects for the
future. She had certainly been distinguished by the Contessa's
marked regard, and her opinion of her charm and ability was of the
very highest . . . No doubt her strange remark about duelling at
dinner had been humorous in intention, but many a true word is

spoken in jest, and the Contessa – perspicacious woman – had seen at once that Major Benjy and Captain Puffin were just the sort of men who might get to duelling (or, at any rate, challenging) about a woman. And her asking which of the ladies the men were most in love with, and her saying that she believed it was Miss Mapp! Miss Mapp had turned nearly as red as poor Diva when that came out, so lightly and yet so acutely . . .

Diva! It had, of course, been a horrid blow to find that Diva had been asked to Mr Wyse's party in the first instance, and an even shrewder one when Diva entered (with such unnecessary fussing and apology on the part of Mr Wyse) in the crimson-lake. Luckily, it would be seen no more, for Diva had promised – if you could trust Diva – to send it to the dyer's; but it was a great puzzle to know why Diva had it on at all, if she was preparing to spend a solitary evening at home. By eight o'clock she ought by rights to have already had her tray, dressed in some old thing; but within three minutes of her being telephoned for she had appeared in the crimson-lake, and eaten so heartily that it was impossible to imagine, greedy though she was, that she had already consumed her tray . . . But in spite of Diva's adventitious triumph, the main feeling in Miss Mapp's mind was pity for her. She looked so ridiculous in that dress with the powder peeling off her red face. No wonder the dear Contessa stared when she came in.

There was her bridge party for the Contessa to consider. The Contessa would be less nervous, perhaps, if there was only one table: that would be more homey and cosy, and it would at the same time give rise to great heartburnings and indignation in the breasts of those who were left out. Diva would certainly be one of the spurned, and the Contessa would not play with Mr Wyse . . . Then there was Major Benjy, he must certainly be asked, for it was evident that the Contessa delighted in him . . .

Suddenly Miss Mapp began to feel less sure that Major Benjy must be of the party. The Contessa, charming though she was, had said several very tropical, Italian things to him. She had told him that she would stop here for ever if the men fought duels about her. She had said 'you dear darling' to him at bridge when, as adversary, he failed to trump her losing card, and she had asked him to ask her to tea ('with no one else, for I have a great deal to say to you'), when the general *macédoine* of sables, *au reservoirs*, and thanks for such a nice evening took place in the hall. Miss Mapp was not, in fact, sure, when she thought it over, that the Contessa was a nice friend for

Major Benjy. She did not do him the injustice of imagining that he would ask her to tea alone; the very suggestion proved that it must be a piece of the Contessa's Southern extravagance of expression. But, after all, thought Miss Mapp to herself, as she writhed at the idea, her other extravagant expressions were proved to cover a good deal of truth. In fact, the Major's chance of being asked to the select bridge party diminished swiftly towards vanishing point.

It was time (and indeed late) to set forth on morning marketings, and Miss Mapp had already determined not to carry her capacious basket with her today, in case of meeting the Contessa in the High Street. It would be grander and Wysier and more magnificent to go basket-less, and direct that the goods should be sent up, rather than run the risk of encountering the Contessa with a basket containing a couple of mutton cutlets, a ball of wool and some tooth-powder. So she put on her Prince of Wales's cloak, and, postponing further reflection over the bridge party till a less busy occasion, set forth in unencumbered gentility for the morning gossip. At the corner of the High Street, she ran into Diva.

'News,' said Diva. 'Met Mr Wyse just now. Engaged to Susan. All over the town by now. Everybody knows. Oh, there's the Padre for the first time.'

She shot across the street, and Miss Mapp, shaking the dust of Diva off her feet, proceeded on her chagrined way. Annoyed as she was with Diva, she was almost more annoyed with Susan. After all she had done for Susan, Susan ought to have told her long ago, pledging her to secrecy. But to be told like this by that common Diva, without any secrecy at all, was an affront that she would find it hard to forgive Susan for. She mentally reduced by a half the sum that she had determined to squander on Susan's wedding-present. It should be plated, not silver, and if Susan was not careful, it shouldn't be plated at all.

She had just come out of the chemist's, after an indignant interview about precipitated chalk. He had deposited the small packet on the counter, when she asked to have it sent up to her house. He could not undertake to deliver small packages. She left the precipitated chalk lying there. Emerging, she heard a loud, foreign sort of scream from close at hand. There was the Contessa, all by herself, carrying a marketing basket of unusual size and newness. It contained a bloody steak and a crab.

'But where is your basket, Miss Mapp?' she exclaimed. 'Algernon told me that all the great ladies of Tilling went marketing in the morning with big baskets, and that if I aspired to be *du monde*, I must have my basket, too. It is the greatest fun, and I have already written to Cecco to say I am just going marketing with my basket. Look, the steak is for Figgis, and the crab is for Algernon and me, if Figgis does not get it. But why are you not *du monde*? Are you *du demi-monde*, Miss Mapp?'

She gave a croak of laughter and tickled the crab . . .

'Will he eat the steak, do you think?' she went on. 'Is he not lively? I went to the shop of Mr Hopkins, who was not there, because he was engaged with Miss Coles. And was that not Miss Coles last night at my brother's? The one who spat in the fire when nobody but I was looking? You are enchanting at Tilling. What is Mr Hopkins doing with Miss Coles? Do they kiss? But your market basket: that disappoints me, for Algernon said you had the biggest market basket of all. I bought the biggest I could find: is it as big as yours?'

Miss Mapp's head was in a whirl. The Contessa said in the loudest possible voice all that everybody else only whispered; she displayed (in her basket) all that everybody else covered up with thick layers of paper. If Miss Mapp had only guessed that the Contessa would have a market basket, she would have paraded the High Street with a leg of mutton protruding from one end and a pair of Wellington boots from the other . . . But who could have suspected that a Contessa . . .

Black thoughts succeeded. Was it possible that Mr Wyse had been satirical about the affairs of Tilling? If so, she wished him nothing worse than to be married to Susan. But a playful face must be put, for the moment, on the situation.

'Too lovely of you, dear Contessa,' she said. 'May we go marketing together tomorrow, and we will measure the size of our baskets? Such fun I have, too, laughing at the dear people in Tilling. But what thrilling news this morning about our sweet Susan and your dear brother, though of course I knew it long ago.'

'Indeed! how was that?' said the Contessa quite sharply.

Miss Mapp was 'nettled' at her tone.

'Oh, you must allow me two eyes,' she said, since it was merely tedious to explain how she had seen them from behind a curtain kissing in the garden. 'Just two eyes.'

'And a nose for scent,' remarked the Contessa very genially.

This was certainly coarse, though probably Italian. Miss Mapp's opinion of the Contessa fluctuated violently like a barometer before a storm and indicated 'Changeable'.

'Dear Susan is such an intimate friend,' she said.

The Contessa looked at her very fixedly for a moment, and then appeared to dismiss the matter.

'My crab, my steak,' she said. 'And where does your nice Captain, no, Major Flint live? I have a note to leave on him, for he has asked me to tea all alone, to see his tiger-skins. He is going to be my flirt while I am in Tilling, and when I go he will break his heart, but I will have told him who can mend it again.'

'Dear Major Benjy!' said Miss Mapp, at her wits' end to know how to deal with so feather-tongued a lady. 'What a treat it will be to him to have you to tea. Today, is it?'

The Contessa quite distinctly winked behind her eyeglass, which she had put up to look at Diva, who whirled by on the other side of the street.

'And if I said "Today",' she remarked, 'you would – what is it that that one says' – and she indicated Diva – 'yes, you would pop in, and the good Major would pay no attention to me. So if I tell you I shall go today, you will know that is a lie, you clever Miss Mapp, and so you will go to tea with him tomorrow and find me there. *Bene!* Now where is his house?'

This was a sort of scheming that had never entered into Miss Mapp's life, and she saw with pain how shallow she had been all these years. Often and often she had, when inquisitive questions were put her, answered them without any strict subservience to truth, but never had she thought of confusing the issues like this. If she told Diva a lie, Diva probably guessed it was a lie, and acted accordingly, but she had never thought of making it practically impossible to tell whether it was a lie or not. She had no more idea when she walked back along the High Street with the Contessa swinging her basket by her side, whether that lady was going to tea with Major Benjy today or tomorrow or when, than she knew whether the crab was going to eat the beef-steak.

'There's his house,' she said, as they paused at the dentist's corner, 'and there's mine next it, with the little bow-window of my garden-room looking out on to the street. I hope to welcome you there, dear Contessa, for a tiny game of bridge and some tea one of these days very soon. What day do you think? Tomorrow?'

(Then she would know if the Contessa was going to tea with Major Benjy tomorrow . . . unfortunately the Contessa appeared to know that she would know it, too.)

'My flirt!' she said. 'Perhaps I may be having tea with my flirt tomorrow.'

Better anything than that.

'I will ask him, too, to meet you,' said Miss Mapp, feeling in some awful and helpless way that she was playing her adversary's game. 'Adversary?' did she say to herself? She did. The inscrutable Contessa was 'up to' that too.

'I will not amalgamate my treats,' she said. 'So that is his house! What a charming house! How my heart flutters as I ring the bell!'

Miss Mapp was now quite distraught. There was the possibility that the Contessa might tell Major Benjy that it was time he married, but on the other hand she was making arrangements to go to tea with him on an unknown date, and the hero of amorous adventures in India and elsewhere might lose his heart again to somebody quite different from one whom he could hope to marry. By daylight the dear Contessa was undeniably plain: that was something, but in these short days, tea would be conducted by artificial light, and by artificial light she was not so like a rabbit. What was worse was that by any light she had a liveliness which might be mistaken for wit, and a flattering manner which might be taken for sincerity. She hoped men were not so easily duped as that, and was sadly afraid that they were. Blind fools!

*   *   *

The number of visits that Miss Mapp made about teatime in this week before Christmas to the postbox at the corner of the High Street, with an envelope in her hand containing Mr Hopkins's bill for fish (and a postal order enclosed), baffles computation. Naturally, she did not intend, either by day or night, to risk being found again with a blank unstamped envelope in her hand, and the one enclosing Mr Hopkins's bill and the postal order would have passed scrutiny for correctness, anywhere. But fair and calm as was the exterior of that envelope, none could tell how agitated was the hand that carried it backwards and forwards until the edges got crumpled and the inscription clouded with much fingering. Indeed, of all the tricks that Miss Mapp had compassed for others, none was so sumptuously contrived as that in which she had now entangled herself.

For these December days were dark, and in consequence not only would the Contessa be looking her best (such as it was) at teatime, but from Miss Mapp's window it was impossible to tell whether she had gone to tea with him on any particular afternoon, for there had been a strike at the gasworks, and the lamp at the corner, which, in happier days, would have told all, told nothing whatever. Miss Mapp

must therefore trudge to the letter-box with Mr Hopkins's bill in
her hand as she went out, and (after a feint of posting it) with it in her
pocket as she came back, in order to gather from the light in the
windows, from the sound of conversation that would be audible as
she passed close beneath them, whether the Major was having tea
there or not, and with whom. Should she hear that ringing laugh
which had sounded so pleasant when she revoked, but now was so
sinister, she had quite determined to go in and borrow a book or a
tiger-skin – anything. The Major could scarcely fail to ask her to tea,
and, once there, wild horses should not drag her away until she had
outstayed the other visitor. Then, as her malady of jealousy grew
more feverish, she began to perceive, as by the ray of some dreadful
dawn, that lights in the Major's room and sounds of elfin laughter
were not completely trustworthy as proofs that the Contessa was
there. It was possible, awfully possible, that the two might be sitting
in the firelight, that voices might be hushed to amorous whisperings,
that pregnant smiles might be taking the place of laughter. On one
such afternoon, as she came back from the letter-box with patient
Mr Hopkins's overdue bill in her pocket, a wild certainty seized her,
when she saw how closely the curtains were drawn, and how still it
seemed inside his room, that firelight dalliance was going on.

She rang the bell, and imagined she heard whisperings inside while
it was being answered. Presently the light went up in the hall, and
the Major's Mrs Dominic opened the door.

'The Major is in, I think, isn't he, Mrs Dominic?' said Miss Mapp,
in her most insinuating tones.

'No, miss; out,' said Dominic uncompromisingly. (Miss Mapp
wondered if Dominic drank.)

'Dear me! How tiresome, when he told me – ' said she, with
playful annoyance. 'Would you be very kind, Mrs Dominic, and just
see for certain that he is not in his room? He may have come in.'

'No, miss, he's out,' said Dominic, with the parrotlike utterance of
the determined liar. 'Any message?'

Miss Mapp turned away, more certain than ever that he was in and
immersed in dalliance. She would have continued to be quite certain
about it, had she not, glancing distractedly down the street, caught
sight of him coming up with Captain Puffin.

Meantime she had twice attempted to get up a cosy little party of
four (so as not to frighten the Contessa) to play bridge from tea till
dinner, and on both occasions the Faradiddleony (for so she had
become) was most unfortunately engaged. But the second of these

disappointing replies contained the hope that they would meet at their marketings tomorrow morning, and though poor Miss Mapp was really getting very tired with these innumerable visits to the postbox, whether wet or fine, she set forth next morning with the hopes anyhow of finding out whether the Contessa had been to tea with Major Flint, or on what day she was going ... There she was, just opposite the post-office, and there – oh, shame! – was Major Benjy on his way to the tram, in light-hearted conversation with her. It was a slight consolation that Captain Puffin was there too.

Miss Mapp quickened her steps to a little tripping run.

'Dear Contessa, so sorry I am late,' she said. 'Such a lot of little things to do this morning. (Major Benjy! Captain Puffin!) Oh, how naughty of you to have begun your shopping without me!'

'Only been to the grocer's,' said the Contessa. 'Major Benjy has been so amusing that I haven't got on with my shopping at all. I have written to Cecco to say that there is no one so witty.'

(Major Benjy! thought Miss Mapp bitterly, remembering how long it had taken her to arrive at that. 'And witty.' She had not arrived at that yet.)

'No, indeed!' said the Major. 'It was the Contessa, Miss Mapp, who has been so entertaining.'

'I'm sure she would be,' said Miss Mapp, with an enormous smile. 'And, oh, Major Benjy, you'll miss your tram unless you hurry, and get no golf at all, and then be vexed with us for keeping you. You men always blame us poor women.'

'Well, upon my word, what's a game of golf compared with the pleasure of being with the ladies?' asked the Major, with a great fat bow.

'I want to catch that tram,' said Puffin quite distinctly, and Miss Mapp found herself more nearly forgetting his inebriated insults than ever before.

'You poor Captain Puffin,' said the Contessa, 'you shall catch it. Be off, both of you, at once. I will not say another word to either of you. I will never forgive you if you miss it. But tomorrow afternoon, Major Benjy.'

He turned round to bow again, and a bicycle luckily (for the rider) going very slowly, butted softly into him behind.

'Not hurt?' called the Contessa. 'Good! Ah, Miss Mapp, let us get to our shopping! How well you manage those men! How right you are about them! They want their golf more than they want us, whatever they may say. They would hate us, if we kept them from their golf. So sorry not to have been able to play bridge with you yesterday, but an engagement. What a busy place Tilling is. Let me see! Where is the list of things that Figgis told me to buy? That Figgis! A roller-towel for his pantry, and some blacking for his boots, and some flannel I suppose for his fat stomach. It is all for Figgis. And there is that swift Mrs Plaistow. She comes like a train with a red light in her face and wheels and whistlings. She talks like a telegram – Good-morning, Mrs Plaistow.'

'Enjoyed my game of bridge, Contessa,' panted Diva. 'Delightful game of bridge yesterday.'

The Contessa seemed in rather a hurry to reply. But long before she could get a word out Miss Mapp felt she knew what had happened . . .

'So pleased,' said the Contessa quickly. 'And now for Figgis's towels, Miss Mapp. Ten and sixpence apiece, he says. What a price to give for a towel! But I learn housekeeping like this, and Cecco will delight in all the economies I shall make. Quick, to the draper's, lest there should be no towels left.'

In spite of Figgis's list, the Contessa's shopping was soon over, and Miss Mapp having seen her as far as the corner, walked on, as if to her own house, in order to give her time to get to Mr Wyse's, and then fled back to the High Street. The suspense was unbearable: she had to know without delay when and where Diva and the Contessa had played bridge yesterday. Never had her eye so rapidly scanned the movement of passengers in that entrancing thoroughfare in order to pick Diva out, and learn from her precisely what had happened . . . There she was, coming out of the dyer's with her basket completely filled by a bulky package, which it needed no ingenuity to identify as the late crimson-lake. She would have to be pleasant with Diva, for much as that perfidious woman might enjoy telling her where this furtive bridge party had taken place, she might enjoy even more torturing her with uncertainty. Diva could, if put to it, give no answer whatever to a direct question, but, skilfully changing the subject, talk about something utterly different.

'The crimson-lake,' said Miss Mapp, pointing to the basket. 'Hope it will turn out well, dear.'

There was rather a wicked light in Diva's eyes.

'Not crimson-lake,' she said. 'Jet-black.'

'Sweet of you to have it dyed again, dear Diva,' said Miss Mapp. 'Not very expensive, I trust?'

'Send the bill in to you, if you like,' said Diva.

Miss Mapp laughed very pleasantly.

'That would be a good joke,' she said. 'How nice it is that the dear Contessa takes so warmly to our Tilling ways. So amusing she was about the commissions Figgis had given her. But a wee bit satirical, do you think?'

This ought to put Diva in a good temper, for there was nothing she liked so much as a few little dabs at somebody else. (Diva was not very good-natured.)

'She is rather satirical,' said Diva.

'Oh, tell me some of her amusing little speeches!' said Miss Mapp enthusiastically. 'I can't always follow her, but you are so quick! A little coarse too, at times, isn't she? What she said the other night when she was playing Patience, about the queens and kings, wasn't quite – was it? And the toothpick.'

'Yes. Toothpick,' said Diva.

'Perhaps she has bad teeth,' said Miss Mapp; 'it runs in families, and Mr Wyse's, you know – We're lucky, you and I.'

Diva maintained a complete silence, and they had now come nearly as far as her door. If she would not give the information that she knew Miss Mapp longed for, she must be asked for it, with the uncertain hope that she would give it then.

'Been playing bridge lately, dear?' asked Miss Mapp.

'Quite lately,' said Diva.

'I thought I heard you say something about it to the Contessa. Yesterday, was it? Whom did you play with?'

Diva paused, and, when they had come quite to her door, made up her mind.

'Contessa, Susan, Mr Wyse, me,' she said.

'But I thought she never played with Mr Wyse,' said Miss Mapp.

'Had to get a four,' said Diva. 'Contessa wanted her bridge. Nobody else.'

She popped into her house.

There is no use in describing Miss Mapp's state of mind, except by saying that for the moment she quite forgot that the Contessa was almost certainly going to tea with Major Benjy tomorrow.

Chapter Twelve

'Peace on earth and mercy mild,' sang Miss Mapp, holding her head back with her uvula clearly visible. She sat in her usual seat close below the pulpit, and the sun streaming in through a stained-glass window opposite made her face of all colours, like Joseph's coat. Not knowing how it looked from outside, she pictured to herself a sort of celestial radiance coming from within, though Diva, sitting opposite, was reminded of the iridescent hues observable on cold boiled beef. But then, Miss Mapp had registered the fact that Diva's notion of singing alto was to follow the trebles at the uniform distance of a minor third below, so that matters were about square between them. She wondered between the verses if she could say something very tactful to Diva, which might before next Christmas induce her not to make that noise . . .

Major Flint came in just before the first hymn was over, and held his top-hat before his face by way of praying in secret, before he opened his hymn-book. A piece of loose holly fell down from the window ledge above him on the exact middle of his head, and the jump that he gave was, considering his baldness, quite justifiable. Captain Puffin, Miss Mapp was sorry to see, was not there at all. But he had been unwell lately with attacks of dizziness, one of which had caused him, in the last game of golf that he had played, to fall down on the eleventh green and groan. If these attacks were not due to his lack of perseverance, no right-minded person could fail to be very sorry for him.

There was a good deal more peace on earth as regards Tilling than might have been expected considering what the week immediately before Christmas had been like. A picture by Miss Coles (who had greatly dropped out of society lately, owing to her odd ways) called 'Adam', which was certainly Mr Hopkins (though no one could have guessed) had appeared for sale in the window of a dealer in pictures and curios, but had been withdrawn from public view at Miss Mapp's personal intercession and her revelation of whom, unlikely as it sounded, the picture represented. The unchivalrous dealer had told the artist the history of its withdrawal, and it had come to Miss Mapp's ears (among many other things) that quaint Irene had imitated the scene of intercession with such piercing fidelity that her servant,

Lucy-Eve, had nearly died of laughing. Then there had been clandestine bridge at Mr Wyse's house on three consecutive days, and on none of these occasions was Miss Mapp asked to continue the instruction which she had professed herself perfectly willing to give to the Contessa. The Contessa, in fact – there seemed to be no doubt about it – had declared that she would sooner not play bridge at all than play with Miss Mapp, because the effort of not laughing would put an unwarrantable strain on those muscles which prevented you from doing so . . . Then the Contessa had gone to tea quite alone with Major Benjy, and though her shrill and senseless monologue was clearly audible in the street as Miss Mapp went by to post her letter again, the Major's Dominic had stoutly denied that he was in, and the notion that the Contessa was haranguing all by herself in his drawing-room was too ridiculous to be entertained for a moment . . . And Diva's dyed dress had turned out so well that Miss Mapp gnashed her teeth at the thought that she had not had hers dyed instead. With some green chiffon round the neck, even Diva looked quite distinguished – for Diva.

Then, quite suddenly, an angel of Peace had descended on the distracted garden-room, for the Poppits, the Contessa and Mr Wyse all went away to spend Christmas and the New Year with the Wyses of Whitchurch. It was probable that the Contessa would then continue a round of visits with all that coronetted luggage, and leave for Italy again without revisiting Tilling. She had behaved as if that was the case, for taking advantage of a fine afternoon, she had borrowed the Royce and whirled round the town on a series of calls, leaving p.p.c. calling cards everywhere, and saying only (so Miss Mapp gathered from Withers), 'Your mistress not in? So sorry,' and had driven away before Withers could get out the information that her mistress was very much in, for she had a bad cold.

But there were the p.p.c. cards, and the Wyses with their future connections were going to Whitchurch, and after a few hours of rage against all that had been going on, without revenge being now possible, and of reaction after the excitement of it, a different reaction set in. Odd and unlikely as it would have appeared a month or two earlier, when Tilling was seething with duels, it was a fact that it was possible to have too much excitement. Ever since the Contessa had arrived, she had been like an active volcano planted down among dangerously inflammable elements, and the removal of it was really a matter of relief. Miss Mapp felt that she would be dealing again with materials whose properties she knew, and since, no doubt, the strain of Susan's marriage would soon follow, it was a merciful dispensation that the removal of the volcano granted Tilling a short restorative pause. The young couple would be back before long, and with Susan's approaching elevation certainly going to her head, and making her talk in a manner wholly intolerable about the grandeur of the Wyses of Whitchurch, it was a boon to be allowed to recuperate for a little, before settling to work afresh to combat Susan's pretensions. There was no fear of being dull: for plenty of things had been going on in Tilling before the Contessa flared on the High Street, and plenty of things would continue to go on after she had taken her explosions elsewhere.

By the time that the second lesson was being read the sun had shifted from Miss Mapp's face, and enabled her to see how ghastly dear Evie looked when focused under the blue robe of Jonah, who was climbing out of the whale. She had had her disappointments to contend with, for the Contessa had never really grasped at all who she was. Sometimes she mistook her for Irene, sometimes she did not seem to see her, but never had she appeared fully to identify her as Mr Bartlett's wee wifey. But then, dear Evie was very insignificant even when she squeaked her loudest. Her best friends, among whom was Miss Mapp, would not deny that. She had been wilted by non-recognition; she would recover again, now that they were all left to themselves.

The sermon contained many repetitions and a quantity of split infinitives. The Padre had once openly stated that Shakespeare was good enough for him, and that Shakespeare was guilty of many split infinitives. On that occasion there had nearly been a breach between him and Mistress Mapp, for Mistress Mapp had said, 'But then you are not Shakespeare, dear Padre.' And he could find nothing better to reply than 'Hoots!' . . . There was nothing more of interest about the sermon.

At the end of the service Miss Mapp lingered in the church looking at the lovely decorations of holly and laurel, for which she was so largely responsible, until her instinct assured her that everybody else had shaken hands and was wondering what to say next about Christmas. Then, just then, she hurried out.

They were all there, and she came like the late and honoured guest (poor Diva).

'Diva, darling,' she said. 'Merry Christmas! And Evie! And the Padre. Padre dear, thank you for your sermon! And Major Benjy! Merry Christmas, Major Benjy. What a small company we are, but not the less Christmassy. No Mr Wyse, no Susan, no Isabel. Oh, and no Captain Puffin. Not quite well again, Major Benjy? Tell me about him. Those dreadful fits of dizziness. So hard to understand.'

She beautifully succeeded in detaching the Major from the rest. With the peace that had descended on Tilling, she had forgiven him for having been made a fool of by the Contessa.

'I'm anxious about my friend Puffin,' he said. 'Not at all up to the mark. Most depressed. I told him he had no business to be depressed. It's selfish to be depressed, I said. If we were all depressed it would be a dreary world, Miss Elizabeth. He's sent for the doctor. I was to have had a round of golf with Puffin this afternoon, but he doesn't feel up to it. It would have done him much more good than a host of doctors.'

'Oh, I wish I could play golf, and not disappoint you of your round, Major Benjy,' said she.

Major Benjy seemed rather to recoil from the thought. He did not profess, at any rate, any sympathetic regret.

'And we were going to have had our Christmas dinner together tonight,' he said, 'and spend a jolly evening afterwards.'

'I'm sure quiet is the best thing for Captain Puffin with his dizziness,' said Miss Mapp firmly.

A sudden audacity seized her. Here was the Major feeling lonely as regards his Christmas evening: here was she delighted that he should not spend it 'jollily' with Captain Puffin . . . and there was plenty of plum-pudding.

'Come and have your dinner with me,' she said. 'I'm alone too.'

He shook his head.

'Very kind of you, I'm sure, Miss Elizabeth,' he said, 'but I think I'll hold myself in readiness to go across to poor old Puffin, if he feels up to it. I feel lost without my friend Puffin.'

'But you must have no jolly evening, Major Benjy,' she said. 'So bad for him. A little soup and a good night's rest. That's the best thing. Perhaps he would like me to go in and read to him. I will gladly. Tell him so from me. And if you find he doesn't want anybody, not even you, well, there's a slice of plum-pudding at your neighbour's, and such a warm welcome.'

She stood on the steps of her house, which in summer were so crowded with sketchers, and would have kissed her hand to him had not Diva been following close behind, for even on Christmas Day poor Diva was capable of finding something ill-natured to say about the most tender and womanly action . . . and Miss Mapp let herself into her house with only a little wave of her hand . . .

Somehow the idea that Major Benjy was feeling lonely and missing the quarrelsome society of his debauched friend was not entirely unpleasing to her. It was odd that there should be anybody who missed Captain Puffin. Who would not sooner play golf all alone (if that was possible) than with him, or spend an evening alone rather than with his companionship? But if Captain Puffin had to be missed, she would certainly have chosen Major Benjy to be the person who missed him. Without wishing Captain Puffin any unpleasant experience, she would have borne with equanimity the news of his settled melancholia, or his permanent dizziness, for Major Benjy with his bright robustness was not the sort of man to prove a willing comrade to a chronically dizzy or melancholic friend. Nor would it be right that he should be so. Men in the prime of life were not meant for that. Nor were they meant to be the victims of designing women, even though Wyses of Whitchurch . . . He was saved from that by their most opportune departure.

In spite of her readiness to be interrupted at any moment, Miss Mapp spent a solitary evening. She had pulled a cracker with Withers, and severely jarred a tooth over a threepenny-piece in the plum-pudding, but there had been no other events. Once or twice, in order to see what the night was like, she had gone to the window of the garden-room, and been aware that there was a light in Major Benjy's house, but when half-past ten struck, she had despaired of company and gone to bed. A little carol-singing in the streets gave her a Christmas feeling, and she hoped that the singers got a nice supper somewhere.

Miss Mapp did not feel as genial as usual when she came down to breakfast next day, and omitted to say good-morning to her rainbow of piggies. She had run short of wool for her knitting, and Boxing Day appeared to her a very ill-advised institution. You would have imagined, thought Miss Mapp, as she began cracking her egg, that the tradespeople had had enough relaxation on Christmas Day, especially when, as on this occasion, it was immediately preceded by Sunday, and would have been all the better for getting to work again. She never relaxed her efforts for a single day in the year, and why –

An overpowering knocking on her front door caused her to stop cracking her egg. That imperious summons was succeeded by but a moment of silence, and then it began again. She heard the hurried step of Withers across the hall, and almost before she could have been supposed to reach the front door, Diva burst into the room.

'Dead!' she said. 'In his soup. Captain Puffin. Can't wait!'

She whirled out again and the front door banged.

Miss Mapp ate her egg in three mouthfuls, had no marmalade at all, and putting on the Prince of Wales's cloak tripped down into the High Street. Though all shops were shut, Evie was there with her market basket, eagerly listening to what Mrs Brace, the doctor's wife, was communicating. Though Mrs Brace was not, strictly speaking, 'in society', Miss Mapp waived all social distinctions, and pressed her hand with a mournful smile.

'Is it all too terribly true?' she asked.

Mrs Brace did not take the smallest notice of her, and, dropping her voice, spoke to Evie in tones so low that Miss Mapp could not catch a single syllable except the word soup, which seemed to imply that Diva had got hold of some correct news at last. Evie gave a shrill little scream at the concluding words, whatever they were, as Mrs Brace hurried away.

Miss Mapp firmly cornered Evie, and heard what had happened. Captain Puffin had gone up to bed last night, not feeling well, without having any dinner. But he had told Mrs Gashly to make him some soup, and he would not want anything else. His parlour-maid had brought it to him, and had soon afterwards opened the door to Major Flint, who, learning that his friend had gone to bed, went away. She called her master in the morning, and found him sitting, still dressed, with his face in the soup which he had poured out into a deep soup-plate. This was very odd, and she had called Mrs Gashly. They settled that he was dead, and rang up the doctor, who agreed with them. It was clear that Captain Puffin had had a stroke of some sort, and had fallen forward into the soup which he had just poured out . . .

'But he didn't die of his stroke,' said Evie in a strangled whisper. 'He was drowned.'

'Drowned, dear?' said Miss Mapp.

'Yes. Lungs were full of ox-tail, oh, dear me! A stroke first, and he fell forward with his face in his soup-plate and got his nose and mouth quite covered with the soup. He was drowned. All on dry land and in his bedroom. Too terrible. What dangers we are all in!'

She gave a loud squeak and escaped, to tell her husband.

*   *   *

Diva had finished calling on everybody, and approached rapidly.

'He must have died of a stroke,' said Diva. 'Very much depressed lately. That precedes a stroke.'

'Oh, then, haven't you heard, dear?' said Miss Mapp. 'It is all too terrible! On Christmas Day, too!'

'Suicide?' asked Diva. 'Oh, how shocking!'

'No, dear. It was like this . . . '

*   *   *

Miss Mapp got back to her house long before she usually left it. Her cook came up with the proposed bill of fare for the day.

'That will do for lunch,' said Miss Mapp. 'But not soup in the evening. A little fish from what was left over yesterday, and some toasted cheese. That will be plenty. Just a tray.'

Miss Mapp went to the garden-room and sat at her window.

'All so sudden,' she said to herself.

She sighed.

'I dare say there may have been much that was good in Captain Puffin,' she thought, 'that we knew nothing about.'

She wore a wintry smile.

'Major Benjy will feel very lonely,' she said.

Epilogue

Miss Mapp went to the garden-room and sat at her window . . .

It was a warm, bright day of February, and a butterfly was enjoying itself in the pale sunshine on the other window, and perhaps (so Miss Mapp sympathetically interpreted its feelings) was rather annoyed that it could not fly away through the pane. It was not a white butterfly, but a tortoiseshell, very pretty, and in order to let it enjoy itself more, she opened the window and it fluttered out into the garden. Before it had flown many yards, a starling ate most of it up, so the starling enjoyed itself too.

Miss Mapp fully shared in the pleasure first of the tortoiseshell and then of the starling, for she was enjoying herself very much too, though her left wrist was terribly stiff. But Major Benjy was so cruel: he insisted on her learning that turn of the wrist which was so important in golf.

'Upon my word, you've got it now, Miss Elizabeth,' he had said to her yesterday, and then made her do it all over again fifty times more. ('Such a bully!') Sometimes she struck the ground, sometimes she struck the ball, sometimes she struck the air. But he had been very much pleased with her. And she was very much pleased with him. She forgot about the butterfly and remembered the starling.

It was idle to deny that the last six weeks had been a terrific strain, and the strain on her left wrist was nothing to them. The worst tension of all, perhaps, was when Diva had bounced in with the news that the Contessa was coming back. That was so like Diva: the only foundation for the report proved to be that Figgis had said to her Janet that Mr Wyse was coming back, and either Janet had misunderstood Figgis, or Diva (far more probably) had misunderstood Janet, and Miss Mapp only hoped that Diva had not done so on purpose, though it looked like it. Stupid as poor Diva undoubtedly was, it was hard for Charity itself to believe that she had thought that Janet really said that. But when this report proved to be totally unfounded, Miss Mapp rose to the occasion, and said that Diva had spoken out of stupidity and not out of malice towards her . . .

Then in due course Mr Wyse had come back and the two Poppits had come back, and only three days ago one Poppit had become a Wyse, and they had all three gone for a motor-tour on the Continent in the Royce. Very likely they would go as far south as Capri, and Susan would stay with her new grand Italian connections. What she would be like when she got back Miss Mapp forbore to conjecture, since it was no use anticipating trouble; but Susan had been so grandiose about the Wyses, multiplying their incomes and their acreage by fifteen or twenty, so Miss Mapp conjectured, and talking so much about county families, that the liveliest imagination failed to picture what she would make of the Faragliones. She already alluded to the Count as 'my brother-in-law Cecco Faraglione', but had luckily heard Diva say 'Faradiddleony' in a loud aside, which had made her a little more reticent. Susan had taken the insignia of the Member of the British Empire with her, as she at once conceived the idea of being presented to the Queen of Italy by Amelia, and going to a court ball, and Isabel had taken her manuscript book of Malaprops and Spoonerisms. If she put down all the Italian malaprops that Mrs Wyse would commit, it was likely that she would bring back two volumes instead of one.

Though all these grandeurs were so rightly irritating, the departure of the 'young couple' and Isabel had left Tilling, already shocked and shattered by the death of Captain Puffin, rather flat and purposeless. Miss Mapp alone refused to be flat, and had never been so full of purpose. She felt that it would be unpardonably selfish of her if she regarded for a moment her own loss, when there was one in Tilling who suffered so much more keenly, and she set herself with admirable singleness of purpose to restore Major Benjy's zest in life, and fill the gap. She wanted no assistance from others in this: Diva, for instance, with her jerky ways would be only too apt to jar on him, and her black dress might remind him of his loss if Miss Mapp had asked her to go shares in the task of making the Major's evenings less lonely. Also the weather, during the whole of January, was particularly inclement, and it would have been too much to expect of Diva to come all the way up the hill in the wet, while it was but a step from the Major's door to her own. So there was little or nothing in the way of winter-bridge as far as Miss Mapp and the Major were concerned. Piquet with a single sympathetic companion who did not mind being rubiconned at threepence a hundred was as much as he was up to at present.

With the end of the month a balmy foretaste of spring (such as had encouraged the tortoiseshell butterfly to hope) set in, and the Major used to drop in after breakfast and stroll round the garden with her, smoking his pipe. Miss Mapp's sweet snowdrops had begun to appear, and green spikes of crocuses pricked the black earth, and the sparrows were having such fun in the creepers. Then one day the Major, who was going out to catch the 11.20 tram, had a 'golf-stick', as Miss Mapp so foolishly called it, with him, and a golf-ball, and after making a dreadful hole in her lawn, she had hit the ball so hard that it rebounded from the brick-wall, which was quite a long way off, and came back to her very feet, as if asking to be hit again by the golf-stick – no, golf club. She learned to keep her wonderfully observant eye on the ball and bought one of her own. The Major lent her a mashie – and before anyone would have thought it possible, she had learned to propel her ball right over the bed where the snowdrops grew, without beheading any of them in its passage. It was the turn of the wrist that did that, and Withers cleaned the dear little mashie afterwards, and put it safely in the corner of the garden-room.

Today was to be epoch-making. They were to go out to the real links by the 11.20 tram (consecrated by so many memories), and he was to call for her at eleven. He had *quai-hai*ed for porridge fully an hour ago.

After letting out the tortoiseshell butterfly from the window looking into the garden, she moved across to the post of observation on the street, and arranged snowdrops in a little glass vase. There were a few over when that was full, and she saw that a reel of cotton was close at hand, in case she had an idea of what to do with the remainder. Eleven o'clock chimed from the church, and on the stroke she saw him coming up the few yards of street that separated his door from hers. So punctual! So manly!

Diva was careering about the High Street as they walked along it, and Miss Mapp kissed her hand to her.

'Off to play golf, darling,' she said. 'Is that not grand? *Au reservoir.*'

Diva had not missed seeing the snowdrops in the Major's button-hole, and stood stupefied for a moment at this news. Then she caught sight of Evie, and shot across the street to communicate her suspicions. Quaint Irene joined then and the Padre.

'Snowdrops, i'fegs!' said he . . .

LUCIA IN LONDON

Chapter One

CONSIDERING THAT PHILIP LUCAS'S AUNT who died early in April was no less than eighty-three years old, and had spent the last seven of them bedridden in a private lunatic asylum, it had been generally and perhaps reasonably hoped among his friends and those of his wife that the bereavement would not be regarded by either of them as an intolerable tragedy. Mrs Quantock, in fact, who, like everybody else at Riseholme, had sent a neat little note of condolence to Mrs Lucas, had, without using the actual words 'happy release', certainly implied it or its close equivalent.

She was hoping that there would be a reply to it, for though she had said in her note that her dear Lucia mustn't dream of answering it, that was a mere figure of speech, and she had instructed her parlour maid who took it across to The Hurst immediately after lunch to say that she didn't know if there was an answer, and would wait to see, for Mrs Lucas might perhaps give a little hint ever so vaguely about what the expectations were concerning which everybody was dying to get information . . .

While she waited for this, Daisy Quantock was busy, like everybody else in the village on this beautiful afternoon of spring, with her garden, hacking about with a small but destructive fork in her flower-beds. She was a gardener of the ruthless type, and went for any small green thing that incautiously showed a timid spike above the earth, suspecting it of being a weed. She had had a slight difference with the professional gardener who had hitherto worked for her on three afternoons during the week, and had told him that his services were no longer required. She meant to do her gardening herself this year, and was confident that a profusion of beautiful flowers and a plethora of delicious vegetables would be the result. At the end of her garden path was a barrow of rich manure, which she proposed, when she had finished the slaughter of the innocents, to dig into the depopulated beds. On the other side of her paling her neighbour Georgie Pillson was rolling his strip of lawn, on which during the summer he often played croquet on a small scale. Occasionally they shouted remarks to each other, but as they got more and more out of breath with their exertions the remarks got fewer. Mrs Quantock's last question had been 'What do you do with slugs, Georgie?' and Georgie had panted out, 'Pretend you don't see them.'

Mrs Quantock had lately grown rather stout owing to a diet of sour milk, which with plenty of sugar was not palatable; but sour milk and pyramids of raw vegetables had quite stopped all the symptoms of consumption which the study of a small but lurid medical manual had induced. Today she had eaten a large but normal lunch in order to test the merits of her new cook, who certainly was a success, for her husband had gobbled up his food with great avidity instead of turning it over and over with his fork as if it was hay. In consequence, stoutness, surfeit, and so much stooping had made her feel rather giddy, and she was standing up to recover, wondering if this giddiness was a symptom of something dire, when de Vere, for such was the incredible name of her parlour-maid, came down the steps from the dining-room with a note in her hand. So Mrs Quantock hastily took off her gardening gloves of stout leather, and opened it.

There was a sentence of formal thanks for her sympathy which Mrs Lucas immensely prized, and then followed these ridiculous words:

> It has been a terrible blow to my poor Peppino and myself. We trusted that Auntie Amy might have been spared us for a few years yet.
>
>   Ever, dear Daisy, your sad
>
>   Lucia

And not a word about expectations! ... Lucia's dear Daisy crumpled up the absurd note, and said 'Rubbish,' so loud that Georgie Pillson in the next garden thought he was being addressed.

'What's that?' he said.

'Georgie, come to the fence a minute,' said Mrs Quantock. 'I want to speak to you.'

Georgie, longing for a little gossip, let go of the handle of his roller, which, suddenly released, gave a loud squeak and rapped him smartly on the elbow.

'Tarsome thing!' said Georgie.

He went to the fence and, being tall, could look over it. There was Mrs Quantock angrily poking Lucia's note into the flower-bed she had been weeding.

'What is it?' said Georgie. 'Shall I like it?'

His face red, and moist with exertion, appearing just over the top of the fence, looked like the sun about to set below the flat grey horizon of the sea.

'I don't know if you'll like it,' said Daisy, 'but it's your Lucia. I sent her a little note of condolence about the aunt, and she says it has been a terrible blow to Peppino and herself. They hoped that the old lady might have been spared them a few years yet.'

'No!' said Georgie, wiping the moisture off his forehead with the back of one of his beautiful pearl-grey gloves.

'But she did,' said the infuriated Daisy, 'they were her very words. I could show you if I hadn't dug it in. Such a pack of nonsense! I hope that long before I've been bedridden for seven years, somebody will strangle me with a bootlace, or anything handy. Why does Lucia pretend to be sorry? What does it all mean?'

Georgie had long been devoted henchman to Lucia (Mrs Lucas, wife of Philip Lucas, and so Lucia), and though he could criticise her in his mind, when he was alone in his bed or his bath, he always championed her in the face of the criticism of others. Whereas Daisy criticised everybody everywhere . . .

'Perhaps it means what it says,' he observed with the delicate sarcasm that never had any effect on his neighbour.

'It can't possibly do that,' said Mrs Quantock. 'Neither Lucia nor Peppino have set eyes on his aunt for years, nor spoken of her. Last time Peppino went to see her she bit him. Sling for a week afterwards, don't you remember, and he was terrified of blood-poisoning. How can her death be a blow, and as for her being spared – '

Mrs Quantock suddenly broke off, remembering that de Vere was still standing there and drinking it all in.

'That's all, de Vere,' she said.

'Thank you, ma'am,' said de Vere, striding back towards the house. She had high-heeled shoes on, and each time she lifted her foot, the heel which had been embedded by her weight in the soft lawn came out with the sound of a cork being drawn. Then Daisy came closer to the fence, with the light of inductive reasoning, which was much cultivated at Riseholme, veiling the fury of her eye.

'Georgie, I've got it,' she said. 'I've guessed what it means.'

Now though Georgie was devoted to his Lucia, he was just as devoted to inductive reasoning, and Daisy Quantock was, with the exception of himself, far the most powerful logician in the place.

'What is it, then?' he asked.

'Stupid of me not to have thought of it at once,' said Daisy. 'Why, don't you see? Peppino is Auntie's heir, for she was unmarried, and he's the only nephew, and probably he has been left piles and piles. So naturally they say it's a terrible blow. Wouldn't do to be exultant. They must say it's a terrible blow, to show they don't care about the money. The more they're left, the sadder it is. So natural. I blame myself for not having thought of it at once. Have you seen her since?'

'Not for a quiet talk,' said Georgie. 'Peppino was there, and a man who, I think, was Peppino's lawyer. He was frightfully deferential.'

'That proves it,' said Daisy. 'And nothing said of any kind?'

Georgie's face screwed itself up in the effort to remember.

'Yes, there was something,' he said, 'but I was talking to Lucia, and the others were talking rather low. But I did hear the lawyer say something to Peppino about pearls. I do remember the word pearls. Perhaps it was the old lady's pearls.'

Mrs Quantock gave a short laugh.

'It couldn't have been Peppino's,' she said. 'He has one in a tie-pin. It's called pear-shaped, but there's little shape about it. When do wills come out?'

'Oh, ages,' said Georgie. 'Months. And there's a house in London, I know.'

'Whereabouts?' asked Daisy greedily.

Georgie's face assumed a look of intense concentration.

'I couldn't tell you for certain,' he said, 'but I know Peppino went up to town not long ago to see about some repairs to his aunt's house, and I think it was the roof.'

'It doesn't matter where the repairs were,' said Daisy impatiently. 'I want to know where the house was.'

'You interrupt me,' said Georgie. 'I was telling you. I know he went to Harrod's afterwards and walked there, because he and Lucia were dining with me and he said so. So the house must have been close to Harrod's, quite close I mean, because it was raining, and if it had been any reasonable distance he would have had a taxi. So it might be Knightsbridge.'

Mrs Quantock put on her gardening gloves again.

'How frightfully secretive people are,' she said. 'Fancy his never having told you where his aunt's house was.'

'But they never spoke of her,' said Georgie. 'She's been in that nursing-home so many years.'

'You may call it a nursing-home,' observed Mrs Quantock, 'or, if

LUCIA IN LONDON 441

you choose, you may call it a post-office. But it was an asylum. And they're just as secretive about the property.'

'But you never talk about the property till after the funeral,' said Georgie. 'I believe it's tomorrow.'

Mrs Quantock gave a prodigious sniff.

'They would have, if there hadn't been any,' she said.

'How horrid you are,' said Georgie. 'How – '

His speech was cut off by several loud sneezes. However beautiful the sleeve-links, it wasn't wise to stand without a coat after being in such a heat.

'How what?' asked Mrs Quantock, when the sneezing was over.

'I've forgotten now. I shall get back to my rolling. A little chilly. I've done half the lawn.'

A telephone bell had been ringing for the last few seconds, and Mrs Quantock localised it as being in his house, not hers. Georgie was rather deaf, however much he pretended not to be.

'Your telephone bell's ringing, Georgie,' she said.

'I thought it was,' said Georgie, who had not heard it at all.

'And come in presently for a cup of tea,' shouted Mrs Quantock.

'Should love to. But I must have a bath first.'

Georgie hurried indoors, for a telephone call usually meant a little gossip with a friend. A very familiar voice, though a little husky and broken, asked if it was he.

'Yes, it's me, Lucia,' he said in soft firm tones of sympathy. 'How are you?'

Lucia sighed. It was a long, very audible, intentional sigh. Georgie could visualise her putting her mouth quite close to the telephone, so as to make sure it carried. 'Quite well,' she said. 'And so is my Peppino, thank heaven. Bearing up wonderfully. He's just gone.'

Georgie was on the point of asking where, but guessed in time.

'I see,' he said. 'And you didn't go. I'm very glad. So wise.'

'I felt I couldn't,' she said, 'and he urged me not. It's tomorrow. He sleeps in London tonight – '

(Again Georgie longed to say 'where', for it was impossible not to wonder if he would sleep in the house of unknown locality near Harrod's.)

'And he'll be back tomorrow evening,' said Lucia without pause. 'I wonder if you would take pity on me and come and dine. Just something to eat, you know: the house is so upset. Don't dress.'

'Delighted,' said Georgie, though he had ordered oysters. But they could be scolloped for tomorrow . . . 'Love to come.'

'Eight o'clock then? Nobody else of course. If you care to bring our Mozart duet.'

'Rather,' said Georgie. 'Good for you to be occupied, Lucia. We'll have a good go at it.'

'Dear Georgie,' said Lucia faintly. He heard her sigh again, not quite so successfully, and replace the earpiece with a click.

Georgie moved away from the telephone, feeling immensely busy: there was so much to think about and to do. The first thing was to speak about the oysters, and, his parlour-maid being out, he called down the kitchen-stairs. The absence of Foljambe made it necessary for him to get his bath ready himself, and he turned the hot-water tap half on, so that he could run downstairs again and out into the garden (for there was not time to finish the lawn if he was to have a bath and change before tea) in order to put the roller back in the shed. Then he had to get his clothes out, and select something which would do for tea and also for dinner, as Lucia had told him not to dress. There was a new suit which he had not worn yet, rather daring, for the trousers, dark fawn, were distinctly of Oxford cut, and he felt quite boyish as he looked at them. He had ordered them in a moment of reckless sartorial courage, and a quiet tea with Daisy Quantock, followed by a quiet dinner with Lucia, was just the way to make a beginning with them, far better than wearing them for the first time at church on Sunday, when the whole of Riseholme simultaneously would see them. The coat and waistcoat were very dark blue: they would look blue at tea and black at dinner; and there were some grey silk socks, rather silvery, and a tie to match them. These took some time to find, and his search was interrupted by volumes of steam pouring into his bedroom from his bathroom; he ran in to find the bath full nearly to the brim of boiling water. It had been little more than lukewarm yesterday, and his cook had evidently taken to heart his too-sharp words after breakfast this morning. So he had to pull up the plug of his bath to let the boiling contents subside, and fill up with cold.

He went back to his bedroom and began undressing. All this news about Lucia and Peppino, with Daisy Quantock's penetrating comments, was intensely interesting. Old Miss Lucas had been in this nursing-home or private asylum for years, and Georgie didn't suppose that the inclusive charges could be less than fifteen pounds a week, and fifteen times fifty-two was a large sum. That was income too, and say it was at five per cent, the capital it represented was considerable. Then there was that house in London. If it was freehold, that meant a great deal more capital: if it was on lease it meant a great deal more income. Then there were rates and taxes, and the wages of a caretaker, and no doubt a margin. And there were the pearls.

Georgie took a half-sheet of paper from the drawer in a writing-table where he kept half-sheets and pieces of string untied from parcels, and began to calculate. There was necessarily a good deal of guesswork about it, and the pearls had to be omitted altogether, since nobody could say what 'pearls' were worth without knowing their quantity or quality. But even omitting these, and putting quite a low figure on the possible rent of the house near Harrod's, he was astounded at the capital which these annual outgoings appeared to represent.

'I don't put it at a penny less than fifty thousand pounds,' he said to himself, 'and the income at two thousand six hundred.'

He had got a little chilly as he sat at his figures, and with a luxurious foretaste of a beautiful hot bath, he hurried into his bathroom. The whole of the boiling water had run out.

'How tarsome! Damn!' said Georgie, putting in the plug and turning on both taps simultaneously.

His calculations, of course, had only been the materials on which his imagination built, and as he dressed it was hard at work, between glances at his trousers as reflected in the full-length mirror which stood in his window. What would Lucia and Peppino do with this vast increase of fortune? Lucia already had the biggest house in Riseholme and the most Elizabethan decor, and a motor, and as many new clothes as she chose. She did not spend much on them because her lofty mind despised clothes, but Georgie permitted himself to indulge cynical reflections that the pearls might make her dressier. Then she already entertained as much as she felt disposed; and more money would not make her wish to give more dinners. And she went up to London whenever there was anything in the way of pictures or plays or music which she felt held the seed of culture. Society (so-called) she despised as thoroughly as she despised clothes, and always said she came back to Riseholme feeling intellectually starved. Perhaps she would endow a permanent fund for holding Mayday revels on the village green, for Lucia had said she meant to have Mayday revels every year. They had been a great success last year, though fatiguing, for everybody dressed up in sixteenth-century costume, and danced Morris dances till they all hobbled home dead lame at the merciful sunset. It had all been wonderfully Elizabethan, and Georgie's jerkin had hurt him very much.

Lucia was a wonderful character, thought Georgie, and she would find a way to spend two or three thousand a year more in an edifying and cultured manner. (Were Oxford trousers meant to turn up at the bottom? He thought not: and how small these voluminous folds made your feet look.) Georgie knew what he himself would do with two or three thousand a year more: indeed he had often considered whether he would not try to do it without. He wanted, ever so much, to have a little flat in London (or a couple of rooms would serve), just for a dip every now and then in the life which Lucia found so vapid. But he knew he wasn't a strong, serious character like Lucia, whose only frivolities were artistic or Elizabethan.

His eye fell on a large photograph on the table by his bedside in a silver frame, representing Brünnhilde. It was signed 'Olga to beloved Georgie', and his waistcoat felt quite tight as, drawing in a long breath, he recalled that wonderful six months when Olga Bracely, the prima-donna, had bought Old Place, and lived here, and had altered all the values of everything. Georgie believed himself to have been desperately in love with her, but it had been a very exciting time for more reasons than that. Old values had gone: she had thought Riseholme the most splendid joke that had ever been made; she loved them all and laughed at them all, and nobody minded a bit, but followed her whims as if she had been a Pied Piper. All but Lucia, that is to say, whose throne had, quite unintentionally on Olga's part, been pulled smartly from under her, and her sceptre flew in one direction, and her crown in another. Then Olga had gone off for an operatic tour in America, and, after six triumphant months there, had gone on to Australia. But she would be back in England by now, for she was singing in London this season, and her house at Riseholme, so long closed, would be open again . . . And the coat buttoned beautifully, just the last button, leaving the rest negligently wide and a little loose. Georgie put an amethyst tie-pin in his grey tie, which gave a pretty touch of colour, brushed his hair back from his forehead, so that the *toupée* was quite indistinguishable from his own hair, and hurried downstairs to go out to tea with Daisy Quantock.

Daisy was seated at her writing-table when he entered, very busy with a pencil and piece of paper and counting something up on her fingers. Her gardening-fork lay in the grate with the fire-irons, on the carpet there were one or two little sausages of garden-mould, which no doubt had peeled off from her boots, and her gardening gloves were on the floor by her side. Georgie instantly registered the conclusion that something important must have occurred, and that she had come indoors in a great hurry, because the carpet was nearly new, and she always made a great fuss if the smallest atom of cigarette ash dropped on it.

'Thirty-seven, forty-seven, fifty-two, and carry five,' she muttered, as Georgie stood in front of the fire, so that the entire new suit should be seen at once. 'Wait a moment, Georgie – and seventeen and five's twenty-three – no, twenty-two, and that's put me out: I must begin again. That can't be right. Help yourself, if de Vere has brought in tea, and if not ring – Oh, I left out the four, and altogether it's two thousand five hundred pounds.'

Georgie had thought at first that Daisy was merely doing some belated household accounts, but the moment she said two thousand five hundred pounds he guessed, and did not even go through the formality of asking what was two thousand five hundred pounds.

'I made it two thousand six hundred,' he said. 'But we're pretty well agreed.'

Naturally Daisy understood that he understood.

'Perhaps you reckoned the pearls as capital,' she said, 'and added the interest.'

'No I didn't,' he said. 'How could I tell how much they were worth? I didn't reckon them in at all.'

'Well, it's a lot of money,' said Daisy. 'Let's have tea. What will she do with it?'

She seemed quite blind to the Oxford trousers, and Georgie wondered whether that was from mere feebleness of vision. Daisy was short-sighted, though she steadily refused to recognise that, and would never wear spectacles. In fact, Lucia had made an unkind little epigram about it at a time when there was a slight coolness between the two, and had said 'Dear Daisy is too short-sighted to see how short-sighted she is.' Of course it was unkind, but very brilliant, and Georgie had read through *The Importance of Being Earnest* which Lucia had gone up to town to see, in the hopes of discovering it . . . Or was Daisy's unconsciousness of his trousers merely due to her preoccupation with Lucia's probable income? . . . Or were the trousers, after all, not so daring as he had thought them?

He sat down with one leg thrown carelessly over the arm of his chair, so that Daisy could hardly fail to see it. Then he took a piece of teacake.

'Yes, do tell me what you think she will do with it?' he asked. 'I've been puzzling over it too.'

'I can't imagine,' said Daisy. 'She's got everything she wants now.

Perhaps they'll just hoard it, in order that when Peppino dies we may all see how much richer he was than we ever imagined. That's too posthumous for me. Give me what I want now, and a pauper's funeral afterwards.'

'Me too,' said Georgie, waving his leg. 'But I don't think Lucia will do that. It did occur to me – '

'The house in London, you mean,' said Daisy, swiftly interrupting. 'Of course if they kept both houses open, with a staff in each, so that they could run up and down as they chose, that would make a big hole in it. Lucia has always said that she couldn't live in London, but she may manage it if she's got a house there.'

'I'm dining with her tonight,' said Georgie. 'Perhaps she'll say something.'

Mrs Quantock was very thirsty with her gardening, and the tea was very hot. She poured it into her saucer and blew on it.

'Lucia would be wise not to waste any time,' she said, 'if she intends to have any fun out of it, for, you know, Georgie, we're beginning to get old. I'm fifty-two. How old are you?'

Georgie disliked that barbarous sort of question. He had been the young man of Riseholme so long that the habit was engrained, and he hardly believed that he was forty-eight.

'Forty-three,' he said, 'but what does it matter how old we are, as long as we're busy and amused? And I'm sure Lucia has got all the energy and life she ever had. I shouldn't be a bit surprised if she made a start in London, and went in for all that. Then, of course, there's Peppino, but he only cares for writing his poetry and looking through his telescope.'

'I hate that telescope,' said Daisy. 'He took me up on to the roof the other night and showed me what he said was Mars, and I'll take my oath he said that the same one was Venus only a week before. But as I couldn't see anything either time, it didn't make much difference.'

The door opened, and Mr Quantock came in. Robert was like a little round brown sarcastic beetle. Georgie got up to greet him, and stood in the full blaze of the light. Robert certainly saw his trousers, for his eyes seemed unable to quit the spreading folds that lay round Georgie's ankles: he looked at them as if he was Cortez and they some new planet. Then without a word he folded his arms and danced a few steps of what was clearly meant to be a sailor's hornpipe.

'Heave-ho, Georgie,' he said. 'Belay there and avast.'

'What is he talking about?' said Daisy.

Georgie, quite apart from his general good nature, always strove to propitiate Mr Quantock. He was far the most sarcastic person in Riseholme and could say sharp things straight off, whereas Georgie had to think a long time before he got a nasty edge to any remark, and then his good nature generally forbade him to slash with it.

'He's talking about my new clothes,' he said, 'and he's being very naughty. Any news?'

'Any news?' was the general gambit of conversation in Riseholme. It could not have been bettered, for there always was news. And there was now.

'Yes, Peppino's gone to the station,' said Mr Quantock. 'Just like a large black crow. Waved a black hand. Bah! Why not call a release a release and have done with it? And if you don't know – why, I'll tell you. It's because they're rolling in riches. Why, I've calculated – '

'Yes?' said Daisy and Georgie simultaneously.

'So you've been calculating too?' said Mr Quantock. 'Might have a sweepstake for the one who gets nearest. I say three thousand a year.'

'Not so much,' said Georgie and Daisy again simultaneously.

'All right. But that's no reason why I shouldn't have a lump of sugar in my tea.'

'Dear me, no,' said Daisy genially. 'But how do you make it up to three thousand?'

'By addition,' said this annoying man. 'There'll be every penny of that. I was at the lending library after lunch, and those who could add made it all that.'

Daisy turned to Georgie.

'You'll be alone with Lucia then tonight,' she said.

'Oh, I knew that,' said Georgie. 'She told me Peppino had gone. I expect he's sleeping in that house tonight.'

Mr Quantock produced his calculations, and the argument waxed hot. It was still raging when Georgie left in order to get a little rest before going on to dinner, and to practise the Mozart duet. He and Lucia hadn't tried it before, so it was as well to practise both parts, and let her choose which she liked. Foljambe had come back from her afternoon out, and told him that there had been a trunk call for him while he was at tea, but she could make nothing of it.

'Somebody in a great hurry, sir,' she said, 'and kept asking if I was – excuse me, sir, if I was Georgie – I kept saying I wasn't, but I'd fetch you. That wouldn't do, and she said she'd telegraph.'

'But who was it?' asked Georgie.

'Couldn't say, sir. She never gave a name, but only kept asking.'

'She?' asked Georgie.

'Sounded like one!' said Foljambe.

'Most mysterious,' said Georgie. It couldn't be either of his sisters, for they sounded not like a she but a he. So he lay down on his sofa to rest a little before he took a turn at the Mozart.

*   *   *

The evening had turned chilly, and he put on his blue cape with the velvet collar to trot across to Lucia's house. The parlour-maid received him with a faint haggard smile of recognition, and then grew funereal again, and preceding him, not at her usual brisk pace, but sadly and slowly, opened the door of the music-room and pronounced his name in a mournful whisper. It was a gay cheerful room, in the ordinary way; now only one light was burning, and from the deepest of the shadows, there came a rustling, and Lucia rose to meet him.

'Georgie, dear,' she said. 'Good of you.'

Georgie held her hand a moment longer than was usual, and gave it a little extra pressure for the conveyance of sympathy. Lucia, to acknowledge that, pressed a little more, and Georgie tightened his grip again to show that he understood, until their respective finger-nails grew white with the conveyance and reception of sympathy. It was rather agonising, because a bit of skin on his little finger had got caught between two of the rings on his third finger, and he was glad when they quite understood each other.

Of course it was not to be expected that in these first moments Lucia should notice his trousers. She herself was dressed in deep mourning, and Georgie thought he recognised the little cap she wore as being that which had faintly expressed her grief over the death of Queen Victoria. But black suited her, and she certainly looked very well. Dinner was announced immediately, and she took Georgie's arm, and with faltering steps they went into the dining-room.

Georgie had determined that his role was to be sympathetic, but bracing. Lucia must rally from this blow, and her suggestion that he should bring the Mozart duet was hopeful. And though her voice was low and unsteady, she did say, as they sat down, 'Any news?'

'I've hardly been outside my house and garden all day,' said Georgie. 'Rolling the lawn. And Daisy Quantock – did you know? – has had a row with her gardener, and is going to do it all herself. So there she was next door with a fork and a wheelbarrow full of manure.'

Lucia gave a wan smile.

'Dear Daisy!' she said. 'What a garden it will be! Anything else?'

'Yes, I had tea with them, and while I was out, there was a trunk call for me. So tarsome. Whoever it was couldn't make any way, and she's going to telegraph. I can't imagine who it was.'

'I wonder!' said Lucia in an interested voice. Then she recollected herself again. 'I had a sort of presentiment, Georgie, when I saw that telegram for Peppino on the table, two days ago, that it was bad news.'

'Curious,' said Georgie. 'And what delicious fish! How do you always manage to get better things than any of us? It tastes of the sea. And I am so hungry after all my work.'

Lucia went firmly on.

'I took it to poor Peppino,' she said, 'and he got quite white. And then – so like him – he thought of me. "It's bad news, darling," he said, "and we've got to help each other to bear it!"'

'So like Peppino,' said Georgie. 'Mr Quantock saw him going to the station. Where is he going to sleep tonight?'

Lucia took a little more fish.

'In Auntie's house in Brompton Square,' she said.

'So *that's* where it is!' thought Georgie. If there was a light anywhere in Daisy's house, except in the attics, he would have to go in for a minute, on his return home, and communicate the news.

'Oh, she had a house there, had she?' he said.

'Yes, a charming house,' said Lucia, 'and full, of course, of dear old memories to Peppino. It will be very trying for him, for he used to go there when he was a boy to see Auntie.'

'And has she left it him?' asked Georgie, trying to make his voice sound unconcerned.

'Yes, and it's a freehold,' said Lucia. 'That makes it easier to dispose of if Peppino settles to sell it. And beautiful Queen Anne furniture.'

'My dear, how delicious!' said Georgie. 'Probably worth a fortune.'

Lucia was certainly rallying from the terrible blow, but she did not allow herself to rally too far, and shook her head sadly.

'Peppino would hate to have to part with Auntie's things,' she said. 'So many memories. He can recollect her sitting at the walnut bureau (one of those tall ones, you know, which let down in front, and the handles of the drawers all original), doing her accounts in the morning. And a picture of her with her pearls over the fireplace by Sargent; quite an early one. Some fine Chinese Chippendale chairs in the dining-room. We must try to keep some of the things.'

Georgie longed to ask a hundred questions, but it would not be wise, for Lucia was so evidently enjoying letting these sumptuous details leak out mingled with memories. He was beginning to feel sure that Daisy's cynical suggestion was correct, and that the stricken desolation of Peppino and Lucia cloaked a very substantial inheritance. Bits of exultation kept peeping out, and Lucia kept poking them back.

'But where will you put all those lovely things, if you sell the house?' he asked. 'Your house here is so perfect already.'

'Nothing is settled yet,' said Lucia. 'Neither he nor I can think of anything but dear Auntie. Such a keen intelligent mind she had when Peppino first remembered her. Very good-looking still in the Sargent picture. And it was all so sudden; when Peppino saw her last she was so full of vigour.'

('That was the time she bit him,' thought Georgie.) Aloud he said: 'Of course you must feel it dreadfully. What is the Sargent? A kit-cat or a full length?'

'Full length, I believe,' said Lucia. 'I don't know where we could put it here. And a William III whatnot. But of course it is not possible to think about that yet. A glass of port?'

'I'm going to give you one,' said Georgie, 'it's just what you want after all your worries and griefs.'

Lucia pushed her glass towards him.

'Just half a glass,' she said. 'You are so dear and understanding, Georgie; I couldn't talk to anyone but you, and perhaps it does me good to talk. There is some wonderful port in Auntie's cellar, Peppino says.'

She rose.

'Let us go into the music-room,' she said. 'We will talk a little more, and then play our Mozart if I feel up to it.'

'That'll do you good too,' said Georgie.

Lucia felt equal to having more illumination than there had been when she rose out of the shadows before dinner, and they established themselves quite cosily by the fire.

'There will be a terrible lot of business for Peppino,' she said. 'Luckily his lawyer is the same firm as Auntie's, and quite a family friend. Whatever Auntie had, so he told us, goes to Peppino, though we haven't really any idea what it is. But with death duties and succession duties, I know we shall have to be prepared to be very poor until they are paid off, and the duties increase so iniquitously in proportion to the inheritance. Then everything in Brompton Square has to be valued, and we have to pay on the entire contents, the very carpets and rugs are priced, and some are beautiful Persians. And then there's the valuer to pay, and all the lawyer's charges. And when all that has been paid and finished, there is the higher supertax.'

'But there's a bigger income,' said Georgie.

'Yes, that's one way of looking at it,' said Lucia. 'But Peppino says that the charges will be enormous. And there's a beautiful music-room.'

Lucia gave him one of her rather gimlet-like looks.

'Georgino, I suppose everybody in Riseholme is all agog to know what Peppino has been left. That is so dreadfully vulgar, but I suppose it's natural. Is everybody talking about it?'

'Well, I have heard it mentioned,' said Georgie. 'But I don't see why it's vulgar. I'm interested in it myself. It concerns you and Peppino, and what concerns one's friends must be of interest to one.'

'*Caro*, I know that,' said Lucia. 'But so much more than the actual money is the responsibility it brings. Peppino and I have all we want for our quiet little needs, and now this great increase of wealth is coming to us – great, that is, compared to our modest little income now – and, as I say, it brings its responsibilities. We shall have to use wisely and without extravagance whatever is left after all these immense expenses have been paid. That meadow at the bottom of the garden, of course, we shall buy at once, so that there will no longer be any fear of its being built over and spoiling the garden. And then perhaps a new telescope for Peppino. But what do I want in Riseholme beyond what I've got? Music and friends, and the power to entertain them, my books and my flowers. Perhaps a library, built on at the end of the wing, where Peppino can be undisturbed, and perhaps every now and then a string-quartet down from London. That will give a great deal of pleasure, and music is more than pleasure, isn't it?'

Again she turned the gimlet-look on to Georgie.

'And then there's the house in Brompton Square,' she said, 'where Auntie was born. Are we to sell that?'

Georgie guessed exactly what was in her mind. It had been in his too, ever since Lucia had alluded to the beautiful music-room. Her voice had lingered over the beautiful music-room: she had seemed to underline it, to caress it, to appropriate it.

'I believe you are thinking of keeping the house and partly living there,' he said.

Lucia looked round, as if a hundred eavesdroppers had entered unaware.

'Hush, Georgie,' she said, 'not a word must be said about that. But it has occurred to both Peppino and me.'

'But I thought you hated London,' he said. 'You're always so glad to get back, you find it so common and garish.'

'It is, compared to the exquisite peace and seriousness of our Riseholme,' she said, 'where there never is a jarring note, at least hardly ever. But there is in London a certain stir and movement which we lack here. In the swim, Georgie, in the middle of things! Perhaps we get too sensitive here where everything is full of harmony and culture, perhaps we are too much sheltered. If I followed my inclination I would never leave our dear Riseholme for a single day. Oh, how easy everything would be if one only followed one's inclination! A morning with my books, an afternoon in my garden, my piano after tea, and a friend like you to come in to dine with my Peppino and me and scold me well, as you'll soon be doing for being so bungling over Mozartino.'

Lucia twirled round the Elizabethan spit that hung in the wide chimney, and again fixed him rather in the style of the Ancient Mariner. Georgie could not choose but hear . . . Lucia's eloquent well-ordered sentences had nothing impromptu about them; what she said was evidently all thought out and probably talked out. If she and Peppino had been talking of nothing else since the terrible blow had shattered them, she could not have been more lucid and crystal-clear.

'Georgie, I feel like a leisurely old horse who has been turned out to grass being suddenly bridled and harnessed again. But there is work and energy in me yet, though I thought that I should be permitted to grow old in the delicious peace and leisure of our dear quiet humdrum Riseholme. But I feel that perhaps that is not to be. My conscience is cracking the whip at me, and saying "You've got to trot again, you lazy old thing." And I've got to think of Peppino. Dear, contented Peppino would never complain if I refused to budge. He would read his paper, and potter in the garden, and write his dear little poems – such a sweet one, "Bereavement", he began it yesterday, a sonnet – and look at the stars. But is it a life for a man?'

Georgie made an uneasy movement in his chair, and Lucia hastened to correct the implied criticism.

'You're different, my dear,' she said. 'You've got that wonderful power of being interested in everything. Everything. But think what London would give Peppino! His club: the Astronomer-Royal is a member, his other club, political, and politics have lately been quite an obsession with him. The reading-room at the British Museum. No, I should be very selfish if I did not see all that. I must and I do think of Peppino. I mustn't be selfish, Georgie.'

This idea of Lucia's leaving Riseholme was a live bomb. At the moment of its explosion, Georgie seemed to see Riseholme fly into a thousand disintegrated fragments. And then, faintly, through the smoke he seemed to see Riseholme still intact. Somebody, of course, would have to fill the vacant throne and direct its affairs. And the thought of Beau Nash at Bath flitted across the distant horizon of his mind. It was a naughty thought, but its vagueness absolved it from treason. He shook it off.

'But how on earth are we to get on without you?' he asked.

'Sweet of you to say that, Georgie,' said she, giving another twirl to the spit. (There had been a leg of mutton roasted on it last Mayday, while they all sat round in jerkins and stomachers and hose, and all the perfumes of Arabia had hardly sufficed to quell the odour of roast meat which had pervaded the room for weeks afterwards.) 'Sweet of you to say that, but you mustn't think that I am deserting Riseholme. We should be in London perhaps (though, as I say, nothing is settled) for two or three months in the summer, and always come here for weekends, and perhaps from November till Christmas, and a little while in the spring. And then Riseholme would always be coming up to us. Five spare bedrooms, I believe, and one of them quite a little suite with a bathroom and sitting-room attached. No, dear Georgie, I would never desert my dear Riseholme. If it was a choice between London and Riseholme, I should not hesitate in my choice.'

'Then would you keep both houses open?' asked Georgie, thrilled to the marrow.

'Peppino thought we could manage it,' she said, utterly erasing the impression of the shattered nephew. 'He was calculating it out last night, and with board wages at the other house, if you understand, and vegetables from the country, he thought that with care we could live well within our means. He got quite excited about it, and I heard him walking about long after I had gone to bed. Peppino has such a head for detail. He intends to keep a complete set of things, clothes and sponge and everything in London, so that he will have no luggage. Such a saving of tips and small expenses, in which as he so truly says, money leaks away. Then there will be no garage expenses in London: we shall leave the motor here, and rough it with tubes and taxis in town.'

Georgie was fully as excited as Peppino, and could not be discreet any longer.

'Tell me,' he said, 'how much do you think it will all come to? The money he'll come into, I mean.'

Lucia also threw discretion to the winds, and forgot all about the fact that they were to be so terribly poor for a long time.

'About three thousand a year, Peppino imagines, when everything is paid. Our income will be doubled, in fact.'

Georgie gave a sigh of pure satisfaction. So much was revealed, not only of the future, but of the past, for no one hitherto had known what their income was. And how clever of Robert Quantock to have made so accurate a guess!

'It's too wonderful for you,' he said. 'And I know you'll spend it beautifully. I had been thinking over it this afternoon, but I never thought it would be as much as that. And then there are the pearls. I do congratulate you.'

Lucia suddenly felt that she had shown too much of the silver (or was it gold?) lining to the cloud of affliction that had over-shadowed her.

'Poor Auntie!' she said. 'We don't forget her through it all. We hoped she might have been spared us a little longer.'

That came out of her note to Daisy Quantock (and perhaps to others as well), but Lucia could not have known that Georgie had already been told about that.

'Now, I've come here to take your mind off these sad things,' he said. 'You mustn't dwell on them any longer.'

She rose briskly.

'You've been ever so good to me,' she said. 'I should just have moped if I had been alone.'

She lapsed into the baby-language which they sometimes spoke, varying it with easy Italian.

'Ickle music, Georgie?' she said. 'And you must be kindy-kindy to me. No practice all these days. You brought Mozart? Which part is easiest? Lucia wants to take easiest part.'

'Lucia shall take which ever part she likes,' said Georgie, who had had a good practice at both.

'Treble then,' said Lucia. 'But oh, how diffy it looks! Hundreds of ickle notes. And me so stupid at reading! Come on then. You begin, *Uno, due, tre.*'

The light by the piano was not very good, but Georgie did not want to put on his spectacles unless he was obliged, for he did not think

Lucia knew that he wore them, and somehow spectacles did not seem to 'go' with Oxford trousers. But it was no good, and after having made a miserable hash of the first page, he surrendered.

'Me must put on speckies,' he said. 'Me a blind old man.'

Then he had an immense surprise.

'And me a blind old woman,' said Lucia. 'I've just got speckies too. Oh, Georgie, aren't we getting *vecchio*? Now we'll start again. *Uno, due* – '

The Mozart went beautifully after that, and each of them inwardly wondered at the accuracy of the other's reading. Lucia suspected that Georgie had been having a try at it, but then, after all, she had had the choice of which part she would take, and if Georgie had practised already, he would have been almost certain to have practised the treble; it never entered her head that he had been so thorough as to practise both. Then they played it through again, changing parts, and again it went excellently. It was late now, and soon Georgie rose to go.

'And what shall I say if anybody who knows I've been dining with you, asks if you've told me anything?' he asked.

Lucia closed the piano and concentrated.

'Say nothing of our plans about the house in Brompton Square,' she said, 'but there's no reason why people shouldn't know that there is a house there. I hate secretiveness, and after all, when the will comes out, everyone will know. So say there is a house there, full of beautiful things. And similarly they will know about the money. So say what Peppino thinks it will come to.'

'I see,' said Georgie.

She came with him to the door, and strolled out into the little garden in front where the daffodils were in flower. The night was clear, but moonless, and the company of stars burned brightly.

'Aldebaran!' said Lucia, pointing inclusively to the spangled arch of the sky. 'That bright one. Oh, Georgie, how restful it is to look at Aldebaran if one is worried and sad. It lifts one's mind above petty cares and personal sorrows. The patens of bright gold! Wonderful Shakespeare! Look in tomorrow afternoon, won't you, and tell me if there is any news. Naturally, I shan't go out.'

'Oh, come and have lunch,' said Georgie.

'No, dear Georgie: the funeral is at two. Putney Vale. *Buona notte.*'

'*Buona notte*, dear Lucia,' he said.

*　　*　　*

Georgie hurried back to his house, and was disappointed to see that there were no lights in Daisy's drawing-room nor in Robert Quantock's study. But when he got up to his bedroom, where Foljambe had forgotten to pull down the blinds, he saw a light in Daisy's bedroom. Even as he looked the curtains there were drawn back, and he saw her amply clad in a dressing-gown, opening windows at top and bottom, for just now the first principle of health consisted in sleeping in a gale. She too must have seen his room was lit, and his face at the window, for she made violent signs to him, and he threw open the casement.

'Well?' she said.

'In Brompton Square,' said George. 'And three thousand a year!'

'No!' said Daisy.

Chapter Two

This simple word 'No' connoted a great deal in the Riseholme vernacular. It was used, of course, as a mere negative, without emphasis, and if you wanted to give weight to your negative you added 'Certainly not.' But when you used the word 'No' with emphasis, as Daisy had used it from her bedroom window to Georgie, it was not a negative at all, and its signification briefly put was 'I never heard anything so marvellous, and it thrills me through and through. Please go on at once, and tell me a great deal more, and then let us talk it all over.'

On that occasion Georgie did not go on at once, for having made his climax he, with supreme art, shut the window and drew down the blind, leaving Daisy to lie awake half the night and ponder over this remarkable news, and wonder what Peppino and Lucia would do with all that money. She arrived at several conclusions: she guessed that they would buy the meadow beyond the garden, and have a new telescope, but the building of a library did not occur to her. Before she went to sleep an even more important problem presented itself, and she scribbled a note to Georgie to be taken across in the morning early, in which she wrote, 'And did she say anything about the house? What's going to happen to it? And you didn't tell me the number,' exactly as she would have continued the conversation if he had not shut his window so quickly and drawn down the blind, ringing down the curtain on his magnificent climax.

Foljambe brought up this note with Georgie's early-morning tea and the glass of very hot water which sometimes he drank instead of it if he suspected an error of diet the night before, and the little glass gallipot of Kruschen salts, which occasionally he added to the hot water or the tea. Georgie was very sleepy, and, only half awake, turned round in bed, so that Foljambe should not see the place where he wore the *toupée*, and smothered a snore, for he would not like her to think that he snored. But when she said 'Telegram for you, sir,' Georgie sat up at once in his pink silk pyjamas.

'No!' he said with emphasis.

He tore the envelope open, and a whole sheaf of sheets fell out. The moment he set eyes on the first words, he knew so well from whom it came that he did not even trouble to look at the last sheet where it would be signed.

Beloved Georgie [it ran] – I rang you up till I lost my temper and so send this. Most expensive, but terribly important. I arrived in London yesterday and shall come down for weekend to Rise-holme. Shall dine with you Saturday all alone to hear about everything. Come to lunch and dinner Sunday, and ask everybody to one or other, particularly Lucia. Am bringing cook, but order sufficient food for Sunday. Wonderful American and Australian tour, and I'm taking house in London for season. Shall motor down. Bless you.

OLGA

Georgie sprang out of bed, merely glancing through Daisy's pencilled note and throwing it away. There was nothing to be said to it in any case, since he had been told not to divulge the project with regard to the house in Brompton Square, and he didn't know the number. But in Olga's telegram there was enough to make anybody busy for the day, for he had to ask all her friends to lunch or dinner on Sunday, order the necessary food, and arrange a little meal for Olga and himself tomorrow night. He scarcely knew what he was drinking, tea or hot water or Kruschen salts, so excited was he. He foresaw too, that there would be call for the most skilled diplomacy with regard to Lucia. She must certainly be asked first, and some urging might be required to make her consent to come at all, either to lunch or dinner, even if due regard was paid to her deep mourning, and the festivity limited to one or two guests of her own selection. Yet somehow Georgie felt that she would stretch a point and be persuaded, for everybody else would be going some time on Sunday to Olga's, and it would be tiresome for her to explain again and again in the days that followed that she had been asked and had not felt up to it. And if she didn't explain carefully every time, Riseholme would be sure to think she hadn't been asked. 'A little diplomacy' thought George, as he trotted across to her house after breakfast with no hat, but a fur tippet round his neck.

He was shown into the music-room, while her maid went to fetch her. The piano was open, so she had evidently been practising, and there was a copy of the Mozart duet which she had read so skilfully last night on the music rest. For the moment Georgie thought he must have forgotten to take his copy away with him, but then looking at it more carefully he saw that there were pencilled marks for the fingering scribbled over the more difficult passages in the treble, which certainly he had never put there. At the moment he saw Lucia through the window coming up the garden, and he hastily took a chair far away from the piano and buried himself in *The Times*.

They sat close together in front of the fire, and Georgie opened his errand.

'I heard from Olga this morning,' he said, 'a great long telegram. She is coming down for the weekend.'

Lucia gave a wintry smile. She did not care for Olga's coming down. Riseholme was quite silly about Olga.

'That will be nice for you, Georgie,' she said.

'She sent you a special message,' said he.

'I am grateful for her sympathy,' said Lucia. 'She might perhaps have written direct to me, but I'm sure she was full of kind intentions. As she sent the message by you verbally, will you verbally thank her? I appreciate it.'

Even as she delivered these icy sentiments, Lucia got up rather hastily and passed behind him. Something white on the music rest of the piano had caught her eye.

'Don't move, Georgie,' she said, 'sit and warm yourself and light your cigarette. Anything else?'

She walked up the room to the far end where the piano stood, and Georgie, though he was a little deaf, quite distinctly heard the rustle of paper. The most elementary rudiments of politeness forbade him to look round. Besides he knew exactly what was happening. Then there came a second rustle of paper, which he could not interpret.

'Anything else, Georgie?' repeated Lucia, coming back to her chair.

'Yes. But Olga's message wasn't quite that,' he said. 'She evidently hadn't heard of your bereavement.'

'Odd,' said Lucia. 'I should have thought perhaps that the death of Miss Amy Lucas – however, what was her message then?'

'She wanted you very much – she said "particularly Lucia" – to go to lunch or dine with her on Sunday. Peppino, too, of course.'

'So kind of her, but naturally quite impossible,' said Lucia.

'Oh, but you mustn't say that,' said Georgie. 'She is down for just that day, and she wants to see all her old friends. Particularly Lucia, you know. In fact she asked me to get up two little parties for her at lunch and dinner. So, of course, I came to see you first, to know which you would prefer.'

Lucia shook her head.

'A party!' she said. 'How do you think I could?'

'But it wouldn't be *that* sort of party,' said Georgie. 'Just a few of your friends. You and Peppino will have seen nobody tonight and all tomorrow. He will have told you everything by Sunday. And so bad to sit brooding.'

The moment Lucia had said it was quite impossible she had been longing for Georgie to urge her, and had indeed been prepared to encourage him to urge her if he didn't do so of his own accord. His last words had given her an admirable opening.

'I wonder!' she said. 'Perhaps Peppino might feel inclined to go, if there really was no party. It doesn't do to brood: you are right, I mustn't let him brood. Selfish of me not to think of that. Who would there be, Georgie?'

'That's really for you to settle,' he said.

'You?' she asked.

'Yes,' said Georgie, thinking it unnecessary to add that Olga was dining with him on Saturday, and that he would be at lunch and dinner on Sunday. 'Yes: she asked me to come.'

'Well, then, what if you asked poor Daisy and her husband?' said Lucia. 'It would be a treat for them. That would make six. I think six would be enough. I will do my best to persuade Peppino.'

'Capital,' said Georgie. 'And would you prefer lunch or dinner?'

Lucia sighed.

'I think dinner,' she said. 'One feels more capable of making the necessary effort in the evening. But, of course, it is all conditional on Peppino's feeling.'

She glanced at the clock.

'He will just be leaving Brompton Square,' she said. 'And then, afterwards, his lawyer is coming to lunch with him and have a talk. Such a lot of business to see to.'

Georgie suddenly remembered that he did not yet know the number of the house.

'Indeed there must be,' he said. 'Such a delightful square, but rather noisy, I should think, at the lower end.'

'Yes, but deliciously quiet at the top end,' said Lucia. 'A curve you know, and a cul-de-sac. Number twenty-five is just before the beginning of the curve. And no houses at the back. Just the peaceful old churchyard – though sad for Peppino to look out on this morning – and a footpath only up to Ennismore Gardens. My music-room looks out at the back.'

Lucia rose.

'Well, Georgie, you will be very busy this morning,' she said, 'getting all the guests for Sunday, and I mustn't keep you. But I should like to play you a morsel of Stravinski which I have been trying over. Terribly modern, of course, and it may sound hideous to you at first, and at best it's a mere little tinkle if you compare it with the immortals. But there is something about it, and one mustn't condemn all modern work unheard. There was a time no doubt when even Beethoven's greatest sonatas were thought to be modern and revolutionary.'

She led the way to the piano, where on the music rest was the morsel of Stravinski, which explained the second and hitherto un-intelligible rustle.

'Sit by me, Georgie,' she said, 'and turn over quick, when I nod. Something like this.'

Lucia got through the first page beautifully, but then everything seemed to go wrong. Georgie had expected it all to be odd and aimless, but surely Stravinski hadn't meant quite what Lucia was playing. Then he suddenly saw that the key had been changed, but in a very inconspicuous manner, right in the middle of a bar, and Lucia had not observed this. She went on playing with amazing agility, nodded at the end of the second page, and then luckily the piece changed back again into its original clef. Would it be wise to tell her? He thought not: next time she tried it, or the time after, she would very likely notice the change of key.

A brilliant roulade consisting of chromatic scales in contrary directions, brought this firework to an end, and Lucia gave a little shiver.

'I must work at it,' she said, 'before I can judge of it . . .'

Her fingers strayed about the piano, and she paused. Then with the wistful expression Georgie knew so well, she played the first movement of the 'Moonlight Sonata'. Georgie set his face also into the Beethoven-expression, and at the end gave the usual little sigh.

'Divine,' he said. 'You never played it better. Thank you, Lucia.'

She rose.

'You must thank immortal Beethoven,' she said.

*   *   *

Georgie's head buzzed with inductive reasoning, as he hurried about on his vicariously hospitable errands. Lucia had certainly determined to make a second home in London, for she had distinctly said 'my music-room' when she referred to the house in Brompton Square. Also it was easy to see the significance of her deigning to touch Stravinski with even the tip of one finger. She was visualising herself in the modern world, she was going to be up-to-date: the music-room in Brompton Square was not only to echo with the first movement of the 'Moonlight' . . . 'It's too thrilling,' said Georgie, as, warmed with this mental activity, he quite forgot to put on his fur tippet.

His first visit, of course, was to Daisy Quantock, but he meant to stay no longer than just to secure her and her husband for dinner on Sunday with Olga, and tell her the number of the house in Brompton Square. He found that she had dug a large trench round her mulberry tree, and was busily pruning the roots with the wood-axe by the light of Nature: in fact she had cut off all their ends, and there was a great pile of chunks of mulberry root to be transferred in the wheelbarrow, now empty of manure, to the woodshed.

'Twenty-five, that's easy to remember,' she said. 'And are they going to sell it?'

'Nothing settled,' said Georgie. 'My dear, you're being rather drastic, aren't you? Won't it die?'

'Not a bit,' said Daisy. 'It'll bear twice as many mulberries as before. Last year there was one. You should always prune the roots of a fruit tree that doesn't bear. And the pearls?'

'No news,' said Georgie, 'except that they come in a portrait of the aunt by Sargent.'

'No! By Sargent?' asked Daisy.

'Yes. And Queen Anne furniture and Chinese Chippendale chairs,' said Georgie.

'And how many bedrooms?' asked Daisy, wiping her axe on the grass.

'Five spare, so I suppose that means seven,' said Georgie, 'and one with a sitting-room and bathroom attached. And a beautiful music-room.'

'Georgie, she means to live there,' said Daisy, 'whether she told you or not. You don't count the bedrooms like that in a house you're going to sell. It isn't done.'

'Nothing settled, I tell you,' said Georgie. 'So you'll dine with Olga on Sunday, and now I must fly and get people to lunch with her.'

'No! A lunch-party too?' asked Daisy.

'Yes. She wants to see everybody.'

'And five spare rooms, did you say?' asked Daisy, beginning to fill in her trench.

Georgie hurried out of the front gate, and Daisy shovelled the earth back and hurried indoors to impart all this news to her husband. He had a little rheumatism in his shoulder, and she gave him Coué treatment before she counter-ordered the chicken which she had bespoken for his dinner on Sunday.

Georgie thought it wise to go first to Olga's house, to make sure that she had told her caretaker that she was coming down for the weekend. That was the kind of thing that prima-donnas sometimes forgot. There was a man sitting on the roof of Old Place with a coil of wire, and another sitting on the chimney. Though listening-in had not yet arrived at Riseholme, Georgie at once conjectured that Olga was installing it, and what would Lucia say? It was utterly un-Elizabethan to begin with, and though she countenanced the telephone, she had expressed herself very strongly on the subject of listening-in. She had had an unfortunate experience of it herself, for on a visit to London not long ago, her hostess had switched it on, and the company was regaled with a vivid lecture on pyorrhea by a hospital nurse . . . Georgie, however, would see Olga before Lucia came to dinner on Sunday and would explain her abhorrence of the instrument.

Then there was the delightful task of asking everybody to lunch. It was the hour now when Riseholme generally was popping in and out of shops, and finding out the news. It was already known that Georgie had dined with Lucia last night and that Peppino had gone to his aunt's funeral, and everyone was agog to ascertain if anything definite had yet been ascertained about the immense fortune which had certainly come to the Lucases . . . Mrs Antrobus spied Georgie going into Olga's house (for the keenness of her eyesight made up for her deafness), and there she was with her ear-trumpet adjusted, looking at the view just outside Old Place when Georgie came out. Already the popular estimate had grown like a gourd.

'A quarter of a million, I'm told, Mr Georgie,' said she, 'and a house in Grosvenor Square, eh?'

Before Georgie could reply, Mrs Antrobus's two daughters, Piggy and Goosie, came bounding up hand in hand. Piggy and Goosie never walked like other people: they skipped and gambolled to show how girlish an age is thirty-four and thirty-five.

'Oh stop, Mr Georgie,' said Piggy. 'Let us all hear. And are the pearls worth a queen's ransom?'

'Silly thing,' said Goosie. 'I don't believe in the pearls.'

'Well, I don't believe in Grosvenor Square,' said Goosie. 'So silly yourself!'

When this ebullition of high spirits had subsided, and Piggy had slapped Goosie on the back of her hands, they both said 'Hush!' simultaneously.

'Well, I can't say about the pearls,' said Georgie.

'Eh, what can't you say?' said Mrs Antrobus.

'About the pearls,' said Georgie, addressing himself to the end of Mrs Antrobus's trumpet. It was like the trunk of a very short elephant, and she waved it about as if asking for a bun.

'About the pearls, mamma,' screamed Goosie and Piggy together. 'Don't interrupt Mr Georgie.'

'And the house isn't in Grosvenor Square, but in Brompton Square,' said Georgie.

'But that's quite in the slums,' said Mrs Antrobus. 'I am disappointed.'

'Not at all, a charming neighbourhood,' said Georgie. This was not at all what he had been looking forward to: he had expected cries of envious surprise at his news. 'As for the fortune, about three thousand a year.'

'Is that all?' said Piggy with an air of deep disgust.

'A mere pittance to millionaires like Piggy,' said Goosie, and they slapped each other again.

'Any more news?' asked Mrs Antrobus.

'Yes,' said Georgie, 'Olga Bracely is coming down tomorrow – '

'No!' said all the ladies together.

'And her husband?' asked Piggy.

'No,' said Georgie without emphasis. 'At least she didn't say so. But she wants all her friends to come to lunch on Sunday. So you'll all come, will you? She told me to ask everybody.'

'Yes,' said Piggy. 'Oh, how lovely! I adore Olga. Will she let me sit next her?'

'Eh?' said Mrs Antrobus.

'Lunch on Sunday, mamma, with Olga Bracely,' screamed Goosie.

'But she's not here,' said Mrs Antrobus.

'No, but she's coming, mamma,' shouted Piggy. 'Come along, Goosie. There's Mrs Boucher. We'll tell her about poor Mrs Lucas.'

Mrs Boucher's bath-chair was stationed opposite the butcher's, where her husband was ordering the joint for Sunday. Piggy and Goosie had poured the tale of Lucia's comparative poverty into her ear, before Georgie got to her. Here, however, it had a different reception, and Georgie found himself the hero of the hour.

'An immense fortune. I call it an immense fortune,' said Mrs Boucher, emphatically, as Georgie approached. 'Good-morning, Mr Georgie, I've heard your news, and I hope Mrs Lucas will use it well. Brompton Square, too! I had an aunt who lived there once, my mother's sister, you understand, not my father's, and she used to say that she would sooner live in Brompton Square than in Buckingham Palace. What will they do with it, do you suppose? It must be worth its weight in gold. What a strange coincidence that Mr Lucas's aunt and mine should both have lived there! Any more news?'

'Yes,' said Georgie. 'Olga is coming down tomorrow – '

'Well, that's a bit of news!' said Mrs Boucher, as her husband came out of the butcher's shop. 'Jacob, Olga's coming down tomorrow, so Mr Georgie says. That'll make you happy! You're madly in love with Olga, Jacob, so don't deny it. You're an old flirt, Jacob, that's what you are. I shan't get much of your attention till Olga goes away again. I should be ashamed at your age, I should. And young enough to be your daughter or mine either. And three thousand a year, Mr Georgie says. I call it an immense fortune. That's Mrs Lucas, you know. I thought perhaps two. I'm astounded. Why, when old Mrs Toppington – not the wife of the young Mr Toppington who married the niece of the man who invented laughing gas – but of his father, or perhaps his uncle, I can't be quite sure which, but when old Mr Toppington died, he left his son or nephew, whichever it was, a sum that brought him in just about that, and he was considered a very rich man. He had the house just beyond the church at Scroby Windham where my father was rector, and he built the new wing with the billiard-room – '

Georgie knew he would never get through his morning's work if he listened to everything that Mrs Boucher had to say about young Mr Toppington, and broke in.

'And she wants you and the Colonel to lunch with her on Sunday,' he said. 'She told me to ask all her old friends.'

'Well, I do call that kind,' said Mrs Boucher, 'and of course we'll go . . . Jacob, the joint. We shan't want the joint. I was going to give you a veal cutlet in the evening, so what's the good of a joint? Just a bit of steak for the servants, a nice piece. Well, that will be a treat, to lunch with our dear Olga! Quite a party, I dare say.'

Mrs Quantock's chicken, already countermanded, came in nicely for Georgie's dinner for Olga on Saturday, and by the time all his errands were done the morning was gone, without any practice at his piano, or work in his garden, or a single stitch in his new piece of embroidery. Fresh amazements awaited him when he made his fatigued return to his house. For Foljambe told him that Lucia had sent her maid to borrow his manual on auction bridge. He was too tired to puzzle over that now, but it was strange that Lucia, who despised any form of cards as only fit for those who had not the intelligence to talk or to listen, should have done that. Cards came next to crossword puzzles in Lucia's index of inanities. What did it mean?

Neither Lucia nor Peppino were seen in public at all till Sunday morning, though Daisy Quantock had caught sight of Peppino on his arrival on Friday afternoon, walking bowed with grief and with a faltering gait through the little paved garden in front of The Hurst, to his door. Lucia opened it for him, and they both shook their heads sadly and passed inside. But it was believed that they never came out the whole of Saturday, and their first appearance was at church on Sunday, though indeed, Lucia could hardly be said to have appeared, so impenetrable was her black veil. But that, so to speak, was the end of all mourning (besides, everybody knew that she was dining with Olga that night), and at the end of the service, she put up her veil, and held a sort of little reception standing in the porch, and shaking hands with all her friends as they went out. It was generally felt that this signified her re-entry into Riseholme life.

Hardly less conspicuous a figure was Georgie. Though Robert had been so sarcastic about his Oxford trousers, he had made up his mind to get it over, and after church he walked twice round the green quite slowly and talked to everybody, standing a little away so that they should get a complete view. The odious Piggy, it is true, burst into a squeal of laughter and cried, 'Oh, Mr Georgie, I see you've gone into long frocks,' and her mother put up her ear-trumpet as she approached as if to give a greater keenness to her general perceptions. But apart from the jarring incident of Piggy, Georgie was pleased with his trousers' reception. They were beautifully cut too, and fell in charming lines, and the sensation they created was quite a respectful one. But it had been an anxious morning, and he was pleased when it was over.

And such a talk he had had with Olga last night, when she dined alone with him, and sat so long with her elbows on the table that Foljambe looked in three times in order to clear away. Her own adventures, she said, didn't matter; she could tell Georgie about the American tour and the Australian tour, and the coming season in London any time at leisure. What she had to know about with the utmost detail was exactly everything that had happened at Riseholme since she had left it a year ago.

'Good heavens!' she said. 'To think that I once thought that it was a quiet backwatery place where I could rest and do nothing but study. But it's a whirl! There's always something wildly exciting going on. Oh, what fools people are not to take an interest in what they call little things. Now go on about Lucia. It's his aunt, isn't it, and mad?'

'Yes, and Peppino's been left her house in Brompton Square,' began Georgie.

'No! That's where I've taken a house for the season. What number?'

'Twenty-five,' said Georgie.

'Twenty-five?' said Olga. 'Why, that's just where the curve begins. And a big – '

'Music-room built out at the back,' said Georgie.

'I'm almost exactly opposite. But mine's a small one. Just room for my husband and me, and one spare room. Go on quickly.'

'And about three thousand a year and some pearls,' said Georgie. 'And the house is full of beautiful furniture.'

'And will they sell it?'

'Nothing settled,' said Georgie.

'That means you think they won't. Do you think that they'll settle altogether in London?'

'No, I don't think that,' said Georgie very carefully.

'You are tactful. Lucia has told you all about it, but has also said firmly that nothing's settled. So I won't pump you. And I met Colonel Boucher on my way here. Why only one bulldog?'

'Because the other always growled so frightfully at Mrs Boucher. He gave it away to his brother.'

'And Daisy Quantock? Is it still spiritualism?'

'No; that's over, though I rather think it's coming back. After that it was sour milk, and now it's raw vegetables. You'll see tomorrow at dinner. She brings them in a paper bag. Carrots and turnips and celery. Raw. But perhaps she may not. Every now and then she eats like anybody else.'

'And Piggy and Goosie?'

'Just the same. But Mrs Antrobus has got a new ear-trumpet. But what I want to know is, why did Lucia send across for my manual on auction bridge? She thinks all card-games imbecile.'

'Oh, Georgie, that's easy!' said Olga. 'Why, of course, Brompton Square, though nothing's settled. Parties, you know, when she wants people who like to play bridge.'

Georgie became deeply thoughtful.

'It might be that,' he said. 'But it would be tremendously thorough.'

'How else can you account for it? By the way, I've had a listening-in put up at Old Place.'

'I know. I saw them at it yesterday. But don't turn it on tomorrow night. Lucia hates it. She only heard it once, and that time it was a lecture on pyorrhea. Now tell me about yourself. And shall we go into the drawing-room? Foljambe's getting restless.'

Olga allowed herself to be weaned from subjects so much more entrancing to her, and told him of the huge success of the American tour, and spoke of the eight weeks' season which was to begin at Covent Garden in the middle of May. But it all led back to Riseholme.

'I'm singing twice a week,' she said. 'Brünnhilde and Lucrezia and Salome. Oh, my dear, how I love it! But I shall come down here every single weekend. To go back to Lucia: do you suppose she'll settle in London for the season? I believe that's the idea. Fresh worlds to conquer.'

Georgie was silent a moment.

'I think you may be right about the auction bridge,' he said at length. 'And that would account for Stravinski too.'

'What's that?' said Olga greedily.

'Why, she played me a bit of Stravinski yesterday morning,' said Georgie. 'And before she never would listen to anything modern. It all fits in.'

'Perfect,' said Olga.

* * *

Georgie and the Quantocks walked up together the next evening to dine with Olga, and Daisy was carrying a little paper parcel. But that proved to be a disappointment, for it did not contain carrots, but only evening shoes. Lucia and Peppino, as usual, were a little late, for it was Lucia's habit to arrive last at any party, as befitted the Queen of Riseholme, and to make her gracious round of the guests. Everyone of course was wondering if she would wear the pearls, but again there was a disappointment, for her only ornaments were two black bangles, and the brooch of entwined sausages of gold containing a lock of Beethoven's hair. (As a matter of fact Beethoven's hair had fallen out some years ago, and she had replaced it with a lock of Peppino's which was the same colour . . . Peppino had never told anybody.) From the first it was evident that though the habiliments of woe still decked her, she had cast off the numb misery of the bereavement.

'So kind of you to invite us,' she said to Olga, 'and so good,' she added in a whisper, 'for my poor Peppino. I've been telling him he must face the world again and not mope. Daisy, dear! Sweet to see you, and Mr Robert. Georgie! Well, I do think this is a delicious little party.'

Peppino followed her: it was just like the arrival of Royal Personages, and Olga had to stiffen her knees so as not to curtsey.

Having greeted those who had the honour to meet her, Lucia became affable rather than gracious. Robert Quantock was between her and Olga at dinner, but then at dinner, everybody left Robert alone, for if disturbed over that function, he was apt to behave rather like a dog with a bone and growl. But if left alone, he was in an extremely good temper afterwards.

'And you're only here just for two days, Miss Olga,' she said, 'at least so Georgie tells me, and he usually knows your movements. And then London, I suppose, and you'll be busy rehearsing for the opera. I must certainly manage to be in London for a week or two this year, and come to *Siegfried*, and the *Valkyrie*, in which, so I see in the papers, you're singing. Georgie, you must take me up to London when the opera comes on. Or perhaps – '

She paused a moment.

'Peppino, shall I tell all our dear friends our little secret?' she said. 'If you say "no", I shan't. But, please, Peppino – '

Peppino, however, had been instructed to say 'yes', and accordingly did so.

'You see, dear Miss Olga,' said Lucia, 'that a little property has come to us through that grievous tragedy last week. A house has been left to Peppino in Brompton Square, all furnished, and with a beautiful music-room. So we're thinking, as there is no immediate hurry about selling it, of spending a few weeks there this season, very quietly of course, but still perhaps entertaining a few friends. Then we shall have time to look about us, and as the house is there, why not use it in the interval? We shall go there at the end of the month.'

This little speech had been carefully prepared, for Lucia felt that if she announced the full extent of their plan, Riseholme would suffer a terrible blow. It must be broken to Riseholme by degrees: Riseholme must first be told that they were to be up in town for a week or two, pending the sale of the house. Subsequently Riseholme would hear that they were not going to sell the house.

She looked round to see how this section of Riseholme took it. A chorus of the emphatic 'No' burst from Georgie, Mrs Quantock and Olga, who, of course, had fully discussed this disclosure already; even Robert, very busy with his dinner, said 'No' and went on gobbling.

'So sweet of you all to say "No",' said Lucia, who knew perfectly well that the emphatic interjection meant only surprise, and the desire to hear more, not the denial that such a thing was possible, 'but there it is. Peppino and I have talked it over – *non e vero, carissimo* – and we feel that there is a sort of call to us to go to London. Dearest Aunt Amy, you know, and all her beautiful furniture! She never would have a stick of it sold, and that seems to point to the fact that she expected Peppino and me not to wholly desert the dear old family home. Aunt Amy was born there, eighty-three years ago.'

'My dear! How it takes one back!' said Georgie.

'Doesn't it?' said Olga.

Lucia had now, so to speak, developed her full horsepower. Peppino's presence stoked her, Robert was stoking himself and might be disregarded, while Olga and Georgie were hanging on her words.

'But it isn't the past only that we are thinking of,' she said, 'but the present and the future. Of course our spiritual home is here – like Lord Haldane and Germany – and oh, how much we have learned at Riseholme, its lovely seriousness and its gaiety, its culture, its absorption in all that is worthy in art and literature, its old customs, its simplicity.'

'Yes,' said Olga. (She had meant long ago to tell Lucia that she had taken a house in Brompton Square exactly opposite Lucia's, but who could interrupt the splendour that was pouring out on them?)

Lucia fumbled for a moment at the brooch containing Beethoven's hair. She had a feeling that the pin had come undone. 'Dear Miss Olga,' she said, 'how good of you to take an interest, you with your great mission of melody in the world, in our little affairs! I am encouraged. Well, Peppino and I feel – don't we? *sposo mio* – that now that this opportunity has come to us, of perhaps having a little salon in London, we ought to take it. There are modern movements in the world we really know nothing about. We want to educate ourselves. We want to know what the cosmopolitan mind is thinking about. Of course we're old, but it is never too late to learn. How we shall treasure all we are lucky enough to glean, and bring it back to our dear Riseholme.'

There was a slight and muffled thud on the ground, and Lucia's fingers went back where the brooch should have been.

'Georgino, my brooch, the Beethoven brooch,' she said; 'it has fallen.'

Georgie stooped rather stiffly to pick it up: that work with the garden roller had found out his lumbar muscles. Olga rose.

'Too thrilling, Mrs Lucas!' she said. 'You must tell me much more. Shall we go? And how lovely for me: I have just taken a house in Brompton Square for the season.'

'No!' said Lucia. 'Which?'

'Oh, one of the little ones,' said Olga. 'Just opposite yours. Forty-two A.'

'Such dear little houses!' said Lucia. 'I have a music-room. Always yours to practise in.'

'Capital good dinner,' said Robert, who had not spoken for a long time.

Lucia put an arm round Daisy Quantock's ample waist, and thus tactfully avoided the question of precedence. Daisy, of course, was far, far the elder, but then Lucia was Lucia.

'Delicious indeed,' she said. 'Georgie, bring the Beethoven with you.'

'And don't be long,' said Olga.

Georgie had no use for the society of his own sex unless they were young, which made him feel young too, or much older than himself, which had the same result. But Peppino had an unpleasant habit of saying to him 'When we come to our age' (which was an unreasonable assumption of juvenility), and Robert of sipping port with the sound of many waters for an indefinite period. So when Georgie had let Robert have two good glasses, he broke up this symposium and trundled them away into the drawing-room, only pausing to snatch up his embroidery tambour, on which he was working at what had been originally intended for a bedspread, but was getting so lovely that he now thought of putting it when finished on the top of his piano. He noticed that Lucia had brought a portfolio of music, and peeping inside saw the morsel of Stravinski . . .

And then, as he came within range of the conversation of the ladies, he nearly fell down from sheer shock.

'Oh, but I adore it,' Lucia was saying. 'One of the most marvellous inventions of modern times. Were we not saying so last night, Peppino? And Miss Olga is telling me that everyone in London has a listening-in apparatus. Pray turn it on, Miss Olga; it will be a treat to hear it! Ah, the Beethoven brooch: thank you, Georgie – *mille grazie*.'

Olga turned a handle or a screw or something, and there was a short pause: the next item presumably had already been announced. And then, wonder of wonders, there came from the trumpet the first bars of the 'Moonlight Sonata'.

Now the 'Moonlight Sonata' (especially the first movement of it) had an almost sacred significance in Riseholme. It was Lucia's tune, much as God Save the King is the King's tune. Whatever musical entertainment had been going on, it was certain that if Lucia was present she would sooner or later be easily induced to play the first movement of the 'Moonlight Sonata'. Astonished as everybody already was at her not only countenancing but even allowing this mechanism, so lately abhorred by her, to be set to work at all, it was infinitely more amazing that she should permit it to play Her tune. But there she was composing her face to her well-known Beethoven expression, leaning a little forward, with her chin in her hand, and her eyes wearing the faraway look from which the last chord would recall her. At the end of the first movement everybody gave the little sigh which was its due, and the wistful sadness faded from their faces, and Lucia, with a gesture, hushing all attempt at comment or applause, gave a gay little smile to show she knew what was coming next. The smile broadened, as the Scherzo began, into a little ripple of laughter, the hand which had supported her chin once more sought the Beethoven brooch, and she sat eager and joyful and alert, sometimes just shaking her head in wordless criticism, and once saying 'Tut-tut' when the clarity of a run did not come up to her standard, till the sonata was finished.

'A treat,' she said at the end, 'really most enjoyable. That dear old tune! I thought the first movement was a little hurried: Cortot, I remember, took it a little more slowly, and a little more *legato*, but it was very creditably played.'

Olga, at the machine, was out of sight of Lucia, and during the performance Georgie noticed that she had glanced at the Sunday paper. And now when Lucia referred to Cortot, she hurriedly chucked it into a window seat and changed the subject.

'I ought to have stopped it,' she said, 'because we needn't go to the wireless to hear that. Do show us what you mean, Mrs Lucas, about the first movement.'

Lucia glided to the piano.

'Just a bar or two, shall I?' she said.

Everybody gave a sympathetic murmur, and they had the first movement over again.

'Only just my impression of how Cortot plays it,' she said. 'It coincides with my own view of it.'

'Don't move,' said Olga, and everybody murmured 'Don't,' or 'Please.' Robert said 'Please' long after the others, because he was drowsy. But he wanted more music, because he wished to doze a little and not to talk.

'How you all work me!' said Lucia, running her hands up and down the piano with a butterfly touch. 'London will be quite a rest after Riseholme. *Peppino mio*, my portfolio on the top of my cloak; would you? . . . Peppino insisted on my bringing some music: he would not let me start without it.' (This was a piece of picturesqueness during Peppino's absence: it would have been more accurate to say he was sent back for it, but less picturesque.) 'Thank you, *carissimo*. A little morsel of Stravinski; Miss Olga, I am sure, knows it by heart, and I am terrified. Georgie, would you turn over?'

The morsel of Stravinski had improved immensely since Friday: it was still very odd, very modern, but not nearly so odd as when, a few days ago, Lucia had failed to observe the change of key. But it was strange to the true Riseholmite to hear the arch-priestess of Beethoven and the foe of all modern music, which she used to account sheer Bolshevism, producing these scrannel staccato tinklings that had so often made her wince. And yet it all fitted in with her approbation of the wireless and her borrowing of Georgie's manual on auction bridge. It was not the morsel of Stravinski alone that Lucia was practising (the performance though really improved might still be called practice): it was modern life, modern ideas on which she was engaged preparatory to her descent on London. Though still in harbour at Riseholme, so to speak, it was generally felt that Lucia had cast off her cable, and was preparing to put to sea.

'Very pretty: I call that very pretty. Honk!' said Robert when the morsel was finished, 'I call that music.'

'Dear Mr Robert, how sweet of you,' said Lucia, wheeling round on the music-stool. 'Now positively, I will not touch another note. But may we, might we, have another little tune on your wonderful wireless, Miss Olga! Such a treat! I shall certainly have one installed at Brompton Square, and listen to it while Peppino is doing his crossword puzzles. Peppino can think of nothing else now but auction bridge and crossword puzzles, and interrupts me in the middle of my practice to ask for an Athenian sculptor whose name begins with P and is of ten letters.'

'Ah, I've got it,' said Peppino, 'Praxiteles.'

Lucia clapped her hands.

'Bravo,' she said. 'We shall not sit up till morning again.'

There was a splendour in the ruthlessness with which Lucia bowled over, like ninepins, every article of her own Riseholme creed, which saw Bolshevism in all modern art, inanity in crossword puzzles and bridge, and aimless vacuity in London . . . Immediately after the fresh tune on the wireless began, and most unfortunately, they came in for the funeral March of a Marionette. A spasm of pain crossed Lucia's face, and Olga abruptly turned off this sad reminder of unavailing woe.

'Go on: I like that tune!' said the drowsy and thoughtless Robert, and a hurried buzz of conversation covered this melancholy coincidence.

It was already late, and Lucia rose to go.

'Delicious evening!' she said. 'And lovely to think that we shall so soon be neighbours in London as well. My music-room always at your disposal. Are you coming, Georgie?'

'Not this minute,' said Georgie firmly.

Lucia was not quite accustomed to this, for Georgie usually left any party when she left. She put her head in the air as she swept by him, but then relented again.

'Dine tomorrow, then? We won't have any music after this feast tonight,' said she, forgetting that the feast had been almost completely of her own providing. 'But perhaps a little game of cut-throat, you and Peppino and me.'

'Delightful,' said Georgie.

*   *   *

Olga hurried back after seeing off her other guests.

'Oh, Georgie, what richness,' she said. 'By the way, of course it *was* Cortot who was playing the "Moonlight" faster than Cortot plays it.'

Georgie put down his tambour.

474 MAPP AND LUCIA: VOLUME ONE

'I thought it probably would be,' he said. 'That's the kind of thing that happens to Lucia. And now we know where we are. She's going to make a circle in London and be its centre. Too thrilling! It's all as clear as it can be. All we don't know about yet is the pearls.'

'I doubt the pearls,' said Olga.

'No, I think there are pearls,' said Georgie, after a moment's intense concentration. 'Otherwise she wouldn't have told me they appeared in the Sargent portrait of the aunt.'

Olga suddenly gave a wild hoot of laughter.

'Oh, why does one ever spend a single hour away from Riseholme?' she said.

'I wish you wouldn't,' said Georgie. 'But you go off tomorrow?'

'Yes, to Paris. My excuse is to meet my Georgie – '

'Here he is,' said Georgie.

'Yes, bless him. But the one who happens to be my husband. Georgie, I think I'm going to change my name and become what I really am, Mrs George Shuttleworth. Why should singers and actresses call themselves Madame Macaroni or Signora Semolina? Yes, that's my excuse, as I said when you interrupted me, and my reason is gowns. I'm going to have lots of new gowns.'

'Tell me about them,' said Georgie. He loved hearing about dress.

'I don't know about them yet; I'm going to Paris to find out. Georgie, you'll have to come and stay with me when I'm settled in London. And when I go to practise in Lucia's music-room you shall play my accompaniments. And shall I be shingled?'

Georgie's face was suddenly immersed in concentration.

'I wouldn't mind betting – ' he began.

Olga again shouted with laughter.

'If you'll give me three to one that I don't know what you were going to say, I'll take it,' she said.

'But you can't know,' said Georgie.

'Yes I do. You wouldn't mind betting that Lucia will be shingled.'

'Well, you are quick,' said Georgie admiringly.

*   *   *

It was known, of course, next morning, that Lucia and Peppino were intending to spend a few weeks in London before selling the house, and who knew what *that* was going to mean? Already it was time to begin rehearsing for the next May Day revels, and Foljambe, that paragon of all parlour-maids, had been overhauling Georgie's jerkin and hose and dainty little hunting boots with turn-down flaps in order to be ready. But when Georgie, dining at The Hurst next evening, said something about May Day revels (Lucia, of course, would be Queen again) as they played cut-throat with the manual on auction bridge handy for the settlement of such small disputes as might arise over the value of the different suits, she only said: 'Those dear old customs! So quaint! And fifty to me above, Peppino, or is it a hundred? I will turn it up while you deal, Georgie!'

This complete apathy of Lucia to May Day revels indicated one of two things, that either mourning would prevent her being Queen, or absence. In consequence of which Georgie had his jerkin folded up again and put away, for he was determined that nobody except Lucia should drive him out to partake in such a day of purgatory as had been his last year . . . Still, there was nothing conclusive about that: it might be mourning. But evidence accumulated that Lucia meant to make a pretty solid stay in London, for she certainly had some cards printed at Ye Signe of Ye Daffodil on the village green where Peppino's poems were on sale, with the inscription

Mr and Mrs Philip Lucas

request the pleasure of the company of

at .... on ....

25 Brompton Square *R.S.V.P.*

Daisy Quantock had found that out, for she saw the engraved copperplate lying on the counter, and while the shopman's back was turned, had very cleverly read it, though it was printed the wrong way round, and was very confusing. Still she managed to do so, and the purport was plain enough: that Lucia contemplated formally asking somebody to something some time at 25 Brompton Square. 'And would she,' demanded Daisy, with bitter irony, 'have had cards printed like that, if they were only meaning to go up for a week or two?' And if that was not enough Georgie saw a postcard on Lucia's writing-table with 'From Mrs Philip Lucas, 25 Brompton Square, SW3', plainly printed on the top.

It was getting very clear then (and during this week Riseholme naturally thought of nothing else) that Lucia designed a longer residence in the garish metropolis than she had admitted. Since she chose to give no information on the subject, mere pride and scorn of vulgar curiosity forbade anyone to ask her, though of course it was quite proper (indeed a matter of duty) to probe the matter to the bottom by every other means in your power, and as these bits of evidence pieced themselves together, Riseholme began to take a very gloomy view of Lucia's real nature. On the whole it was felt that Mrs Boucher, when she paused in her bath-chair as it was being wheeled round the green, nodding her head very emphatically, and bawling into Mrs Antrobus's ear-trumpet, reflected public opinion.

'She's deserting Riseholme and all her friends,' said Mrs Boucher, 'that's what she's doing. She means to cut a dash in London, and lead London by the nose. There'll be fashionable parties, you'll see, there'll be paragraphs, and then when the season's over she'll come back and swagger about them. For my part I shall take no interest in them. Perhaps she'll bring down some of her smart friends for a Saturday till Monday. There'll be dukes and duchesses at The Hurst. That's what she's meaning to do, I tell you, and I don't care who hears it.'

That was lucky, as anyone within the radius of a quarter of a mile could have heard it.

'Well, never mind, my dear,' said Colonel Boucher, who was pushing his wife's chair.

'Mind? I should hope not, Jacob,' said Mrs Boucher. 'And now let us go home, or we'll be late for lunch and that would never do, for I expect the Prince of Wales and the Lord Chancellor, and we'll play bridge and crossword puzzles all afternoon.'

Such fury and withering sarcasm, though possibly excessive, had, it was felt, a certain justification, for had not Lucia for years given little indulgent smiles when anyone referred to the cheap delights and restless apish chatterings of London? She had always come back from her visits to that truly provincial place which thought itself a centre, wearied with its false and foolish activity, its veneer of culture, its pseudo-Athenian rage for any new thing. They were all busy enough at Riseholme, but busy over worthy objects, over Beethoven and Shakespeare, over high thinking, over study of the true master-pieces. And now, the moment that Aunt Amy's death gave her and Peppino the means to live in the fiddling little ant-hill by the Thames they were turning their backs on all that hitherto had made existence so splendid and serious a reality, and were training, positively training for frivolity by exercises in Stravinski, auction bridge and crossword puzzles. Only the day before the fatal influx of fortune had come to them, Lucia, dropping in on Colonel and Mrs Boucher about teatime, had found them very cosily puzzling out a children's crossword in the evening paper, having given up the adult conundrum as too difficult, had pretended that even this was far beyond her poor wits, and had gone home the moment she had swallowed her tea in order to finish a canto of Dante's *Purgatorio* . . . And it was no use Lucia's saying that they intended only to spend a week or two in Brompton Square before the house was sold: Daisy's quickness and cleverness about the copperplate at Ye Signe of Ye Daffodil had made short work of that. Lucia was evidently the prey of a guilty conscience too: she meant, so Mrs Boucher was firmly convinced, to steal away, leaving the impression she was soon coming back.

Vigorous reflections like these came in fits and spurts from Mrs Boucher as her husband wheeled her home for lunch.

'And as for the pearls, Jacob,' she said, as she got out, hot with indignation, 'if you asked me, actually asked me what I think about the pearls, I should have to tell you that I don't believe in the pearls. There may be half a dozen seed pearls in an old pillbox: I don't say there are not, but that's all the pearls we shall see. Pearls!'

Chapter Three

Georgie had only just come down to breakfast and had not yet opened his *Times*, one morning at the end of this hectic week, when the telephone bell rang. Lucia had not been seen at all the day before and he had a distinct premonition, though he had not time to write it down, that this was she. It was: and her voice sounded very brisk and playful.

'Is that Georgino?' she said. 'Zat oo, Georgie?'

Georgie had another premonition, stronger than the first.

'Yes, it's me,' he said.

'Georgie, is oo coming round to say Ta-ta to poor Lucia and Peppino?' she said.

('I knew it,' thought Georgie.)

'What, are you going away?' he asked.

'Yes, I told you the other night,' said Lucia in a great hurry, 'when you were doing crosswords, you and Peppino. Sure I did. Perhaps you weren't attending. But – '

'No, you never told me,' said Georgie firmly.

'How cwoss oo sounds. But come round, Georgie, about eleven

and have 'ickle chat. We're going to be very stravvy and motor up, and perhaps keep the motor for a day or two.'

'And when are you coming back?' asked Georgie.

'Not quite settled,' said Lucia brightly. 'There's a lot of bizz-bizz for poor Peppino. Can't quite tell how long it will take. Eleven, then?'

Georgie had hardly replaced the receiver when there came a series of bangs and rings at his front door, and Foljambe coming from the kitchen with his dish of bacon in one hand, turned to open it. It was only de Vere with a copy of *The Times* in her hand.

'With Mrs Quantock's compliments,' said de Vere, 'and would Mr Pillson look at the paragraph she has marked, and send it back? Mrs Quantock will see him whenever he comes round.'

'That all?' said Foljambe rather crossly. 'What did you want to knock the house down for then?'

De Vere vouchsafed no reply, but turned slowly in her high-heeled shoes and regarded the prospect.

Georgie also had come into the hall at this battering summons, and Foljambe gave him the paper. There were a large blue pencil mark and several notes of exclamation opposite a short paragraph.

'Mr and Mrs Philip Lucas will arrive today from The Hurst, Riseholme, at 25 Brompton Square.'

'No!' said Georgie. 'Tell Mrs Quantock I'll look in after breakfast,' and he hurried back, and opened his copy of *The Times* to see if it were the same there. It was: there was no misprint, nor could any other interpretation be attached to it. Though he knew the fact already, print seemed to bring it home. Print also disclosed the further fact that Lucia must have settled everything at least before the morning post yesterday, or this paragraph could never have appeared today. He gobbled up his breakfast, burning his tongue terribly with his tea . . .

'It isn't only deception,' said Daisy the moment he appeared without even greeting him, 'for that we knew already, but it's funk as well. She didn't dare tell us.'

'She's going to motor up,' said Georgie, 'starting soon after eleven. She's just asked me to come and say goodbye.'

'That's more deception then,' said Daisy, 'for naturally, having read that, we should have imagined she was going up by the afternoon train, and gone round to say goodbye after lunch, and found her gone. If I were you, I shouldn't dream of going to say goodbye to her after this. She's shaking the dust of Riseholme off her London shoes . . . But we'll have no May Day revels if I've got anything to do with it.'

'Nor me,' said Georgie. 'But it's no use being cross with her. Besides, it's so terribly interesting. I shouldn't wonder if she was writing some invitations on the cards you saw – '

'No, I never saw the cards,' said Daisy, scrupulously. 'Only the plate.'

'It's the same thing. She may be writing invitations now, to post in London.'

'Go a little before eleven then, and see,' said Daisy. 'Even if she's not writing them then, there'll be envelopes lying about perhaps.'

'Come too,' said Georgie.

'Certainly not,' said Daisy. 'If Lucia doesn't choose to tell me she's going away, the only dignified thing to do is to behave as if I knew nothing whatever about it. I'm sure I hope she'll have a very pleasant drive. That's all I can say about it; I take no further interest in her movements. Besides, I'm very busy: I've got to finish weeding my garden, for I've not been able to touch it these last days, and then my planchette arrived this morning. And a ouija board.'

'What's that?' said Georgie.

'A sort of planchette, but much more – much more powerful. Only it takes longer, as it points at letters instead of writing,' said Daisy. 'I shall begin with planchette and take it up seriously, because I know I'm very psychic, and there'll be a little time for it now that we shan't be traipsing round all day in ruffs and stomachers over those May Day revels. Perhaps there'll be May Day revels in Brompton Square for a change. I shouldn't wonder: nothing would surprise me about Lucia now. And it's my opinion we shall get on very well without her.'

Georgie felt he must stick up for her: she was catching it so frightfully hot all round.

'After all, it isn't criminal to spend a few weeks in London,' he observed.

'Whoever said it was?' said Daisy. 'I'm all for everybody doing exactly as they like. I just shrug my shoulders.'

She heaved up her round little shoulders with an effort.

'Georgie, how do you think she'll begin up there?' she said. 'There's that cousin of hers with whom she stayed sometimes, Aggie Sandeman, and then, of course, there's Olga Bracely. Will she just pick up acquaintances, and pick up more from them, like one of those charity snowballs? Will she be presented? Not that I take the slightest interest in it.'

Georgie looked at his watch and rose.

'I do,' he said. 'I'm thrilled about it. I expect she'll manage. After all, we none of us wanted to have May Day revels last year but she got us to. She's got drive.'

'I should call it push,' said Daisy. 'Come back and tell me exactly what's happened.'

'Any message?' asked Georgie.

'Certainly not,' said Daisy again, and began untying the string of the parcel that held the instruments of divination.

Georgie went quickly down the road (for he saw Lucia's motor already at the door) and up the paved walk that led past the sundial, round which was the circular flower-border known as Perdita's border, for it contained only the flowers that Perdita gathered. Today it was all a-bloom with daffodils and violets and primroses, and it was strange to think that Lucia would not go gassing on about Perdita's border, as she always did at this time of the year, but would have to be content with whatever flowers there happened to be in Brompton Square: a few sooty crocuses perhaps and a periwinkle . . . She was waiting for him, kissed her hand through the window, and opened the door.

'Now for little chat,' she said, adjusting a very smart hat, which Georgie was sure he had never seen before. There was no trace of mourning about it: it looked in the highest spirits. So, too, did Lucia.

'Sit down, Georgie,' she said, 'and cheer me up. Poor Lucia feels ever so sad at going away.'

'It is rather sudden,' he said. 'Nobody dreamed you were off today, at least until they saw *The Times* this morning.'

Lucia gave a little sigh.

'I know,' she said, 'but Peppino thought that was the best plan. He said that if Riseholme knew when I was going, you'd all have had little dinners and lunches for us, and I should have been completely worn out with your kindness and hospitality. And there was so much to do, and we weren't feeling much like gaiety. Seen anybody this morning? Any news?'

'I saw Daisy,' said Georgie.

'And told her?'

'No, it was she who saw it in *The Times* first, and sent it round to me,' said Georgie. 'She's got a ouija board, by the way. It came this morning.'

'That's nice,' said Lucia. 'I shall think of Riseholme as being ever so busy. And everybody must come up and stay with me, and you first of all. When will you be able to come?'

'Whenever you ask me,' said Georgie.

'Then you must give me a day or two to settle down, and I'll write to you. You'll be popping across though every moment of the day to see Olga.'

'She's in Paris,' said Georgie.

'No! What a disappointment! I had already written her a card, asking her to dine with us the day after tomorrow, which I was taking up to London to post there.'

'She may be back by then,' said Georgie.

Lucia rose and went to her writing-table, on which, as Georgie was thrilled to observe, was a whole pile of stamped and directed envelopes.

'I think I won't chance it,' said Lucia, 'for I had enclosed another card for Signor Cortese which I wanted her to forward, asking him for the same night. He composed *Lucrezia* you know, which I see is coming out in London in the first week of the Opera Season, with her, of course, in the name-part. But it will be safer to ask them when I know she is back.'

Georgie longed to know to whom all the other invitations were addressed. He saw that the top one was directed to an MP, and guessed that it was for the member for the Riseholme district, who had lunched at The Hurst during the last election.

'And what are you going to do tonight?' he asked.

'Dining with dear Aggie Sandeman. I threw myself on her mercy, for the servants won't have settled in, and I hoped we should have just a little quiet evening with her. But it seems that she's got a large dinner party on. Not what I should have chosen, but there's no help for it now. Oh, Georgie, to think of you in dear old quiet Riseholme and poor Peppino and me gabbling and gobbling at a huge dinner party.'

She looked wistfully round the room.

'Goodbye, dear music-room,' she said, kissing her hand in all directions. 'How glad I shall be to get back! Oh, Georgie, your manual on auction bridge got packed by mistake. So sorry. I'll send it back. Come in and play the piano sometimes, and then it won't feel lonely. We must be off, or Peppino will get fussing. Say goodbye to everyone for us, and explain. And Perdita's border! Will sweet Perdita forgive me for leaving all her lovely flowers and running away to London? After all, Georgie, Shakespeare wrote *The Winter's Tale* in London, did he not? Lovely daffies! And violets dim. Let me give you 'ickle violet, Georgie, to remind you of poor Lucia tramping about in long unlovely streets, as Tennyson said.'

Lucia, so Georgie felt, wanted no more comments or questions about her departure, and went on drivelling like this till she was safely in the motor. She had expected Peppino to be waiting for her and beginning to fuss, but so far from his fussing he was not there at all. So she got in a fuss instead.

'Georgino, will you run back and shout for Peppino?' she said. 'We shall be so late, and tell him that I am sitting in the motor waiting. Ah, there he is! Peppino, where have you been? Do get in and let us start, for there are Piggy and Goosie running across the green, and we shall never get off if we have to begin kissing everybody. Give them my love, Georgie, and say how sorry we were just to miss them. Shut the door quickly, Peppino, and tell him to drive on.'

The motor purred and started. Lucia was gone. 'She had a bad conscience too,' thought Georgie, as Piggy and Goosie gambolled up rather out of breath with pretty playful cries, 'and I'm sure I don't wonder.'

The news that she had gone of course now spread rapidly, and by lunchtime Riseholme had made up its mind what to do, and that was hermetically to close its lips for ever on the subject of Lucia. You might think what you pleased, for it was a free country, but silence was best. But this counsel of perfection was not easy to practise next day when the evening paper came. There, for all the world to read, were two quite long paragraphs, in 'Five o'clock Chit-Chat', over the renowned signature of Hermione, entirely about Lucia and 25 Brompton Square, and there for all the world to see was the reproduction of one of her most elegant photographs, in which she gazed dreamily outwards and a little upwards, with her fingers still pressed on the last chord of (probably) the 'Moonlight Sonata' . . . She had come up, so Hermione told countless readers, from her Elizabethan country seat at Riseholme (where she was a neighbour of Miss Olga Bracely) and was settling for the season in the beautiful little house in Brompton Square, which was the freehold property of her husband, and had just come to him on the death of his aunt. It was a veritable treasure house of exquisite furniture, with a charming music-room where Lucia had given Hermione a cup of tea from her marvellous Worcester tea service . . . (At this point Daisy, whose hands were trembling with passion, exclaimed in a loud and injured voice, 'The very day she arrived!') Mrs Lucas (one of the Warwickshire Smythes by birth) was, as all the world knew, a most accomplished musician and Shakespearian scholar, and had made Riseholme a centre of culture and art. But nobody would suspect the bluestocking in the brilliant, beautiful and witty hostess whose presence would lend an added gaiety to the London season.

Daisy was beginning to feel physically unwell. She hurried over the few remaining lines, and then ejaculating 'Witty! Beautiful!' sent de Vere across to Georgie's with the paper, bidding him to return it, as she hadn't finished with it. But she thought he ought to know . . . Georgie read it through, and with admirable self-restraint, sent Foljambe back with it and a message of thanks – nothing more – to Mrs Quantock for the loan of it. Daisy, by this time feeling better, memorised the whole of it.

Life under the new conditions was not easy, for a mere glance at the paper might send any true Riseholmite into a paroxysm of chattering rage or a deep disgusted melancholy. *The Times* again recorded the fact that Mr and Mrs Philip Lucas had arrived at 25 Brompton Square, there was another terrible paragraph headed 'Dinner', stating that Mrs Sandeman entertained the following to dinner. There was an Ambassador, a Marquis, a Countess (dowager), two Viscounts with wives, a Baronet, a quantity of Honourables and Knights, and Mr and Mrs Philip Lucas. Every single person except Mr and Mrs Philip Lucas had a title. The list was too much for Mrs Boucher, who, reading it at breakfast, suddenly exclaimed: 'I didn't think it of them. And it's a poor consolation to know that they must have gone in last.'

Then she hermetically sealed her lips again on this painful subject, and when she had finished her breakfast (her appetite had quite gone) she looked up every member of that degrading party in Colonel Boucher's *Who's Who*.

*   *   *

The announcement that Mr and Mrs Philip Lucas had arrived at 25 Brompton Square was repeated once more, in case anybody had missed it (Riseholme had not), and Robert Quantock observed that at this rate the three thousand pounds a year would soon be gone, with nothing to show for it except a few press-cuttings. That was very clever and very withering, but anyone could be withering over such a subject. It roused, it is true, a faint and unexpressed hope that the arrival of Lucia in London had not spontaneously produced the desired effect, or why should she cause it to be repeated so often? But that brought no real comfort, and a few days afterwards, there fell a further staggering blow. There was a Court, and Mrs Agnes Sandeman presented Mrs Philip Lucas. Worse yet, her gown was minutely described, and her ornaments were diamonds and pearls.

The vow of silence could no longer be observed: human nature was human nature, and Riseholme would have burst unless it had spoken. Georgie, sitting in his little back parlour overlooking the garden, and lost in exasperated meditation, was roused by his name being loudly called from Daisy's garden next door, and looking out, saw the unprecedented sight of Mrs Boucher's bath-chair planted on Daisy's lawn.

'She must have come in along the gravel path by the back door,' he thought to himself. 'I shouldn't have thought it was wide enough.' He looked to see if his tie was straight, and then leaned out to answer.

'Georgie, come round a minute,' called Daisy. 'Have you seen it?'

'Yes,' said Georgie, 'I have. And I'll come.'

Mrs Boucher was talking in her loud emphatic voice, when he arrived.

'As for pearls,' she said, 'I can't say anything about them, not having seen them. But as for diamonds, the only diamonds she ever had were two or three little chips on the back of her wristwatch. That I'll swear to.'

The two ladies took no notice of him: Daisy referred to the description of Lucia's dress again.

'I believe it was her last dinner-gown with a train added,' she said. 'It was a sort of brocade.'

'Yes, and plush is a sort of velvet,' said Mrs Boucher. 'I've a good mind to write to *The Times*, and say they're mistaken. Brocade! Bunkum! It's pushing and shoving instead of diamonds and pearls. But I've had my say, and that's all. I shouldn't a bit wonder if we saw that the King and Queen had gone to lunch quite quietly at Brompton Square.'

'That's all very well,' said Daisy, 'but what are we to do?'

'Do?' said Mrs Boucher. 'There's plenty to do in Riseholme, isn't there? I'm sure I never suffered from lack of employment, and I should be sorry to think that I had fewer interests now than I had before last Wednesday week. Wednesday, or was it Thursday, when they slipped away like that? Whichever it was, it makes no difference to me, and if you're both disengaged this evening, you and Mr Georgie, the Colonel and I would be very glad if you would come and take your bit of dinner with us. And Mr Quantock too, of course. But as for diamonds and pearls, well, let's leave that alone. I shall wear my emerald tiara tonight and my ruby necklace. My sapphires have gone to be cleaned.'

But though Riseholme was justifiably incensed over Lucia's worldliness and all this pushing and shoving and this self-advertising publicity, it had seldom been so wildly interested. Also, after the first pangs of shame had lost their fierceness, a very different sort of emotion began to soothe the wounded hearts: it was possible to see Lucia in another light. She had stepped straight from the sheltered and cultured life of Riseholme into the great busy feverish world, and already she was making her splendid mark there. Though it might have been she who had told Hermione what to say in those fashionable paragraphs of hers (and those who knew Lucia best were surely best competent to form just conclusions about that) still Hermione had said it, and the public now knew how witty and beautiful Lucia was, and what a wonderful house she had. Then on the very night of her arrival she had been a guest at an obviously superb dinner party, and had since been presented at Court. All this, to look at it fairly, reflected glory on Riseholme, and if it was impossible in one mood not to be ashamed of her, it was even more impossible in other moods not to be proud of her. She had come, and almost before she had seen, she was conquering. She could be viewed as a sort of ambassadress, and her conquests in that light were Riseholme's conquests. But pride did not oust shame, nor shame pride, and shuddering anticipations as to what new enormity the daily papers might reveal were mingled with secret and delighted conjectures as to what Riseholme's next triumph would be.

It was not till the day after her presentation that any news came to Riseholme direct from the ambassadress's headquarters. Every day Georgie had been expecting to hear, and in anticipation of her summons to come up and stay in the bedroom with the bathroom and sitting-room attached, had been carefully through his wardrobe, and was satisfied that he would present a creditable appearance. His small portmanteau, Foljambe declared, would be ample to hold all that he wanted, including the suit with the Oxford trousers, and his cloth-topped boots. When the long-expected letter came, he therefore felt prepared to start that very afternoon, and tore it open with the most eager haste and propped it against his teapot.

GEORGINO MIO – Such a whirl ever since we left, that I haven't had a moment. But tonight (Oh such a relief) Peppino and I have dined alone quite *à la* Riseholme, and for the first time I have had half an hour's quiet practice in my music-room, and now sit down to write to you. (You'd have scolded me if you'd heard me play, so stiff and rusty have I become.)

Well, now for my little chronicles. The very first evening we were here, we went out to a big dinner at dearest Aggie's. Some interesting people: I enjoyed a pleasant talk with the Italian Ambassador, and called on them the day after, but I had no long conversation with anyone, for Aggie kept bringing up fresh people to introduce me to, and your poor Lucia got quite confused with so many, till Peppino and I sorted them out afterwards. Everyone seemed to have heard of our coming up to town, and I assure you that ever since the tiresome telephone has been a perfect nuisance, though all so kind. Would we go to lunch one day, or would we go to dinner another, and there was a private view here, and a little music in the afternoon there: I assure you I have never been so petted and made so much of.

We have done a little entertaining too, already, just a few old friends like our member of Parliament, Mr Garroby-Ashton. ('She met him once,' thought Georgie in parenthesis.) He insisted also on our going to tea with him at the House of Commons. I knew that would interest Peppino, for he's becoming quite a politician, and so we went. Tea on the terrace, and a pleasant little chat with the Prime Minister who came and sat at our table for ever so long. How I wanted you to be there and make a sketch of the Thames: just the sort of view you do, so beautifully! Wonderful river, and I repeated to myself, 'Sweet Thames, run softly, till I end my song.' Then such a scurry to get back to dine somewhere or other and go to a play. Then dearest Aggie (such a good soul) had set her heart on presenting me and I couldn't disappoint her. Did you see the description of my dress? How annoyed I was that it appeared in the papers! So vulgar, all that sort of thing, and you know how I hate publicity, but they tell me I must just put up with it and not mind.

The house is getting into order, but there are lots of little changes and furbishings up to be done before I venture to show it to anyone as critical as you, Georgino. How you would scream at the carpet in the dining-room! I know it would give you indigestion. But when I get the house straight, I shall insist on your coming, whatever your engagements are, and staying a long, long time. We will fix a date when I come down for some weekend.

Your beloved Olga is back, but I haven't seen her yet. I asked Signor Cortese to dine and meet her one night, and I asked her to meet him. I thought that would make a pleasant little party, but they were both engaged. I hope they have not quarrelled. Her house, just opposite mine, looks very tiny, but I dare say it is quite large enough for her and her husband. She sings at the opening

night of the opera next week, in *Lucrezia*. I must manage to go
even if I can only look in for an act or two. Peppino (so extravagant
of him) has taken a box for two nights in the week. It is his birthday
present to me, so I couldn't scold the dear! And after all, we shall
give a great deal of pleasure to friends, by letting them have it
when we do not want it ourselves.

Love to everybody at dear Riseholme. I feel quite like an exile,
and sometimes I long for its sweet peace and quietness. But there
is no doubt that London suits Peppino very well, and I must make
the best of this incessant hustle. I had hoped to get down for next
Sunday, but Mrs Garroby-Ashton (I hear he will certainly be raised
to the peerage when the birthday honours come out) has made a
point of our spending it with them ... Good-night, dear Georgino.
Me so so sleepy.

LUCIA

Georgie swallowed this letter at a gulp, and then, beginning again,
took it in sips. At first it gave him an impression of someone wholly
unlike her, but when sipped, every sentence seemed wonderfully
characteristic. She was not adapting herself to new circumstances,
she was adapting new circumstances to herself with all her old
ingenuity and success, and with all her invincible energy. True, you
had sometimes to read between the lines, and divide everything by
about three in order to allow for exaggerations, and when Lucia
spoke of not disappointing dearest Aggie, who had set her heart on
presenting her at Court, or of Mrs Garroby-Ashton making a point
of her going down for the weekend which she had intended to spend
at Riseholme, Georgie only had to remember how she had been
forced (so she said) to be Queen at those May Day revels. By sheer
power of will she had made each of them become a Robin Hood or
a Maid Marian, or whatever it was, and then, when she had got them
all at work she said it was she who was being worked to death over
their May Day revels. They had forced her to organise them, they
had insisted that she should be Queen, and lead the dances and sing
louder than anybody, and be crowned and curtseyed to. They had
been wax in her hands, and now in new circumstances, Georgie felt
sure that dearest Aggie had been positively forced to present her,
and no doubt Mrs Garroby-Ashton, cornered on that terrace of the
House of Commons, while sweet Thames flowed softly, had had no
choice but to ask her down for a Sunday. Will-power, indomitable
perseverance now, as always, was getting her just precisely what she

had wanted: by it she had become Queen of Riseholme, and by it she was firmly climbing away in London, and already she was saying that everybody was insisting on her dining and lunching with them, whereas it was her moral force that made them powerless in her grip. Riseholme she had no use for now: she was busy with something else; she did not care to be bothered with Georgie, and so she said it was the dining-room carpet.

'Very well,' said Georgie bitterly. 'And if she doesn't want me, I won't want her. So that's that.'

He briskly put the letter away, and began to consider what he should do with himself all day. It was warm enough to sit out and paint: in fact, he had already begun a sketch of the front of his house from the green opposite; there was his piano if he settled to have a morning of music; there was the paper to read, there was news to collect, there was Daisy Quantock next door who would be delighted to have a sitting with the planchette, which was really beginning to write whole words instead of making meaningless dashes and scribbles, and yet none of these things which, together with plenty of conversation and a little housekeeping and manicuring, had long made life such a busy and strenuous performance, seemed to offer an adequate stimulus. And he knew well enough what rendered them devoid of tonic: it was that Lucia was not here, and however much he told himself he did not want her, he like all the rest of Riseholme was beginning to miss her dreadfully. She aggravated and exasperated them: she was a hypocrite (all that pretence of not having read the Mozart duet, and desolation at Auntie's death), a poseuse, a sham and a snob, but there was something about her that stirred you into violent though protesting activity, and though she might infuriate you, she prevented your being dull. Georgie enjoyed painting, but he knew that the fact that he would show his sketch to Lucia gave spice to his enjoyment, and that she, though knowing no more about it than a rhinoceros, would hold it at arm's length with her head a little on one side and her eyes slightly closed, and say:

'Yes, Georgie, very nice, very nice. But have you got the value of your middle-distance quite right? And a little more depth in your distance, do you think?'

Or if he played his piano, he knew that what inspired his nimbleness would be the prospect of playing his piece to her, and if he was practising on the sly a duet for performance with her, the knowledge that he was stealing a march on her and would astonish her (though she might suspect the cause of his facility). And as for conversation,

it was useless to deny that conversation languished in Riseholme if
the subject of Lucia, her feats and her frailties was tabooed.

'We've got to pull ourselves together,' thought Georgie, 'and start
again. We must get going and learn to do without her, as she's
getting on so nicely without us. I shall go and see how the planchette
is progressing.'

Daisy was already at it, and the pencil was getting up steam. A day
or two ago it had written not once only but many times a strange sort
of hieroglyphic, which might easily be interpreted to be the mystic
word Abfou. Daisy had therefore settled (what could be more obvious?)
that the name of the control who guided these strange gyrations was
Abfou, which sounded very Egyptian and antique. Therefore, she
powerfully reasoned, the scribbles which could not be made to fit
any known configuration of English letters might easily be Arabic.
Why Abfou should write his name in English characters and his
communications in Arabic was not Daisy's concern, for who knew
what were the conditions on the other side? A sheet was finished just
as Georgie came in, and though it presented nothing but Arabic
script, the movements of the planchette had been so swift and eager
that Daisy quite forgot to ask if there was any news.

'Abfou is getting in more direct touch with me every time I sit,'
said Daisy. 'I feel sure we shall have something of great importance
before long. Put your hand on the planchette too, Georgie, for I
have always believed that you have mediumistic powers. Concentrate
first: that means you must put everything else out of your head. Let
us sit for a minute or two with our eyes shut. Breathe deeply. Relax.
Sometimes slight hypnosis comes on, so the book says, which means
you get very drowsy.'

There was silence for a few moments: Georgie wanted to tell
Daisy about Lucia's letter, but that would certainly interrupt Abfou,
so he drew up a chair, and after laying his hand on Daisy's closed his
eyes and breathed deeply. And then suddenly the most extraordinary
things began to happen.

The planchette trembled: it vibrated like a kettle on the boil, and
began to skate about the paper. He had no idea what its antic motions
meant: he only knew that it was writing something, Arabic perhaps,
but something firm and decided. It seemed to him that so far from
aiding its movement, he almost, to be on the safe side, checked it. He
opened his eyes, for it was impossible not to want to watch this
manifestation of psychic force, and also he wished to be sure (though
he had no real suspicions on the subject) that his collaborator was

not, to put it coarsely, pushing. Exactly the same train of thought
was passing in Daisy's mind, and she opened her eyes too.

'Georgie, my hand is positively being dragged about,' she said
excitedly. 'If anything, I try to resist.'

'Mine too; so do I,' said Georgie. 'It's too wonderful. Do you
suppose it's Arabic still?'

The pencil gave a great dash, and stopped.

'It isn't Arabic,' said Daisy as she examined the message, 'at least,
there's heaps of English too.'

'No!' said Georgie, putting on his spectacles in his excitement, and
not caring whether Daisy knew he wore them or not. 'I can see it
looks like English, but what a difficult handwriting! Look, that's
"Abfou", isn't it? And that is "Abfou" again there.'

They bent their heads over the script.

'There's an "L",' cried Daisy, 'and there it is again. And then
there's "L from L". And then there's "Dead" repeated twice. It can't
mean that Abfou is dead, because this is positive proof that he's alive.
And then I can see "Mouse"?'

'Where?' said Georgie eagerly. 'And what would "dead mouse"
mean?'

'There!' said Daisy pointing. 'No: it isn't "dead mouse". It's "dead"
and then a lot of Arabic, and then "mouse".'

'I don't believe it is "Mouse",' said Georgie, 'though of course,
you know Abfou's handwriting much better than I do. It looks to me
far more like "Museum".'

'Perhaps he wants me to send all the Arabic he's written up to the
British Museum,' said Daisy with a flash of genius, 'so that they can
read it and say what it means.'

'But then there's "Museum" or "Mouse" again there,' said Georgie,
'and surely that word in front of it – It is! It's Riseholme! Riseholme
Mouse or Riseholme Museum! I don't know what either would mean.'

'You may depend upon it that it means something,' said Daisy,
'and there's another capital "L". Does it mean Lucia, do you think?
But "dead" . . .'

'No: dead's got nothing to do with the "L",' said Georgie. 'Museum
comes in between, and quantities of Arabic.'

'I think I'll just record the exact time; it would be more scientific,'
said Daisy. 'A quarter to eleven. No, that clock's three minutes fast
by the church time.'

'No, the church time is slow,' said Georgie.

Suddenly he jumped up.

'I've got it,' he said. 'Look! "L from L". That means a letter from Lucia. And it's quite true. I heard this morning, and it's in my pocket now.'

'No!' said Daisy, 'that's just a sign Abfou is giving us, that he really is with us, and knows what is going on. Very evidential.'

The absorption of them both in this script may be faintly appreciated by the fact that neither Daisy evinced the slightest curiosity as to what Lucia said, nor Georgie the least desire to communicate it.

'And then there's "dead",' said Georgie, looking out of the window. 'I wonder what that means.'

'I'm sure I hope it's not Lucia,' said Daisy with stoical calmness, 'but I can't think of anybody else.'

Georgie's eyes wandered over the green; Mrs Boucher was speeding round in her bath-chair, pushed by her husband, and there was the vicar walking very fast, and Mrs Antrobus and Piggy and Goosie . . . nobody else seemed to be dead. Then his eye came back to the foreground of Daisy's front garden.

'What has happened to your mulberry tree?' he said parenthetically. 'Its leaves are all drooping. You ought never to have pruned its roots without knowing how to do it.'

Daisy jumped up.

'Georgie, you've got it!' she said. 'It's the mulberry tree that's dead. Isn't that wonderful?'

Georgie was suitably impressed.

'That's very curious: very curious indeed,' he said. 'Letter from Lucia, and the dead mulberry tree. I do believe there's something in it. But let's go on studying the script. Now I look at it again I feel certain it is Riseholme Museum, not Riseholme Mouse. The only difficulty is that there isn't a Museum in Riseholme.'

'There are plenty of mice,' observed Daisy, who had had some trouble with these little creatures. 'Abfou may be wanting to give me advice about some kind of ancient Egyptian trap . . . But if you aren't very busy this morning, Georgie, we might have another sitting and see if we get anything more definite. Let us attain collectedness as the directions advise.'

'What's collectedness?' asked Georgie.

Daisy gave him the directions. Collectedness seemed to be a sort of mixture of intense concentration and complete vacuity of mind.

'You seem to have to concentrate your mind upon nothing at all,' said he after reading it.

'That's just it,' said Daisy. 'You put all thoughts out of your head,

MAPP AND LUCIA: VOLUME ONE

and then focus your mind. We have to be only the instrument through which Abfou functions.'

They sat down again after a little deep breathing and relaxation, and almost immediately the planchette began to move across the paper with a firm and steady progression. It stopped sometimes for a few minutes, which was proof of the authenticity of the controlling force, for in spite of all efforts at collectedness, both Daisy's and Georgie's minds were full of things which they longed for Abfou to communicate, and if either of them was consciously directing those movements, there could have been no pause at all. When finally it gave that great dash across the paper again, indicating that the communication was finished, they found the most remarkable results.

Abfou had written two pages of foolscap in a tall upright hand, which was quite unlike either Daisy's or Georgie's ordinary script, and this was another proof (if proof were wanted) of authenticity. It was comparatively easy to read, and, except for a long passage at the end in Arabic, was written almost entirely in English.

'Look, there's Lucia written out in full four times,' said Daisy eagerly. 'And "Pepper". What's Pepper?'

Georgie gasped. 'Why Peppino, of course,' he said. 'I do call that odd. And see how it goes on – "Muck company", no, "Much company, much grand company, higher and higher".'

'Poor Lucia!' said Daisy. 'How sarcastic! That's what Abfou thinks about it all. By the way, you haven't told me what she says yet; never mind, this is far more interesting . . . Then there's a little Arabic, at least I think it's Arabic, for I can't make anything out of it, and then – why, I believe those next words are "From Olga". Have you heard from Olga?'

'No,' said Georgie, 'but there's something about her in Lucia's letter. Perhaps that's it.'

'Very likely. And then I can make out Riseholme, and it isn't "mouse", it's quite clearly "Museum", and then – I can't read that, but it looks English, and then "opera", that's Olga again, and "dead", which is the mulberry tree. And then "It is better to work than to be idle. Think not – " something – '

' "Bark",' said Georgie. 'No, "hard".'

'Yes. "Think not hard thoughts of any, but turn thy mind to improving work." – Georgie, isn't that wonderful? – and then it goes off into Arabic, what a pity! It might have been more about the museum. I shall certainly send all the first Arabic scripts to the British Museum.'

Georgie considered this.

'Somehow I don't believe that is what Abfou means,' said he. 'He says Riseholme Museum, not British Museum. You can't possibly get "British" out of that word.'

Georgie left Daisy still attempting to detect more English among Arabic passages and engaged himself to come in again after tea for fresh investigation. Within a minute of his departure Daisy's telephone rang.

'How tiresome these interruptions are,' said Daisy to herself, as she hurried to the instrument. 'Yes, yes. Who is it?'

Georgie's voice had the composure of terrific excitement.

'It's me,' he said. 'The second post has just come in, and a letter from Olga. "From Olga", you remember.'

'No!' said Daisy. 'Do tell me if she says anything about – '

But Georgie had already rung off. He wanted to read his letter from Olga, and Daisy sat down again quite awestruck at this further revelation. The future clearly was known to Abfou as well as the past, for Georgie knew nothing about Olga's letter when the words "From Olga" occurred in the script. And if in it she said anything about "opera" (which really was on the cards) it would be more wonderful still.

The morning was nearly over, so Daisy observed to her prodigious surprise, for it had really gone like a flash (a flash of the highest illuminative power), and she hurried out with a trowel and a rake to get half an hour in the garden before lunch. It was rather disconcerting to find that though she spent the entire day in the garden, often not sitting down to her planchette till dusk rendered it impossible to see the mazes of cotton threads she had stretched over newly sown beds, to keep off sparrows (she had on one occasion shattered with a couple of hasty steps the whole of those defensive fortifications) she seemed, in spite of blistered hands and aching back, to be falling more and more into arrears over her horticulture. Whereas that ruffian Simkinson, whom she had dismissed for laziness when she found him smoking a pipe in the potting-shed and doing a crossword puzzle when he ought to have been working, really kept her garden in very good order by slouching about it for three half-days in the week. To be sure, she had pruned the roots of the mulberry tree, which had taken a whole day (and so incidentally had killed the mulberry tree) and though the death of that antique vegetable had given Abfou a fine opportunity for proving himself, evidence now was getting so abundant that Daisy almost wished it hadn't happened. Then, too, she was beginning to have secret qualms that she had torn up as weeds a quantity of seedlings which the indolent Simkinson had just pricked out, for though the beds were now certainly weedless, there was no sign of any other growth there. And either Daisy's little wooden labels had got mixed, or she had sown Brussels sprouts in the circular bed just outside the dining-room window instead of Phlox Drummondi. She thought she had attached the appropriate label to the seed she had sown, but it was very dark at the time, and in the morning the label certainly said 'Brussels sprouts'. In which case there would be a bed of Phlox at the far end of the little strip of kitchen garden. The seeds in both places were sprouting now, so she would know the worst or the best before long.

Then, again, there was the rockery she had told Simkinson to build, which he had neglected for crossword puzzles, and though Daisy had been working six or eight hours a day in her garden ever since, she had not found time to touch a stone of it, and the fragments lying like a moraine on the path by the potting-shed still rendered any approach to the latter a mountaineering feat. They consisted of fragments of mediaeval masonry, from the site of the ancient abbey, finials and crockets and pieces of mullioned windows which had been turned up when a new siding of the railway had been made, and everyone almost had got some with the exception of Mrs Boucher, who called them rubbish. Then there were some fossils, ammonites and spar and curious flints with holes in them and bits of talc, for Lucia one year had commandeered them all into the study of geology and they had got hammers and whacked away at the face of an old quarry, detaching these petrified relics and hitting themselves over the fingers in the process. It was that year that the Roman camp outside the village had been put under the plough and Riseholme had followed it like a bevy of rooks, and Georgie had got several trays full of fragments of iridescent glass, and Colonel Boucher had collected bits of Samian ware, and Mrs Antrobus had found a bronze fibula or safety-pin. Daisy had got some chunks of Roman brickwork, and a section of Roman drain-pipe, which now figured among the materials for her rockery; and she had bought, for about their weight in gold, quite a dozen bronze coins. These, of course, would not be placed in the rockery, but she had put them somewhere very carefully, and had subsequently forgotten where that was. Now as these archaeological associations came into her mind from the contemplation of the materials for the rockery, she suddenly thought she remembered that she had put them at the back of the drawer in her card-table.

The sight of these antique fragments disgusted Daisy; they littered the path, and she could not imagine them built up into a rockery that should have the smallest claim to be an attractive object. How could the juxtaposition of a stone mullion, a drain-pipe and an ammonite present a pleasant appearance? Besides, who was to juxtapose them? She could not keep pace with the other needs of the garden, let alone a rockery, and where, after all, was the rockery to stand? The asparagus-bed seemed the only place, and she preferred asparagus.

Robert was bawling out from the dining-room window that lunch was ready, and as she retraced her steps to the house, she thought that perhaps it would be better to eat humble pie and get Simkinson to return. It was clear to Daisy that if she was to do her duty as medium between ancient Egypt and the world of today, the garden would deteriorate even more rapidly than it was doing already, and no doubt Robert would consent to eat the humble pie for her, and tell Simkinson that they couldn't get on without him, and that when she had said he was lazy, she had meant industrious, or whatever else was necessary.

Robert was in a very good temper that day because Roumanian oils, which were the main source of his fortunes, had announced a higher dividend than usual, and he promised to seek out Simkinson and explain what lazy meant, and if he didn't understand to soothe his injured feelings with a small tip.

'And tell him he needn't make a rockery at all,' said Daisy. 'He always hated the idea of a rockery. He can dig a pit and bury the fossils and the architectural fragments and everything. That will be the easiest way of disposing of them.'

'And what is he to do with the earth he takes out of the pit, my dear?' asked Robert.

'Put it back, I suppose,' said Daisy rather sharply. Robert was so pleased at having 'caught' her, that he did not even explain that she had been caught . . .

*   *   *

After lunch Daisy found the coins; it was odd that, having forgotten where she had put them for so long, she should suddenly remember, and she was inclined to attribute this inspiration to Abfou. The difficulty was to know what, having found them, to do with them next. Some of them obviously bore signs of once having had profiles of Roman emperors stamped on them, and she was sure she had heard that some Roman coins were of great value, and probably these were the ones. Perhaps when she sent the Arabic script to the British Museum she might send these too for identification . . . And then she dropped them all on the floor as the great idea struck her.

She flew into the garden, calling to Georgie, who was putting up croquet-hoops.

'Georgie, I've got it!' she cried. 'It's as plain as plain. What Abfou wants us to do is to start a Riseholme Museum. He wrote Riseholme Museum quite distinctly. Think how it would pay too, when we're overrun with American tourists in the summer! They would all come to see it. A shilling admission I should put it at, and sixpence for the catalogue.'

'I wonder if Abfou meant that,' said Georgie.

'He said it,' said Daisy. 'You can't deny that!'

'But what should we put in the Museum?' asked he.

'My dear, we should fill it with antiquities and things which none of us want in our houses. There are those beautiful fragments of the Abbey which I've got, and which are simply wasted in my garden with no one to see them, and my drain-pipe. I would present them all to the Museum, and the fossils, and perhaps some of my coins. And my Roman brickwork.'

Georgie paused with a hoop in his hand.

'That is an idea,' he said. 'And I've got all those lovely pieces of iridescent glass, which are always tumbling about. I would give them.'

'And Colonel Boucher's Samian ware,' cried Daisy. 'He was saying only the other day how he hated it, but didn't quite want to throw it away. It will be a question of what we leave out, not of what we put in. Besides, I'm sure that's what Abfou meant. We must form a committee at once. You and Mrs Boucher and I, I should think, would be enough. Large committees are a great mistake.'

'Not Lucia?' asked Georgie, with lingering loyalty.

'No. Certainly not,' said Daisy. 'She would only send us orders from London, as to what we were to do and want us to undo all we had done when she came back, besides saying she had thought of it, and making herself President!'

'There's something in that,' said Georgie.

'Of course there is, there's sense,' said Daisy. 'Now I shall go straight and see Mrs Boucher.'

Georgie dealt a few smart blows with his mallet to the hoop he was putting in place.

'I shall come too,' he said. 'Riseholme Museum! I believe Abfou did mean that. We *shall* be busy again.'

Chapter Four

The committee met that very afternoon, and the next morning and the next afternoon, and the scheme quickly took shape. Robert, rolling in golden billows of Roumanian oil, was called in as financial adviser, and after calculation, the scheme strongly recommended itself to him. All the summer the town was thronged with visitors, and enquiring American minds would hardly leave unvisited the Museum at so Elizabethan a place.

'I don't know what you'll have in your Museum,' he said, 'but I expect they'll go to look, and even if they don't find much they'll have paid their shillings. And if Mrs Boucher thinks her husband will let you have that big tithe-barn of his, at a small rent, I dare say you'll have a paying proposition.'

The question of funds therefore in order to convert the tithe-barn into a museum was instantly gone into. Robert professed himself perfectly ready to equip the tithe-barn with all necessary furniture and decoration, if he might collar the whole of the receipts, but his willingness to take all financial responsibilities made the committee think that they would like to have a share in them, since so shrewd a business man clearly saw the probability of making something out of it. Up till then, the sordid question of money had not really occurred to them: there was to be a museum which would make them busy again, and the committee was to run it. They were quite willing to devote practically the whole of their time to it, for Riseholme was one of those happy places where the proverb that Time is money was a flat fallacy, for nobody had ever earned a penny with it. But since Robert's financial judgement argued that the Museum would be a profitable investment, the committee naturally wished to have a hand in it, and the three members each subscribed fifty pounds, and co-opted Robert to join the board and supply the rest. Profits (if any) would be divided up between the members of the committee in proportion to their subscriptions. The financial Robert would see to all that, and the rest of them could turn their attention to the provision of curiosities.

There was evidently to be no lack of them, for everyone in Rise-holme had stores of miscellaneous antiquities and 'specimens' of various kinds which encumbered their houses and required a deal of dusting, but which couldn't quite be thrown away. A very few striking objects were only lent: among these were Daisy's box of coins, and Mrs Antrobus's fibula, but the most of them, like Georgie's glass and Colonel Boucher's pieces of Samian ware, were fervently bestowed. Objects of all sorts poured in, the greater portion of a spinning-wheel, an Elizabethan pestle and mortar, no end of Roman tiles, a large wooden post unhesitatingly called a whipping-post, some indecipherable documents on parchment with seals attached, belonging to the vicar, an ordnance map of the district, numerous collections of fossils and of carved stones from the site of the Abbey, ancient quilts, a baby's cradle, worm-eaten enough to be Anglo-Saxon, queer-shaped bottles, a tiger-ware jug, fire-irons too ponderous for use, and (by special vote of the Parish Council) the stocks which had hitherto stood at the edge of the pond on the green. All Riseholme was busy again, for fossils had to be sorted out (it was early realised that even a museum could have too many ammonites), curtains had to be stitched for the windows, labels to be written, Samian ware to be pieced together, cases arranged, a catalogue prepared. The period of flatness consequent on Lucia's desertion had passed off, and what had certainly added zest to industry was the thought that Lucia had nothing to do with the Museum. When next she deigned to visit her discarded kingdom, she would find how busily and successfully and originally they had got on without her, and that there was no place for her on the committee, and probably none in the Museum for the Elizabethan turnspit which so often made the chimney of her music-room to smoke.

Riseholme, indeed, was busier than ever, for not only had it the Museum feverishly to occupy it so that it might be open for the tourist season this year, and, if possible, before Lucia came down for one of her promised weekends, but it was immersed in a wave of psychical experiments. Daisy Quantock had been perfectly honest in acknowledging that the idea of the Museum was not hers at all, but Abfou's, her Egyptian guide. She had, it is true, been as ingenious as Joseph in interpreting Abfou's directions, but it was Abfou to whom all credit was due, and who evidently took such a deep interest in the affairs of Riseholme. She even offered to present the Museum with the sheet of foolscap on which the words 'Riseholme Museum' (not mouse) were written, but the general feeling of the committee, while thanking her for her munificence, was that it would not be tactful to display it, since the same Sibylline sheet contained those sarcastic remarks about Lucia. It was proved also that Abfou had meant the Museum to be started, for subsequently he several times said, 'Much pleased with your plans for the Museum. Abfou approves.' So everybody else wanted to get into touch with Abfou too, and no less than four planchettes or ouija-boards were immediately ordered by various members of Riseholme society. At present Abfou did not manifest himself to any of them, except in what was possibly Arabic script (for it certainly bore a strong resemblance to his earlier efforts of communication with Daisy), and while she encouraged the scribes to persevere in the hope that he might soon regale them with English, she was not really very anxious that he should. With her he was getting Englisher and Englisher every day, and had not Simkinson, after having had the true meaning of the word 'lazy' carefully explained to him, consented to manage her garden again, it certainly would have degenerated into primeval jungle, for she absolutely had not a minute to attend to it.

Simkinson, however, was quite genial.

'Oh yes, ma'am, very pleased to come back,' he said. 'I knew you wouldn't be able to get on long without me, and I want no explanations. Now let's have a look round and see what you've been doing. Why, whatever's happened to my mulberry tree?'

That was Simkinson's way: he always talked of 'my flowers' and 'my asparagus' when he meant hers.

'I've been pruning its roots,' she said.

'Well, ma'am, you've done your best to do it in,' said Simkinson. 'I don't think it's dead though, I dare say it'll pull round.'

Abfou had been understood to say it was dead, but perhaps he meant something else, thought Daisy, and they went on to the small circular bed below the dining-room windows.

'Phlox,' said Daisy hopefully.

'Broccoli,' said Simkinson examining the young green sprouts. 'And the long bed there. I sowed a lot of annuals there, and I don't see a sign of anything coming up.'

He fixed her with a merry eye.

'I believe you've been weeding, ma'am,' he said. 'I shall have to get you a lot of young plants if you want a bit of colour there. It's too late for me to put my seeds in again.'

Daisy rather wished she hadn't come out with him, and changed the subject to something more cheerful.

'Well, I shan't want the rockery,' she said. 'You needn't bother about that. All these stones will be carted away in a day or two.'

'Glad of that, ma'am. I'll be able to get to my potting-shed again. Well, I'll try to put you to rights. I'd best pull up the broccoli first, you won't want it under your windows, will you? You stick to rolling the lawn, ma'am, if you want to garden. You won't do any harm then.'

It was rather dreadful being put in one's place like this, but Daisy did not dare risk a second quarrel, and the sight of Georgie at the dining-room window (he had come across to 'weedj', as the psychical processes, whether ouija or planchette, were now called) was rather a relief. Weeding, after all, was unimportant compared with weedjing.

'And I don't believe I ever told you what Olga wrote about,' said Georgie, as soon as she was within range. 'We've talked of nothing but museum. Oh, and Mrs Boucher's planchette has come. But it broke in the post, and she's gumming it together.'

'I doubt if it will act,' said Daisy. 'But what did Olga say? It quite went out of my head to ask you.'

'It's too heavenly of her,' said he. 'She's asked me to go up and stay with her for the first night of the opera. She's singing Lucrezia, and has got a stall for me.'

'No!' said Daisy, making a trial trip over the blotting-paper to see if the pencil was sharp. 'That will be an event! I suppose you're going.'

'Just about,' said Georgie. 'It's going to be broadcasted, too, and I shall be listening to the original.'

'How interesting!' said Daisy. 'And there you'll be in Brompton Square, just opposite Lucia. Oh, you heard from her? What did she say?'

'Apparently she's getting on marvellously,' said Georgie. 'Not a moment to spare. Just what she likes.'

Daisy pushed the planchette aside. There would be time for that when she had had a little talk about Lucia.

'And are you going to stay with her too?' she asked

Georgie was quite determined not to be ill-natured. He had taken no part (or very little) in this trampling on Lucia's majesty, which had been so merrily going on.

'I should love to, if she would ask me,' he observed. 'She only says she's going to. Of course, I shall go to see her.'

'I wouldn't,' said Daisy savagely. 'If she asked me fifty times I should say "no" fifty times. What's happened is that she's dropped us. I wouldn't have her on our museum committee if – if she gave her pearls to it and said they belonged to Queen Elizabeth. I wonder you haven't got more spirit.'

'I've got plenty of spirit,' said Georgie, 'and I allow I did feel rather hurt at her letter. But then, after all, what does it matter?'

'Of course it doesn't if you're going to stay with Olga,' said Daisy. 'How she'll hate you for that!'

'Well, I can't help it,' he said. 'Lucia hasn't asked me and Olga has. She's twice reminded Olga that she may use her music-room to practise in whenever she likes. Isn't that kind? She would love to be able to say that Olga's always practising in her music-room. But aren't we ill-natured? Let's weedj instead.'

*   *   *

Georgie found, when he arrived next afternoon in Brompton Square, that Olga had already had her early dinner, and that he was to dine alone at seven and follow her to the opera house.

'I'm on the point of collapse from sheer nerves,' she said. 'I always am before I sing, and then out of desperation I pull myself together. If – I say "if" – I survive till midnight, we're going to have a little party here. Cortese is coming, and Princess Isabel, and one or two other people. Georgie, it's very daring of you to come here, you know, because my husband's away, and I'm an unprotected female alone with Don Juan. How's Riseholme? Talk to me about Riseholme. Are you engaged to Piggy yet? And is it broccoli or phlox in Daisy's round bed? Your letter was so mysterious too. I know nothing about the Museum yet. What Museum? Are you going to kill and stuff Lucia and put her in the hall? You simply alluded to the Museum as if I knew all about it. If you don't talk to me, I shall scream.'

Georgie flung himself into the task, delighted to be thought capable of doing anything for Olga. He described at great length and with much emphasis the whole of the history of Riseholme from the first epiphany of Arabic and Abfou on the planchette-board down to the return of Simkinson. Olga lost herself in these chronicles, and when her maid came in to tell her it was time to start, she got up quite cheerfully.

'And so it was broccoli,' she said. 'I was afraid it was going to be phlox after all. You're an angel, Georgie, for getting me through my bad hour. I'll give you anything you like for the Museum. Wait for me afterwards at the stage door. We'll drive back together.'

From the moment Olga appeared, the success of the opera was

secure. Cortese, who was conducting, had made his music well; it thoroughly suited her, and she was singing and looking and acting her best. Again and again after the first act the curtain had to go up, and not until the house was satisfied could Georgie turn his glances this way and that to observe the audience. Then in the twilight of a small box on the second tier he espied a woman who was kissing her hand somewhere in his direction, and a man waving a programme, and then he suddenly focused them and saw who they were. He ran upstairs to visit them, and there was Lucia in an extraordinarily short skirt with her hair shingled, and round her neck three short rows of seed pearls.

'Georgino *mio*!' she cried. 'This is a surprise! You came up to see our dear Olga's triumph. I do call that loyalty. Why did you not tell me you were coming?'

'I thought I would call tomorrow,' said Georgie, with his eyes still going backwards and forwards between the shingle and the pearls and the legs.

'Ah, you are staying the night in town?' she asked. 'Not going back by the midnight train? The dear old midnight train, and waking in Riseholme! At your club?'

'No, I'm staying with Olga,' said Georgie.

Lucia seemed to become slightly cataleptic for a moment, but recovered.

'No! Are you really?' she said. 'I think that is unkind of you, Georgie. You might have told me you were coming.'

'But you said that the house wasn't ready,' said he. 'And she asked me.'

Lucia put on a bright smile.

'Well, you're forgiven,' she said. 'We're all at sixes and sevens yet. And we've seen nothing of dearest Olga – or Mrs Shuttleworth, I should say, for that's on the bills. Of course we'll drive you home, and you must come in for a chat, before Mrs Shuttleworth gets home, and then no doubt she will be very tired and want to go to bed.'

Lucia as she spoke had been surveying the house with occasional little smiles and wagglings of her hand in vague directions.

'Ah, there's Elsie Garroby-Ashton,' she said, 'and who is that with her, Peppino? Lord Shrivenham, surely. So come back with me and have 'ickle talk, Georgie. Oh, there's the Italian Ambassadress. Dearest Gioconda! Such a sweet. And look at the Royal Box. What a gathering! That's the Royal Box, Georgie, away to the left – that large one – in the tier below. Too near the stage for my taste: so little illusion – '

Lucia suddenly rose and made a profound curtsey.

'I think she saw us, Peppino,' she said, 'perhaps you had better bow. No, she's looking somewhere else now: you did not bow quick enough. And what a party in dearest Aggie's box. Who can that be? Oh yes, it's Toby Limpsfield. We met him at Aggie's, do you remember, on the first night we were up. So join us at the grand entrance, Georgie, and drive back with us. We shall be giving a lift to somebody else, I'll be bound, but if you have your motor, it is so ill-natured not to pick up friends. I always do it: they will be calling us the "Lifts of London", as Marcia Whitby said.'

'I'm afraid I can't do that,' said Georgie. 'I'm waiting for Olga, and she's having a little party, I believe.'

'No! Is she really?' asked Lucia, with all the old Riseholme vivacity. 'Who is coming?'

'Cortese, I believe,' said Georgie, thinking it might be too much for Lucia if he mentioned a princess, 'and one or two of the singers.'

Lucia's mouth watered, and she swallowed rapidly. That was the kind of party she longed to be asked to, for it would be so wonderful and glorious to be able casually to allude to Olga's tiny, tiny little party after the first night of the opera, not a party at all really, just a few *intimes*, herself and Cortese and so on. How could she manage it, she wondered? Could she pretend not to know that there was a party, and just drop in for a moment in neighbourly fashion with enthusiastic congratulations? Or should she pretend her motor had not come, and hang about the stage door with Georgie – Peppino could go home in the motor – and get a lift? Or should she hint very violently to Georgie how she would like to come in just for a minute. Or should she, now that she knew there was to be a party, merely assert that she had been to it? Perhaps a hint to Georgie was the best plan . . .

Her momentary indecision was put an end to by the appearance of Cortese threading his way among the orchestra, and the lowering of the lights. Georgie, without giving her any further opportunity, hurried back to his stall, feeling that he had had an escape, for Lucia's beady eye had been fixing him, just in the way it always used to do when she wanted something and, in consequence, meant to get it. He felt he had been quite wrong in ever supposing that Lucia had changed. She was just precisely the same, translated into a larger sphere. She had expanded: strange though it seemed, she had only been in bud at Riseholme. 'I wonder what she'll do?' thought Georgie as he settled himself into his stall. 'She wants dreadfully to come.'

The opera came to an end in a blaze of bouquets and triumph and recalls, and curtseys. It was something of an occasion, for it was the first night of the opera, and the first performance of *Lucrezia* in London, and it was late when Olga came florally out. The party, which was originally meant to be no party at all, but just a little supper with Cortese and one or two of the singers, had marvellously increased during the evening, for friends had sent round messages and congratulations, and Olga had asked them to drop in, and when she and Georgie arrived at Brompton Square, the whole of the curve at the top was packed with motors.

'Heavens, what a lot of people I seem to have asked,' she said, 'but it will be great fun. There won't be nearly enough chairs, but we'll sit on the floor, and there won't be nearly enough supper, but I know there's a ham, and what can be better than a ham? Oh, Georgie, I am happy.'

Now from opposite, across the narrow space of the square, Lucia had seen the arrival of all these cars. In order to see them better she had gone on to the balcony of her drawing-room, and noted their occupants with her opera-glasses. There was Lord Limpsfield, and the Italian Ambassadress, and Mr Garroby-Ashton, and Cortese, and some woman to whom Mr Garroby-Ashton bowed and Mrs Garroby-Ashton curtseyed. Up they streamed. And there was the Duchess of Whitby (Marcia, for Lucia had heard her called that) coming up the steps, and curtseying too, but as yet Olga and Georgie quite certainly had not come. It seemed strange that so many brilliant guests should arrive before their hostess, but Lucia saw at once that this was the most chic informality that it was possible to conceive. No doubt Mr Shuttleworth was there to receive them, but how wonderful it all was! . . . And then the thought occurred to her that Olga would arrive, and with her would be Georgie, and she felt herself turning bright green all over with impotent jealousy. Georgie in that crowd! It was impossible that Georgie should be there, and not she, but that was certainly what would happen unless she thought of something. Georgie would go back to Riseholme and describe this gathering, and he would say that Lucia was not there: he supposed she had not been asked.

Lucia thought of something; she hurried downstairs and let herself out. Motors were still arriving, but perhaps she was not too late. She took up her stand in the central shadow of a gas lamp close to Olga's door and waited.

Up the square came yet another car, and she could see it was full of flowers. Olga stepped out, and she darted forward.

'Oh, Mrs Shuttleworth,' she said. 'Splendid! Glorious! Marvellous! If only Beethoven was alive! I could not think of going to bed, without just popping across to thank you for a revelation! Georgie, dear! Just to shake your hand: that is all. All! I won't detain you. I see you have a party! You wonderful Queen of Song.'

Olga at all times was good-natured. Her eye met Georgie's for a moment.

'Oh, but come in,' she said. 'Do come in. It isn't a party: it's just anybody. Georgie, be a dear, and help to carry all those flowers in. How nice of you to come across, Mrs Lucas! I know you'll excuse my running on ahead, because all – at least I hope all – my guests have come, and there's no one to look after them.'

Lucia, following closely in her wake, and taking no further notice of Georgie, slipped into the little front drawing-room behind her. It was crammed, and it was such a little room. Why had she not foreseen this, why had she not sent a note across to Olga earlier in the day, asking her to treat Lucia's house precisely as her own, and have her party in the spacious music-room? It would have been only neigh-bourly. But the bitterness of such regrets soon vanished in the extraordinary sweetness of the present, and she was soon in con-versation with Mrs Garroby-Ashton, and distributing little smiles and nods to all the folk with whom she had the slightest acquaintance. By the fireplace was standing the Royal lady, and that for the moment was the only chagrin, for Lucia had not the vaguest idea who she was. Then Georgie came in, looking like a flower-stall, and then came a slight second chagrin, for Olga led him up to the Royal lady, and introduced him. But that would be all right, for she could easily get Georgie to tell her who she was, without exactly asking him, and then poor Georgie made a very awkward sort of bow, and dropped a large quantity of flowers, and said 'tarsome'.

Lucia glided away from Mrs Garroby-Ashton and stood near the Duchess of Whitby. Marcia did not seem to recognise her at first, but that was quickly remedied, and after a little pleasant talk, Lucia asked her to lunch to meet Olga, and fixed in her mind that she must ask Olga to lunch on the same day to meet the Duchess of Whitby. Then edging a little nearer to the centre of attraction, she secured Lord Limpsfield by angling for him with the bait of dearest Aggie, to whom she must remember to telephone early next morning, to ask her to come and meet Lord Limpsfield.

That would do for the present, and Lucia abandoned herself to the joys of the moment. A move was made downstairs to supper, and

Lucia, sticking like a limpet to Lord Limpsfield, was wafted in azure to Olga's little tiny dining-room, and saw at once that there were not nearly enough seats for everybody. There were two small round tables, and that was absolutely all: the rest would have to stand and forage at the narrow buffet which ran along the wall.

'It's musical chairs,' said Olga cheerfully, 'those who are quick get seats, and the others don't. Tony, go and sit next the Princess, and Cortese, you go the other side. We shall all get something to eat sometime. Georgie, go and stand by the buffet, there's a dear, and make yourself wonderfully useful, and oh, rush upstairs first, and bring the cigarettes; they stay the pangs of hunger. Now we're getting on beautifully. Darling Marcia, there's just one chair left. Slip into it.'

Lucia had lingered for a moment at the door to ask Olga to lunch the day after tomorrow, and Olga said she would be delighted, so there was a wonderful little party arranged for. To complete her content it was only needful to be presented to the hitherto anonymous Princess and learn her name. By dexterously picking up her fan for her and much admiring it, as she made a low curtsey, she secured a few precious words with her, but the name was still denied her. To ask anybody what it was would faintly indicate that she didn't know it, and that was not to be thought of.

*   *   *

Georgie popped in, as they all said at Riseholme, to see Lucia next morning when Olga had gone to a rehearsal at Covent Garden, and found her in her music-room, busy over Stravinski. Olga's party had not been in *The Times*, which was annoying, and Lucia was still unaware what the Princess's name was. Though the previous evening had been far the most rewarding she had yet spent, it was wiser to let Georgie suppose that such an affair was a very ordinary occurrence, and not to allude to it for some time.

'Ah, Georgino!' she said. 'How nice of you to pop in. By *buona fortuna* I have got a spare hour this morning, before Sophy Alingsby – dear Sophy, such a brain – fetches me to go to some private view or other, so we can have a good chat. Yes, this is the music-room, and before you go, I must trot you round to see the rest of our little establishment. Not a bad room – those are the famous Chippendale chairs – as soon as we get a little more settled, I shall give an evening party or two with some music. You must come.'

'Should love to,' said Georgie.

'Such a whirl it has been, and it gets worse every day,' went on Lucia. 'Sometimes Peppino and I go out together, but often he dines at one house and I at another – they do that in London, you know – and sometimes I hardly set eyes on him all day. I haven't seen him this morning, but just now they told me he had gone out. He enjoys it so much that I do not mind how tired I get. Ah! that telephone, it never ceases ringing. Sometimes I think I will have it taken out of the house altogether, for I get no peace. Somebody always seems to be wanting Peppino or me.'

She hurried, all the same, with considerable alacrity to the machine, and really there was no thought in her mind of having the telephone taken out, for it had only just been installed. The call, however, was rather a disappointment, for it only concerned a pair of walking-shoes. There was no need, however, to tell Georgie that, and pressing her finger to her forehead she said, 'Yes, I can manage half-past three' (which meant nothing), and quickly rang off.

'Not a moment's peace,' said Lucia. 'Ting-a-ting-a-ting from morning till night. Now tell me all about Riseholme, Georgie; that will give me such a delicious feeling of tranquillity. Dear me, who is this coming to interrupt us now?'

It was only Peppino. He seemed leisurely enough, and rather unnecessarily explained that he had only been out to get a toothbrush from the chemist's in Brompton Road. This he carried in a small paper parcel.

'And there's the man coming about the telephone this morning, Lucia,' he said. 'You want the extension to your bedroom, don't you?'

'Yes, dear, as we have got it in the house we may as well have it conveniently placed,' she said. 'I'm sure the miles I walk up and down stairs, as I was telling Georgie – '

Peppino chuckled.

'She woke them up, Georgie,' he said. 'None of their leisurely London ways for Lucia. She had the telephone put into the house in record time. Gave them no peace till she got it done.'

'Very wise,' said Georgie tactfully. 'That's the way to get things. Well, about Riseholme. We've really been very busy indeed.'

'Dear old place!' said Lucia. 'Tell me all about it.'

Georgie rapidly considered with himself whether he should mention the Museum. He decided against it, for, put it as you might, the Museum, apart from the convenience of getting rid of interesting rubbish, was of a conspiratorial nature, a policy of revenge against Lucia for her desertion, and a demonstration of how wonderfully well and truly they all got on without her. It was, then, the mark of a highly injudicious conspirator to give information to her against whom this plot was directed.

'Well, Daisy has been having some most remarkable experiences,' he said. 'She got a ouija-board and a planchette – we use the planchette most – and very soon it was quite clear that messages were coming through from a guide.'

Lucia laughed with a shrill metallic note of rather hostile timbre.

'Dear Daisy,' she said. 'If only she would take common sense as her guide. I suppose the guide is a Chaldean astrologer or King Nebuchadnezzar.'

'Not at all,' said Georgie. 'It's an Egyptian called Abfou.'

A momentary pang of envy shot through Lucia. She could well imagine the quality of excitement which thrilled Riseholme, how Georgie would have popped in to tell her about it, and how she would have got a ouija-board too, and obtained twice as many messages as Daisy. She hated the thought of Daisy having Abfou all her own way, and gave another little shrill laugh.

'Daisy is priceless,' she said. 'And what has Abfou told her?'

'Well, it was very odd,' said Georgie. 'The morning I got your letter Abfou wrote "L from L", and if that doesn't mean "Letter from Lucia", I don't know what else it could be.'

'It might just as well mean "Lozenges from Leamington",' said Lucia witheringly. 'And what else?'

Georgie felt the conversation was beginning to border rather dangerously on the Museum, and tried a light-hearted sortie into another subject.

'Oh, just things of that sort,' he said. 'And then she had a terrible time over her garden. She dismissed Simkinson for doing crossword puzzles instead of the lawn, and determined to do it all herself. She sowed sprouts in that round bed under the dining-room window.'

'No!' said Peppino, who was listening with qualms of homesickness to these chronicles.

'Yes, and the phlox in the kitchen garden,' said Georgie.

He looked at Lucia, and became aware that her gimlet-eye was on him, and was afraid he had made the transition from Abfou to horticulture rather too eagerly. He went volubly on.

'And she dug up all the seeds that Simkinson had planted, and pruned the roots of her mulberry tree and probably killed it,' he said. 'Then in that warm weather last week, no, the week before, I got out my painting things again, and am doing a sketch of my house from the green. Foljambe is very well, and, and . . .' he could think of nothing else except the Museum.

Lucia waited till he had quite run down.

'And what more did Abfou say?' she asked. 'His message of "L to L" would not have made you busy for very long.'

Georgie had to reconsider the wisdom of silence. Lucia clearly suspected something, and when she came down for her weekend, and found the affairs of the Museum entirely engrossing the whole of Riseholme, his reticence, if he persisted in it, would wear a very suspicious aspect.

'Oh yes, the Museum,' he said with feigned lightness. 'Abfou told us to start a museum, and it's getting on splendidly. That tithe-barn of Colonel Boucher's. And Daisy's given all the things she was going to make into a rockery, and I'm giving my Roman glass and two sketches, and Colonel Boucher his Samian ware and an ordnance map, and there are lots of fossils and some coins.'

'And a committee?' asked Lucia.

'Yes. Daisy and Mrs Boucher and I, and we co-opted Robert,' he said with affected carelessness.

Again some nameless pang shot through Lucia. Absent or present, she ought to have been the chairman of the committee and told them exactly what to do, and how to do it. But she felt no doubt that she could remedy all that when she came down to Riseholme for a weekend. In the meantime, it was sufficient to have pulled his secret out of Georgie, like a cork, with a loud pop, and an effusion of contents.

'Most interesting,' she said. 'I must think what I can give you for your museum. Well, that's a nice little gossip.'

Georgie could not bring himself to tell her that the stocks had already been moved from the village green to the tithe-barn, for he seemed to remember that Lucia and Peppino had presented them to the Parish Council. Now the Parish Council had presented them to the Museum, but that was a reason the more why the Parish Council and not he should face the donors.

'A nice little gossip,' said Lucia. 'And what a pleasant party last night. I just popped over, to congratulate dear Olga on the favourable, indeed the very favourable reception of *Lucrezia*, for I thought she would be hurt – artists are so sensitive – if I did not add my little tribute, and then you saw how she refused to let me go, but insisted that I should come in. And I found it all most pleasant: one met many friends, and I was very glad to be able to look in.'

This expressed very properly what Lucia meant to convey. She did not in the least want to put Olga in her place, but to put herself, in Georgie's eyes, in her own place. She had just, out of kindness, stepped across to congratulate Olga, and then had been dragged in. Unfortunately Georgie did not believe a single word of it: he had already made up his mind that Lucia had laid an ambush for Olga, so swiftly and punctually had she come out of the shadow of the gas lamp on her arrival. He answered her therefore precisely in the spirit in which she had spoken. Lucia would know very well . . .

'It was good of you,' he said enthusiastically. 'I'm sure Olga appreciated your coming immensely. How forgetful of her not to have asked you at first! And as for *Lucrezia* just having a favourable reception, I thought it was the most brilliant success it is possible to imagine.'

Lucia felt that her attitude hadn't quite produced the impression she had intended. Though she did not want Georgie (and Riseholme) to think *she* joined in the uncritical adulation of Olga, she certainly did not want Georgie to tell Olga that she didn't. And she still wanted to hear the Princess's name.

'No doubt, dear Georgie,' she said, 'it was a great success. And she was in wonderful voice, and looked most charming. As you know, I am terribly critical, but I can certainly say that. Yes. And her party delicious. So many pleasant people. I saw you having great jokes with the Princess.'

Peppino having been asleep when Lucia came back last night, and not having seen her this morning, had not heard about the Princess.

'Indeed, who was that?' he asked Lucia.

Very tiresome of Peppino. But Lucia's guide (better than poor Daisy's Abfou) must have been very attentive to her needs that morning, for Peppino had hardly uttered these awkward words, when the telephone rang. She could easily therefore trip across to it, protesting at these tiresome interruptions, and leave Georgie to answer.

'Yes, Mrs Lucas,' said Lucia. 'Covent Garden? Yes. Then please put me through . . . Dearest Olga is ringing up. No doubt about the *Valkyrie* next week . . . '

Georgie had a brainwave. He felt sure Lucia would have answered Peppino's question instantly if she had known what the Princess's name was. He had noticed that Lucia in spite of her hangings about had not been presented to the illustrious lady last night, and the brainwave that she did not know the illustrious lady's name swept over him. He also saw that Lucia was anxiously listening not to the telephone only, but to him. If Lucia (and there could be no doubt about that) wanted to know, she must eat her humble pie and ask him . . .

'Yes, dear Diva, it's me,' said Lucia. 'Couldn't sleep a wink: *Lucrezia* running in my head all night. Marvellous. You rang me up?'

Her face fell.

'Oh, I am disappointed you can't come,' she said. 'You are naughty. I shall have to give you a little engagement book to put things down in . . .'

Lucia's guide befriended her again, and her face brightened. It grew almost to an unearthly brightness as she listened to Olga's apologies and a further proposal.

'Sunday evening?' she said. 'Now let me think a moment: yes, I am free on Sunday. So glad you said Sunday, because all other nights are full. Delightful. And how nice to see Princess Isabel again. Goodbye.'

She snapped the receiver back in triumph.

'What was it you asked me, Peppino?' she said. 'Oh, yes: it was Princess Isabel. Dear Olga insists on my dining with her on Sunday to meet her again. Such a nice woman.'

'I thought we were going down to Riseholme for the Sunday,' said Peppino.

Lucia made a little despairing gesture.

'My poor head!' she said. 'It is I who ought to have an engagement book chained to me. What am I to do? I hardly like to disappoint dear Olga. But you go down, Peppino, just the same. I know you are longing to get a breath of country air. Georgie will give you dinner one night, I am sure, and the other he will dine with you. Won't you, Georgie? So dear of you. Now who shall I get to fill my Olga's place at lunch tomorrow? Mrs Garroby-Ashton, I think. Dear me, it is close on twelve, and Sophy will scold me if I keep her waiting. How the morning flashes by! I had hardly begun my practice, when Georgie came, and I've hardly had a word with him before it is time to go out. What will happen to my morning's post I'm sure I don't know. But I insist on your getting your breath of country air on Sunday, Peppino. I shall have plenty to do here, with all my arrears.'

There was one note Lucia found she had to write before she went out, and she sent Peppino to show Georgie the house while she scribbled it, and addressing it to Mr Stephen Merriall at the office of the *Evening Gazette*, sent it off by hand. This was hardly done when Mrs Alingsby arrived, and they went off together to the private view of the Post-Cubists, and revelled in the works of those remarkable artists. Some were portraits and some landscapes, and it was usually easy to tell which was which, because a careful scrutiny revealed an eye or a stray mouth in some, and a tree or a house in others. Lucia was specially enthusiastic over a picture of Waterloo Bridge, but she had mistaken the number in the catalogue, and it proved to be a portrait of the artist's wife. Luckily she had not actually read out to Sophy that it was Waterloo Bridge, though she had said something about the river, but this was easily covered up in appreciation.

'Too wonderful,' she said. 'How they get to the very soul of things! What is it that Wordsworth says? "The very pulse of the machine". Pulsating, is it not?'

Mrs Alingsby was tall and weird and intense, dressed rather like a bird-of-paradise that had been out in a high gale, but very well connected. She had long straight hair which fell over her forehead, and sometimes got in her eyes, and she wore on her head a scarlet jockey-cap with an immense cameo in front of it. She hated all art that was earlier than 1923, and a considerable lot of what was later. In music, on the other hand, she was primitive, and thought Bach decadent: in literature her taste was for stories without a story, and poems without metre or meaning. But she had collected round her a group of interesting outlaws, of whom the men looked like women, and the women like nothing at all, and though nobody ever knew what they were talking about, they themselves were talked about. Lucia had been to a party of hers, where they all sat in a room with black walls, and listened to early Italian music on a spinet while a charcoal brazier on a blue hearth was fed with incense . . . Lucia's general opinion of her was that she might be useful up to a point, for she certainly excited interest.

'Wordsworth?' she asked. 'Oh, yes, I remember who you mean. About the Westmoreland Lakes. Such a kill-joy.'

She put on her large horn spectacles to look at the picture of the artist's wife, and her body began to sway with a lithe circular motion.

'Marvellous! What a rhythm!' she said. 'Sigismund is the most rhythmical of them all. You ought to be painted by him. He would make something wonderful of you. Something *andante*, *adagio* almost. He's coming to see me on Sunday. Come and meet him. Breakfast about half-past twelve. Vegetarian with cocktails.'

Lucia accepted this remarkable invitation with avidity: it would be an interesting and progressive meal. In these first weeks, she was designedly experimental; she intended to sweep into her net all there was which could conceivably harbour distinction, and sort it out by degrees. She was no snob in the narrow sense of the word; she would have been very discontented if she had only the high-born on her visiting list. The high-born, of course, were safe – you could not make a mistake in having a duchess to tea, because in her own line a duchess had distinction – but it would not have been enough to have all the duchesses there were: it might even have been a disappointing tea-party if the whole room was packed with them. What she wanted was the foam of the wave, the topmost, the most sunlit of the billows that rode the sea. Anything that had proved itself billowish was her game, and anything which showed signs of being a billow, even if it entailed a vegetarian lunch with cocktails and the possible necessity of being painted like the artist's wife with an eyebrow in one corner of the picture and a substance like desiccated cauliflower in the centre. That had always been her way: whatever those dear funny folk at Riseholme had thought of, a juggler, a professor of Yoga, a geologist, a psychoanalyst, had been snapped up by her and exploited till he exploded.

But Peppino was not as nimble as she. The incense at Sophy's had made him sneeze, and the primitive tunes on the spinet had made him snore; that had been all the uplift they had held for him. Thus, though she did not mind tiring herself to death, because Peppino was having such an interesting time, she didn't mind his going down to Riseholme for the Sunday to rest, while she had a vegetarian lunch with Post-Cubists, and a dinner with a princess. Literally, she could scarcely tell which of the two she looked forward to most; the princess was safe, but the Post-Cubists might prove more perilously paying. It was impossible to make a corner in princesses for they were too independent, but already, in case of Post-Cubism turning out to be the rage, she could visualise her music-room and even the famous Chippendale chairs being painted black, and the Sargent picture of Auntie being banished to the attic. She could not make them the rage, for she was not (as yet) the supreme arbiter here that she had been at Riseholme, but should they become the rage, there was no one surely more capable than herself of giving the impression that she had discovered them.

Lucia spent a strenuous afternoon with correspondence and telephonings, and dropped into Mrs Sandeman's for a cup of tea, of which she stood sorely in need. She found there was no need to tell dearest Aggie about the party last night at Olga's, for the *Evening Gazette* had come in, and there was an account of it, described in Hermione's matchless style. Hermione had found the bijou residence

of the prima-donna in Brompton Square full of friends – *très intimes* –
who had been invited to celebrate the huge success of *Lucrezia* and to
congratulate Mrs Shuttleworth. There was Princess Isabel, wearing
her wonderful turquoises, chatting with the composer, Signor Cortese
(Princess Isabel spoke Italian perfectly), and among other friends
Hermione had noticed the Duchess of Whitby, Lord Limpsfield,
Mrs Garroby-Ashton, and Mrs Philip Lucas.

Chapter Five

The mystery of that Friday evening in the last week in June became
portentous on the ensuing Saturday morning . . .

A cab had certainly driven from the station to The Hurst late on
Friday evening, but owing to the darkness it was not known who got
out of it. Previously the windows of The Hurst had been very
diligently cleaned all Friday afternoon. Of course the latter might be
accounted for by the mere fact that they needed cleaning, but if it
had been Peppino or Lucia herself who had arrived by the cab (if
both of them, they would almost certainly have come by their motor),
surely some sign of their presence would have manifested itself either
to Riseholme's collective eye, or to Riseholme's ear. But the piano,
Daisy felt certain, had not been heard, nor had the telephone tinkled
for anybody. Also, when she looked out about half-past ten in the
evening, and again when she went upstairs to bed, there were no
lights in the house. But somebody had come, and as the servants'
rooms looked out on to the back, it was probably a servant or servants.
Daisy had felt so terribly interested in this that she came restlessly
down, and had a quarter of an hour's weedjing to see if Abfou could
tell her. She had been quite unable to form any satisfactory conjecture
herself, and Abfou, after writing 'Museum' once or twice, had relapsed
into rapid and unintelligible Arabic. She did not ring up Georgie to
ask his help in solving this conundrum, because she hoped to solve it
unaided and be able to tell him the answer.

She went upstairs again, and after a little deep-breathing and
bathing her feet in alternate applications of hot and cold water in
order to produce somnolence, found herself more widely awake than
ever. Her well-trained mind cantered about on scents that led nowhere, and she was unable to find any that seemed likely to lead
anywhere. Of Lucia nothing whatever was known except what was
accessible to anybody who spent a penny on the *Evening Gazette*. She

had written to nobody, she had given no sign of any sort, and, but for the *Evening Gazette*, she might, as far as Riseholme was concerned, be dead. But the *Evening Gazette* showed that she was alive, painfully alive in fact, if Hermione could be trusted. She had been seen here, there and everywhere in London: Hermione had observed her chatting in the Park with friends, sitting with friends in her box at the opera, shopping in Bond Street, watching polo (why, she did not know a horse from a cow!) at Hurlingham, and even in a punt at Henley. She had been entertaining in her own house too: there had been dinner parties and musical parties, and she had dined at so many houses that Daisy had added them all up, hoping to prove that she had spent more evenings than there had been evenings to spend, but to her great regret they came out exactly right. Now she was having her portrait painted by Sigismund, and not a word had she written, not a glimpse of herself had she vouchsafed, to Riseholme . . . Of course Georgie had seen her, when he went up to stay with Olga, but his account of her had been far from reassuring. She had said that she did not care how tired she got while Peppino was enjoying London so tremendously. Why then, thought Daisy with a sense of incredulous indignation, had Peppino come down a few Sundays ago, all by himself, and looking a perfect wreck? . . . 'Very odd, *I* call it,' muttered Daisy, turning over to her other side.

It was odd, and Peppino had been odd. He had dined with Georgie one night, and on the other Georgie had dined with him, but he had said nothing about Lucia that Hermione had not trumpeted to the world. Otherwise, Peppino had not been seen at all on that Sunday except when Mrs Antrobus, not feeling very well in the middle of the Psalms on Sunday morning, had come out, and observed him standing on tiptoe and peering into the window of the Museum that looked on to the Roman Antiquities. Mrs Antrobus (feeling much better as soon as she got into the air) had come quite close up to him before he perceived her, and then with only the curtest word of greeting, just as if she was the Museum Committee, he had walked away so fast that she could not but conclude that he wished to be alone. It was odd too, and scarcely honourable, that he should have looked into the window like that, and clearly it was for that purpose that he had absented himself from church, thinking that he would be unobserved. Daisy had not the smallest doubt that he was spying for Lucia, and had been told merely to collect information and to say nothing, for though he knew that Georgie was on the committee, he had carefully kept off the subject of the Museum on both their tête-à-tête dinners. Probably he had begun his spying the moment church began, and if Mrs Antrobus had not so providentially felt faint, no one would have known anything about it. As it was, it was quite likely that he had looked into every window by the time she saw him, and knew all that the Museum contained. Since then, the Museum had been formally opened by Lady Ambermere, who had lent (not presented) some mittens which she said belonged to Queen Charlotte (it was impossible to prove that they hadn't), and the committee had put up some very baffling casement curtains which would make an end to spying for ever.

Now this degrading espionage had happened three weeks ago (come Sunday), and therefore for three weeks (come Monday), Lucia must have known all about the Museum. But not a word had she transmitted on that or any other subject; she had not demanded a place on the committee, nor presented the Elizabethan spit which so often made the chimney of her music-room to smoke, nor written to say that they must arrange it all quite differently. That she had a plan, a policy about the Museum, no one who knew Lucia could possibly doubt, but her policy (which thus at present was wrapped in mystery) might be her complete and eternal ignoring of it. It would indeed be dreadful if she intended to remain unaware of it, but Daisy doubted if anyone in her position and of her domineering character could be capable of such inhuman self-control. No: she meant to do something when she came back, but nobody could guess what it was, or when she was coming.

Daisy tossed and turned as she revolved these knotty points. She was sure Lucia would punish them all for making a museum while she was away, and not asking her advice and begging her to be president, and she would be ill with chagrin when she learned how successful it was proving. The tourist season, when charabancs passed through Riseholme in endless procession, had begun, and whole parties after lunching at the Ambermere Arms went to see it. In the first week alone there had been a hundred and twenty-six visitors, and that meant a corresponding take of shillings without reckoning sixpenny catalogues. Even the committee paid their shillings when they went in to look at their own exhibits, and there had been quite a scene when Lady Ambermere with a party from The Hall tried to get in without paying for any of them on the ground that she had lent the Museum Queen Charlotte's mittens. Georgie, who was hanging up another picture of his, had heard it all and hidden behind a curtain. The small boy in charge of the turnstile (bought from a bankrupt circus for a mere song) had, though trembling with fright, absolutely refused to let the turnstile turn until the requisite number of shillings had been paid, and didn't care whose mittens they were which Lady Ambermere had lent, and when, snatching up a catalogue without paying for it, she had threatened to report him to the committee, this intrepid lad had followed her, continuing to say 'Sixpence, please, my lady,' till one of the party, in order to save brawling in a public place, had produced the insignificant sum. And if Lucia tried to get in without paying, on the ground that she and Peppino had given the stocks to the Parish Council, which had lent them to the Museum, she would find her mistake. At length, in the effort to calculate what would be the total receipts of the year if a hundred and twenty-six people per week paid their shillings, Daisy lapsed into an uneasy arithmetical slumber.

Next morning (Saturday), the mystery of that arrival at The Hurst the evening before grew infinitely more intense. It was believed that only one person had come, and yet there was no doubt that several pounds of salmon, dozens ('Literally dozens,' said Mrs Boucher, 'for I saw the basket') of eggs, two chickens, a leg of lamb, as well as countless other provisions unidentified were delivered at the back door of The Hurst; a positive frieze of tradesmen's boys was strung across the green. Even if the mysterious arrival was Lucia herself, she could not, unless the whirl and worldliness of her London life had strangely increased her appetite, eat all that before Monday. And besides, why had she not rung up Georgie, or somebody, or opened her bedroom window on this hot morning? Or could it be Peppino again, sent down here for a rest-cure and a stuffing of his emaciated frame? But then he would not have come down without some sort of attendant to look after him . . . Riseholme was completely baffled; never had its powers of inductive reasoning been so non-plussed, for though so much went into The Hurst, nobody but the tradesmen's boys with empty baskets came out. Georgie and Daisy stared at each other in blankness over the garden paling, and when, in despair of arriving at any solution, they sought the oracles of Abfou, he would give them nothing but hesitating Arabic.

'Which shows,' said Daisy, as she put the planchette away in disgust, 'that even he doesn't know, or doesn't wish to tell us.' Lunchtime arrived, and there were very poor appetites in Riseholme (with the exception of that Gargantuan of whom nothing was known). But as for going to The Hurst and ringing the bell and asking if Mrs Lucas was at home all Riseholme would sooner have died lingering and

painful deaths, rather than let Lucia know that they took the smallest
interest in anything she had done, was doing or would do.

About three o'clock Georgie was sitting on the green opposite his
house, finishing his sketch, which the affairs of the Museum had
caused him sadly to neglect. He had got it upside down on his easel
and was washing some more blue into the sky, when he heard the
hoot of a motor. He just looked up, and what he saw caused his hand
to twitch so violently that he put a large dab of cobalt on the middle
of his red-brick house. For the motor had stopped at The Hurst, not
a hundred yards away, and out of it got Lucia and Peppino. She gave
some orders to her chauffeur, and then without noticing him (*perhaps*
without seeing him) she followed Peppino into the house. Hardly
waiting to wash the worst of the cobalt off his house, Georgie hurried
into Daisy's, and told her exactly what had happened.

'No!' said Daisy, and out they came again, and stood in the shadow
of her mulberry tree to see what would happen next. The mulberry
tree had recovered from the pruning of its roots (so it wasn't it which
Abfou had said was dead), and gave them good shelter.

Nothing happened next.

'But it's impossible,' said Daisy, speaking in a sort of conspiratorial
whisper. 'It's queer enough her coming without telling any of us, but
now she's here, she surely must ring somebody up.'

Georgie was thinking intently.

'The next thing that will happen,' he said, 'will be that servants and
luggage will arrive from the station. They'll be here any minute; I
heard the three-twenty whistle just now. She and Peppino have driven
down.'

'I shouldn't wonder,' said Daisy. 'But even now, what about the
chickens and all those eggs? Georgie, it must have been her cook
who came last night – she and Peppino were dining out in London –
and ordered all those provisions this morning. But there were enough
to last them a week. And three pints of cream, so I've heard since,
and enough ice for a skating rink and – '

It was then that Georgie had the flash of intuition that was for ever
memorable. It soared above inductive reasoning.

'She's having a weekend party of some of her smart friends from
London,' he said slowly. 'And she doesn't want any of us.'

Daisy blinked at this amazing light. Then she cast one withering
glance in the direction of The Hurst.

'She!' she said. 'And her shingles. And her seed pearls! That's all.'

A minute afterwards the station cab arrived pyramidal with luggage.

Four figures disembarked, three female and one male.

'The major-domo,' said Daisy, and without another word marched back into her house to ask Abfou about it all. He came through at once, and wrote 'Snob' all over the paper.

There was no reason why Georgie should not finish his sketch, and he sat down again and began by taking out the rest of the misplaced cobalt. He felt so certain of the truth of his prophecy that he just let it alone to fulfil itself, and for the next hour he never worked with more absorbed attention. He knew that Daisy came out of her house, walking very fast, and he supposed she was on her way to spread the news and forecast the sequel. But beyond the fact that he was perfectly sure that a party from London was coming down for the weekend, he could form no idea of what would be the result of that. It might be that Lucia would ask him or Daisy, or some of her old friends to dine, but if she had intended to do that she would probably have done it already. The only alternative seemed to be that she meant to ignore Riseholme altogether. But shortly before the arrival of the fast train from London at half-past four, his prophetical calm began (for he was but human) to be violently agitated, and he took his tea in the window of his drawing-room, which commanded a good view of the front garden of The Hurst, and put his opera-glasses ready to hand. The window was a big bow, and he distinctly saw the end of Robert's brass telescope projecting from the corresponding window next door.

Once more a motor-horn sounded, and the Lucases' car drew up at the gate of The Hurst. There stepped out Mrs Garroby-Ashton, followed by the weird bright thing which had called to take Lucia to the private view of the Post-Cubists. Georgie had not time for the moment to rack his brain as to the name he had forgotten, for observation was his primary concern, and next he saw Lord Limps-field, whom he had met at Olga's party. Finally there emerged a tall, slim, middle-aged man in Oxford trousers, for whom Georgie instantly conceived a deep distrust. He had thick auburn hair, for he wore no hat, and he waved his hands about in a silly manner as he talked. Over his shoulder was a little cape. Then Lucia came tripping out of the house with her short skirts and her shingles, and they all chattered together, and kissed and squealed, and pointed in different directions, and moved up the garden into the house. The door was shut, and the end of Robert's brass telescope withdrawn.

*   *   *

Hardly had these shameful events occurred when Georgie's telephone bell rang. It might be Daisy wanting to compare notes, but it might be Lucia asking him to tea. He felt torn in half at the idea: carnal curiosity urged him with clamour to go, dignity dissuaded him. Still halting between two opinions, he went towards the instrument, which continued ringing. He felt sure now that it was Lucia, and what on earth was he to say? He stood there so long that Foljambe came hurrying into the room, in case he had gone out.

'See who it is, Foljambe,' he said.

Foljambe with amazing calm took off the receiver.

'Trunk call,' she said.

He glued himself to the instrument, and soon there came a voice he knew.

'No! Is it you?' he asked. 'What is it?'

'I'm motoring down tomorrow morning,' said Olga, 'and Princess Isabel is probably coming with me, though she is not absolutely certain. But expect her, unless I telephone tomorrow. Be a darling and give us lunch, as we shall be late, and come and dine. Terrible hurry: goodbye.'

'No, you must wait a minute,' screamed Georgie. 'Of course I'll do that, but I must tell you, Lucia's just come with a party from London and hasn't asked any of us.'

'No!' said Olga. 'Then don't tell her I'm coming. She's become such a bore. She asks me to lunch and dinner every day. How thrilling though, Georgie! Whom has she got?'

Suddenly the name of the weird bright female came back to Georgie.

'Mrs Alingsby,' he said.

'Lor!' said Olga. 'Who else?'

'Mrs Garroby-Ashton – '

'What?'

'Garr-o-by Ash-ton,' said Georgie very distinctly; 'and Lord Limpsfield. And a tall man in Oxford trousers with auburn hair.'

'It sounds like your double, Georgie,' said Olga. 'And a little cape like yours?'

'Yes,' said Georgie rather coldly.

'I think it must be Stephen Merriall,' said Olga after a pause.

'And who's that?' asked he.

'Lucia's lover,' said Olga quite distinctly.

'No!' said Georgie.

'Of course he isn't. I only meant he was always there. But I believe he's Hermione. I'm not sure, but I think so. Georgie, we shall have a hectic Sunday. Goodbye, tomorrow about two or three for lunch, and two or three *for* lunch. What a gossip you are.'

He heard that delicious laugh, and the click of her receiver.

Georgie was far too thrilled to gasp. He sat quite quiet, breathing gently. For the honour of Riseholme he was glad that a Princess was perhaps coming to lunch with him, but apart from that he would really have much preferred that Olga should be alone. The 'affaire Lucia' was so much more thrilling than anything else, but Princess Isabel might feel no interest in it, and instead they would talk about all sorts of dull things like kings and courts . . . Then suddenly he sprang from his chair: there was a leg of lamb for Sunday lunch, and an apple tart, and nothing else at all. What was to be done? The shops by now would be shut.

He rang for Foljambe.

'Miss Olga's coming to lunch and possibly – possibly a friend of hers,' he said. 'What are we to do?'

'A leg of lamb and an apple tart's good enough for anybody, isn't it?' said Foljambe severely.

This really seemed true as soon as it was pointed out, and Georgie made an effort to dismiss the matter from his mind. But he could not stop still: it was all so exciting, and after having changed his Oxford trousers in order to minimise the likeness between him and that odious Mr Merriall, he went out for a constitutional, round the green from all points of which he could see any important development at The Hurst. Riseholme generally was doing the same, and his stroll was interrupted by many agreeable stoppages. It was already known that Lucia and Peppino had arrived, and that servants and luggage had come by the three-twenty, and that Lucia's motor had met the half-past four and returned laden with exciting people. Georgie therefore was in high demand, for he might supply the names of the exciting people, and he had the further information to divulge that Olga was arriving tomorrow, and was lunching with him and dining at her own house. He said nothing about a possible Princess: she might not come, and in that case he knew that there would be a faint suspicion in everybody's mind that he had invented it; whereas if she did, she would no doubt sign his visitors' book for everyone to see.

Feeling ran stormy high against Lucia, and as usual when Riseholme felt a thing deeply there was little said by way of public comment, though couples might have been observed with set and angry faces and gabbling mouths. But higher yet ran curiosity and surmise as to what Lucia would do, and what Olga would do. Not a sign had come for anyone from The Hurst, not a soul had been asked to lunch, dinner, or even tea, and if Lucia seemed to be ashamed of Riseholme society before her grand friends, there was no doubt that Riseholme society was ashamed of Lucia . . .

And then suddenly a deadly hush fell on these discussions, and even those who were walking fastest in their indignation came to a halt, for out of the front door of The Hurst streamed the 'exciting people' and their hosts. There was Lucia, hatless and shingled and short-skirted, and the Bird-of-Paradise and Mrs Garroby-Ashton, and Peppino and Lord Limpsfield and Mr Merriall all talking shrilly together, with shrieks of hollow laughter. They came slowly across the green towards the little pond round which Riseholme stood, and passed within fifty yards of it, and if Lucia had been the Gorgon, Riseholme could not more effectually have been turned into stone. She too, appeared not to notice them, so absorbed was she in conversation, and on they went straight towards the Museum. Just as they passed Colonel Boucher's house, Mrs Boucher came out in her bath-chair, and without pause was wheeled straight through the middle of them. She then drew up by the side of the green below the large elm.

The party passed into the Museum. The windows were open, and from inside them came shrieks of laughter. This continued for about ten minutes, and then . . . they all came out again. Several of them carried catalogues, and Mr Merriall was reading out of one in a loud voice.

'Pair of worsted mittens,' he announced, 'belonging to Queen Charlotte, and presented by the Lady Ambermere.'

'Don't,' said Lucia. 'Don't make fun of our dear little Museum, Stephen.'

As they retraced their way along the edge of the green, movement came back to Riseholme again. Lucia's policy with regard to the Museum had declared itself. Georgie strolled up to Mrs Boucher's bath-chair. Mrs Boucher was extremely red in the face, and her hands were trembling.

'Good-evening, Mr Georgie,' said she. 'Another party of strangers, I see, visiting the Museum. They looked very odd people, and I hope we shan't find anything missing. Any news?'

That was a very dignified way of taking it, and Georgie responded in the same spirit.

'Not a scrap that I know of,' he said, 'except that Olga's coming down tomorrow.'

'That will be nice,' said Mrs Boucher. 'Riseholme is always glad to see *her*.'

Daisy joined them.

'Good-evening, Mrs Quantock,' said Mrs Boucher. 'Any news?'

'Yes, indeed,' said Daisy rather breathlessly. 'Didn't you see them? Lucia and her party?'

'No,' said Mrs Boucher firmly. 'She is in London surely. Anything else?'

Daisy took the cue. Complete ignorance that Lucia was in Riseholme at all was a noble manoeuvre.

'It must have been my mistake,' she said. 'Oh, my mulberry tree has quite come round.'

'No!' said Mrs Boucher in the Riseholme voice. 'I am pleased. I dare say the pruning did it good. And Mr Georgie's just told me that our dear Olga, or I should say Mrs Shuttleworth, is coming down tomorrow, but he hasn't told me what time yet.'

'Two or three, she said,' answered Georgie. 'She's motoring down, and is going to have lunch with me whenever she gets here.'

'Indeed! Then I should advise you to have something cold that won't spoil by waiting. A bit of cold lamb, for instance. Nothing so good on a hot day.'

'What an excellent idea!' said Georgie. 'I was thinking of hot lamb. But the other's much better. I'll have it cooked tonight.'

'And a nice tomato salad,' said Mrs Boucher, 'and if you haven't got any, I can give you some. Send your Foljambe round, and she'll come back with half a dozen ripe tomatoes.'

Georgie hurried off to see to these new arrangements, and Colonel Boucher having strolled away with Piggy, his wife could talk freely to Mrs Quantock . . . She did.

*   *   *

Lucia waking rather early next morning found she had rather an uneasy conscience as her bedfellow, and she used what seemed very reasonable arguments to quiet it. There would have been no point in writing to Georgie or any of them to say that she was bringing down some friends for the weekend and would be occupied with them all Sunday. She could not with all these guests play duets with Georgie, or get poor Daisy to give an exhibition of ouija, or have Mrs Boucher in her bath-chair to tea, for she would give them all long histories of purely local interest, which could not conceivably amuse people like Lord Limpsfield or weird Sophy. She had been quite wise to keep

Riseholme and Brompton Square apart, for they would not mix. Besides, her guests would go away on Monday morning, and she had determined to stop over till Tuesday and be extremely kind, and not the least condescending. She would have one or two of them to lunch, and one or two more to dinner, and give Georgie a full hour of duets as well. Naturally, if Olga had been here, she would have asked Olga on Sunday but Olga had been singing last night at the opera. Lucia had talked a good deal about her at dinner, and given the impression that they were never out of each other's houses either in town or here, and had lamented her absence.

'Such a pity,' she had said. 'For dearest Olga loves singing in my music-room. I shall never forget how she dropped in for some little garden-party and sang the awakening of Brünnhilde. Even you, dear Sophy, with your passion for the primitive, would have enjoyed that. She sang *Lucrezia* here, too, before anyone had heard it. Cortese brought the score down the moment he had finished it – ah, I think that was in her house – there was just Peppino and me, and perhaps one or two others. We would have had dearest Olga here all day tomorrow if only she had been here . . . '

So Lucia felt fairly easy, having planned these treats for Riseholme on Monday, as to her aloofness today, and then her conscience brought up the question of the Museum. Here she stoutly defended herself: she knew nothing about the Museum (except what Peppino had seen through the window a few Sundays before); she had not been consulted about the Museum, she was not on the committee, and it was perfectly proper for her to take her party to see it. She could not prevent them bursting into shrieks of laughter at Queen Charlotte's mittens and Daisy's drain-pipes, nor could she possibly prevent herself from joining in those shrieks of laughter herself, for surely this was the most ridiculous collection of rubbish ever brought together. A glass case for Queen Charlotte's mittens, a heap of fossils such as she had chipped out by the score from the old quarry, some fragments of glass (Georgie ought to have known better), some quilts, a dozen coins, lent, only lent, by poor Daisy! In fact the only object of the slightest interest was the pair of stocks which she and Peppino had bought and set up on the village green. She would see about that when she came down in August, and back they should go on to the village green. Then there was the catalogue: who could help laughing at the catalogue which described in most pompous language the contents of this dustbin? There was nothing to be uneasy about over that. And as for Mrs Boucher having driven right through her party without a glance of recognition, what did that matter? On her own side also, Lucia had given no glance of recognition to Mrs Boucher: if she had, Mrs Boucher would have told them all about her asparagus or how her Elizabeth had broken a plate. It was odd, perhaps, that Mrs Boucher hadn't stopped . . . and was it rather odd also that, though from the corner of her eye she had seen all Riseholme standing about on the green, no one had made the smallest sign of welcome? It was true that she had practically cut them (if a process conducted at the distance of fifty yards can be called a cut), but she was not quite sure that she enjoyed the same process herself. Probably it meant nothing; they saw she was engaged with her friends, and very properly had not thrust themselves forward.

Her guests mostly breakfasted upstairs, but by the middle of the morning they had all straggled down. Lucia had brought with her yesterday her portrait by Sigismund, which Sophy declared was a masterpiece of *adagio*. She was advising her to clear all other pictures out of the music-room and hang it there alone, like a wonderful slow movement, when Mr Merriall came in with the Sunday paper.

'Ah, the paper has come,' said Lucia. 'Is not that Riseholmish of us? We never get the Sunday paper till midday.'

'Better late than never,' said Mr Merriall, who was rather addicted to quoting proverbial sayings. 'I see that Mrs Shuttleworth's coming down here today. Do ask her to dine and perhaps she'll sing to us.'

Lucia paused for a single second, then clapped her hands.

'Oh, what fun that would be!' she said. 'But I don't think it can be true. Dearest Olga popped in – or did I pop in – yesterday morning in town, and she said nothing about it. No doubt she had not made up her mind then whether she was coming or not. Of course I'll ring her up at once and scold her for not telling me.'

Lucia found from Olga's caretaker that she and a friend were expected, but she knew they couldn't come to lunch with her, as they were lunching with Mr Pillson. She 'couldn't say, I'm sure' who the friend was, but promised to give the message that Mrs Lucas hoped they would both come and dine . . . The next thing was to ring up Georgie and be wonderfully cordial.

'Georgino *mio*, is it 'oo?' she asked.

'Yes,' said Georgie. He did not have to ask who it was, nor did he feel inclined for baby-talk.

'Georgino, I never caught a glimpse of you yesterday,' she said. 'Why didn't 'oo come round and see me?'

'Because you never asked me,' said Georgie firmly, 'and because you never told me you were coming.'

'Me so sorry,' said Lucia. 'But me was so fussed and busy in town. Delicious to be in Riseholme again.'

'Delicious,' said Georgie.

Lucia paused a moment.

'Is Georgino cross with me?' she asked.

'Not a bit,' said Georgie brightly. 'Why?'

'I didn't know. And I hear my Olga and a friend are lunching with you. I am hoping they will come and dine with me tonight. And do come in afterwards. We shall be eight already, or of course I should ask you.'

'Thanks so much, but I'm dining with her,' said Georgie.

A pause.

'Well, all of you come and dine here,' said Lucia. 'Such amusing people, and I'll squeeze you in.'

'I'm afraid I can't accept for Olga,' said Georgie. 'And I'm dining with her, you see.'

'Well, will you come across after lunch and bring them?' said Lucia. 'Or tea?'

'I don't know what they will feel inclined to do,' said Georgie. 'But I'll tell them.'

'Do, and I'll ring up at lunchtime again, and have ickle talk to my Olga. Who is her friend?'

Georgie hesitated: he thought he would not give that away just yet. Lucia would know in heaps of time.

'Oh, just somebody whom she's possibly bringing down,' he said, and rang off.

Lucia began to suspect a slight mystery, and she disliked mysteries, except when she made them herself. Olga's caretaker was 'sure she couldn't say', and Georgie (Lucia was sure) wouldn't. So she went back to her guests, and very prudently said that Olga had not arrived at present, and then gave them a wonderful account of her little *intime* dinner with Olga and Princess Isabel. Such a delightful amusing woman: they must all come and meet Princess Isabel some day soon in town.

Lucia and her guests, with the exception of Sophy Alingsby who continued to play primitive tunes with one finger on the piano, went for a stroll on the green before lunch. Mrs Quantock hurried by with averted face, and naturally everybody wanted to know who the Red Queen from *Alice in Wonderland* was. Lucia amused them by a bright version of poor Daisy's ouija-board and the story of the mulberry tree.

'Such dears they all are,' she said. 'But too killing. And then she planted broccoli instead of phlox. It's only in Riseholme that such things happen. You must all come and stay with me in August, and we'll enter into the life of the place. I adore it, simply adore it. We are always wildly excited about something . . . And next door is Georgie Pillson's house. A lamb! I'm devoted to him. He does embroidery, and gave those broken bits of glass to the Museum. And that's dear Olga's house at the end of the road . . .'

Just as Lucia was kissing her hand to Olga's house, her eagle eye had seen a motor approaching, and it drew up at Georgie's house. Two women got out, and there was no doubt whatever who either of them were. They went in at the gate, and he came out of his front door like the cuckoo out of a clock and made a low bow. All this Lucia saw, and though for the moment petrified, she quickly recovered, and turned sharply round.

'Well, we must be getting home again,' she said, in a rather strangled voice. 'It is lunchtime.'

Mr Merriall did not turn so quickly, but watched the three figures at Georgie's door.

'Appearances are deceptive,' he said. 'But isn't that Olga Shuttleworth and Princess Isabel?'

'No! Where?' said Lucia, looking in the opposite direction.

'Just gone into that house; Georgie Pillson's, didn't you say?'

'No, really?' said Lucia. 'How stupid of me not to have seen them. Shall I pop in now? No, I think I will ring them up presently, unless we find that they have already rung me up.'

Lucia was putting a brave face on it, but she was far from easy. It looked like a plot: it did indeed, for Olga had never told her she was coming to Riseholme, and Georgie had never told her that Princess Isabel was the friend she was bringing with her. However, there was lunchtime in which to think over what was to be done. But though she talked incessantly and rather satirically about Riseholme, she said no more about the prima-donna and the Princess . . .

*   *   *

Lucia might have been gratified (or again she might not) if she had known how vivacious a subject of conversation she afforded at Georgie's select little luncheon-party. Princess Isabel (with her mouth now full of Mrs Boucher's tomatoes) had been subjected during this last week to an incessant bombardment from Lucia, and had heard on quite good authority that she alluded to her as 'Isabel, dear Princess Isabel'.

'And I will not go to her house,' she said. 'It is a free country, and I do not choose to go to her kind house. No doubt she is a very good woman. But I want to hear more of her, for she thrills me. So does your Riseholme. You were talking of the Museum.'

'Georgie, go on about the Museum,' said Olga.

'Well,' said Georgie, 'there it was. They all went in, and then they all came out again, and one of them was reading my catalogue – I made it – aloud, and they all screamed with laughter.'

'But I dare say it was a very funny catalogue, Georgie,' said Olga.

'I don't think so. Mr Merriall read out about Queen Charlotte's mittens presented by Lady Ambermere.'

'No!' said Olga.

'Most interesting!' said the Princess. 'She was my aunt, big aunt, is it? No, great-aunt – that is it. Afterwards we will go to the Museum and see her mittens. Also, I must see the lady who kills mulberry trees. Olga, can't you ask her to bring her planchette and prophesy?'

'Georgie, ring up Daisy, and ask her to come to tea with me,' said Olga. 'We must have a weedj.'

'And I must go for a drive, and I must walk on the green, and I must have some more delicious apple pie,' began the Princess.

Georgie had just risen to ring up Daisy, when Foljambe entered with the news that Mrs Lucas was on the telephone and would like to speak to Olga.

'Oh, say we're still at lunch, please, Foljambe,' said she. 'Can she send a message? And you say Stephen Merriall is there, Georgie?'

'No, you said he was there,' said Georgie. 'I only described him.'

'Well, I'm pretty sure it is he, but you will have to go sometime this afternoon and find out. If it is, he's Hermione, who's always writing about Lucia in the *Evening Gazette*. Priceless! So you must go across for a few minutes, Georgie, and make certain.'

Foljambe came back to ask if Mrs Lucas might pop in to pay her respects to Princess Isabel.

'So kind of her, but she must not dream of troubling herself,' said the Princess.

Foljambe retired and appeared for the third time with a faint, firm smile.

'Mrs Lucas will ring up Mrs Shuttleworth in a quarter of an hour,' she said.

The Princess finished her apple tart.

'And now let us go and see the Museum,' she said.

*   *   *

Georgie remained behind to ring up Daisy, to explain when Lucia telephoned next that Olga had gone out, and to pay his visit to The Hurst. To pretend that he did not enjoy that, would be to misunderstand him altogether. Lucia had come down here with her smart party and had taken no notice of Riseholme, and now two people a million times smarter had by a clearly providential dealing come down at the same time and were taking no notice of her. Instead they were hobnobbing with people like himself and Daisy whom Lucia had slighted. Then she had laughed at the Museum, and especially at the catalogue and the mittens, and now the great-niece of the owner of the mittens had gone to see them. That was a stinger, in fact it was all a stinger, and well Lucia deserved it.

He was shown into the music-room, and he had just time to observe that there was a printed envelope on the writing-table addressed to the *Evening Gazette*, when Lucia and Mr Merriall came hurrying in.

'Georgino *mio*,' said Lucia effusively. 'How nice of you to come in. But you've not brought your ladies? Oh, this is Mr Merriall.'

(Hermione, of the *Evening Gazette*, it's proved, thought Georgie.)

'They thought they wouldn't add to your big party,' said Georgie sumptuously. (That was another stinger.)

'And was it Princess Isabel I saw at your door?' asked Mr Merriall with an involuntary glance at the writing-table. (Lucia had not mentioned her since.)

'Oh yes. They just motored down and took pot luck with me.'

'What did you give them?' asked Lucia, forgetting her anxieties for a moment.

'Oh, just cold lamb and apple tart,' said Georgie.

'No!' said Lucia. 'You ought to have brought them to lunch here. Oh, Georgie, my picture, look. By Sigismund.'

'Oh yes,' said Georgie. 'What's it of?'

'*Cattivo!*' said Lucia. 'Why, it's a portrait of me. Sigismund, you know, he's the great rage in London just now. Everyone is crazy to be painted by him.'

'And they look crazy when they are. It's a mad world, my masters,' said Mr Merriall.

'Naughty,' said Lucia. 'Is it not wonderful, Georgie?'

'Yes. I expect it's very clever,' said Georgie. 'Very clever indeed.'

'I should so like to show it dearest Olga,' said Lucia, 'and I'm sure the Princess would be interested in it. She was talking about modern art the other day when I dined with Olga. I wonder if they would look in at teatime, or indeed any other time.'

'Not very likely, I'm afraid,' said Georgie, 'for Daisy Quantock's coming to tea, I know. We're going to weedj. And they're going out for a drive sometime.'

'And where are they now?' asked Lucia. It was terrible to have to get news of her intimate friends from Georgie, but how else was she to find out?

'They went across to see the Museum,' said he. 'They were most interested in it.'

Mr Merriall waved his hands, just in the same way as Georgie did.

'Ah, that Museum!' he said. 'Those mittens! Shall I ever get over those mittens? Lucia said she would give it the next shoelace she broke.'

'Yes,' said Georgie. 'The Princess wanted to see those mittens. Queen Charlotte was her great-aunt. I told them how amused you all were at the mittens.'

Lucia had been pressing her finger to her forehead, a sign of concentration. She rose as if going back to her other guests.

'Coming into the garden presently?' she asked, and glided from the room.

'And so you're going to have a sitting with the ouija-board,' said Mr Merriall. 'I am intensely interested in ouija. Very odd phenomena certainly occur. Strange but true.'

A fresh idea had come into Georgie's head. Lucia certainly had not appeared outside the window that looked into the garden, and so he walked across to the other one which commanded a view of the green. There she was heading straight for the Museum.

'It is marvellous,' he said to Mr Merriall. 'We have had some curious results here, too.'

Mr Merriall was moving daintily about the room, and Georgie wondered if it would be possible to convert Oxford trousers into an ordinary pair. It was dreadful to think that Olga, even in fun, had suggested that such a man was his double. There was the little cape as well.

'I have quite fallen in love with your Riseholme,' said Mr Merriall.

'We all adore it,' said Georgie, not attending very much because his whole mind was fixed on the progress of Lucia across the green.

Would she catch them in the Museum, or had they already gone? Smaller and smaller grew her figure and her twinkling legs, and at last she crossed the road and vanished behind the belt of shrubs in front of the tithe-barn.

'All so homey and intimate. "Home, Sweet Home", in fact,' said Mr Merriall. 'We have been hearing how Mrs Shuttleworth loves singing in this room.'

Georgie was instantly on his guard again. It was quite right and proper that Lucia should be punished, and of course Riseholme would know all about it, for indeed Riseholme was administering the punishment. But it was a very different thing to let her down before those who were not Riseholme.

'Oh yes, she sings here constantly,' he said. 'We are all in and out of each other's houses. But I must be getting back to mine now.'

Mr Merriall longed to be asked to this little ouija party at Olga's, and at present his hostess had been quite unsuccessful in capturing either of the two great stars. There was no harm in trying . . .

'You couldn't perhaps take me to Mrs Shuttleworth's for tea?' he asked.

'No, I'm afraid I could hardly do that,' said Georgie. 'Goodbye. I hope we shall meet again.'

* * *

Nemesis meantime had been dogging Lucia's footsteps, with more success than Lucia was having in dogging Olga's. She had arrived, as Georgie had seen, at the Museum, and again paid a shilling to enter that despised exhibition. It was rather full, for visitors who had lunched at the Ambermere Arms had come in, and there was quite a crowd round Queen Charlotte's mittens, among whom was Lady Ambermere herself who had driven over from The Hall with two depressed guests whom she had forced to come with her. She put up her glasses and stared at Lucia.

'Ah, Mrs Lucas!' she said with the singular directness for which she was famous. 'For the moment I did not recognise you with your hair like that. It is a fashion that does not commend itself to me. You have come in, of course, to look at Her late Majesty's mittens, for really there is very little else to see.'

As a rule, Lucia shamelessly truckled to Lady Ambermere, and schemed to get her to lunch or dinner. But today she didn't care two straws about her, and while these rather severe remarks were being addressed to her, her eyes darted eagerly round the room in search of those for whom she would have dropped Lady Ambermere without the smallest hesitation.

'Yes, dear Lady Ambermere,' she said. 'So interesting to think that Queen Charlotte wore them. Most good of you to have presented them to our little Museum.'

'Lent,' said Lady Ambermere. 'They are heirlooms in my family. But I am glad to let others enjoy the sight of them. And by a remarkable coincidence I have just had the privilege of showing them to a relative of their late owner. Princess Isabel. I offered to have the case opened for her, and let her try them on. She said, most graciously, that it was not necessary.'

'Yes, dear Princess Isabel,' said Lucia, 'I heard she had come down. Is she here still?'

'No. She and Mrs Shuttleworth have just gone. A motor drive, I understand, before tea. I suggested, of course, a visit to The Hall, where I would have been delighted to entertain them. Where did they lunch?'

'At Georgie Pillson's,' said Lucia bitterly.

'Indeed. I wonder why Mr Pillson did not let me know. Did you lunch there too?'

'No. I have a party in my own house. Some friends from London, Lord Limpsfield, Mrs Garroby-Ashton – '

'Indeed!' said Lady Ambermere. 'I had meant to return to The Hall for tea, but I will change my plans and have a cup of tea with you, Mrs Lucas. Perhaps you would ask Mrs Shuttleworth and her distinguished guest to drop in. I will present you to her. You have a pretty little garden, I remember. Quaint. You are at liberty to say that I am taking tea with you. But stay! If they have gone out for a drive, they will not be back quite yet. It does not matter: we will sit in your garden.'

Now in the ordinary way this would have been a most honourable event, but today, though Lady Ambermere had not changed, her value had. If only Olga had not come down bringing her whom Lucia could almost refer to as that infernal Princess, it would have been rich, it would have been glorious, to have Lady Ambermere dropping in to tea. Even now she would be better than nothing, thought Lucia, and after inspecting the visitors' book of the Museum, where Olga and the Princess had inscribed their names, and where now Lady Ambermere wrote hers, very close to the last one, so as to convey the impression that they were one party, they left the place.

Outside was drawn up Lady Ambermere's car, with her companion, the meek Miss Lyall, sitting on the front seat nursing Lady Amber-mere's stertorous pug.

'Let me see,' said she. 'How had we best arrange? A walk would be good for Pug before he has his tea. Pug takes lukewarm milk with a biscuit broken up into it. Please put Pug on his leash, Miss Lyall, and we will all walk across the green to Mrs Lucas's little house. The motor shall go round by the road and wait for us there. That is Mrs Shuttleworth's little house, is it not? So you might kindly step in there, Mrs Lucas, and leave a message for them about tea, stating that I shall be there. We will walk slowly and you will soon catch us up.'

The speech was thoroughly Ambermerian: everybody in Riseholme had a 'little house' compared with The Hall: everybody had a 'little garden'. Equally Ambermerian was her complete confidence that her wish was everybody else's pleasure, and Lucia dismally reflected that she, for her part, had never failed to indicate that it was. But just now, though Lady Ambermere was so conspicuously second-best, and though she was like a small luggage-engine with a Roman nose and a fat dog, the wretched Lucia badly wanted somebody to 'drop in', and by so doing give her some sort of status – alas, that one so lately the Queen of Riseholme should desire it – in the sight of her guests. She could say what a bore Lady Ambermere was the moment she had gone.

Wretched also was her errand: she knew that Olga and the infernal Princess were to have a ouija with Daisy and Georgie, and that her invitation would be futile, and as for that foolish old woman's suggestion that her presence at The Hurst would prove an attraction to Olga, she was aware that if anything was needful to make Olga refuse to come, it would be that Lady Ambermere was there. Olga had dined at The Hall once, and had been induced to sing, while her hostess played Patience and talked to Pug.

Lucia had a thought: not a very bright one, but comparatively so. She might write her name in the Princess's book: that would be something. So, when her ring was answered, and she ascertained, as she already knew, that Olga was out, and left the hopeless invitation that she and her guest would come to tea, where they would meet Lady Ambermere, she asked for the Princess's book.

Olga's parlour-maid looked puzzled.

'Would that be the book of crossword puzzles, ma'am?' she asked. 'I don't think her Highness brought any other book, and that she's taken with her for her drive.'

Lucia trudged sadly away. Halfway across the green she saw Georgie and Daisy Quantock with a large sort of drawing-board under her arm coming briskly in her direction. She knew where they were going, and she pulled her shattered forces together.

'Dearest Daisy, not set eyes on you!' she said. 'A few friends from London, how it ties one! But I shall pop in tomorrow, for I stop till Tuesday. Going to have a ouija party with dear Piggy and Goosie? Wish I could come, but Lady Ambermere has quartered herself on me for tea, and I must run on and catch her up. Just been to your delicious Museum. Wonderful mittens! Wonderful everything. Peppino and I will look out something for it!'

'Very kind,' said Daisy. It was as if the North Pole had spoken.

Pug and Miss Lyall and Lady Ambermere and her two depressed guests had been admitted to The Hurst before Lucia caught them up, and she found them all seated stonily in the music-room, where Stephen Merriall had been finishing his official correspondence. Well Lucia knew what he had been writing about: there might perhaps be a line or two about The Hurst, and the party weekending there, but that, she was afraid, would form a mere little postscript to more exalted paragraphs. She hastily introduced him to Lady Ambermere and Miss Lyall, but she had no idea who Lady Ambermere's guests were, and suspected they were poor relations, for Lady Ambermere introduced them to nobody.

Pug gave a series of wheezy barks.

'Clever little man,' said Lady Ambermere. 'He is asking for his tea. He barks four times like that for his tea.'

'And he shall have it,' said Lucia. 'Where are the others, Stephen?'

Mr Merriall exerted himself a little on hearing Lady Ambermere's name: he would put in a sentence about her . . .

'Lord Limpsfield and Mrs Garroby-Ashton have gone to play golf,' he said. 'Barbarously energetic of them, is it not, Lady Ambermere? What a sweet little dog.'

'Pug does not like strangers,' said Lady Ambermere. 'And I am disappointed not to see Lord Limpsfield. Do we expect Mrs Shuttleworth and the Princess?'

'I left the message,' said Lucia.

Lady Ambermere's eyes finished looking at Mr Merriall and proceeded slowly round the room.

'What is that curious picture?' she said. 'I am completely puzzled.'

Lucia gave her bright laugh: it was being an awful afternoon, but she had to keep her flag flying.

'Striking, is it not?' she said. 'Dear Benjy Sigismund insisted on painting me. Such a lot of sittings.'

Lady Ambermere looked from one to the other.

'I do not see any resemblance,' she said. 'It appears to me to resemble nothing. Ah, here is tea. A little lukewarm milk for Pug, Miss Lyall. Mix a little hot water with it, it does not suit him to have it quite cold. And I should like to see Mr Georgie Pillson. No doubt he could be told that I am here.'

This was really rather desperate: Lucia could not produce Olga or the Princess, or Lord Limpsfield or Mrs Garroby-Ashton for Lady Ambermere, and she knew she could not produce Georgie, for by that time he would be at Olga's. All that was left for her was to be able to tell Lord Limpsfield and Mrs Garroby-Ashton when they returned that they had missed Lady Ambermere. As for Riseholme . . . but it was better not to think how she stood with regard to Riseholme, which, yesterday, she had settled to be of no account at all. If only, before coming down, she had asked them all to lunch and tea and dinner . . .

The message came back that Mr Pillson had gone to tea with Mrs Shuttleworth. Five minutes later came regrets from Olga that she had friends with her, and could not come to tea. Lady Ambermere ate seed cake in silence. Mrs Alingsby meantime had been spending the afternoon in her bedroom, and she now appeared in a chintz wrapper and morocco slippers. Her hair fell over her eyes like that of an Aberdeen terrier, and she gave a shrill scream when she saw Pug.

'I can't bear dogs,' she said. 'Take that dog away, dear Lucia. Burn it, drown it! You told me you hadn't got any dogs.'

Lady Ambermere turned on her a face that should have instantly petrified her, if she had had any proper feeling. Never had Pug been so blasphemed. She rose as she swallowed the last mouthful of seed cake.

'We are inconveniencing your guests, Mrs Lucas,' she said. 'Pug and I will be off. Miss Lyall, Pug's leash. We must be getting back to The Hall. I shall look in at Mrs Shuttleworth's, and sign my name in the Princess's book. Goodbye, Mrs Lucas. Thank you for my tea.'

She pointedly ignored Mrs Alingsby, and headed the gloomy frieze that defiled through the door. The sole bright spot was that she would find only a book of crossword puzzles to write her name in.

Chapter Six

Lucia's guests went off by the early train next morning and she was left, like Marius among the ruins of Carthage. But, unlike that weak-hearted senator, she had no intention of mourning: her first function was to rebuild, and presently she became aware that the work of rebuilding had to begin from its very foundations. There was as background the fact that her weekend party had not been a triumphant success, for she had been speaking in London of Riseholme being such a queer dear old-fashioned little place, where everybody adored her, and where Olga kept incessantly running in to sing acts and acts of the most renowned operas in her music-room; she had also represented Princess Isabel as being a dear and intimate friend, and these two cronies of hers had politely but firmly refused all invitations to pop in. Lady Ambermere, it is true, had popped in, but nobody had seemed the least impressed with her, and Lucia had really been very glad when after Sophy's painful remarks about Pug, she had popped out, leaving that astonished post-cubist free to enquire who that crashing old hag was. Of course all this could be quickly lived down again when she got to London, but it certainly did require obliteration.

What gave her more pause for thought was the effect that her weekend had produced on Riseholme. Lucia knew that all Riseholme knew that Olga and the Princess had lunched off cold lamb with Georgie, and had never been near The Hurst, and Riseholme, if she knew Riseholme at all, would have something to talk about there. Riseholme knew also that Lucia and her party had shrieked with laughter at the Museum, while the Princess had politely signed her name in the visitors' book after reverently viewing her great-aunt's mittens. But what else had been happening, whether Olga was here still, what Daisy and her ouija-board had been up to, who had dined (if anyone except Georgie) at Olga's last night, Lucia was at present ignorant, and all that she had to find out, for she had a presentiment that nobody would pop in and tell her. Above all, what was Riseholme saying about her? How were they taking it all?

Lucia had determined to devote this day to her old friends, and she rang up Daisy and asked her and Robert to lunch. Daisy regretted that she was engaged, and rang off with such precipitation that (so it was easy to guess) she dropped the receiver on the floor, said 'Drat,' and replaced it. Lucia then rang up Mrs Boucher and asked her and the Colonel to lunch. Mrs Boucher with great emphasis said that she had got friends to lunch. Of course that might mean that Daisy Quantock was lunching there; indeed it seemed a very natural explanation, but somehow it was far from satisfying Lucia.

She sat down to think, and the unwelcome result of thought was a faint suspicion that just as she had decided to ignore Riseholme while her smart party from London was with her, Riseholme was malignant enough to retaliate. It was very base, it was very childish, but there was that possibility. She resolved to put a playful face on it and rang up Georgie. From the extraordinary celerity with which he answered, she wondered whether he was expecting a call from her or another.

'Georgino *mio!*' she said.

The eagerness with which Georgie had said 'Yes. Who is it?' seemed to die out of his voice.

'Oh, it's you, is it?' he said. 'Good-morning.'

Lucia was not discouraged.

'Me coming round to have good long chat,' she said. 'All my tiresome guests have gone, Georgie, and I'm staying till *domani*. So lovely to be here again.'

'*Si,*' said Georgie; just '*si*'.

The faint suspicion became a shade more definite.

'Coming at once then,' said Lucia.

Lucia set forth and emerging on to the green, was in time to see Daisy Quantock hurry out of Georgie's house and bolt into her own like a plump little red-faced rabbit. Somehow that was slightly disconcerting: it required very little inductive reasoning to form the theory that Daisy had popped in to tell Georgie that Lucia had asked her to lunch, and that she had refused. Daisy must have been present also when Lucia rang Georgie up and instead of waiting to join in the good long chat had scuttled home again. A slight effort therefore was needed to keep herself up to the gay playful level and be quite unconscious that anything unpropitious could possibly have occurred. She found Georgie with his sewing in the little room which he called his study because he did his embroidery there. He seemed somehow to Lucia to be encased in a thin covering of ice, and she directed her full effulgence to the task of melting it.

'Now that is nice!' she said. 'And we'll have a good gossip. So lovely to be in Riseholme again. And isn't it naughty of me? I was almost glad when I saw the last of my guests off this morning, and promised myself a real Riseholme day. Such dears, all of them, too, and tremendously in the movement; such arguments and discussions as we had! All day yesterday I was occupied, talks with one, strolls with another, and all the time I was longing to trot round and see you and Daisy and all the rest. Any news, Georgie? What did you do with yourself yesterday?'

'Well, I was very busy too,' said Georgie. 'Quite a rush. I had two guests at lunch, and then I had tea at Olga's – '

'Is she here still?' asked Lucia. She did not intend to ask that, but she simply could not help it.

'Oh yes. She's going to stop here two or three days, as she doesn't sing in London again till Thursday.'

Lucia longed to ask if the Princess was remaining as well, but she had self-control enough not to. Perhaps it would come out some other way . . .

'Dear Olga,' said Lucia effusively. 'I reckon her quite a Rise-holmite.'

'Oh quite,' said Georgie, who was determined not to let his ice melt. 'Yes: I had tea at Olga's, and we had the most wonderful weedj. Just she and the Princess and Daisy and I.'

Lucia gave her silvery peal of laughter. It sounded as if it had 'turned' a little in this hot weather, or got a little tarnished.

'Dear Daisy!' she said. 'Is she not priceless? How she adores her conjuring tricks and hocus-pocuses! Tell me all about it. An Egyptian guide: Abfou, was it not?'

Georgie thought it might be wiser not to tell Lucia all that Abfou had vouchsafed, unless she really insisted, for Abfou had written the most sarcastic things about her in perfect English at top speed. He had called her a snob again, and said she was too grand now for her old friends, and had been really rude about her shingled hair.

'Yes, Abfou,' he said. 'Abfou was in great form, and Olga has telegraphed for a planchette. Abfou said she was most psychical, and had great mediumistic gifts. Well, that went on a long time.'

'What else did Abfou say?' asked Lucia, fixing Georgie with her penetrating eye.

'Oh, he talked about Riseholme affairs,' said Georgie. 'He knew the Princess had been to the Museum, for he had seen her there. It was he, you know, who suggested the Museum. He kept writing Museum, though we thought it was Mouse at first.'

Lucia felt perfectly certain in her own mind that Abfou had been saying things about her. But perhaps, as it was Daisy who had been operating, it was better not to ask what they were. Ignorance was not bliss, but knowledge might be even less blissful. And Georgie was not thawing: he was polite, he was reserved, but so far from chatting, he was talking with great care. She must get him in a more confidential mood.

'That reminds me,' she said. 'Peppino and I haven't given you anything for the Museum yet. I must send you the Elizabethan spit from my music-room. They say it is the most perfect spit in existence. I don't know what Peppino didn't pay for it.'

'How kind of you,' said Georgie. 'I will tell the committee of your offer. Olga gave us a most magnificent present yesterday: the manuscript of *Lucrezia*, which Cortese had given her. I took it to the Museum directly after breakfast, and put it in the glass case opposite the door.'

Again Lucia longed to be as sarcastic as Abfou, and ask whether a committee meeting had been held to settle if this should be accepted. Probably Georgie had some perception of that, for he went on in a great hurry.

'Well, the weedj lasted so long that I had only just time to get home to dress for dinner and go back to Olga's,' he said.

'Who was there?' asked Lucia.

'Colonel and Mrs Boucher, that's all,' said Georgie. 'And after dinner Olga sang too divinely. I played her accompaniments. A lot of Schubert songs.'

Lucia was beginning to feel sick with envy. She pictured to herself the glory of having taken her party across to Olga's after dinner last night, of having played the accompaniments instead of Georgie (who was a miserable accompanist), of having been persuaded afterwards to give them the little morsel of Stravinski, which she had got by heart. How brilliant it would all have been; what a sumptuous paragraph Hermione would have written about her weekend! Instead of which Olga had sung to those old Bouchers, neither of whom knew one note from another, nor cared the least for the distinction of hearing the prima-donna sing in her own house. The bitterness of it could not be suppressed.

'Dear old Schubert songs!' she said with extraordinary acidity. 'Such sweet old-fashioned things. "Wiedmung", I suppose.'

'No, that's by Schumann,' said Georgie, who was nettled by her tone, though he guessed what she was suffering.

Lucia knew he was right, but had to uphold her own unfortunate mistake.

'Schubert, I think,' she said. 'Not that it matters. And so, as dear old Pepys said, and so to bed?'

Georgie was certainly enjoying himself.

'Oh no, we didn't go to bed till terribly late,' he said. 'But you would have hated to be there, for what we did next. We turned on the gramophone –'

Lucia gave a little wince. Her views about gramophones, as being a profane parody of music, were well known.

'Yes, I should have run away then,' she said.

'We turned on the gramophone and danced!' said Georgie firmly.

This was the worst she had heard yet. Again she pictured what yesterday evening might have been. The idea of having popped in with her party after dinner, to hear Olga sing, and then dance impromptu with a prima-donna and a princess . . . It was agonising: it was intolerable.

She gave a dreadful little titter.

'How very droll!' she said. 'I can hardly imagine it. Mrs Boucher in her bath-chair must have been an unwieldy partner, Georgie. Are you not very stiff this morning?'

'No, Mrs Boucher didn't dance,' said Georgie with fearful literalness. 'She looked on and wound up the gramophone. Just we four danced: Olga and the Princess and Colonel Boucher and I.'

Lucia made a great effort with herself. She knew quite well that Georgie knew how she would have given anything to have brought her party across, and it only made matters worse (if they could be made worse) to be sarcastic about it and pretend to find it all ridiculous. Olga certainly had left her and her friends alone, just as she herself had left Riseholme alone, in this matter of her weekend party. Yet it was unwise to be withering about Colonel Boucher's dancing. She had made it clear that she was busy with her party, and but for this unfortunate accident of Olga's coming down, nothing else could have happened in Riseholme that day except by her dispensing. It was unfortunate, but it must be lived down, and if dear old Riseholme was offended with her, Riseholme must be propitiated.

'Great fun it must have been,' she said. 'How delicious a little impromptu thing like that is! And singing too: well, you had a nice evening, Georgie. And now let us make some delicious little plan for today. Pop in presently and have 'ickle music and bit of lunch.'

'I'm afraid I've just promised to lunch with Daisy,' said he.

This again was rather ominous, for there could be no doubt that

Daisy, having said she was engaged, had popped in here to effect an engagement.

'How gay!' said Lucia. 'Come and dine this evening then! Really, Georgie, you are busier than any of us in London.'

'Too tarsome,' said Georgie, 'because Olga's coming in here.'

'And the Princess?' asked Lucia before she could stop herself.

'No, she went away this morning,' said Georgie.

That was something, anyhow, thought Lucia. One distinguished person had gone away from Riseholme. She waited, in slowly diminishing confidence, for Georgie to ask her to dine with him instead. Perhaps he would ask Peppino too, but if not, Peppino would be quite happy with his telescope and his crosswords all by himself. But it was odd and distasteful to wait to be asked to dinner by anybody in Riseholme instead of everyone wanting to be asked by her.

'She went away by the ten-thirty,' said Georgie, after an awful pause.

Lucia had already learned certain lessons in London. If you get a snub – and this seemed very like a snub – the only possible course was to be unaware of it. So, though the thought of being snubbed by Georgie nearly made her swoon, she was unaware of it.

'Such a good train,' she said, magnificently disregarding the well-known fact that it stopped at every station, and crawled in between.

'Excellent,' said Georgie with conviction. He had not the slightest intention of asking Lucia to dine, for he wanted his tête-à-tête with Olga. There would be such a lot to talk over, and besides it would be tiresome to have Lucia there, for she would be sure to gabble away about her wonderful life in London, and her music-room and her Chippendale chairs, and generally to lay down the law. She must be punished too, for her loathsome conduct in disregarding her old friends when she had her party from London, and be made to learn that her old friends were being much smarter than she was.

Lucia kept her end up nobly.

'Well, Georgie, I must trot away,' she said. 'Such a lot of people to see. Look in, if you've got a spare minute. I'm off again tomorrow. Such a whirl of things in London this week.'

Lucia, instead of proceeding to see lots of people, went back to her house and saw Peppino. He was sitting in the garden in very old clothes, smoking a pipe, and thoroughly enjoying the complete absence of anything to do. He was aware that officially he loved the bustle of London, but it was extremely pleasant to sit in his garden and smoke a pipe, and above all to be rid of those rather hectic people who had talked quite incessantly from morning till night all Sunday. He had given up the crossword, and was thinking over the material for a sonnet on Tranquillity, when Lucia came out to him.

'I was wondering, Peppino,' she said, 'if it would not be pleasanter to go up to town this afternoon. We should get the cool of the evening for our drive, and really, now all our guests have gone, and we are going tomorrow, these hours will be rather tedious. We are spoilt, *caro*, you and I, by our full life up there, where any moment the telephone bell may ring with some delightful invitation. Of course in August we will be here, and settle down to our quaint old life again, but these little odds and ends of time, you know.'

Peppino was reasonably astonished. Half an hour ago Lucia had set out, burning with enthusiasm to pick up the 'old threads', and now all she seemed to want to do was to drop the old threads as quickly as possible. Though he knew himself to be incapable of following the swift and antic movements of Lucia's mind, he was capable of putting two and two together. He had been faintly conscious all yesterday that matters were not going precisely as Lucia wished, and knew that her efforts to entice Olga and her guest to the house had been as barren as a fig tree, but there must have been something more than that. Though not an imaginative man (except in thinking that words rhymed when they did not), it occurred to him that Riseholme was irritated with Lucia, and was indicating it in some unusual manner.

'Why, my dear, I thought you were going to have people in to lunch and dinner,' he said, 'and see about sending the spit to the Museum, and be tremendously busy all day.'

Lucia pulled herself together. She had a momentary impulse to confide in Peppino and tell him all the ominous happenings of the last hour, how Daisy had said she was engaged for lunch and Mrs Boucher had friends to lunch, and Georgie had Olga to dinner and had not asked her, and how the munificent gift of the spit was to be considered by the Museum committee before they accepted it. But to have done that would be to acknowledge not one snub but many snubs, which was contrary to the whole principle of successful attainment. Never must she confess, even to Peppino, that the wheels of her chariot seemed to drive heavily, or that Riseholme was not at the moment agape to receive the signs of her favour. She must not even confess it to herself, and she made a rapid and complete *volte face*.

'It shall be as you like, *caro*,' she said. 'You would prefer to spend a quiet day here, so you shall. As for me, you've never known me yet otherwise than busy, have you? I have a stack of letters to write, and there's my piano looking, oh, so reproachfully at me, for I haven't touched the dear keys since I came, and I must just glance through *Henry VIII*, as we're going to see it tomorrow. I shall be busy enough, and you will have your day in the sun and the air. I only thought you might prefer to run up to town today, instead of waiting till tomorrow. Now don't keep me chatting here any longer.'

Lucia proved her quality on that dismal day. She played her piano with all her usual concentration, she read *Henry VIII*, she wrote her letters, and it was not till the *Evening Gazette* came in that she allowed herself a moment's relaxation. Hurriedly she turned the pages, stopping neither for crossword nor record of international interests, till she came to Hermione's column. She had feared (and with a gasp of relief she saw how unfounded her fears had been) that Hermione would have devoted his picturesque pen to Olga and the Princess, and given her and her party only the fag-end of his last paragraph, but she had disquieted herself in vain. Olga had taken no notice of him, and now (what could be fairer?) he took no notice of Olga. He just mentioned that she had a 'pretty little cottage' at Riseholme, where she came occasionally for weekends, and there were three long sumptuous paragraphs about The Hurst, and Mr and Mrs Philip Lucas who had Lord Limpsfield and the wife of the member, Mrs Garroby-Ashton, and Mrs Alingsby staying with them. Lady Ambermere and her party from The Hall had come to tea, and it was all glorious and distinguished. Hermione had proved himself a true friend, and there was not a word about Olga and the Princess going to lunch with Georgie, or about Daisy and her absurd weedj . . . Lucia read the luscious lines through twice, and then, as she often did, sent her copy across to Georgie, in order to help him to readjust values. Almost simultaneously Daisy sent de Vere across to him with her copy, and Mrs Boucher did the same, calling attention to the obnoxious paragraphs with blue and red pencil respectively, and a great many exclamation marks in both cases.

*　　*　　*

Riseholme settled back into its strenuous life again when Lucia departed next morning to resume her vapid existence in London. It was not annoyed with her any more, because it had 'larned' her, and was quite prepared to welcome her back if (and when) she returned in a proper spirit and behaved herself suitably. Moreover,

even with its own perennial interests to attend to, it privately missed
the old Lucia, who gave them a lead in everything, even though she
domineered, and was absurd, and pretended to know all about
everything, and put her finger into every pie within reach. But it did
not miss the new shingled Lucia, the one who had come down with
a party of fresh friends, and had laughed at the Museum, and had
neglected her old friends altogether, till she found out that Olga
and a Princess were in the place: the less seen of her the better. It
was considered also that she had remained down here this extra day
in order to propitiate those whom she had treated as pariahs, and
condescend to take notice of them again, and if there was one thing
that Riseholme could not stand, and did not mean to stand from
anybody, it was condescension. It was therefore perfectly correct
for Daisy and Mrs Boucher to say they were engaged for lunch, and
for Georgie to decline to ask her to dinner . . . These three formed
the committee of the Museum, and they met that morning to audit
the accounts for the week and discuss any other business connected
or unconnected with their office. There was not, of course, with so
small and intimate a body, any need to have a chairman, and they all
rapped the table when they wanted to be listened to.

Mrs Boucher was greedily counting the shillings which had been
taken from the till, while Georgie counted the counterfoils of the
tickets.

'A hundred and twenty-three,' he said. 'That's nearly the best
week we've had yet.'

'And fifteen and four is nineteen,' said Mrs Boucher, 'and four is
twenty-three which makes exactly six pounds three shillings. Well, I
do call that good. And I hear we've had a wonderful bequest made.
Most generous of our dear Olga. I think she ought not only to be
thanked, but asked to join the committee. I always said – '

Daisy rapped the table.

'Abfou said just the same,' she interrupted. 'I had a sitting this
morning, and he kept writing "committee". I brought the paper
along with me, because I was going to propose that myself. But
there's another thing first, and that's about insurance. Robert told
me he was insuring the building and its contents separately for a
thousand pounds each. We shall have to pay a premium, of course.
Oh, here's Abfou's message. "Committee", you see "committee"
written three times. I feel quite sure he meant Olga.'

'He spells it with only one "m",' said Georgie, 'but I expect he
means that. There's one bit of business that comes before that, for I

have been offered another object for the Museum, and I said I would refer the offer to the committee before I accepted it. Lucia came to see me yesterday morning and asked – '

'The Elizabethan spit,' said Mrs Boucher. 'I don't see what we want with it, for my part, and if I had to say what I thought, I should thank her most politely, and beg that she would keep it herself. Most kind of her, I'm sure. Sorry to refuse, which was just what I said when she asked me to lunch yesterday. There'd have been legs of cold chickens of which her friends from London had eaten wings.'

'She asked me too,' said Daisy, 'and I said "no". Did she leave this morning?'

'Yes, about half-past ten,' said Georgie. 'She wanted me to ask her to dinner last night.'

Daisy had been writing 'committee' again and again on her blotting-paper. It looked very odd with two 'm's and she would certainly have spelt it with one herself.

'I think Abfou is right about the way to spell "committee",' she said, 'and even if he weren't the meaning is clear enough. But about the insurance. Robert only advises insurance against fire, for he says no burglar in his senses – '

Mrs Boucher rapped the table.

'But there wasn't the manuscript of *Lucrezia* then,' she said. 'And I should think that any burglar whether in his senses or out of them would think *that* worth taking. If it was a question of insuring an Elizabethan spit – '

'Well, I want to know what the committee wishes me to say about that,' said Georgie. 'Oh, by the way, when we have a new edition of the catalogue, we must bring it up to date. There'll be the manuscript of *Lucrezia*.'

'And if you ask me,' said Mrs Boucher, 'she only wanted to get rid of the spit because it makes her chimney smoke. Tell her to get her chimney swept and keep the spit.'

'There's a portrait of her in the music-room,' said Georgie, 'by Sigismund. It looks like nothing at all – '

'Of course everybody has a right to have their hair shingled,' said Mrs Boucher, 'whatever their age, and there's no law to prevent you.'

Daisy rapped the table.

'We were considering as to whether we should ask Mrs Shuttleworth to join the committee,' she said.

'She sang too, beautifully, on Sunday night,' said Georgie, 'and what fun we had dancing. Oh, and Lucia asked for the Princess's book to sign her name in, and the only book she had brought was a book of crossword puzzles.'

'No!' said both ladies together.

'She did, because Olga's parlour-maid told Foljambe, and – '

'Well I never!' said Daisy. 'That served her out. Did she write Lucia across, and Peppino down?'

'I'm sure I've nothing to say against her,' said Mrs Boucher, 'but people usually get what they deserve. Certainly let us have the Museum insured if that's the right thing to do, and as for asking Olga to be on the committee, why we settled that hours ago, and I have nothing more to say about the spit. Have the spit if you like, but I would no more think of insuring it, than insuring a cold in the head. I've as much use for one as the other. All that stuff too about the gracious *châtelaine* at The Hurst in the *Evening Gazette*! My husband read it, and what he said was, "Faugh!" Tush and faugh, was what he said.'

Public opinion was beginning to boil up again about Lucia, and Georgie intervened.

'I think that's all the business before the meeting,' he said, 'and so we accept the manuscript of *Lucrezia* and decline the spit. I'm sure it was very kind of both the donors. And Olga's to be asked to join the committee. Well, we have got through a good morning's work.'

* * *

Lucia meanwhile was driving back to London, where she intended to make herself a busy week. There would be two nights at the opera, on the second of which Olga was singing in *The Valkyrie*, and so far from intending to depreciate her singing, or to refrain from going, by way of revenge for the slight she had suffered, she meant, even if Olga sang like a screech-owl and acted like a stick, to say there had never been so perfect a presentation of Brünnhilde. She could not conceive doing anything so stupid as snubbing Olga because she had not come to her house or permitted her to enter Old Place: that would have been the height of folly.

At present, she was (or hoped to be) on the upward road, and the upward road could only be climbed by industry and appreciation. When she got to the top, it would be a different matter, but just now it was an asset, a score to allude to dear Olga and the hoppings in and out that took place all day at Riseholme: she knew too, a good deal that Olga had done on Sunday and that would all be useful. 'Always appreciate, always admire,' thought Lucia to herself as she woke

Peppino up from a profound nap on their arrival at Brompton Square. 'Be busy: work, work, work.'

She knew already that there would be hard work in front of her before she got where she wanted to get, and she whisked off like a disturbing fly which impeded concentration the slight disappointment which her weekend had brought. If you meant to progress, you must never look back (the awful example of Lot's wife!) and never, unless you are certain it is absolutely useless, kick down a ladder which has brought you anywhere, or might in the future bring you anywhere. Already she had learned a lesson about that, for if she had only told Georgie that she had been coming down for a weekend, and had bidden him to lunch and dinner and anything else he liked, he would certainly have got Olga to pop in at The Hurst, or have said that he couldn't dine with Olga on that fateful Sunday night because he was dining with her, and then no doubt Olga would have asked them all to come in afterwards. It had been a mistake to kick Riseholme down, a woeful mistake, and she would never do such a thing again. It was a mistake also to be sarcastic about anybody till you were sure they could not help you, and who could be sure of that? Even poor dear Daisy with her ridiculous Abfou had proved such an attraction at Old Place, that Georgie had barely time to get back and dress for dinner, and a benignant Daisy instead of a militant and malignant Daisy would have helped. Everything helps, thought Lucia, as she snatched up the tablets which stood by the telephone and recorded the ringings up that had taken place in her absence.

She fairly gasped at the amazing appropriateness of a message that had been received only ten minutes ago. Marcia Whitby hoped that she could dine that evening: the message was to be delivered as soon as she arrived. Obviously it was a last-moment invitation: somebody had thrown her over, and perhaps that made them thirteen. There was no great compliment in it, for Marcia, so Lucia conjectured, had already tried high and low to get another woman, and now in despair she tried Lucia . . . Of course there were the tickets for *Henry VIII*, and it was a first night, but perhaps she could get somebody to go with Peppino . . . Ah, she remembered Aggie Sanderson lamenting that she had been able to secure a seat! Without a pause she rang up the Duchess of Whitby, and expressed her eager delight at coming to dine tonight. So lucky, so charmed. Then having committed herself, she rang up Aggie and hoped for the best, and Aggie jumped at the idea of a ticket for *Henry VIII*, and then she told Peppino all about it.

'*Caro*, I had to be kind,' she said, tripping off into the music-room where he was at tea. 'Poor Marcia Whitby in despair.'

'Dear me, what has happened?' asked Peppino.

'One short, one woman short, evidently, for her dinner tonight: besought me to go. But you shall have your play all the same, and a dear sweet woman to take to it. Guess! No. I'll tell you: Aggie. She was longing to go, and so it's a kindness all round. You will have somebody more exciting to talk to than your poor old *sposa*, and dearest Aggie will get her play, and Marcia will be ever so grateful to me. I shall miss the play, but I will go another night unless you tell me it is no good . . . '

Of course the *Evening Gazette* would contain no further news of the *châtelaine* at The Hurst, but Lucia turned to Hermione's column with a certain eagerness, for there might be something about the Duchess's dinner this evening. Hermione did not seem to have heard of it, but if Hermione came to lunch tomorrow, he would hear of it then. She rang him up . . .

*   *   *

Lucia's kindness to Marcia Whitby met with all sorts of rewards. She got there, as was her custom in London, rather early, so that she could hear the names of all the guests as they arrived, and Marcia, feeling thoroughly warm-hearted to her, for she had tried dozens of women to turn her party from thirteen into fourteen, called her Lucia instead of Mrs Lucas. It was no difficulty to Lucia to reciprocate this intimacy in a natural manner, for she had alluded to the Duchess as Marcia behind her back, for weeks, and now the syllables tripped to her tongue with the familiarity of custom.

'Sweet of you to ask me, dear Marcia,' she said. 'Peppino and I only arrived from Riseholme an hour or two ago, and he took Aggie Sandeman to the theatre instead of me. Such a lovely Sunday at Riseholme: you must spare a weekend and come down and vegetate. Olga Shuttleworth was there with Princess Isabel, and she sang too divinely on Sunday evening, and then, would you believe it, we turned on the gramophone and danced.'

'What a coincidence!' said Marcia, 'because I've got a small dance tonight, and Princess Isabel is coming. But not nearly so chic as your dance at Riseholme.'

She moved towards the door to receive the guests who were beginning to arrive, and Lucia, with ears open for distinguished names, had just a moment's qualm for having given the impression which she meant to give, that she had been dancing to Olga's gramophone. It was no more than momentary, and presently the Princess arrived, and was led round by her hostess, to receive curtseys.

'And of course you know Mrs Lucas,' said Marcia. 'She's been telling me about your dancing to the gramophone at her house on Sunday.'

Lucia recovered from her curtsey.

'No, dear Marcia,' she said. 'It was at Olga's, in fact – '

The Princess fixed her with a Royal eye before she passed on, as if she seemed to understand.

But that was the only catastrophe, and how small a one! The Princess liked freaks, and so Marcia had asked a star of the movies and a distinguished novelist, and a woman with a skin like a kipper from having crossed the Sahara twice on foot, or having swum the Atlantic twice, or something of the sort, and a society caricaturist and a slim young gentleman with a soft voice, who turned out to be the bloodiest pugilist of the century, and the Prime Minister, two ambassadresses, and the great Mrs Beaucourt who had just astounded the world by her scandalous volume of purely imaginary reminiscences. Each of these would furnish a brilliant centre for a dinner party, and the idea of spreading the butter as thick as that seemed to Lucia almost criminal: she herself, indeed, was the only bit of bread to be seen anywhere. Before dinner was over she had engaged both her neighbours, the pugilist and the cinema star, to dine with her on consecutive nights next week, and was mentally running through her list of friends to settle whom to group round them. Alf Watson, the pugilist, it appeared, when not engaged in knocking people out, spent his time in playing the flute to soothe his savage breast, while Marcelle Periscope, when not impersonating impassioned lovers, played with his moderately tame lion-cub. Lucia begged Alf to bring his flute, and they would have some music, but did not extend her invitation to the lion-cub, which sounded slightly Bolshevistic . . . Later in the evening she got hold of Herbert Alton, the social caricaturist, who promised to lunch on Sunday, but failed to do business with the lady from the Sahara, who was leaving next day to swim another sea, or cross another desert. Then the guests for the dance began to arrive, and Lucia, already half-intoxicated by celebrities, sank rapt in a chair at the top of the staircase and listened to the catalogue of sonorous names. Up trooped stars and garters and tiaras, and when she felt stronger, she clung firmly to Lord Limpsfield, who seemed to know everybody and raked in introductions.

Lucia did not get home till three o'clock (for having given up her play out of kindness to Marcia, she might as well do it thoroughly), but she was busy writing invitations for her two dinner parties next week by nine in the morning. Peppino was lunching at his club, where he might meet the Astronomer-Royal, and have a chat about the constellations, but he was to ring her up about a quarter past two and ascertain if she had made any engagement for him during the afternoon. The idea of this somehow occupied her brain as she filled up the cards of invitation in her small exquisite handwriting. There was a telephone in her dining-room, and she began to visualise to herself Peppino's ringing her up, while she and the two or three friends who were lunching with her would be still at table. It would be at the end of lunch: they would be drinking their coffee, which she always made herself in a glass machine with a spirit-lamp which, when it appeared to be on the point of exploding, indicated that coffee was ready. The servants would have left the room, and she would go to the telephone herself . . . She would hear Peppino's voice, but nobody else would. They would not know who was at the other end, and she might easily pretend that it was not Peppino, but . . . She would give a gabbling answer, audible to her guests, but she could divert her mouth a little away so that Peppino could not make anything out of it, and then hang up the receiver again . . . Peppino no doubt would think he had got hold of a wrong number, and presently call her up again, and she would then tell him anything there was to communicate. As she scribbled away the idea took shape and substance: there was an attraction about it, it smiled on her.

She came to the end of her dinner-invitations grouped round the cinema star and the fluting prizefighter, and she considered whom to ask to meet Herbert Alton on Sunday. He was working hard, he had told her, to finish his little gallery of caricatures with which he annually regaled London, and which was to open in a fortnight. He was a licensed satirist, and all London always flocked to his show to observe with glee what he made of them all, and what witty and pungent little remarks he affixed to their monstrous effigies. It was a distinct cachet, too, to be caricatured by him, a sign that you attracted attention and were a notable figure. He might (in fact, he always did) make you a perfect guy, and his captions invariably made fun of something characteristic, but it gave you publicity. She wondered whether he would take a commission: she wondered whether he might be induced to do a caricature of Peppino or herself or of them both, at a handsome price, with the proviso that it was to be on view at his exhibition. That could probably be ascertained, and then she might approach the subject on Sunday. Anyhow, she would ask one or two pleasant people to meet him, and hope for the best.

*   *   *

Lucia's little lunch-party that day consisted only of four people. Lunch, Lucia considered, was for *intimes*: you sat with your elbows on the table, and all talked together, and learned the news, just as you did on the green at Riseholme. There was something unwieldy about a large lunch-party; it was a distracted affair, and in the effort to assimilate more news than you could really digest, you forgot half of it. Today, therefore, there was only Aggie Sandeman who had been to the play last night with Peppino, and was bringing her cousin Adele Brixton (whom Lucia had not yet met, but very much wanted to know), and Stephen Merriall. Lady Brixton was a lean, intelligent American of large fortune who found she got on better without her husband. But as Lord Brixton preferred living in America and she in England, satisfactory arrangements were easily made. Occasionally she had to go to see relatives in America, and he selected such periods for seeing relatives in England.

She explained the situation very good-naturedly to Lucia who rather rashly asked after her husband.

'In fact,' she said, 'we blow kisses to each other from the decks of Atlantic liners going in opposite directions, if it's calm, and if it's rough, we're sick into the same ocean.'

Now that would never have been said at Riseholme, or if it was, it would have been very ill thought of, and a forced smile followed by a complete change of conversation would have given it a chilly welcome. Now, out of habit, Lucia smiled a forced smile, and then remembered that you could not judge London by the chaste standards of Riseholme. She turned the forced smile into a genial one.

'Too delicious!' she said. 'I must tell Peppino that.'

'Pep what?' asked Lady Brixton.

This was explained; it was also explained that Aggie had been with Peppino to the play last night; in fact there was rather too much explanation going on for social ease, and Lucia thought it was time to tell them all about what she had done last night. She did this in a characteristic manner.

'Dear Lady Brixton,' she said, 'ever since you came in I've been wondering where I have seen you. Of course it was last night, at our darling Marcia's dance.'

This seemed to introduce the desirable topic, and though it was not in the least true, it was a wonderfully good shot.

'Yes, I was there,' said Adele. 'What a crush. Sheer Mormonism: one man to fifty women.'

'How unkind of you! I dined there first; quite a small party. Princess Isabel, who had been down at our dear little Riseholme on Sunday, staying with Olga – such a coincidence –' Lucia stopped just in time; she was about to describe the impromptu dance at Olga's on Sunday night, but remembered that Stephen knew she had not been to it. So she left the coincidence alone, and went rapidly on:

'Dear Marcia insisted on my coming,' she said, 'and so, really, like a true friend I gave up the play and went. Such an amusing little dinner. Marcelle – Marcelle Periscope, the Prime Minister and the Italian Ambassadress, and Princess Isabel of course, and Alf, and a few more. There's nobody like Marcia for getting up a wonderful unexpected little party like that. Alf was too delicious.'

'Not Alf Watson?' asked Lady Brixton.

'Yes, I sat next him at dinner, and he's coming to dine with me next week, and is bringing his flute. He adores playing the flute. Can't I persuade you to come, Lady Brixton? Thursday, let me see, is it Thursday? Yes, Thursday. No party at all, just a few old friends, and some music. I must find some duets for the piano and flute: Alf made me promise that I would play his accompaniments for him. And Dora: Dora Beaucourt. What a lurid life! And Sigismund: no, I don't think Sigismund was there; it was at Sophy's. Such a marvellous portrait he has done of me: is it not marvellous, Stephen? You remember it down at Riseholme. How amusing Sophy was, insisting that I should move every other picture out of my music-room. I must get her to come in after dinner on Thursday; there is something primitive about the flute.' So Theocritan!

Lucia suddenly remembered that she mustn't kick ladders down, and turned to Aggie. Aggie had been very useful when first she came up to London, and she might quite easily be useful again, for she knew quantities of solid people, and if her parties lacked brilliance, they were highly respectable. The people whom Sophy called 'the old crusted' went there.

'Aggie dear, as soon as you get home, put down Wednesday for dining with me,' she said, 'and if there's an engagement there already, as there's sure to be, cross it out and have pseudo-influenza. Marcelle – Marcelle Periscope is coming, but I didn't ask the lion-cub. A lion-cub: so quaint of him – and who else was there last night? Dear me, I get so mixed up with all the people one runs across.'

Lucia, of course, never got mixed up at all: there was no one so clear-headed, but she had to spin things out a little, for Peppino was rather late ringing up. The coffee-equipage had been set before her, and she kept drawing away the spirit-lamp in an absent manner just before it boiled, for they must still be sitting in the dining-room when he rang up. But even as she lamented her muddled memory, the tinkle of the telephone bell sounded. She rapidly rehearsed in her mind what she was going to say.

'Ah, that telephone,' she said, rising hastily, so as to get to it before one of the servants came back. 'I often tell Peppino I shall cut it out of the house, for one never gets a moment's peace. Yes, yes, who is it?'

Lucia listened for a second, and then gave a curtsey.

'Oh, is it you, ma'am?' she said, holding the mouthpiece a little obliquely. 'Yes, I'm Mrs Lucas.'

A rather gruff noise, clearly Peppino's voice, came from the instrument, but she trusted it was inaudible to the others, and she soon broke in again talking very rapidly.

'Oh, that is kind of you, your Highness,' she said. 'It would be too delightful. Tomorrow: charmed. Delighted.'

She replaced the mouthpiece, and instantly began to talk again from the point at which she had left off.

'Yes, and of course Herbert Alton was there,' she said. 'His show opens in a fortnight, and how we shall all meet there at the private view and laugh at each other's caricatures! What is it that Rousseau – is it Rousseau? – says, about our not being wholly grieved at the misfortunes of our friends? So true! Bertie is rather wicked sometimes though, but still one forgives him everything. Ah, the coffee is boiling at last.'

Peppino, as Lucia had foreseen, rang up again almost immediately, and she told him he had missed the most charming little lunch-party, because he would go to his club. Her guests, of course, were burning to know to whom she had curtseyed, but Lucia gave no information on the point. Adele Brixton and Aggie presently went off to a matinée, but Stephen remained behind. That looked rather well, Lucia thought, for she had noticed that often a handsome and tolerably young man lingered with the hostess when other guests had gone. There was something rather chic about it; if it happened very constantly, or if at another house they came together or went away together, people would begin to talk, quite pleasantly of course, about his devotion to her. Georgie had been just such a *cavaliere servente*. Stephen, for his part, was quite unconscious of any such scintillations in Lucia's mind: he merely knew that it was certainly convenient for an unattached man to have a very pleasant house always to go to, where he would be sure of hearing things that interested Hermione.

'Delicious little lunch-party,' he said. 'What a charming woman Lady Brixton is.'

'Dear Adele,' said Lucia dreamily. 'Charming, isn't she? How pleased she was at the thought of meeting Alf! Do look in after dinner that night, Stephen. I wish I could ask you to dine, but I expect to be crammed as it is. Dine on Wednesday, though: let me see, Marcelle comes that night. What a rush next week will be!'

Stephen waited for her to allude to the voice to which she had curtseyed, but he waited in vain.

Chapter Seven

This delicious little luncheon-party had violently excited Adele Brixton: she was thrilled to the marrow at Lucia's curtsey to the telephone.

'My dear, she's marvellous,' she said to Aggie. 'She's a study. She's cosmic. The telephone, the curtsey! I've never seen the like. But why in the name of wonder didn't she tell us who the Highness was? She wasn't shy of talking about the other folk she'd met. Alf and Marcelle and Marcia and Bertie. But she made a mistake over Bertie. She shouldn't have said "Bertie". I've known Herbert Alton for years, and never has anybody called him anything but Herbert. "Bertie" was a mistake, but don't tell her. I adore your Lucia. She'll go far, mark my words, and I bet you she's talking of me as Adele this moment. Don't you see how wonderful she is? I've been a climber myself and I know. But I was a snail compared to her.'

Aggie Sandeman was rather vexed at not being asked to the Alf party.

'You needn't tell me how wonderful she is,' she observed with some asperity. 'It's not two months since she came to London first, and she didn't know a soul. She dined with me the first night she came up, and since then she has annexed every single person she met at my house.'

'She would,' said Adele appreciatively. 'And who was the man who looked as if he had been labelled "Man" by mistake when he was born, and ought to have been labelled "Lady"? I never saw such a perfect lady, though I only know him as Stephen at present. She just said, "Stephen, do you know Lady Brixton?" '

'Stephen Merriall,' said Aggie. 'Just one of the men who go out to tea every day – one of the unattached.'

'Well then, she's going to attach him,' said Adele. 'Dear me, aren't I poisonous, when I'm going to her house to meet Alf next week! But I don't feel poisonous; I feel wildly interested: I adore her. Here we are at the theatre: what a bore! And there's Tony Limpsfield. Tony, come and help me out. We've been lunching with the most marvellous – '

'I expect you mean Lucia,' said Tony. 'I spent Sunday with her at Riseholme.'

'She curtseyed to the telephone,' began Adele.

'Who was at the other end?' asked Tony eagerly.

'That's what she didn't say,' said Adele.

'Why not?' asked Tony.

Adele stepped briskly out of her car, followed by Aggie.

'I can't make out,' she said. 'Oh, do you know Mrs Sandeman?'

'Yes, of course,' said Tony. 'And it couldn't have been Princess Isabel.'

'Why not? She met her at Marcia's last night.'

'Yes, but the Princess fled from her. She fled from her at Riseholme too, and said she would never go to her house. It can't have been she. But she got hold of that boxer – '

'Alf Watson,' said Adele. 'She called him Alf, and I'm going to meet him at her house on Thursday.'

'Then it's very unkind of you to crab her, Adele,' said Tony.

'I'm not: I'm simply wildly interested. Anyhow, what about you? You spent a Sunday with her at Riseholme.'

'And she calls you Tony,' said Aggie vituperatively, still thinking about the Alf party.

'No, does she really?' said Tony. 'But after all, I call her Lucia when she's not there. The bell's gone, by the way: the curtain will be up.'

Adele hurried in.

'Come to my box, Tony,' she said, 'after the first act. I haven't been so interested in anything for years.'

Adele paid no attention whatever to the gloomy play of Chekhov's.

Her whole mind was concentrated on Lucia, and soon she leaned across to Aggie, and whispered: 'I believe it was Peppino who rang her up.'

Aggie knitted her brows for a moment.

'Couldn't have been,' she said. 'He rang her up directly afterwards.'

Adele's face fell. Not being able to think as far ahead as Lucia she didn't see the answer to that, and relapsed into Lucian meditation, till the moment the curtain fell, when Tony Limpsfield slid into their box.

'I don't know what the play has been about,' he said, 'but I must tell you why she was at Marcia's last night. Some women chucked Marcia during the afternoon and made her thirteen – '

'Marcia would like that,' said Aggie.

Tony took no notice of this silly joke.

'So she rang up everybody in town – ' he continued.

'Except me,' said Aggie bitterly.

'Oh, never mind that,' said Tony. 'She rang up everybody, and couldn't get hold of anyone. Then she rang up Lucia.'

'Who instantly said she was disengaged, and rang me up to go to the theatre with Peppino,' said Aggie. 'I suspected something of the sort, but I wanted to see the play, and I wasn't going to cut off my nose to spite Lucia's face.'

'Besides, she would have got someone else, or sent Peppino to the play alone,' said Tony. 'And you've got hold of the wrong end of the stick, Aggie. Nobody wants to spite Lucia. We all want her to have the most glorious time.'

'Aggie's vexed because she thinks she invented Lucia,' observed Adele. 'That's the wrong attitude altogether. Tell me about Pep.'

'Simply nothing to say about him,' said Tony. 'He has trousers and a hat, and a telescope on the roof at Riseholme, and when you talk to him you see he remembers what the leading articles in *The Times* said that morning. Don't introduce irrelevant matters, Adele.'

'But husbands are relevant – all but mine,' said Adele. 'Part of the picture. And what about Stephen?'

'Oh, you always see him handing buns at tea-parties. He's irrelevant too.'

'He might not be if her husband is,' said Adele.

Tony exploded with laughter.

'You are off the track,' he said. 'You'll get nowhere if you attempt to smirch Lucia's character. How could she have time for a lover to begin with? And you misunderstand her altogether, if you think that.'

'It would be frightfully picturesque,' said Adele.

'No, it would spoil it altogether . . . Oh, there's this stupid play beginning again . . . Gracious heavens, look there!'

They followed his finger, and saw Lucia followed by Stephen coming up the central aisle of the stalls to two places in the front row. Just as she reached her place she turned round to survey the house, and caught sight of them. Then the lights were lowered, and her face slid into darkness.

*   *   *

This little colloquy in Adele's box was really the foundation of the secret society of the Luciaphils, and the membership of the Luciaphils began swiftly to increase. Aggie Sandeman was scarcely eligible, for complete goodwill towards Lucia was a *sine qua non* of membership, and there was in her mind a certain asperity when she thought that it was she who had given Lucia her gambit, and that already she was beginning to be relegated to second circles in Lucia's scale of social precedence. It was true that she had been asked to dine to meet Marcelle Periscope, but the party to meet Alf and his flute was clearly the smarter of the two. Adele, however, and Tony Limpsfield were real members, so too, when she came up a few days later, was Olga. Marcia Whitby was another who greedily followed her career, and such as these, whenever they met, gave eager news to each other about it. There was, of course, another camp, consisting of those whom Lucia bombarded with pleasant invitations, but who (at present) firmly refused them. They professed not to know her and not to take the slightest interest in her, which showed, as Adele said, a deplorable narrowness of mind. Types and striking characters like Lucia, who pursued undaunted and indefatigable their aim in life, were rare, and when they occurred should be studied with reverent affection . . . Sometimes one of the old and original members of the Luciaphils discovered others, and if when Lucia's name was mentioned an eager and a kindly light shone in their eyes, and they said in a hushed whisper 'Did you hear who was there on Thursday?' they thus disclosed themselves as Luciaphils . . . All this was gradual, but the movement went steadily on, keeping pace with her astonishing career, for the days were few on which some gratifying achievement was not recorded in the veracious columns of Hermione.

*   *   *

Lucia was driving home one afternoon after a day passed in the Divorce Court. She had made the acquaintance of the President not long ago, and had asked him to dinner on the evening before this trial, which was the talk of the town, was to begin, and at the third attempt had got him to give her a seat in the court. The trial had already lasted three days, and really no one seemed to think about anything else, and the papers had been full of soulful and surprising evidence. Certainly, Babs Shyton, the lady whose husband wanted to get rid of her, had written very odd letters to Woof-dog, otherwise known as Lord Middlesex, and he to her: Lucia could not imagine writing to anybody like that, and she would have been very much surprised if anyone had written to her as Woof-dog wrote to Babs. But as the trial went on, Lucia found herself growing warm with sympathy for Babs. Her husband, Colonel Shyton, must have been an impossible person to live with, for sometimes he would lie in bed all day, get up in the evening, have breakfast at eight o'clock, lunch a little after midnight, and dine heavily at half-past eight in the morning. Surely with a husband like that, any woman would want some sort of a Woof-dog to take care of her. Both Babs and he, in the extracts from the remarkable correspondence between them which were read out in court, alluded to Colonel Shyton as the S. P., which Babs (amid loud laughter) frankly confessed meant Stinkpot; and Babs had certainly written to Woof-dog to say that she was in bed and very sleepy and cross, but wished that Woof-dog was thumping his tail on the hearthrug. That was indiscreet, but there was nothing incriminating about it, and as for the row of crosses which followed Babs's signature, she explained quite frankly that they indicated that she was cross. There were roars of laughter again at this, and even the judge wore a broad grin as he said that if there was any more disturbance he should clear the court. Babs had produced an excellent impression, in fact: she had looked so pretty and had answered so gaily, and the Woof-dog had been just as admirable, for he was a strong silent Englishman, and when he was asked whether he had ever kissed Babs he said 'That's a lie' in such a loud fierce voice that you felt that the jury had better believe him unless they all wanted to be knocked down. The verdict was expected next day, and Lucia meant to lose no time in asking Babs to dinner if it was in her favour.

The court had been very hot and airless, and Lucia directed her chauffeur to drive round the Park before going home. She had asked one or two people to tea at five, and one or two more at half-past,

but there was time for a turn first, and, diverting her mind from the
special features of the case to the general features of such cases, she
thought what an amazing and incomparable publicity they gave any
woman. Of course, if the verdict went against her, such publicity
would be extremely disagreeable, but, given that the jury decided
that there was nothing against her, Lucia could imagine being almost
envious of her. She did not actually want to be placed in such a
situation herself, but certainly it would convey a notoriety that could
scarcely be accomplished by years of patient effort. Babs would feel
that there was not a single person in any gathering who did not know
who she was, and all about her, and, if she was innocent, that would
be a wholly delightful result. Naturally, Lucia only envied the outcome of such an experience, not the experience itself, for it would
entail a miserable life with Peppino, and she felt sure that dinner at
half-past eight in the morning would be highly indigestible, but it
would be wonderful to be as well-known as Babs.

Another point that had struck her, both in the trial itself and in the
torrents of talk that for the last few days had been poured out over
the case, was the warm sympathy of the world in general with Babs,
whether guilty or innocent. 'The world always loves a lover,' thought
Lucia, and Woof-dog thumping his tail on the rug by her bedroom
fire was a beautiful image.

Her thoughts took a more personal turn. The idea of having a real
lover was, of course, absolutely abhorrent to her whole nature, and
besides, she did not know whom she could get. But the reputation of
having a lover was a wholly different matter, presenting no such
objections or difficulties, and most decidedly it gave a woman a
certain cachet, if a man was always seen about with her and was
supposed to be deeply devoted to her. The idea had occurred to her
vaguely before, but now it took more definite shape, and as to her
choice of this sort of lover, there was no difficulty about that.
Hitherto, she had done nothing to encourage the notion, beyond
having Stephen at the house a good deal, but now she saw herself
assuming an air of devoted proprietorship of him; she could see
herself talking to him in a corner, and even laying her hand on his
sleeve, arriving with him at an evening party, and going away with
him, for Peppino hated going out after dinner . . .

But caution was necessary in the first steps, for it would be hard to
explain to Stephen what the proposed relationship was, and she could
not imagine herself saying 'We are going to pretend to be lovers, but
we aren't.' It would be quite dreadful if he misunderstood, and

unexpectedly imprinted on her lips or even her hand a hot lascivious kiss, but up till now he certainly had not shown the smallest desire to do anything of the sort. She would never be able to see him again if he did that, and the world would probably say that he had dropped her. But she knew she couldn't explain the proposed position to him and he would have to guess: she could only give him a lead and must trust to his intelligence, and to the absence in him of any unsuspected amorous proclivities. She would begin gently, anyhow, and have him to dinner every day that she was at home. And really it would be very pleasant for him, for she was entertaining a great deal during this next week or two, and if he only did not yield to one of those rash and turbulent impulses of the male, all would be well. Georgie, until (so Lucia put it to herself) Olga had come between them, had done it beautifully, and Stephen was rather like Georgie. As for herself, she knew she could trust her firm slow pulses never to beat wild measures for anybody.

*   *   *

She reached home to find that Adele had already arrived, and pausing only to tell her servant to ring up Stephen and ask him to come round at once, she went upstairs.

'Dearest Adele,' she said, 'a million pardons. I have been in the Divorce Court all day. Too thrilled. Babs, dear Babs Shyton, was wonderful. They got nothing out of her at all – '

'No: Lord Middlesex has got everything out of her already,' observed Adele.

'Ah, how can you say that?' said Lucia. 'Lord Middlesex – Woof-dog, you know – was just as wonderful. I feel sure the jury will believe them. Dear Babs! I must get her to come here some night soon and have a friendly little party for her. Think of that horrid old man who had lunch in the middle of the night! How terrible for her to have to go back to him. Dear me, what is her address?'

'She may not have to go back to him,' said Adele. 'If so, "care of Woof-dog" would probably find her.'

Adele had been feeling rather cross. Her husband had announced his intention of visiting his friends and relations in England, and she did not feel inclined to make a corresponding journey to America. But as Lucia went on, she forgot these minor troubles, and became enthralled. Though she was still talking about Babs and Woof-dog, Adele felt sure these were only symbols, like the dreams of psychoanalysts.

'My sympathy is entirely with dear Babs,' she said. 'Think of her position with that dreadful old wretch. A woman surely may be pardoned, even if the jury don't believe her for – '

'Of course she may,' said Adele with a final spurt of ill-temper. 'What she's not pardoned for is being found out.'

'Now you're talking as everybody talked in that dreadful play I went to last night,' said Lucia. 'Dear Olga was there: she is singing tomorrow, is she not? And you are assuming that Babs is guilty. How glad I am, Adele, that you are not on the jury! I take quite the other view: a woman with a wretched home like that must have a man with whom she is friends. I think it was a pure and beautiful affection between Babs and Woof-dog, such as any woman, even if she was happily married, might be proud to enjoy. There can be no doubt of Lord Middlesex's devotion to her, and really – I hope this does not shock you – what their relations were concerns nobody but them. George Sands and Chopin, you know. Nelson and Lady Hamilton. Sir Andrew Moss – he was the judge, you know – dined here the other night; I'm sure he is broad-minded. He gave me an admission card to the court . . . Ah, Stephen, there you are. Come in, my dear. You know Lady Brixton, don't you? We were talking of Babs Shyton. Bring up your chair. Let me see, no sugar, isn't it? How you scolded me when I put sugar into your tea by mistake the other day!'

She held Stephen's hand for as long as anybody might, or, as Browning says, 'so very little longer', and Adele saw a look of faint surprise on his face. It was not alarm, it was not rapture, it was just surprise.

'Were you there?' he said. 'No verdict yet, I suppose.'

'Not till tomorrow, but then you will see. Adele has been horrid about her, quite horrid, and I have been preaching to her. I shall certainly ask Babs to dine some night soon, and you shall come, if you can spare an evening, but we won't ask Adele. Tell me the news, Stephen. I've been in court all day.'

'Lucia's quite misunderstood me,' said Adele. 'My sympathy is entirely with Babs: all I blame her for is being found out. If you and I had an affair, Mr Merriall, we should receive the envious sympathy of everybody, until we were officially brought to book. But then we should acquiesce in even our darling Lucia's cutting us. And if you had an affair with anybody else – I'm sure you've got hundreds – I and everybody else would be ever so pleased and interested, until – Mark that word "until". Now I must go, and leave you two to talk me well over.'

Lucia rose, making affectionate but rather half-hearted murmurs to induce her to stop.

'Must you really be going, Adele?' she said. 'Let me see, what am I doing tomorrow – Stephen, what is tomorrow, and what am I doing? Ah yes, Bertie Alton's private view in the morning. We shall be sure to meet there, Adele. The wretch has done two caricatures of Peppino and me. I feel as if I was to be flayed in the sight of all London. *Au revoir*, then, dear Adele, if you're so tired of us. And then the opera in the evening: I shall hardly dare to show my face. Your motor's here, is it? Ring, Stephen, will you. Such a short visit, and I expect Olga will pop in presently. All sorts of messages to her, I suppose. Look in again, Adele: propose yourself.'

* * *

On the doorstep Adele met Tony Limpsfield. She hurried him into her motor, and told the chauffeur not to drive on.

'News!' she said. 'Lucia's going to have a lover.'

'No!' said Tony in the Riseholme manner.

'But I tell you she is. He's with her now.'

'They won't want me then,' said Tony. 'And yet she asked me to come at half-past five.'

'Nonsense, my dear. They will want you, both of them . . . Oh Tony, don't you see? It's a stunt.'

Tony assumed the rapt expression of Luciaphils receiving intelligence.

'Tell me all about it,' he said.

'I'm sure I'm right,' said she. 'Her poppet came in just now, and she held his hand as women do, and made him draw his chair up to her, and said he scolded her. I'm not sure that he knows yet. But I saw that he guessed something was up. I wonder if he's clever enough to do it properly . . . I wish she had chosen you, Tony, you'd have done it perfectly. They have got – don't you understand? – to have the appearance of being lovers, everyone must think they are lovers, while all the time there's nothing at all of any sort in it. It's a stunt: it's a play: it's a glory.'

'But perhaps there is something in it,' said Tony. 'I really think I had better not go in.'

'Tony, trust me. Lucia has no more idea of keeping a real lover than of keeping a chimpanzee. She's as chaste as snow, a kiss would scorch her. Besides, she hasn't time. She asked Stephen there in order to show him to me, and to show him to you. It's the most wonderful plan; and it's wonderful of me to have understood it so quickly. You must go in: there's nothing private of any kind: indeed, she thirsts for publicity.'

Her confidence inspired confidence, and Tony was naturally consumed with curiosity. He got out, told Adele's chauffeur to drive on, and went upstairs. Stephen was no longer sitting in the chair next to Lucia, but on the sofa at the other side of the tea-table. This rather looked as if Adele was right: it was consistent anyhow with their being lovers in public, but certainly not lovers in private.

'Dear Lord Tony,' said Lucia – this appellation was a halfway house between Lord Limpsfield and Tony, and she left out the 'Lord' except to him – 'how nice of you to drop in. You have just missed Adele. Stephen, you know Lord Limpsfield?'

Lucia gave him his tea, and presently getting up, reseated herself negligently on the sofa beside Stephen. She was a shade too close at first, and edged slightly away.

'Wonderful play of Tchekov's the other day,' she said. 'Such a strange, unhappy atmosphere. We came out, didn't we, Stephen, feeling as if we had been in some remote dream. I saw you there, Lord Tony, with Adele who had been lunching with me.'

Tony knew that: was not that the birthday of the Luciaphils?

'It was a dream I wasn't sorry to wake from,' he said. 'I found it a boring dream.'

'Ah, how can you say so? Such an experience! I felt as if the woe of a thousand years had come upon me, some old anguish which I had forgotten. With the effect, too, that I wanted to live more fully and vividly than ever, till the dusk closed round.'

Stephen waved his hands, as he edged a little further away from Lucia. There was something strange about Lucia today. In those few minutes when they had been alone she had been quite normal, but both before, when Adele was here, and now after Lord Limpfield's entry, she seemed to be implying a certain intimacy, to which he felt he ought to respond.

'Morbid fancies, Lucia,' he said, 'I shan't let you go to a Tchekov play again.'

'Horrid boy,' said Lucia daringly. 'But that's the way with all you men. You want women to be gay and bright and thoughtless, and have no other ideas except to amuse you. I shan't ever talk to either of you again about my real feelings. We will talk about the trial today. My entire sympathies are with Babs, Lord Tony. I'm sure yours are too.'

Lord Limpsfield left Stephen there when he took his leave, after a quarter of an hour's lighter conversation, and as nobody else dropped in, Lucia only asked her lover to dine on two or three nights the next week, to meet her at the private view of Herbert Alton's exhibition next morning, and let him go in a slightly bewildered frame of mind.

*   *   *

Stephen walked slowly up the Brompton Road, looking into the shop windows, and puzzling this out. She had held his hand oddly, she had sat close to him on the sofa, she had waved a dozen of those little signals of intimacy which gave colour to a supposition which, though it did not actually make his blood run cold, certainly did not make it run hot . . . He and Lucia were excellent friends, they had many tastes in common, but Stephen knew that he would sooner never see her again than have an intrigue with her. He was no hand, to begin with, at amorous adventures, and even if he had been he could not conceive a woman more ill-adapted to dally with than Lucia. 'Galahad and Artemis would make a better job of it than Lucia and me,' he muttered to himself, turning hastily away from a window full of dainty under-clothing for ladies. In vain he searched the blameless records of his intercourse with Lucia: he could not accuse himself of thought, word or deed which could possibly have given rise to any disordered fancy of hers that he observed her with a lascivious eye.

'God knows I am innocent,' he said to himself, and froze with horror at the sudden sight of a large news-board on which was printed in large capitals 'Babs wants Woof-dog on the hearthrug.'

He knew he had no taste for gallantry, and he felt morally certain that Lucia hadn't either . . . What then could she mean by those little tweaks and pressures? Conning them over for the second time, it struck him more forcibly than before that she had only indulged in these little licentiousnesses when there was someone else present. Little as he knew of the ways of lovers, he always imagined that they exchanged such tokens chiefly in private, and in public only when their passions had to find a small safety-valve. Again, if she had had designs on his virtue, she would surely, having got him alone, have given a message to her servants that she was out and not have had Lord Limpsfield admitted . . . He felt sure she was up to something, but to his dull male sense, it was at present wrapped in mystery. He did not want to give up all those charming hospitalities of hers, but he must needs be very circumspect.

It was, however, without much misgiving that he awaited her next morning at the doors of the little Rutland Gallery, for he felt safe in so public a place as a private view. Only a few early visitors had come in when Lucia arrived, and as she passed the turnstile showing the two cards of invitation for herself and Peppino, impersonated by Stephen, she asked for hers back, saying that she was only going to make a short visit now and would return later. She had not yet seen the caricature of herself and Peppino, for which Bertie Alton (she still stuck to this little mistake) had accepted a commission, and she made her way at once to Numbers 39 and 40, which her catalogue told her were of Mr and Mrs Philip Lucas. Subjoined to their names were the captions, and she read with excitement that Peppino was supposed to be saying 'At whatever personal inconvenience I must live up to Lucia,' while below Number 40 was the enticing little legend 'Oh, these duchesses! They give one no peace!' . . . And there was Peppino, in the knee-breeches of levee dress, tripping over his sword which had got entangled with his legs, and a cocked-hat on the back of his head, with his eyes very much apart, and no nose, and a small agonised hole in his face for a mouth . . . And there was she with a pile of opened letters on the floor, and a pile of unopened letters on the table. There was not much of her face to be seen, for she was talking into a telephone, but her skirt was very short, and so was her hair, and there was a wealth of weary resignation in the limpness of her carriage.

Lucia examined them both carefully, and then gave a long sigh of perfect happiness. That was her irrepressible comment: she could not have imagined anything more ideal. Then she gave a little peal of laughter.

'Look, Stephen,' she said. 'Bobbie – I mean Bertie – really is too wicked for anything! Really, outrageous! I am furious with him, and yet I can't help laughing. Poor Peppino, and poor me! Marcia will adore it. She always says she can never get hold of me nowadays.'

Lucia gave a swift scrutiny to the rest of the collection, so as to be able to recognise them all without reference to her catalogue, when she came back, as she intended to do later in the morning. There was hardly anyone here at present, but the place would certainly be crowded an hour before lunchtime, and she proposed to make a *soi-disant* first visit then, and know at once whom all the caricatures represented (for Bertie in his enthusiasm for caricature sometimes omitted likenesses), and go into peals of laughter at those of herself and Peppino, and say she must buy them, which of course she had already done. Stephen remained behind, for Hermione was going to say a good deal about the exhibition, but promised to wait till Lucia came back. She had not shown the smallest sign of amorousness this morning. His apprehensions were considerably relieved, and it looked as if no storm of emotion was likely to be required of him.

'Hundreds of things to do!' she said. 'Let me see, half-past eleven, twelve – yes, I shall be back soon after twelve, and we'll have a real look at them. And you'll lunch? Just a few people coming.'

Before Lucia got back, the gallery had got thick with visitors, and Hermione was busy noting those whom he saw chatting with friends or looking lovely, or being very pleased with the new house in Park Lane, or receiving congratulations on the engagement of a daughter. There was no doubt which of the pictures excited most interest, and soon there was a regular queue waiting to look at Numbers 39 and 40. People stood in front of them regarding them gravely and consulting their catalogues and then bursting into loud cracks of laughter and looking again till the growing weight of the queue dislodged them. One of those who lingered longest and stood her ground best was Adele, who, when she was eventually shoved on, ran round to the tail of the queue and herself shoved till she got opposite again. She saw Stephen.

'Ah, then Lucia won't be far off,' she observed archly. 'Doesn't she adore it? Where is Lucia?'

'She's been, but she's coming back,' he said. 'I expect her every minute. Ah! there she is.'

This was rather stupid of Stephen. He ought to have guessed that Lucia's second appearance was officially intended to be her first. He grasped that when she squeezed her way through the crowd and greeted him as if they had not met before that morning.

'And dearest Adele,' she said. 'What a crush! Tell me quickly, where are the caricatures of Peppino and me? I'm dying to see them; and when I see them no doubt I shall wish I was dead.'

The light of Luciaphilism came into Adele's intelligent eyes.

'We'll look for them together,' she said. 'Ah, thirty-nine and forty. They must be somewhere just ahead.'

Lucia exerted a steady indefatigable pressure on those in front, and presently came into range.

'Well, I never!' she said. 'Oh, but so like Peppino! How could Bertie have told he got his sword entangled just like that? And look what he says . . . Oh, and then Me! Just because I met him at Marcia's party and people were wanting to know when I had an evening free! Of all the impertinences! How I shall scold him!'

Lucia did it quite admirably in blissful unconsciousness that Adele knew she had been here before. She laughed, she looked again and laughed again. ('Mrs Lucas and Lady Brixton in fits of merriment over the cartoon of Mr Lucas and herself,' thought Hermione.)

'Ah, and there's Lord Hurtacombe,' she said. 'I'm sure that's Lord Hurtacombe, though you can't see much of him, and, look, Olga surely, is it not? How does he do it?'

That was a very clever identification for one who had not previously studied the catalogue, for Olga's face consisted entirely of a large open mouth and the tip of a chin; it might have been the face of anybody yawning. Her arms were stretched wide, and she towered above a small man in shorts.

'The last scene in *Siegfried*, I'm sure,' said Lucia. 'What does the catalogue say, Stephen? Yes, I am right. "Siegfried! Brünnhilde!" How wicked, is it not? But killing! Who could be cross with him?'

This was all splendid stuff for Luciaphils; it was amazing how at a first glance she recognised everybody. The gallery, too, was full of dears and darlings of a few weeks' standing, and she completed a little dinner party for next Tuesday long before she had made the circuit. All the time she kept Stephen by her side, looked over his catalogue, put a hand on his arm to direct his attention to some picture, took a speck of alien material off his sleeve, and all the time the entranced Adele felt increasingly certain that she had plumbed the depth of the adorable situation. Her sole anxiety was as to whether Stephen would plumb it too. He might – though he didn't look like it – welcome these little tokens of intimacy as indicating something more, and when they were alone attempt to kiss her, and that would ruin the whole exquisite design. Luckily his demeanour was not that of a favoured swain; it was, on the other hand, more the demeanour of a swain who feared to be favoured, and if that shy thing took fright, the situation would be equally ruined . . . To think that the most perfect piece of Luciaphilism was dependent on the just perceptions of Stephen! As the three made their slow progress, listening to Lucia's brilliant identifications, Adele willed Stephen to understand; she projected a perfect torrent of suggestion towards his mind. He must, he should understand . . .

Fervent desire, so every psychist affirms, is never barren. It conveys something of its yearning to the consciousness to which it is directed, and there began to break on the dull male mind what had been so obvious to the finer feminine sense of Adele. Once again, and in the blaze of publicity, Lucia was full of touches and tweaks, and the significance of them dawned, like some pale, austere sunrise, on his darkened senses. The situation was revealed, and he saw it was one with which he could easily deal. His gloomy apprehensions brightened, and he perceived that there would be no need, when he went to stay at Riseholme next, to lock his bedroom door, a practice which was abhorrent to him, for fear of fire suddenly breaking out in the house. Last night he had had a miserable dream about what had happened when he failed to lock his door at The Hurst, but now he dismissed its haunting. These little intimacies of Lucia's were purely a public performance.

'Lucia, we must be off,' he said loudly and confidently. 'Peppino will wonder where we are.'

Lucia sighed.

'He always bullies me like that, Adele,' she said. 'I must go: *au revoir*, dear. Tuesday next: just a few intimes.'

Lucia's relief was hardly less than Stephen's. He would surely not have said anything so indiscreet if he had been contemplating an indiscretion, and she had no fear that his hurry to be off was due to any passionate desire to embrace her in the privacy of her car. She believed he understood, and her belief felt justified when he proposed that the car should be opened.

*   *   *

Riseholme, in the last three weeks of social progress, had not occupied the front row of Lucia's thoughts, but the second row, so to speak, had been entirely filled with it, for, as far as the future dimly outlined itself behind the present, the plan was to go down there early in August, and remain there, with a few brilliant excursions, till autumn peopled London again. She had hoped for a dash to Aix, where there would be many pleasant people, but Peppino had told her summarily that the treasury would not stand it. Lucia had accepted that with the frankest good nature: she had made quite a gay little lament about it, when she was asked what she was going to do in August. 'Ah, all you lucky rich people with money to throw about; we've got to go and live quietly at home,' she used to say. 'But I shall love it, though I shall miss you all dreadfully. Riseholme, dear Riseholme, you know, adorable, and all the delicious funny friends down there who spoil me so dreadfully. I shall have lovely tranquil days, with a trot across the green to order fish, and a chat on the way, and my books and my piano, and a chair in the garden, and an early bedtime instead of all these late hours. An anchorite life, but if you have a weekend to

spare between your Aix and your yacht and your Scotland, ah, how
nice it would be if you just sent a postcard!'

Before they became anchorites, however, there was a long weekend
for her and Peppino over the August bank-holiday, and Lucia looked
forward to that with unusual excitement. Adele was the hostess, and
the scene that immense country-house of hers in Essex. The whole
world, apparently, was to be there, for Adele had said the house
would be full; and it was to be a final reunion of the choicest spirits
before the annual dispersion. Mrs Garroby-Ashton had longed to be
bidden, but was not, and though Lucia was sorry for dear Millicent's
disappointment, she could not but look down on it, as a sort of perch
far below her that showed how dizzily she herself had gone upwards.
But she had no intention of dropping good kind Millie who was
hopping about below: she must certainly come to The Hurst for a
Sunday: that would be nice for her, and she would learn all about
Adele's party.

There were yet ten days before that, and the morning after the
triumphant affair at the Rutland Gallery, Lucia heard a faint rumour,
coming from nowhere in particular, that Marcia Whitby was going
to give a very small and very wonderful dance to wind up the season.
She had not seen much of Marcia lately, in other words she had seen
nothing at all, and Lucia's last three invitations to her had been
declined, one through a secretary, and two through a telephone.
Lucia continued, however, to talk about her with unabated familiarity
and affection. The next day the rumour became slightly more solid:
Adele let slip some allusion to Marcia's ball, and hurriedly covered it
up with talk of her own weekend. Lucia fixed her with a penetrating
eye for a moment, but the eye failed apparently to penetrate: Adele
went on gabbling about her own party, and took not the slightest
notice of it.

But in truth Adele's gabble was a frenzied and feverish manoeuvre
to get away from the subject of Marcia's ball. Marcia was no true
Luciaphil; instead of feeling entranced pleasure in Lucia's successes
and failures, her schemes and attainments and ambitions, she had
lately been taking a high severe line about her.

'She's beyond a joke, Adele,' she said. 'I hear she's got a scrapbook,
and puts in picture postcards and photographs of country-houses,
with dates below them to indicate she has been there – '

'No!' said Adele. 'How heavenly of her. I must see it, or did you
make it up?'

'Indeed I didn't,' said the injured Marcia. 'And she's got in it a picture postcard of the moat-garden at Whitby with the date of the Sunday before last, when I had a party there and didn't ask her. Besides, she was in London at the time. And there's one of Buckingham Palace Garden, with the date of the last garden-party. Was she asked?'

'I haven't heard she was,' said Adele.

'Then you may be sure she wasn't. She's beyond a joke, I tell you, and I'm not going to ask her to my dance. I won't, I won't – I will not. And she asked me to dine three times last week. It isn't fair: it's bullying. A weak-minded person would have submitted, but I'm not weak-minded, and I won't be bullied. I won't be forcibly fed, and I won't ask her to my dance. There!'

'Don't be so unkind,' said Adele. 'Besides, you'll meet her down at my house only a few days afterwards, and it will be awkward. Everybody else will have been.'

'Well, then she can pretend she has been exclusive,' said Marcia snappily, 'and she'll like that . . . '

The rumours solidified into fact, and soon Lucia was forced to the dreadful conclusion that Marcia's ball was to take place without her. That was an intolerable thought, and she gave Marcia one more chance by ringing her up and inviting her to dinner on that night (so as to remind her she knew nothing about the ball), but Marcia's stony voice replied that most unfortunately she had a few people to dinner herself. Wherever she went (and where now did Lucia not go?) she heard talk of the ball, and the plethora of princes and princesses that were to attend it.

For a moment the thought of princesses lightened the depression of this topic. Princess Isabel was rather seriously ill with influenza, so Lucia, driving down Park Lane, thought it would not be amiss to call and enquire how she was, for she had noticed that sometimes the papers recorded the names of enquirers. She did not any longer care in the least how Princess Isabel was; whether she died or recovered was a matter of complete indifference to her in her present embittered frame of mind, for the princess had not taken the smallest notice of her all these weeks. However, there was the front door open, for there were other enquirers on the threshold, and Lucia joined them. She presented her card, and asked in a trembling voice what news there was, and was told that the Princess was no better. Lucia bowed her head in resignation, and then, after faltering a moment in her walk, pulled herself together, and with a firmer step went back to her motor.

After this interlude her mind returned to the terrible topic. She was due at a drawing-room meeting at Sophy Alingsby's house to hear a lecture on psychoanalysis, and she really hardly felt up to it. But there would certainly be a quantity of interesting people there, and the lecture itself might possibly be of interest, and so before long she found herself in the black dining-room, which had been cleared for the purpose. With the self-effacing instincts of the English the audience had left the front-row chairs completely unoccupied, and she got a very good place. The lecture had just begun, and so her entry was not unmarked. Stephen was there, and as she seated herself, she nodded to him, and patted the empty chair by her side with a beckoning gesture. Her lover, therefore, sidled up to her and took it.

Lucia whistled her thoughts away from such ephemeral and frivolous subjects as dances, and tried to give Professor Bonstetter her attention. She felt that she had been living a very hectic life lately; the world and its empty vanities had been too much with her, and she needed some intellectual tonic. She had seen no pictures lately, except Bobbie (or was it Bertie?) Alton's, she had heard no music, she had not touched the piano herself for weeks, she had read no books, and at the most had skimmed the reviews of such as had lately appeared in order to be up to date and be able to reproduce a short but striking criticism or two if the talk became literary. She must not let the mere froth of living entirely conceal by its winking headiness of foam the true beverage below it. There was Sophy, with her hair over her eyes and her chin in her hand, dressed in a faded rainbow, weird beyond description, but rapt in concentration, while she herself was letting the notion of a dance to which she had not been asked and was clearly not to be asked, drive like a mist between her and these cosmic facts about dreams and the unconscious self. How curious that if you dreamed about boiled rabbit, it meant that sometime in early childhood you had been kissed by a poacher in a railway-carriage, and had forgotten all about it! What a magnificent subject for excited research psychoanalysis would have been in those keen intellectual days at Riseholme . . . She thought of them now with a vague yearning for their simplicity and absorbing earnestness; of the hours she had spent with Georgie over piano duets, of Daisy Quantock's ouija-board and planchette, of the Museum with its mittens. Riseholme presented itself now as an abode of sweet peace, where there were no disappointments or heartburnings, for sooner or later she had always managed to assert her will and constitute herself priestess of the current interests . . . Suddenly the solution of her present difficulty flashed upon her. Riseholme. She would go to

Riseholme: that would explain her absence from Marcia's stupid ball.

The lecture came to an end, and with others she buzzed for a little while round Professor Bonstetter, and had a few words with her hostess.

'Too interesting: marvellous, was it not, dear Sophy? Boiled rabbit! How curious! And the outcropping of the unconscious in dreams. Explains so much about phobias: people who can't go in the tube. So pleased to have heard it. Ah, there's Aggie. Aggie darling! What a treat, wasn't it? Such a refreshment from our bustlings and runnings-about to get back into origins. I've got to fly, but I couldn't miss this. Dreadful overlapping all this afternoon, and poor Princess Isabel is no better. I just called on my way here, but I wasn't allowed to see her. Stephen, where is Stephen? See if my motor is there, dear. *Au revoir!* dear Sophy. We must meet again very soon. Are you going to Adele's next week? No? How tiresome! Wonderful lecture! Calming!'

Lucia edged herself out of the room with these very hurried greetings, for she was really eager to get home. She found Peppino there, having tea peacefully all by himself, and sank exhausted in a chair.

'Give me a cup of tea, strong tea, Peppino,' she said. 'I've been racketing about all day, and I feel done for. How I shall get through these next two or three days I really don't know. And London is stifling. You look worn out too, my dear.'

Peppino acknowledged the truth of this. He had hardly had time even to go to his club this last day or two, and had been reflecting on the enormous strength of the weaker sex. But for Lucia to confess herself done for was a portentous thing: he could not remember such a thing happening before.

'Well, there are not many more days of it,' he said. 'Three more this week, and then Lady Brixton's party.'

He gave several loud sneezes.

'Not a cold?' asked Lucia.

'Something extraordinarily like one,' said he.

Lucia became suddenly alert again. She was sorry for Peppino's cold, but it gave her an admirable gambit for what she had made up her mind to do.

'My dear, that's enough,' she said. 'I won't have you flying about London with a bad cold coming on. I shall take you down to Riseholme tomorrow.'

'Oh, but you can't, my dear,' said he. 'You've got your engagement book full for the next three days.'

'Oh, a lot of stupid things,' said she. 'And really, I tell you quite honestly, I'm fairly worn out. It'll do us both good to have a rest for a day or two. Now don't make objections. Let us see what I've got to do.'

The days were pretty full (though, alas, Thursday evening was deplorably empty) and Lucia had a brisk half-hour at the telephone. To those who had been bidden here, and to those to whom she had been bidden, she gave the same excuse, namely, that she had been advised (by herself) two or three days' complete rest.

She rang up The Hurst, to say that they were coming down tomorrow, and would bring the necessary attendants, she rang up Georgie (for she was not going to fall into *that* error again) and in a mixture of baby-language and Italian, which he found very hard to understand, asked him to dine tomorrow night, and finally she scribbled a short paragraph to the leading morning papers to say that Mrs Philip Lucas had been ordered to leave London for two or three days' complete rest. She had hesitated a moment over the wording of that, for it was Peppino who was much more in need of rest than she, but it would have been rather ludicrous to say that Mr and Mrs Philip Lucas were in need of a complete rest . . . These announcements she sent by hand so that there might be no mis-carriage in their appearance tomorrow morning. And then, as an afterthought, she rang up Daisy Quantock and asked her and Robert to lunch tomorrow.

She felt much happier. She would not be at the fell Marcia's ball, because she was resting in the country.

Chapter Eight

A few minutes before Lucia and Peppino drove off next morning from Brompton Square, Marcia observed Lucia's announcement in the *Morning Post*. She was a good-natured woman, but she had been goaded, and now that Lucia could goad her no more for the present, she saw no objection to asking her to her ball. She thought of telephoning, but there was the chance that Lucia had not yet started, so she sent her a card instead, directing it to 25 Brompton Square, saying that she was At Home, dancing, to have the honour to meet a string of exalted personages. If she had telephoned, no one knows what would have happened, whether Daisy would have had any lunch that day or Georgie any dinner that night, and what excuse Lucia would have made to them . . . Adele and Tony Limpsfield, the most adept of all the Luciaphils, subsequently argued the matter out with much heat, but never arrived at a solution that they felt was satisfactory. But then Marcia did not telephone . . .

The news that the two were coming down was, of course, all over Riseholme a few minutes after Lucia had rung Georgie up. He was in his study when the telephone bell rang, in the fawn-coloured Oxford trousers, which had been cut down from their monstrous proportions and fitted quite nicely, though there had been a sad waste of stuff. Robert Quantock, the wag who had danced a hornpipe when Georgie had appeared in the original voluminousness, was waggish again, when he saw the abbreviated garments, and *à propos* of nothing in particular had said 'Home is the sailor, home from sea,' and that was the epitaph on the Oxford trousers.

Georgie had been busy indoors this afternoon, for he had been attending to his hair, and it was not quite dry yet, and the smell of the auburn mixture still clung to it. But the telephone was a trunk call, and, whether his hair was dry or not, it must be attended to. Since Lucia had disappeared after that weekend party, he had had a line from her once or twice, saying that they must really settle when he would come and spend a few days in London, but she had never descended to the sordid mention of dates.

A trunk call, as far as he knew, could only be Lucia or Olga, and one would be interesting and the other delightful. It proved to be the interesting one, and though rather difficult to understand because of the aforesaid mixture of baby-talk and Italian, it certainly conveyed the gist of the originator's intention.

'Me so tired,' Lucia said, 'and it will be divine to get to Riseholme again. So come to 'ickle quiet din-din with me and Peppino tomorrow, Georgino. Shall want to hear all *novelle* – '

'What?' said Georgie.

'All the news,' said Lucia.

Georgie sat in the draught – it was very hot today – until the auburn mixture dried. He knew that Daisy Quantock and Robert were playing clock-golf on the other side of his garden paling, for their voices had been very audible. Daisy had not been weeding much lately but had taken to golf, and since all the authorities said that matches were entirely won or lost on the putting-green, she with her usual wisdom devoted herself to the winning factor in the game. Presently she would learn to drive and approach and niblick and that sort of thing, and then they would see . . . She wondered how good Miss Wethered really was.

Georgie, now dry, tripped out into the garden and shouted, 'May I come in?' That meant, of course, might he look over the garden paling and talk.

Daisy missed a very short putt, owing to the interruption.

'Yes, do,' she said icily. 'I supposed you would give me that, Robert.'

'You supposed wrong,' said Robert, who was now two up.

Georgie stepped on a beautiful pansy.

'Lucia's coming down tomorrow,' he said.

Daisy dropped her putter.

'No!' she exclaimed.

'And Peppino,' went on Georgie. 'She says she's very tired.'

'All those duchesses,' said Daisy. Robert Alton's cartoon had been reproduced in an illustrated weekly, but Riseholme up to this moment had been absolutely silent about it. It was beneath notice.

'And she's asked me to dinner tomorrow,' said Georgie.

'So she's not bringing down a party?' said Daisy.

'I don't know,' remarked Robert, 'if you are going on putting, or if you give me the match.'

'Pouf!' said Daisy, just like that. 'But tired, Georgie? What does that mean?'

'I don't know,' said Georgie, 'but that's what she said.'

'It means something else,' said Daisy, 'I can't tell you what, but it doesn't mean that. I suppose you've said you're engaged.'

'No I haven't,' said Georgie.

De Vere came out from the house. In this dry weather her heels made no indentations on the lawn.

'Trunk call, ma'am,' she said to Daisy.

'These tiresome interruptions,' said Daisy, hurrying indoors with great alacrity.

Georgie lingered. He longed to know what the trunk call was, and was determined to remain with his head on the top of the paling till Daisy came back. So he made conversation.

'Your lawn is better than mine,' he said pleasantly to Robert.

Robert was cross at this delay.

'That's not saying much,' he observed.

'I can't say any more,' said Georgie, rather nettled. 'And there's the leather-jacket grub I see has begun on yours. I dare say there won't be a blade of grass left presently.'

Robert changed the conversation: there were bare patches. 'The Museum insurance,' he said. 'I got the fire-policy this morning. The contents are the property of the four trustees, me and you and Daisy and Mrs Boucher. The building is Colonel Boucher's, and that's insured separately. If you had a spark of enterprise about you, you would take a match, set light to the mittens, and hope for the best.'

'You're very tarsome and cross,' said Georgie. 'I should like to take a match and set light to you.'

Georgie hated rude conversations like this, but when Robert was in such a mood, it was best to be playful. He did not mean, in any case, to cease leaning over the garden paling till Daisy came back from her trunk call.

'Beyond the mittens,' began Robert, 'and, of course, those three sketches of yours, which I dare say are masterpieces – '

Daisy bowled out of the dining-room and came with such speed down the steps that she nearly fell into the circular bed where the broccoli had been. (The mignonette there was poorish.)

'At half-past one or two,' said she, bursting with the news and at the same time unable to suppress her gift for withering sarcasm. 'Lunch tomorrow. Just a picnic, you know, as soon as she happens to arrive. So kind of her. More notice than she took of me last time.'

'Lucia?' asked Georgie.

'Yes. Let me see, I was putting, wasn't I?'

'If you call it putting,' said Robert. He was not often two up and he made the most of it.

'So I suppose you said you were engaged,' said Georgie.

Daisy did not trouble to reply at all. She merely went on putting. That was the way to deal with inquisitive questions.

This news, therefore, was very soon all over Riseholme, and next morning it was supplemented by the amazing announcement in *The Times*, *Morning Post*, *Daily Telegraph* and *Daily Mail* that Mrs Philip Lucas had left London for two or three days' complete rest. It sounded incredible to Riseholme, but of course it might be true and, as Daisy had said, that the duchesses had been too much for her. (This was nearer the mark than the sarcastic Daisy had known, for it was absolutely and literally true that one Duchess had been too much for her . . .) In any case, Lucia was coming back to them again, and though Riseholme was still a little dignified and reticent, Georgie's acceptance of his dinner-invitation, and Daisy's of her lunch-invitation, were symptomatic of Riseholme's feelings. Lucia had foully deserted them, she had been down here only once since that fatal accession to fortune, and on that occasion had evidently intended to see nothing of her old friends while that Yahoo party ('Yahoo' was the only word for Mrs Alingsby) was with her; she had laughed at their Museum, she had courted the vulgar publicity of the press to record her movements in London, but Riseholme was really perfectly willing to forget and forgive if she behaved properly now. For, though no one would have confessed it, they missed her more and more. In spite of all her bullying monarchical ways, she had initiative, and though the excitement of the Museum and the sagas from Abfou had kept them going for a while, it was really in relation to Lucia that these enterprises had been interesting. Since then, too, Abfou had been full of vain repetitions, and no one could go on being excited by his denunciation of Lucia as a snob, indefinitely. Lucia had personality, and if she had been here and had taken to golf Riseholme would have been thrilled at her skill, and have exulted over her want of it, whereas Daisy's wonderful scores at clock-golf (she was off her game today) produced no real interest. Degrading, too, as were the records of Lucia's movements in the columns of Hermione, Riseholme had been thrilled (though disgusted) by them, because they were about Lucia, and though she was coming down now for complete rest (whatever that might mean), the mere fact of her being here would make things hum. This time too she had behaved properly (perhaps she had learned wisdom) and had announced her coming, and asked old friends in.

Forgiveness, therefore, and excitement were the prevalent emotions in the morning parliament on the green next day. Mrs Boucher alone expressed grave doubts on the situation.

'I don't believe she's ill,' she said. 'If she's ill, I shall be very sorry, but I don't believe it. If she is, Mr Georgie, I'm all for accepting her gift of the spit to the Museum, for it would be unkind not to. You can write and say that the committee have reconsidered it and would be very glad to have it. But let's wait to see if she's ill first. In fact, wait to see if she's coming at all, first.'

Piggy came whizzing up with news, while Goosie shouted it into her mother's ear-trumpet. Before Piggy could come out with it, Goosie's announcement was audible everywhere.

'A cab from the station has arrived at The Hurst, mamma,' she yelled, 'with the cook and the housemaid, and a quantity of luggage.'

'Oh, Mrs Boucher, have you heard the news?' panted Piggy.

'Yes, my dear, I've just heard it,' said Mrs Boucher, 'and it looks as if they were coming. That's all I can say. And if the cook's come by half-past eleven, I don't see why you shouldn't get a proper lunch, Daisy. No need for a cup of strong soup or a sandwich which I should have recommended if there had been no further news since you were asked to a picnic lunch. But if the cook's here now . . . '

Daisy was too excited to go home and have any serious putting and went off to the Museum. Mr Rushbold, the vicar, had just presented his unique collection of walking-sticks to it, and though the committee felt it would be unkind not to accept them, it was difficult to know how to deal with them. They could not all be stacked together in one immense stick-stand, for then they could not be appreciated. The handles of many were curiously carved, some with gargoyle-heads of monsters putting out their tongues and leering, some with images of birds and fish, and there was one rather indelicate one, of a young man and a girl passionately embracing . . . On the other hand, if they were spaced and leaned against the wall, some slight disturbance upset the equilibrium of one and it fell against the next, and the whole lot went down like ninepins. In fact, the boy at the turnstile said his entire time was occupied with picking them up. Daisy had a scheme of stretching an old lawn-tennis net against the wall, and tastefully entangling them in its meshes . . .

Riseholme lingered on the green that morning long after one o'clock, which was its usual lunchtime, and at precisely twenty-five minutes past they were rewarded. Out of the motor stepped Peppino in a very thick coat and a large muffler. He sneezed twice as he held out his arm to assist Lucia to alight. She clung to it, and leaning heavily on it went with faltering steps past Perdita's garden into the house. So she was ill.

Ten minutes later, Daisy and Robert Quantock were seated at lunch with them. Lucia certainly looked very well and she ate her lunch very properly, but she spoke in a slightly faded voice, as befitted one who had come here for complete rest. 'But Riseholme, dear Riseholme will soon put me all right again,' she said. 'Such a joy to be here! Any news, Daisy?'

Really there was very little. Daisy ran through such topics as had interested Riseholme during those last weeks, and felt that the only thing which had attracted true, feverish, Riseholme-attention was the record of Lucia's own movements. Apart from this there was only her own putting, and the embarrassing gift of walking-sticks to the Museum . . . But then she remembered that the committee had authorised the acceptance of the Elizabethan spit, if Lucia seemed ill, and she rather precipitately decided that she was ill enough.

'Well, we've been busy over the Museum,' she began.

'Ah, the dear Museum,' said Lucia wistfully.

That quite settled it.

'We should so like to accept the Elizabethan spit, if we may,' said Daisy. 'It would be a great acquisition.'

'Of course; delighted,' said Lucia. 'I will have it sent over. Any other gifts?'

Daisy went on to the walking-sticks, omitting all mention of the indelicate one in the presence of gentlemen, and described the difficulty of placing them satisfactorily. They were eighty-one (including the indelicacy) and a lawn-tennis net would barely hold them. The invalid took but a wan interest in this, and Daisy's putting did not rouse much keener enthusiasm. But soon she recovered a greater animation and was more herself. Indeed, before the end of lunch it had struck Daisy that Peppino was really the invalid of the two. He certainly had a prodigious cold, and spoke in a throaty wheeze that was scarcely audible. She wondered if she had been a little hasty about accepting the spit, for that gave Lucia a sort of footing in the Museum.

*   *   *

Lucia recovered still further when her guests had gone, and her habitual energy began to assert itself. She had made her impressive invalid entry into Riseholme, which justified the announcement in the papers, and now, quietly, she must be on the move again. She might begin by getting rid, without delay, of that tiresome spit.

'I think I shall go out for a little drive, Peppino,' she said, 'though if I were you I would nurse my cold and get it all right before Saturday when we go to Adele's. The gardener, I think, could take the spit out of the chimney for me, and put it in the motor, and I would drop it at the Museum. I thought they would want it before long . . . And that clock-golf of Daisy's; it sounds amusing; the sort of thing for Sunday afternoon if we have guests with us. I think she said that you could get the apparatus at the Stores. Little tournaments might be rather fun.'

The spit was easily removed, and Lucia, having written to the Stores for a set of clock-golf, had it loaded up on the motor, and conveyed to the Museum. So that was done. She waved and fluttered a hand of greeting to Piggy and Goosie who were gambolling on the green, and set forth into the country, satisfied that she had behaved wisely in leaving London rather than being left out in London. Apart from that, too, it had been politic to come down to Riseholme again like this, to give them a taste of her quality before she resumed, in August, as she entirely meant to do, her ancient sway. She guessed from the paucity of news which that arch-gossip, dear Daisy, had to give, that things had been remarkably dull in her absence, and though she had made a sad mistake over her weekend party, a little propitiation would soon put that right. And Daisy had had nothing to say about Abfou: they seemed to have got a little tired of Abfou. But Abfou might be revived: clock-golf and a revival of ouija would start August very pleasantly. She would have liked Aix better, but Peppino was quite clear about that . . .

Georgie was agreeably surprised to find her so much herself when he came over for dinner. Peppino, whose cold was still extremely heavy, went to bed very soon after, and he and Lucia settled themselves in the music-room.

'First a little chat, Georgie,' she said, 'and then I insist on our having some music. I've played nothing lately, you will find me terribly out of practice, but you mustn't scold me. Yes, the spit has gone: dear Daisy said the Museum was most anxious to get it, and I took it across myself this afternoon. I must see what else I can find worthy of it.'

This was all rather splendid. Lucia had a glorious way of completely disregarding the past, and pushing on ahead into the future.

'And have you been playing much lately?' she asked.

'Hardly a note,' said Georgie, 'there is nobody to play with. Piggy wanted to do some duets, but I said "No, thanks".'

'Georgie, you've been lazy,' she said, 'there's been nobody to keep you up to the mark. And Olga? Has Olga been down?'

'Not since – not since that Sunday when you were both down together,' said he.

'Very wrong of her to have deserted Riseholme. But just as wrong of me, you will say. But now we must put our heads together and make great plans for August. I shall be here to bully you all August. Just one visit, which Peppino and I are paying to dear Adele Brixton on Saturday, and then you will have me here solidly. London? Yes, it has been great fun, though you and I never managed to arrange a date for your stay with us. That must come in the autumn when we go up in November. But, oh, how tired I was when we settled to leave town yesterday. Not a kick left in me. Lots of engagements, too, and I just scrapped them. But people must be kind to me and forgive me. And sometimes I feel that I've been wasting time terribly. I've done nothing but see people, people, people. All sorts, from Alf Watson the pugilist – '

'No!' said Georgie, beginning to feel the thrill of Lucia again.

'Yes, he came to dine with me, such a little duck, and brought his flute. There was a great deal of talk about my party for Alf, and how the women buzzed round him!'

'Who else?' said Georgie greedily.

'My dear, who *not* else? Marcelle – Marcelle Periscope came another night, Adele, Sophy Alingsby, Bertie Alton, Aggie – I must ask dear Aggie down here; Tony – Tony Limpsfield; a thousand others. And then of course dear Marcia Whitby often. She is giving a ball tomorrow night. I should like to have been there, but I was just *finito*. Ah, and your friend Princess Isabel. Very bad influenza. You should ring up her house, Georgie, and ask how she is. I called there yesterday. So sad! But let us talk of more cheerful things. Daisy's clock-golf: I must pop in and see her at it tomorrow. She is wonderful, I suppose. I have ordered a set from the Stores, and we will have great games.'

'She's been doing nothing else for weeks,' said Georgie. 'I dare say she's very good, but nobody takes any interest in it. She's rather a bore about it – '

'Georgie, don't be unkind about poor Daisy,' said Lucia. 'We must start little competitions, with prizes. Do you have partners? You and I will be partners at mixed putting. And what about Abfou?'

It seemed to Georgie that this was just the old Lucia, and so no doubt it was. She was intending to bag any employments that happened to be going about and claim them as her own. It was larceny, intellectual and physical larceny, no doubt, but Lucia breathed life into those dead bones and made them interesting. It was weary work to watch Daisy dabbing away with her putter and then trying to beat her score without caring the least whether you beat it or not. And Daisy even telephoned her more marvellous feats, and nobody cared how marvellous they were. But it would be altogether different if Lucia was the goddess of putting . . .

'I haven't Abfou'd for ages,' said Georgie. 'I fancy she has dropped it.'

'Well, we must pick everything up again,' said Lucia briskly, 'and you shan't be lazy any more, Georgie. Come and play duets. My dear piano! What shall we do?'

They did quantities of things, and then Lucia played the slow movement of the 'Moonlight Sonata', and Georgie sighed as usual, and eventually Lucia let him out and walked with him to the garden-gate. There were quantities of stars, and as usual she quoted 'See how the floor of heaven is thick inlaid . . .' and said she must ring him up in the morning, after a good night's rest.

There was a light in Daisy's drawing-room, and just as he came opposite it she heard his step, for which she had long been listening, and looked out.

'Is it Georgie?' she said, knowing perfectly well that it must be.

'Yes,' said Georgie. 'How late you are.'

'And how is Lucia?' asked Daisy.

Georgie quite forgot for the moment that Lucia was having complete rest.

'Excellent form,' he said. 'Such a talk, and such a music.'

'There you are, then!' said Daisy. 'There's nothing the matter with her. She doesn't want rest any more – than the moon. What does it mean, Georgie? Mark my words: it means something.'

*   *   *

Lucia, indeed, seemed in no need whatever of complete rest the next day. She popped into Daisy's very soon after breakfast, and asked to be taught how to putt. Daisy gave her a demonstration, and told her how to hold the putter and where to place her feet, and said it was absolutely essential to stand like a rock and to concentrate. Nobody could putt if anyone spoke. Eventually Lucia was allowed to try, and she stood all wrong and grasped her putter like an umbrella, and holed out of the longest of putts in the middle of an uninterrupted sentence. Then they had a match, Daisy proposing to give her four strokes in the round, which Lucia refused, and Daisy, dithering with excitement and superiority, couldn't putt at all. Lucia won easily, with Robert looking on, and she praised Daisy's putter, and said it was beautifully balanced, though where she picked that up Daisy couldn't imagine.

'And now I must fly,' said Lucia, 'and we must have a return match sometime. So amusing! I have sent for a set, and you will have to give me lessons. Goodbye, dear Daisy, I'm away for the Sunday at dear Adele Brixton's, but after that how lovely to settle down at Riseholme again! You must show me your ouija-board too. I feel quite rested this morning. Shall I help you with the walking-sticks later on?'

Daisy went uneasily back to her putting: it was too awful that

Lucia in that amateurish manner should have beaten a serious exponent of the art, and already, in dark anticipation, she saw Lucia as the impresario of clock-golf, popularising it in Riseholme. She herself would have to learn to drive and approach without delay, and make Riseholme take up real golf, instead of merely putting.

Lucia visited the Museum next, and arranged the spit in an empty and prominent place between Daisy's fossils and Colonel Boucher's fragments of Samian ware. She attended the morning parliament on the green, and walked beside Mrs Boucher's bath-chair. She shouted into Mrs Antrobus's ear-trumpet, she dallied with Piggy and Goosie, and never so much as mentioned a duchess. All her thoughts seemed wrapped up in Riseholme; just one tiresome visit lay in front of her, and then, oh, the joy of settling down here again! Even Mrs Boucher felt disarmed; little as she would have thought it, there was something in Lucia beyond mere snobbery.

Georgie popped in that afternoon about teatime. The afternoon was rather chilly, and Lucia had a fire lit in the grate of the music-room, which, now that the spit had been removed, burned beautifully. Peppino, drowsy with his cold, sat by it, while the other two played duets. Already Lucia had taken down Sigismund's portrait and installed Georgie's watercolours again by the piano. They had had a fine tussle over the Mozart duet, and Georgie had promised to practise it, and Lucia had promised to practise it, and she had called him an idle boy, and he had called her a lazy girl, quite in the old style, while Peppino dozed. Just then the evening post came in, with the evening paper, and Lucia picked up the latter to see what Hermione had said about her departure from London. Even as she turned back the page her eye fell on two or three letters which had been forwarded from Brompton Square. The top one was a large square envelope, the sort of fine thick envelope that contained a rich card of invitation, and she opened it. Next moment she sprang from her seat.

'Peppino, dear,' she cried. 'Marcia! Her ball. Marcia's ball tonight!'

Peppino roused himself a little.

'Ball? What ball?' he said. 'No ball. Riseholme.'

Lucia pushed by Georgie on the treble music-stool, without seeming to notice that he was there.

'No dear, of course you won't go,' she said. 'But do you know, I think I shall go up and pop in for an hour. Georgie will come to dine with you, won't you, Georgie, and you'll go to bed early. Half-past six! Yes, I can be in town by ten. That will be heaps of time. I shall dress at Brompton Square. Just a sandwich to take with me and eat it in the car.'

She wheeled round to Georgie, pressing the bell in her circum-volution.

'Marcia Whitby,' she said. 'Winding up the season. So easy to pop up there, and dear Marcia would be hurt if I didn't come. Let me see, shall I come back tomorrow, Peppino? Perhaps it would be simpler if I stayed up there and sent the car back. Then you could come up in comfort next day, and we would go on to Adele's together. I have a host of things to do in London tomorrow. That party at Aggie's. I will telephone to Aggie to say that I can come after all. My maid, my chauffeur,' she said to the butler, rather in the style of Shylock. 'I want my maid and my chauffeur and my car. Let him have his dinner quickly – no, he can get his dinner at Brompton Square. Tell him to come round at once.'

Georgie sat positively aghast, for Lucia ran on like a thing demented. Mozart, ouija, putting, the Elizabethan spit, all the simple joys of Riseholme fizzled out like damp fireworks. Gone, too, utterly gone was her need of complete rest; she had never been so full of raw, blatant, savage vitality.

'Dear Marcia,' she said. 'I felt it must be an oversight from the first, but naturally, Georgie, though she and I are such friends, I could not dream of reminding her. What a blessing that my delicious day at Riseholme has so rested me: I feel I could go to fifty balls without fatigue. Such a wonderful house, Georgie; when you come up to stay with us in the autumn, I must take you there. Peppino, is it not lucky that I only brought down here just enough for a couple of nights, and left everything in London to pick up as we came through to go to Adele's? What a sight it will be, all the Royal Family almost I believe, and the whole of the Diplomatic corps: my Gioconda, I know, is going. Not a large ball though at all: not one of those great promiscuous affairs, which I hate so. How dear Marcia was besieged for invitations! how vulgar people are and how pushing! Goody-bye, mind you practise your Mozart, Georgie. Oh, and tell Daisy that I shan't be able to have another of those delicious puttings with her tomorrow. Back on Tuesday after the weekend at Adele's, and then weeks and weeks of dear Riseholme. How long they are! I will just go and hurry my maid up.'

Georgie tripped off, as soon as she had gone, to see Daisy, and narrated to her open-mouthed disgust this amazing scene.

'And the question is,' he said, 'about the complete rest that

was ordered her. I don't believe she was ordered any rest at all. I
believe –'

Daisy gave a triumphant crow: inductive reasoning had led her to
precisely the same point at precisely the same moment.

'Why, of course!' she said. 'I always felt there was something behind
that complete rest. I told you it meant something different. She
wasn't asked, and so –'

'And so she came down here for rest,' said Georgie in a loud
voice. He was determined to bring that out first. 'Because she wasn't
asked –'

'And the moment she was asked she flew,' said Daisy. 'Nothing
could be plainer. No more rest, thank you.'

'She's wonderful,' said Georgie. 'Too interesting!'

*   *   *

Lucia sped through the summer evening on this errand of her own
reprieve, too excited to eat, and too happy to wonder how it had
happened like this. How wise, too, she had been to hold her tongue
and give way to no passionate laments at her exclusion from the
paradise towards which she was now hastening. Not one word of
abuse had she uttered against Marcia: she had asked nobody to
intercede: she had joined in all the talk about the ball as if she was
going, and finally had made it impossible for herself to go by
announcing that she had been ordered a few days of complete rest.
She could (and would) explain her appearance perfectly: she had felt
much better – doctors were such fussers – and at the last moment
had made just a little effort, and here she was.

A loud explosion interrupted these agreeable reflections and the
car drew up. A tyre had burst, but they carried an extra wheel, and
though the delay seemed terribly long they were soon on their way
again. They traversed another ten miles, and now in the north-east
the smouldering glow of London reddened the toneless hue of the
summer night. The stars burned bright, and she pictured Peppino at
his telescope – no, Peppino had a really bad cold, and would not be
at his telescope. Then there came another explosion – was it those
disgusting stars in their courses that were fighting against her? – and
again the car drew up by the side of the empty road.

'What has happened?' asked Lucia in a strangled voice.

'Another tyre gone, ma'am,' said the chauffeur. 'Never knew such
a thing.'

Lucia looked at her clock. It was ten already, and she ought now to be in Brompton Square. There was no further wheel that could be put on, and the tyre had to be taken off and mended. The minutes passed like seconds . . . Lucia, outwardly composed, sat on a rug at the edge of the road, and tried unsuccessfully not to curse Almighty Providence. The moon rose, like a gelatine lozenge.

She began to count the hours that intervened between the tragic present and, say, four o'clock in the morning, and she determined that whatever further disasters might befall, she would go to Whitby House, even if it was in a dustman's cart, so long as there was a chance of a single guest being left there. She would go . . .

And all the time, if she had only known it, the stars were fighting not against her but for her. The tyre was mended, and she got to Brompton Square at exactly a quarter past eleven. Cupboards were torn open, drawers ransacked, her goaded maid burst into tears. Aunt Amy's pearls were clasped round her neck, Peppino's hair in the shrine of gold sausage that had once been Beethoven's was pinned on, and at five minutes past twelve she hurried up the great stairs at Whitby House. Precisely as she came to the door of the ballroom there emerged the head of the procession going down to supper. Marcia for a moment stared at her as if she was a ghost, but Lucia was so busy curtseying that she gave no thought to that. Seven times in rapid succession did she curtsey. It almost became a habit, and she nearly curtseyed to Adele who (so like Adele) followed immediately after.

'Just up from Riseholme, dearest Adele,' she said. 'I felt quite rested – How are you, Lord Tony? – and so I made a little effort. Peppino urged me to come. How nice to see your Excellency! Millie! Dearest Olga! What a lot of friends! How is poor Princess Isabel? Marcia looked so handsome. Brilliant! Such a delicious drive: I felt I had to pop in . . .'

Chapter Nine

Poor Peppino's cold next day, instead of being better, was a good deal worse. He had aches and pains, and felt feverish, and sent for the doctor, who peremptorily ordered him to go to bed. There was nothing in the least to cause alarm, but it would be the height of folly to go to any weekend party at all. Bed.

Peppino telegraphed to Lady Brixton with many regrets for the unavoidable, and rang up Lucia. The state of his voice made it difficult to catch what he said, but she quite understood that there was nothing to be anxious about, and that he hoped she would go to Adele's without him. Her voice on the other hand was marvellously distinct, and he heard a great deal about the misfortunes which had come to so brilliant a conclusion last night. There followed a string of seven Christian names, and Lucia said a flashlight photograph had been permitted during supper. She thought she was in it, though rather in the background.

Lucia was very sorry for Peppino's indisposition, but, as ordered, had no anxiety about him. She felt too, that he wouldn't personally miss very much by being prevented from coming to Adele's party, for it was to be a very large party, and Peppino – bless him – occasionally got a little dazed at these brilliant gatherings. He did not grasp who people were with the speed and certainty which were needful, and he had been known to grasp the hand of an eminent author and tell him how much he had admired his fine picture at the Academy. (Lucia constantly did that sort of thing herself, but then she got herself out of the holes she had herself digged with so brilliant a manoeuvre that it didn't matter, whereas Peppino was only dazed the more by his misfortunes.) Moreover she knew that Peppino's presence somehow hampered her style: she could not be the brilliant *mondaine*, when his patient but proud eye was on her, with quite the dash that was hers when he was not there. There was always the sense that he knew her best in her Riseholme incarnation, in her duets with Georgie, and her rendering of the slow movement of the 'Moonlight Sonata', and her grabbing of all Daisy's little stunts. She electrified him as the superb butterfly, but the electrification was accompanied by slight shocks and surprises. When she referred by her Christian name to some woman with whom her only bond was that she had refused to dine at Brompton Square, that puzzled Peppino . . . In the autumn she must be a little more serious, have some quiet dinner parties of ordinary people, for really up till now there had scarcely been an 'ordinary' person at Brompton Square at all, such noble lions of every species had been entrapped there. And Adele's party was to be of a very leonine kind; the smart world was to be there, and some highbrows and some politicians, and she was aware that she herself would have to do her very best, and be allusive, and pretend to know what she didn't know, and seem to swim in very distinguished currents. Dear Peppino wasn't up to that sort of thing, he couldn't grapple with it, and she grappled with it best without

him . . . At the moment of that vainglorious thought, it is probable
that Nemesis fixed her inexorable eye on Lucia.

Lucia, unconscious of this deadly scrutiny, turned to her immediate
affairs. Her engagement book pleasantly informed her that she had
many things to do on the day when the need for complete rest
overtook her, and now she heralded through the telephone the glad
tidings that she could lunch here and drop in there, and dine with
Aggie. All went well with these restorations, and the day would be
full, and tomorrow also, down to the hour of her departure for
Adele's. Having despatched this agreeable business, she was on the
point of ringing up Stephen, to fit him in for the spare three-quarters
of an hour that was left, when she was rung up and it was Stephen's
voice that greeted her.

'Stephano *mio*,' she said. 'How did you guess I was back?'

'Because I rang up Riseholme first,' said he, 'and heard you had
gone to town. Were you there last night?'

There was no cause to ask where 'there' was. There had only been
one place in London last night.

'Yes; delicious dance,' said Lucia. 'I was just going to ring you up
and see if you could come round for a chat at a quarter to five. I am
free till half-past five. Such fun it was. A flashlight photograph.'

'No!' said Stephen in the Riseholme manner. 'I long to hear about
it. And were there really seven of them?'

'Quite,' said Lucia magnificently.

'Wonderful! But quarter to five is no use for me. Can't you give
me another time?'

'My dear, impossible,' said Lucia. 'You know what London is in
these last days. Such a scrimmage.'

'Well, we shall meet tomorrow then,' said he.

'But, alas, I go to Adele's tomorrow,' she said.

'Yes, but so do I,' said Stephen. 'She asked me this morning. I was
wondering if you would drive me down, if you're going in your car.
Would there be room for you and Peppino and me?'

Lucia rapidly reviewed the situation. It was perfectly clear to her
that Adele had asked Stephen, at the last moment, to fill Peppino's
place. But naturally she had not told him that, and Lucia determined
not to do so either. It would spoil his pleasure (at least it would have
spoiled hers) to know that . . . And what a wonderful entry it would
make for her – rather daring – to drive down alone with her lover.
She could tell him about Peppino's indisposition tomorrow, as if it
had just occurred.

'Yes, Stephano, heaps of room,' she said. 'Delighted. I'll call for you, shall I, on my way down, soon after three.'

'Angelic,' he said. 'What fun we shall have.'

And it is probable that Nemesis at that precise moment licked her dry lips. 'Fun!' thought Nemesis.

* * *

Marcia Whitby was of the party. She went down in the morning, and lunched alone with Adele. Their main topic of conversation was obvious.

'I saw her announcement in the *Morning Post*,' said the infuriated Marcia, 'that she had gone for a few days' complete rest into the country, and naturally I thought I was safe. I was determined she shouldn't come to my ball, and when I saw that, I thought she couldn't. So out of sheer good nature I sent her a card, so that she could tell everybody she had been asked. Never did I dream that there was a possibility of her coming. Instead of which, she made the most conspicuous entry that she could have made. I believe she timed it: I believe she waited on the stairs till she saw we were going down to supper.'

'I wonder!' said Adele. 'Genius, if it was that. She curtseyed seven times, too. I can't do that without loud cracks from my aged knees.'

'And she stopped till the very end,' said Marcia. 'She was positively the last to go. I shall never do a kind thing again.'

'You're horrid about her,' said Adele. 'Besides, what has she done? You asked her and she came. You don't rave at your guests for coming when they're asked. You wouldn't like it if none of them came.'

'That's different,' said Marcia. 'I shouldn't wonder if she announced she was ordered complete rest in order that I should fall into her trap.'

Adele sighed, but shook her head.

'Oh, my dear, that *would* have been magnificent,' she said. 'But I'm afraid I can't hope to believe that. I dare say she went into the country because you hadn't asked her, and that was pretty good. But the other: no. However, we'll ask Tony what he thinks.'

'What's Tony got to do with it?' said Marcia.

'Why, he's even more wrapped up in her than I am,' said Adele. 'He thinks of nothing else.'

Marcia was silent a moment. Then a sort of softer gleam came into her angry eye.

'Tell me some more about her,' she said.

Adele clapped her hands.

'Ah, that's splendid,' she said. 'You're beginning to feel kinder. What we would do without our Lucia I can't imagine. I don't know what there would be to talk about.'

'She's ridiculous!' said Marcia, relapsing a little.

'No, you mustn't feel that,' said Adele. 'You mustn't laugh at her ever. You must just richly enjoy her.'

'She's a snob!' said Marcia, as if this was a tremendous discovery.

'So am I: so are you: so are we all,' said Adele. 'We all run after distinguished people like – like Alf and Marcelle. The difference between you and Lucia is entirely in her favour, for you pretend you're not a snob, and she is perfectly frank and open about it. Besides, what is a duchess like you for except to give pleasure to snobs? That's your work in the world, darling; that's why you were sent here. Don't shirk it, or when you're old you will suffer agonies of remorse. And you're a snob too. You liked having seven – or was it seventy? – Royals at your dance.'

'Well, tell me some more about Lucia,' said Marcia, rather struck by this ingenious presentation of the case.

'Indeed I will: I long for your conversion to Luciaphilism. Now today there are going to be marvellous happenings. You see Lucia has got a lover – '

'Quite absolutely impossible!' said Marcia firmly.

'Oh, don't interrupt. Of course he is only an official lover, a public lover, and his name is Stephen Merriall. A perfect lady. Now Peppino, Lucia's husband, was coming down with her today, but he's got a very bad cold and has put me off. I'm rather glad: Lucia has got more – more dash when he's not there. So I've asked her lover instead – '

'No!' said Marcia. 'Go on.'

'My dear, they are much better than any play I have ever seen. They do it beautifully: they give each other little glances and smiles, and then begin to talk hurriedly to someone else. Of course, they're both as chaste as snow, chaster if possible. I think poor Babs's case put it into Lucia's head that in this naughty world it gave a cachet to a woman to have the reputation of having a lover. So safe too: there's nothing to expose. They only behave like lovers strictly in public. I was terrified when it began that Mr Merriall would think she meant something, and try to kiss her when they were alone, and so rub the delicate bloom completely off, but I'm sure he's tumbled to it.'

'How perfect!' said Marcia.

'Isn't it? Aren't you feeling more Luciaphil? I'm sure you are. You must enjoy her: it shows such a want of humour to be annoyed with her. And really I've taken a great deal of trouble to get people she will revel in. There's the Prime Minister, there's you, there's Greatorex the pianist who's the only person who can play Stravinski, there's Professor Bonstetter the psychoanalyst, there's the Italian Ambassador, there's her lover, there's Tony . . . I can't go on. Oh, and I must remember to tell her that Archie Singleton is Babs's brother, or she may say something dreadful. And then there are lots who will revel in Lucia, and I the foremost. I'm devoted to her; I am really, Marcia. She's got character, she's got an iron will, and I like strong talkative women so much better than strong silent men.'

'Yes, she's got will,' said Marcia. 'She determined to come to my ball, and she came. I allow I gave her the chance.'

'Those are the chances that come to gifted people,' said Adele. 'They don't come to ordinary people.'

'Suppose I flirted violently with her lover?' said Marcia.

Adele's eyes grew bright with thought.

'I can't imagine what she would do,' she said. 'But I'm sure she would do something that scored. Otherwise she wouldn't be Lucia. But you mustn't do it.'

'Just one evening,' said Marcia. 'Just for an hour or two. It's not poaching, you see, because her lover isn't her lover. He's just a stunt.'

Adele wavered.

'It would be wonderful to know what she would do,' she said. 'And it's true that he's only a stunt. Perhaps for an hour or two tomorrow, and then give him back.'

* * *

Adele did not expect any of her guests till teatime, and Marcia and she both retired for after-lunch siestas. Adele had been down here for the last four or five days, driving up to Marcia's ball and back in the very early morning, and had three days before settled everything in connection with her party, assigning rooms, discussing questions of high importance with her chef, and arranging to meet as many trains as possible! It so happened, therefore, that Stephen Merriall, since the house was full, was to occupy the spacious dressing-room, furnished as a bedroom, next Lucia's room, which had been originally allotted to Peppino. Adele had told her butler that Mr Lucas was not coming, but that his room would be occupied by Mr Merriall, thought no more about it, and omitted to substitute a new card on his door. These two rooms were halfway down a long corridor of bedrooms and bathrooms that ran the whole length of the house, a spacious oak-boarded corridor, rather dark, with the broad staircase coming up at the end of it. Below was the suite of public rooms, a library at the end, a big music-room, a long gallery of a drawing-room, and the dining-room. These all opened on to a paved terrace overlooking the gardens and tennis-courts, and it was here, with the shadow of the house lying coolly across it, that her guests began to assemble. In ones and twos they gathered, some motoring down from London, others arriving by train, and it was not till there were some dozen of them, among whom were the most fervent Luciaphils, that the object of their devotion, attended by her lover, made her appearance, evidently at the top of her form.

'Dearest Adele,' she said. 'How delicious to get into the cool country again. Marcia dear! Such adventures I had on my way up to your ball: two burst tyres: I thought I should never get there. How are you, your Excellency? I saw you at the Duchess's, but couldn't get a word with you. Aggie darling! Ah, Lord Tony! Yes, a cup of tea would be delicious; no sugar, Stephen, thanks.'

Lucia had not noticed quite everybody. There were one or two people rather retired from the tea-table, but they did not seem to be of much importance, and certainly the Prime Minister was not among them. Stephen hovered, loverlike, just behind her chair, and she turned to the Italian Ambassador.

'I was afraid of a motor accident all the way down,' she said, 'because last night I dreamed I broke a looking-glass. Quaint things dreams are, though really the psychoanalysts who interpret them are quainter. I went to a meeting at Sophy's, dear Sophy Alingsby, the other day – your Excellency I am sure knows Sophy Alingsby – and heard a lecture on it. Let me see: boiled rabbit, if you dream of boiled rabbit – '

Lucia suddenly became aware of a sort of tension. Just a tension. She looked quickly round, and recognised one of the men she had not paid much attention to. She sprang from her chair.

'Professor Bonstetter,' she said. 'How are you? I know you won't remember me, but I did have the honour of shaking hands with you after your enthralling lecture the other day. Do come and tell his Excellency and me a little more about it. There were so many questions I longed to ask you.'

Adele wanted to applaud, but she had to be content with catching Marcia's eye. Was Lucia great, or was she not? Stephen too: how exactly right she was to hand him her empty cup when she had finished with it, without a word, and how perfectly he took it! 'More?' he said, and Lucia just shook her head without withdrawing her attention from Professor Bonstetter. Then the Prime Minister arrived, and she said how lovely Chequers must be looking. She did not annex him, she just hovered and hinted, and made no direct suggestion, and sure enough, within five minutes he had asked her if she knew Chequers. Of course she did, but only as a tourist – and so one thing led on to another. It would be a nice break in her long drive down to Riseholme on Tuesday to lunch at Chequers, and not more than forty miles out of her way.

People dispersed and strolled on the terrace, and gathered again, and some went off to their rooms. Lucia had one little turn up and down with the Ambassador, and spoke with great tact of Mussolini, and another with Lord Tony, and not for a long time did she let Stephen join her. But then they wandered off into the garden, and were seen standing very close together and arguing publicly about a flower, and Lucia seeing they were observed, called to Adele to know if it wasn't Dropmore Borage. They came back very soon, and Stephen went up to his room while Lucia remained downstairs. Adele showed her the library and the music-room, and the long drawing-room, and then vanished. Lucia gravitated to the music-room, opened the piano, and began the slow movement of the 'Moonlight Sonata'.

About halfway through it, she became aware that somebody had come into the room. But her eyes were fixed dreamily on the usual point at the edge of the ceiling, and her fingers faultlessly doled out the slow triplets. She gave a little sigh when she had finished, pressed her fingers to her eyes, and slowly awoke, as from some melodious anaesthetic.

It was a man who had come in and who had seated himself not far from the keyboard.

'Charming!' he said. 'Thank you.'

Lucia didn't remember seeing him on the terrace: perhaps he had only just arrived. She had a vague idea, however, that whether on the terrace or elsewhere, she had seen him before. She gave a pretty little start. 'Ah, had no idea I had an audience,' she said. 'I should never have ventured to go on playing. So dreadfully out of practice.'

'Please have a little more practice then,' said the polite stranger.

She ran her hands, butterfly fashion, over the keys.

'A little morsel of Stravinski?' she said.

It was in the middle of the morsel that Adele came in and found Lucia playing Stravinski to Mr Greatorex. The position seemed to be away, away beyond her orbit altogether, and she merely waited with undiminished faith in Lucia, to see what would happen when Lucia became aware to whom she was playing . . . It was a longish morsel, too: more like a meal than a morsel, and it was also remarkably like a muddle. Finally, Lucia made an optimistic attempt at the double chromatic scale in divergent directions which brought it to an end, and laughed gaily.

'My poor fingers,' she said. 'Delicious piano, dear Adele. I love a Bechstein; that was a little morsel of Stravinski. Hectic perhaps, do you think? But so true to the modern idea: little feverish excursions: little bits of tunes, and nothing worked out. But I always say that there is something in Stravinski, if you study him. How I worked at that little piece, and I'm afraid it's far from perfect yet.'

Lucia played one more little run with her right hand, while she cudgelled her brain to remember where she had seen this man before, and turned round on the music-stool. She felt sure he was an artist of some kind, and she did not want to ask Adele to introduce him, for that would look as if she did not know everybody. She tried pictures next.

'In art I always think that the Stravinski school is represented by the Post-Cubists,' she said. 'They give us pattern in lines, just as Stravinski gives us patterns in notes, and the modern poet patterns in words. At Sophy Alingsby's the other night we had a feast of patterns. Dear Sophy – what a curious mixture of tastes! She cares only for the ultra-primitive in music, and the ultra-modern in art. Just before you came in, Adele, I was trying to remember the first movement of Beethoven's "Moonlight"; those triplets though they look easy have to be kept so level. And yet Sophy considers Beethoven a positive decadent. I ought to have taken her to Diva's little concert – Diva Dalrymple – for I assure you really that Stravinski sounded classical compared to the rest of the programme. It was very creditably played, too. Mr – ' what was his name? – 'Mr Greatorex.'

She had actually said the word before her brain made the connection. She gave her little peal of laughter.

'Ah, you wicked people,' she cried. 'A plot: clearly a plot. Mr Greatorex, how could you? Adele told you to come in here when she heard me begin my little strummings, and told you to sit down and encourage me. Don't deny it, Adele! I know it was like that. I shall tell everybody how unkind you've been, unless Mr Greatorex sits down instantly and magically restores to life what I have just murdered.'

Adele denied nothing. In fact there was no time to deny anything, for Lucia positively thrust Mr Greatorex on to the music-stool, and instantly put on her rapt musical face, chin in hand, and eyes looking dreamily upwards. There was Nemesis, you would have thought, dealing thrusts at her, but Nemesis was no match for her amazing quickness. She parried and thrust again, and here – what richness of future reminiscence – was Mr Greatorex playing Stravinski to her, before no audience but herself and Adele, who really didn't count, for the only tune she liked was 'Land of Hope and Glory' . . . Great was Lucia!

Adele left the two, warning them that it was getting on for dressing time, but there was some more Stravinski first, for Lucia's sole ear. Adele had told her the direction of her room, and said her name was on the door, and Lucia found it at once. A beautiful room it was, with a bathroom on one side, and a magnificent Charles II bed draped at the back with wool-work tapestry. It was a little late for Lucia's Elizabethan taste, and she noticed that the big wardrobe was Chippendale, which was later still. There was a Chinese paper on the wall, and fine Persian rugs on the floor, and though she could have criticised it was easy to admire. And there for herself was a very smart dress, and for decoration Aunt Amy's pearls, and the Beethoven brooch. But she decided to avoid all possible chance of competition, and put the pearls back into her jewel-case. The Beethoven brooch, she was sure, need fear no rival.

Lucia felt that dinner, as far as she went, was a huge success. Stephen was seated just opposite her, and now and then she exchanged little distant smiles with him. Next her on one side was Lord Tony, who adored her story about Stravinski and Greatorex. She told him also what the Italian Ambassador had said about Mussolini, and the Prime Minister about Chequers: she was going to pop in to lunch on her way down to Riseholme after this delicious party. Then conversation shifted, and she turned left, and talked to the only man whose identity she had not grasped. But, as matter of public knowledge, she began about poor Babs, and her own admiration of her demeanour at that wicked trial, which had ended so disastrously. And once again there was slight tension.

Bridge and mah-jong followed, and rich allusive conversation and the sense, so dear to Lucia, of being in the very centre of everything that was distinguished. When the women went upstairs she hurried to her room, made a swift change into greater simplicity, and, by invitation, sought out Marcia's room, at the far end of the passage, for a chat. Adele was there, and dear (rather common) Aggie was there, and Aggie was being just a shade sycophantic over the six rows of Whitby pearls. Lucia was glad she had limited her splendours to the Beethoven brooch.

'But why didn't you wear your pearls, Lucia?' asked Adele. 'I was hoping to see them.' (She had heard talk of Aunt Amy's pearls, but had not noticed them on the night of Marcia's ball.)

'My little seedlings!' said Lucia. 'Just seedlings, compared to Marcia's marbles. Little trumperies!'

Aggie had seen them, and she knew Lucia did not overstate their minuteness. Like a true Luciaphil, she changed a subject that might prove embarrassing.

'Take away your baubles, Marcia,' said Aggie. 'They are only diseases of a common shellfish which you eat when it's healthy and wear when it's got a tumour ... How wretched it is to think that all of us aren't going to meet day after day as we have been doing! There's Adele going to America, and there's Marcia going to Scotland – what a foul spot, Marcia, come to Marienbad instead with me. And what are you going to do, Lucia?'

'Oh, my dear, how I wanted to go to Aix or Marienbad,' she said. 'But my Peppino says it's impossible. We've got to stop quiet at Riseholme. Shekels, tiresome shekels.'

'There she goes, talking about Riseholme as if it was some dreadful penance to go there,' said Adele. 'You adore Riseholme, Lucia, at least if you don't, you ought to. Olga raves about it. She says she's never really happy away from it. When are you going to ask me there?'

'Adele, as if you didn't know that you weren't always welcome,' said Lucia.

'Me, too,' said Marcia.

'A standing invitation to both of you always,' said Lucia. 'Dear Marcia, how sweet of you to want to come! I go there on Tuesday, and there I remain. But it's true, I do adore it. No balls, no parties, and such dear Arcadians. You couldn't believe in them without seeing them. Life at its very simplest, dears.'

'It can't be simpler than Scotland,' said Marcia. 'In Scotland you kill birds and fish all day, and eat them at night. That's all.'

Lucia through these months of strenuous effort had never perhaps felt herself so amply rewarded as she was at this moment. All evening she had talked in an effortless deshabille of mind to the great ones of the country, the noble, the distinguished, the accomplished, and now here she was in a duchess's bedroom having a good-night talk. This was nearer Nirvana than even Marcia's ball. And the three women there seemed to be grouped round her: they waited – there was no mistaking it – listening for something from her, just as Riseholme used to wait for her lead. She felt that she was truly attaining, and put her chin in her hand and looked a little upwards.

'I shall get tremendously put in my place when I go back to Riseholme again,' she said. 'I'm sure Riseholme thinks I have been wasting my time in idle frivolities. It sees perhaps in an evening paper that I have been to Aggie's party, or Adele's house or Marcia's ball, and I assure you it will be very suspicious of me. Just as if I didn't know that all these delightful things were symbols.'

Adele had got the cataleptic look of a figure in a stained-glass window, so rapt she was. But she wanted to grasp this with full appreciation.

'Lucia, don't be so dreadfully clever,' she said. 'You're talking high over my head: you're like the whirr of an aeroplane. Explain what you mean by symbols.'

Lucia was toying with the string of Whitby pearls, which Marcia still held, with one hand. The other she laid on Adele's knee. She felt that a high line was expected of her.

'My dear, you know,' she said. 'All our runnings-about, all our gaieties are symbols of affection: we love to see each other because we partake of each other. Interesting people, distinguished people, obscure people, ordinary people, we long to bring them all into our lives in order to widen our horizons. We learn, or we try to learn, of other interests beside our own. I shall have to make Riseholme understand that dear little Alf, playing the flute at my house, or half a dozen princes eating quails at Marcia's mansion, it's all the same, isn't it? We get to know the point of view of prizefighters and princes. And it seems to me, it seems to me – '

Lucia's gaze grew a shade more lost and aloof.

'It seems to me that we extend our very souls,' she said, 'by letting them flow into other lives. How badly I put it! But when Eric Greatorex – so charming of him – played those delicious pieces of Stravinski to me before dinner, I felt I was stepping over some sort of frontier *into* Stravinski. Eric made out my passport. A multiplication of experience: I think that is what I mean.'

None of those present could have said with any precision what
Lucia had meant, but the general drift seemed to be that an hour
with a burglar or a cannibal was valuable for the amplification of the
soul.

'Odd types too,' she said. 'How good for one to be put into touch
with something quite remote. Marcelle – Marcelle Periscope – you
met him at my house, didn't you, Aggie – '

'Why wasn't I asked?' said Marcia.

Lucia gave a little quick smile, as at some sweet child's interruption.

'Darling Marcia, why didn't you propose yourself? Surely you
know me well enough to do that. Yes, Marcelle, a cinema artist. A
fresh horizon, a fresh attitude towards life. So good for me: it helps
me not to be narrow. *Dio mio!* how I pray I shall never be narrow. To
be shocked, too! How shocking to be shocked. If you all had fifty
lovers apiece, I should merely think it a privilege to know about
them all.'

Marcia longed, with almost the imperativeness of a longing to
sneeze, to allude directly to Stephen. She raised her eyes for a half
second to Adele, the priestess of this cult in which she knew she was
rapidly becoming a worshipper, but if ever an emphatic negative was
wordlessly bawled at a tentative enquirer, it was bawled now. If
Lucia chose to say anything about Stephen it would indeed be manna,
but to ask – never! Aggie, seated sideways to them, had not seen this
telegraphy, and spoke unwisely with her lips.

'If an ordinary good-looking woman,' she said, 'tells me that she
hasn't got a lover or a man who wants to be her lover, I always say
"You lie!" So she does. You shall begin, Lucia, about your lovers.'

Nothing could have been more unfortunate. Adele could have
hurled the entire six rows of the Whitby pearls at Aggie's face.
Lucia had no lover, but only the wraith of a lover, on whom direct
light must never be flashed. Such a little reflection should have
shown Aggie that. The effect of her carelessness was that Lucia
became visibly embarrassed, looked at the clock, and got up in a
violent hurry.

'Good gracious me!' she said. 'What a time of night! Who could
have thought that our little chat had lasted so long? Yes, dear Adele,
I know my room, on the left with my name on the door. Don't
dream of coming to show it me.'

*   *   *

Lucia distributed little pressures and kisses and clingings, and holding her very smart pale blue wrapper close about her, slid noiselessly out in her slippers into the corridor. It was late, the house was quite quiet, for a quarter of an hour ago they had heard the creaking of men's footsteps going to their rooms. The main lights had been put out, only here and there down the long silent aisle there burned a single small illumination. Past half a dozen doors Lucia tiptoed, until she came to one on which she could just see the name Philip Lucas preceded by a dim hieroglyph which of course was 'Mrs'. She turned the handle and went in.

Two yards in front of her, by the side of the bed, was standing Stephen, voluptuous in honey-coloured pyjamas. For one awful second – for she felt sure this was her room (*and so did he*) – they stared at each other in dead silence.

'How dare you?' said Stephen, so agitated that he could scarcely form the syllables.

'And how dare *you*?' hissed Lucia. 'Go out of my room instantly.'

'Go out of mine!' said Stephen.

Lucia's indignant eye left his horror-stricken face and swept round the room. There was no Chinese paper on the wall, but a pretty Morris paper: there was no Charles II bed with tapestry, but a brass-testered couch; there was no Chippendale wardrobe, but something useful from Tottenham Court Road. She gave one little squeal, of a pitch between the music of the slate-pencil and of the bat, and closed his door again. She staggered on to the next room where again the legend 'Philip Lucas' was legible, popped in, and locked the door. She hurried to the door of communication between this and the fatal chamber next it, and as she locked that also she heard from the other side of it the bolt violently pulled forward.

She sat down on her bed in a state of painful agitation. Her excursion into the fatal chamber had been an awful, a hideous mistake: none knew that better than herself, but how was she to explain that to her lover? For weeks they had been advertising the guilt of their blameless relationship, and now it seemed to her impossible ever to resume it. Every time she gave Stephen one of those little smiles or glances, at which she had become so perfect an adept, there would start into her mind that moment of speechless horror, and her smile would turn to a tragic grimace, and her sick glance recoil from him. Worse than that, how was she ever to speak of it to him, or passionately protest her innocence? He had thought that she had come to his room (indeed she had) when the house was quiet, on the sinister errand of love, and though, when he had repudiated her, she had followed suit, she saw the recoiling indignation of her lover. If only, just now, she had kept her head, if only she had said at once, 'I beg your pardon, I mistook my room,' all might have been well, but how nerve herself to say it afterwards? And in spite of the entire integrity of her moral nature, which was puritanical to the verge of prudishness, she had not liked (no woman could) his unfeigned horror at her irruption.

Stephen next door was in little better plight. He had had a severe shock. For weeks Lucia had encouraged him to play the lover, and had (so he awfully asked himself) this pleasant public stunt become a reality to her, a need of her nature? She had made it appear, when he so rightly repulsed her, that she had come to his room by mistake, but was that pretence? Had she really come with a terrible motive? It was her business, anyhow, to explain, and insist on her innocence, if she was innocent, and he would only be too thankful to believe her. But at present and without that, the idea of resuming the public loverlike demeanour was frankly beyond him. She might be encouraged again . . . Though now he was safe with locked and bolted doors, he knew he would not be able to sleep, and he took a large dose of aspirin.

Lucia was far more thorough: she never shelved difficulties, but faced them. She still sat on the edge of her bed, long after Stephen's nerves were quieted, and as she herself calmed down, thought it all out. For the present, loverlike relations in public were impossible, and it was lucky that in a couple of days more she would be interned at Riseholme. Then with a flash of genius there occurred to her the interesting attitude to adopt in the interval. She would give the impression that there had been a lovers' quarrel. The more she thought of that, the more it commended itself to her. People would notice it, and wonder what it was all about, and their curiosity would never be gratified, for Lucia felt sure, from the horror depicted on Stephen's face, that he as well as she would be for ever dumb on the subject of that midnight encounter. She must not look unhappy: she must on the other hand be more vivid and eager than ever, and just completely ignore Stephen. But there would be no lift for him in her car back to London: he would have to go by train.

*   *   *

The ex-lovers both came down very late next day, for fear of meeting each other alone, and thus they sat in adjoining rooms half the morning. Stephen had some Hermione-work on hand, for this party would run to several paragraphs, but, however many it ran to, Hermione was utterly determined not to mention Lucia in any of them. Hermione knew, however, that Mr Stephen Merriall was there, and said so . . . By one of those malignant strokes which are rained on those whom Nemesis desires to chastise, they came out of their rooms at precisely the same moment, and had to walk downstairs together, coldly congratulating each other on the beauty of the morning. Luckily there were people on the terrace, among whom was Marcia. She thought this was an excellent opportunity for beginning her flirtation with Stephen, and instantly carried him off to the kitchen garden, for unless she ate gooseberries on Sunday morning she died. Lucia seemed sublimely unaware of their departure, and joined a select little group round the Prime Minister. Between a discussion on the housing problem with him, a stroll with Lord Tony, who begged her to drop the 'lord', and a little more Stravinski alone with Greatorex, the short morning passed very agreeably. But she saw when she went into lunch rather late that Marcia and Stephen had not returned from their gooseberrying. There was a gap of just three places at the table, and it thus became a certainty that Stephen would sit next her.

Lunch was fully half over before they appeared, Marcia profusely apologetic.

'Wretchedly rude of me, dear Adele,' she said, 'but we had no idea it was so late, did we, Mr Merriall? We went to the gooseberries, and – and I suppose we must have stopped there. Your fault, Mr Merriall; you men have no idea of time.'

'Who could, Duchess, when he was with you?' said Stephen most adroitly.

'Sweet of you,' said she. 'Now do go on. You were in the middle of telling me something quite thrilling. And please, Adele, let nobody wait for us. I see you are all at the end of lunch, and I haven't begun, and gooseberries, as usual, have given me an enormous appetite. Yes, Mr Merriall?'

Adele looked in vain, when throughout the afternoon Marcia continued in possession of Lucia's lover, for the smallest sign of resentment or uneasiness on her part. There was simply none; it was impossible to detect a thing that had no existence. Lucia seemed completely unconscious of any annexation, or indeed of Stephen's existence. There she sat, just now with Tony and herself, talking of Marcia's ball, and the last volume of risky memoirs, of which she had

read a review in the Sunday paper, and Sophy's black room and Alf:
never had she been more equipped at all points, more prosperously
central. Marcia, thought Adele, was being wonderfully worsted, if
she imagined she could produce any sign of emotion on Lucia's part.
The lovers understood each other too well . . . Or, she suddenly
conjectured, had they quarrelled? It really looked rather like it.
Though she and Tony were having a good Luciaphil meeting, she
almost wanted Lucia to go away, in order to go into committee over
this entrancing possibility. And how naturally she Tony'd him: she
must have been practising on her maid.

Somewhere in the house a telephone bell rang, and a footman
came out on to the terrace.

'Lucia, I know that's for you,' said Adele. 'Wherever you are,
somebody wants you on the telephone. If you were in the middle of
the Sahara, a telephone would ring for you from the sands of the
desert. Yes? Who is it for?' she said to the footman.

'Mrs Lucas, my lady,' he said.

Lucia got up, quite delighted.

'You're always chaffing me, Adele,' she said. 'What a nuisance the
telephone is. One never gets a rest from it. But I won't be a moment.'
She tripped off.

'Tony, there's a great deal to talk about,' said Adele quickly. 'Now
what's the situation between the lovers? Perfect understanding or a
quarrel? And who has been ringing her up? What would you bet that
it was – '

'Alf,' said Tony.

'I wonder. Tony, about the lovers. There's something. I never
saw such superb indifference. How I shall laugh at Marcia. She's
producing no effect at all. Lucia doesn't take the slightest notice. I
knew she would be great. Last night we had a wonderful talk in
Marcia's room, till Aggie was an ass. There she is again. Now we
shall know.'

Lucia came quickly along the terrace.

'Adele dear,' she said. 'Would it be dreadful of me if I left this
afternoon? They've rung me up from Riseholme. Georgie rang me
up. My Peppino is very far from well. Nothing really anxious, but
he's in bed and he's alone. I think I had better go.'

'Oh my dear,' said Adele, 'of course you shall do precisely as you
wish. I'm dreadfully sorry: so shall we all be if you go. But if you feel
you would be easier in your mind – '

Lucia looked round on all the brilliant little groups. She was leaving the most wonderful party: it was the highest perch she had reached yet. On the other hand she was leaving her lover, which was a compensation. But she truly didn't think of any of these things.

'My poor old Peppino,' she said. 'I must go, Adele.'

Chapter Ten

Today, the last of August, Peppino had been allowed for the first time to go out and have a half-hour's quiet strolling in the garden and sit in the sun. His illness which had caused Lucia to recall herself had been serious, and for a few days he had been dangerously ill with pneumonia. After turning a bad corner he had made satisfactory progress.

Lucia, who for these weeks had been wholly admirable, would have gone out with him now, but the doctor, after his visit, had said he wanted to have a talk with her, and for twenty minutes or so they had held colloquy in the music-room. Then, on his departure, she sat there a few minutes more, arranged her ideas, and went out to join Peppino.

'Such a good cheering talk, *caro*,' she said. 'There never was such a perfect convalescer – my dear, what a word – as you. You're a prize patient. All you've got to do is to go on exactly as you're going, doing a little more, and a little more every day, and in a month's time you'll be ever so strong again. Such a good constitution.'

'And no sea-voyage?' asked Peppino. The dread prospect had been dangled before him at one time.

'Not unless they think a month or two on the Riviera in the winter might be advisable. Then the sea-voyage from Dover to Calais, but no more than that. Now I know what you're thinking about. You told me that we couldn't manage Aix this August because of expense, so how are we to manage two months of Cannes?'

Lucia paused a moment.

'That delicious story of dear Marcia's,' she said, 'about those cousins of hers who had to retrench. After talking everything over they decided that all the retrenchment they could possibly make was to have no coffee after lunch. But we can manage better than that . . . '

Lucia paused again. Peppino had had enough of movement under his own steam, and they had seated themselves in the sunny little arbour by the sundial, which had so many appropriate mottoes carved on it.

'The doctor told me too that it would be most unwise of you to attempt to live in London for any solid period,' she said. 'Fogs, sunlessness, damp darkness: all bad. And I know again what's in your kind head. You think I adore London, and can spend a month or two there in the autumn, and in the spring, coming down here for weekends. But I haven't the slightest intention of doing anything of the kind. I'm not going to be up there alone. Besides, where are the dibs, as that sweet little Alf said, where are the dibs to come from for our Riviera?'

'Let the house for the winter then?' said Peppino.

'Excellent idea, if we could be certain of letting it. But we can't be certain of letting it, and all the time a stream of rates and taxes, and caretakers. It would be wretched to be always anxious about it, and always counting the dibs. I've been going into what we spent there this summer, *caro*, and it staggered me. What I vote for is to sell it. I'm not going to use it without you, and you're not going to use it at all. You know how I looked forward to being there for your sake, your club, the Reading Room at the British Museum, the Astronomer-Royal, but now that's all kaput, as Tony says. We'll bring down here anything that's particularly connected with dear Auntie: her portrait by Sargent, of course, though Sargents are fetching immense prices; or the walnut bureau, or the Chippendale chairs or that little worsted rug in her bedroom; but I vote for selling it all, freehold, furniture, everything. As if I couldn't go up to Claridge's now and then, when I want to have a luncheon-party or two of all our friends! And then we shall have no more anxieties, and if they say you must get away from the cold and the damp, we shall know we're doing nothing on the margin of our means. That would be hateful: we mustn't do that.'

'But you'll never be able to be content with Riseholme again,' said Peppino. 'After your balls and your parties and all that, what will you find to do here?'

Lucia turned her gimlet-eye on him.

'I shall be a great fool if I don't find something to do,' she said. 'Was I so idle and unoccupied before we went to London? Good gracious, I was always worked to death here. Don't you bother your head about that, Peppino, for if you do it will show you don't understand me at all. And our dear Riseholme, let me tell you, has got very slack and inert in our absence, and I feel very guilty about that. There's nothing going on: there's none of the old fizz and bubble and Excelsior there used to be. They're vegetating, they're dry-rotting, and Georgie's getting fat. There's never any news. All that happens is that Daisy slashes a golf-ball about the green for practice in the morning, and then goes down to the links in the afternoon, and positively the only news next day is whether she has been round under a thousand strokes, whatever that means.'

Lucia gave a little indulgent sigh.

'Dear Daisy has ideas sometimes,' she said, 'and I don't deny that. She had the idea of ouija, she had the idea of the Museum, and though she said that came from Abfou, she had the idea of Abfou. Also she had the idea of golf. But she doesn't carry her ideas out in a vivid manner that excites interest and keeps people on the boil. On the boil! That's what we all ought to be, with a thousand things to do that seem immensely important and which are important because they seem so. You want a certain touch to give importance to things, which dear Daisy hasn't got. Whatever poor Daisy does seems trivial. But they shall see that I've come home. What does it matter to me whether it's Marcia's ball, or playing Alf's accompaniments, or playing golf with Daisy, or playing duets with poor dear Georgie, whose fingers have all become thumbs, so long as I find it thrilling? If I find it dull, *caro*, I shall be, as Adele once said, a bloody fool. Dear Adele, she has always that little vein of coarseness.'

Lucia encountered more opposition from Peppino than she anticipated, for he had taken a huge pride in her triumphant summer campaign in London, and though at times he had felt bewildered and buffeted in this high gale of social activity, and had, so to speak, to close his streaming eyes and hold his hat on, he gloried in the incessant and tireless blowing of it, which stripped the choicest fruits from the trees. He thought they could manage, without encroaching on financial margins, to keep the house open for another year yet, anyhow: he acknowledged that he had been unduly pessimistic about going to Aix, he even alluded to the memories of Aunt Amy which were twined about 25 Brompton Square, and which he would be so sorry to sever. But Lucia, in that talk with his doctor, had made up her mind: she rejected at once the idea of pursuing her victorious career in London if all the time she would have to be careful and thrifty, and if, far more importantly, she would be leaving Peppino down at Riseholme. That was not to be thought of: affection no less than decency made it impossible, and so having made up her mind, she set about the attainment of her object with all her usual energy. She knew, too, the value of incessant attack: smash little Alf, for instance, when he had landed a useful blow on his opponent's face, did not wait for him to recover, but instantly followed it up with another and yet another till his victim collapsed and was counted out. Lucia behaved in precisely the same way with Peppino: she produced rows of figures to show they were living beyond their means: she quoted (or invented) something the Prime Minister had said about the probability of an increase in income-tax: she assumed that they would go to the Riviera for certain, and was appalled at the price of tickets in the Blue Train, and of the tariff at hotels.

'And with all our friends in London, Peppino,' she said in the decisive round of these combats, 'who are longing to come down to Riseholme and spend a week with us, our expenses here will go up. You mustn't forget that. We shall be having a succession of visitors in October, and indeed till we go south. Then there's the meadow at the bottom of the garden: you've not bought that yet, and on that I really have set my heart. A spring garden there. A profusion of daffodils, and a paved walk. You promised me that. I described what it would be like to Tony, and he is wildly jealous. I'm sure I don't wonder. Your new telescope too. I insist on that telescope, and I'm sure I don't know where the money's to come from. My dear old piano also: it's on its very last legs, and won't last much longer, and I know you don't expect me to live, literally keep alive, without a good piano in the house.'

Peppino, was weakening. Even when he was perfectly well and strong he was no match for her, and this rain of blows was visibly staggering him.

'I don't want to urge you, *caro*,' she continued. 'You know I never urge you to do what you don't feel is best.'

'But you are urging me,' said Peppino.

'Only to do what you feel is best. As for the memories of Aunt Amy in Brompton Square, you must not allow false sentiment to come in. You never saw her there since you were a boy, and if you brought down here her portrait, and the wool-work rug which you remember her putting over her knees, I should say, without urging you, mind, that that was ample . . . What a sweet morning! Come to the end of the garden and imagine what the meadow will look like with a paved walk and a blaze of daffodils . . . The Chippendale chairs, I think I should sell.'

Lucia did not really want Aunt Amy's portrait either, for she was aware she had said a good deal from time to time about Aunt Amy's pearls, which were there, a little collar of very little seeds, faultlessly portrayed. But then Georgie had seen them on that night at the opera, and Lucia felt that she knew Riseholme very poorly if it was not perfectly acquainted by now with the nature and minuteness of Aunt Amy's pearls. The pearls had better be sold too, and also, she thought, her own portrait by Sigismund, for the Post-Cubists were not making much of a mark.

The determining factor in her mind, over this abandonment of her London career, to which in a few days, by incessant battering, she had got Peppino to consent, was Peppino himself. He could not be with her in London, and she could not leave him week after week (for nothing less than that, if you were to make any solid progress in London, was any good) alone in Riseholme. But a large factor, also, was the discovery of how little at present she counted for in Riseholme, and that could not be tolerated. Riseholme had deposed her, Riseholme was not intending to be managed by her from Brompton Square. The throne was vacant, for poor Daisy, and for the matter of that poor Georgie were not the sort of people who could occupy thrones at all. She longed to queen it there again, and though she was aware that her utmost energies would be required, what were energies for except to get you what you wanted?

Just now she was nothing in Riseholme: they had been sorry for her because Peppino had been so ill, but as his steady convalescence proceeded, and she began to ring people up, and pop in, and make plans for them, she became aware that she mattered no more than Piggy and Goosie . . . There on the green, as she saw from the window of her hall, was Daisy, whirling her arms madly, and hitting a ball with a stick which had a steel blade at the end, and Georgie, she was rather horrified to observe, was there too, trying to do the same. Was Daisy reaping the reward of her persistence, and getting somebody interested in golf? And, good heavens, there were Piggy and Goosie also smacking away. Riseholme was clearly devoting itself to golf.

'I shall have to take to golf,' thought Lucia. 'What a bore! Such a foolish game.'

At this moment a small white ball bounded over her yew-hedge, and tapped smartly against the front door.

'What an immense distance to have hit a ball,' she thought. 'I wonder which of them did that?'

It was soon clear, for Daisy came tripping through the garden after it, and Lucia, all smiles, went out to meet her.

'Good-morning, dear Daisy,' she said. 'Did you hit that ball that immense distance? How wonderful! No harm done at all. But what a splendid player you must be!'

'So sorry,' panted Daisy, 'but I thought I would have a hit with a driver. Very wrong of me; I had no idea it would go so far or so crooked.'

'A marvellous shot,' said Lucia. 'I remember how beautifully you putted. And this is all part of golf too? Do let me see you do it again.'

Daisy could not reproduce that particular masterpiece, but she sent the ball high in the air, or skimming along the ground, and explained that one was a lofted shot, and the other a windcheater.

'I like the windcheater best,' said Lucia. 'Do let me see if I can do that.'

She missed the ball once or twice, and then made a lovely windcheater, only this time Daisy called it a top. Daisy had three clubs, two of which she put down when she used the third, and then forgot about them, so that they had to go back for them . . . And up came Georgie, who was making windcheaters too.

'Good-morning, Lucia,' he said. 'It's so tarsome not to be able to hit the ball, but it's great fun if you do. Have you put down your clock-golf yet? There, didn't that go?'

Lucia had forgotten all about the clock-golf. It was somewhere in what was called the 'game-cupboard', which contained bowls (as being Elizabethan) and some old tennis rackets, and a cricket bat Peppino had used at school.

'I'll put it down this afternoon,' she said. 'Come in after lunch, Georgie, and play a game with me. You too, Daisy.'

'Thanks, but Georgie and I were going to have a real round on the links,' said Daisy, in a rather superior manner.

'What fun!' said Lucia sycophantically. 'I shall walk down and look at you. I think I must learn. I never saw anything so interesting as golf.'

This was gratifying: Daisy was by no means reluctant to show Lucia the way to do anything, but behind that, she was not quite sure whether she liked this sudden interest in golf. Now that practically the whole of Riseholme was taking to it, and she herself could beat them all, having had a good start, she was hoping that Lucia would despise it, and find herself left quite alone on these lovely afternoons. Everybody went down to the little nine-hole course now after lunch, the vicar (Mr Rushbold) and his wife, the curate, Colonel Boucher, Georgie, Mrs Antrobus (who discarded her ear-trumpet for these athletics and never could hear you call 'Fore') and Piggy and Goosie, and often Mrs Boucher was wheeled down in her bath-chair, and

applauded the beautiful putts made on the last green. Indeed, Daisy
had started instruction classes in her garden, and Riseholme stood in
rows and practised swinging and keeping its eye on a particular blade
of grass: golf in fact promised to make Riseholme busy and happy
again just as the establishment of the Museum had done. Of course,
if Lucia was wanting to learn (and not learn too much) Daisy would
be very happy to instruct her, but at the back of Daisy's mind was a
strange uneasiness. She consoled herself, however, by supposing that
Lucia would go back to London again in the autumn, and by giving
Georgie an awful drubbing.

Lucia did not accompany them far on their round, but turned back
to the little shed of a clubhouse, where she gathered information
about the club. It was quite new, having been started only last spring
by the tradesmen and townspeople of Riseholme and the neighbouring little town of Blitton. She then entered into pleasant conversation with the landlord of the Ambermere Arms, who had just
finished his round and said how pleased they all were that the gentry
had taken to golf.

'There's Mrs Quantock, ma'am,' said he. 'She comes down every
afternoon and practises on the green every morning. Walking over
the green now of a morning, is to take your life in your hand. Such
keenness I never saw, and she'll never be able to hit the ball at all.'

'Oh, but you mustn't discourage us, Mr Stratton,' said Lucia. 'I'm
going to devote myself to golf this autumn.'

'You'll make a better hand at it, I'll be bound,' said Mr Stratton
obsequiously. 'They say Mrs Quantock putts very nicely when she
gets near the hole, but it takes her so many strokes to get there. She's
lost the hole, in a manner of speaking, before she has a chance of
winning it.'

Lucia thought hard for a minute.

'I must see about joining at once,' she said. 'Who – who are the
committee?'

'Well, we are going to reconstitute it next October,' he said, 'seeing
that the ladies and gentlemen of Riseholme are joining. We should
like to have one of you ladies as President, and one of the gentlemen
on the committee.'

Lucia made no hesitation about this.

'I should be delighted,' she said, 'if the present committee did me
the honour to ask me. And how about Mr Pillson? I would sound
him if you like. But we must say nothing about it, till your committee
meets.'

That was beautifully settled then; Mr Stratton knew how gratified the committee would be, and Lucia, long before Georgie and Daisy returned, had bought four clubs, and was having a lesson from a small wiry caddie.

Every morning while Daisy was swanking away on the green, teaching Georgie and Piggy and Goosie how to play, Lucia went surreptitiously down the hill and learned, while after tea she humbly took her place in Daisy's class and observed Daisy doing everything all wrong. She putted away at her clock-golf, she bought a beautiful book with pictures and studied them, and all the time she said nothing whatever about it. In her heart she utterly despised golf, but golf just now was the stunt, and she had to get hold of Riseholme again . . .

Georgie popped in one morning after she had come back from her lesson, and found her in the act of holing out from the very longest of the stations.

'My dear, what a beautiful putt!' he said. 'I believe you're getting quite keen on it.'

'Indeed I am,' said she. 'It's great fun. I go down sometimes to the links and knock the ball about. Be very kind to me this afternoon and come round with me.'

Georgie readily promised to do so.

'Of course I will,' he said, 'and I should be delighted to give you a hint or two, if I can. I won two holes from Daisy yesterday.'

'How clever of you, Georgie! Any news?'

Georgie said the sound that is spelt 'tut'.

'I quite forgot,' he said. 'I came round to tell you. Neither Mrs Boucher nor Daisy nor I know *what* to do.'

('That's the Museum Committee,' thought Lucia.)

'What is it, Georgie?' she said. 'See if poor Lucia can help.'

'Well,' said Georgie, 'you know Pug?'

'That mangy little thing of Lady Ambermere's?' asked Lucia.

'Yes. Pug died, I don't know what of – '

'Cream, I should think,' said Lucia. 'And cake.'

'Well, it may have been. Anyhow, Lady Ambermere had him stuffed, and while I was out this morning, she left him in a glass case at my house, as a present for the Museum. There he is lying on a blue cushion, with one ear cocked, and a great watery eye, and the end of his horrid tongue between his lips.'

'No!' said Lucia.

'I assure you. And we don't know what to do. We can't put him in the Museum, can we? And we're afraid she'll take the mittens away if we don't. But, how can we refuse? She wrote me a note about "her precious Pug".'

Lucia remembered how they had refused an Elizabethan spit, though they had subsequently accepted it. But she was not going to remind Georgie of that. She wanted to get a better footing in the Museum than an Elizabethan spit had given her.

'What a dreadful thing!' she said. 'And so you came to see if your poor old Lucia could help you.'

'Well, we all wondered if you might be able to think of something,' said he.

Lucia enjoyed this: the Museum was wanting her . . . She fixed Georgie with her eye.

'Perhaps I can get you out of your hole,' she said. 'What I imagine is, Georgie, that you want *me* to take that awful Pug back to her. I see what's happened. She had him stuffed, and then found he was too dreadful an object to keep, and so thought she'd be generous to the Museum. We – I should say "you", for I've got nothing to do with it – you don't care about the Museum being made a dump for all the rubbish that people don't want in their houses. Do you?'

'No, certainly not,' said Georgie. (Did Lucia mean anything by that? Apparently she did.) She became brisk and voluble.

'Of course, if you asked my opinion,' said Lucia, 'I should say that there has been a little too much dumping done already. But that is not the point, is it? And it's not my business either. Anyhow, you don't want any more rubbish to be dumped. As for withdrawing the mittens – only lent, are they? – she won't do anything of the kind. She likes taking people over and showing them. Yes, Georgie, I'll help you: tell Mrs Boucher and Daisy that I'll help you. I'll drive over this afternoon – no, I won't, for I'm going to have a lovely game of golf with you – I'll drive over tomorrow and take Pug back, with the committee's regrets that they are not taxidermists. Or, if you like, I'll do it on my own authority. How odd to be afraid of poor old Lady Ambermere! Never mind: I'm not. How all you people bully me into doing just what you want! I always was Rise-holme's slave. Put Pug's case in a nice piece of brown paper, Georgie, for I don't want to see the horrid little abortion, and don't think anything more about it. Now let's have a good little putting match till lunchtime.'

Georgie was nowhere in the good little putting match, and he was even less anywhere when it came to their game in the afternoon.

Lucia made magnificent swipes from the tee, the least of which, if she happened to hit it, must have gone well over a hundred yards, whereas Daisy considered eighty yards from the tee a most respectable shot, and was positively pleased if she went into a bunker at a greater distance than that, and said the bunker ought to be put further off for the sake of the longer hitters. And when Lucia came near the green, she gave a smart little dig with her mashie, and, when this remarkable stroke came off, though she certainly hit the ground, the ball went beautifully, whereas when Daisy hit the ground the ball didn't go at all. All the time she was light-hearted and talkative, and even up to the moment of striking, would be saying 'Now oo naughty ickle ball: Lucia's going to give you such a spank!' whereas when Daisy was playing, her opponent and the caddies had all to be dumb and turned to stone, while she drew a long breath and waved her club with a pendulum-like movement over the ball.

'But you're marvellous,' said Georgie as, three down, he stood on the fourth tee, and watched Lucia's ball sail away over a sheep that looked quite small in the distance. 'It's only three weeks or so since you began to play at all. You are clever! I believe you'd nearly beat Daisy.'

'Georgie, I'm afraid you're a flatterer,' said Lucia. 'Now give your ball a good bang, and then there's something I want to talk to you about.'

'Let's see; it's slow back, isn't it?' said Georgie. 'Or is it quick back? I believe Daisy says sometimes one and sometimes the other.'

Daisy and Piggy, starting before them, were playing in a parallel and opposite direction. Daisy had no luck with her first shot, and very little with her second. Lucia just got out of the way of her third and Daisy hurried by them.

'Such a slice!' she said. 'How are you getting on, Lucia? How many have you played to get there?'

'One at present, dear,' said Lucia. 'But isn't it difficult?'

Daisy's face fell.

'One?' she said.

Lucia kissed her hand.

'That's all,' she said. 'And has Georgie told you that I'll manage about Pug for you?'

Daisy looked round severely. She had begun to address her ball and nobody must talk.

Lucia watched Daisy do it again, and rejoined Georgie who was in a 'tarsome' place, and tufts of grass flew in the air.

'Georgie, I had a little talk with Mr Stratton the other day,' she said. 'There's a new golf-committee being elected in October, and they would so like to have you on it. Now be good-natured and say you will.'

Georgie had no intention of saying anything else.

'And they want poor little me to be President,' said Lucia. 'So shall I send Mr Stratton a line and say we will? It would be kind, Georgie. Oh, by the way, do come and dine tonight. Peppino – so much better, thanks – Peppino told me to ask you. He would enjoy it. Just one of our dear little evenings again.'

Lucia, in fact, was bringing her batteries into action, and Georgie was the immediate though not the ultimate objective. He longed to be on the golf-committee, he was intensely grateful for the promised removal of Pug, and it was much more amusing to play golf with Lucia than to be dragooned round by Daisy who told him after every stroke what he ought to have done and could never do it herself. A game should not be a lecture.

Lucia thought it was time to confide in him about the abandoning of Brompton Square. Georgie would love knowing what nobody else knew yet. She waited till he had failed to hole a short putt, and gave him the subsequent one, which Daisy never did.

'I hope we shall have many of our little evenings, Georgie,' she said. 'We shall be here till Christmas. No, no more London for us, though it's a secret at present.'

'What?' said Georgie.

'Wait a moment,' said Lucia, teeing up for the last hole. 'Now ickle ballie, fly away home. There! . . .' and ickle ballie flew at about right angles to home, but ever such a long way.

She walked with him to cover-point, where he had gone too.

'Peppino must never live in London again,' she said. 'All going to be sold, Georgie. The house and the furniture and the pearls. You must put up with your poor old Lucia at Riseholme again. Nobody knows yet but you, but now it is all settled. Am I sorry? Yes, Georgie, course I am. So many dear friends in London. But then there are dear friends in Riseholme. Oh, what a beautiful bang, Georgie. You nearly hit Daisy. Call "Five!" isn't that what they do?'

Lucia was feeling much surer of her ground. Georgie, bribed by a place on the golf-committee and by her admiration of his golf, and by her nobility with regard to Pug, was trotting back quick to her, and that was something. Next morning she had a hectic interview with Lady Ambermere . . .

Lady Ambermere was said to be not at home, though Lucia had seen her majestic face at the window of the pink saloon. So she asked for Miss Lyall, the downtrodden companion, and waited in the hall. Her chauffeur had deposited the large brown-paper parcel with Pug inside on the much-admired tessellated pavement.

'Oh, Miss Lyall,' said Lucia. 'So sad that dear Lady Ambermere is out, for I wanted to convey the grateful thanks of the Museum Committee to her for her beautiful gift of poor Pug. But they feel they can't . . . Yes, that's Pug in the brown-paper parcel. So sweet. But will you, on Lady Ambermere's return, make it quite clear?'

Miss Lyall, looking like a mouse, considered what her duty was in this difficult situation. She felt that Lady Ambermere ought to know Lucia's mission and deal with it in person.

'I'll see if Lady Ambermere has come in, Mrs Lucas,' she said. 'She may have come in. Just out in the garden, you know. Might like to know what you've brought. Oh dear me!'

Poor Miss Lyall scuttled away, and presently the door of the pink saloon was thrown open. After an impressive pause Lady Ambermere appeared, looking vexed. The purport of this astounding mission had evidently been conveyed to her.

'Mrs Lucas, I believe,' she said, just as if she wasn't sure.

Now Lucia after all her duchesses was not going to stand that. Lady Ambermere might have a Roman nose, but she hadn't any manners.

'Lady Ambermere, I presume,' she retorted. So there they were.

Lady Ambermere glared at her in a way that should have turned her to stone. It made no impression.

'You have come, I believe, with a message from the committee of your little Museum at Riseholme, which I may have misunderstood.'

Lucia knew she was doing what neither Mrs Boucher nor Daisy in their most courageous moments would have dared to do. As for Georgie . . .

'No, Lady Ambermere,' she said. 'I don't think you've misunderstood it. A stuffed dog on a cushion. They felt that the Museum was not quite the place for it. I have brought it back to you with their thanks and regrets. So kind of you and – and sorry of them. This is the parcel. That is all, I think.'

It wasn't quite all . . .

'Are you aware, Mrs Lucas,' said Lady Ambermere, 'that the mittens of the late Queen Charlotte are my loan to your little Museum?'

Lucia put her finger to her forehead.

'Mittens?' she said. 'Yes, I believe there are some mittens. I think I have seen them. No doubt those are the ones. Yes?'

That was brilliant: it implied complete indifference on the part of the committee (to which Lucia felt sure she would presently belong) as to what Lady Ambermere might think fit to do about mittens.

'The committee shall hear from me,' said Lady Ambermere, and walked majestically back to the pink saloon.

Lucia felt sorry for Miss Lyall: Miss Lyall would probably not have a very pleasant day, but she had no real apprehensions, so she explained to the committee, who were anxiously awaiting her return on the green, about the withdrawal of these worsted relics.

'Bluff, just bluff,' she said. 'And even if it wasn't – Surely, dear Daisy, it's better to have no mittens and no Pug than both. Pug – I caught a peep of him through a hole in the brown paper – Pug would have made your Museum a laughing-stock.'

'Was she very dreadful?' asked Georgie.

Lucia gave a little silvery laugh.

'Yes, dear Georgie, quite dreadful. You would have collapsed if she had said to you "Mr Pillson, I believe." Wouldn't you, Georgie? Don't pretend to be braver than you are.'

'Well, I think we ought all to be much obliged to you, Mrs Lucas,' said Mrs Boucher. 'And I'm sure we are. I should never have stood up to her like that! And if she takes the mittens away, I should be much inclined to put another pair in the case, for the case belongs to us and not to her, with just the label "These mittens did not belong to Queen Charlotte, and were not presented by Lady Ambermere." That would serve her out.'

Lucia laughed gaily again. 'So glad to have been of use,' she said. 'And now, dear Daisy, will you be as kind to me as Georgie was yesterday and give me a little game of golf this afternoon? Not much fun for you, but so good for me.'

Daisy had observed some of Lucia's powerful strokes yesterday, and she was rather dreading this invitation for fear it should not be, as Lucia said, much fun for her. Luckily, she and Georgie had already arranged to play today, and she had, in anticipation of the dread event, engaged Piggy, Goosie, Mrs Antrobus and Colonel Boucher to play with her on all the remaining days of that week. She meant to practise like anything in the interval. And then, like a raven croaking disaster, the infamous Georgie let her down.

'I'd sooner not play this afternoon,' he said. 'I'd sooner just stroll out with you.'

'Sure, Georgie?' said Lucia. 'That will be nice then. Oh, how nervous I shall be.'

Daisy made one final effort to avert her downfall, by offering, as they went out that afternoon, to give Lucia a stroke a hole. Lucia said she knew she could do it, but might they, just for fun, play level? And as the round proceeded, Lucia's kindness was almost intolerable. She could see, she said, that Daisy was completely off her game, when Daisy wasn't in the least off her game: she said, 'Oh, that was bad luck!' when Daisy missed short putts: she begged her to pick her ball out of bushes and not count it . . . At half-past four Riseholme knew that Daisy had halved four holes and lost the other five. Her short reign as Queen of Golf had come to an end.

*   *   *

The Museum Committee met after tea at Mrs Boucher's (Daisy did not hold her golfing-class in the garden that day) and tact, Georgie felt, seemed to indicate that Lucia's name should not be suggested as a new member of the committee so swiftly on the heels of Daisy's disaster. Mrs Boucher, privately consulted, concurred, though with some rather stinging remarks as to Daisy's having deceived them all about her golf, and the business of the meeting was chiefly concerned with the proposed closing down of the Museum for the winter. The tourist season was over, no charabancs came any more with visitors, and for three days not a soul had passed the turnstile.

'So where's the use,' asked Mrs Boucher, 'of paying a boy to let people into the Museum when nobody wants to be let in? I call it throwing money away. Far better close it till the spring, and have no more expense, except to pay him a shilling a week to open the windows and air it, say on Tuesday and Friday, or Wednesday and Saturday.'

'I should suggest Monday and Thursday,' said Daisy, very decisively. If she couldn't have it all her own way on the links, she could make herself felt on committees.

'Very well, Monday and Thursday,' said Mrs Boucher. 'And then there's another thing. It's getting so damp in there, that if you wanted a cold bath, you might undress and stand there. The water's pouring off the walls. A couple of oil-stoves, I suggest, every day except when it's being aired. The boy will attend to them, and make it half a crown instead of a shilling. I'm going to Blitton tomorrow, and if that's your wish I'll order them. No: I'll bring them back with me, and I'll have them lit tomorrow morning. But unless you want to have nothing to show next spring but mildew, don't let us delay about it. A crop of mildew won't be sufficient attraction to visitors, and there'll be nothing else.'

Georgie rapped the table.

'And I vote we take the manuscript of *Lucrezia* out, and that one of us keeps it till we open again,' he said.

'I should be happy to keep it,' said Daisy.

Georgie wanted it himself, but it was better not to thwart Daisy today. Besides, he was in a hurry, as Lucia had asked him to bring round his planchette and see if Abfou would not like a little attention. Nobody had talked to Abfou for weeks.

'Very well,' he said, 'and if that's all – '

'I'm not sure I shouldn't feel happier if it was at the bank,' said Mrs Boucher. 'Supposing it was stolen.'

Georgie magnanimously took Daisy's side: he knew how Daisy was feeling. Mrs Boucher was outvoted, and he got up.

'If that's all then, I'll be off,' he said.

Daisy had a sort of conviction that he was going to do something with Lucia, perhaps have a lesson at golf.

'Come in presently?' she said.

'I can't, I'm afraid,' he said. 'I'm busy till dinner.'

And of course, on her way home, she saw him hurrying across to The Hurst with his planchette.

Chapter Eleven

Lucia made no allusion whatever to her athletic triumph in the afternoon when Georgie appeared. That was not her way: she just triumphed, and left other people to talk about it. But her principles did not prevent her speaking about golf in the abstract.

'We must get more businesslike when you and I are on the committee, Georgie,' she said. 'We must have competitions and handicaps, and I will give a small silver cup, the President's Cup, to be competed for. There's no organisation at present, you see: great fun, but no organisation. We shall have to put our heads together over that. And foursomes: I have been reading about foursomes, when two people on one side hit the ball in turn. Peppino, I'm sure, would give a little cup for foursomes, the Lucas Cup . . . And you've brought the planchette? You must teach me how to use it. What a good employment for winter evenings, Georgie. And we must have some bridge tournaments. Wet afternoons, you know, and then tea, and then some more bridge. But we will talk about all that presently, only I warn you I shall expect you to get up all sorts of diversions for Peppino.'

Lucia gave a little sigh.

'Peppino adored London,' she said, 'and we must cheer him up, Georgie, and not let him feel dull. You must think of lots of little diversions: little pleasant bustling things for these long evenings: music, and bridge, and some planchette. Then I shall get up some Shakespeare readings, selections from plays, with a small part for Peppino and another for poor Daisy. I foresee already that I shall have a very busy autumn. But you must all be very kind and come here for our little entertainments. Madness for Peppino to go out after sunset. Now let us get to our planchette. How I do chatter, Georgie!'

Georgie explained the technique of planchette, how important it was not to push, but on the other hand not to resist its independent motions. As he spoke Lucia glanced over the directions for planchette which he had brought with him.

'We may not get anything,' he said. 'Abfou was very disappointing sometimes. We can go on talking: indeed, it is better not to attend to what it does.'

'I see,' said Lucia, 'let us go on talking then. How late you are, Georgie. I expected you half an hour ago. Oh, you said you might be detained by a Museum Committee meeting.'

'Yes, we settled to shut the Museum up for the winter,' he said. 'Just an oil-stove or two to keep it dry. I wanted – and so did Mrs Boucher, I know – to ask you – '

He stopped, for planchette had already begun to throb in a very extraordinary manner.

'I believe something is going to happen,' he said.

'No! How interesting!' said Lucia. 'What do we do?'

'Nothing,' said Georgie. 'Just let it do what it likes. Let's concentrate: that means thinking of nothing at all.'

Georgie of course had noticed and inwardly applauded the lofty reticence which Lucia had shown about Daisy's disaster this afternoon. But he had the strongest suspicion of her wish to weedj, and he fully expected that if Abfou 'came through' and talked anything but Arabic, he would express his scorn of Daisy's golf. There would be scathing remarks, corresponding to 'snob' and those rude things about Lucia's shingling of her hair, and then he would feel that Lucia had pushed. She might say she hadn't, just as Daisy said she hadn't, but it would be very unconvincing if Abfou talked about golf. He hoped it wouldn't happen, for the very appositeness of Abfou's remarks before had strangely shaken his faith in Abfou. He had been willing to believe that it was Daisy's subconscious self that had inspired Abfou – or at any rate he tried to believe it – but it had been impossible to dissociate the complete Daisy from these violent criticisms.

Planchette began to move.

'Probably it's Arabic,' said Georgie. 'You never quite know. Empty your mind of everything, Lucia.'

She did not answer, and he looked up at her. She had that faraway expression which he associated with renderings of the 'Moonlight Sonata'. Then her eyes closed.

Planchette was moving quietly and steadily along. When it came near the edge of the paper, it ran back and began again, and Georgie felt quite sure he wasn't pushing: he only wanted it not to waste its energy on the tablecloth. Once he felt almost certain that it traced out the word 'drive', but one couldn't be sure. And was that 'committee'? His heart rather sank: it would be such a pity if Abfou was only talking about the golf club which no doubt was filling Lucia's subconscious as well as conscious mind . . . Then suddenly he got rather alarmed, for Lucia's head was sunk forward, and she breathed with strange rapidity.

'Lucia!' he said sharply.

Lucia lifted her head, and planchette stopped.

'Dear me, I felt quite dreamy,' she said. 'Let us go on talking, Georgie. Lady Ambermere this morning: I wish you could have seen her.'

'Planchette has been writing,' said Georgie.

'No!' said Lucia. 'Has it? May we look?'

Georgie lifted the machine. There was no Arabic at all, nor was it Abfou's writing, which in quaint little ways resembled Daisy's when he wrote quickly.

'Vittoria,' he read. 'I am Vittoria.'

'Georgie, how silly,' said Lucia, 'or is it the Queen?'

'Let's see what she says,' said Georgie. 'I am Vittoria. I come to Riseholme. For proof, there is a dog and a Vecchia – '

'That's Italian,' said Lucia excitedly. 'You see, Vittoria is Italian. Vecchia means – let me see; yes, of course, it means "old woman". "A dog, and an old woman who is angry." Oh Georgie, you did that! You were thinking about Pug and Lady Ambermere.'

'I swear I wasn't,' said Georgie. 'It never entered my head. Let's see what else. "And Vittoria comes to tell you of fire and water, of fire and water. The strong elements that burn and soak. Fire and water and moonlight."'

'Oh Georgie, what gibberish,' said Lucia. 'It's as silly as Abfou. What does it mean? Moonlight! I suppose you would say I pushed and was thinking of the "Moonlight Sonata".'

That base thought had occurred to Georgie's mind, but where did fire and water come in? Suddenly a stupendous interpretation struck him.

'It's most extraordinary!' he said. 'We had a Museum Committee meeting just now, and Mrs Boucher said the place was streaming wet. We settled to get some oil-stoves to keep it dry. There's fire and water for you!' Georgie had mentioned this fact about the Museum Committee, but so casually that he had quite forgotten he had done so. Lucia did not remind him of it.

'Well, I do call that remarkable!' she said. 'But I dare say it's only a coincidence.'

'I don't think so at all,' said Georgie. 'I think it's most curious, for I wasn't thinking about that a bit. What else does it say? "Vittoria bids you keep love and loyalty alive in your hearts. Vittoria has suffered, and bids you be kind to the suffering."'

'That's curious!' said Lucia. 'That might apply to Peppino, mightn't it? . . . Oh Georgie, why, of course, that was in both of our minds: we had just been talking about it. I don't say you pushed intentionally, and you mustn't say I did, but that might easily have come from us.'

'I think it's very strange,' said Georgie. 'And then, what came over you, Lucia? You looked only half-conscious. I believe it was what the planchette directions call light hypnosis.'

'No!' said Lucia. 'Light hypnosis, that means half-asleep, doesn't it? I did feel drowsy.'

'It's a condition of trance,' said Georgie. 'Let's try again.'

Lucia seemed reluctant.

'I think I won't, Georgie,' she said. 'It is so strange. I'm not sure that I like it.'

'It can't hurt you if you approach it in the right spirit,' said Georgie, quoting from the directions.

'Not again this evening, Georgie,' said she. 'Tomorrow perhaps. It is interesting, it is curious, and somehow I don't think Vittoria would hurt us. She seems kind. There's something noble, indeed, about her message.'

'Much nobler than Abfou,' said Georgie, 'and much more powerful. Why, she came through at once, without pages of scribbles first! I never felt quite certain that Abfou's scribbles were Arabic.'

Lucia gave a little indulgent smile.

'There didn't seem much evidence for it from what you told me,' she said. 'All you could be certain of was that they weren't English.'

Georgie left his planchette with Lucia, in case she would consent to sit again tomorrow, and hurried back, it is unnecessary to state, not to his own house, but to Daisy's. Vittoria was worth two of Abfou, he thought . . . that communication about fire and water, that kindness to the suffering, and, hardly less, the keeping of loyalty alive. That made him feel rather guilty, for certainly loyalty to Lucia had flickered somewhat in consequence of her behaviour during the summer.

He gave a short account of these remarkable proceedings (omitting the loyalty) to Daisy, who took a superior and scornful attitude.

'Vittoria, indeed!' she said, 'and Vecchia. Isn't that Lucia all over, lugging in easy Italian like that? And Pug and the angry old lady. Glorifying herself, I call it. Why, that wasn't even subconscious: her mind was full of it.'

'But how about the fire and water?' asked Georgie. 'It does apply to the damp in the Museum and the oil-stoves.'

Daisy knew that her position as priestess of Abfou was tottering. It was true that she had not celebrated the mysteries of late, for Riseholme (and she) had got rather tired of Abfou, but it was gall and wormwood to think that Lucia should steal (steal was the word) her invention and bring it out under the patronage of Vittoria as something quite new.

'A pure fluke,' said Daisy. 'If she'd written mutton and music, you would have found some interpretation for it. Such far-fetched nonsense!'

Georgie was getting rather heated. He remembered how when Abfou had written 'death' it was held to apply to the mulberry tree which Daisy believed she had killed by amateur root-pruning, so if it came to talking about far-fetched nonsense, he could have something to say. Besides, the mulberry tree hadn't died at all, so that if Abfou meant that he was wrong. But there was no good in indulging in recriminations with Daisy, not only for the sake of peace and quietness, but because Georgie could guess very well all she was feeling.

'But she didn't write about mutton and music,' he observed, 'so we needn't discuss that. Then there was moonlight. I don't know what that means.'

'I should call it moonshine,' said Daisy brightly.

'Well, it wrote moonlight,' said Georgie. 'Of course there's the "Moonlight Sonata" which might have been in Lucia's mind, but it's all curious. And I believe Lucia was in a condition of light hypnosis – '

'Light fiddlesticks!' said Daisy . . . (Why hadn't she thought of going into a condition of light hypnosis when she was Abfouing? So much more impressive!) 'We can all shut our eyes and droop our heads.'

'Well, I think it was light hypnosis,' said Georgie firmly. 'It was very curious to see. I hope she'll consent to sit again. She didn't much want to.'

Daisy profoundly hoped that Lucia would not consent to sit again, for she felt Abfouism slipping out of her fingers. In any case, she would instantly resuscitate Abfou, for Vittoria shouldn't have it all her own way. She got up.

'Georgie, why shouldn't we see if Abfou has anything to say about it?' she asked. 'After all, Abfou told us to make a museum, and that hasn't turned out so badly. Abfou was practical; what he suggested led to something.'

Though the notion that Daisy had thought of the Museum and pushed flitted through Georgie's mind, there was something in what she said, for certainly Abfou had written museum (if it wasn't 'mouse') and there was the Museum which had turned out so profitably for the committee.

'We might try,' he said.

Daisy instantly got out her planchette, which sadly wanted dusting, and it began to move almost as soon as they laid their hands on it: Abfou was in a rather inartistic hurry. And it really wasn't very wise of Daisy to close her eyes and snort: it was indeed light fiddlesticks to do that. It was a sheer unconvincing plagiarism from Lucia, and his distrust of Daisy and of Abfou immeasurably deepened. Furiously the pencil scribbled, going off the paper occasionally and writing on the table till Georgie could insert the paper under it: it was evident that Abfou was very indignant about something, and there was no need to enquire what that was. For some time the writing seemed to feel to Georgie like Arabic, but presently the pencil slowed down, and he thought some English was coming through. Finally Abfou gave a great scrawl, as he usually did when the message was complete, and Daisy looked dreamily up. 'Anything?' she said.

'It's been writing hard,' said Georgie.

They examined the script. It began, as he had expected, with quantities of Arabic, and then (as he had expected) dropped into English, which was quite legible.

'Beware of charlatans,' wrote Abfou, 'beware of southern charlatans. All spirits are not true and faithful like Abfou, who instituted your Museum. False guides deceive. A warning from Abfou.'

'Well, if that isn't convincing, I don't know what is,' said Daisy.

Georgie thought it convincing too.

The din of battle began to rise. It was known that very evening, for Colonel and Mrs Boucher dined with Georgie, that he and Lucia (for Georgie did not give all the credit to Lucia) had received that remarkable message from Vittoria about fire and water and the dog and the angry old woman, and it was agreed that Abfou cut a very poor figure, and had a jealous temper. Why hadn't Abfou done something better than merely warn them against southern charlatans?

'If it comes to that,' said Mrs Boucher, 'Egypt is in the south, and charlatans can come from Egypt as much as from Italy. Fire and water! Very remarkable. There's the water there now, plenty of it, and the fire will be there tomorrow. I must get out my planchette again, for I put it away. I got sick of writing nothing but Arabic, even if it was Arabic. I call it very strange. And not a word about golf from Vittoria. I consider that's most important. If Lucia had been pushing, she'd have written about her golf with Daisy. Abfou and Vittoria! I wonder which will win.'

That summed it up pretty well, for it was felt that Abfou and Vittoria could not both direct the affairs of Riseholme from the other world, unless they acted jointly; and Abfou's remarks about the southern charlatan and false spirits put the idea of a coalition out of the question. All the time, firm in the consciousness of Riseholme, but never under any circumstances spoken of, was the feeling that Abfou and Vittoria (as well as standing for themselves) were pseudonyms: they stood also for Daisy and Lucia. And how much finer and bigger, how much more gifted of the two in every way was Vittoria-Lucia. Lucia quickly got over her disinclination to weedj, and messages, not very definite, but of high moral significance came from this exalted spirit. There was never a word about golf, and there was never a word about Abfou, nor any ravings concerning inferior and untrustworthy spirits. Vittoria was clearly above all that (indeed, she was probably in some sphere miles away above Abfou), whereas Abfou's pages (Daisy sat with her planchette morning after morning and obtained sheets of the most voluble English) were blistered with denunciations of low and earth-born intelligences and dark with awful warnings for those who trusted them.

Riseholme, in fact, had never been at a higher pitch of excited activity; even the arrival of the *Evening Gazette* during those weeks when Hermione had recorded so much about Mrs Philip Lucas hadn't roused such emotions as the reception of a new message from Abfou or Vittoria. And it was Lucia again who was the cause of it all: no one for months had cared what Abfou said, till Lucia became the recipient of Vittoria's messages. She had invested planchette with the interest that attached to all she did. On the other hand it was felt that Abfou (though certainly he lowered himself by these pointed recriminations) had done something. Abfou-Daisy had invented the Museum, whereas Vittoria-Lucia, apart from giving utterance to high moral sentiments, had invented nothing (high moral sentiments couldn't count as an invention). To be sure there was the remarkable piece about Pug and angry Lady Ambermere, but the facts of that were already known to Lucia, and as for the communication about fire, water and moon-light, though there were new oil-stoves in the damp Museum, that was not as remarkable as inventing the Museum, and moonlight unless it meant the Sonata was quite unexplained. Over this cavilling objection, rather timidly put forward by Georgie, who longed for some striking vindication of Vittoria, Lucia was superb.

'Yes, Georgie, I can't tell you what it means,' she said. 'I am only the humble scribe. It is quite mysterious to me. For myself, I am content to be Vittoria's medium. I feel it a high honour. Perhaps some day it will be explained, and we shall see.'

They saw.

Meanwhile, since no one can live entirely on messages from the unseen, other interests were not neglected. There were bridge parties at The Hurst, there was much music, there was a reading of *Hamlet* at which Lucia doubled several of the principal parts and Daisy declined to be the Ghost. The new committee of the golf club was formed, and at the first meeting Lucia announced her gift of the President's Cup, and Peppino's of the Lucas Cup for foursomes. Notice of these was duly put up in the clubhouse, and Daisy's face was of such a grimness when she read them that something very savage from Abfou might be confidently expected. She went out for a round soon after with Colonel Boucher, who wore a scared and worried look when he returned. Daisy had got into a bunker, and had simply hewed her ball to pieces . . . Peppino's convalescence proceeded well; Lucia laid down the law a good deal at auction bridge, and the oil-stoves at the Museum were satisfactory. They were certainly making headway against the large patches of damp on the walls, and Daisy, one evening, recollecting that she had not made a personal inspection of them, went in just before dinner to look at them. The boy in charge of them had put them out, for they only burned during the day, and certainly they were doing their work well. Daisy felt she would not be able to bring forward any objection to them at the next committee meeting, as she had rather hoped to do. In order to hurry on the drying process, she filled them both up and lit them so that they should burn all night. She spilt a little paraffin, but that would soon evaporate. Georgie was tripping back across the green from a visit to Mrs Boucher, and they walked homeward together.

* * *

Georgie had dined at home that night, and working at a crossword puzzle was amazed to see how late it was. He had pored long over a map of South America, trying to find a river of seven letters with pt in the middle, but he determined to do no more at it tonight.

'The tarsome thing,' he said, 'if I could get that, I'm sure it would give me thirty-one across.'

He strolled to the window and pushed aside the blind. It was a moonlight night with a high wind and a few scudding clouds. Just as he was about to let the blind drop again he saw a reddish light in the sky, immediately above his tall yew-hedge, and wondered what it was. His curiosity combined with the fact that a breath of air was always pleasant before going to bed, led him to open the front door and look out. He gave a wild gasp of dismay and horror.

The windows of the Museum were vividly illuminated by a red glow. Smoke poured out of one which apparently was broken, and across the smoke shot tongues of flame. He bounded to his telephone, and with great presence of mind rang up the fire-station at Blitton. 'Riseholme,' he called. 'House on fire: send engine at once.' He ran into his garden again, and seeing a light still in the drawing-room next door (Daisy was getting some sulphurous expressions from Abfou) tapped at the pane. 'The Museum's burning,' he cried, and set off across the green to the scene of the fire.

By this time others had seen it too, and were coming out of their houses, looking like little black ants on a red tablecloth. The fire had evidently caught strong hold, and now a piece of the roof fell in, and the flames roared upwards. In the building itself there was no apparatus for extinguishing fire, nor, if there had been, could anyone have reached it. A hose was fetched from the Ambermere Arms, but that was not long enough, and there was nothing to be done except wait for the arrival of the fire-engine from Blitton. Luckily the Museum stood well apart from other houses, and there seemed little danger of the fire spreading.

Soon the bell of the approaching engine was heard, but already it was clear that nothing could be saved. The rest of the roof crashed in, a wall tottered and fell. The longer hose was adjusted, and the stream of water directed through the windows, now here, now there, where the fire was fiercest, and clouds of steam mingled with the smoke. But all efforts to save anything were absolutely vain: all that could be done, as the fire burned itself out, was to quench the glowing embers of the conflagration . . . As he watched, three words suddenly repeated themselves in Georgie's mind. 'Fire, water, moonlight,' he said a loud in an awed tone . . . Victorious Vittoria!

The committee, of course, met next morning, and Robert as financial adviser was specially asked to attend. Georgie arrived at Mrs Boucher's house where the meeting was held before Daisy and Robert got there, and Mrs Boucher could hardly greet him, so excited was she.

'I call it most remarkable,' she said. 'Dog and angry old woman never convinced me, but this is beyond anything. Fire, water, moon-light! It's prophecy, nothing less than prophecy. I shall believe anything Vittoria says, for the future. As for Abfou – well – '

She tactfully broke off at Daisy's and Robert's entrance.

'Good-morning,' she said. 'And good-morning, Mr Robert. This is a disaster, indeed. All Mr Georgie's sketches, and the walking-sticks, and the mittens and the spit. Nothing left at all.'

Robert seemed amazingly cheerful.

'I don't see it as such a disaster,' he said. 'Lucky I had those insurances executed. We get two thousand pounds from the company, of which five hundred goes to Colonel Boucher for his barn – I mean the Museum.'

'Well, that's something,' said Mrs Boucher. 'And the rest? I never could understand about insurances. They've always been a sealed book to me.'

'Well, the rest belongs to those who put the money up to equip the Museum,' he said. 'In proportion, of course, to the sums they advanced. Altogether four hundred and fifty pounds was put up; you and Daisy and Georgie each put in fifty. The rest, well, I advanced the rest.'

There were some rapid and silent calculations made. It seemed rather hard that Robert should get such a lot. Business always seemed to favour the rich. But Robert didn't seem the least ashamed of that. He treated it as a perfect matter of course.

'The – the treasures in the Museum almost all belonged to the committee,' he went on. 'They were given to the Museum, which was the property of the committee. Quite simple. If it had been a loan collection now – well, we shouldn't be finding quite such a bright lining to our cloud. I'll manage the insurance business for you, and pay you pleasant little cheques all round. The company, no doubt, will ask a few questions as to the origin of the fire.'

'Ah, there's a mystery for you,' said Mrs Boucher. 'The oil-stoves were always put out in the evening, after burning all day, and how a fire broke out in the middle of the night beats me.'

Daisy's mouth twitched. Then she pulled herself together.

'Most mysterious,' she said, and looked carelessly out of the window to where the debris of the Museum was still steaming. Simultaneously, Georgie gave a little start, and instantly changed the subject, rapping on the table.

'There's one thing we've forgotten,' said he. 'It wasn't entirely our property. Queen Charlotte's mittens were only on loan.'

The faces of the committee fell slightly.

'A shilling or two,' said Mrs Boucher hopefully. 'I'm only glad we didn't have Pug as well. Lucia got us out of that!'

Instantly the words of Vittoria about the dog and the angry old woman, and fire and water and moonlight occurred to everybody. Most of all they occurred to Daisy, and there was a slight pause, which might have become awkward if it had continued. It was broken by the entry of Mrs Boucher's parlour-maid, who carried a letter in a large square envelope with a deep mourning border, and a huge coronet on the flap.

'Addressed to the Museum Committee, ma'am,' she said.

Mrs Boucher opened it, and her face flushed.

'Well, she's lost no time,' she said. 'Lady Ambermere. I think I had better read it.'

'Please,' said everybody in rather strained voices.

Mrs Boucher read:

'Ladies and Gentlemen of the Committee of Riseholme Museum
    Your little Museum, I hear, has been totally destroyed with all
its contents by fire. I have to remind you therefore that the mittens
of her late Majesty Queen Charlotte were there on loan, as lent by
me. No equivalent in money can really make up for the loss of so
irreplaceable a relic, but I should be glad to know, as soon as
possible, what compensation you propose to offer me.
    The figure that has been suggested to me is £50, and an early
cheque would oblige.
    Faithfully yours,

CORNELIA AMBERMERE.'

A dead silence succeeded, broken by Mrs Boucher as soon as her
indignation allowed her to speak.

'I would sooner,' she said, 'go to law about it, and appeal if it went
against us, and carry it up to the House of Lords, than pay fifty
pounds for those rubbishy things. Why, the whole contents of the
Museum weren't worth more than – well, leave it at that.'

The figure at which the contents of the Museum had been insured
floated into everybody's mind, and it was more dignified to 'leave it
at that', and not let the imagination play over the probable end of
Mrs Boucher's sentence.

The meeting entirely concurred, but nobody, not even Robert,
knew what to do next.

'I propose offering her ten pounds,' said Georgie at last, 'and I call
that handsome.'

'Five,' said Daisy, like an auction reversed.

Robert rubbed the top of his head, as was his custom in perplexity.
'Difficult to know what to do,' he said. 'I don't know of any standard
of valuation for the old clothes of deceased queens.'

'Two,' said Mrs Boucher, continuing the auction, 'and that's a fancy
price. What would Pug have been, I wonder, if we're asked fifty
pounds for two old mittens. A pound each, I say, and that's a monstrous
price. And if you want to know who suggested to Lady Ambermere to
ask fifty, I can tell you, and her name was Cornelia Ambermere.'

This proposal of Lady Ambermere's rather damped the secret
exaltation of the committee, though it stirred a pleasant feeling of
rage. Fifty pounds was a paltry sum compared to what they would
receive from the insurance company, but the sense of the attempt to
impose on them caused laudable resentment. They broke up, to

consider separately what was to be done, and to poke about the ashes
of the Museum, all feeling very rich. The rest of Riseholme were
there, of course, also poking about, Piggy and Goosie skipping over
smouldering heaps of ash, and Mrs Antrobus, and the vicar and the
curate, and Mr Stratton. Only Lucia was absent, and Georgie, after
satisfying himself that nothing whatever remained of his sketches,
popped in to The Hurst.

Lucia was in the music-room reading the paper. She had heard, of
course, about the total destruction of the Museum, that ridiculous
invention of Daisy and Abfou, but not a shadow of exultation betrayed
itself.

'My dear, too sad about the Museum,' she said. 'All your beautiful
things. Poor Daisy, too, her idea.'

Georgie explained about the silver lining to the cloud.

'But what's so marvellous,' he said, 'is Vittoria. Fire, water, moonlight. I never heard of anything so extraordinary, and I thought it
only meant the damp on the walls, and the new oil-stoves. It was
prophetical, Lucia, and Mrs Boucher thinks so too.'

Lucia still showed no elation. Oddly enough, she had thought it
meant damp and oil-stoves, too, for she did remember what Georgie
had forgotten that he had told her just before the epiphany of Vittoria.
But now this stupendous fulfilment of Vittoria's communication of
which she had never dreamed, had happened. As for Abfou, it was a
mere waste of time to give another thought to poor dear malicious
Abfou. She sighed.

'Yes, Georgie, it was strange,' she said. 'That was our first sitting,
wasn't it? When I got so drowsy and felt so queer. Very strange
indeed: convincing, I think. But whether I shall go on sitting now, I
hardly know.'

'Oh, but you must,' said Georgie. 'After all the rubbish – '

Lucia held up a finger.

'Now, Georgie, don't be unkind,' she said. 'Let us say, "Poor
Daisy", and leave it there. That's all. Any other news?'

Georgie retailed the monstrous demand of Lady Ambermere.

'And, as Robert says, it's so hard to know what to offer her,' he
concluded.

Lucia gave the gayest of laughs.

'Georgie, what would poor Riseholme do without me?' she said. 'I
seem to be made to pull you all out of difficulties. That mismanaged
golf club, Pug, and now there's this. Well, shall I be kind and help
you once more?'

She turned over the leaves of her paper.

'Ah, that's it,' she said. 'Listen, Georgie. Sale at Pemberton's auction-rooms in Knightsbridge yesterday. Various items. Autograph of Crippen the murderer. Dear me, what horrid minds people have! Mother-of-pearl brooch belonging to the wife of the poet Mr Robert Montgomery; a pair of razors belonging to Carlyle, all odds and ends of trumpery, you see . . . Ah yes, here it is. Pair of riding gaiters, in good condition, belonging to His Majesty King George IV. That seems a sort of guide, doesn't it, to the value of Queen Charlotte's mittens. And what do you think they fetched? A terrific sum, Georgie; fifty pounds is nowhere near it. They fetched ten shillings and sixpence.'

'No!' said Georgie. 'And Lady Ambermere asked fifty pounds!'

Lucia laughed again.

'Well, Georgie, I suppose I must be good-natured,' she said. 'I'll draft a little letter for your committee to Lady Ambermere. How you all bully me and work me to death! Why, only yesterday I said to Peppino that those months we spent in London seemed a holiday compared to what I have to do here. Dear old Riseholme! I'm sure I'm very glad to help it out of its little holes.'

Georgie gave a gasp of admiration. It was but a month or two ago that all Riseholme rejoiced when Abfou called her a snob, and now here they all were again (with the exception of Daisy) going to her for help and guidance in all those employments and excitements in which Riseholme revelled. Golf competitions and bridge tournaments, and duets, and real séances, and deliverance from Lady Ambermere, and above all, the excitement supplied by her personality.

'You're too wonderful,' he said, 'indeed, I don't know what we should do without you.'

Lucia got up.

'Well, I'll scribble a little letter for you,' she said, 'bringing in the price of George IV's gaiters in good condition. What shall we – I mean what shall you offer? I think you must be generous, Georgie, and not calculate the exact difference between the value of a pair of gaiters in good condition belonging to a king, and that of a pair of moth-eaten mittens belonging to a queen consort. Offer her the same; in fact, I think I should enclose a treasury note for ten shillings and six stamps. That will be more than generous, it will be munificent.'

Lucia sat down at her writing-table, and after a few minutes' thought, scribbled a couple of sides of notepaper in that neat handwriting that bore no resemblance to Vittoria's. She read them through, and approved.

'I think that will settle it,' she said. 'If there is any further bother with the Vecchia, let me know. There's one more thing, Georgie, and then let us have a little music. How do you think the fire broke out?'

Georgie felt her penetrating eye was on him. She had not asked that question quite idly. He tried to answer it quite idly.

'It's most mysterious,' he said. 'The oil-stoves are always put out quite early in the evening, and lit again next morning. The boy says he put them out as usual.'

Lucia's eye was still on him.

'Georgie, how do you think the fire broke out?' she repeated.

This time Georgie felt thoroughly uncomfortable. Had Lucia the power of divination? . . .

'I don't know,' he said. 'Have you any idea about it?'

'Yes,' said Lucia. 'And so have you. I'll tell you my idea if you like. I saw our poor misguided Daisy coming out of the Museum close on seven o'clock last night.'

'So did I,' said Georgie in a whisper.

'Well, the oil-stoves must have been put out long before that,' said Lucia. 'Mustn't they?'

'Yes,' said Georgie.

'Then how was it that there was a light coming out of the Museum windows? Not much of a light, but a little light; I saw it. What do you make of that?'

'I don't know,' said Georgie.

Lucia held up a censuring finger.

'Georgie, you must be very dull this morning,' she said. 'What I make of it is that our poor Daisy lit the oil-stoves again. And then probably in her fumbling way, she spilt some oil. Something of the sort, anyhow. In fact, I'm afraid Daisy burned down the Museum.'

There was a terrible pause.

'What are we to do?' said Georgie.

Lucia laughed.

'Do?' she said. 'Nothing, except never know anything about it. We know quite well that poor Daisy didn't do it on purpose. She hasn't got the pluck or the invention to be an incendiary. It was only her muddling, meddling ways.'

'But the insurance money?' said Georgie.

'What about it? The fire was an accident, whether Daisy confessed what she had done or not. Poor Daisy! We must be nice to Daisy, Georgie. Her golf, her Abfou! Such disappointments. I think I will ask her to be my partner in the foursome for the Lucas Cup. And perhaps if there was another place on the golf-committee, we might propose her for it.'

Lucia sighed, smiling wistfully.

'A pity she is not a little wiser,' she said.

Lucia sat looking wistful for a moment. Then to Georgie's immense surprise she burst out into peals of laughter.

'My dear, what is the matter?' said Georgie.

Lucia was helpless for a little, but she gasped and recovered and wiped her eyes.

'Georgie, you *are* dull this morning!' she said. 'Don't you see? Poor Daisy's meddling has made the reputation of Vittoria and crumpled up Abfou. Fire, water, moonlight: Vittoria's prophecy. Vittoria owes it all to poor dear Daisy!'

Georgie's laughter set Lucia off again, and Peppino coming in found both at it.

'Good-morning, Georgie,' he said. 'Terrible about the Museum. A sad loss. What are you laughing at?'

'Nothing, *caro*,' said Lucia. 'Just a little joke of Daisy's. Not worth repeating, but it amused Georgie and me. Come, Georgie, half an hour's good practice of celestial Mozartino. We have been lazy lately.'